HARD TO RESIST

VOLUME II

S.L. SCOTT

S.L. SCOTT

The Redemption Copyright © S. L. Scott 2014
The Redemption ISBN: 978-1-940071-25-1
Cover photographer: Kari Branch
Cover model: John Humphrey
Interior Design: Fictional Formats
Content Edits: Heather Maven
Marla Esposito of Proofing Style

The Revolution Copyright © S. L. Scott 2016
The Revolution ISBN: 978-1-940071-42-8
Interior Design: Fictional Formats
Cover Image: Scott Hoover
Featured on the Front Cover: Richard Rocco
Editors: Making Manuscripts
Marla Esposito of Proofing Style

The Rebellion Copyright © S. L. Scott 2017
The Rebellion ISBN: 978-1-940071-50-3
Cover Image: Scott Hoover
Editing: Evident Ink
Marion Making Manuscripts
Marla Esposito, Proofing Style
Virginia Carey, Proofreading
Kristen Johnson, Proofreader

~

Hard to Resist Volume II Cover Design:
Mr. Scott

These books are dedicated to the women who put their hearts on the line to fight for love and the soul mates that will do anything for them.

Audiobooks are available on major retailers

To keep up to date with her writing and more, visit S.L. Scott's website: **www.slscottauthor.com**

To receive the newsletter about all of her publishing adventures, free books, giveaways, steals and more: https://geni.us/intheknow

Follow me on TikTok: https://geni.us/SLTikTok
Follow on IG: https://geni.us/IGSLS
Follow on Bookbub: https://geni.us/SLScottBB

Join S.L.'s Facebook group here: S.L. Scott Books

THE REDEMPTION

Three years ago, Rochelle Floros was living her dream come true... then lost it all. On the worst day of her life, the last person she expected to be there for her was a rock star and tabloid favorite. Dex Caggiano is everything she never wanted. Yet, she can't stop thinking about those soulful, amber eyes.

While trying to rebuild her life after the tragedy that destroyed her fairytale, she's caught between the grief that shrouds her heart in the past and the charismatic man that makes it race in the present.

Can what she wants really be what she needs? With his rhythm and her passion, can they make music together? Or will their harmony be lost forever?

The Redemption is about finding the pulse of your soul in the most unlikely places and giving love a chance to grow.

PROLOGUE

Sadness surrounds me and I feel bad for not feeling worse.

I stand at the back, near a tree, separate from the families and friends that have gathered. I stay back here, away from the crowd, and watch her. She tries to hide her devastation and tears behind big sunglasses that she slipped down over her eyes minutes before.

Her hair is down, hanging over her shoulders and longer than I remember from the last time I saw her. It's been too long since then. But even in the middle of a sea of black, she still stands out, strikingly beautiful and I'm drawn to her, wanting to be with her in ways I can't.

With all of these people around, I'm finding it hard to swallow despite being outdoors. A lump formed in my throat earlier this week, making me wonder what caused it. *Maybe guilt.* Squeezing my hand tightly around the coin, I realize a tragedy has given me hope where none existed before. And despite one of my closest friends dying, an uncertain future, and the realization that with his death, my life has been forever changed, I can't stop thinking about the woman he left behind.

1

ROCHELLE FLOROS

THE FUNERAL WAS... it was what it was. Johnny and Holli drove me and the kids home. There were too many people staring at me, waiting for my breakdown. I needed the silence of the ride to be able to face the waiting mourners at my house, and they gave that to me. Just after we park, Johnny turns to me and says, "The Resistance is a family. We take care of one another. I'll always be here for you, Rochelle."

I nod, not sure I can speak under the weight of my emotions. I want today to become a distant memory sooner than I should. I don't want to remember Cory's death. I want to remember his life, his life with me, his life with our four-year-old. It's a life that our newborn will never get to experience and the significance of that drags me under. I rush out of the car right before the first tear slips down, but I wipe it away before anybody can see.

But he sees.

Antonio Dexter Caggiano sees right through the facade I put on for everyone else, but doesn't move from Neil's side. He knows where he's needed without me saying. They sit on the tire swing together, spinning slowly, talking, bonding in a way that seems almost abnormal for the man I've always known Dex to be. A magic trick reveals a pair of drumsticks and Dex hands them to Neil. My oldest son starts banging on the tire and up the chains, happily distracted from the sadness of the day.

Staring across the lawn—faded black jeans, long, shaggy hair, bandana back in place after we left the cemetery—I find the most unlikely ally on such a depressing day. He's just here, silently supportive without asking anything of me.

Dex is kind to spend time with the boys. He has a playful smile on his face, and assuming from Neil's laughter, which I hear echoing across the yard, Dex is also funny. He left his ego at home, an anomaly from every other day. He's fascinating to watch. Kids are genuine in their emotions and Neil seems to like Dex.

Neil deserves laughter and fun, but he also deserves his father. I get up and move to the side of the yard where I plant my small garden each year. My tears water the lettuce that is just starting to grow. Cory planted that. I wanted strawberries.

I stomp on it. With both feet, I jump up and land down on the plant because he didn't live to see it grow. "Damn you!" Picking it up, I rip it from the ground and throw it against the fence. "Damn you, Cory!"

A burning regret coats my insides as I panic and rush to pick it up. Through watery-vision, I drop to my knees and take it in hand, holding it to my chest. Suddenly strong arms wrap around me from behind, pulling me into his lap. Dex's body against mine feels so foreign and yet, like the only place safe for me to grieve.

The sobs break free, the ones that I've been holding back all day, and my body is wracked with every emotion that I don't want anyone else to see. My breakdown feels like a failure. I should be the one to comfort others today. Pressing my head against his shoulder, the light hum in his chest is soothing. "He left me, Dex. He left me here all by myself to raise the boys on my own. I can't do it."

"You can. You will. I'll be here for you."

He's the least expected person to find comfort in, but he's the only one that feels right. I nod. My head is tucked under his chin while his fingers gently but firmly open my fisted hand. He takes the lettuce that is destroyed and sad, just like me, and says, "It's gonna be okay. Maybe not for the lettuce, but you're gonna be okay."

We sit there a few minutes, the slight breeze feeling good against my hot face. Maybe he's right. Maybe I will be okay. It's hard to tell right now. With a deep breath and even heavier exhale, I look up into his eyes and all that he said is repeated in his expression. I get up and start walking to the backyard again. He follows, but he stops and plants the lettuce back into the garden, and says, "It's worth a shot."

"Yeah, it's worth a shot."

We come from around the corner and Dex goes inside without another word and I join Neil on the swing. No one's the wiser that I almost fell apart, or that Dex held me together. My strength is back on display for everyone else. His bad boy reputation as the drummer for one of the biggest bands in the world is back intact.

Six months later...

It's hot in here. I need fresh air; the crowded party is steamy from all the bodies crammed into the living room. Looking out at the pool area, it's not any better. "I'm gonna walk around," I say, leaving the safety of Johnny's side.

"I'll be here," he replies before taking a drink of his beer. Johnny Outlaw may be one of the most famous musicians in the world and the lead singer of The Resistance, but he's also been a shoulder for me to cry on. He's like the brother I never had. Along with that role, he's become very protective of me in public settings and these types of situations. Holli, his wife, is usually here to keep me company, but she had a business trip and is out of town. So I'm here with the guys from the band. That's a lot of testosterone to be around while drinking your sorrows away.

Remembering there's a small balcony off the master bedroom, I head for the stairs. The balcony has a great vantage point overlooking the pool. Dex is the master of throwing awesome parties and he's gone all out for his birthday. Everyone from Academy Award winning Directors to young starlets jumping at any casting couch opportunity that comes along is here. Current rock musicians are mingling with Pop Princesses, and I just spotted Tommy, the tour manager with some of our roadies at the bar. I used to be more of a free spirit, comfortable in social settings... when Cory was alive. But my happiness died when he did. I never imagined I would be expected to live in a world without my heart. I'd gotten good at hiding my sadness, but lately I've been struggling to put on a happy face for others.

Dex's party is a sea of beautiful people and definitely intimidating. The heat and drinks making my mind blur into a mixture of emotions. I start walking faster, hoping to stave off the panic attack I feel coming on.

I pass some familiar faces, saying hi as I walk by. Seeing other people, the ones I don't know, makes me want to lower my gaze to the floor and block out the stares. Sometimes the stares bother me. I was relatively unrecognizable before Cory's death, but I made headlines as the 'Poor Widow' and my photo was everywhere. So I see the looks, the sideways glances, and feel the sympathy lying heavy from their curiosity. Nights like this usually help me escape the sadness of losing the only man I ever loved. Alcohol also helps, so I down a shot and slowly make my way upstairs, trying not to let the liquor knock me off-balance.

The double doors of the master bedroom are closed along with the other bedroom doors down the hall. Taking the knob in hand, I turn slowly. It opens and I'm greeted with darkness. I'm hoping no one is in here doing something I don't want to see or hear, so I enter with caution. Although there is no light except for the moonlight coming in from the balcony doors, I walk in when I hear silence. Closing the door behind me, I don't bother looking around. I just go to the French doors and open them wide. The night is clearer up here, the miles of LA lights laid out before me with a stunning view of the city. The area around the pool below is more crowded than I realized when I was in the mix of it.

A heavy exhale of smoke draws my gaze to the left. Dex sits forward resting his elbows on his knees and eyes me.

He doesn't look bothered that I'm here, but I feel the need to explain anyway. "I wanted... I needed to get away."

"From what?" he asks while stubbing his cigarette into an ashtray on the Spanish tile.

I lean against the doorframe, my head resting back, my eyes lulled closed by the voices carrying up from below. Over the last six months, we haven't spent a lot of time together, but he's stopped by a few times to talk, reminisce, or just sit with someone who knows what he's going through, empathizing through moments of silent understanding. He makes it easy to just be, to be whatever I need to be. "Everything... from me."

"It's hard to escape yourself."

"I know. I've tried."

"Me too." The ice in his glass shifts, clanging against the walls of the double old-fashioned. I look just as he sets it down, and asks, "Drink?"

"Sure," I reply. "Why are you trying to escape?"

"Sometimes being the bad guy sucks."

"You're not a bad guy."

"Everyone else thinks I am."

"I like to think you just play one on TV... or in your case, on stage. The infamous bad boy drummer of The Resistance isn't all that bad, you know."

He hands me his glass and I hold it up to toast him. "Happy birthday, Dex." The straight bourbon feels thick as it slides down my throat.

His expression changes and he stands, moving behind me, his chest against my back. "Do I get a birthday wish?"

I feel his every breath coming in and out, each one hot against my neck. My heart starts beating faster, the air that felt freer moments before now ripe with innuendoes. This tension between us is new, but I like it. The hesitation I thought I would feel drowned with the last gulp of his drink. I take one last breath before turning, my gaze now meeting his. "Make a wish."

The warmth of his hand covers my cheek and his lips are pressed to mine and mine to his, connecting us like never before. I would have thought I'd get careful, gentle, tentative. I get pressure swarmed with confidence, a wanting that feels more lustful, caressed in need. My body reacts, moving closer, edging into the kiss, wanting it, needing it. I'm pulled inside, the doors shut behind and he whispers, "Too many people can see up here."

I nod, though I'm not sure he can see as I stand in the shadows of the curtain. He's seen clearly, the window panes reflecting an abstract design across his body. Taking a sip, his eyes find mine. There's nothing hurried about his movements as he takes me in. While setting his glass down on the table nearby, he says, "I've wanted to kiss you longer than you'll understand, longer than I had a right to."

Licking my lips, the action involuntary, I'm starting to think that maybe I've wanted to kiss him longer than I had the right to as well. But I see him. I've always seen the real him and not the showman or the manwhore he wants everyone else to see. I see the way the light reflects in his brown eyes, giving them more life than one would expect when labeled just "brown." The liquid tone of where sand meets the ocean at night might do them more justice. His eyes are lighter than mine, and hold a history completely different. But they draw me in, his body wagering me closer.

When I go, I lift up this time to kiss him. With a tilt of our heads, our mouths open and our tongues meet. I shouldn't want him like I do. It's wrong to feel this way, but every physical urge I have overrides my thoughts and deepens as our breaths become each others.

Immersed in a passion that alleviates other burdens I've carried for too long, I enjoy the loss of control, my tension slipping away as he maneuvers me back toward the bed. I go willingly in all ways, wanting to grab hold of this feeling of freedom and release it sexually. I sit as he stands in front of me. The expression on his face highlights his handsome structure—a cut jaw, strong when juxtaposed against his soft gaze. I realize he hides behind his sunglasses so much that I'd forgotten how truly striking he is. His hair is shorter than a year ago, but still hits just below his chin in a jagged-style, carefree and uncalculated.

He slips his shirt off, dropping it to his feet before leaning down and popping open the front of my jeans. I let him as I lean back on my elbows. My shoes come off and then my jeans, slowly, but with no doubt. Neither of us are naïve to what's happening or what's to come. I sit up and take my shirt off before lying back down and asking for the drink. When he hands it to me, I finish the amber liquid and take an ice cube into my mouth, finishing the remaining traces.

Standing up, I demand, "Take your jeans off and lay down." I set the glass back on the dresser across the room and when I return, his lean, muscular body, all six-foot-three of him is on the bed. Crawling up the large mattress, I sit down on his middle, his hardness feeling so good between my legs. I take the ice from my mouth and it drips on his abs, making them twitch. Another drip and another.

"You like to tease," he says, not a question, just an observation.

I lean down and run my tongue over each drop, my chest pressed to his erection.

Lifting my eyes up to watch him, I drag my tongue lower and slower before hearing him mutter, "Fuck."

His head falls back and his eyes close. I drag my fingers over the ups and downs of his defined muscles, appreciating every sit up he does for this exact reason. When I blow across his stomach, his reaction is felt everywhere. Sitting up, he pulls me by my arms and flips me under him in one smooth move. Desperate lips are pressed against mine as his hips flex down, his knees maneuvering my legs apart. Ten inches taller than me, but our bodies seem to fit in so many ways. He kisses my neck and I moan unexpectedly, well aware I just made the only sound in the room. Lifting up, he looks at my face as his hand gently squeezes my left breast. "You're beautiful. The most beautiful woman I've ever seen."

If I thought the moan was unexpected… that tops it.

Never knowing he thought this about me, I'm not sure what to say, so I lift up and kiss him instead. I let the bourbon take over for a bit and enjoy the other ten inches he has on me. His hips come down again, and my body tingles from the contact, my hips reacting by moving against him.

My chest presses against his as his body weighs down on top of mine. Another moan escapes me as our tongues caress. The slightly rough skin of his hand slides under my bra and he takes me firmly, massaging and peaking my nipples. Rolling onto our sides, our mouths part and our eyes meet again. With a soft whisper between us, he asks, "You sure?"

I reply with a kiss to his cheek before I roll onto my back and unfasten my bra. After dropping it to the floor, I lift my hips up, removing my thong. The moonlight streaks in, accentuating the want found in his eyes as he stares at my body. Boxer briefs are removed and he lies next to me. When I look over at him, the reality of the situation is clear even through the wavy goggles of alcohol. His penis is long, thickly attractive, smooth, but hard. He reaches for a packet from a drawer next to the bed and rolls a condom on before turning to me and staring at me without reservation. His gaze is heavy enough to feel as it envelops me in desire. The way his tongue slides over his bottom lip while looking at me makes me anxious for more. But I remain still, letting his lust linger between us, building, just like my yearning for him.

Patience has no concept of time, but cravings do, so I touch his arms, encouraging him closer... closer... until he's centered on top of me. He leans down resting on his elbows and kisses me. Pushing in, my body welcomes the stretch and burn, desiring the long lost sensation. Deep inside our bodies, our feelings emulate the intensity of the act. Our pace picks up in a frenzy of kisses and caresses. Heated bodies move together in sync, out of sync, and everything else that feels good and natural. A bite to my neck, a nibble to his earlobe. We cover each other in panting breaths over skin that becomes slick with passion.

Every thrust elicits sounds from our mouths we can't contain. Guttural. Sensual. Every thrust purposeful and rough, sexy, and caring. Our connection is not casual but filled with an unbridled passion I wasn't aware lay deep beneath the surface.

Pushing his hair back with my hands, I look up at him as a sheen of sweat starts dotting his forehead. His body moves fluidly, his experience showing. I push him over and readjust on top, slipping down slowly. His three gun tattoos wrap around the muscles of his arm and flex when he steadies me on top of him. Our pace slows. I don't want this to end too soon, but my insides urge for more. I close my eyes, willing the darkness behind my lids toward the imploding light I know is buried, longing to be seen.

Fingers rub assuredly, a confidence in the action. I feel. Feel. Feel. My head drops back as his touch drives me closer. I want. Want. Want. I move, rocking on top of him, increasingly selfish in pursuit of my own ecstasy. With a gasp, I catch that elusive sensation that makes me feel Heaven and Hell equally. "Oh God! Cory!"

Everything stops.

Just when I peak, I fall back into reality, well aware of the damage I just caused. I open my eyes, seeking his out. It's not a soft gaze I find but a glare cloaked in hurt and shock. I'm still, afraid to move at all, but the words come tripping out. "I'm sorry. I'm sorry. So sorry."

Then shame fills my racing heart. "Oh my God! What have I done?" I'm swift to my feet as disgust fills my soul. "What have I done?" I mumble again. Cory's face flashes in my head, memories of his laughter ringing in my ears as a torturous reminder. "Shit. Shit. Shit." Not sure what to do, I stand there mortified.

"You wanted this," Dex says, sitting up. His voice sounds as confused as I feel. "You fucking wanted this. You wanted me."

His words are messing with my head as guilt slithers in, drenching me on the inside. How could I betray Cory like this and with Dex, his friend? "Fuck. I've gotta go." I run for my jeans, pulling them on, then drop to my knees to feel for my shirt. I slip it over my head and stand, my thoughts are like broken nerves, the pain of what I've done covering the raw ends like pinpricks of shame. I feel Dex's gaze heavy on my backside as I put my shoes on and run out of the bedroom, slamming the door behind me.

Down the staircase and through the party-goers, I run for the front door, not bothering to shut it or look back this time.

Outside, I stand on the stairs that led me away from his bedroom and the disgrace, hoping I can escape the cramping in my chest. I hate Hollywood and their fucking valets and mansions. Humiliation like this needs a quick escape, but I have to wait for my car to be pulled around. When it is, I jump inside, relieved that I didn't run into anyone I know while waiting. I leave through the gates of the neighborhood and speed home. My hands are shaking, so I hold the wheel tighter.

What would Cory say? I've disrespected his memory. *What will Johnny say? He barely tolerates him since his drug use almost destroyed the band. He would never support me and Dex being together.* Shame coats me. *And Holli? Will she be disgusted that I gave into a physical desire instead of using my head and mourning quietly like I've done for the last six months? Will I be able to face them if they find out? What if Dex tells them?* I'll become one of his many, but this time with a face, a name for them to judge. *Will I be able to face myself? Look in the mirror without feeling disgusted for a lapse in judgment?*

I flip the visor down and open the mirror. The lights are bright, making me squint. When my eyes adjust, mascara is smeared on the left corner. My cheeks are flushed, not from the night or the rash exit, but from sex and lust, desire, and dishonor—everything I had managed to avoid until tonight.

Flipping the mirror back up, my eyes fill with heavy tears. I hope to find physical safety in the distance from him before they fall. But no distance will protect me from betraying the memory of the man I loved so much.

2

ROCHELLE

One month later...

THE PHONE CALL comes just as I return to my car after dropping Neil at preschool. I'm strapping CJ's carrier into the base when the ringer sounds. I double check the straps before answering and climbing into the driver's seat. "Hello?"

Tommy sounds panicked as he asks, "Rochelle, I need a favor. Can you meet me at your house in thirty minutes?"

"What's up? What's wrong?" I can't lie, my heart is thundering in my chest, knowing something is wrong.

"It's Dex. I need you to come with me."

There's no question I'll go because I'd do anything for the guys. I drop CJ off at his grandmother's. Luckily, I had already arranged the visit and I can run my errands tomorrow. I drive back home and spot Tommy's silver Mercedes G-Class parked at the curb. The gate closes behind me and I take my purse from the passenger's seat and walk toward him. I get in the SUV and buckle in. He says, "He's been missing for three days—"

"What? Why am I just hearing about this? Where is he? Is he okay?"

"He's fucked up, Rochelle. Johnny can't know. We just hired the new guys and are talking shows and tours for the first time..." He turns back to the road and I see his hands tighten around the wheel. "...since Cory's death. If Dex blows this, the tour will never happen and the band will be done."

"Damn it, Tommy. Why didn't you tell me before?"

We hit the highway and he's off, way over the speed limit. "I know what happened... between you two. He told me. His head's all messed up... I should have seen this coming."

I stare out the windshield, watching as we pass car after car after truck, staying quiet. I don't want to talk about that night or what happened.

"Rochelle?"

When I turn and look at Tommy, he says, "It's okay. I understand. And I won't tell anyone."

"Thank you," I whisper. Setting my elbow on the door, I tilt my head, resting it against the glass. "Where are we going?"

"Barstow."

I sit straight up. "Barstow? I can't go to Barstow today. I have a meeting in three hours."

"Dex needs us."

Closing my eyes, I exhale, knowing he would do it for me, just like I would do it for any of the guys if they needed me to. "I'll reschedule." I call my part-time assistant and ask her to move the meeting to tomorrow or Wednesday. Then I call Cory's mom to pick up Neil for me after school. When I hang up, I ask, "What's he doing in Barstow?"

"He wasn't clear on the phone when he called. I think he called me by accident."

I'm still in shock over hearing this news. I feel so bad for not knowing, for not noticing. "He's relapsed?"

Tommy hesitates to answer. I only know of two reasons why: one, because he doesn't know or two, because he doesn't want to tell me. I'm thinking it's more the latter. His large fingers turn the dial of the air conditioning up so it gets cooler inside the vehicle, then he replies, "By the way he sounded, my guess would be yes."

"And your gut?"

"Same answer."

"How can I help him?"

"I'm hoping he'll listen to you, so I need your help to either get him home or checked into rehab."

"Why me?" I ask, but I think I know the answer already. My hunch is confirmed when he remains silent. I sigh, letting the burden of the situation be heard. "What is he trying to do to himself? What is he trying to prove?" Tommy doesn't answer because he knows I'm not asking him.

The miles pass as I return emails and phone calls, set more appointments and touch base with Johnny. It's been our thing since Cory died. "So you doing okay?" Johnny asks.

"I'm okay." Fine and well aren't answers either of us can give these days. He sounds better since he and Holli moved to Ohai a few months ago. He's writing music, playing his guitar and moving forward with the band.

My sadness and guilt haven't left my side or my heart. My kids are daily reminders of their father's death. I don't know if I'll ever be enough for them, if I can fill the role of both parents the way they deserve. But I get out of bed and try my damndest every day despite my secret fears.

Johnny says, "I'll drive us to the cemetery tomorrow."

He goes with us sometimes. I like the company. "Okay. Pick us up at 4?"

"See you then."

"Bye." I see a mileage sign just as I look up from the phone. "Ten miles to Barstow."

Tommy says, "Ten miles. Johnny doing okay today?"

"Getting by."

"And you?"

I reply, "Getting by."

Tommy has never been one for forced conversation, which I've come to appreciate over the years. He may not have started with the band back in the day, but he's been with us for eight years, so he is one of us. He's also someone we all can rely on even when it's not band related.

A sand colored motel with blue doors is visible up on the right. When we pull into a parking space, I wonder if it's painted that way or if it used to be white and the surrounding desert colored it naturally. "Which room?" I ask.

"Twenty-two." He leans forward over the steering wheel and points to the top right.

"How do you know?"

"I don't. It's either the girl's age or the room number. We're about to find out."

A sick, sinking feeling fills my stomach and I push open the door and step out. "Great," I reply sarcastically.

Tommy follows me up the side stairs to the second floor. Room twenty-two's door is cracked open. The music is loud and I recognize it as Jane's Addiction's "Summertime Rolls." We glance at each other, take a deep breath, and then he moves in front of me before pushing the door open further. Our eyes struggle to adjust to the darkness of the room after being blinded by the brightness of the desert.

The curtains are drawn on the only window, which resides next to the door. A broken coffee table is in front of the loveseat that has some girl with long brown hair asleep on it. She's in what looks like Dex's T-shirts and by the way it rides up, I can tell nothing else. The bathroom light is on, the door to it closed, the sound of the shower coming from inside. Dex's shoes are on the ground and two empty bottles of Jack Daniels and Fireball are on the floor next to them. White powdery residue is on the nightstand. Dex is passed out on the bed next to it, lying on his back. He's wearing his leather jacket, revealing a shield tattoo on his chest, one that he's become known to show at concerts when he plays. His jeans on with the button fly are wide open. His hair covers his eyes, his signature bandana fallen and knotted tightly around his neck. My heart breaks seeing him broken like this. This is not the man I've know all these years. This is the shell of what remains when someone sells their soul to the devil.

I push down my emotions and rely on logic. Besides immediately wanting to check and see if he's even alive, my second thought is to look for needles. My third, for condoms. No needles are found, but I see three condoms near the trash bin. That relieves me for some reason.

Tommy looks at me and says, "Stay outside the door."

I see the concern in his eyes, so I step back without asking questions. Peeking inside, I watch as Tommy goes to the bed and shakes Dex. Dex doesn't respond, so he calls his name, grabbing his face to look at him. Dex shifts, but doesn't come to. Tommy grabs his phone and turns off the music right when the door to the bathroom opens. I lean back, not knowing who to expect. A female comes out with a towel wrapped around her body and stops when she sees Tommy. As if this is a normal situation, nonchalantly she says, "He's been out like that for a while. Is he okay?"

"How long?" Tommy asks, watching her.

"Two hours maybe. I think he had a seizure poor guy. Jenny and I didn't know what to do. It really freaked us out. I think he just wanted another shot, so we gave it to him. But we need to get back to campus. We have evening classes and a test to study for. Can you drive us back?"

Knowing they won't hurt me, I hurry to Dex's side. I hear the girl asking who I am, but neither of us bothers with her. "Dex? It's me. Can you hear me?" When he doesn't respond, I lean down, resting my cheek to his. He reeks of alcohol and sweat, but I don't care. His cheek is warm and he's alive. While rubbing my hand over his tattooed heart, I whisper into his ear, "Dex, it's Rochelle. Please wake up. Wake up for me, Dex. I'll take you home."

I feel his hand cover mine and his breath against my skin. "Rochelle, beautiful Rochelle." His other arm comes up and wraps around me.

"I'm here, Dex."

The words just murmurs, but I hear him say, "Stay with me."

"I'm here with you. Can you sit up?" I lean back to find his brown eyes dull and bloodshot, so unlike the roguish ones I'm used to. Running my hand over his cheek, I say, "I want to get you out of here. Okay?" He nods, and when I try to move him, I feel every pound of his muscular body. "Help me, Dex."

Tommy snakes an arm under him and says, "Hey man, it's Tommy. We're gonna help you."

Dex nods again, talking seeming like too much of a chore for him.

When he's standing, the girl on the couch wakes up. "Are you our ride?"

"No," I snap. "I'll call a car for you if you promise never to repeat what happened here again." We get Dex to his feet, an arm over each of our shoulders.

Tommy says, "He's able to walk. Get his stuff and let's move him to the car."

"A ride? That's it?" the one girl says, putting her hand on her hip.

Pissed, I glare at her. "You left him here on the bed to die and you expect what exactly?"

"We were just having a good time. He didn't seem that out of it," she protests.

I don't say anything else because I need to control my anger, which I'm struggling to do. With Dex's boots and wallet in hand, I walk out, leaving the girls for Tommy to come back to handle. Catching up to them on the stairs, I help by holding Dex's waist. Dex's arm comes around and he holds me tight. "I've missed you."

"I've missed you too," I say, meaning every word.

We get him into the back seat where he lays down. Tommy runs back upstairs and is gone a few minutes before heading to the motel office. I assume he's paying the bill and for the damage to the room.

As soon as Tommy pulls back onto the highway, Dex puts his forearm over his eyes. I gulp, hearing the pain in his voice, the strain of the death that has destroyed us winning the battle when he says, "Cory was my best friend and I slept with the woman he loved."

Tommy reaches over just as my tears begin to fall and squeezes my shoulder. I'm reminded that everyone grieves differently and Dex might kill himself in the process. Even though it's obvious to us he's hitting bottom, hitting his lowest, the worst stage in the grieving process, I look out over the flat desert and realize my turn is coming.

3

ROCHELLE

It was the harder decision to make, but Tommy and I made it while driving back to LA. Dex had passed out again and we refused to second guess ourselves. It will leak to the press by tomorrow, but we can't worry about that. Dex needs help. If he had died... we're not equipped to give him what he needs right now.

He's not talking to us anymore. Sitting in the backseat, he's staring blankly out the window, quiet for the last hour. Before that, he was talking a mile a minute trying to convince us that what we were about to do was wrong. Empty promises he can't guarantee were being made. Anything he could think of saying to change our minds, he tried. We're holding strong.

My heart starts racing after entering through the large wrought iron gates of the rehab in Santa Barbara. The cobblestone driveway is lined with short pristine grass and flowering bushes. It winds around a large fountain and there's a bench off to the right that overlooks a large ocean vista. With doubts and the possibility of regret seeping in, I glance back to Dex. When he finally turns and looks at me—his own pain and regrets are showing. I'm betraying him, but I can't help but think this is seated in the best of reasoning. I apologize anyway. "I'm sorry."

He looks away from me again and as soon as the car comes to a stop he gets out without hesitation, then slams the car door shut. Tommy sighs, glancing at me before he reluctantly gets out.

When I get out, I overhear Tommy say, "It's only two weeks, man. You need to clean up, clean out. You know the deal with the band. If you're using, you're out."

Dex pushes past him and spits, "Fuck off, Tommy."

He treats me worse. The glare he gives me comes without any words at all.

A woman walks out with a clipboard and a fake smile to greet him. He doesn't look back before the door is slammed shut. From this point on it's up to him.

One and a half years later...

The curtains puff like sails of a ship as the wind slips in through the small crack of the open door. The weather is turning from cool to warm as spring settles in, reminding me that the grass needs to be mowed again. I should call the lawn service in the morning and get them back on a regular schedule.

My mind can't rest despite how much I wish to sleep, so I roll over and grab the journal I've come to rely too much on and begin writing.

Dear Cory,

The night is always the hardest—nightmares plague my sleep. I go to bed hoping for the best, but the best has become the worst.

CLOSING MY EYES, I squeeze my lids tight, hoping to stop the inevitable. But when I release them, the tears I've become too acquainted with are there for their encore—night after night the memories come back.

· · ·

I SEE you in my dreams. I'm transported back to when we were seventeen and I taught you how to play guitar. The way you looked at me, the way you learned the notes by studying my fingers, and when I caught you stealing glances... this perfect moment in our lives has become a nightly haunting for me. In the last two years, my memories have stilted my ability to play guitar without you. My loneliness is most exposed at this dark hour.

I miss you so much. All the time.

XO

SITTING UP, I grab for his pillow beside me and hold it to my nose, inhaling. His scent is gone. It used to be strong and comforted me when he traveled. His smell has left me, just like he did. So I throw the pillow across the room.

The curtains blow again, so I get up and slam the door shut before stepping over the pillow and crawling back in bed. The tightening in my chest starts to ease; the heartache of losing my soulmate lessens as I begin to drift off.

"I'M TIRED, Neil. Can you please have some cereal this morning instead?" I look over at my seven-year-old and my heart momentarily stops altogether. At least once a day this happens. Neil has my eye coloring and olive skin, but his hair and the way he smiles is just like Cory. I turn back to the counter quickly before I get lost, staring at him 'again' as he puts it. He doesn't even have to beg, these kids own me. "Fine, I'll make you scrambled eggs."

"Thanks, Mom," he replies, a drumstick beating against the top of his thigh.

A sleepy little guy leans his head against my leg, one of Cory's T-shirts in hand. It's become a security blanket for him. With my free hand, I rub the top of his light brown hair, and say, "Good morning, buddy."

My three-year-old looks up and says, "Morning." His blue eyes flash with an inner happiness.

"Are you hungry, CJ? I'm making eggs."

He nods as he makes his way to the table. I finish the morning routine and take them to their schools. After drop-off, I head back home and shower. Working for the band allows me flexibility in time management and attire, so I pull on jeans, a cream colored blouse, and flats before heading out with the contracts I printed off last night.

Twenty-minutes later, I knock on the door. Dex answers, no greeting. He just sways his arm in front of him allowing me entrance. With little eye contact, I walk past him, and say, "I see the month on the road hasn't sullied your sparkling personality."

"It's before noon," he replies with an annoyed sigh. "It better be fucking good."

We've never quite recovered from that night. He has no patience for me, but I deserve that. Looking back, I wish I could change things, so many things.

I walk to the kitchen and sit down on a barstool. This is what we do—we can be around each other, but we tend to pretend the other isn't there—parallel universes. When it's just the two of us, like it is now, that's impossible to do. The coffee machine is started and he stares at the mug. I'm sure to keep from looking at me. "What brings you by, Rochelle?" He glances my way briefly before returning his gaze to the brewing coffee again.

"I need you to sign off on these contracts. The other guys all signed them last week when you were in Toronto. Why didn't you? You don't like the deal?"

"I don't understand the deal—"

"Oh. No problem. I can explain. So the video game characters will be modeled—"

He turns suddenly, his glare burning into me. "I understand that part. What I don't get is when we became *that* band."

"What band?"

"The one that sells out. The one that does video games and deodorant ads."

Tilting my head, with a smirk I say, "You've never been offered a deodorant ad."

"Fuck that! You know what I mean." He walks to the large window that overlooks the patio and pool. "When did it stop being about the music?"

"It's still about the music, Dex. The band is changing, growing, evolving. There's a vision we all have that will set you guys up for life. So if one day you develop carpal tunnel and can't play or Johnny has throat issues and can't sing, you'll not worry about money. This is about The Resistance, the brand."

"When you walked into that club on Sunset, you didn't ask me if I was interested in building a brand." With his back to me, he says, "You asked me if I would play drums for a band you put together that had a gig down on Ventura in some dive pizza parlor." He turns around with his arms crossed over his chest. "Did I go?"

I eye him, wondering where this is going. "You did."

"You're damn right I did. I took my sticks at intermission and left a paying gig to go meet your boys. Do you know why I did that?"

"No. Why?"

"Because I was better than a cover band drummer on a Tuesday night in Hollywood, even with the pay."

I nod. I'm following his train of thought as he drives his point home.

"So stop treating me like I am. We're The motherfucking Resistance and we're better than this year's video game simulation that followed some cheesy, hair-band from the 80's in last year's edition."

I gather my papers and slip off the stool. As I start to leave, he grabs my wrist as I pass, and I stop, my breath caught in my throat just from his touch. His grip loosens, and I try to steady my voice when I say, "I got the message. I'll talk to the guys, but majority rules. You agreed to that when you left that other band."

He releases my wrist and my skin is left bare, his touch feeling better than I remember.

I open the door, and step out, but stop. Looking over my shoulder, I add, "I like the shorter hair on you. You look good." Closing the door behind me, I don't wait for a response. The boy I convinced to leave a dead-end band on Sunset way back then has turned into a man and a force to be reckoned with—mentally and physically. Memories of our night together before I screwed up come flashing back, but the humiliation of my mistake overtakes the warmth I'm feeling.

I should have gone with my gut. I convinced myself that we were wrong before I even gave the alternative a chance. My instincts told me to stay with him despite my mistake of calling him Cory. My head said to run. My more logical side seems to always get in the way.

"Wait up, Rochelle." I hear him behind me.

When I look back, he's leaning against the door opening, his eyes set on me. Even at rest, his muscles are defined. His arms carved from strength and power. Despite being hidden under the cotton of his T-shirt, his abs tease me as I remember how I once licked them. "What's up?" I turn the focus back on business, trying to sound indifferent.

"It's been a long time, a couple months since I saw you." He pauses. "It's good to see you again."

"Thanks. It's good to be seen again," I joke, trying to cover my nervous excitement.

He nods, a small smile tugging at the corners of his mouth as he stands upright. "You should come to the show in New York. The band always has fun there."

I open my car door and step up on the running board, looking at him over the top of my SUV. "Yeah, I'll give it some thought."

"Yeah, okay."

With a small smile of my own, I give a little wave. "See ya around."

I start to step into the vehicle, but I stop when I hear him say, "See ya around. Oh, and Rochelle?"

Popping back up, I answer, "Yes?"

"You look good, too."

My smile isn't little anymore. It's full on ridiculous. "Thanks."

If I wasn't so aware of every nerve in my body and beat of my heart when I get inside the Escalade, I might have missed how my heart just leaped.

While pulling out of Dex's gated community, I call Johnny. It's only ten-thirty, so I'm not surprised he doesn't answer. I leave a message, warning him that Dex may not sign and I might just agree with him.

I call my nanny, Beth, and let her know that she'll need to pick up the boys today. With all the thoughts crowding my head, I need therapy. So I call one of my best friends, Lara, to meet me. I met her in yoga years before it became trendy. We quit after two weeks, preferring to cocktail together rather than work out. We've been great friends ever since. "Shopping?" I ask, when she answers.

"Beverly Center, Melrose, or the boutiques down near the beach."

Today is about shopping for me, so I reply, "Suru on Melrose?"

"Suru. For sure. They just got in their new collection."

"I'll see you there in twenty."

"It will take me thirty."

"Cool." We disconnect, and I smile, excited to see her. She's always up to go out and I like that.

Just over an hour later, I'm standing near the far wall of Suru in front of newly altered frocks, and I say, "I think I like Dex." I peek over at her.

Her head remains down, focused on finding her size in a stack of jeans. "I like him too. He's always been cool. Haven't seen him in a while."

"He got his hair cut."

She looks up, so I look down. "Really? I liked the medium length on him. He could pull it off."

"It's shorter. Short now."

When I look up again, she's staring at me. "Why are we having a full-blown conversation about Dex's hair?"

I shrug it off. "No reason. I just saw him this morning about some contracts. Just making chitchat."

"Ooookaay," she replies like I'm crazy before returning her attention to the clothes in front of her. "The boys are good?"

"They're great. Dating much?"

"Too much. It sucks. Be glad you've decided to stay single."

My hand stops on a blue dress. "I didn't decide to stay single."

"Oh no, I didn't mean it like that. I just meant that since... well, you know his death—"

"You can say his name. Cory."

There's an awkward pause that I would rather avoid. I'm glad she doesn't leave it to build. "Since Cory's death, you've remained unattached. You're strong like that."

"We're all tested in life. I just got tested in the worst of ways. Anyway, I haven't chosen to stay single. I just haven't dated."

"Do you think you're ready?"

"I'm not sure. How will I know?"

"Maybe if you start getting that feeling, the tingly one deep inside when you meet someone." She comes over and puts her hand on my shoulder. "If you are ready, I'll help anyway I can. If you're not, that's fine too. You know what's best for you."

"Thanks. I'm just..." I sigh. "I don't know what I want."

She nods toward the door. "Come on. Let's cut the shopping short and get a drink."

WHILE SITTING at the café inside Fred Segal, I smile. "We should have just started here."

She laughs. "I thought you actually wanted to go shopping. Next time just say you want a drink."

We order salads and a bottle of white wine before sitting back and easing into talk of our lives. After taking two sips, her hands go into the air, and she continues the story she's been retelling, "So I told them, 'Honey, the 90's have to leave before they can make a come-back.' I got the job and she burned the valances that afternoon."

"Beverly Hills is a lot different from Hollywood style-wise."

Lara is an interior decorator and has a huge celebrity clientele. I've watched her grow from working out of her spare bedroom to buying a large house with an entire floor dedicated to her business and five employees. She's very animated when she talks, passionate about what she does. "Totally. In Hollywood, they like clean and modern. The celebrities I've worked for all give me carte blanche. They're adventurous. Not so much in Beverly Hills. This new project will be fun though, something different for me to tackle."

"Let's toast to that. To your new project."

Our glasses clink right as our salads are served.

She smothers the lettuce in dressing, very un-L.A. like, and asks, "I have a job in New York next week. Want to come with me. We can move our 'shopping' to the other coast."

Dex's words replay in my mind. "You're the second one to mention going to New York next week."

"Oh really? Who was the other?"

"Dex. They're playing there. He said I should come."

Dragging her fork through the vegetables on her plate, she lowers her gaze. "Interesting."

"What's interesting?"

"Oh nothing." Her eyebrows go up and her eyes go wide, her expression hopeful. "So is that a yes?"

"It might be fun. Maybe I can get Cory's mom, Janice, to watch the boys for a few days. They'd love that. She spoils them rotten."

"That's what Grandma's are supposed to do."

"Yeah, we're lucky to have her living so close by."

"So that settles it. They get Grammie and we paint the Big Apple red. Yay! It will be awesome," she adds with another tap of her glass against mine.

4

ROCHELLE

MY THOUGHTS WANDER to Dex a lot over the next few days, but why? It's Dex, after all. He sleeps with everyone he can and has a temper to rival the titans. He smokes too much and drinks heavily. He lives off junk food and is moody. He swears too much but has a wicked sense of humor. His new haircut emphasizes a strong jaw that sometimes looks a little too sexy when it has a day or two's growth on it. His eyes are the most unique color, so close to caramel, but more soulful. Wait...

What? Why am I thinking of him? When did I start thinking of him? Or like the little sweet nothings we've been sharing? This is something that's crept up on me when I wasn't looking.

I drop my head to the mattress and cover myself under the pillow. No. I refuse to think of him that way. But I can't help it. Somehow over the last week, things have changed, shifted into something different, something new, something exciting.

And then the tingles began...

I know what it is, recognizing the feeling that's sneaking in without my permission. And now I wonder if these small gestures and occurrences aren't so random. I felt safe in his arms. The warmth between us is new, but I felt safe and wanted. It's the *wanted* that scares me most. Liking the thought that Dex might want me leaves me restless and I roll over, hiding beneath the covers

---

DEAR CORY,

It never bothered me before, but now I hate flying. My therapist... I know. I know. Yes, I have a therapist. I think that officially makes me an Angeleno now. Anyway, she once told me that it was a natural fear since you died in a plane crash. But she also gave me the statistics of car crashes, death by mosquitoes, and lightning to help put it in perspective. Not sure if it worked since I shudder just thinking about mosquitoes and hide under my covers during storms. I'm in my car too much and have a false sense of safety there.

I have a flight to see the band in NYC tomorrow, so I should get some sleep. I miss you.

XO.

MY HANDS ARE SWEATING and my knee is bouncing, anxiety getting the best of me. I wish I had something to take to calm me, but for now, the shot of whiskey will have to do. Staring out the window, I try to think of happy things like my kids, the beautiful weather California has been having, and try not think about plane crashes, mosquitoes, or cars. Adjusting my neck pillow, I move to lean back in my chair and turn up my music. I close my eyes and lose myself in the music.

Once I arrive at the hotel, the same one where the guys are staying, I shut the door to my room and flop back on the bed. Not even five minutes later, a light knock on the door makes me sit up and go. Expecting the bellhop, I open the door wide, then walk back inside, signaling for him to come in. "Just put the suitcases there please."

"Sorry, no luggage. Just a shit ton of baggage."

Surprised, I turn back to find Dex standing in the middle of the doorway. I quirk a grin and reply, "Well, get your ass and all your baggage in here anyway."

As he walks by, he says, "I wanted to see how you're doing?" I'm sure my face is showing my confusion, his unexpected concern taking me by surprise. He laughs. "I know. I know. I have this tough exterior, but believe it or not, I have a heart buried deep down in here somewhere. I just haven't felt it in a while."

"Well, I hope you do soon because I'd hate to think of you going through life without a heartbeat."

"A lifeline."

I nod.

He asks, "So how are you?"

"I'm good."

His eyes lock with mine, holding me steady just through a look. "No, how are you really?"

Tilting my head, I remark, "I appreciate it, but I'm not sure where all the concern is coming from."

"Just a friend checking on a friend."

I sit in a chair by the window and start swiveling back and forth. "Are we friends?"

"Are we not?" With his eyebrows up, he seems genuinely surprised.

"Sometimes, I'm not sure."

"We're friends, Rochelle. I'm sorry if I gave the impression we weren't."

With all of this apologizing going on, I take a chance. "I'm sorry for the past stuff."

"You don't have to be."

"I am though." This is the most we've ever broached the topic and the whole conversation catches me off-guard. I used to have planned rebuttals, but today, with our defenses down, I don't worry about those and just go with it.

He looks around as if searching for an escape in case he needs one, but it's just us here in this hotel room with one door in and the same door out. No other escapes, not even the luxury of an interruption.

"I wanted to know if you wanted to go out after the show... with the band?"

"Yeah, that will be fun. My friend Lara will be with me tonight."

"Cool." He nervously shoves his hands in his pockets like a seventeen-year-old. The vulnerability on his face is quite charming. "I should go."

"I appreciate the welcome wagon."

"No problem," he says with a short chuckle. "I'll catch ya later."

"At the show. Break a leg."

"I'm not superstitious."

"I am," I reply.

"Good to know." He opens the door and the bellhop is standing there with his hand raised as if he was about to knock. Handing the kid some money as he passes, Dex says, "That's for her."

"Thank you, Sir."

As the bellhop carries my case inside the room, I'm left standing there baffled by what just happened. Dex has always been hard to figure out, but this time, he's near impossible.

THE NIGHT STARTED off innocent enough. Lara and I had dinner and drinks, then headed to see The Resistance. In the past, New Yorkers have always been crazy and fun at their shows. I assume they won't disappoint tonight.

Feeling sexy in my new black jeans and tank top, I decided my high-heeled knee boots, silver and black necklaces would complement. The outfit is a departure from my normal California style, which tends to be very laidback and more free-flowing with some Mom mixed in. Tonight's theme is sex appeal and rock n'roll. Lara was influential in the ensemble.

She looks amazing—effortless, but always at the edge of fashion.

Together, we are both beauty *and* brains. We learned a long time ago that we can be sexy without coming off like bimbos.

Clutching her purse under her arm, she glances my way. "So I've been thinking about our conversation last week. Maybe it's time for you to start dating again."

There's a quiet between us as we both take that in. Finally, I say, "And why do you think that?"

"Seems like you might be more ready than you think."

I shrug. "I dunno. I don't think about it much."

"Tonight seems like a good time to start."

"Start what? Thinking about it or dating?"

She shrugs this time. "Maybe both."

With a laugh, I say, "I can tell you're gonna be trouble with a capital T tonight."

"Is there any other way to be?"

Shaking my head, I laugh again. I love her spirit and energy too much to deny her the possibility of the fun in store for us. I also feel my more adventurous side revealing itself. It feels good to let loose. It's been too long and the rush of adrenaline hypes me up after so many years. Taking her hand, I pull her into the massive crowd toward the doors.

When we enter, I realize it's also been forever since I've been on this side of a concert. The T-shirts, buttons, posters, and passion displayed for the band makes me smile. But I'm soon tugged to the left by Lara when she spots a bar. "Shot time."

While we wait in line, I ask, "You're gonna get me wasted, aren't you?"

"If my plan works."

"Fine. First round is on me." I bump her hip with mine. "If we're gonna do it, we're gonna go big."

After two shots and a Jack and Coke to-go, we make our way backstage, flashing our badges when necessary. I leave the guys alone, not wanting to interrupt their pre-performance routine. I lead her down to the VIP area off to the side of the crowd next to the media. "This is great," she says, squeezing in next to me.

The anticipation builds just like it always did when I used to come to their shows. I would watch Cory, my eyes fixed on him. Tonight I stare at the spot where he used to stand to start the show, but he's not there. I take the other shot, wanting to drown out the memories and live in the here and now. The music being piped in overhead stops and the arena goes black. My heart starts thundering in my chest from excitement. This is how The Resistance has started every show since the first tour, and for tradition, they still do. With one loud hit on the drums, the entire place goes quiet. Dex is at his kit, doing a countdown even though the arena lies trapped in darkness. I smile.

I can't see, but I know Kaz and Derrick should be in place. Dex kicks into the opening solo and we start screaming along with everyone else. Like I've seen so many times before, a spotlight hits Johnny center stage, his guitar hanging upside down on his back, his hands gripping the microphone in such a seductive way, the way that made him the star he is.

His voice carries over the screams. The girls next to me start to cry and the guys holler. Johnny's pitch is flawless, something that's always come so easily for him. Dex is in the background—sunglasses on, no headband anymore like he used to wear when his hair was long, ripped shirt where the sleeves used to be, and a rhythm that no other drummer on the music scene can rival. I close my eyes, the alcohol and song melding perfectly together. For a minute, I forget all that's happened in the last three years. For a moment in time, I feel, just like I used to feel when I played guitar and wrote songs with the guys. When I open my eyes, a wave of emotion takes hold and I finish the drink in my hands, dropping the plastic cup to the floor and throw my arms in the air, letting the melody wash through me, over me, taking me whole.

The only thing more powerful than music is love. The music will have to be enough for now.

Five songs in and the audience is much drunker and less aware of their bodies. Lara and I follow as the vibe of the night carries us. I spin, dancing my ass off, and embracing the freedom. Before the band breaks for the encore, we sneak backstage again and make a cocktail. The guys have a full bar setup back here. They don't drink before or during the shows anymore, but after, I know they like to have the option. With fresh drinks in hand, we go to the dressing room and plop down on the couch together. It only takes one look in each other's direction and we start giggling. "You're a mess," I tease.

Poking me in the arm, she says, "Look who's talking."

The door swings open and the guys come in one-by-one. Dex smiles when he sees me—cocky and annoyingly sexy. The rest of them greet us before retreating to different parts of the room. Johnny makes a call. Kaz goes into the bathroom, and Derrick hops up on the counter, his back against the mirror, and starts playing on his phone.

Dex sits next to me, a bottle of soda in his hands. He takes a long swig, his eyes steady on me and asks, "Are you drunk?"

Leaning my head back, I reply, "A little."

"Don't get wasted... yet. We're going out later." He stands up and heads for the door. But he stops to look in the mirror and run his hands through his hair first. He puts his sunglasses back on and leaves with a bodyguard in tow.

I'm left there with my mouth hanging open and very much looking forward to later.

Derrick gets up, looking annoyed. "Damn Kaz, hogging the toilet." He walks out. I guess in search of another bathroom.

Johnny hangs up, then grabs a water from the fridge. "It's a good crowd tonight. Holliday says hi."

"New York," I reply as if that's the only answer needed. "Tell her hi."

"I'm glad you flew out, Ro. It's good to have you back on the road again."

"Thanks."

When he leaves, I turn to Lara. "You still up for going out?"

"Umm. Have you met me?"

"Silly question. What was I thinking?" I laugh, then ask, "Where exactly are we going out tonight? Any idea?"

"Hopefully not to jail."

"So that's our goal? Just to stay out of trouble?"

"No one said anything about trouble. Trouble is definitely still on the agenda."

IT'S BEEN a long time since I've hung out with the band in public. My mind has blocked the chaos that came along with it. But I'm quickly reminded when we get out of the SUV and have to walk one block up to a private restaurant and bar. Derrick and Kaz went to party across town with some friends of theirs. Johnny went to the hotel. Tommy and Lara lead the way inside while Dex walks next to me. Our hands accidentally touch a couple of times and I notice each one, wanting more. My desire is fulfilled in a different way when we go inside the bar. His hand presses lightly against my lower back, guiding me in, and making me wonder if he's ever done that to me in the past. I don't think he has because that one caring gesture is felt throughout my entire body. I think I would remember this sensation. Once inside, the crowd is subdued, calm is being restored as the adrenaline starts wearing off. So does the booze, so I tell Dex, "I'm ready for a drink."

With a smile that reaches his eyes, he says, "I'm ready for a few myself. Our table's over here."

The music is exotic—seductive, the lights dim, and the crowd stylish. I recognize a few celebrities, some I've met before—one is an actor, Chad Spears, who hit it big in the last year and hit on me at an after-party of an awards show a couple years back. He was young and cute then. He's more man and more handsome these days. Sitting on a white leather couch, he has his arm draped over a woman who is either a model or a wannabe actress. Chad's gaze meets mine and a wry grin appears. With a nod, we acknowledge each other just as Dex's hand slips to my side, redirecting me to the corner where our booth is located.

We settle in and order drinks. Tommy jokes about a screw up backstage while Dex eyes me. "You look good tonight."

"Good?" I tease with a nudge to his side, liking the fact that he's looking at me.

"Better than good. Hot."

I tap my head lightly to his shoulder. "Aww, thank you. You look go—"

A smooth voice interrupts us, "Hey, Rochelle." I know it's Chad before I even look up. Glancing past him to the VIP table he was recently occupying, I notice the girl is gone. "Good to see you."

"Hi," I reply just as our drinks are delivered.

"Chad," Dex says with a harsh emphasis on the name.

"Interesting to see you here... in a bar, Dexter. How's post-rehab working out for you?" Chad eyes Dex's drink insinuating everything.

Dex is calm considering the insult, and says, "I don't do drugs anymore, so it's working out just peachy." Dex is about to say something else, but bites his bottom lip as he looks away. Picking up his glass, he drinks like he's got a point to prove.

Chad bumps his leg against mine, making me look back up. He straightens his suit jacket and puts a smile on for me. "We should catch up. Can I buy you a drink?" I start to say no, but he cuts me off. "Just one. Please."

He holds his hand out for me. Feeling it would be rude not to, I take it. Dex grabs me by the belt loop and stops me. "Stay."

"Just one drink," Chad interjects. "Relax, I'm not gonna steal your date."

"Stay." There's a plea in Dex's eyes that makes me start to pull my hand back from Chad, but Chad tightens his grip and pulls me to my feet.

"Just one drink," he says. I can tell he's trying to charm me. "He'll be okay without you. He gets plenty of company. I want a little time with you."

"I made plans with my friends tonight. It would be rude if I left."

"Maybe later then."

"Yeah, maybe later," I reply and sit back down.

As he walks away, Dex's hand covers my knee. "Stay away from him. He's an asshole."

"That was uncomfortable. What's the history between you two?"

Dex sits back and looks over his shoulder at Chad across the room. "We went to high school together."

"You did?"

"Yeah. He was an asshole then, too."

"Let me guess. Star quarterback, dated all the hot girls, Class President?"

He chuckles. "Something like that."

"Tell me about you," I say. "Give me all the dirty details of when you were younger."

"The past doesn't matter, Rochelle. Only tonight."

His words and his eyes, the way they've latched onto mine, possession taking hold, I'm shocked I'm still upright. My body is flooded with want for him and I quickly reach for my drink to cool myself down. I close my eyes and sip. When I open them, I find myself gravitating even closer to him, pressed to his side. I whisper, "You can't say things like that to me, Dex."

His hand warms my leg and he leans in until I feel his words cover my skin. "Why not?"

Just as I'm about to answer with that there is no reason or maybe with a kiss, we're interrupted by a group of women. "You're with The Resistance. Can we have your autograph and a picture?"

She shoves a napkin and a pen in front of him. As he scribbles his name, my gaze meets Lara's across the table and our silent conversation begins. Her lips purse and her eyebrows are raised. She signals toward Dex with a nod, questioning.

He's hot and I don't know, I guess I like his attention. I like him. I say all that through a guilty smile and a playful shrug.

Looking at Tommy, she leans in and tells him something. He jumps and sits on top of the booth. "You need another?" He asks me from across the table.

"Yes. Thanks."

Slipping out of the booth, he leans in when he passes and says, "You guys be careful. Okay? You know what happened last time."

I'm not sure if he's giving me advice or warning me. I know he cares about both of us and his concern is showing tonight. Understandable worry since he's had to watch Dex and I flirt so much tonight.

Suddenly I have a bare midriff with a temporary tattoo of gold hearts circling her belly button pressing against my shoulder as one of the girls pushes in. She's trying to get closer to Dex... as if I'm not even here. When I turn, my head jerks back. I get more than an eyeful of breasts because of her low cut shirt. I lean closer to Dex to get away from her, but she presses in even more.

Jealousy wells up inside and I shake my head, trying to rid myself of it. It's ridiculous I feel anything remotely close to that emotion when it comes to him. This is Dex. He's a free man. Our flirtations were harmless, just hanging out like we have for years. Then I realize we haven't really hung out like this before. Sure, we've partied many times in the same group of friends and I've gone out a million times with the band, but this is different. This is me hanging out with Dex specifically... and Lara and Tommy, of course, but I know deep down I wanted to spend time with Dex.

Lara taps my shoulder. "Let's go to the bathroom."

We slip out of the booth and with the girl vying for Dex's attention, I'm not even sure he notices we're leaving, which bothers me. *Ugh.* I follow Lara to the restroom where girls line the hallway, waiting impatiently.

"What's going on?" she asks. "You seem upset."

I lie. "I'm not upset."

She looks at me and then bursts out laughing. "So that girl hanging on Dex's every breath doesn't bother you at all?"

Tweaking my lips to the side, I say, "Nope."

We move up a few spots in line. "Okay, keep telling yourself that. Maybe you'll start to believe it."

"I'm not lying to myself. Dex is Dex. I've known him for years and he's definitely not someone I should get involved with."

She stands on her tiptoes and looks ahead. Only two more people until we're at the front of the line. When she spins around, she says, "Look, you mention him all faux-casual while shopping the other day. Now we're here with him tonight. I saw how you watched him during the show and how he looked at you backstage. If you guys aren't attracted to each other, then I have no idea what's going on. But if you ask me, you have feelings for him. I know you feel guilty for having them, but your heart doesn't feel guilt. That's all in your head. You aren't doing anything wrong. If anything, you're doing what's right."

"So follow my heart?"

Shrugging, she says, "Beats letting the guilt win."

The line moves and my boldness peaks. "You're right. I may regret this in the morning, but I'm ready to see if there's more between us."

"He's also damn sexy. You were right. That haircut is making him even more irresistible."

When we walk out of the bathroom, I'm feeling determined. The only thing that holds me back, stopping me in my tracks is the girl who has slid into the booth next to him taking my spot. She's so close with her arm around the back of him, and I detour, letting Lara return without me. I stop behind a column and peek back, not spying, just checking to see if it's safe to return. Lara's looking for me and Dex downs his drink.

"Couldn't hide his stripes for long." Chad is next to me, both of us watching Dex from afar. "Dex may not be snorting his fortune anymore, but he's still the same guy, Rochelle."

"Not now, Chad," I say, starting to walk away.

He stops me, by taking my hand in his. "Hey, I know you've had a hard time the last few years, but Dex isn't the answer. He's the problem. You deserve better—"

Rolling my eyes, I retort, "You mean someone like you?"

He laughs. "I'm not perfect, but at least you know what you're getting with me."

His arrogance is getting on my nerves, but his cockiness still fascinates me equally. "And what is that exactly?"

Rubbing his chest with pride, he says, "The rumors are true."

"The rumors? And which rumors would those be?"

"I'm the best fuck in Hollywood—"

"What did you just say, Spears?" Dex startles us, his body hard against my back, his breathing jagged.

Chad stands, his ego making him brave. "Fuck off, Caggiano. Go back to your whores and hookers. The grown-ups are trying to have a conversation here."

"You've always been such a fucking prick, but now you're just a sad asshole too."

"This sad asshole gets more pussy than you can dream of."

Dex looks at me and if I'm not mistaken, I see disappointment residing there. "C'mon, Rochelle. I'm ready to leave."

Taking my own stance on the matter, I say, "Maybe I'm not."

His eyes narrow on me, puzzled. "You want to stay here with him?"

"Beats being the third wheel over there."

My words shake him, taking him aback like a slap across the face. He leans down, eye-to-eye with me. "You could never be a third wheel. Not to me." My breath catches from his intensity and he adds, "Do you understand me?"

"Yes," I reply, believing the truth I see in his eyes.

"I will always treat you how you deserve." With promises swirling around us, Chad and the other girl are forgotten and our own world seems to form. "I want you to come with me," Dex says, sincerity on his face and heard in his words.

I take his hand and we leave together not knowing where this will lead to, but knowing that right now, tonight, this is right.

5

———————

ROCHELLE

DEX PUTS two fingers in his mouth and blows, hailing a cab.

"You sure are good at that considering you're a Cali kid," I say, giving him a smile. The way his hand is possessively around mine suddenly feels like we're more than friends. And I like it.

"I've spent enough time in the city, enough to learn how to get a cab when I need one," he says.

The cab pulls up, the door opens, and we climb inside. "The Bowery," he tells the driver as he sits back. Our hands drop to the space between us.

"Why did you want to leave, Dex?"

He looks at me with all the confidence in the world backing him. "Because I want to be alone with you." He nods as if that's all the response needed, and suddenly it is. It's good enough.

When we arrive, we don't talk or hold hands. I'm sure we don't even seem like we're together as we walk through the lobby of the hotel and take the elevator up. Trying to appear normal to the outside world, like things aren't about to get heated in a sexual way is harder than it seems. I try to avoid eye contact but we catch each other's in the trim of the door. "Where are we going?" I ask, whispering though we're alone.

"My room."

"Why?" I ask to be clear.

"I already told you. I want to be alone with you."

"Why?"

A smirk appears. "Good question."

The elevator doors open and he walks out without further explanation. Reaching back in, he takes my hand again and pulls me out of the vestibule. "Come with me."

It's not like I'm going to say no or anything, but still... *Why?* He holds the hotel room door wide, letting me enter. Looking around, it looks very similar to my room, but larger. The door slams shut and I'm spun around. My face is taken between his hands as his lips meet mine. Two beats pass before I close my eyes, relaxing under his touch, and return the kiss.

"I want you," he whispers. "All of you this time."

"I'm yours. With you, Dex," I reply between kisses and caught breaths.

His hips press against me as my body finds purchase against the wall. Hands move with speed and diligence, finding the backside of my bra as warm breath covers my skin and his lips cover my neck. I slide my fingers up his back and into his hair, holding him there as my body squirms from his touch.

Just when I think we might have sex against this wall, a female voice scares us in the dark. "I wanted to surprise you... guess I'm the one who's surprised."

"What the fuck?" Dex is in front of me, his hand on my hip, holding me protectively behind him.

The lamp on the nightstand is turned on and a woman I recognize not only as one of Dex's ex-girlfriends, but also as a popular lingerie model, stands next to the bed. I've never met her before, but saw the tabloid stories. She's dressed in a red lace bra and matching g-string, and her hair rivals Bridgette Bardot's sex kitten do. I try to swallow down the fact that she makes me look like I just got rescued after being stranded on an island for six months with my mismatched underwear and my messy hair.

With her hands on her hips, she looks offended by our intrusion. "Dex? Who is she?" Her accent is thick—Eastern European, I think.

"How'd you get in here, Alexia?" he asks. His tone firm but tinged with an authority that makes me take a step back, closer to the door.

She points at me while looking over his shoulder, making me feel short and unattractive compared to the supermodel standing before me. I'm usually in jeans and my hair is messy most days. She wears skin-tight dresses and her locks always look professionally styled. "I'm here," she says with a stamp of her high heel. "She can go now."

I take another step toward the door. "I'm gonna leave."

"No," he says with authority, turning to face me. "She's leaving." His expression is stern, leaving no room to argue.

I need to escape this fiasco though. "I want to," I add with a little less strength.

"I don't want you to." He lowers his voice and says, "Stay, Rochelle. I want you to stay with me." He reaches for my hand, but when we hear *her* demand his attention, he looks back and I reach for the door.

"Dex!" We turn to see her arms crossed over her chest and a look of determination on her face. "You told me to come here, so I'm here."

"That was when we were together. We've been broken up for months. So I want you out, Alexia. I want you to get the fuck out right now." When he turns back to me, his tone softens again. "I'll come to your room after I settle this."

With three quick nods, I leave the room. The heavy door shuts behind me and I remain leaning against it for support while I right my senses. Dropping my head back, I close my eyes. "Damn. Damn. Damn. Damn. Damn." Then I push off the wood and head down the hall to my room.

Once inside, I lock the bolt and flip the safety slider over. Now I'm pissed. I can't compete with a supermodel. These are the women he's dated... dates. Not a five-foot-three mom of two young sons who eats salad for lunch six days a week to keep most of the cellulite at bay. I flip on the bathroom light and lean forward. My brown hair is in disarray, the colors of summer not yet affecting it. My skin is more pale than olive these days and my eyeliner is smeared from the gropes in the dark. The alcohol sloshes around in my stomach, rattling my thoughts and self-esteem, or maybe it was the glamazon lying across his bed in nothing but lingerie like a gift being presented to Dex that has me shaken.

There's a soft knock on the door and I look down, trying to collect my thoughts back together. With a deep breath, I turn and go to open it. I unlock the bolt but leave the slider in place. Three inches of visual is all I'm allowing in the state I'm in. The offense is caught in his expression. The subtle message that he knows this is going nowhere is now obvious.

"Hey, what's going on?" he asks, keeping his voice low.

"I'm gonna go to bed."

"What about we try this again?"

I shake my head, looking away from him. "I'm tired." My heart pounds but I know what's best for me.

"Roch—"

"No, it's too much. It's... it's just not meant to be."

"Bullshit. You're scared."

I don't deny that. I can't. I am scared. Looking at him, I try to hold the eye contact that will tell him I'm strong, not weak, how I really feel inside. "I had a good time, but I'm tired. I think it's best if we both just go to bed. Goodnight, Dex."

I start to shut the door, but his palm goes flat against the thick wood, causing a loud thud. "No, don't do this. I don't know how she got in. But she wasn't there because I wanted her there. Don't let this ruin something good," he says, his free hand signaling between us.

After a deep sigh, all reality hits, and I respond, "She can't ruin what's not there. We're an illusion that's never supposed to be real."

"Don't do this, Rochelle. Please." I see the desperation in his eyes, a panic and sadness. Maybe disappointment in me. "You're convincing yourself that I'm the bad guy, that I don't care, and you know that's lies, lies you're telling yourself to avoid anything that might actually be real."

Wanting this door closed. Wanting the emotions welled up like a fist lingering in my chest to subside. Wanting the tears to stay at bay, I say what I shouldn't to make it all go away. "I don't have to convince myself that you're the bad guy. You do a fine job of that all on your own." With my weight behind me, I slam the door shut, knowing what I said is wrong and unwarranted, knowing that all the good strides he's made over the years to clean up his life—I just took that away in that one line, in a sad attempt to protect my heart. Because no matter what he says to me today, he'll break my heart tomorrow. *That* I do know.

MY HEAD IS POUNDING from dehydration and not enough food. I break into the mini-bar to get a bottle of water. After fishing two ibuprofen from my purse, I swallow them and lay back down. With my forearm draped over my eyes, I try to sleep again. It's not working. Tonight was so good... then it wasn't. Damn supermodel in matching lingerie exes. There is nothing wrong with a little cotton every now and again.

Rolling to my side, I try my hardest to block out my confrontation with Dex and what almost was. When that doesn't work, I turn on the TV and watch infomercials until the sun starts to rise. Then I get up and get dressed. After washing my face, I pull my hair back before heading downstairs and outside. Two blocks down and one street over, I find a Starbucks.

I retrieve my coffee when my name is called and find a chair in the corner near the window. With my back to the line that's forming, I drop my head into my hands. *What am I doing here?* I don't have the luxury of being irresponsible. I have children who rely on me to be the exact opposite.

"Stop beating yourself up."

With my back to him, I sigh, not sure how I feel about the intrusion into my head.

"Can I join you?" Dex asks.

Per usual, my heart reacts to the sound of his voice. I slowly look up and nod, giving in. "Why are you up so early?"

He sits across from me, our knees bumping under the tiny round table. "I don't think I actually went to sleep." Disappointment settles on my face, but he's quick to correct my assumption. "I was alone all night."

"I'm sorry."

"Don't be. If I couldn't be with you, I didn't want to be with anyone else." He leans forward, pushing his coffee to the side, and whispers, "We weren't doing anything wrong. Rochelle, you're a widow, but that doesn't take away the fact that you're young, you have needs. I'm sure you don't want to spend the rest of your life alone."

Sitting up straight, this topic feels heavy for seven-thirty in the morning. "My needs come second to my kids and I don't think my kids need the disruption right now."

"You're a great mother, but you're also a woman. You have feelings and deserve a life of your own as well."

"Dex, why are you here? Why do you want this to happen? Two years ago it was sex in a weak moment. Last night, I was drunk and you're too good looking. But this can't be. I don't understand why you act like it can."

His mouth hangs open enough for me to know I've shocked him. When he gets up, the chair bumps against the window in his haste, but he stops, tapping twice on the table in front of me. I glance up and see once again that I've hurt him when all I meant to do was give him an out. "You know," he starts. "One day, I hope you'll see me for more than a coked-up drummer who used to sleep around."

Just as he starts to leave again, I grab his hand. He looks back at me, the connection slipping from my grip. "I do, Dex. It's me. It's not you."

His hand leaves mine and he disappears, and I'm left with the chiming of the bell above the door echoing in my heart. Memories of him holding me after the funeral come rushing back and the feeling that in that moment, I felt safe, like everything would be okay one day. I found that in *his* arms.

Cory used to be my safe haven, but with him gone... I get up, feeling all wrong that he's gone because he's right. No matter what changes I recognize in him now, I'm still holding his past against him. And I'm still holding onto a future that can never be with Cory. I'm alone. No matter how much I wish I wasn't, I am. That's the reality I need to accept.

I have a guy, a great guy, willing to take a chance on me and maybe it's time I put myself out there and give him that chance. But I have conditions—two, in fact—a brown-eyed and a blue-eyed— conditions that will always come first in my life.

I run after him, out the door and across the street. "Dex?" I call just before he enters the hotel. "Wait up."

He stops one block ahead of me, and turns back. Hands shoved in pockets, head tilted down, but his curious eyes look up to watch me run toward him. Stopping with a few feet between us and with harsh breaths from running, I say, "You're right."

The hope his voice held earlier is all but gone when he asks, "About what?"

"About us."

"What about us?"

"The truth is, I can't be frivolous with my emotions, but you're right, we aren't wrong. What we did isn't wrong. You've changed and though not everyone can see it, I do. It's been amazing to watch your transformation from the guy I knew years ago to the man you are now. But I need time—"

"I understand."

"No, I don't know that you do. I loved Cory. I'm not saying that to hurt your feelings, but it's something I struggle with every day. He's not here anymore, but I am and I don't want to be alone."

"He left us all. I've tried to hold back, for your sake. To not require you to think about me, but I fucking miss him, every single day. I miss my friend. I know you loved him. So did I. He was the only one in my life I could always rely on. That void will never be filled, Rochelle. I'm not trying to fill his shoes. I'm not him. All I can be is me and hope it's good enough."

"Oh Dex. I'm sorry. I know his death has affected everyone. But it's time I focused on my family. I have to put my kids first. I want to. They deserve that much and more." He nods as I continue. "So I have an offer for you. I'll understand if you're not ready to take us all on. I promise I will. But what if we start off slowly? Maybe you can spend some time at my house when the tour's over?"

"What do you mean? Like hang out?"

"Yes, let's start off as friends, real friends, friends who spend time together because I come as a package deal. You're young and not responsible for anyone else, but when you date me, you date my boys. So what if you maybe came over for lunch or dinner one night? It will give you a chance to see the reality of what you're getting into before things get too deep."

"Your boys know who I am, Rochelle."

"But they don't know you. It's the only offer I can make."

"So two steps back and we slow things down?" A section of his hair falls forward and as much as I want to touch the soft strands again, I don't. "You tell me when," he says, "and I'll be there."

"Deal." I stick out my hand, another offer of my sincerity to give him the chance he deserves.

He accepts the offer. "Deal."

We shake on it, his warmth coursing through my body. When we part, I go to him and wrap my arms around his middle because despite the deal we just made, he needs to know that our time together mattered to me. I tilt my mouth up toward his ear, and whisper, "Just in case you think I'm being completely selfless here, I'm not. I remember every kiss we shared and everything we did that night."

I see his mouth broaden into a smile and he kisses me on the forehead. "Good to know I'm not alone."

"You're not. I'm just not as brave as you."

He pulls back to look me in the eyes. "You're braver than you know yourself to be."

"I'm only brave because you give me strength." I glance down and when I look back up, I feel like we might just kiss again. Licking my bottom lip, I take in a deep breath, but when I release it, he says, "Two steps back for now, but one day, Rochelle Floros, I'm gonna be the man of your dreams."

I don't dare mention that I've already had a few dreams of the naughty variety about him. "What about my reality?"

He walks backward a couple of steps, a self-assured grin on his face. With a cocked eyebrow and two thumbs to his chest, he replies, "Right here. Reality and fantasy all rolled into one, baby."

Putting my hand on my hip, I can't stop the smile he brings out of me. "A bit cocky, aren't we?"

"I'm very cocky, but you already know that from the first time we fuc—"

"Oh my God, I meant arrogant, not your, your—"

"That works too."

"Pfft. Go. Go before I feel the need to knock that chip off your shoulder."

He reaches the door and pulls it open. "We'll be knocking, but it will have nothing to do with chips."

"What about shoulders?" I tease.

"I always knew you were a kinky girl." He goes inside and I'm left standing there like a fool in the middle of the sidewalk with a huge goofy grin on my face.

I pull my phone out and check the calendar. The band gets back to LA in eleven days, so I text *Dex: **How about lunch in twelve days?***

*Dex: **Going out or staying in?***

I type back: ***I'll cook for you.***

*Dex: **What are you going to cook?***

*Me: **Are you coming over or what?***

*Dex: **I love when you beg. It's sexy.***

*Me: **I'm not begging. I'm asking.***

*Dex: **Since you're asking so nicely, the answer is yes.***

*Me: **You're incorrigible.***

*Dex: **I've been called worse.***

*Me: **I just bet you have.***

*Dex: **Stop bugging me. I need some beauty sleep before we leave for Boston. You think I wake up this hot naturally? Oh wait, that's right, I do.***

I burst out laughing and reply: *LOL. On that note, Mr. Humble, sweet dreams.*

Dex: Forget sweet. I'm hoping for wet if I have my way, sweetheart.

My eyes go wide and my mouth drops open. I quickly shove my phone into my back pocket and hurry inside the hotel. Within minutes, I'm knocking on the door.

He opens his door wide and with a wry smile while acting innocent, he asks, "And to what do I owe the pleasure?"

I walk under his arm and slip inside his room. "I could use some sleep too."

As I strip off my shirt and jeans, he suddenly gets this cocky expression on his face as he lets the door slam shut. "Don't let me stop you from getting naked or anything, but what happened to two steps back?"

In just my bra and thong, I sit down on the edge of the bed. He moves closer as if he has no other choice. His eyes trace up and down my body leaving a trail of goosebumps in the wake of his heated gaze. I lean back on my elbows while he stands between my legs, his fingertips touching the tops of my thighs and slowly sliding down on the inside.

My thighs tighten in response and he smirks. With a teasing smirk of my own, I crawl up the bed, giving him full view of my ass, climb under the covers, and snuggle in before we cross a line we know we shouldn't. I hear his heavy, impatient sigh as I pat the bed next to me. "Well, c'mon. Let's get our sleep on."

His shirt is over his head and off, his jeans dropped just as fast. He slips under the covers and I immediately move to lie against his side. We lay there in silence for a few minutes. I find comfort when I hear his steady heartbeat, then whisper, "How about just one step back?"

"Deal," he says, then kisses the top of my head. He stretches and turns off the bedside lamp and gets more comfortable while I stay wrapped around him. "I think I'm gonna like this stepping back friends business."

6

ROCHELLE

THIS NEW PLAN, the deal I made with Dex, seemed like such a good idea at first. But when I woke up in his arms just before noon, I wanted to stay. I couldn't though. He had to get up to catch a flight to Boston for the next show and I needed to get back to LA.

This was only supposed to be a short trip when I planned it. But something about having his body wrapped around me made me want to see if Janice wouldn't mind keeping the boys another night.

"You should probably go," Dex says, his voice husky with sleep.

"What?" I tilt up to find him smirking down at me. "Why do you say that?"

"Because this feels too good. And if you're not careful, I might have to steal you away and take you with me."

"What if I came voluntarily?"

"That's the plan." The double meaning is exaggerated by his hand slowly running up the side of my body and back down again. He sits up and rubs his face before pushing his hair back. "So you gonna come?"

"And you call me dirty."

He laughs, then says, "Not dirty, kinky." He leans in really close, his lips against my ear. "There's a difference and I'm more than happy to explore that kinky side with you... and the dirty side."

"You're too kind," I say in response to his words tickling my neck and making me tingle in other ways. "Thanks for volunteering."

And there's that smile again, the one that shoots straight to my heart when he says, "I'm here to please, sweetheart."

I really shouldn't like his arrogant side as much as I do, but I don't bother hiding it. "You're making it very hard to leave this bed."

"Then don't. Stay with me. Stay in bed with me. We'll catch a later flight or rent a car and drive together."

"You're making me an offer I'm finding hard to resist. I want to go. I really do, but I need to check. It would only be for one night—"

"I'll take one more night over nothing."

"You have a show tonight. Sound check, meetings—"

His fingers run along my cheekbone, pushing back strands of hair that lie across my cheek. "Don't think about the time we don't have. Think of what we have when we're together."

I close my eyes under his soothing touch. "I'm scared, Dex. What if this doesn't work out?"

"Don't be scared." After drawing in a slow breath, he says, "If all we ever have is one more night together, the rest of the nights won't matter."

I can tell he wants to kiss me as we stare into each other's eyes. I'm not opposed to the idea myself as our breaths mingle between us. I close my eyes and lean forward, but instead of a kiss, he whispers, "One step back." A gentle reminder of what I put in place as he drags his fingertip lightly over my lips, his gaze savoring them.

"And what if I don't want to take a step back?" I sulk, rejection covering my heart.

"That's my good cuddling skills talking right there. Once I let you leave, you'll realize you were just under my spell."

Now my cynical side comes out. "Cuddling skills, really?" I roll onto my back.

"Yeah, cuddling skills. I'm a master, but it's not something I work on. It's like a gift the ladies can't resist." My silence must speak for me because he adds, "Trust me, once you leave my arms, you'll realize how powerless you really were while in the throes of my amazing cuddles."

"I didn't know guys cuddled?"

"Damn right guys cuddle, but I just happen to be a master, an artiste, an expert in the field."

"Does that make you a cudster or an arddle?"

"I'm thinking it makes me more of a perddle, but that's just a personal preference."

I sit up. "I'm gonna get up now and see if my common sense comes back."

"Wait." He grabs my waist. "Just one more time."

I tilt my head, then start to laugh. "Okay, I'll let you cuddle me one more time." I snuggle into his side and his arms tighten around me. When my body relaxes, my eyes start to close again.

"I win. I'm the cuddle king."

Even though I love being with him this way, I roll my eyes and sarcastically repeat after him, "You win, Oh great cuddler." A minute more in his arms and I finally look up. "Are we still doing this?"

"You're welcome to stay as long as you like. I'm happy to oblige."

"What about Boston? Do I get these kinds of snuggles there?"

"If you come to Boston, I'll give you whatever you like."

"Tempting." When his erection presses against my leg, I say, "So are you. Too tempting most of the time."

He drags his finger slowly down my neck and over my collarbone, stopping just at the top of my right breast. "I'm struggling here, but for you, I'll live with tempting for now."

"C'MON, I have a surprise for you," Dex says. We arrived in Boston just over an hour ago and went straight to the arena for sound check.

Typically, no one would take notice of us because they're so used to seeing us around, but not today. While I follow Dex down the hall, I see the stares, the looks, the curiosity in their eyes as the stagehands go about their jobs, setting up for the performance tonight. But I'm not bothered by it. He leads me onto the stage where a single chair with a guitar on it sits with a spotlight shining down, lighting the area. "What is this?" I ask.

"I want you to play." There's a spark in his eyes that I bet gets women to do whatever he asks of them.

But with the fear beginning to rise inside of me I can't think about that. With wide eyes, I ask, "You want me to play for you?"

"No, I want you to play for you."

"On stage? Why?"

"Because I don't think you do anymore and you should."

I stare at him, my stomach tying up in knots, then I try to defend myself. "I'm busy is all. No biggie." I shrug to add to the casualness I'm trying to portray.

"No biggie? You used to love to play," he says. "I remember watching you in the studio on the last album. You come alive when you play."

"I'm busy. I'm tired. I don't have the same passion for it that I used to."

This time he stares at me like he's trying to work through some complicated equation... or maybe he already has me all figured out. Maybe he can see through the façade I try so hard to put on every day. "I don't have to prove anything, Dex." I cross my arms, adamant.

"Nope, you don't have anything to prove. Not to me or anyone else, except maybe yourself."

"I don't understand what you're doing?"

"Don't you?"

"No, I don't."

A loud thud behind me causes me to look over my shoulder. Johnny sits in a chair near the other, guitar in hand. "You lead. I'll follow," he says.

I can't hide my panic. "No. I don't have time for music anymore."

"Wow," Johnny says, looking disappointed. "That's pretty damn sad, Rochelle."

"Sad as it may be, I have different priorities these days."

Johnny leans forward resting his elbows on his knees, chin in hand, rubbing it in thought. "Music isn't something that comes in and out of our lives when it's convenient. Music defines us, filling the holes that others have left behind."

My hands start shaking. "I can't. I just can't." Walking around Dex, I head for the side of the stage and rush down the steps to the exit doors. The sun blinds me when the door flies open. I move to the side, away from the door, and into the shadows. It's been well over a year since I last played and I remember every second of it. The studio recordings took every ounce of what was left of me. The guys wouldn't take no for an answer, so I filled in for Cory on the last record. But once we were done, I was done as well. The nightmares started and I haven't gone near any of the guitars in our house since. That part of my life has been packed away just like the instruments.

"It's times like these that I still wish I smoked."

I spy Johnny out of the corner of my eye and my shoulders drop in ease from seeing my friend. "You don't?" I ask.

He leans against the cinderblock wall and shakes his head. "Holliday would kick my ass. She has this seventh sense that alerts her when I'm screwing up."

"She wants you to live a long life."

"Yeah, I guess she does," he says with a smile that's more reflective of his love for his wife than for me.

"Holli loves you."

"We all have the capacity to love more than we think we're capable of."

"Are you talking about Holli or me?"

"Might be about you."

"Since when did my love life become the band's pet project?" I lightly kick his foot with mine.

"When did you stop playing?"

"The day I left the studio."

"Why?"

Taking a moment, I look down at my shoes, noticing all the scuff marks on them. "Music was something I did with Cory, for him, because of him."

"You played before you met him."

"I messed around."

"No, you're just forgetting the details." He pushes off the wall and reaches for the doorknob. "That passion still lives inside you." He pats his chest over his heart.

"Then how do I find it again?"

"It will find you when you're ready." The door closes and I'm left there in awe. His lyrics speak so justly of the man behind them and Johnny Outlaw sure knows how to deliver a line.

I go back inside and find Dex in the dressing room waiting on sound check to begin. "Hey, gotta sec?" I sit down next to him.

"For you." He leans back on the couch, his sticks in hand while tapping rhythmically on his leg.

"I want to thank you for what you did. It was very thoughtful."

"We've had some good sessions over the years. We should do that again... maybe when I come over in a few weeks."

Bouncing my palm lightly on his knee, I say, "Maybe. I might need some more time with that too."

His drumsticks pause and he says, "Time is something we take for granted."

"I think I know that better than anyone."

The beat continues as he starts up again and says, "I lost my dad when I was eight years old."

Taken by surprise by the admission, I exhale. I knew his dad had died before I met him, but I didn't know Dex was so young. My heart thumps in my chest and I place my hand over his hand, stilling his rhythm. His sticks stop and he takes them in one hand, then covers mine with the other.

A guy opens the door and I pull my hand away reflexively. He says, "Sound check is up. The new snare is on the kit and tested, but they want final approval."

I lay back and push Dex up. "Go. I'll be around later after the show."

With that smile that drives me wild, he asks, "You sure you don't want to join us on stage?"

"I'm positive. Thanks for the offer though."

I watch his ass as he walks out the door, simply because he has a great ass. Then I kick my feet up on the coffee table and drop my head back while closing my eyes. The panic has subsided and my heart becomes all mushy thinking about his sweet gesture. Shaking my head, I smile. Dex is a very unexpected, but a wonderful surprise in my life.

I HEAD BACK to the hotel to change before the show. Lara traveled to Boston on an earlier flight than us and is checked into our room already. Having her there helps keep the drunken lines with Dex from blurring. She knows to hold me accountable for my actions.

After my shower, I lay on the bed as she digs through her suitcase. With a shirt in her hands, she asks, "What do you think about the red, one shoulder number for tonight?"

"With the dark jeans? Sexy."

"Black ankle boots or black shimmer heels?"

"Ankle boots."

"Sex with Dex or kissing only?"

I stare at the back of her head, surprised by her question, but not shocked. When she turns around, she grins with her hand on her hip. "I can tell you're into him. You can't hide the truth from me."

"I like him, but it feels self-indulgent."

She sits on the edge of the bed and I move over to give her more space. "Since when is happiness self-indulgent?"

"You know what I mean."

"Yes, I do, but here's the reality. You are a single woman, whether you wanted to be or not. It's been years. You don't have to forget, but don't do your heart the injustice of never letting it race again either."

"What will people say if Dex and I do end up dating?"

"What people? Because everyone that is important in your life wants you to be happy. If it's happy with Mr. Smooth and Sexy, then even better."

"You think he's sexy?"

"God, Rochelle. You were totally right. He's hot, hotter than even I remembered and I remember him being pretty damn hot. I think his old hairstyle, that ratty bandana, and sunglasses hid that sexy man for too long."

"He smells good too."

Her eyebrows shoot up. "Oh really?"

"Yep," I say, nodding. "He does."

She giggles and that makes me giggle too. It feels good to talk to someone about Dex. It feels good to be unburdened from the guilt that's weighed me down for so long and just feel giddy again.

"Did you sleep with him yet?"

No one knows of our one night years ago, except Tommy, and I'm not telling now. "Lara!"

"I'll take that as a yes. I'm not judging by the way. I'd drop my panties for those captivating brown eyes any day."

She gets up and grabs the red top again.

To move this topic along to something else, I say, "We need to leave in thirty if we're gonna make it to the show in time."

JOHNNY LOOKS BACK at Dex sitting on his pedestal as he beats down the end of the song on his drum kit, closing the show. Dex gets up, walks to the edge of the stage and the crowd goes nuts. He launches the drumsticks into the audience and I shake my head. He pays a fine every time he does that, but he still does it because he knows how much the fans love it. He's been warned a million times not to do it, but I kind of love that he still does. Johnny exits the stage first, then Dex, Kaz, and Derrick trailing.

"Good show," I say as they pass. They're usually moody or high-strung after a performance, so I like to give them space until they're grounded again. Lara and I walk to the exit, wanting some fresh air because it smells backstage. A lot of sweaty men moving heavy equipment and lights around will do that.

With my back against the grey wall, I slide down and balance as Lara lights a cigarette. The doors open again and Kaz and Dex are there. They nod in acknowledgment, but continue talking about some screw up that pissed off Johnny. Dex winks at me before telling Kaz, "Fuck, just hit the riff. It's not hard. You do it in rehearsal." Dex lights up, then brings the cigarette to his mouth and inhales. The action is sexier than it should be. I'm not sure if it's the way he holds it or the way his lips caress it, but either way, I can't stop staring.

Through smoke-filled exhales, Kaz says, "No one notices that shit."

"Everybody fucking notices," Dex snaps, aggravated. "Fans know these songs inside and out. How the fuck do you mess up a song you've been playing for two years?"

"Fuck you," Kaz gripes. "Maybe it wasn't a mess up but my own fucking spin on it."

Dex is quick with his response, "Nobody wants your spin on it, man. They want Cory's."

Kaz takes a drag and then says, "Fuck that music. That music is dead just like him. It's time for us to make our own."

I'm on my feet, moving to the door.

Kaz grabs my arm. "Oh fuck, Rochelle. I'm sorry. I didn't mean it like that."

I yank my arm free and go inside, not running though it's all I want to do. I can't breakdown in front of them. I can't show my weakness, or how affected I still get. I go as fast as I can, now running despite all the strength I try to pretend to have. But I'm stopped and pulled into a dark doorway. I gasp, the sudden impact a surprise and I look up into sympathetic, but warm eyes.

My own eyes start to water, the tears forcing themselves out. Dex pulls me against him. His scent—sweat from the show under a clean shirt—sexy and strong, masculine, but overpowering. His large hand covers the back of my head and he strokes. I breathe him in, finding the comfort I need.

"Rochelle."

We jump apart when Kaz appears. "Rochelle, I'm sorry. I really am. You know Cory was my idol."

Slowly stepping back into the light, I clear my throat and steady myself. "Then treat him with the respect he deserves. He wrote that song, the one you were complaining about, when he was nineteen. It came from somewhere deep inside, somewhere slightly dark. You don't get that. You play notes that you feel forced to play, so you're pushing back. I *do* get that. But The Resistance isn't about you, Kaz. It's about the music and a band as a whole. You play over an hour of new songs. The encore will always be about the hits and what the fans love. So do us all the courtesy of setting your ego aside and playing for them instead of yourself."

I push past him and head for the dressing room, the anger hitting its stride by the time I open the door. "Rochelle?" I hear Dex calling my name, but I walk past Johnny and Kaz, and grab my bag from the floor.

When I turn around, I run right into Dex's chest, his arms around me again and I'm suddenly all too aware of the other guys watching us.

Johnny stands. "What happened?"

Feeling my face heat from them being privy to the intimacy between me and Dex, I free myself. Just a glance at Johnny, then to Kaz, and I see the expressions on their face, the disapproval on Johnny's, confusion on Kaz.

"What the fuck, Dex?" Johnny asks—protective brother voice in place as he straightens his shoulders back.

I try to ease things between them before I leave. "It's okay, Johnny. He didn't do anything. It's me. I just need to go. I'll see you back in LA."

"Rochelle? Wait up," he says, catching up to me in the corridor.

"Dude, really. I'm okay. I just don't want to be here right now." I see Dex out of the corner of my eye, Lara just beyond him coming inside with Kaz. "I'll be fine. I'll see you at home."

Johnny nods, knowing when to back off. "Be safe."

"I will." I walk in the opposite direction, leaving them all behind. With a quick glance back over my shoulder, the scene fades to black as I focus ahead of me.

As I pack my clothes, a light knock on the hotel door makes me pause and sigh. I'm guessing it's Lara or Dex. I'm hoping it's not Johnny. He sees right through me and I don't have the energy to lie to him.

When I open the door, Dex is there. I smile automatically while leaning against the wall. "What are you doing here? Shouldn't you be out partying after the show?"

"I didn't want to go." An urgent kiss lands on my lips, the sweet pressure trapped between desperation and passion. I find the line often blurs when I kiss him as well. "I don't want you to go either." Sliding my hands down his arms to his wrists, he lifts them to caress my neck. "Sometimes we're assholes. It was Kaz's turn tonight. I'm sorry."

"I know he didn't mean it, but when he said it... I don't know anymore," I say, shrugging. "I don't want him forgotten."

"He won't be. He's a legend, Rochelle." His lips replace his hands on my neck. "But let's leave all that for now. Right here together, we can be us—no baggage, no past, no witnesses. Just us, here together."

I kiss him, needing him close. When our lips part, I look into his eyes just as he opens his. I whisper, "No past. Just us with no judgments or expectations."

He kisses me again, then says, "Back in LA, we have to be responsible and do what's right. Once there, we can go back to square one, not for me, but for Neil and CJ. We'll start over, the way we should have two years ago."

"You're okay with that?"

"No," he replies, making me laugh. "But I'll do whatever it takes to spend more time with you. Anyway, your boys seem pretty cool. I mean Neil is named after one of the best drummers in the world, after all. The kid can't be that bad."

I giggle, the lighthearted moment easing the heavy from before. Dropping my forehead to his chest, I ask, "What about tonight?"

"Tonight, you're mine."

Is this too much too fast? Am I the only one who's concerned about what the future holds? "Are you worried?"

"Shit yeah, I worry. I worry that this may be the last time I get to kiss you or feel your breath on my skin. I worry that I'll never get to hear your heart racing because you're near me. So yeah, I worry. But tonight, let's not talk about tomorrow or what happens after. Let's just live in the here—"

"Live in the now." I pull him inside by his shirt and let the door slam closed, deciding to do just that. I kiss him again and again while walking backward into the room, leaving yesterday to the past and tomorrow to be dealt with another day.

We tumble onto the bed, our bodies entwined, his lips pressed to the skin of my collarbone. With one knee between his legs and his knee between mine, we move together in a flurry of overdue movements. I tug at his collar, trailing kisses across his shoulder. His strong hands flex and grip as he holds me at the waist and slides them up, his thumb rubbing gentle circles against the side of my breasts.

He moves on top of me, his erection against my stomach, his lips finding and caressing mine. Breathless, I drop my head back. "I want you. I want you so much, Dex. So much."

His hands stop flexing, his lips stop kissing, his body stills while his breathing remains jagged over my cheek. I'm about to say something just as he pauses and looks away. His fingers tap lightly across my ribs and he leans down to whisper, "You deserve more than this."

"No." I release my breath and hold him by the jaw, making him look at me. "I'm good. This is good. The here and now, remember. Tonight is all that matters."

"Rochelle, you deserve dates and flowers, romantic dinners, and for me to show you that I'm good enough to spend time with your family."

"You're good enough, Dex. It wasn't about you not being good enough for me or my ki—" He kisses me, ending my plea. As soon as our lips part, I continue, "Kids. So please don't think otherwise."

Chuckling, he runs his finger down my nose and lingers on my lips, stopping me from talking. "Here's the truth of the matter. If we do this... again, there's no going back to square one tomorrow. Not for me. I won't be able to act like I don't care about you, like I haven't thought about you every day since we were together last. So it's easier to stop now than later."

With a discouraged sigh, I say, "You're stronger than me, Dex."

"No, I just know my greatest weakness is the woman beneath me right now." He rolls over sighing in a way that shows frustration has set in. Turning his head to me, he says, "I want to fuck you so bad, but I also want to do all that making love stuff too. And if we do that, I can't pretend it didn't happen." He sits up and walks to the other side of the room, leaning his back against the wall.

I prop myself up on my elbows, caught by the heaviness of the emotions I'm suddenly feeling for him.

"Go to sleep tonight. Fly home tomorrow." He walks into the shadow of the entryway. "I'll see you in a few weeks."

I hear the door open as I fall back on the bed, my own sexual frustration setting in. But just when I hear the door close, the weight of his body lands on top of me and he kisses me hard. Surprised, my eyes fly open, but then I go for it just like him and kiss him back with just as much passion. He pushes off of me again and stands between my legs. "I make very few promises in life, but this one I can make to you. Rochelle Floros, I'm coming for you. It's our time, so get ready for me." He turns abruptly and leaves me sitting there stunned... and tingly... and then smiling, my heart full of happiness and so much more for that man.

7

―――――

ROCHELLE

LARA CAME BACK to the room this morning and found me asleep. She's been giving me a hard time on our morning flight back to LA ever since. "That grin on your face sure was unexpected."

"I wasn't grinning. I was sleeping."

"Well, whatever you were dreaming about had you smiling like a fool in your sleep."

I roll my eyes. "And what did you do after the concert last night?"

She looks away briefly before she says, "Met some friends at the bar downstairs. Once you texted me you were going to bed, I thought it best not to bring the party up to the room."

"Thank you."

"You're welcome. Now what brought on that smile? It was polar opposite of what I expected to find when you left the show."

I figure the truth will hush her up. "I had three orgasms last night."

Her eyes go wide. "Eh, er... wow. Umm, okay. Huh." She adjusts in her seat and says, "I'm impressed. Did you have these on your own or did someone special, someone like Dex, induce these?"

"All on my own." I just don't mention that Dex was the inspiration behind each one. Seems every time I close my eyes, I can still feel his lips on me and the gentle sucking he did to my collarbone.

"Ew, are you gonna cum again right now? Wipe that expression off your face."

I burst out laughing and slap her arm. "Stop teasing me. You wanted the truth. Well, you got it."

"I love a great masturbation session."

"Oh my God, keep your voice down, Lara."

An older woman in the seat in front of us peers back through the crack between the seats. When my eyes meet her judgy ones, she frowns and turns back around quickly.

Lara shrugs not caring if she's heard by everyone on the plane or not. "Wouldn't it be hot to have sex with the pilot while he was flying the plane?"

Shaking my head, I say, "I'm not really partial to planes."

Her hand covers mine on the shared armrest. "I'm sorry."

"It's okay."

"So maybe you're more a mailman type of gal. You know, a guy who can really deliver his package?"

My head goes back and I scrunch my nose. "What 80's porn have you been watching?"

"Not porn, just my imagination... Okay, some porn, but we all watch porn every now and then."

"Maybe I should watch some," I say, actually considering the idea.

"If you had three orgasms all by yourself, I don't think you need porn. Your dirty thoughts are good enough."

"I have some good references."

She leans closer. "Do tell."

"No, I think I'll hold onto them a little longer."

"If it makes a difference, I saw how Dex looks at you over the last few days. You could have him if you wanted."

Looking out the window of the plane into the great blue yonder, I reply, "It makes all the difference in the world." Three more hours on the flight left to go, so I lean my head against the window and close my eyes. "I'm gonna try to get some sleep."

AFTER THANKING Janice for keeping my kids, I drag my suitcase into the bedroom. The boys follow me in and we all lay on my king size bed together, cartoons on the large flat screen hanging on the wall. Despite that they were engrossed in the show, I'm instantly smothered in kisses and hugs and I love it. My boys take the opportunity to bounce on the bed, and despite the no jumping rule usually in place, I let them. Their happy faces are worth the potential for broken springs.

"Mama, I love you," CJ says, and I grab him mid-jump and snuggle him to my side.

"Come here, buddy," I say to Neil.

He bounces to his knees and then drops to my open arm, which I close around him. I kiss each of their heads and smile. "I missed you guys so much. Did you miss me?"

"Yes," they say in unison. Then Neil adds, "You were with Uncle Johnny on tour?"

"Yes," I reply, wanting to reintroduce them to Dex soon hopefully. "And Dex, the drummer. Do you remember him?"

"He gave me the drumsticks."

"Yes, that's right."

"I don't member," CJ says.

I rough up his hair. "You'll see him soon and you'll remember. You've met him many times." I reach over and declare, "Ticklefest."

After lots of giggles and catching up on their days while I was away, I start dinner. I want to make something that shows how much I love them, warming their souls while filling their tummies. I decide on homemade lasagna, which they devour, making me happy. We read books and then I tuck them in.

When I lay down in my bed, I turn on the TV. My mind drifts away from the match-making show and I think of Dex, wondering what he's doing tonight. It was a travel day for them and no performance, so I don't know if he's going out or staying in and resting up. It makes me realize that I don't really know him—his habits, his hobbies, his routine—at all. But I want to and this time I don't feel bad for that.

I roll to my side and smile before catching up on the show, my nightmares a little less this night.

WHY DOES a simple text seem monumental right now? This should be easy, I tell myself as I pace my kitchen. Looking down at the phone in my hand, the screen glows bright white waiting for me to type something. I feel like I'm asking Dex out on a date. Wait, *am I?* What seemed like a casual get-to-know-you-better plan has suddenly turned into a big date. Oh no. I turn my phone off, not ready for this at all.

Two hours later while lying on the couch, I kick my feet up on the arm and go to my message app again. This time I'm determined. I start to type: *Hi Stranger, just wondering if...* Ugh! Delete. Delete. Delete. *Stranger? Really?* Ugh!

Hi, hope you're doing well. I know you probably need some down time when you get home next week, but I was wondering if you want to come over for a meal. I can cook for you. I'm sure it's been a while since you've had food not delivered by room service. I'll deliver it to the table though and all you have to do is show up. We can hang out, maybe play a board game with the boys. Tag is also a big favorite of theirs. Anyway, let me know.

I hit send before I can chicken out. Staring down at the rambling message, I'm so embarrassed. If there was a way to take that back, I would.

My phone buzzes in my hand when a message appears. It's a lot sooner than I expected. *Long time, no talk, Stranger. It's good to hear from you. What day?*

I laugh at the 'stranger' then type: *You get back on Monday. How about Wednesday?*

Dex: How about Tuesday?

I might be blushing that he wants to see me as much as I want to see him. *Tuesday is great.*

Dex: *What time?*

Me: *5 p.m.?*

Dex: *I'll be there.*

Me: *See you then.*

Dex: *Feel free to text me anytime, dollface.*

Dollface? Now my cheeks really heat. Me: *Text soon, champ.*

Champ!!! What the hell am I doing? He's making me senseless.

Dex: *Lol. Okay, champ is interesting...*

Me: *Ignore me. Just carry on with your day like that never happened.*

Dex: *I'll try, but it'll be hard.*

My eyebrows rise up when I read 'It'll be hard.'

Dex: *Did I just type that?*

Me: *You did.*

Dex: *I'll forget about champ, but you need to forget about things being hard over here in Dallas.*

Me: *Now that will be 'hard' to do.*

Dex: *Are you sexting me?*

Me: *You're the one sexting I believe. You started it first.*

Dex: *I'll be happy to finish it too. See you next Tuesday.*

Me: *Another funny. Like C U Next Tuesday.*

Dex: *Let's stop while we're a'head'*

Me: *You're right. Stop.*

I laugh and set my phone down on the couch cushion next to me, but it buzzes again. I look at the screen and read: *Just in case I wasn't clear, I'm really looking forward to seeing you again.*

Me: *Me too.*

ONCE AGAIN, I find myself pacing in the kitchen, nervous. I'm roasting a chicken and I don't even know if Dex eats meat. How have I known him this long and I don't know if he eats meat or not. I think he does, but it's been a long time since we had a proper meal together. What if he's gone Vegan in that time? I poke the parsnips with a fork to check for tenderness and then decide that I should make a salad. It's a healthy meal all around and if he's gone Vegan then he'll have the two sides, at least.

The doorbell rings and the kids go running. I throw the fork on the counter and dash for the door, hoping to beat them to it. Dex knows the code to the yard gate, but I still want to be the one who greets him. "Wait, wait, wait. Let me answer it."

The boys stop and let me in front of them. I take a deep breath and straighten my shirt before opening the door. "Hi," I say a little breathless. I'm hoping he thinks it's sexy. Though I was expecting him, I'm still caught off guard by how attractive he is. I waver a bit, grasping the doorknob tightly to ground me.

"Hi," Dex says smiling at me. He's holding a bouquet of flowers made up of lilacs, peonies, and miniature white roses. "These are for you." Leaning in, he kisses me on the cheeks. "You look beautiful."

"Thank you," I reply, impressed by the romantic gesture and look away as I feel my cheeks heat.

Turning back to his touch, his hand rubbing my arm, I see he has come bearing more gifts. He whips out some Fun Dips for the kids, shaking them in the air. "Brought these too."

"Yay!" The kids jump up and down in excitement, snatching them from his hands.

"That was nice," I say, then turn to the kids. "You can have them after dinner. Not before."

After a round of disappointed grumblings from them, Dex says, "No biggie."

"I'll let you deal with the sugar high later." With a laugh, I turn and nod toward the kitchen. "Come on in. I need to check on the chicken." But I stop and turn around abruptly. "Do you eat chicken? I don't even know if you eat chicken."

"I eat chicken." Relieved, I start back to the kitchen, but he stops me and takes my pinky, and says, "It's good to see you again." Slowly tugging me closer, he wraps his arms around me and hugs me.

I relish the closeness as I wrap my arms around him. "It's good to see you too. Thanks for coming over." I hear him gulp and I gulp in response, but his arms around me feel too good to get hung up in the newness and unknown of what's ahead for us. So I take a deep breath, breathing him in, and smile. "You smell good."

"So do you. You smell like roasted chicken." He chuckles.

Pushing off of him playfully, I say, "That's because I'm roasting a chicken."

"Cool."

"Drink?"

"What are you having?"

I enter the kitchen, but sneak a peek back at him. He's wearing a white T-shirt that highlights his tan arms, fitted around the muscles of his biceps. His jeans are a loose, but not baggy and he has on lace-up Vans. To top it off, I can tell he's freshly showered, not just from inhaling his clean, manliness back in the living room, but his hair is shiny and kind of enviable. But it's the devilish smile on his face and devious look in his eyes that makes me reply, "Wine. You? I have beer, cocktails, soda, water, milk?"

"Did you just offer me milk?"

"Yeah, it's a popular beverage around here."

He just continues smiling. "How about a soda?"

"Sure."

I make our drinks and tend to dinner one more time before leading Dex outside where the boys are running around on the swings chasing each other. We sit in patio chairs and watch for a few minutes before CJ comes over, and says, "I member you."

With a big smile that shows off Dex's dimples, he says, "I member you too, big guy."

"Why are you here?"

I lean forward, taking CJ by the arm and pull him in front of me. Holding him by the waist, I wiggle him. "Dex is here for dinner and to play with us."

CJ's eyes light up. "We like Marco Polo, but Mama doesn't let us play much since we run into things and get boo-boos."

"Ahh," Dex responds. "I can understand. How about tag or hide-and-go-seek?"

"Hide seek," my little guy says, jumping up in excitement. "Let's play. Neil, Hide seek."

Dex stands up, offering me a hand up. I take it, catching his eye on me as I stand. He looks out over the yard and announces, "I'm it. I'll count to twenty and then I'm gonna come find you." He turns to go to the door, pinching my side as he does. "Better hide fast. I'm coming for you."

The words echo the ones he told me back in Boston before I left. And I like hearing them again.

As soon as he hides his face in his hands, the boys and I run for cover. The boys go for the bushes in the corners. They're tiny and can hide in there easily. There aren't many spots for me, so I run to the side of the house and squat down on the other side of the garden. I hear him announce, "Twenty. Ready or not, here I come," and I don't know what it is about this game, but butterflies fill my stomach as I sit in anticipation of being found and trying to make it back to home base untagged.

Peeking toward the corner of the house, waiting, I hear little joyful screams and Neil yell, "I'm safe!" That makes me smile. I know very well that Dex could catch him if he wanted. To my right, I see a Dandelion growing. Just as I reach for it, I'm grabbed, hand over my mouth as I scream, his other arm holding me to him. When he uncovers my mouth, his finger goes to his and he says, "Shhhhh."

I slide up, my back against the wood, and he leans forward. With his arms on either side of my head and his chest barely touching mine, his breath warms me over as if the sun wasn't doing a good enough job of it. "Square one is gonna be hard to do with you looking so edible."

My breath is rough as I breathe in his words. "Square one?"

His eyes crinkle at the corners and being this close to him makes my knees weak. He's so close, so close that I could kiss him. His nose runs along the side of my nose and his lips brush against mine. But he pulls back, and says, "Yes, remember? Square one." Nodding his head, he smiles, knowing damn well I'd kiss him if I had the chance. "We're starting back at square one."

I can't hide my disappointment. "Oh yeah, that's right."

He steps back and looks down at the garden. The last time we were here was on that day I don't like to think about. He says, "I knew it would all be okay." Following his gaze, I see the sprouts of new lettuce growing there. "By the way," he adds, tapping my arm. "You're it." Dex takes off running toward home base, leaving me standing there, my insides twisted in a new emotion, my body already missing his touch.

Instead of dwelling on the fact that I came up with this stupid square one idea, I run around and try to find my CJ. "Where are you, cutie pie?"

Giggles alert me to the corner bush, but the opposite one he ran for earlier. I hurry over and go to the back side, so he can make a break for home base, which he does. Thanks to my slow-motion running, he makes it safely there, grabbing onto Dex's leg and laughing. Dex rubs the top of his head, and kneels down. "You're safe, buddy. Your Mom's still it."

Breathless, I reach the patio. I think we have time for one more round before dinner, so I start to count and everyone else scatters. This time I tag Dex first, making him it, and I'm really starting to think he just might be *it* in more ways than one.

I ALWAYS WONDERED why people drank coffee at night, until now. I don't want this night to end. I don't want to miss a thing, not even a moment, so I make us coffee to make it last.

Tonight, I don't get the Dex who filled the tabloids with stories of drug abuse, legal issues, and a myriad of women. And it's not the Dex I knew five years ago or even three. This Dex is attentive and considerate, quiet at times, and contemplative. Our conversations have been lively and his outlook on his life fascinating. He's changed over the years. It's been inevitable with the fame and the money, but he's matured and has this gentle side to him that he's showing me that I'm finding very hard to resist.

But even coffee can't make the night last forever despite my best efforts. Tomorrow has requirements that come along with the new day that I can't delay. Realizing the time, I say, "Wow, it's getting late."

"It is?" He says, looking at me. Dex is lying across the couch, his lids much heavier than they were an hour ago, his smile lazy, but so attractive.

"It's just gone ten. It's quite the life I'm living here in the Valley."

"It's a good life. I've had a good time." He sits up and stretches and that V, the one that I remember so vividly from before, is exposed. "Hey, eyes up here."

Busted. "Sorry," I say, though I'm not really.

"It's okay. I like the way you look at me."

Tilting my head, I grin, feeling flirty. "How do I look to you?"

"How *I* look at you."

And with that, silence infiltrates, leaving me speechless. I want to get up and go to him, everything about him draws me in, but I don't because this is the first of many nights I hope to spend with him. I don't want to risk the perfection of our time together.

Standing up, he says, "Thank you for dinner. I don't think I knew you were such a good cook."

"Sheer necessity."

"You can afford a chef."

"I like to cook for my family."

"It's a good skill to have." Taking another step, he adds, "I guess I should get going."

I don't want him to though I know it's the right thing to do. I stand up as well, and ask, "So the first half of the tour's over. Got any plans for your month off?"

"Sleep."

"Eh, c'mon, you get a ton of sleep."

"I don't sleep well on the road. I never have."

I nod, and agree. "I never did either."

"At least you had someone," he says so easily.

I know he doesn't mean anything more than the words themselves, but the reminders are hard to live with sometimes. "Yeah."

Dex comes closer and tugs at my shirt. "Did I just make it awkward?"

"No... okay, maybe a little, but it's real and I can't deny a real moment. Cory was in my life. He's not anymore. I didn't have a say in the decision. But for the record, I still struggle all the time, but it's good for you to see, to know who I am now. I'm not the same girl you met ten years ago."

"No," he whispers, pushing my hair back over my shoulders. "You're not. You're the woman that..." Looking away from me, he backs up suddenly. "I should go."

"Dex?" I turn and follow after him. "What were you going to say?"

He scrapes his teeth across his bottom lip and it's entirely distracting and more than a little teasing. "Square one, remember?"

"I'm beginning to hate square one." I open the door for him, deflated, maybe defeated inside.

With a chuckle, he leans in and kisses me on the forehead. It's quick and gentle, not illicit in the least, though I could use some illicit right about now. "Go to bed and get some rest. And before I go, how's Thursday looking for you?"

"What time?"

"Five o'clock."

"I'll be here with the boys."

He smiles and asks, "How about the three of you come to dinner at my house?"

"Really?"

"Really."

I lift up on my tiptoes and hug him. "We'd love to."

"See you then and if you get lonely, feel free to sext me anytime."

"I'll keep that in mind." I give him a little wink because really, what else can you do but camp it up.

After locking the door and setting the security system, I lean against the wall. I'm all smiles and full of feel-goods from the night and from the man who just left. But I'm left wondering on Thursday, *do we get to move to square two?*

8

ROCHELLE

WEDNESDAY DRAGS. I try to appreciate each day we're given, but it's hard when all I want is for it to be Thursday already. Since it's not, I do what I totally shouldn't do according to dating rules. *I text Dex.*

   Me: Is it Thursday yet?

Five minutes later…

Dex: I wish.
   Me: Me too.
   Dex: Want to go to lunch?
Too excited, I rush my answer, not caring about old dating rules.
Me: Yes.
   Dex: I'll pick you up in an hour.
   Me: I'll be ready.
Now I try to play it cool and settle the giddiness that has built up inside me while hurrying to my closet to figure out what to wear. Dex makes me want to dress cool like he does, but aside from clothes that tend to lend themselves more for evening wear, I don't own much 'cool' anymore. Not sure where we're going to eat, so I pull a long striped skirt on and a fitted tank top because it's comfortable. It's also

warm out, so this way I won't get all sweaty. The last thing I want to be around Dex, is sweaty. Images of the last few times we got sweaty together cross my mind, but I quickly shake them away, well aware that that kind of workout won't be happening today. No matter how much I kind of wish it could.

I finish getting ready and am going to the kitchen to retrieve my purse when the doorbell rings. After grabbing my bag, I'm greeted by Dex's smile, and just like that, my breath catches as my heart skips a beat. "Hi," I say, feeling that familiar heat rise to my cheeks.

His grin grows wider and he says, "Hi. You ready to go?"

"Yep."

In the driveway sits his 1976 Challenger. He opens the door for me then shuts it after I slide onto the leather seat. "The car's looking good," I say when he gets in.

"Sitting in a driveway for almost six months doesn't do any car good, but this Challenger is reliable."

"Where are we going?" I ask.

"Rodeo Drive."

"I didn't take you for the Beverly Hills crowd."

He pulls off my street and says, "I'm not, but my mother is. I need to pick up a birthday present from her favorite jeweler. Mind going with me before lunch?"

"Not at all." I look out the window, then turn to him again. "How are you?"

His fingers stretch over the steering wheel and I see the right side of his lips curl up. "I'm good. I'm glad to see you... too."

"I guess I'm not good at pretending, playing it cool and all that." I roll my eyes, feeling foolish.

"You don't have to be. You only have to be yourself around me. At this stage in our lives, it feels like we've known each other longer than we have."

Dragging my hands down the front of my thighs, I say, "I think we've just lived more life in the time we've known each other than before we met."

"I thought life was so fucking hard back then."

"It's much harder now."

He nods, leaning his head against the seatback, he sighs. "Let's not ever grow up."

I laugh at the irony before the humor is gone. "I think it's too late."

"It's never too late to live in Neverland."

"I thought Neverland was only for boys."

"Hmm... I don't think so." He contemplates the thought before adding, "Wendy was there."

"Wendy wasn't supposed to be there though. Peter took her there."

"Maybe we can just pretend she was meant to be there all along."

Looking down at my lap, I twist the hem of my shirt. His words always seem to have a meaning deeper than what's spoken. "I'll be Wendy," I whisper, playing along with what I hope is the right assumption. "You can show me your world, Peter."

He glances over at me, then back to the road, his brown eyes revealing how he feels. "You look beautiful." Reaching forward he turns on some music. The Nirvana song is loud, the words sad, but like the man sitting next to me, complex and completely captivating.

When we near the store, he slows down, and asks, "Do you want to wait here or come with me?"

"I'll come with you."

He pulls up to the curb and the attendant opens my door. Dex moves to the sidewalk, giving the keys to the valet as he passes. I could be mistaken but it looks as if he's reaching for my hand, then quickly tucks it into his pocket instead. When I'm by his side, I ask, "Hey, what was that?"

While checking out the surrounding area, he says, "That was the realization that Neverland only exists when we're alone. The rest of the world owns everything else."

His strides are long and determined to reach the shop, so I pick up my pace to keep up with him. "It doesn't have to be like that, Dex. Cory and I—"

He stops and looks at me. His demeanor patient, but his expression tainted when he asks, "What about you and Cory?"

Eeks. Touchy subject. "Um, I was just going to say that we managed to elude them most times when we went out."

Staring into my eyes, his narrow, but suddenly he checks his watch. "We're going to be late."

"Late for what?"

"Lunch," he says as the door to the jeweler opens and he walks in.

A few minutes later, he's inspecting a brooch in the shape of a cat. "My mother loves cats as companions. I think it's because they're aloof like she is. She disagrees."

"I love fireflies."

With a smile, he says, "Why fireflies? They're ugly."

"But at night they transform. They're magical. I've seen them on the East Coast, but I don't think I've ever seen them here in LA."

"I don't think I have either. It's probably too smoggy." He hands his credit card to the salesperson after approving the custom piece.

"I bet there are fireflies in Neverland."

His hand brushes against mine. "I bet there are."

"You're taking me home for lunch?"

"No, I'm taking you to my mother's."

"In Beverly Hills?"

"Yes," he responds and turns left.

"You're a rich kid, aren't you, Dexter?"

He takes a right, obviously a short cut he knows by heart. "As the band's business manager, you know how much money I've made."

"You're right. I do, but I mean, you come from money. How did I never know this before?"

"I guess you had your mind on other things."

That hits hard. "I guess I did. I'm sorry for not asking about you before now. I should have. I want to know all about you and your family."

Pulling up to the white gate of the nearest driveway, he punches in a code on the keypad. As the big gates open before us, he says,

"We're here." After he parks, he takes the gift from the seat between us and looks at me. "My Mother can be intimidating. Don't take her shit."

My wide eyes must show my fear. "How about I just stick close to you?"

"That's good." The mood lightens and we get out.

A butler is standing at the open front door when we approach. "Sir, good to see you again," he says.

"Good to see you, Charles. You know I prefer Dex to Sir. This is my friend, Rochelle Floros."

"Ms. Floros. It's a pleasure to meet you," he greets me with a slight bow.

"Rochelle is fine," I say, sticking my hand out to shake his. He hesitates before accepting it. I know it goes against their formal training to accept the handshake, but I haven't been around butlers and such since I lived in Boston. Housekeepers, yes. But formally trained butlers, no.

I smile at Dex, so curious as to how he went from this fancy estate to where I met him at that dive down on Sunset. As we follow Charles inside, I whisper, "We've known each other for almost eleven years."

"Eleven next month."

"You knew that?"

"I—"

"Antonio," a woman calls as she comes toward us, the sound bouncing off the marble floors, echoing. She's dressed in a maid's uniform.

I'm kind of blown away by how different everything is here from his house in the Hills, and how I know Dex to be. But we're all shaped from our childhood so I'm interested to see if any of the rich kid from Beverly Hills still remains.

"Judith." His arms open wide. Looking at me over her shoulder, he adds, "Judith was my nanny when I was young. She stayed on as housekeeper afterward." He pulls back and smiles at her. "You're looking good. You working out?"

He's such a flirt.

She blushes with a hand on her hip, and replies, "I have a new boyfriend, so there might be a little workout involved."

"You dirty girl!" he says with a look of approval.

"Stop it." She swats his arm and he playfully ducks out of reach. "Anyway, you're here for lunch with your mother, but unfortunately, she's not here."

The good-natured moment has evaporated and a staleness fills the air. "Where is she?"

"It doesn't matter, Antonio. I've got a wonderful meal and I see you've brought a friend. Hello, I'm Judith." A warm, welcoming smile crosses her face as she reaches for my hand.

"I'm Rochelle. It's very nice to meet you."

She covers the back of my hand with her free one and asks, "Are you hungry?"

Dex cuts in before I can respond, "We're not staying."

Judith rubs his arm. "Don't let her upset you."

"She already did. Where'd she go?"

Judith hesitates then glances to me before she answers him, "The club."

He nods as he walks toward me. "She always did enjoy spending more time with a martini than her own son. Did Gage call her?"

"No, he was due in court today."

"We're gonna go." His pain evident.

"Antonio…" I hear the sadness in Judith's voice. It sounds a lot like the ache in my chest I'm feeling for him.

He takes my hands and starts walking back out the door.

Judith hurries behind us, and says, "I'm sorry she's not here."

"Not your fault. Always good to see you and go easy on your new boyfriend. Not everyone can handle a sex kitten like you in the sack," he jokes.

She laughs. "More like cougar. I haven't been a kitten for many years."

In the car, we wait at the bottom of the driveway for the gates to open. The tension in the car is building but I just want to make it go away and heal the hurt he's feeling. "I'm sorry you won't get to see your mother."

"We're gonna see her."

"We are?"

He nods, not adding to the conversation. Certain topics control his mood like a pendulum. He can be the happiest guy around and then fall to the other side when a heaviness replaces the joy. His mother is obviously one of these topics. Cory being another…

Ten minutes of listening to the engine roar as the wind blows through the open windows of the car, and we're there. Security waves him through. "Are you a member of this country club?" I ask.

"My family has generational privileges."

"Makes sense and very fancy, Mr. Caggiano. I didn't think you golfed."

He pulls into a parking spot and says, "Actually, I do golf. I even played in high school on the team for a year before I quit."

"Why'd you quit?"

"Because I hate golf clothes almost as much as I hate Chad Spears and he was Team Captain."

"Why do you hate Chad so much?"

His irritation is apparent. "Spears is a spoiled asshole." His eyes hook to his right onto mine and he says, "Listen, stay away from him. He's shiny on the outside, all packaged up and manufactured by his producer parents and Hollywood, but he's bad news."

"Are you jealous?" I tease. Wrong move on my part.

Cutting the engine, he stares at me. "I'm not jealous. The girls he dates, they're different when he's done with him. He's a user of drugs, people, and connections. He gets high off of building himself up by destroying others. Bad news, Rochelle. Don't trust him. Okay?"

I've never seen him so serious before. "Fine."

"Promise me?"

"Okay, I promise," I reply.

I'm learning there's a long history there. I mentally note that Chad Spears is another one of those hot topics for Dex.

We walk inside the main building and I follow as he begins

walking faster, taking big strides to the patio on the other side. The place is busy, the ladies who lunch dressed in tennis clothes, Diane Von Furstenberg, or silk dresses. I feel out of place, definitely under-dressed now.

There's a beautiful woman, flawless skin with chestnut colored hair that is reminiscent of Jackie O. She's laughing with three friends, martini glasses in front of each. He sets the present down in front of her and says, "Happy Birthday, Mother." With that out of the way, he turns around and starts walking away.

She doesn't seem surprised in the least as she calls, "Antonio. Come back here." Her tone is not demanding, but lilted with a smile, maybe to keep up appearances.

"Dex," I whisper, taking hold of his arm before he passes me. "Stop." I nod behind me and add, "It can be different. Give her a chance."

His hardened glare softens before my eyes as he looks at me. When his hand touches my face, he whispers, "You're so damn beautiful." He leaves me standing there in awe of his sweet words and twisted from the sad event.

Her voice reminds me of Katherine Hepburn and other women of society back East, not California at all. "Are you with my son?" she asks, fluffing the bottom of her bob hairstyle.

With big curious eyes on me, I reply, "I am." Maybe more than I'm ready to acknowledge.

"Please send my gratitude for the gift."

Her sentiment feels cold despite the words. "I think it would mean more coming from you."

She's uncomfortable in the conversation by how she shifts on her feet. "He doesn't take my calls," she states with one hand on her hip.

"Maybe because you stand him up. Excuse me. I need to catch up with him." I hurry away, rushing through the clubhouse and out the doors. Dex is sitting in his car, windows down, the engine off. When I approach, he slides his sunglasses down over his eyes and looks straight ahead. Choosing to let this all die down, his emotions showing in his slumped shoulders, I lean my palms on the open window, and say, "Hey, you still owe me lunch."

With a tilt of his head in my direction, I see a slight smile cross his face. "You're right. Get in."

"I DIDN'T KNOW Beverly Hills had burger joints." I take another big bite of my burger.

"It's a little secret. Most people don't realize that not everyone in Beverly Hills proper is wealthy. There are pockets of average working Joes."

Related, but my thoughts veering, I state, "I've thought about moving."

His head jolts and he's facing me. "Where?"

"I'm not sure. Just somewhere else."

Setting his burger down, he appears to have lost his appetite. He pushes his plastic basket away from him and looks out at the nearby street. "LA?"

"There are a lot of memories tied up in LA, but I feel it might be time for a change of scenery."

When he turns back to me, there's an earnestness found in his unwavering confession. "I don't want you to leave."

His honesty strikes me, causing me to take him seriously. "I have the boys, Dex."

Leaning forward, his whispered words don't hide his irritation, "You keep reminding me like I don't realize you're a package deal."

"I remind you so you can get out before it's too late."

"It's already too late."

His words take my breath, a silent gasp held hostage while I stare into the sincerity of his comforting eyes. Two beats of my pulse and I'm revived, and reply, "You don't know what you're saying."

Under the table, he finds my hand and holds it. "My feelings for you are real. But for you, I'll be your Peter Pan and you can pretend to be Wendy and we'll stay in Neverland until you're ready to see that Neverland doesn't have to live only in our imaginations."

"Dex?" I say, looking down. It's all too much and I push my burger away, feeling a lump forming in my throat. "You say these things in broad daylight—"

"I say what I feel and I feel so much for you."

I sigh. "Please—"

"Please what?"

Sitting up, our fingers falling away from each other, I say, "Please leave the future out there in the distance for just a little longer. I have things that I need to sort through first, right here in the present."

"I'll wait."

Getting up, I set my napkin on the table and walk around the booth to his side. Sliding in next to him, I take his face between my hands and ask, "Did Wendy and Peter ever kiss?"

With a smug smile in place, he says, "All the fucking time."

My smile is unstoppable as I lift up to kiss him on the lips. His strong hands cover my sides, holding me to him, but he pulls back. "We shouldn't do this here."

"I'm sorry."

"Don't be."

"Good. Because I'm really not."

He leans forward this time and kisses my forehead. "Let's go. I need to get you back to the Valley before the kids are out of school." Hearing him say that makes me think that maybe he does realize what comes along with dating me.

In the car, I want to ask him about his mother, but I'm not sure how to broach the subject. I decide direct is best. "Your Mother said to tell you thank you."

Silence.

"Dex?"

"I haven't seen my brother, Gage, in almost a year. He's married and lives in Thousand Oaks. LA's big, but it's not that big."

"Why haven't you seen him?"

"He's a lawyer, a partner at a firm with a steady job and all that, former pride of my family, but he took money from me and I found out three years ago."

"He stole from you?"

Dex's fingers tighten around the wheel, his knuckles going white. "He set up this account and had me sign a contract that I thought was for IRS reporting. It blew up in his face when the IRS contacted my accountant wanting their money. Like I wouldn't find out."

I shift my back against the door, so I can see him better. "Why didn't I know about this?"

With a glance, he says, "You were kind of busy three years ago."

The plane crash. The funeral. My darkest year.

"I'm sorry." I say it because my heart aches for him and his betrayal.

With a reassuring smile, he says, "Why are you sorry? You have no reason to be."

"I'm sorry I couldn't be there for you."

"There was nothing anybody could do. I dealt with my shitty brother. Per her usual MO, my Mother didn't take my side—"

"She took his?"

"No, she tried to play Switzerland, but I know deep down if the roles had been reversed, she would have sided with him. He was always her favorite. It was easy to see it. Each summer, I was shipped off to my grandfather's. She took him to the South of France."

"Doesn't sound like it was all bad if you ask me. I mean, how much sun and beautiful azure-colored water can you really stare at all day?"

His laugh is heard over the wind that whistles through the car. "True." When his hand finds mine, he says, "You have a really unique way of looking at situations, Wendy."

"It's a gift, I guess. I just learned that you see a situation how you want to see it, whether it's the truth or not."

"Your beauty shines through."

"Well I'm also learning that you're not just a pretty face and kickass drummer."

Chuckling, he says, "Nope, I also have other talents." He waggles his tongue, and at the sight of that, I clench my legs together. If he wasn't so damn sexy, I might be offended.

Pulling up into my driveway, I say, "Can't wait to see that in action, you big tease."

"It's not about seeing. It's about feeling. And trust me, I'm struggling to wait too." He looks past me, and says, "You're home."

I'm too stunned and now too turned on to think clearly, so I just sit there for a few seconds trying to collect myself from the puddle I turned into on the floorboard of his Challenger. The name of the car feels way too apropos right now. "Yeah, I should go... home, inside, the place I live," I start rambling.

One more stunning smile in my direction, and he adds, "I'll see you tomorrow."

"Yes, um, right. Tomorrow."

I get out and stumble a bit, left a little off balance from his words and a lot off balance by how much he affects me. And just like how the day started, I'm left impatiently waiting for Thursday to get here.

9

ANTONIO DEXTER CAGGIANO

SHE'S BECOME AN ADDICTION, and something I obsess over. Living the life I have, living it hard, I've become an expert at both addiction and obsession. I know the difference. Rochelle is the first person I've felt both over.

Now that she's let me in, I never want to go. I've waited so long for this chance. I have to pretend to act normal, but I feel anything but that when I'm around her. I don't want to scare her. I want... I want... I want so much with her, from her, that it scares me. But I play it cool, keeping my deepest thoughts to myself. I'm good like that, the quiet one. I've been called moody, but it's not that. That's an emotion someone wears for show. My moods aren't for show, but to hide, to protect what I don't want any of them to see. If they know how I really feel, rejection can follow and I've had too much of that in my life to survive a rejection from her.

I lie on the couch in the middle of my dark house, letting her invade my thoughts and crawl under my skin, becoming a part of me. She's the sun when it sets and my moon when it rises. My day begins and ends with her on my mind. She asks about me but all I want to do is hear about her. Her days are mundane to her, but are envious to me. Routine. She has this amazing life, her routine as she calls it, and

I just want to be there, be a staple, a part of her daily routine. Too much.

Obsessed.

I'm obsessed.

This girl, this light, walked into my life and I just had to follow it. At nineteen, she was beautiful. She had brown hair with that just come from the beach look—chin length, a little wild, a little off. Her big brown eyes reminded me of the sun tea that would sit in the window sill when I was a kid. Rochelle didn't belong in that bar, but she owned it the minute she walked in, under-aged and full of confidence.

From behind the drumkit, I watched her, changing my beat to match the rhythm of her vibe. She was unique in the middle of a crowd of trite. As she put her straw to her mouth, my gaze wrapped around her wrist and followed the floral tattoo that had been started but not yet finished. When the band took a break, she climbed right up on stage and said, "You're good. You ever consider playing rock?"

"We play some rock covers sometimes."

"What about rock music that you help create? Original stuff."

Leaning back on my stool, I cross my arms over my chest. "I don't own my drums. It's me and the sticks for now."

She shrugs. "That's cool. It's your talent that caught my ear. Anyway, the bassist has a set of drums you can use if you want to join our band."

Suddenly, she had my undivided attention. Well, she had it before, but now she's talking drums and a real band. "Why does a bassist have a drum kit?"

"He used to think he wanted to be a drummer, but his talent lies in the guitar."

"And what do you play?" I ask, so damn curious by this tenacious girl.

"Guitar. I'm not in the band, but two of the best guitarists around are. They're gonna be big. This is your chance."

I stand and notice the height difference. She's short and really fucking cute. "Why aren't you in the band if you play guitar?"

"If you wanna sit around here all night yapping, then I'll let you get back to playing cover songs from the seventies that should have never been made in the first place. But if you want in on the next big thing, then come with me."

"You want me to meet them tonight? Right now?"

With a smile, she says, "Yeah, right now. We have a gig in an hour and no drummer."

"You want me to play a gig with them tonight?"

Nodding, she looks at me like I'm the crazy one. "Yep. I saw how you hit. You're good. You've got natural skill. Not all drummers do."

"You actually want me to leave before the end of this gig to go play *your* gig?"

"I sure do. Is that a yes?" She turns and looks around the club. "I mean, I understand how karaoke—"

"Covers."

"I stand corrected. Covers. I totally get that playing covers can sometimes be cool and all, but I'm giving you the chance to be a part of something great."

"Promise?" I smirk.

"Promise. C'mon. I hate being late."

She hops off the stage and I follow right behind her, hoping that 'something great' will include hooking up with her later. Calling across the room to the old guys I was backing, I say, "Thanks guys. It's been fun, but my work here is done."

They don't seem entirely surprised and raise a pint to me.

Out on the street, she takes a helmet off of a Honda Shadow motorcycle and hands it to me. I recognize it from when I worked as a mechanic last year for a few months. I helped rebuild one similar to this. "This is yours?" I ask.

"Sure is."

"It's in good condition. What year is it?"

"An '87. Ever ridden one before?"

She's a feisty little thing, but I can handle her attitude. "Yeah, but I've never owned one."

"You should. There's nothing that feels more freeing than riding a motorcycle." She tightens the strap under her chin, and adds, "There's always a chance of death when you ride a bike. Makes you appreciate the life you have."

Nodding, I try to relate to this girl. I tuck the drumsticks into my Martens and pull my jeans over them. We get on and she warns, "Hold on tight."

I wrap my arms around her waist and we swerve into traffic. *Holy shit!* The girl's a dare devil. Leaning forward, I ask, "So what's the name of this soon to be big band anyway?"

She speeds up and yells into the wind, "The Resistance."

BECAUSE OF A LAST minute project Neil had due, Thursday turned into dinner at her place again. Rochelle apologized, but I didn't mind. I actually liked it. I'm already attached to the boys, being around them is fun. And anytime I get to spend time with her is good.

"Whatever happened to that motorcycle you had?" I ask Rochelle as we lay on a blanket in the middle of the backyard. The sun has set, the kids are watching a cartoon, and we just finished a bottle of wine.

"I got rid of it a few years ago," she replies. "It's clear enough to see some stars tonight."

I've learned when she changes the subject, not to push. She's not as open as she used to be, but I understand that the harshness of life changes people. It's changed her in ways I wish I could give back to her. I move to the new topic to keep her in the moment, here with me. "I once heard that only those who see the big picture can focus on the details."

Looking tired, but amused, she turns to me. "What does that mean?"

Seeing the sparkle to her eyes, I give her a smile. "If we see things on a grander scale, we're more likely to appreciate the little things that make it up."

When I look at her, there's a small smile on her face when she says, "Sometimes you say the most amazing things and I don't even think you realize it."

"If it makes you smile, my work here is done."

With a giggle, her hand nudges mine between us. As if the thought just came to her, she comments, "You never ask for anything. Not even on your performer's contract rider. No special requests whatsoever."

I want to touch her, to kiss her again, and reinforce that it wasn't a wet dream. We had sex once and the memory still haunts me. As casually as I can, I cover one finger over hers, and reply, "Nothing I want can be put on a tour rider."

From the look in her eyes, she's analyzing the meaning beneath my words, but she knows deep down what I really mean. Knowing we can't quite go there yet, I add, "Anyway, the guys request enough shit for all of us on tour."

"That's true." Moving closer, she uses my chest as a pillow. I wrap my arm around her shoulders and steal a peek at her boys inside. They look content with popcorn and big smiles on their faces, giggling at the kid's movie playing. These two boys that I've watched grow from a distance might become my responsibility one day... and I'm not opposed to this. I see Cory in their faces. They have Rochelle's heart and spunk.

I can give... *What can I give them that matters?* They have money. They have family. Any toy they could ever want for is easily bought. *What role can I play in their lives that add value? How can I make their lives better by being in it?*

Her voice is soft and cuts into my doubts. "If you could have anything, what would it be, Dex?"

I slip my hand down her back and rub while staring up at the sky again. "Time. I'd want time back."

She sits up, leaning over me while looking down, her gaze soft but direct. "And what would you do if you got time back?"

"I wouldn't waste a minute." I sit up and kiss her, running my hand into her hair and holding her close.

"Ew! What are you doing?" Neil says with disgust in his tone.

We part like two teenagers busted by their parents. Rochelle is to her knees and then standing up in a flash. "I, uh, he was helping me look for my earring." She tugs at her earlobe.

"It looked like kissing," Neil adds.

"It was," she starts again, her voice shaking. "It was kissing but like just a friendly goodnight kiss since Dex is leaving. Yeah, so—"

"Yeah, kiddo, I'm leaving." I stand and look between the two of them. "Thanks for having me over." Rochelle's a mess and Neil seems a little protective of his mother in his stance. That's my cue. When I approach, he opens the door nice and wide for me. I walk inside and he follows with Rochelle behind him. "I'm thinking you can come over this week, Neil, and we can play on my drums. I can teach you some beats, easy rhythms. What do you think about that?"

"That'd be cool," he says, his tone lighthearted again.

At the front door, Rochelle says, "Thanks for coming over."

I'm not sure what to say because everything I want to, I can't with Neil between us, so I turn to leave instead. "Thanks again for dinner. Bye, CJ. Bye, Neil. I'll see you in a few days."

"Bye-bye," CJ yells.

Neil nods. "Bye."

And when I see Rochelle, she mouths silently, "I'm sorry." When I start walking away from the door, I hear her say, "C'mon, buddy, let's get you guys to bed." The door shuts and I'm left standing in the dark under a blanket of stars wondering what the fuck I'm doing. I think I just got in trouble by a seven-year-old.

As soon as I walk into my house, I head for the bar. It's stocked just the way I like it because although I don't make requests on the road, I do in my own home. I pour bourbon over ice and watch as the ice begins to melt on contact. It's the same burning that I usually feel, like an addiction reminding me how it has all the control. I give into it every time, realizing I don't need the upper hand. I just need to feel the burn again.

And the sensation is euphoric much like Rochelle—a burning euphoria.

Outside, I sit in a chair, setting my drink down to replace it with a cigarette. Under the same stars, but separated by more than a few miles physically and emotionally. Deep drags calm my insides as I rest my hands on my thighs and close my eyes.

I need to loosen up.

Addiction.

Obsession.

Square One.

There are more cons than pros when it comes to Rochelle. Just when I thought it might be our time after all of these years, life has happened, making it more complicated. She's a mother. Damn, that still blows my mind. She's a good one, not like mine at all. Rochelle's warm. My mother is cold. About the only thing they have in common is money, but my mother comes from undeserved, family funds. Money I've already started to inherit on a monthly basis from my grandfather's estate since I turned thirty. Apparently thirty is the expected age to have one's life figured out and in order.

I'll take his money and try not to think about him too much. But memories are powerful and hard to force down.

THEODORE DEXTER THE FIFTH was a trip. The most formal man I've ever known. He wore suits to dinner and everyone was expected to follow the dress code when in his presence. My mother obliged him when we stayed there. She would stay for a few days before taking my brother on her escapades around the world. Gage was more presentable by nature, the chosen child to represent The Dexter's. I would stay at my grandfathers for at least two weeks each summer without them. I actually liked the time alone, but when visiting, even my play clothes were discarded after one wearing for not being crisp in appearance. Breakfast was at 7 or you got none. Lunch at eleven. Tea at three. Dinner at six. Bed by eight. The name of the city always felt fitting. Expectations ran high in Diablo, California. They ran high back in LA too, but here I missed my friends.

At thirteen, I snuck out of my room after curfew with thoughts of running away, running back home. I figured no one would notice anyway. I cut through the property and passed the guest quarters when I heard some banging. I moved closer, feeling very stealthy at the time. When I got close enough to look in the window, I saw Tres, the handyman I had seen around the house playing drums. I didn't even know he lived here. He was probably in his early twenties and was wearing a black Ramones shirt. A cigarette, or joint, hung from the corner of his mouth. It was dark outside, but he wore his sunglasses anyway. One of the newly hired maids, a blonde who looked like she was his age, danced around with her arms in the air. Her uniform was unbuttoned enough to see her bright pink bra and the skirt rose up as she moved.

My journey that night ended there. I sat down in a chair outside the window—watched and listened for over an hour. I was fixated on that kit and the power he put into hitting it as much as I was on seeing her slowly strip for him. They turned out the lights, but a purple lava lamp lit the room enough to see them as they hit the bed. I'd never seen two people having sex. I had magazines I stole from a convenience store down by the public school near us, but never seen a video, much less two people in real life having sex.

Tres blended into the darkness. But the blonde was hot and as much as I knew I shouldn't watch, I stayed there until she yelled his name long enough to penetrate the walls. I got up after that and went back to my room.

I lied in bed that night, jerked off for the first time to visions of her before falling asleep. When I woke up, I was angry. I had taken piano for five years and I hated it. I hated practicing and the recitals. I hated the formality and having to perform at dinner parties like a chump. I knew it wasn't frowned upon to play piano or any classical instrument, but the drums were, so it made them that much more intriguing

The next morning when I thought no one was around, busy at their jobs, I went back to the guest house and went inside. I spent three hours banging away on that drum kit and that was it. I saw how she reacted to him, turned on by the man behind the drums. That could be me. I could turn her on too. I knew I'd found my passion. The secrecy of it all, this crazy, loud, invasive music just clicked with me.

MY LEGS ARE BURNING, causing me to open my eyes in a hurry. "Shit!" I jump up, the cigarette flung from my hand. I grab my drink and pour a little over my burned skin. The lit end had burned a small hole through my jeans and singed some hair on my leg.

I finish my drink in three gulps and set the glass down on the table before going inside. Up the stairs to my room I go, opening the door, and closing it behind me. I walk into the bathroom and turn on the shower, debating if it should be hot or cold; I have a good argument for each right now. I decide on hot, wanting to relieve some pressure. Stripping down, I then move under the water. My muscles not relaxing like I hoped.

My body is tense. I want to fuck. I want to fuck hard. I want to fuck and come and not wonder what the fuck I'm doing chasing Rochelle. I have a phone full of numbers I could call. I don't want them. They are a thousand numbers that are meaningless to me. They aren't her and my hand is a better option than a poor substitute.

Leaning my head against the slate wall, I close my eyes, remembering her body on top of mine, and how it was wrapped around my cock like a warm blanket. My grip tightens. She was so fucking wet, wet for me. Kisses to her neck became licks of ecstasy. I tasted her sweat, her sweetness before wanting her to come so I could taste all of her.

But Cory's name shocks me back to reality just like it did that day and my dick goes soft. "Fuck!" I slam the shower off and get out, dripping across the floor while walking to the cabinet and retrieving a towel.

After drying off, I get into bed angry. I sit up and punch the fuck out the pillow next to me before throwing it across the room and hearing it hit the door with a thud when it falls. So fucking anticlimactic for how I'm feeling.

Getting out of bed, I grab boxer brief from my dresser and pull them on. I go outside onto my balcony and sit down. The lighter and pack of cigarettes are on the table. I light up, resisting the urge for another drink. I look out over the city of Los Angeles all lit up in the distance frustrated that the best thing that ever happened to me sometimes feels like the worst.

10

ROCHELLE

I REACH FOR MY JOURNAL, but stop when I realize what I want to write is not what I'm ready to share with Cory. I grab my laptop instead. I write to get it out, to help unburden my heart.

Love finds most of us fast and unexpectedly, but when it came to me and Dex, it was slow and calculated as if it knew to hold on and wait. I'm caught in the middle of developing feelings for a man that has shown me more than his heart. He's shown me his soul.

Feeling much like lyrics, I title it 'Dex' and save the document in my Songs folder. The one thing I've learned about giving a part of yourself away is that you may not get it back. Love is a risk and I'm finding that I'm more willing to take it with him. I'm still left questioning if I'm as ready as I think I am, if I'm prepared to have someone in my life that is also a regular fixture in the boys' lives. I have no room for casual when it comes to them, so I need to be sure before jumping into something that could leave us devastated again.

Me: Hi.

Thirty minutes go by on this Friday evening before he replies: *Hi.*

What to say? What to say? *Me: How are you?*

Dex: Good. You?

I'm not feeling very liked right now. *Me: I'm fine. What are you up to?*

Dex: I'm out. You want to join us?

Me: Us?

Dex: Some friends of mine. You should come.

"Beth?" I call from my office.

The boys' nanny comes in. "Yes?"

"Can you work late tonight?"

A sly smile works its way across her face. "You going out?"

"I'm thinking I might."

She's always supportive of me. "I'll stay. I could use the extra money and I owe CJ a foot race in the backyard. He's convinced he can outrun me just because I'm a girl."

"Make sure to win big. We can't have them growing up thinking women are the weaker sex."

With a laugh, she says, "Nope, we can't have that. Now you get ready and I'll go tell the boys we get to make ice cream sundaes."

"Thanks for staying."

"No problem at all."

I close my email and shut down my computer before going into my bedroom, phone in hand. *Me: Text me where you'll be in an hour.*

Dex: I'm glad you're coming out. It's been too long since I've seen you.

Me: You saw me yesterday.

Dex: Like I said, it's been too long.

And I swoon, holding the phone to my chest as the happy emotions bubble up inside.

Just over an hour later, I'm walking into the outside patio of a restaurant that's located at the back of a well-known hotel. It's a private place that's hard to get into unless you're famous or you're with someone famous, so celebrities like to hang out here.

Dex is seated at a table on the far side of the garden. There are four other people with him—three guys and a girl. With a cigarette in his mouth, he turns my way and a smile appears. Smoke fills the air above his head as he exhales, then stubs out the butt. Standing up, his chair is pushed back. He takes my hand and kisses my cheek, then whispers, "Glad you're here."

"Me too," I reply.

"Sit here. I'll get another chair."

When I sit, the conversation ceases, so I lift my hand awkwardly, and say, "Hi, I'm Rochelle." I recognize two of the guys from parties or somewhere in the past. But the other man and the woman I don't.

She smiles, but it's tight-lipped while she scopes me out to see if I'm competition for whomever she has her eye on at the table. This happens a lot in LA. Men hold all the cards here and too many women indulge that power by presenting it on a silver platter to them. "Enchante," she says, putting her hand toward me like I should kiss it. I take the limp hand, dropping it as quickly as I can.

Dex brings a chair, setting it at the corner of the crowded table. Tilting his head, he looks at me and smiles. It's sexual and genuine all in one. "It's good to see you." When he looks back to the group, he starts the introductions, "Toby, Keith, but not the country singer, Wes, and Firenza. This is Rochelle."

Firenza? Sounds exotic. Funny, I didn't hear an accent.

Her chair is bumped up to his, and she leans forward, her arm resting on top of Dex's. "You look familiar. How would I know you?"

Dex sits back, moving his arm out from under hers.

Everyone looks at me, waiting for an answer, but Toby replies, "She was married to the guitarist of the band."

"Which band?" Firenza asks.

Dex sits up, looking annoyed. "The Resistance." His answer is clipped.

She ignores his mood and continues in on me. "So you're divorced, but you still hang on... I mean, hang out with Dex?"

"I'm not divorced. Cory and I weren't marrie—"

Dex's hands hit the table, drawing my attention as the metal feet of his chair scrape across the cement when he stands. "I haven't seen the waitress in forever. I'm gonna get a drink from the bar." He leaves so abruptly that we're left staring at his back as he goes inside.

Uncomfortable being left here with her and confused to why he left, I start to get up so I can check on Dex. Persistent Firenza keeps going like nothing unusual happened at all though. "So you were only dating?" She scrunches her nose at me.

Wes touches her arm and she glares at him when he says, "He died. He was the one who died in the plane crash."

Hearing Cory dismissed so easily by her angers me. I stand, my own chair noisy this time. When I look at her, her expression never changes. It's just as cold and bitchy as a moment earlier. "You're dating his band mate now?"

My eyes meet Wes's and I say, "I'm gonna find Dex."

As I'm walking away, I hear her explaining to the others, "So what, she's dating Dex now. Who's next, Johnny Outlaw?"

I let the bad vibes go as the distance grows between us. She wants to package me up and categorize me so it's easier for her to under-stand. But none of this is easy to understand and if I don't, then she won't either. Dex is leaning on the bar talking with a tall brunette. She's laughing. He's smiling. I'm stepping to the side, debating. And now I'm apparently spying. *Ugh!* I make my way through the crowd of cocktail tables and patrons, not wanting to confront him, which is exactly what I'll do if I talk to him now. But I still can't resist sneaking a peek at him. He takes her card and tucks it into his shirt pocket before they say their goodbyes.

Wow. And here I was stupid enough to think he actually wanted me. *Why'd I even bother?* I just don't fit into his world and by watching him, I don't want to. I can't stay here and continue to be hurt by him or these women.

I continue toward the door that will lead me to the valet. Just as I exit, I hear him call after me. I hand the ticket to the valet attendant and step to the side, pretending to be oblivious to Dex. "Rochelle? Why are you leaving?"

He's got two drinks in his hand and he hands one to me. I don't take it, but glance off to the side to see if that's my car being pulled around. It's not. I say, "You left me out there with that woman who seems to think I'm a gold-digger of some sort while you come inside and collect other women's numbers. And you're surprised I'm leaving?"

"I didn't want to be rude. She works for Gucci and wants to talk to me about the potential for a campaign."

"She should be talking to me then. I'm your business manager. Why'd you leave the table?"

He stares at me and I stare right back. Then he sets the drinks down on the valet podium and reaches into his shirt pocket, pulling out his pack of cigarettes. Flicking one up, he takes it and taps it on the inside of his wrist before lighting it and taking a deep inhale. Finally, he says, "I don't want to talk about Cory."

"I didn't bring him up. I was only correcting *Firenza's* rude comment."

"I don't want *you* talking about Cory tonight."

"Then you should have answered for me so I didn't have to."

He inhales again. With a slow exhale above my head, he says, "I wanted you to meet some of my friends. That's all."

"Your friends are assholes."

"Not all of them."

"No Dex, you're right. Not all of them. Just her. And who is she exactly? I seem to be lost on her connection to you."

He drops the cigarette to the ground and says, "We used to fuck."

My heart is set on fire as he crushes me with his flippancy. I glare at him, then spit, "You sure it's past tense?"

"I'm not having sex with her anymore. Why are you so bent out of shape?"

I double blink in shock at his attitude toward me. This is the Dex I've always known, his cocky side getting the best of him. I shouldn't bother, but I do. "By how territorial she seemed during the interrogation I got, she might be under the impression the two of you are still fucking."

With a shrug and an arrogant grin on his face, he says, "What can I say, she wants me."

"Ms. Floros," the valet says, tapping me on the shoulder. "Your car's here."

I turn and take the keys while tipping the valet. "Thank you." Without another word, I begin to leave, but I'm startled and spun around, then pinned against my car by Dex's firm body.

"Don't leave," he whispers just a breath away. "Stay."

"Why?"

"Because I'm not fucking her anymore and the only reason that I'm not is you."

"That's not charming."

"I'm not trying to be charming. I'm trying to be truthful. She knows I like you. You're a threat to her."

"I'm not gonna get into some catfight over you."

"You don't have to. We can ditch them or join them and I'll set her straight. Whatever you want, I'll do. Just stay with me." Our locked stares soften into gazes as our defenses come down, and he whispers, "Please stay."

His vulnerability is a turn on, so several heavy heartbeats later, I lay my conditions down for him. "Fine. I'll stay, but I want you to set her straight. She made me feel like I should be ashamed."

"She doesn't matter to me." He takes my hand in his. "Only you do." Leaning forward he kisses me, taking my breath away along with any doubts I had about us.

And with that, I give my keys back to the valet and we walk inside holding hands. He leads me back to the table, but we remain standing. Looking directly at *her*, he says, "We're not gonna do this anymore."

"I'm sorry, darling," Firenza replies, batting her eyelashes. "Do what?"

The table falls silent and he says, "Fuck. I'm not interested in anyone but Rochelle."

Her face falls when he says it so bluntly, and she starts reaching for anything to keep her in his good graces. "But she's like a groupie, going through the band."

"Shut your mouth," he demands, hitting his hand down on the table. "You know nothing about her. The only reason I'm even bothering to tell you that you and I are over is that I respect her enough to do it." He starts walking with me behind him, his grip wrapped tightly around my hand. "We're leaving. The crowd sucks tonight."

This time at the valet, *he* tips and takes the keys from the attendant. "I'll drive." I slip into the passenger seat and he waits to leave until I'm buckled in. The tension is high in the car, but not sexually like I prefer. He's mad and I'm not sure what to say, so I stay quiet.

By the route he's driving, he's taking me to his house. I hope his mood lightens when we get there. Before we enter his community, he says, "I want you to stay the night with me."

"I don't have a sitter for the night."

He doesn't say anything else the rest of the ride.

When we walk in, it's dark inside, but the pool lights are lit, drawing my eye to the backyard. "It's a beautiful night. We should go for a swim," I suggest, drawn to the blue lagoon.

When I look back to him, his eyebrow is raised and a devious grin lies across his face. "You don't have your suit."

"I can go in my underwear."

"Or go naked."

"Yes, or go naked but I'm thinking my bra and panties will be safer."

He unlocks the doors and opens them wide. "Safe from what?" he asks, following me outside. After kicking off his shoes, he unbuttons his shirt, exposing his sexy abs.

When the shirt is tossed to a nearby chair, I reply, "Safe, safe, safe. What were we talking about again?"

"You were saying how keeping your undies on would be safer."

"Oh yeah, that's right." A new skull and roses tattoo resides on his shoulder and I look at the style of it, reading the words under it—solum bonum decessura. I don't know what it means. I'm distracted again as he undoes each button on his jeans, making me inhale an uneven breath. *Safer.* I'm not sure if he's gonna be safe from my sexual attacks when he's that hot. His words make me look up when he asks, "You gonna get undressed or what?"

"I'm enjoying the show too much. I might just watch you instead."

"Shirt off, woman."

"All right. All right. Fine." I pull my top off and place it neatly on a chaise. Turning my back, I check him out over my shoulder.

He's at the bar and music starts playing though I don't see any speakers. *Nirvana's* "In Bloom." "I never knew you liked grunge so much. Jane's Addiction, now Nirvana."

"Soundgarden, Stone Temple Pilots though it's debatable about their grunginess. Bands of that time like Red Hot Chili Peppers have kick ass drummers. Rock is great but I like the rhythms that straddle the hardcore rock and the grunge era." He pulls bottles of liquor onto the countertop. I pop open the top button of my jeans as he pours two shots of tequila. With his jeans hanging low on his hips and wide open in the front, I feel my self-control slipping away as he comes toward me. "You never did get a drink at the bar."

"Salud," I say, taking the shot and downing it. "No lime?"

"No." His reply is direct, then his tongue drags up the corner of his mouth and I stare. My heart starts thudding in my chest as I move closer to him. He asks, "We should swim, right? It's safer that way."

"We'll end up the same either way."

His right hand touches just where my bra ends and goes lower exploring my waist. "How so?"

When his fingers dip into the back of my jeans, I reply, "Wet."

"*Fuuuck,*" he curses under his breath, looking up and taking a step back.

"I'm trying."

His hands slide into his hair, his frustration scene in the move. "Shit. You can't say things like that and expect me to stand here and not react."

"It's the tequila talking. Ignore me."

"Trust me. I've tried to ignore you. It's impossible."

With a sigh and roll of my neck, I say, "I'm thinking it's hot tub time."

"I'm thinking the pool to cool off." He takes his jeans off and dives in.

I take mine off and walk to the edge and sit down, dangling my feet in. He swims closer and grabs my ankles. Bearing my weight on my wrists I lift up as he tugs me down slowly until the front of my body slides down against his. Dex kisses my stomach as I slip into the chilly water.

"Why do we play these games anyway? I want you, Rochelle. I think that's clear."

Clear is not the word I would use for his erection. Rock hard might fit the situation better. The liquor warms my body as it infiltrates my senses and relaxes me. I wrap my legs around his waist, but lean back on the ledge, keeping my body afloat by holding onto the side.

"It's not just a matter of want between us."

Moving closer, his hands slide to my ass as he presses harder against me. "You're right, but we've got the basics covered. Aren't you ready to try more?"

Slipping my arms around his neck, I readjust, the wiggle making my body tingle. "It's not just about us. It's not even just about the kids. There are things, people involved that I don't want to hurt and you asked me not to talk about that tonight. So let's not. Let's just leave it for another day and have another shot."

There's a gleam in his eye reflecting the pool, maybe more as he looks at me. "Okay, more shots then."

He perches me on the side of the pool and I lay back as he jumps out. Staring up at the sky, I try to orientate myself by the constellations I'm used to seeing at home. Just as I start to think I'm turned around, I find the big dipper and a comfort settles in as does Dex. He sits down next to me and I ask, "What does your tattoo with the skull say?"

In Latin, he says, "Solum bonum decessura."

"What does it mean?"

"Only the good die young."

"When did you get it?"

"About a year ago."

"Do you want to talk about it?"

"No," he says, moving into a push-up, his face over mine. "I'd rather kiss you." He lowers down and kisses me. It's sweet, gentle, and wonderful, which is exactly opposite of how I really want him to kiss me.

I'm going to make figuring out what this is a priority tomorrow. Others may get hurt when I give this a real shot, but I can't live tethered to the past. Just when he's about to get up, I grab him, my hands at the back of his head and bring his lips to mine. I kiss him how I want to be kissed, and how I know he wants me to kiss him.

When our lips part, I intake the night air, savoring him on my lips. When he sits up, I do too before moving into the pool to face him. The shot is set on the edge, we clink our glasses, and finish the drink.

He lies on his stomach, resting his head on his crossed arms. "What time do you have to be home?"

"Midnight."

"That's two hours. Wanna make out?"

A laugh escapes, filling the serene surrounding. "Heck yeah, I do." Lifting up, I get out of the pool as he rolls onto his back. I stand above him, offering him a hand to get up. He accepts and stands, but quickly pulls me over to the hot tub. We climb in one at a time and I sit, settling on his lap. His hands hold onto me as his head dips back a bit, his eyelids growing heavy, as his focus on me intensifies. "You're so fucking sexy." He licks his lips. Watching him makes me clench, wanting those lips on me.

With one hand on my back and the other on my hip, he bucks beneath me, then brings me to him, our lips pressing together. Our words are replaced by the bubbling water, kisses, and soft sighs of pleasure. His tongue is strong and dominant, wanting to be felt, to feel, and I oblige.

Large hands cover my breasts and he squeezes gently. I take control as our kisses find purchase against our craving bodies. I run my fingers through his hair, and my nails down his back. His muscles dance under my touch, each tensing and releasing.

With his arms wrapped around the back of my shoulders, his hips join mine. The friction leading to a deeper desire, a desire I try to lessen to save us both the dissatisfaction we're gonna end up with. But it's impossible to hold back when he's giving so much.

That spot. That spot. That spot. The perfect spot being teased and coaxed until I tug his hair, pressing myself against him as I tighten my legs around him. My head drops back and his breath is warm as he covers me with hot kisses. His hands grab a hold of my hips. "God, Rochelle. I want you to be inside you. I want you so much."

Goosebumps cover my skin as his words become the only air I need. As I'm coming down from my own bliss, I want the same thing. I want him so badly. Before I can say anything his movements become erratic, his fingers digging into the flesh where my hips meet my ass. "So close," he says, his forehead against my collarbone. "Oh fuck. Yes." My shoulders are grabbed again and I'm pushed down on top of him.

His arms fall away as he leans back, closing his eyes. When he opens them, he grins, it's lazy and beautiful. Bringing me closer, he kisses me just like the first kiss tonight—deep and sensual, passionate just like the man.

"Sorry about the hot tub," I tease.

"Don't be. It was hot," he puns.

"The orgasm or the water?"

"Both."

"I agree." Feeling very comfortable here.

My body is relaxed and my eyes heavy as he walks me to my car. "Do you want me to drop you off so you can get your car?"

"No, I'll get it tomorrow."

His hips press into mine, my car solid behind my back. I say, "This was a good night."

"A very good night," he replies, kissing my neck. "When do we get to do it again?"

"Is tomorrow too soon?"

"Not soon enough."

11

ROCHELLE

If Dex didn't already have a piece of my heart, he has it all now. Watching him teach Neil how to play drums is beyond endearing and makes my heart clench. I've not seen Neil's attention on one thing last this long in a while. I can tell he likes Dex and Dex's patience is admirable. I hear Dex say, "Let's try it one more time on this drum. What's it called?"

"Ummmm...the tom-tom?" Neil answers.

"Right. Good job."

CJ runs in, alerting them to our presence. Dex looks up and winks at me, then asks, "You wanna join us? I have an acoustic guitar over here."

"Maybe." I'm still unsure, but being here in his music room makes me want to play... just a little bit.

CJ slips under the drum set and is pounding the bass with his hand until Dex grabs him and tickles him before placing my little whirlwind of energy beside him. He hands him a stick and says, "Hit the middle, not the rim. Okay, CJ?"

CJ bangs once and hits the rim, then asks, "The shiny part is the rim?"

"Yep. Don't hit that part."

I walk behind them, letting my fingers drag over Dex's shoulders as I pass. Picking up the guitar, I strum once, then start tuning it until I'm satisfied. Lots of banging on the drums distracts the boys, but I see Dex sneaking peeks at me while a small, knowing smile crosses his face. His lure worked and I took the guitar bait, too tempted being here in the easiness of his music room to resist. Sitting down on the edge of a recliner, I stroke the neck of the guitar, sliding my fingers up the slick wood and back down again. I position my fingers and start strumming again, but this time a melody I know by heart, my own song that I've been working on in my head and writing down on my laptop.

When I look up, my gaze meets Dex's and I don't stop, fighting the feeling to hide the music away. The notes come to me by memory, easy in their flow, the music dancing in my head, leading my hands. Then I stop. This is the part where I always stop, my head getting in the way of my heart. It's too heavy.

"You okay?" Dex asks, his furrowed brow showing his concern.

My breaths quicken as I struggle to control my emotions. Trying to halt the panic, I close my eyes and forcefully slow my breathing. I block out the fact that I know Dex is watching me freak out and try to concentrate on regulating each breath instead. When I reopen my eyes, Dex is kneeling before me. His hand covers my knee, but he doesn't say anything.

"I'm okay."

He nods, then stands up. "C'mon guys, let's go get cookies in the kitchen." Drumsticks are dropped with a careless clang and both boys race for the kitchen. Dex says, "I'll give you a few minutes."

As soon as he's gone, I take a deep breath and then another. Standing up, I pick up the drumsticks so it's not messy in here, having a strong desire to busy myself. I place the guitar back on the stand and turn out the lights. When I return to the living room, I see them outside, the boys running in the large grassy area to the left of the pool. Dex is sitting under the patio, two juiceboxes and two glasses on the table next to him.

I walk out the open door and laugh, "You have juiceboxes?"

As I sit across the table from him, he turns to me, his sunglasses covering his eyes. "I stocked up on kid essentials. I have popsicles too."

His sweet gesture sweeps me up in the moment and I smile. "Thank you."

"No thanks needed." We turn our attention to watching the kids, but he asks, "How long have you been getting panic attacks?"

"I'm not sure you want to hear about it."

"If I'm asking, I want to hear about it."

"I had my first when I went into labor with CJ."

His attention is now fully on me. Turning in his chair, he rests his elbows on the table. "Do you know what brought it on?"

"Hindsight says I do..."

He lifts his sunglasses to the top of his head and looks at me, really looks at me. "You know, I was thinking about Cory. I know I've said it before, but I feel I need to say it again." He glances away briefly then back to me. "I'm sorry. I'm sorry he died. I think about him all the time. I hear him when I play. It's still hard for me to talk about him, but he was a great man, Rochelle." I feel the tears welling up in the corners of my eyes, so I look away. After a calming breath, I feel strong enough to look back at him. When I do, he adds, "He was lucky to have you."

Turning back around, I say, "Dex—"

"I never told you this before, but as much as I loved him..." He pauses and gulps, his Adam's apple bobbing twice in his throat.

I cut him off this time. "Don't say it, okay?"

We stare into each other's eyes, holding the moment a few seconds longer. Pulling his sunglasses back down over his eyes, he gives a small nod before sitting back and looking out over the yard. From his profile, I can see his mood shift through his expression. He stands suddenly, grabbing his glass and going inside.

Following him in, I say, "I'm sorry. It just feels too personal—"

Anger covers his words. "It is fucking personal. It's personal to me. You go back and forth between square one and practically having sex with me in the hot tub the other night. Maybe I'm unclear as to what the fuck is going on between us, but I know how I feel. So I guess you need to figure your shit out and let me know so this doesn't end up messier than it needs to be."

"Shit? It's not shit, Dex. It's my life. I don't have to explain this to you. I owe you nothing."

When I turn to leave, he says to my backside, "Go ahead. Leave. It's safer that way, much like wearing your underwear in a hot tub."

"You're an ass, Dex."

His comeback is swift and tinged with arrogance. "A sexy one if I interpreted the way you stared at me the other night correctly."

I give my best pointed look. "You can interpret my stares however you like, but that doesn't change the fact that I think there's more truth to the tabloid tales than you like to admit."

"Really, Rochelle? We're going there? Because how I see it, we can skirt the issue all we want but somehow we keep ending up..." He steps closer and I stay strong, unwavering as his hands grab my hips and our mouths are only separated by our height difference. In a whisper, he says, "Right. Back. Here." His lips press against mine, and my eyelids close as my mouth meets his in the middle.

"You're right," I say as my heels touch the ground again, my anger subsiding. Every time. Every time, he proves over and over how weak I am to him. I give in feeding his ego and say, "Fine. I like you." I add a shrug to make it come off more casual, but he sees right through me.

A huge, obnoxiously cocky grin appears. "What? Rochelle Floros, did you just say you like me? I think I just kissed the pissiness right out of you."

His teasing and the poke to my side makes me roll my eyes and smile. "Yeah, don't hold it against me. I'm weak to a good kiss."

Swiveling my hips against his, he raises an eyebrow and says, "It won't be your like for me that I hold against you. Trust me on that."

I swat his chest. "You are so bad."

Leaning down, he kisses my neck, then whispers in my ear, "Which is what you 'like' so much about me."

"Mama, I fell down." Surprised by CJ, I turn just as he tugs the bottom of my shirt. "I need Band-aid."

Dex bends down and picks him up. "I got one, buddy."

"It hwerts," CJ replies, then pouts his bottom lip out.

Dex sets him on the counter and pulls out a first aid kit from the cabinet. "Show me the damage," Dex says.

I lean against the counter and watch, fascinated to see how this goes. CJ points to a small pinkish scrap on his left knee. There's no blood, but Dex treats it like a medical emergency, all for show, for CJ. "Oh man, I think we'll be able to save the leg, but we definitely need a Band-Aid on the situation. Let's get you all fixed up."

And there goes my heart, melting for the sweetness of this man. First he cleans the boo-boo, then he puts antibiotic ointment on, topped with a big Band-aid. "Better?"

"Mama kisses it. Makes it heal faster."

I smile hearing my youngest say that, but it works. Dex bends down and kisses the bandage. "You think you'll be able to run like that?"

CJ smiles and nods. Then he melts my heart by leaning forward and hugging Dex. I see the surprise on Dex's face, but he takes my son and hugs him back, his expression one of appreciation. My heart blooms with emotion in the moment. CJ turns to me when they part and says, "Do we have time to play?"

"Ten more minutes, then we need to go. Okay?"

I watch as he runs off yelling to Neil how they scored ten more minutes.

Dex asks, "Only ten?"

"I need to get them to bed on time tonight. They start day camp tomorrow."

While cleaning up the medical mess, he asks, "What about you?"

"I have two meetings tomorrow. Proposals for a tour next year. The events team wants to do something different."

He turns, his eyes narrowed with irritation. "Next year? We don't even know if we'll tour next year. Damn, we leave to finish this tour off in two days."

"Tours take a lot of time to plan. It's good to hear the ideas. Doesn't mean the band is doing it."

With a heavy sigh, he puts the kit away, then looks at me. "So I'm leaving. Eight shows left."

The topic of him leaving is not one I like to think about right now, but I try to convince myself otherwise. "Only eight shows. It'll be okay."

"You're better at this than I am."

"I've had more practice."

"I've had none."

"None?" I ask. "You've never left a girlfriend before? That can't be right."

Walking around me he stops in front of the back door. "I've never cared about anyone enough when I left to tour."

"So what you're saying is that you like me too."

He chuckles. "Yes, I like you, as if that wasn't already clear."

———

THE NEXT DAY EVERYTHING CHANGED. It's strange and kind of amazing how that happens. You think you're finally figuring things out, but you're not and stuff gets twisted... and tainted. No matter how you fight against the inevitable, fate finds you just to make sure you never forget the pain of the past.

It all started off with a knock on the door just as I was about to load the boys into the car to take them to camp. Janice stood there, a frown on her face. Tears in her eyes.

"Janice," the name rushes from my mouth. "What's wrong?"

Her eyes settle on the kids behind me. "I forgot about camp. Can we talk when you get back?"

"Yes. Yes. I won't be long." I call the boys to come with me as Janice hugs them each before we leave. "I'll be right back."

The day camp is just down the street from my neighborhood, so it doesn't take long to get there, but my thoughts are consumed with worry. I've not seen Janice so distraught since... since her son died. I gulp, the lump in my throat heavy with fear. The fear is something I try to swallow down in front of the boys. I don't want to scare them.

After checking them in and making sure they're all set, I head back home. When I open the door, Janice is pacing the living room. She looks up, and the devastation I saw earlier has morphed into anger. "How could you do it? How could you disrespect my son like this? Hurt your children?"

"What?" I ask, taken aback as the door closes behind me. "What are you talking about?"

"It's on the internet."

"What is?"

Another knock disrupts and I look at her like she might know who it is. Janice crosses her arms over her chest, and turns her back to me. The knocks turn to pounding and I rush to answer the door. It can only be someone who has my code, so I don't expect to be surprised again, but I am when I open it. "*Dex?* Hi."

"Hi," he replies looking uneasy.

"What are you doing here?"

Janice's voice carries over my head. "You chose him, a drug-addict over my son!"

"What?" Shocked by her statement, I turn back to her. "I don't understand—"

Dex says, "Rochelle, she knows about us."

Glancing back to him, I ask, "What does she know?"

Janice screams. "I saw the pictures online. Do you know how humiliated and hurt I am by what you've done?"

I'm shaking my head, my hands starting to follow suit. My breathing quickens, shallowing when all I want is to take a deep one.

Dex steps forward. "Janice, I know you don't like me, but my feelings for Rochelle are genuine." He enters my house with his hands up in surrender.

She continues to shout, the anguish she's feeling heard. "I don't care about your feelings. I care about my son!"

Dex still approaches her slowly. "I loved Cory like a brother—"

"Don't you dare insert your despicable self into my family like that when you have done nothing but cause the band trouble! Cory was always there cleaning up your mess of a life and this is how you repay him?"

Her anger and Cory being dragged into this stabs my heart. My thoughts start to twist, so I reach for the nearest wall for balance. With my palm flat against the sheetrock, I close my eyes, but hear Dex say, "I'm not the same person I was before, Janice. You only know what you read and that's not the truth anymore. Believe me. Our kiss was innocent, but sincere."

My world is spinning—guilt, anger, sympathy, Dex, Cory, Janice, the kids as she yells, "I saw the posts with you and Rochelle kissing in public like it doesn't matter, like you don't care about anyone but yourselves or how this would make me or the boys feel. So much damage was done with your 'innocent' kiss."

I collapse to my knees on the cold tile, my hands falling forward as my mind begins to blur.

12

ROCHELLE

A STEADY BEAT infiltrates my dreams. I fight the awareness that brings me from the darkness to a more lucid state, the sound louder. *Beep. Beep. Beep.*

My eyelids flutter open at the sound of the machine next to me. The soft light above feels too bright until my eyes slowly adjust. Janice is there, her hand on mine. "Rochelle. Dear."

The last moments before I blacked out come rushing back to me. The beeping picks up as my heart does. "Dex." I cough to clear my throat. "Where is he?"

Her hand leaves mine. "Rochelle, you shouldn't be thinking of him. There are photographers outside the hospital, waiting for you to comment on this 'story.' It's time to end this crazy behavior. You need to think of your children."

"What story?" I start to sit up.

"That's why I came over this morning. There are pictures of you and Dex kissing outside a hotel."

"No."

"Yes, there are. And do you know how much that hurt to see? My son has not been gone that long and here you are gallivanting around

LA at seedy motels like he never existed." A tear falls down her cheek.

My body aches, but my mind is stronger. "Janice, I can't believe you think that. You know I loved Cory."

"Loved? Past tense? Well, I still love him, present tense, and always will."

My hand goes to my head as it starts to throb. "You're twisting my words."

She steps back, appalled. "Your actions are twisting your reality. You have small children to raise. If you prefer to sleep with a drug-addict playboy, then do so, but I won't sit by and let my grandchildren bear witness to it." She walks out, her heels clicking loudly down the corridor.

There's a pang in my chest, the pain of her words hit me hard. Maybe she's right. I'm being selfish right now. *What am I doing? Choosing to do what I want seems in complete opposite of what I should do for the boys, or does it? Has Dex changed? I mean really changed?*

A nurse walks in and asks, "Ms. Floros, I'm Anne. Do you know why you're here?"

"I'm thinking I had a panic attack, but this one felt more like a heart-attack."

She leans against the foot of the bed. "I see you've taken medicine for them before. The doctor has already called in a new prescription for you." With her clipboard down at her side, she asks, "Do you know what might have brought this one on? It was severe enough for your loved ones to bring you to the hospital."

"People were fighting..."

With a small nod of understanding, she asks, "Are there ways to eliminate some of that stress?"

I gulp, then reach for the water pitcher. She comes around and pours a glass for me. "I don't know. Maybe. I'm not sure. I guess I didn't realize... I'll give it some thought."

"Take this seriously, Ms. Floros, and consider ways to reduce stress and conflicts. Those are some common triggers for panic attacks. Make sure to eat healthy and to exercise regularly." She removes the IV. "Exercise can help reduce the toll that emotional stress can cause. I don't want to see you back in here again."

"Does that mean I'm free to go?"

Swabbing the area, she covers it with a small white bandage. "You are. You just need to sign a few forms at the desk first. Your ride is waiting for you at the nurse's station."

Wondering who's waiting for me, I look up and ask, "Who's my ride?"

She looks down at her clipboard. "Dex Caggiano."

———

It's LA, so the hospital has a private back drive for these types of media situations. I'm thankful for that. We sneak out that way. The dark tinting of his black Bronco keeps the paps on the street from getting any photos worth using when we pass.

We don't speak until the coast seems clear, then begin to relax though an awkwardness stretches between us that's never existed before. Pushing through, thinking about what the nurse said, I start, "Dex, we should talk before we get to my house."

"Yeah," he replies, sounding resolved. "You might have more paps there, so I shouldn't stay."

"I mean, we need to talk about today, the panic attack. Janice. This. Us."

His hesitation is heard when he replies, "Okay."

"I can't hurt her like that. She's been there for me since Cory's death. I was there for her. It wasn't easy, but she was the only one who seemed to truly get how I felt. She's wonderful to my kids and loves them. I've never seen her like she was this morning. She was distraught and *I* did that to her. I hurt her like that by betraying her."

"You didn't betray her by kissing me. She wants you to keep playing the role you've played for years—the widow, but you're more than that, Rochelle. You're a woman, a mother, a musician, a business manager. You are more than a one-dimensional person. She needs to recognize that. It's not just about her."

"I need to focus on my kids, Dex. They don't have a father. I have to be both mom and dad for them, and lately, I feel like I'm failing."

"Us dating—"

"I hadn't had a panic attack in years and now I've basically had two in the last two days. Both times were with you. Do you find that coincidental? Because I don't."

He pulls over to the side of a street that leads to mine. "You're building this up in your head like you being happy goes against feeling bad that Cory died. They aren't related."

"Janice—"

"Janice is turning what we shared into something bad. You're letting her into your head." He takes my hand, holding it as if it might be the last time—firm grip, thumb trying to soothe.

I pull my hand away slowly, leaving all the feelings we were developing behind in the palm of his hand. "The timing is wrong."

"Bullshit!"

Startled, I jump in my seat.

Lowering his voice, he says, "That's a cop out. I know you feel something for me. I see how you react because I also feel it when I'm around you. There's something here and you're just scared."

"Scared of what?"

"Scared to have a life without Cory and thinking you have to justify it to others. The problem with that is when you start justifying it, it will make you feel like your love for Cory was less. It wasn't. It's just different. He's not here, Rochelle."

"Stop it. Stop talking about Cory and take me home."

"Now you want to stop talking about him?" He looks surprised. "I can't win with you when it comes to him." He shifts the car into drive.

"This is not a competition, Dex."

Disappointment slides onto his face. "Then why is he being shoved in my face every time we make a move?"

"This is one of the reasons why we won't work. We see things very differently."

"One of the reasons? Name another because from where I sit, we fit like two puzzle pieces clicking together."

"You're a *supposed* recovering addict. You have sex with anyone who offers. You—"

"That's it. Right there. You play like you know who I am, but you don't. That's why the lies are so easily believed. I can tell what you're doing. You're giving me an out that I don't want. You're allowing yourself to believe the worst about me to ease your conscience, but it won't—"

"You know what. Not everything is about you and your past. You lost a band mate and friend, but I lost my soulmate!"

My breath chokes in my throat after I say the one thing that would hurt him most. His eyes die inside as he stares at me. As usual, I'm the one who needs to make him feel better about everything. But I can't this time. I'm too tired to help anyone else right now. "I was the one left in the wake of this tragedy to pick up the pieces for everyone around me, and pretend that everything is all right so they can go about their days not worrying about me." I shift in my seat, taking a breath, then hit my hands against my thighs as I yell, "Everything is not all right! *I* am not all right!"

I see the street in front of my house is clear. *Thank God!* But right when Dex pulls up in front of the locked gate, a car parks right in front of us with a long lens aimed in our direction, so I react by ducking down. "Oh my God! That's exactly why we can't do this. They don't want me. They just want your latest conquest. Well, guess what? That's one role I don't want to play. I have to think about two little boys and protect their future."

"Protect their future from me? Protect them from me? You're twisting this. I care about those boys. I love them. I would never hurt them!" Throwing the SUV in reverse, he backs up around the corner, then turns, heading in the opposite direction from the paparazzi. "I can protect you from them. You just won't try. You're protecting your heart so hard that you're losing the ability to feel anything except numb."

Unfortunately, they're right behind us when I peek up and over the back of the seat. My head hurts, my heart is racing, and my eyes have filled with tears. "This is the stress I can't have in my life. I can't have you, Dex. I'm sorry. We can't happen. It's not good for me. *You're* not good for me. We're not good for each other."

He struggles to keep his tone steady, but I hear the shake in it. "Don't make rash decisions, Rochelle. You just got released from the hospital. You're tired. In the grand scheme of things, this is nothing, but *we're* something. We matter."

I grab either side of my head while shaking it. "Stop saying that. We don't. I can't think of only myself and enjoy it while hurting others in the process. It doesn't work like that." I look up and add, "Just like now. Just like I'm hurting you. But it's you or everyone else. That's how I see it and the only options I have to choose from."

He makes the block and then pulls up to my driveway and punches in the code. "Are you telling me that you don't want to date me because it will upset others or because you don't believe I've changed? Because you've said both, which makes me think you're reaching for anything and hoping it sticks." The gate closes behind him and he parks.

"Don't belittle my reasons."

"They're not reasons. They're excuses and you know it, but I'm gonna let you go live with those excuses. Just remember these are the choices *you* made. I was here, wholeheartedly for you." His breath deepens, a mixture of anger and sadness battling in his eyes. "This fence isn't tall enough. You should go before they come back."

I open the door, determined to walk away without damaging him anymore. When I step one foot out, he adds, "Go find this happy-ever-after you're so desperately searching for that I can't give you. And maybe one day you'll see that you're throwing away that ending before you even realized you had it."

His words make me panic, worried he's right. "Dex, it doesn't—"

"I can't make you believe in me." He revs the engine while gripping the steering wheel. Looking away from me, he says, "You either do or you don't." He backs up and the gate starts to reopen.

I release a heavy sigh, feeling the anxiety of the paparazzi showing up again and the weight of the pain caused from this conversation. His window is down, so I walk the few feet to him and start to lean in to say, "Pleas—"

"Go inside. This conversation is fucking over. Just like we are!"

The shock of his words coaxes my anger back up as I stand there. He leaves skid marks on the street from peeling out so fast. Pissed, I turn my back and go inside before any photographers show up.

As soon as the door closes behind me I see Beth. She's sitting on the couch reading a book to CJ and they both look up. "Hey, are you okay?" she asks. "Janice called me."

"No. I'm not. Can you stay a bit longer so I can clean up?"

"Sure, no problem."

I kiss CJ on the head. "Hi, Sweetie. Where's Neil?"

Beth answers, "In his room, practicing on that drum pad Dex left for him earlier."

Dex. "I'm gonna take a bath."

"Okay, the boys have eaten. There's still some casserole in there if you're hungry."

"Thank you."

I stop by Neil's room on the way to mine. "Hi Buddy."

He doesn't look up. "Hi Mom."

"Did you have fun today at camp?" I ask, seeing the black and grey pad on the floor in front of him.

"Yeah. Now I'm practicing my rhythms. They're para somethings but I can't remember, so Dex told me to call them rhythms. He says if I learn these three, I get to start on a song next time."

"Oh." Looking into the hopeful face of my sweet son makes my whole body ache. I almost tell him there won't be a next time with Dex, but I don't, not wanting to upset him. No need to have all of us crying over Dex. "I'm gonna take a bath if you need me."

"'Kay."

I start the hot water on the tub before stopping to look at myself in the mirror. It's hard though. Breaking people's hearts is not something I enjoy doing and I feel ashamed for hurting him. I take my clothes off and slip into the tub, hoping to wash away the pain of breaking my own heart in the process of Dex's.

The water soothes, but it doesn't relieve. When I get out twenty minutes later, the pain is more than skin deep. It can't be washed away that easily. I'll leave it up to time to heal the rest while I focus on my family.

DEAR CORY,

I can't control my heart. As much as I try, the beat goes on. There's no power in that. The heart holds not only the power over our souls but the key to it.

I had this epiphany at three in the morning. I wish I could sleep, but my brain has other plans like torturing me with too many thoughts, regrets, and memories. Why this doesn't happen at three in the afternoon boggles my mind. It is what it is though.

XO

BY SEVEN, I was tired and a bit delirious. I missed Dex already and it hadn't even been twenty-four hours. Not only that, but he was right. I *was* thinking of him fondly. When we let go of the anger, we find clarity in the remains.

Beth was here early to take the kids to camp and I was drinking my coffee before getting dressed for my meetings that got moved from yesterday to today. A trip to the hospital is usually an acceptable excuse to reschedule.

Janice's voice travels from the living room, calling my name. I put my makeup brush down and go out there. I haven't called her since the hospital, but I'm still hurt by what she said. When I walk out there, she's standing near the door, timid. With a half-smile she says, "I'm sorry about yesterday."

I love this woman, so it's hard to stay mad at her. Walking to her, I open my arms. When we hug, she says, "You're a wonderful mother to Neil and Cory Junior. I was upset thinking you were over my son."

Stepping back, I say, "I will never be 'over' Cory. But he needs to live in my heart because he's not here to live in our home. To be truthful with you, I'm lonely, Janice, and doing something for myself doesn't make me a bad mother. It makes me human. I can't wear black for the rest of my life. I still wear the ring, but I'm almost thirty and I don't want to spend my life alone."

"Just don't pick him."

"Dex?"

"Yes, you have to be careful who you bring around the kids, Rochelle. He's a bad influence."

"He's not. You're wrong, he's changed. You're reading tabloids and gossip magazines and believing them blindly. I know the real him."

She steps closer and takes my arms gently. "I love you like a daughter. I care about you, but I also know you're in a vulnerable state and can be easily taken advantage of if not careful. Dex is no good. There's always some truth found in those stories."

"Hearing you repeat it doesn't change how I feel about him. I can't help who I fall in love..." I stop, gasping. My hand covers my mouth and I turn away from her.

"You *love* him?" The words hit me in the back like tiny daggers.

The air is sucked from my chest as my own words sink in. "I... I might," I reply more for myself than her.

Upon this realization, I'm on the move. I run to the front door and slip on my Havianas. "I have to go."

"Where?"

Looking at her, seeing the shock in her eyes, makes me want to stay, but I can't. I'll talk myself out of doing this or she will. "We'll talk later. I'm sorry."

I run outside to my car. I'm five minutes down the road before I realize I didn't finish putting on my makeup, but I know he won't care. I see the way he looks at me. He more than likes me. He practically said yesterday. I'm not sure I would call my feelings full blown star-crossed lovers love yet, but it sure feels like the beginning of something 'spectacular.' I need to talk to him, to talk this through with him, to apologize for everything I said. His plane for the last leg of the tour leaves in an hour, so I know he'll be up, but I've got to hurry.

After tapping in the code to his gate, I park next to a white convertible BMW. Makes me wonder if he got a new car though I've never thought of him as a BMW kind of guy. That will throw the paps off his trail for sure. I knock twice before finding the door unlocked. When no one answers, I walk in. I see a martini glass with a few shot glasses on the coffee table and get a sick feeling in my stomach, making me pause at the bottom of the stairs. I ascend them slowly, my gut telling me to go back to my car and call first. I go, my curiosity winning out. When I reach the second level, I walk to his room, finding the door cracked open. I push it the rest of the way open with one finger and my jaw drops along with my heart.

Platinum blonde hair, long, tan legs stretch across his bed, her breast exposed though the sheet does me the favor of keeping the rest of her body covered. *Firenza.*

Her blue eyes look up from the phone she's been reading, and she smiles. Elbowing Dex's back, she says, "We have company, Tiger."

"Rochelle?" His voice follows me as I turn and run down the stairs, but Dex catches me before I reach the front door. Looking down, I make sure he's not naked, not needing the gross reminder of what he was doing, which was very clear as he likes to say. "Let go of me, you bastard."

He has the nerve to be angry with me when he asks, "What are you doing here? You wanted nothing to do with me, so why are you here?"

Like a sucker punch, his words hit me in the gut, making me nauseous. Stepping back, he releases me. When I look up at him, his eyes are glazed and bloodshot.

"I came over here to tell you I was wrong. That I thought that maybe we were meant to be like you led me to believe."

A different emotion takes over his expression completely, and he says, "Rochelle... please." He gulps while reaching for me again. "I didn—"

"You didn't what, Dex?" All the adrenaline, the anger I had a minute before has left, leaving me defeated and deflated. "I thought you were right, but Janice was. Guess a 'tiger' can't change his stripes after all."

"Don't do this. You told me you didn't want to be with me. You said I was bad when all I've done is bend over backwards to prove to you that I'm good. You pushed me away."

I'm tired of crying, but they come anyway. "Not judgment, disbelief that one argument led to this. I stayed home and cried, hurt, confused, but alone. You call a fuck buddy over after telling me 'We matter.' We obviously don't or you wouldn't have had sex with her, and *her* of all people."

"It's just push and fucking pull with you. I get you've been hurt, but you chose to live with the pain than to move past it with me. I'm only doing what you and Cory's mother say I do. It's like manifest motherfucking destiny or some shit. So fuck this. I'm done."

We stare into each other's eyes, neither of us relenting until a cleared throat grabs our attention and we look up. Firenza stands on the top of the staircase in a tank that looks a lot like one of Dex's. "Come back to bed, Antonio."

When I look back to him, the disgust I feel far outweighs my weak emotions that I once felt for him. "And here I thought you were the good guy..."

There's a shift in his demeanor. I may be physically right here, but he knows my heart is already gone. Reaching for me, his voice wavers when he says, "Rochelle?" Regret colors him. "I didn't mean..."

Fear takes over in his eyes as I back away. The pain in my chest makes me want to run, but I won't let them win, refusing to let either of them see me breakdown. I open the door and start to leave, making it halfway to my car before I stop, and say, "As your business manager, I should remind you that your flight leaves in thirty minutes."

"Fuck!" I hear him yell before the door slams closed.

I get in my car and yell the same thing but for entirely different reasons.

13

***

ROCHELLE

WHEN I OPEN the door to my house, Janice is there and stands from the couch. I thought she'd be gone, wishing she had. I swipe at my eyes, hoping she doesn't see my tears. "Rochelle? Are you okay?"

"No," I reply, walking past her and going to my room. I slam the door closed and lay down on the bed, wishing for this day to go away, wishing I could go away for a few hours from myself.

I'm tired of being strong. Curling into a ball on my side, I finally drop the act I've put on for everyone else and cry. I give myself an hour to recover, but my heart is refusing the deadline. No matter how much I remind myself that I have to get ready for the meetings, I still struggle to pull myself together. This ache in my chest makes me think I'm mourning more than just the loss of Dex. Cory is always on my mind. I used to be happy. I used to carefree. I used to have a heart full of love. Now... I miss him. I miss the ease of our life together.

I went numb while holding my newborn. I should have gotten to enjoy my sweet baby being born. But that was ripped away from me when I was told of the plane crash. A numbness took over, then anger that welled up inside of me, squeezing the life out of me, making each breath hard to take as if the world was lacking oxygen.

The anger is so easily to identify with, but I pushed it down, not wanting to upset anyone, not wanting anyone to think I didn't love Cory. I loved him with all of my being. But he left me in a world I don't feel equipped to live in or maybe it's just my emotions that are hard to live with. I reach for the framed photo of me and Cory that sits on the nightstand. Taking it in hand, I run my finger over the glass. I see love when it was pure and simple. He made it so damn easy to love him. When I smile, I have a moment of clarity—Johnny, Dex, and Tommy mourned Cory's death. His family has mourned. Mourning doesn't mean forgetting... I will never forget him, but I need to mourn him.

Now I'm left questioning whether it was fair to start things with Dex under these conditions. Not being in the right state of mind, I'm in no mood to have to justify my reaction today. We had sex. We made out. We were coupling. That much is fact. So for him to jump into bed with someone else after a fight... I don't know if I can forgive him for that.

Thinking about him, makes me want to call him. And wanting to call him makes me feel pathetic. I check for any messages, just in case before setting my phone back down. Now I'm even more disappointed that he hasn't called or texted me. *Ugh!*

I try to convince myself that it's because he's on his flight, but deep down I know it's not. What pisses me off the most is that I want to hear from him. I want him to tell me this is all a misunderstanding and that what I walked in on wasn't what it looked like. But I know better no matter how much I try to change the image in my head. He also didn't deny it. I need to stop being stupid and focus on business.

BY THE SECOND meeting of the day, I'm bored. "These ideas are unoriginal," I start in. "I don't want the band doing the festival circuit. Anyway, I'm not seeing a need for them to tour next summer unless they have a new album out and right now they aren't due to go back into the studio for three months. Give them another two months to work through the tracks that haven't even been written and then we might have new music for them to promote. But it's going to be a hard sell to talk them into it now without tour ideas that wow them."

Nick is the home base assistant to Tommy. He says, "They're tired right now. Getting burned out like all bands nearing the end of a lengthy tour. Tommy says we shouldn't even pitch the idea to them until they're home and rested."

"I wouldn't even broach the subject unless we're solid with something original," I say, "Johnny likes real ideas, something he can visualize. We'd need to present it on paper, through art. Also, this tour needs a better concept for the drum kit. Dex..." My heart starts beating heavy in my chest. I clear my throat while looking down. Focus. "Umm... Dex likes his platform rounded and it's been square the last two tours."

MaryLee, the set designer, leans forward and asks, "Why does he like a rounded platform?"

I turn my attention to her, trying to hold any personal reaction I might have. "He thinks it shows off his drum set better. The curves highlight the curve of the kit. It's a personal thing, not something I think makes a difference to most, but he'll want input when it comes to the drum arrangement on stage."

She taps a pen against the table, looking to others for additional suggestions. When none come, she says, "What about we highlight Dex on the tour. He can have a sliding stage that moves front and center when he has a solo, then moves back into place?"

Nick agrees, "I like that idea."

I add, "It can move up and down maybe."

MaryLee sits ups. "That's a fantastic idea. We can showcase him."

Nodding, I say, "Get more ideas going. The album will set the theme, but we need these new concepts to really pull it off and get them enthused to sign on."

MaryLee asks, "When do you want the concepts?"

"We have time. Two months. I want a model made to see how the platform will work and to show the guys. Thanks for your time. We'll talk soon." I get up and leave, restraining myself from rushing to the elevators. As I ride down, I begin to wonder if I've screwed up my job now as well by sleeping with Dex. Any idiot would know this outcome was predictable, but I still fell for his act. That's just it. He said it himself—He was trying to prove how good he was. It doesn't come second nature to him. That's why he has to prove it. Good people don't have to prove it because they show through their every day behavior.

As soon as I'm in my car, I think about the time under the stars—big and little pictures—the details, and the kiss before we were caught.

I was a fool for going to his place. The second he had a chance, he dropped the good guy act and slipped right back into his wolfish self. He's probably breathing easier now that he's taken off the sheep's clothing.

Needing gas, I pull off to a gas station on La Cienega Boulevard. After it begins pumping, my thoughts drift back to the gathering at my house after the funeral. So vividly, I remember how he felt wrapped around me, and the smell of his breath against my neck as I cried, when he gave Neil the drumsticks, and how he replanted the lettuce knowing it was more about the metaphor than the vegetable.

Firenza invades the good—her arrogant smile, tearing me apart as she stood there mostly naked and called him by his first name like she has a right to. I almost prefer he fuck a nameless stranger, a groupie, instead of her. She knew I was a passing fancy and nothing more than a challenge he'd taken. Everything about her tone, words, and body language knew she would be with him again.

"Come here often?"

I look up and see Chad Spears standing on the other side of the pump getting gas. "Hi." He repeats himself, "Hi. Sorry to interrupt the deep conversation you seem to be having with yourself."

I laugh, suddenly embarrassed. "Yeah, deeps thoughts and all while getting gas. You know how that goes."

"Sure. I always come up with my best ideas while waiting at the gas pump." He smiles. "You're causing quite the stir these days."

Sighing, I ask, "Online?"

"Seems so. The girl who fought so hard to stay out of the head-lines is now making them."

Glancing at the meter, I have a few more gallons to go before it's full. "LA sucks like that. I guess I'm not sure why there's interest in me at all."

"A beautiful widow, a tragic tale, and a bad boy. Makes for good gossip."

"Tragic is right."

"You still seeing Dex?"

My shoulders tense, my answer clipped. "Nope."

His pump clicks off before mine. He locks up his tank, then comes around to my side and leans his back against my Escalade. "How about that raincheck?"

It's the most sincere I've ever seen him. No guard or pretenses, no audience to perform for or like he's trying to impress me. Just a genuine smile and a gentle tone. He reminds me of teenage guys who haven't been defeated by rejection and not tasted enough success to have an attitude yet.

My pump clicks loudly and I reach for it, but he takes the handle before I can and puts it back in place. As I put the gas cap back on, I waiver, thinking I may have judged him because of Dex and maybe that's not fair. "I do owe you a drink."

Looking down at his watch, he says, "I'm late for a meeting, but how's Friday around three for you?"

I'm tired of trying to please everyone else. Chad Spears is not my future, but he may be fun with no commitment, maybe exactly what I need. Wondering if I'm trading one bad boy for another, I decide I don't care anymore. "That works."

"Cool." He hands me his phone. "What's your number? I'll text you."

"Here. I'll do it." I take the phone and program my number into it.

"So," he says all flirty and looking better than he ever has on a red carpet. "Friday?"

"Yeah, Friday."

With a little wave, he walks back to his sports car and I walk around mine to get in. One more glance in his direction and I smile before he drives off. I follow behind but turn the opposite way on Le Cienega. I immediately turn on music so I don't have the quiet to over think what I just agreed to. It's a drink at three, basically the same as a business meeting. The music gets louder, so I let the date and all the heavy thoughts stop and try to enjoy someone else's rhythm for a while.

SPENDING time with my boys renews me. There are no other beings on earth that bring me more happiness or make me more proud. As Neil reads to his little brother, I hold them on either side of me, loving the sound of their voices and giggles. After 'The End' is read, I give them a bath, letting them play in my jetted tub, which they love. My mind occasionally wanders to Dex, wondering if he's thinking of me, like I have him. Wondering if he cares how much he hurt me.

By eight o'clock, I'm wiped out just like the boys. My mind even more tired than my body. My heart still bruised. I crawl under my covers and check my phone on my nightstand. There's a text from Tommy: *We need to talk. Call me after the show.*

Crap.

I look at the time again. The band is playing in Florida, so they're on Eastern Standard. They should be halfway through the show if they started on time. I text back: *I'll call you in two hours.*

I can only imagine what he needs to talk about at this time of night. I'm sure Dex has told his side of the tale by now and I'm probably the bad guy for breaking his heart. I cringe thinking I might have to talk about this, but they should hear my side before their judgments settle in.

Grabbing my files from the end of the bed, I open them wide, then spread out the contracts for the new offers that were sent over from the main office. Action figures. *No.* Wine... um, *No.* Not their style at all. Private jet company. *Too flashy.* Watches. *Maybe.* A tour book. *Maybe.* A documentary. *Maybe.* A line of athletic wear. *No.* I gather the maybes and stack the rest back up and place them in the No folder. I'm gonna have to present these in the next two weeks to the guys, which means traveling to see them. As much as I think I can be professional around Dex, I also know my heart isn't ready to see him.

His betrayal has tainted our past and all of the things that made us special together. Everything has changed for the worse. We weren't special. *I* wasn't special. I was used like so many before me. He had no intention of love, but I believed his words. Now I believe his actions. They speak louder. I just hope I can bear to be in the same room as him.

Logging onto the tour schedule, I look at the dates and cities. Miami in nine days. Nine days to wean my heart away from him. Nine days to mentally prepare myself to see him after our fight. Nine days to forget the past and try to move forward like we never happened. Nine days.

Ready or not, I'll go because I have to. I'm damn good at what I do and I'm not gonna let little things like broken hearts and hurt feelings get in my way.

My phone rings just after ten-thirty. "Hello?"

Tommy's voice is gruff. "Hey Rochelle, I need talk to you about Dex."

Bracing myself to the mattress the best I can, I wearily reply, "Okay, but I think it's only fair that I get to share my side of it."

"Your side of what?"

"What happened betw—Wait, what were you going to say?"

"His kit got damaged in transport. He got through the show by using a floor model from Guitar Center. It's not gonna work for the tour. It's not made for that kind of stress. I'm sending over the contact information for the set maker. Call them first thing in the morning and see if they can rush the frame, bass, tom-tom, and snare out overnight to the next city. Philly. Philly's next."

"What happened? And what about the rest of the equipment?"

"The hi-hat and other cymbals are fine. A local stagehand put the set down on the dock and a backloader didn't see it. Bent it to shit. Dex is pissed."

"He should be pissed. Will the current set work if the other won't make it?"

"For the next show, yeah. But he was hitting pretty hard tonight. I don't know if it will make it for two shows. It's not as heavy as his usual. Oh and maybe give him a call tomorrow. He seemed out of sorts today. Left his clothes because he was late for the plane. Said he didn't have time to pack. Maybe you can send some clothes too."

"Geez, Tommy, let me just drop everything and go shopping for Dex," I reply sarcastically. "He forgot his clothes? What happened to *you* managing him during the tour?"

"C'mon, Ro. Do me the favors. I can only do so much from here and keeping a tight leash on the guys is doing me in already and it's only the first show of this leg."

"What do you mean?"

"Dex is wasted because he's upset about the drums. Johnny left after the show. Derrick and Kaz are dragging me out with them. I'm thinking I need to go to keep an eye on them. You know how those two are when they party."

"Partying with the guys sounds like real torture, Tommy," I say, rolling my eyes. "But don't worry. I'll handle everything in the morning."

"I knew I could count on you."

"No need to suck up. I already said yes. Don't you have some bars to get to?"

He laughs. "Yup, getting right on that. Thanks for the help."

As soon as the phone disconnects, I lay in bed and turn on the TV, trying to distract myself from the fact that I have to return to Dex's house in the morning. *Damn him.* There's just no escaping. As soon as I decide to get out, I'm dragged right back into the lion's den... or tiger and lair in his case, according to Firenza.

14

ROCHELLE

I'm NOT happy about going back to the scene of the cheating crime, but I'll do it for Tommy. Even though it's really for Dex. I swallow my pain, blaming myself for getting involved with him in the first place, and go inside with a huff.

His house is quiet, the house manager only coming twice a week while he's on tour to check on things, organize mail, and dust. I help pay the bills while the guys are gone, so I know all of this. I know too much these days. I shut the door behind me and stand there, smacked by the conversation I was caught in the last time I stood in this spot. The disappointment that he could give us up so easily, that he could move on so fast, weighs my feet to the spot, hesitant to go further. I steel myself and head upstairs not wanting to waste any more time than necessary here.

His bed is made this time. I'm sure with fresh sheets, but the memory still remains. My senses tormented by the memory. Firenza taints that same bed that I once had sex with him in. My stomach rolls, so I take a deep breath, gripping my arms around me and focus on the job at hand. I direct my gaze to his nightstand where his charger sits, no phone attached, and I wonder if I should pack it. I walk over, reaching behind the stand to unplug it, knowing the answer already. The corner of a photo tucked under a leather book catches my eye.

I reach for it and pull, sliding it out from under its hiding spot. My breath doesn't catch, it stops altogether as I stare down at a photo of me.

I don't remember when or where it was taken. There's a light reflecting in my eyes, the area around me has a red glow, maybe an after party from eight or nine years ago judging by my hairstyle. Two corners are bent and finger prints cover the glossy surface. I don't know why Dex has it, but all that strength I gathered to get through this task suddenly evaporates. I sit on the edge of the bed and stare down at it. It's a smile I don't recognize as one I usually have, not posed for the camera, exposing an inner happiness, one not manufactured *for* others but instead *by* others.

Tucking it back under the well-worn leather book, I'm tempted to open the book. It looks like a journal though so I don't. My thoughts are still on why Dex has this picture of me and it raises questions. Too many to work through right now.

"Ms. Floros, hello?"

I turn around and see his house manager. "Hi, Marguerite. Um…" Suddenly I feel the need to explain why I'm here as she looks at me curiously. "Dex needs clothes overnighted to him. He was running late, so Tommy asked me to come here and pack a case."

"I can help you. I know where everything is."

Relieved, I say, "That would be great."

She goes to his closet and pulls down a duffle bag and has an arm full of T-shirts when she walks back out. "These are his favorites. I keep them together. That way he can find them easily. Maybe three pairs of jeans?" She sets the stuff down on the bed.

"Yes, that will work." I start to put the shirts in the bag as she goes back to the closet for more clothes. Peeking over at her, I say, "I saw a picture on his nightstand."

She stills, her hands stopping on a stack of jeans. She recovers quickly though and says, "Yes," and nothing else.

"It's of me."

"Yes," she replies when she returns. She sets the jeans down, her eyes lowered as well, almost seeming to avoid my questioning ones.

Wanting to pursue it more, I ask, "Can you tell me about it?"

"I'm not sure."

"You clean his room. So you know it's there. Has he ever mentioned it?"

"Ms. Floros—"

"Please call me Rochelle."

Her kind smile reappears. "Rochelle, I've only ever had instructions, not explanations."

"That sounds like Dex. He's not the best at explaining his actions." A dig I should have probably saved for him.

Walking to the dresser, she shuffles around and I continue packing the bag. She looks over at me and says, "It's to remain there."

I stop what I'm doing, and ask, "What is? The photo?"

"Yes, those are my instructions. He wants it there, except when he knows he's going to be having company. Then I'm supposed to put it in the drawer."

"Those are pretty specific instructions."

With a small smile, she says, "Yes, they are."

She doesn't need to explain anymore, the drift is caught in her expression. After adding his boxer briefs into the bag, she puts two handfuls of socks, then disappears into the bathroom. She's not gone long, but long enough for me to slip over to the nightstand and grab the picture. I tuck it into the bag, hidden from view just as she returns with a toiletry case and sets it inside the bag. It's zipped closed. She grabs a little lock from the closet and fastens it. "Women steal his clothes. They all want a piece of him," she says, protectively.

Grabbing it off the bed, I turn and head out of the bedroom. "I'll ship it from the office address so they won't know it's his."

Following me down the stairs, she says, "He cares about you."

I stop with three steps to go and look over my shoulder. She seems like she might want to say more, but I don't. "Thanks for helping me pack, Marguerite."

"You're welcome."

Outside, I toss the bag in the back of my SUV and drive away feeling more confused than when I arrived, as if that was even possible. After I ship the duffle bag, I call the makers of his preferred drums. Cost is not a factor so they'll hit the road themselves and have them delivered and setup for the show tomorrow. He'll be happy. Tommy will be happy. And I can go back to dealing with my work.

DEAR CORY,

I don't want to talk to anyone else about this, so I hope you don't mind my nonsense. I should be working. Should being the operative part of that sentence. But I have so much on my mind. I was just thinking the problem with plans, like working, is that your mind and heart don't care about the day-to-day routines. They care about things that affect them and make them work harder, beat faster.

Today I had a fascinating conversation with Marguerite, Dex's house-keeper. The conversation has played on repeat all afternoon and pretty much the entire next day.

I found this photo he had... I sigh. *You know, I shouldn't bother you with silly stuff like this. I miss you.*

XO

I CLOSE the journal and think on the photo. A photo of me that he keeps on his nightstand only adds to the bewilderment I have over this whole situation. What Marguerite said about the photo makes me think that maybe there is something more to this story. But my more logical side cannot come to any solid conclusion to why he would lie to me. So I am stuck—*do I believe what Marguerite said or do I believe what I saw?*

I ARRIVE at the café a few minutes early, but I'm impressed that Chad Spears has arrived even earlier. "Hello," I say, approaching the table.

"Hi." He stands and comes around to pull my chair out for me. We greet each other Hollywood style—a faux-kiss to the cheek. "You look beautiful," he says.

"Thank you." I sit down as he takes his seat across the small table from me. "Have you been waiting long?"

"No, less than five minutes." The waiter approaches and Chad asks, "Champagne, Rochelle?"

"Are we celebrating?"

"Yes."

"Champagne will be great then."

The waiter walks away in a hurry, eager to please. I'm sure everyone is eager to please Chad since he's famous.

Chad leans his elbows on the table and says, "I'm glad you met me."

"You mean met you as a person or here today? Ha!" I joke.

"Both." He smiles. Holding the menu, he asks, "Have you been here before? It's early, but I'm hungry. Are you?"

"I haven't been here." Looking around, I add, "I like it. And I can always eat."

The bottle of champagne arrives and our glasses are filled as menus are set down in front of us and specials announced. When we're alone, I lift my glass and ask, "So what are we celebrating?"

"Us. To us and finally cashing in that raincheck." He's a charmer all right. Our glasses tap together and we drink. As I'm setting mine down, he asks, "How have you been?"

"Good. Busy with life. You know how it is."

"Yeah, I head out next week—"

The waiter appears and asks, "Do you know what you'd like to order?"

Chad turns to him, but with a glance to me, he asks, "Rochelle?"

"I'll have the Waldorf salad, light on the dressing."

Chad orders plain grilled chicken and steamed veggies before turning his full attention back to me. "So as I was saying, I head out next week to start a project in Toronto."

"Oh," I remark, picking up my glass. I drink and listen as he talks about this movie for some indie director that he thinks could lead to an Oscar nomination for him. My mind wanders, remembering this is why I always got along with musicians better—they are less talk and more action.

My hand is grabbed and I look up at him. He says, "Okay?"

"What?" I ask, surprised. Busted for not listening. Oops.

His brow is furrowed as he pleads, "When she gets here, pretend to be my girlfriend. Okay?"

I realize I had not heard whatever led up to this question and thinking he realizes it too because he says, "This chick, she's all over me all the time. She'll come over here in a minute. Pretend to be my girlfriend. I've been trying to shake her for months."

I feel bad for not paying attention and readily agree. "Oh. Sure. Okay."

When he looks over my shoulder, he says, "She's coming." I start to look back, but he stops me. "Don't look! Keep your eyes on me."

"Chad, darling," I hear over my right shoulder. "I didn't know you were still in town. I would have called."

Looking up, I recognize her as a popular LA socialite who lives to make tabloid headlines and not much else. He stands to greet her, effectively pulling me up with him. They European kiss—one on each cheek. She lingers and he tugs me closer. As she backs up, he wraps his arm around my waist and kisses me on the cheek. "Have you met Rochelle Floros?"

His arm snuggling me close doesn't seem to faze her. Like Dex, maybe he just has a whole slew of fuck buddies. She replies, "I don't believe I have, but I've spent a lot of time in New York and Miami recently. I'm Dotty Greensberg."

Dotty Greensberg? I stifle a laugh and offer a hand instead. "Nice to meet you."

"Rochelle is my girlfriend," Chad states confidently.

I remain quiet, trying to channel the fake girlfriend role I've been asked to play.

"Girlfriend?" she asks as if the word is foreign to her, a glare directed at him. "So this is a new relationship?"

"Yes," he replies. "Well, it was good to see you, Dotty."

The waiter walks up with our plates.

She gives her best smile trying to hide her heartbreak. It's obvious she likes him, but I've learned that it takes two or someone always gets screwed. "Yes, I should go. I'm meeting my agent at the bar."

Chad releases me and I sit down, the charade almost over. They polite kiss each other goodbye and he sits down smiling. Putting his napkin back in his lap, he says, "I think that went well."

"Yeah, seemed like she believed you." Believe. Believe. Charades... Dex. I drop my fork.

Chad asks, "What is it? Your salad?"

Was I set up? Dex wants me to believe he slept with Firenza. Maybe he didn't... or maybe he did. If he didn't, why would he want me to believe a lie? He tried to say something, but I cut him off.

"Rochelle?"

I look back up at Chad.

He says, "You keep disappearing. Am I that boring?"

"No," I say, shaking my head. "I just have a lot on my mind. I'm sorry." Trying to keep my mind from reeling in conspiracy theories, I attempt to keep my attention on Chad.

"No problem. So how's the band business?"

We fall into light conversation, easier than I expected it to be with him. But after spending time with him one-on-one, I have a feeling he doesn't do deep conversation. He loves to talk fashion and gossip. I listen most of the time, not able to add too much to either of those topics. After we eat, I call it a day wanting to go home and think about things.

While waiting for our cars at the valet out front, I say, "Thank you for the meal and drinks."

"Thank you for joining me. So I mentioned I'm leaving soon, next week in fact, but I have this party to go to on Sunday. Would you like to go with me?"

"Oh... *like on a date?*"

"Yeah," he says, smiling. "Kind of like what we just went on."

My head goes back. "Was this a date?"

"Was it not?"

My embarrassment is felt through the heat of my cheeks. "I'm sorry. Yes, of course. I just thought of it as more friends hanging out when you asked me."

"I know you have a lot going on with the band and you know, your other things—"

"My kids?" I fill in the 'other things' for him.

"Yeah, your kids. But I like you—"

"*But* you like me? You mean in spite of my kids?"

"You'll have to give me time. I've not dated anyone with kids before."

I try to end his failed attempt to explain things as the hole he's digging gets deeper. "Chad, I think we both can see there's no romantic chemistry between us. I know about your history with Dex and I don't know if that played into why you asked me here today, but let's just stay friends. I had fun. We don't need to ruin it with starting something that's obviously not gonna work for either of us."

He's not sad. He's not relieved. But he's grateful. "I would have slept with you, you know."

I laugh. "Geez, I appreciate it, but I'm all good in that department."

My car arrives first. "Thank you again." I smile as I walk away. "Break a leg on that new project."

With a nod, he says, "Thanks."

And that was the beginning and end of my relationship with Chad Spears. As soon as Dex came to mind, the date was already over in my mind. So now I need to figure out what the deal is with him and why I'm holding on so tight to the possibility. He's only caused me heartache, but deep down, way deep down, he might be worth the pain.

15

ROCHELLE

I FLY to Miami on a Monday. After a week of meetings, packing, and work, I leave my boys in the care of Janice and take off for Florida. On the plane I go over the files one more time, making sure I can answer any questions the guys might have regarding the deals. The flight is a little turbulent and sickens my stomach. While cleaning up in the bathroom, I look in the mirror. My hands are shaking and I'm a little pale. I should have gotten a prescription, but deep down I know I'm not just upset from the flight.

I've lost a lot of sleep the last few nights. I had nine days and seemed to have squandered them away, not feeling any less hurt than I did then. Screw Dex. I don't owe him anything and he owes me nothing. We are back to being completely platonic. Just how we should have stayed all along.

I flash my pass and go backstage, finding Tommy near the backup amps on stage left. Hugging him, we don't bother talking, since the band is performing, and neither of us wants to shout.

The set change and break happens after this song. As soon as it ends, the band hurries off stage, knowing they have ten minutes to do whatever they need to do—whether it's use the bathroom, get a drink, or make a phone call. They run down the stairs that are near us. Each one of them smiles at me as they pass, except for Dex who eyes me but keeps walking. We follow them into the dressing room, Tommy shutting the door behind. Like a coach, he goes over what's working and what didn't, including one of Johnny's guitars that broke a string while he was playing.

I try to give Dex his space by standing across the room. As much as I kind of want to reach out to him, I don't. I'm conflicted over this whole mess we've found ourselves in and burned he picked someone else up so soon after our fight. *Am I being unreasonable?* I don't even know. I'm a girl and sometimes reason takes a backseat to feelings. Sucks, but I'm not unique this way.

Without my eyes leaving my feet, I feel the weight of his gaze on me, a stare that caresses my curves, reminding me of where his hands once were. When I dare look over, the warmth I'm so used to seeing has left... what is there, I'm unfamiliar with, so I turn away.

"When's the meeting?" Johnny asks me after he finishes drinking his water.

"Lunch tomorrow. My suite."

He nods. "Let's go." They all stand up and Tommy opens the door.

Just as Dex passes, he whispers without looking, "Thanks for the clothes."

"You're welcome."

I don't get any visitors tonight, stuck in my room alone. I chose not to go out with Kaz and Derrick. Tommy called it a night and went to bed as soon as we got back. Johnny was meeting friends for a late dinner and Dex disappeared. I have no idea what happened to him and I try not to spend my night guessing either. That could lead to disastrous thoughts of groupies and drugs. I'm not ready to go there right now, so I turn my attention to the fact that he's made a huge impact on my life in such a short amount of time. When he spent time with Neil after the funeral. The way he 'fixed' CJ's boo boo. When he looks at me like he can't bear to lose me. All of these memories are little Band-aids on my heart. I sigh.

I just can't seem to stop thinking about him despite my better judgment. I was unsuspecting, but not blind and yet, it feels like this man I've known forever came out of nowhere and swept me off my feet.

Maybe I'm being ridiculous or maybe he's made a bigger mark on my heart than I originally thought. *How much pain can one heart bear? Am I willing to take another beating? Is Dex worth it?* The mystery that he's laid out before me makes me wonder what he's up to, which is driving me bizonkers. *Why can't I just get clear-cut answers? Why must it all be a guessing game when it comes to him? Why is he lying to me? Or is he telling the truth?*

I turn on the TV and fall asleep after watching three Friends episodes in a row.

THE NEXT MORNING, I head downstairs to the coffee stand in the lobby. I'm waiting behind three other people desperately in need of caffeine like me. The one at the front can't seem to figure out their cup sizes, so the barista is going through explaining and taking way too long to do so. I check my phone for the fourth time since I have the meeting in less than thirty minutes and at the snail's rate of this line, I might not get my coffee. That doesn't bode well for anybody.

"Can I buy you a cup of Joe?"

I recognize the smooth voice before I see him. Turning around, I say, "Make it a latte and you've got yourself a deal."

Dex doesn't smile, but he doesn't look unhappy to see me either. "You always liked your lattes. Mocha as usual?"

"Yep." I find myself swaying between my anger from his actions and the traitorous side of me that wants to take his side and let him back in, just a little bit.

"Surprised you're talking to me."

"It was only a yep. Don't get your hopes too high." I roll my eyes.

"I'll take one word over the silent treatment."

When I look up, he has the most sincere smile on his face. He's hard to resist. "Anyway, I thought you weren't talking to me after our fight, so we're even."

"I'm sorry."

"Let's not get too deep. Haven't had my first cup yet."

He chuckles lightly. "Maybe later then."

I shrug and looked toward the baked goods display. "Yeah, maybe later."

A guy in line starts saying, "Dude... dude. Oh shit. Dude."

I see him pointing at Dex and Dex instantly tenses, so I offer, "How about I buy you a coffee this time and I'll see you at the meeting?"

"Deal." He steps out of line quickly and hurries away before the fan can fully comprehend that he was standing next to greatness.

"Dude," the guy says again, this time into his phone. "He was right in front of me..."

I finally reach the front of the line and order the coffees. I decide to buy a to-go container for the guys just in case they haven't had any. When I reach my room, I struggle opening the door with my hands full, but Kaz shows up and helps.

We go inside and I situate the coffee in the living room portion of the suite near the couch. He settles in and closes his eyes. I let him rest. I know how touring tears you down physically, remembering the old days when I toured with Cory.

Everyone arrives on time, some not as happy with the ten o'clock meeting time, but it is what it is. And what it is, is business we must get done. I go over the proposals with them and they decide which ones to move forward on and which ones to eliminate.

As a group, they seem satisfied, so I am. When they leave, I start making calls and getting contracts sent over. I log onto the latest batch of paparazzi photos taken of the band members that their press agent sent over. It's the usual boring stuff which I like to see. Nothing salacious. Nothing newsworthy in their personal lives. These are the kinds of pics that don't get bought by tabloids or blogs.

But when I scroll to the fourth page, I see me—me and Chad Spears from our kind-of-sort-of date. *Shit!* My heart starts pounding and my hands start shaking while I reach for my phone. I immediately call Rory, the band's public relations agent.

He picks up on the first ring. "I've been expecting this phone call."

"Can you kill the pics?"

"Too late. They were sold to two sites last night. That's when I found out about them."

"Make them go away, Rory." I beg, "Please."

"Rochelle, you should have given me a heads up. I could have done something then, but now, it's too late. I'm sorry. I can look into the story they'll post with it and try to use some tactics to get them to go easy, but it's Chad Spears. He sells magazines. He gets people clicking online. You being a widow of a famous musician and with him gets *even more* hits."

"I can't... These photos will upset people. Cory's Mother for one."

"And Dex."

The way he says it so casually as if the whole world knows our secret makes me cringe. "What do you know about that?"

"Everything. That story of you kissing at the bar—another time you should have forewarned me."

"I'm new to this. Cut me some slack."

"Slacks been cut. Now it's time to play hardball. I'm gonna send you an email that I usually send my clients when I first bring them on. It's how to stay out of the headlines when you don't want to make headlines. I suggest you memorize it if you don't want the attention. If you do want it, I can help you out there as well, but I'll need some forewarning next time."

"I don't want the attention. How much time do we have before this story comes out?"

"Less than twenty-four hours I would say, but probably closer to an hour. The online blogs are fast with this kind of news and it's already a few days old."

Looking out my room window, I stare at a nearby building that's blocking the sun, casting a shadow over the hotel. Very ominous. Very fitting. I sigh, dropping my head down.

"Hey Rochelle, I'll do my best," he says, his voice sympathetic. "I've already got calls into them."

"Thank you, Rory. I appreciate it."

Shit! What have I done? I need to tell Dex before he hears about it.

A hard knock on the door foreshadows things to come. I stand slowly, the weight of a thousand waves pulling me back, begging me not to answer. I have to though. I peek through the peephole and my fears are confirmed. When I open the door, Dex walks in and straight for the window. His body is stiff as he paces back in forth. I remain standing near the door. "Hi," I say, a fake happy tone failing me.

His eyes hit me like daggers when he asks, "Do you want to talk about anything?"

Cowering a bit, I reply, "Not really."

Turning his back on me, he nods and stares out the window. His voice is alarmingly calm like lava boiling at the base of a volcano. "I only asked you not to date one person." When he looks at me again, he narrows his eyes and asks, "Do you remember who that one person was?"

It's not a question and we both know it. "Chad Spears," I answer begrudgingly.

"God damn it, Rochelle." He closes his eyes as if he can calm himself by not seeing me. When he opens them again, he shakes his head. Instead of saying anything else, he comes toward me, closing the gap in a few long strides. But he doesn't stop. He keeps going and leaves the room. The disappointment I feel is abruptly halted as the door flies open before it has time to latch. His body is pressing against mine and he kisses me. I push back but he holds tightly to him. And just as fast as he kissed me, he stops. Brushing his lips against mine, he whispers, "That was the last time I will ever kiss you."

And then he leaves me standing there breathless and agitated.

16

ROCHELLE

HERE I STAND, just seconds separating us, in shock as my door slams closed, automatically locking with a thud. *The last kiss he'll ever give me?* The last kiss *he'll* ever give me!

His egotism is exasperating.

The nerve of him swooping in here and kissing *me* like I was the one who wanted it. He took it without my permission. It was him... *clearly.* And now I've been rendered speechless while my lips continue to tingle even after he's gone.

The one thing I didn't count on when I was planning this trip was how I would feel about Dex. Sure, I'd let a million scenarios play out in my head, but they were ones based on harsher realities. When I saw him, all of those thunderous emotions weakened. I had somehow forgotten how handsome he was or that he has this innate ability to win people over with just his smile. The boy is gifted and no heart stands a chance against him. Obviously, I'm no different. Compound that with his nerve to threaten me with kisses or lack thereof and my mood sours.

Frustrated, I fist my hands and go to my computer to look up flights. *Screw this!* I don't need this added headache, this added heartache. Tommy can get any additional contracts signed. For my own sanity, I need to get the hell out of here.

A knock matching the last one sounds out and I stomp my way over. I glare at the back of the wood door gathering my anger together and ready to direct it at Dex. I swing the door wide open and spew, "How dare you—"

"How dare I what?" Johnny asks, his eyebrows knitted together.

"Oh!" I lean, easing back. "Hi. I thought you were someone else."

"Clearly."

I roll my eyes when I hear that damn word again.

He walks in like he owns the place. "Are we gonna keep pretending like no one knows what's going on between you and Dex?"

Exhaling heavily, I reply with sarcasm and a tilted grin, "Sounds good to me."

He sits at the desk, kicking his feet up next to my laptop. With a glance over at the screen that shows the different airline options, he asks, "Going somewhere?"

"I'm leaving."

"Tomorrow."

Shaking my head, I say, "No, tonight, Johnny."

"You can't tonight. I don't have anyone to eat dinner with."

"You have the band, Tommy, thirty stagehands, fans, radio DJ's, press—"

He chuckles. "Yeah, sure. I'll call up the press and ask if anyone wants to have dinner with me."

Lowering his feet, he leans forward and looks down. I sit on the edge of the bed, still trying to calm down, and wait. I'm not sure if I'm going to get a lecture or what, but I let him lead the conversation. After a minute or so, he says, "I'd like to have dinner with you and talk." His voice is softer and sincere, more Jack Dalton than Johnny Outlaw. "Will you have dinner with me?"

Our eyes meet and my anger starts to dissipate. "Just like old times. Almost." Cory's not here.

"Yeah," he says, knowing exactly what I mean. "Almost."

Always a sucker for his charming side, I guess I'm staying the night. "I will. But I don't want to talk about Dex, okay?"

"Okay."

"So when did you and Dex start up?" Johnny asks right before taking a bite of his steak.

I set my fork down, but continue chewing the bite in my mouth before speaking. "You said we wouldn't talk about him."

Pointing his fork at me, he says, "No, you said you didn't want to talk about him. I want to talk about what's going on with you. The band knows. Hell, everyone on the tour knows. You guys can't hide your relationship for shit. Like, you're the worst secret lovers that ever were. I mean—"

"All right. All right. Stop it. First of all, we are not in a relationship. Secondly, we are not *secret* lovers."

"I know. That's my point. You suck at hiding these things."

I sigh, rolling my eyes. As much as he's frustrating, he's kind of funny too. "Stop teasing. We aren't lovers at all."

"Have you had sex?"

"Johnny!"

"You've had sex with Dex." His face scrunches in disgust. "And besides that rhyming, gross by the way. I'm totally judging you for that."

"You sound like Holli."

He shrugs, not ashamed. God love him.

As he drinks his beer, I say, "Look, I'll tell you what we're not. We're not lovers, secret or otherwise. We're not friends because we can't seem to do that without other stuff getting in the way—"

"Like your attraction for each other?"

"Settle down, Mr. Quicky with the Comebacks. No, I meant all of this baggage both of us are lugging around."

"Maybe it's time to lighten the load, Rochelle."

"I can't. I'm held to different standards. Impossible standards."

"Not by me. I don't like the idea of you and Dex. I mean Dex can't do better than you, so I see why he's in it. But as for you, Dex is pretty much rock bottom. So what's your excuse?"

I look around the restaurant. It's a traditional steakhouse and dim, candles on the tables, and us in a booth in the corner. I spin my wine glass around a few times before lifting it and taking a sip. He's stopped eating and is waiting for my reply, but I'm not sure what to say, so I go with the truth, tired of hiding my real feelings. "I'm lonely."

And there it is, a soft sigh accompanied with a side of sympathy written all over his face. "That. What you're doing right there, Johnny, that's what I don't want. Not from you. Not from anyone."

Leaning back, he drops his hands to his sides. His eyes fixed on mine. "I want what's best for you and the boys."

"I know. I do too. But I'm starting to feel like what's best for me as a woman may not be what's best for the boys."

"Dex isn't that bad. I mean, he's actually kind of cool. We've kept him around for a reason."

With a light laugh, I say, "I know that too, but Janice doesn't. The tabs don't."

"Fuck the tabs. We don't live our lives to justify our actions to them. Sometimes we fuck up and sometimes the day turns out better than planned. We just have to do the best we can. As for Janice, I know I don't have to explain her angle. You're well aware of that. But she loves you and she loves those kids. You guys are all that remains of her son, so she's gonna be tough on you. Probably not accept some guy strutting in like he's gonna replace Cory."

Looking down at the burgundy table cloth, running my finger along the fold wrinkle, I release a deep breath. "Dex didn't strut, but I treated him like he did."

With a slight nod in understanding, Johnny says, "I have a feeling he's underestimated a lot."

"But we shouldn't. As his friends, we should stick by him. I've seen how much he's changed over the years and I doubted what I knew to be true because of my own fears of being judged."

Johnny shifts when the waiter arrives, and asks, "Would you like to see our dessert menu?"

"No, thank you," he replies and then I repeat the same.

When we're alone again, he leans in. "From where I sit, you have a choice to make."

"I pushed him away," I interrupt. "And then he slept with someone and I caught them, so there's no choice to make anymore."

His face contorts. "Hmmm."

"For some reason my gut tells me he didn't, but he wants me to believe he did."

"What?"

"Exactly. It's a mess." With another sigh, I say, "We're a mess."

"Back up. He slept with someone, but didn't, but wants you to believe he did?"

"I don't know for certain, but something like that."

"You guys are twisted." The check arrives and he glances over it, sets his credit card down in the folder, then scopes out the restaurant. The waiter swipes it from the table, leaving us alone again. Usually by this point at dinner, he gets anxious to leave because word has spread that he's in the restaurant. It will be a miracle if we get out of here without him stopping to take a pic or signing an autograph or twenty. Looking down at his watch, he says, "It's almost eleven, but I'm up for an adventure. How about you?"

His excitement is contagious, so I ask, "Like old times?"

He smirks. "Yeah, but without the cop chase."

Nodding toward the door, I say, "Let's go."

Thirty minutes later, the band—all four members—Tommy and me, are piled into a light blue minivan heading away from South Beach. The food I just ate feels heavy in my stomach, the awkwardness of the situation not sitting well with me. I did not have enough to drink to pretend to be cool.

"Where are we going?" Kaz asks, shifting uncomfortably next to me.

I elbow behind me lightly. "Stop moving. You just jabbed me in the boob." I'm half on his lap and Derrick's right leg. Dex is on the other side of Derrick crammed against the far door.

"Sorry," Derrick mumbles.

Tommy laughs from the front seat. Dex leans forward and hits him on the arm, sneaking a peek at me in the process. Johnny hands his phone to Tommy and tells him to put on some music. Classic Aerosmith starts playing just seconds later; the melody calming the giggles and grunts as we settle in. Music is the thread that stitches us together. I feel Kaz's foot bounce to the beat. Out of the corner of my eye, I spy Dex drumming his fingers on his legs.

The van crosses over a large bridge and then turns off on a small street that veers toward the beach. When Johnny parks, we all stagger out of the van, enjoying that we can stretch our cramped up legs.

The beach is isolated. More of a fisherman's beach than a sunbathers. The headlights shine forward, lighting the water as it crashes down on the sand. I take my shoes off and walk forward wanting to get lost in the sounds of the music, the ocean, and the dark sky above.

Kaz and Tommy are nearby. Derrick is on his phone and walking down the beach. Johnny lays down in the sand halfway between the water's edge and the car. And Dex—I turn back and see him sitting on the hood of the dated rental. He's a silhouette of darkness, smoke wafting into the wind before it has time to settle above his head. He's watching me. Unabashedly. His gaze seeking me out and taking hold, making me want to go to him. The water covers my feet and splashes up the side of my legs. The bottom of my jeans are rolled up but still get wet.

As "Dream On" by Aerosmith kicks in, I trek back. When I pass Johnny, he lazily asks, "You sure?"

"Yeah," I reply and keep walking. Dex's legs are parted, his forearms resting on his knees. He's wearing sunglasses not to hide his eyes, but to hide his emotions. He can't hide though. Just like me, there's more to this, more to us than he can admit. I lean my back against the grill, resting on the bumper and keep my eyes forward.

His knee bumps me and I turn to look at him. In a hurry, he slides down the hood, his feet hitting the sand. I stand and he looks at me. Lifting his sunglasses up, his expression more pissed than any other. With a slight roll of his body, he's pressed against me, his arms on either side of me, his palms flat on the hood. His head is on my shoulder, and he says, "You're inside of me, the blood that fills my veins, the aches that my heart feel, and every good decision I ever made. That's what you mean to me. I can't stay away from you and I don't want to." Lifting up and looking me in the eyes, his lips brush against my cheek without leaving a kiss, and he adds, "You're the melody I can't capture and the notes I can't hit. But I can't fight your pull, always gravitating toward your world, to you." Just when I think he might kiss me, going against his promise from this morning, he pushes off, leaving me in awe of not only his words, but the man himself. The underlying passion we fight so hard against is back in place, denying us both any peace until we give in again.

With my mouth left agape, it's times like these I wish I smoked. I steady myself as I walk back to Johnny and sit down silently next to him. His arm goes out and I lie back, using it as a pillow. Our life experiences have bonded us. He's become the only man I can rely on in my life. One of his best qualities is he knows when and when not to push. He stays quiet, letting the waves fill the air instead.

Derrick is the next to join us, sitting down on the other side of me. Tommy and Kaz leave the laughter down at the water and sit next to Derrick. I see Dex in the distance throwing something into the ocean; a seashell is my guess.

Despite his actions, he still fascinates me. Physically, he's so beautiful, and could easily be mistaken for a model down here in Miami. But his insides are conflicted. He's a lot like me in that way. I know there's good inside. I've seen it in him. But sometimes, we can't fix people. He wants to live one way, but his image comes into play and he battles that demon daily. I realize regardless of our pull, as he calls it, our efforts might not be enough. He might have to be the one who finds his own peace instead of me giving him what he needs. I may not be able to do that.

I sit up just as Dex sits down on the other side of Johnny. No one says anything, and a different song echoes through the windows of the van. Kaz is smoking a joint. The smell reminds me of our days as a garage band. We were all about fucking up just so we could say we lived life to the fullest. Cory was always the most responsible of us.

I look over at Dex and he looks away. It's then that I finally get it. All of this with Dex isn't about him. Sure he has his issues to deal with, but this is about me and my issues as well. I can have fond memories of Cory, which I always will. But he's not here sitting on the beach with us or to guide us to safety anymore.

Dex is.

Dex with his smile that hides the good from the rest of the world and saves it all for me. Dex with his mysterious side and secrets and intriguing reasons for lying to me. I may be glorifying him, but deep down, I feel he's lying to protect me, not to hurt me. Revelations like these make me anxious and want to share them, celebrate them, but not with the guys here. I can't act like an emotional girl around them. I'd lose all my cool kid cred if I do.

I stand up and dust the sand off my ass. "Dex, walk with me." I don't ask. I make my demand as I start walking toward the water again. He's behind me trailing, so I slow down and let him catch up. "I can't keep doing this with you."

Looking over, he's pulling another cigarette from his shirt pocket and a lighter from the front of his jeans. He lights up, then tilts his head back and blows. "It's a self-fulfilling prophecy."

"What is?"

"I am."

Hoping my words are not lost to the wind, I whisper, "You don't have to be."

"I don't know any other way."

I bend down and pick up a seashell. When he squats down next to me, I say, "You do. Just sometimes you get lost."

"I need you to help me find my way back."

My eyes meet his and in the moonlight of Miami, I reply, "Okay."

He nods. It's small, but it's an understanding passing between us, an agreement between two hearts.

17

ROCHELLE

I DIDN'T KNOW what I had agreed to with Dex, but I left Miami knowing it entailed more than just words. Actions and support would be included. In what way, I would soon discover.

Burnout is a big problem for bands on the road. Fortunately, they had a four day break in New Orleans, which I'm sure they needed. The headlines didn't thrill me. Gossip blogs had posted photos of them playing an impromptu concert at Preservation Hall. A few drunken pics on Bourbon Street bothered me. They didn't say Dex hooked up with anyone, but how would they know really.

A knot forms in my stomach just thinking about it. It's a grounded fear since we haven't dealt with the Firenza issue. Something is off with that situation. When I replay that morning back in my head, the whole thing just doesn't sit right with me. Naturally, Dex having sex with *her* doesn't sit right, but something about how he acted toward me in front of her still makes me doubt what I saw with my own eyes.

The way she nudged his back... and how he had his back to her in the first place.

The look in his eyes, the fear, wasn't one of fear of losing me, but more of shame.

He makes me feel weak when I need to be strong because I know he cared about me. But emotionally, I'm in no position to ask the questions that need to be asked, not strong enough to hear the answers. So I need to stop guessing at what his motives were because that's the one thing that was clear. I punch my pillow to fluff it, wishing I could stop thinking about why he hasn't called me either. *I'm weak.*

Resting my head down on the couch, I try to block out my thoughts by listening to the boys playing in Neil's room, hoping to sneak in a quick nap.

But as soon as I close my eyes, I hear, "Mom."

Gradually opening one eye, then the other, I find myself face to face with Neil and CJ. Neil flashes four postcards in front of me. "Dex is home. I want to go to his house and play."

"How do you know?" Sitting up slowly, I take one of the postcards. "What is this?"

"We got letters from him."

"What? You did? When?" I flip Chicago's postcard over and read: *Hey Buddies, I'm in the Windy City today. Looking forward to hanging with you guys again. Take care of your mom, Dex.*

Stunned by what I'm seeing, I anxiously pull the next postcard from his hands—Atlanta—and read: *Neil, the crowd at Chastain Park was so cool. One day I'm gonna bring you to a concert so you can play drums with me on stage. CJ, hope you're keeping up with your alphabet. We'll practice hitting rhythms to the alphabet song when I return. Take care of your mom, Dex.*

The handwriting is messy, but legible—a lot like Dex these days. Grabbing postcard three, I read: Nashville: *Hey Buddies, miss you guys. I've bought you each a surprise, but you have to be good for your mom to get it. I'm gonna check with her too, so no fibbing. Hope you're practicing your paradiddles and rhythms. Take care of your mom, Dex.*

Neil snatches them away from me. "Mom, these are mine. Dex sent 'em to me."

Somewhere while reading postcards two and three, I started holding my breath. My chest now aches as a consequence when I exhale. "When did he send them?" I ask.

"I dunno." CJ grabs Atlanta from Neil and runs around the couch singing his alphabet. Even he knows what they say. Beth or Neil must have read them to him. Neil sits on the coffee table in front of me. "Beth gave them to us."

She leaves my mail in the basket in the kitchen, but I forgot to check it over the last few weeks. Too much other stuff on my mind. "Why didn't you tell me about them sooner?"

"Am I in trouble?"

"No," I reply, shaking my head. "Why would you be in trouble?"

"I dunno. Just asking cuz you're using that voice you use when I'm in trouble."

I relax a little. "Sorry. I'm just kind of blown away that he sent you guys these. What does the last one say?"

Neil turns it over in his hands and my heartbeats pick up when I see the city name on the front—Miami. He reads, "Dear Neil and CJ, almost home for a short break in the tour. One more city to go. Keep practicing. If you have the single paradiddle down, I'll show you something called a fill. See you soon and take care of your mom, Dex." He looks up at me and adds, "See? He should be home."

The only city left is New Orleans. "Did Beth check the mail yesterday?" I ask, standing up.

"I don't think so. Can I?"

"C'mon, let's walk down and get it."

With both boys in tow, we walk down to the other street where the neighborhood mailboxes are situated. I let Neil open it with the key. He feels very important given the task. I reach for all the mail and pull it out, a letter slipping to the ground. CJ picks it up and says, "For you, Mama."

"Thank you, kind Sir."

I flip through the mail and as soon as I see New Orleans on the front of a postcard, Neil grabs it. We start back for the house and I ask Neil to read it to me.

"Hi Buddies, almost home. Can't wait. I'm super tired from traveling. Forget everything I taught you. Go to law school instead."

Neil looks up at me and asks, "What's law school?"

"It's where you learn to become a lawyer." Pointing at the post-card, I say, "I think he's being sarcastic, just joking with you." I wrap my arm around his shoulders and give him a squeeze.

"Oh." Neil looks at the card confused, but then continues reading. "I'm home for four days and then off again. Looking forward to hearing your progress. Take care of your mom, Dex."

Maybe it was the smile on Neil's face and watching CJ gallop down the sidewalk, or maybe it was that Dex was keeping his word to my kids and they were smiling. I'm thinking it's both, but no matter where this warm feeling inside derived from, I love it. Seeing my kids happy makes me happy. As we enter the house, Neil takes off running and says, "Gotta practice. I want to learn what fills are."

"Teach me. Teach me. Fills." CJ runs after him.

I dump the mail on the island in the kitchen and start sorting it. When I come across the letter with my name on it, I glance to the return address. There isn't one.

CJ comes in singing, but stops and says, "That's like the other letters."

"What other letters?"

He points to the basket in the corner that holds the mail that I still need to go through. "Those."

I walk over and look inside the basket, then pull out two other letters that match the one on the island. I see the similarities in hand-writing when they're together like this and I smile, knowing they're from Dex. Each is postmarked to correspond with the tour and cities listed—Chicago, Nashville, and Miami.

I need time to process the fact that he's been writing us for weeks and I'm just now finding out. As much as I want to rip them open and read each and every word, I don't. I won't be able to give them the attention I want with hungry kids begging for food at my feet. My heart is beating out of control, but dinner needs to be made, so I set the letters aside and ask, "CJ, you want to be Mommy's helper with dinner?"

"Yes," he says excitedly.

"Okay, you grab the lettuce and I'll get the carrots and tomatoes from the fridge. You can help with the salad."

***

THE LETTERS CALL to me throughout dinner, a cartoon, and book time in CJ's room. I kiss him on the head and turn out his light before making my way into Neil's room. Snuggling with him, he reads aloud to me from his adventure book. I help on the tough names and big words, but he's a really good reader. When it's time for lights out, he asks, "Will I get to see Dex again?"

His tone makes my heart sting and not knowing how to answer, I go with my gut. Looking up at the stars on his ceiling, I ask, "Do you want to see Dex again?"

"Yes. I like his gameroom. He has cool video games and the drums are awesome."

I slip out of bed and tuck him in. "What else do you like about him?"

"I like that he's a grownup, but cooler. Some grownups talk to me like I'm dumb. He doesn't."

Smiling, I reply, "That is cool. Get some rest and I'll message him." I kiss him on the head, then turn out his lamp. Shutting the door behind me after several I love yous, I leave and head back to the kitchen.

I pour a glass of wine while keeping an eye on the letters that look so harmless sitting there, but taunt me relentlessly. The hotel envelopes only add to the intrigue. After taking a few sips, I grab them and go into my bathroom and start the water. As the tub fills, I set them down on the vanity and undress. I'm shocked by my own willpower. Once the water is high enough to cover me, I take the letters and climb into the tub. I open them in order. The first is from two weeks ago, which makes me realize I should go through my mail more often.

Chicago. The paper is crumpled a bit and the inks slightly smeared near the hotel logo at the top.

. . .

DEAR ROCHELLE,

I don't know what I'm doing, but still feel the urge to do it. What does that say about me? Maybe I can't change. Maybe at thirty, I am who I am.

The thing is, I'm not sure who I am anymore. I've lost interest in my own life. But your life—I can't stop thinking about you. You undoubtedly have my complete attention. Sometimes I damn you for it.

I never told you much about me. I don't know why I'm feeling the need to do it now. It's probably the bourbon talking.

Did you know that I didn't learn to ride my bike until I was eight? I borrowed a neighbor kids' bike and taught myself on the driveway since there was no one else to do it. My brother was too busy with his friends to teach me.

I've got more money than I can blow through. I was never meant to be rich. Besides my money, I'm the son to a mother who inherited more than she could spend in a lifetime and a father who built an empire on the backs of using cheap labor with low expenditures. I never fit into their world. I never belonged.

But I belong in The Resistance.

Sincerely,

Dex

I EXHALE WITH SIGH. Reaching for my wine, I take an unsteady sip to calm the torrential emotions brewing. My heart and head hurt for him. He's exposed himself to me in the short letter and I'm left here in shock and hurting for him.

Nashville. I open the second letter, not knowing what to expect from this one. It's neater—the handwriting and the hotel stationary. Quality paper.

DEAR ROCHELLE,

I've always wondered what it would be like to live somewhere else, somewhere other than LA. Is thirty too young to have a life crisis?

I might be having one.

Nothing seems to stick or gel, or anything else with me these days. Except one.

And Johnny knows.

I didn't tell him. I hope you believe me. He mentioned you in passing, but I know he was really letting on that he knows. I didn't confirm his suspicions. But I didn't deny them either. It felt wrong to do either.

Did you know at fourteen, I found out my mother was raped by her uncle when she was fourteen. I don't even think I knew what rape was at that age, but I found out. I also lost my grandfather later that year. He had a heart attack. My mother refused to attend his funeral, so I went alone. Later, I wished I hadn't gone at all. I got drunk for the first time at fourteen right after his service.

I smoked my first cigarette at fourteen. I lost my virginity at fourteen. I smoked pot for the first time at fourteen. I did coke at fifteen. I totaled my first Porsche at sixteen. My second at seventeen. My third at nineteen and then I was kicked out of the house. I got my first job at nineteen playing back up for a cover band down on Sunset for fifty dollars a night.

You walked into my life at nineteen...

Sincerely,

Dex

DROPPING the letter to the floor, I sink further down into the water not able to process everything he's told me, struggling since the tears slipping from my eyes take precedence. Of all the years I have known him, I never knew even a quarter of what he's shared with me in these two letters. *Why is he telling me now?*

My hands are pruning and the bath water is cold. I stand up and dry off, draining the tub. Carrying the letters into the other room, I set them down on my bed before getting into my pajamas. Checking on the boys, who have both fallen asleep, I kiss each one of them on the head, then tiptoe out afterwards.

But my stomach is twisted and my heart pounding, worried what the last letter will say, so I wait to read it. While I brush my teeth I think about everything he revealed to me. It makes the stuff with Firenza seem petty in comparison. His past defines who he is now just as mine does. And the one thing I've learned is, there is no escaping it.

I climb under the covers and take the letter in hand along with a deep breath. Miami. Stars. Beach. The last kiss ever. Dex has lost his way and I'm not sure if I've helped or hurt him in the last couple of months, so I open the letter and hope for the best.

Miami.

Dear Rochelle,

I thought LA was soulless until I came to Miami. I've been to Miami many times, but never stayed sober before. Just an observation.

I knew you were coming, but I didn't know what to expect. I thought I had a grasp on things, but you stir something in me, emotions I have trouble burying. These little confessionals have been freeing for me.

If you ever need to unload some burdens, I'm here for you. I know I'm probably the last person you would trust with such gravity—I should apologize. I worry my apologies hold no value with you anymore.

I'm going to try anyway. Here goes... Wait for it...

I'm sorry. I'm sorry for so much. If we ever get to that stage of trust again, I won't blow it.

But there was something about Miami. On the beach, you outshined the stars.

Just something else I should have told you then. I was just too distracted by my own ego to say what my heart was feeling.

Something else I should have told you in one of those other letters is I started hanging out with Chad Spears at fourteen. I'm not asking you to stay away from him anymore. I have no right to do that, but know that I'd still like you to.

Sincerely,

Dex

Holy shit! Fourteen. Fourteen. Fourteen. Everything goes back to when he was fourteen. All the bad he's had happen started at fourteen. With my thoughts and heartbeats running rampant, I can't deny the urge to call him any longer. A text will not suffice. I grab my phone from the nightstand and do it before I can change my mind. After three rings, he answers and I can hear the hesitancy in his voice, "Hello?"

"Hi." My own voice shakes a little from the uncertainty that lies between us.

There's a momentary pause. I hear a TV or music in the background being turned down. "Hi."

I blurt, "I got your letters." I anxiously wait to hear his response, but typical Dex it's not what I expect.

"I'm not sure what to say to that."

"You don't have to say anything, Dex. I just want you to know that I got them all tonight. I didn't know any of that in Miami. I wish I had."

Always expect the unexpected with him. "Can I come over?"

"Ummm... I'm in bed already." I regret it as soon as I say it, so I quickly cover with the truth. "If you want."

"It's late," he says, the moment passed. "How about you bring the boys over tomorrow? I promised Neil another lesson."

Feeling like we might be able to find our way back to each other, I relax down onto the mattress after turning out the light, and reply, "How's noon for you? I can bring lunch."

"Noon is good."

"I should get some sleep. I have an early morning phone call to the U.K."

"Goodnight, then."

"Goodnight, Dex."

I hear him take in a breath, then say, "Sweet dreams, Rochelle."

"Sweet dreams."

We both remain on the phone, the silence that felt distancing before now feels bonding. Eventually, I crack and giggle. "Are you going to hang up?"

"No, I like hearing you breathe."

"Funny that. I was listening to you breathe."

"You're weird," he says, "Why would you do that?"

"Why am I the weirdo when you were doing the same thing?"

"Okay," he adds, "We're both weirdoes. Now hang up first."

With a smile on my face, I reply, "Goodnight for real this time."

"Goodnight for real this time."

We both hang up, or at least I think he hung up when I did. I call back just to make sure. "Hello?" he answers like he doesn't know who it is.

"I didn't hang up on you, did I?"

"Yes, you did. Now do it again because I don't want to be the one who does it."

"You're a dork."

Right before I disconnect, I hear him say, "You're beautiful."

I immediately call him back again. When he answers, he laughs. "Yes, I called you beautiful."

"Just checking. Thank you."

"Goodnight, Rochelle."

"Goodnight, Dex."

This time I hang up and set my phone down on the bed. The problem with Dex is that no matter how much I should be mad at him for all the shit he's pulled over the years, I just can't seem to keep myself in that state. He's not the bad guy he likes to portray himself to be. Call me sentimental, but I see through the act to the man himself.

18

ROCHELLE

THE REPORTS WERE EVERYWHERE on TV the next day. *"Chad Spears has been involved in an accident. He's currently recovering from surgery after breaking his leg on the set of his latest movie filming in Toronto. His camp has issued a statement that he is resting comfortably and claim trailer cables were the cause of his fall. They are currently considering a lawsuit..."*

When I told him to break a leg, I didn't mean to literally 'break a leg.' I'd like to say I feel bad, but since our lunch and the tabloid explosion it caused, I don't. Rory found out that Chad was the one who called the paparazzi to stake us out. He's also dating the woman he told me was stalking him. He used me as a pawn for publicity. And I totally fell for it.

Because of his douche move, I opt not to send him a Cheer Up bouquet and head over to Dex's as promised the next day. The kids run in as soon as Marguerite opens the door. She laughs as I justify, "They're excited to be here. Sorry for their poor manners."

She makes it easy on me. "It's good to have happy children."

I take her forearm and give her a gentle squeeze. "Thank you."

"You're welcome. Dex is in the gameroom if you'd like to join him."

"I'll put the food in the kitchen first." I follow her into the other room and set the basket on the table along with my purse. The blue skies outside his window make his backyard paradise even that much more appealing.

"Can I get you anything to drink?" Marguerite asks.

"A glass of water would be great. Thank you." I walk to the back door and stare out over the lagoon like pool and large grassy area beyond it.

A few moments later, she hands me the glass. "Thank you."

"You're welcome. It's so lovely to see you again. How are you doing?"

I turn with a smile. "I'm well." When her eyes soften in the corners sympathetically, I add, "I'm okay... most of the time."

She nods. "I hope it gets better. I know Dex was really looking forward to today."

"I was too."

"You should join them. I'm just gonna tidy up in here."

"Okay. See you later." I slowly make my way through the living room and down the corridor, feeling nervous. When I approach I hear laughter. Dex's first, then the boys. It truly is wonderful to hear all of them happy. I peek around the corner and spy on them for a few minutes, but Dex catches me and winks. With a smile, he says, "C'mon in. See what your muskrats have gotten up to."

I walk in and find a seat, near them, but just out from the spotlight shining down on the drums. Crayons are all over the floor with loose construction paper scattered at their feet. Dex whispers, "Hi."

"Hi."

My gaze is drawn to him and as he strums the acoustic guitar in his hands, he says, "You doing okay?"

"Been better," I reply so only he can hear.

He starts playing a song. Louder than he was before and I suspect he's doing it so the boys won't hear us. "Me too."

CJ holds up his green paper and shouts, "I drew our house in blue and me with the dog I want."

My eyes go wide. "You want a dog?"

He smiles so big and says, "I want a black dog with a long tail. Can we get one?"

Dex adds, "Tell her what you want to name him, CJ."

"Spot."

I look closer at the drawing. "But the dog you drew doesn't have any spots."

He nods as if that says it all. I smile because he's adorable. "I love your drawing. Great job."

Neil holds up a yellow piece of paper and then starts to explain, "This is the tire swing. Dex is on this side and me on the other side."

I point at something, then ask, "What's this?"

"Those are the drumsticks."

A flashback of years earlier crosses my mind and I look to Dex. I see a deeper emotion in his caramel-colored eyes. I just wish I understood the emotion better. I ask Neil, "Are those the drumsticks Dex gave you?"

"Yeah. He just gave me these too." Neil holds up drumsticks that have his name inscribed on the side and The Resistance on the other.

CJ holds a pair up too. His look similar but are less worn. "Me got some too."

I ask, "Wow, did you use these in a show?"

Dex leans forward. "I used CJ's in Denver from the first leg and Neil's are from Atlanta."

"Chastain Park," I say, remembering his postcard.

He nods. "The show was amazing. You should have seen the crowd."

"Maybe that's the difference. You could see the crowd the way the place is setup."

"Yeah, maybe that's it. But I could feel the energy too. It was good."

I love seeing him so excited about a show. After Cory's death, we all went through a transition, including Dex. I was worried about the guys. "You've found your groove," I say.

"When it clicks, it's magic."

Magic. Staring into his eyes, his words seep under my skin, filling holes that felt empty before. And for a brief moment in time, our unbreakable bond suspends us between time and memories, leaving us in the present full of peace and happiness.

"Dex show me a fill," Neil says, our moment interrupted for the best of reasons—the kiddos.

I see Dex sigh and although I know he's happy to work with Neil, his disappointment that the moment is gone is seen. He rubs the top of Neil's head, and says, "Okay. Let's get down to business." He sends a smile my way before giving the kids his full attention.

I stand. "I'll go unpack lunch and get it ready. Meet me in the backyard shortly." I head to the kitchen. Marguerite is in there making fresh orange juice. "Hi," I greet her again. "Would you like to join us for lunch?"

"No, I need to leave and pick up my grandson soon. I've made juice for the boys before I go."

"Thank you." I move over to the counter where she's working, lean against it nonchalantly, and whisper, "About Dex. I've been wondering if you know anything maybe I should—"

"Dexter is a complicated man." She stops juicing and looks at me. "People always want to put him in a box, easily categorized, and he's fighting against it."

"He's complicated for sure," I reply, turning to look out the window for a moment. When I turn back, I dig deeper. "Why is he fighting so hard?"

"Because it's not his box." She starts juicing again. "As for you, you're trying to figure out something when it may not be time."

I bite the inside of my cheek, wanting to stomp my foot and get all the answers now. "Why can't I know? Why won't he let me in?"

"He already has. That's what scares him most."

She makes it sound so simple. *Maybe it is.* If I give him more time, maybe he'll give me the answers I need.

19

ROCHELLE

I FIND myself staring at Dex throughout lunch. He catches me several times and winks, but doesn't seem to mind. I think he actually likes when I watch him.

After lunch, the boys are given the run of the house and take off before he even finishes his sentence. He leans forward on his elbows, the two of us alone outside. That's when I feel it, just like the night before when I was on the phone with him—a little fluttering in my stomach. I stand, taking my glass of water with me, and walk to the edge of the cement patio. "How long have you lived here?"

"Six years," his reply is relaxed, much like him.

I can tell he's watching me now. When I check, my suspicion is verified. "It's very homey. I like it here."

"I like you being here." Sitting down across from him again, I look at him, searching for signs of anything that will give me the answers I need. As soon as I look away, he says, "I didn't have sex with her."

My head jolts back in his direction, the flutters replaced with dread. I tuck my hands under my legs to keep from revealing how this conversation really affects me.

"I feel like shit for lying to you, Rochelle."

"Why would you lie about it? It makes no sense why you would hurt me like that?"

His gaze drifts away and he swallows hard.

I stand, not able to contain my emotions over this anymore. Walking toward the pool, I stop and yell, "I opened my heart to you. And you hurt me, Dex!"

He follows me and even though I want to back away, needing the space, I stay. My conflicting heart spiting me. He stops a few feet away and stares into my eyes. Keeping his voice low, he says, "Let me heal you."

The racing starts, the flutters back, but my rational side takes charge. "I can't. I can't let you back in."

"You already have. You just won't admit it. I'm in there," he says, glancing to my heart, then back up. "I'm in there and I refuse to leave."

It's my turn to gulp heavily, touched by his words. "Why did you lie to me?"

"To protect you. I may be in your life, but it doesn't mean I deserve to be."

"I don't know how to respond when you say things like that."

"I don't need words."

"Then tell me what you need. What do you want from me?"

"Everything."

My breath catches as we stare into each other's eyes. He's serious. He's impossible. He makes me want to give him more than I should. "You want too much from me." Looking down, I shake my head, needing to stand my ground. "I can't give you everything. I don't know how to be enough for you."

"You're enough. I found that out the hard way."

I cross my arms over my chest. "Actually, I found out the hard way. You knew what you were doing when you brought her back here. I'm the one who was blindsided."

"I'm a cliché, Rochelle. I never claimed otherwise."

"You fall back on the perceptions, then complain that no one sees the real person behind the façade. You can't have it both ways." I walk to a nearby chaise and sit, needing the support under such a heavy conversation.

"See?" he says, smiling. "You know me better than anyone. After the letters, you also know more than I've ever shared with another person." He comes and sits next to me. "But what you fail to realize is you're the only person that I want to see the real me. And for you, I'd do anything. So when you told me I wasn't good enough, you're right, I wasn't... and I wanted to prove that by fucking Firenza."

"And?" I glance down, then back up.

"And I discovered that you were in here." He says, touching his chest briefly. "You weren't a fantasy anymore. You had managed to take the one real thing I had left—"

"So you couldn't fuck her because you might lo—"

"Yep, I like you, more than you're ready to hear right now. So we're gonna take this round slower again."

Surprised by his arrogant assumption, I sit upright. "Who says there's going to be another round?"

His fingers take hold of my chin, keeping my face focused on his. "I do."

Backing away, I snap, "That's either extremely romantic like in the movies or totally creepy. I haven't decided yet. Anyway..." I shrug, trying to regain control of the situation. "...You leave in two days."

"We can get into a lot of trouble in two days." Now he shrugs, instigating me by acting like it's not big deal. "You know, if you're up for some fun and stuff. I don't know. Maybe you can't handle fun anymore."

With a challenging eyebrow raised, I say, "I'm not falling for your ploy, Mr. Caggiano. I'm not dumb and I thought we were going to slow this round way down?"

"Friends who get into trouble together don't go slow. They set their own pace. Speaking of trouble, Spears was all over the news."

"I wasn't going to bring him up, but yeah, I heard about the broken leg."

"Karma's a bitch."

"I might have had the same thought." He stands before me and offers me two hands. When I take them, I whisper, "What are we doing, Dex?"

He gently nudges me and smiles. "Hanging out, pretending we can go slow when all I want to do is go fast with you."

Falling for his boyish charms, I nod. "Me too, but let's settle on medium for now."

"Medium it is."

The alarm on my phone chimes, the magic that was returning gone in a flash as reality sets back in. With a heavy sigh, I say, "I need to go. I have a couple of calls and a lot of work to do this afternoon."

His shoulders drop just a little, but I notice, the disappointment apparent though his voice hides it. "I have some errands to do." He starts walking and I go inside with him.

I shut the back door and say, "I wish I could stay. I like when we're this way."

The right side of his mouth lifts, a slight crinkling on the outside of his eyes reveal his inner emotion. "I like when we're this way too." Taking my hand in his, he brings it up and kisses the underside of my wrist. His lips smooth and purposeful as his eyes lock onto mine.

The boys come running through the kitchen, circling us, then back out, but he still has my wrist to his mouth, savoring it. My heart is too weak to be broken again so soon, so I ask, "How many times do we do this before we accept the truth?"

He lowers my hand, but holds onto it. "As many as it takes."

That's when I know we aren't over. But for the safety of my heart, the business, and until I figure out this game of life I'm playing, we need slow bordering on medium.

Walking into the living room, he says, "Guess you need to get going. I'll help wrangle the boys."

I stand there a moment longer watching him walk away and smile at him. His heart connected to mine once again. "Thanks."

LATER IN THE NIGHT, just as I climb into bed, my phone rings. My smile is probably heard over the phone and I'm too tired to hide it. "Hello."

"Good evening, Rochelle," Dex says, his own voice smooth and seductive with a light playful undertone.

If I wasn't smiling already... "How are you?"

"Really good. And you?"

The casual chitchat makes me happy. "Oh, you know, busy but good."

"You're busy right now?"

"No," I reply, "I just got into bed after a busy day."

His voice gets deeper and I hear him settling down. "I like the thought of you doing that."

"The having a busy day part or climbing into bed?" I tease.

He chuckles. "Am I going to see you tomorrow?"

"What'd you have in mind?"

"Take a ride with me. Up the coast."

My lips part and a silent gasp chokes my immediate response. "Dex..."

"As friends," he adds.

I'm pathetic and give in way too easily, wanting to see him more than I've convinced myself otherwise. "What time?"

"I'll pick you up at seven tomorrow evening."

"Okay."

"Goodnight, Rochelle."

"Goodnight, Dex. Sweet dreams."

"Sweet dreams."

The pause makes us both laugh. Knowing we have plans makes it easier to hang up though. "I'll see you tomorrow," I say.

"Tomorrow."

IT FEELS a lot like I'm getting dressed for a date. Beth has preached to me several times this afternoon that, in fact, two friends can hang out together without it getting too deep... or sexual. I'm not fully convinced, but I'm willing to try again. Because he's easy on the eyes. Oh wait, damn it. Okay, I'm not convinced at all that two people who have great sexual chemistry can remain only friends.

I kiss the kids goodnight and say goodbye to Beth just as Dex calls me to meet him outside. After closing the front door behind me, my mouth drops open when I see him. "Oh good lord!" Rolling my eyes, I shake my head. This is gonna be impossible with him looking so damn sexy in his leather jacket and old jeans, tight T-shirt, and motorcycle. What? Rushing forward, I stumble over my words, "What? How? Where'd you get her?"

With two motorcycle helmets in his hands, Dex straddles the bike with a big ole smirk on his face. "Wanna go for a ride, sweetheart?"

"Hell yes, I do." I go through the gate, making sure to set the alarm before shutting the door. I take a helmet and put it on. After securing my license and credit card in my pocket, I zip up my jacket. "I'm ready."

I start to swing my leg over the back, but he stops me. "You're driving."

Lowering my leg back down, I look at him incredulously. "Really?" I ask, hopeful.

"Really. You were once a badass on a bike. Show me that girl again."

"I like your version of trouble."

"Good because I have more where that came from."

"I'm counting on it." I get on and he settles in the seat behind me, then wraps his arms around my middle just as I rev the bike. When we take off, I realize I'd forgotten how exhilarating riding a motorcycle can be. Also, how scary. I'm rusty as I try to balance better.

Gaining speed, a feeling of freedom takes over. It's a similar high I imagine runner's get when they hit their stride—a feeling of invincibility, power, and liberation from your worries. On a bike, I only have to think about my surroundings, to be conscious of others, and let my worries drift into the wind behind me.

About an hour later, Dex has me stop at a public beach past

Malibu, but just shy of Santa Barbara. "The sun is setting. Let's take a walk on the beach." We hang our helmets and kick off our shoes, before I bend over and roll up the bottom of my jeans. The sand is big, gritty, and warm from the hot day today. Walking toward the ocean, Dex stays quiet beside me, seeming to have his mind on things other than the sunset.

"Wanna talk about it?" I ask while pulling my hair back into an elastic band.

"The bike is a gift."

Shocked by his doozie of a statement, I stop walking and turn to him. "For what?"

"I thought you should have it."

Glancing back to it, I feel the debate beginning. "You can't give me a motorcycle, Dex."

"I just did."

"Take it back," I demand, putting my hands on my hips.

"No. Why should I?"

"Because it's too much. We're friends. Friends don't give each other gifts like that."

"What do friends give each other then?"

"I don't know." I shrug. "Like sweaters and stuff. Maybe a trinket box or flowers, but a motorcycle is too expensive."

"I don't even know what a trinket box is." He points back to the bike, and says, "And that bike was not expensive."

"It's like my old one?"

"Yeah. An '87 Honda."

"Okay, it's not expensive but it's still too much."

"The thought is too much?" He laughs and takes my hand in his. "Let's walk." And we do. The sun is dipping into the ocean, reflecting like magic dust on the surface. He adds, "I bought the bike because of what it represents."

"I'm lost, Dex. Tell me what it represents."

"You know what you once told me about riding motorcycles?"

I shake my head. "No, I don't remember. It's been too long since I had one to remember my philosophies on the subject."

"I remember. You said, there's always a chance of death when you ride a bike, so it makes you appreciate the life you have."

Standing just before the water can touch our feet, I say, "That's deep," which makes him chuckle.

"Yeah, it was pretty profound at nineteen. It means more today."

I start to laugh, but I don't continue when I realize he's being serious. Instead, I turn my head to face into the wind and close my eyes. When I reopen them the sun is almost gone. "I got rid of my bike when I got pregnant with Neil."

He nods. "Makes sense."

The horizon is the only bright spot left. "How'd you remember what I said after all these years?"

He comes to stand between me and the view. "Because it changed my life... you changed my life, Rochelle."

"See," I say, backing away. "You do that. You say these things to me and make me feel special when I haven't earned it. I'm not special."

"You're special to me."

"No!" I turn on my heel and stomp my way through the sand, kicking it up in the process.

"You can't just yell no and walk away, Rochelle. It's not that simple. *We're* not that simple."

He's right. We're not. Coming to a halt, I stop with my back to him and drop my head down, feeling the emotions beginning to wash through me. Smothering my weaknesses, I spin around and point my finger at him. "You can't do this to me anymore. We're not together. Dex."

"I was going to have sex with Firenza so you would hate me. So you wouldn't come on rides with me up the coast at sunset or come by with your kids. I wanted to fuck her to make you fuck off." He comes closer and I stand there stabbed by his words. "No one believes in me. No one. They believe in my drumming, but not in me. You're right. I'm no good, Rochelle. I'm no good for you or your kids. I'm not the one you should be standing next to if a photographer snaps your picture."

"I don't understand this back and forth with you."

"I didn't either and then I woke up this morning and realized I've suffered enough. You've suffered enough. But when we're together, it's all good. We stop suffering and the rest of the bullshit falls away and... You need to know that I see you as pure and good. You're loved by everyone. You're perfection to me." He stops in front of me and wipes my tears away. "So this slow or medium or whatever it is, it's okay for now, but one day I'm gonna be good too. I'm gonna be good enough for you."

"Don't tell me these things—"

"I'm not gonna tell you, sweetheart. I'm going to show you. One day I'll deserve to be the one standing here."

No matter the anguish I feel, I'm captivated by this man. "And until then?"

"Stop dating jerks like me." He walks around my stunned body and heads for the bike.

Running to catch up, I say, "So you brought me out here to tell me to stop dating assholes?"

"No. I brought you out here to watch the sunset. The rest is a just a perk."

I don't bother stifling a laugh. He may be cocky, determined, too sexy for his own good, but he's also wise. Tossing him the key as I pass by him, I say, "You can drive back."

"You sure?"

Grabbing my helmet, I say, "I'm sure." And I am. I'll let him drive this relationship for awhile and we can start with the motorcycle.

I wrap myself around him, molding to the back of him, resting my head to the side. I rub the soft leather, then my hands slip inside the unzipped front to find the cotton blowing over his stomach. Squeezing tighter, his shirt waves up, and my hand is against the firm muscles. My legs tighten around him, the rough back of his jeans hitting me and making me want him. I'd forgotten how much motorcycles turned me on, especially when riding with a hot guy.

His hand covers mine and I close my eyes, enjoying the feel of being this at peace again. Letting my mind go back to the beach, I think about what he said and the side effects of our relationship. But I realize, they're not side effects. They're consequences of our actions. And like all actions, we have a choice to make, a price to pay, and a lesson to learn—consequences.

It's not until I'm lying in my room in the middle of the night that I finally connect the pieces Dex has given me. Two to be fastened together, interlocked in this puzzle we call life—Dex will never feel good enough as long as others remind him of his faults. And for me, just like at nineteen, it took a bike to remind me to appreciate the life I have.

I reach over and turn my phone off, the call I wanted never came, but an epiphany or two did. I fall asleep and dream of the beach and a crooked smile that is perfect to me.

20

ROCHELLE

IT WASN'T the merry-go-round of emotions that usually woke me up, my own inner turmoil disturbing any peace I found in sleep. *Nope.* It wasn't even an alarm jolting me awake. Two little wiggly monkeys giggle at my side, under the covers, and I roll over, waking up with a smile. "Good morning, guys."

I'm greeted with more laughs, giggles that tell me they think they're getting away with something. I throw the comforter over my head and trap us all underneath. Wide eyes and big smiles warm my heart. "Who's up for an adventure today?"

"Me," both Neil and CJ repeat several times, vying for my attention.

I flip the covers back down and say, "So what are we waiting for? Let's go."

They take off toward their bedrooms and I go to my closet, pulling on comfy jeans and a T-shirt. After brushing our teeth all lined up in a row in my bathroom, we slip on our shoes and head to the SUV. As soon as we're all inside and buckled, I ask, "Who wants to go to the zoo?" They both start jumping up and down in their seat with excitement. I add, "But first, we're gonna get some doughnuts."

SITTING on a bench watching my monkeys watch the zoo's monkeys makes me smile. They've been to the zoo many times over the years but today feels special—a new sense of freedom is felt that I didn't carry even as recently as yesterday.

It makes me want to call Dex and thank him, but like he said, he's not ready. He needs to find the good in himself, a good that I see so clearly now.

Ultimately, Firenza never mattered. I built her up to be something bigger in my head, someone better than me. She's not. She's just struggling to find the good within herself, just like Dex. She thinks hooking up with celebrities and chasing rich men will make her happy. But I kind of live by the old adage—a woman who marries for money earns every cent. Her happiness won't be found in someone else's wallet.

She is a consequence to mine and Dex's actions. We're at fault equally. But despite this new outlook on life, the bottom line is that Dex didn't have sex with her because deep down, he loves me. He didn't say it, but I feel it. I smile, knowing one day Dex and I will both heal and be whole again. And maybe, just maybe, if the stars align, we'll be together. I walk over and join the kids, being silly, and enjoy the great life I've been given.

DEAR CORY,

The beginning of October came and just like every year in LA, the weather changes to slightly milder from its usual state. Waking up early to get the kids to school never gets easier, but it does free up more of my day for work. Add CJ playing soccer and Neil taking private drumming lessons and my week is full.

Btw – Neil kicks ass on drums. At his age, I can confirm that he's living up to the Neil Peart moniker. You'd be proud.

Despite the crazy, I love the days when I get to play mom and spend time with them, but I'd miss the connection with the band.

I laugh lightly as I write: *Who knew I'd end up in the business world after fighting against it for so long. But you know what? I'm good at my job. Damn good, and that makes me feel great. As silly as it sounds, my family is proud that by all appearances, I'm a respectable member of society these days instead of a 'groupie with tattoos' like they once called me.*

The tour ended over the summer and the band has been writing music again. Johnny told me last week they have five solid songs for the new album, but refused to share until they're "ready." The offers have been pouring in and now the band seems to be doing a lot of appearances. I remember you preferred to stay home. I still do too. Scheduling has fallen on my shoulders to keep them organized. It's a lot of work, but I love the extra responsibility.

We really didn't think they could get much bigger, but the fans proved otherwise. The Resistance earned two gold records and three awards for Band of the Year, Album of the Year, and Sexiest Band of the Year. Yeah, I've had to temper their egos for that last one by reminding them of their awkward teenage years from when I knew them when... You would find it really funny. Anyway, I guess that's it for now.

XO

I TUCK my journal back into my nightstand drawer and lay there, staring up at the ceiling. The quiet leaves too much space to fill and my mind drifts to Dex. I call Holli, hoping for a respite from the wondering.

She answers, always happy to hear from me, "Hey there."

"Hey, it's not too late is it?"

"Nope. Just having a glass of wine outside. It's beautiful out tonight."

"Where's Johnny?"

"He went back into the studio after dinner. Did you want to talk to him?"

"No, I called for you."

She says, "It's good to hear from you. How have you been?"

"I need to talk to someone…"

"Alright. You sound serious. Everything okay?"

I release an unsteady breath, then say, "I miss Dex."

There's a long pause. I'm sure she's taking in the information. "Why do you miss Dex?"

"I need to tell you something, but you can't tell anyone else. Okay?"

"Okay," she answers hesitantly. "You can trust me. You know that."

"I know. That's why I'm calling. Look it's no secret that Dex and I were getting close… I'm sure Johnny told you."

"Johnny didn't tell me, but I heard some roadies talking about it."

"Oh great. Now we're fodder for roadies." I roll my eyes.

"It was all good gossip if there is such a thing as good gossip. As for Johnny, I've wondered why he didn't tell me. I'm thinking he hasn't come to terms with the idea. You know how protective he is of you—"

"And how he used to feel about Dex."

"I think he's made peace with him ever since he completed the last visit to rehab. When it comes to you and Dex being together, that may take more time."

"Here's the thing I don't understand," I start, snuggling under my covers after rolling away from the lamp on the nightstand. "We've struggled, Holli. This doesn't come easy for me and he's just as lost as me. Put us together and sometimes we're like peanut butter and chocolate and other times we're like oil and water."

"Did you just compare your relationship with Dex to food?"

"Don't judge. I'm hungry and I want all the bad things to inhale right now because I feel this crazy sadness, a sadness that's different from the one I had for Cory."

"I know the sadness, Rochelle. I know it well because I feel it too. Every time Dalton tours or has to make an appearance out of LA, I feel it." Her voice gets all girly-mushy on me when she says, "Awwww, you miss Dex."

Naturally, I respond like the girl I am and pout. "I do. I miss him. I don't know what happened, but he pulled away when I thought we were moving forward. We were going slow, but making progress."

Holli sighs softly, then says, "I'm sorry. I wish I knew what was going on with him. I only see him occasionally when the guys practice and record here."

"Can you talk to him about it?"

I think about what I would say to him if I could talk openly. "Maybe. But when I've seen him lately, it's with the boys. He still spends time with them here and there, but never stays to spend time with me."

"Are you worried about him relapsing? Hiding something from you?"

"Not really. I'm more worried about the fact that I can't stop thinking about a man who seems to have stopped thinking about me." I laugh at the end though I'm not really amused, just trying to cover my awkward real emotions.

"When our hearts are involved, we're always at risk. But there's no fun in safe."

"Nope, there's no fun in safe." I look at the ring of flowers wrapped around my wrist and remember how free I felt from the ties of my past. These flowers represented the life I chose, not the one my family had chosen for me. "Yeah, if I'd played it safe, I'd be married to a banker or insurance broker in Boston, attending luncheons in Chanel suits."

She laughs. "I love a good Chanel suit, but not on you. You're way too vibrant for something like that." She pauses, then says, "How long has it been since you spent time together, just the two of you?"

"When he told me he was going to show me how much he cares."

Holli's smile is heard through the phone. "Well, time will only tell, but I have a good feeling about you two."

"I appreciate you listening. Oh, and while I have you on the phone. Lunch soon?"

"Definitely. I'm in town next week, but leave for a week after that for a shoot in New York."

"Awesome. We'll catch up next week."

She says, "Anytime, my friend. Bye."

"Night."

Laying there, I acknowledge my feelings instead of hiding from them. I miss Dex. I miss snuggling with him and taking drives up the coast to watch sunsets. I liked him in my life and I think my heart just got used to him being around. It leaves me thinking about the promise he made to me on the beach in Miami, wondering if it was fleeting in the moment, just like the sunset that night.

I bury my face into the pillow, refusing to sit here and wallow. After a minute, I roll over and turn out the lamp and go to sleep.

21

ROCHELLE

THREE MONTHS after our ride up the coast and two days after my call to Holli, I receive a letter. The return address lists Caggiano as the sender. I flip it over in my hands a few times before sitting down on the couch and dumping the rest of the mail on the coffee table. The letter remains next to me for a good five minutes before I brace myself for the worst and open it.

DEAR ROCHELLE,

I thought the days without you would get easier than being tortured with your untouchable beauty. Each passing day offers a new form of cruelty and I have to stop my reflex of reaching for the phone and calling you, driving to your house, or writing you a letter.

I've failed as you can see. I'm starting to think that it's not about proving myself good enough so I can have more of you, but more about learning to enjoy what simple pleasures I'm given—your smile, for instance. I could write a song about the way your smile brightens my soul, filling it with light and hope, something pure that never existed there before.

Your eyes—the way they pinch at the corner when you're frustrated and widen when you're happy. The golden brown brings new meaning to the word brilliance.

The laugh that makes me want to become a comedian just to hear it more. The olive of your skin that makes me crave to lick every inch as well as caress it. These days I'd settle for a simple touch.

Your beauty exudes all that you are on the inside. I find myself wanting to consume your every breath and mark you as mine. Weaknesses I'm struggling to overcome.

But when you hit bottom, sometimes you're given the gift of clarity. Me without you is never the answer. I need you. The way you make me feel... it's good enough. It makes me better because you're around. It made me realize that when I'm with you, I'm good enough.

Love,

Dex

I REREAD the letter seven times before I run around my couch, my world full of hope again as I hold it to my heart. I love being a mom and responsible, but sometimes it's just good to be a giddy girl again.

"Dance party, Mama," CJ says, running after me.

I bend down and smile, then kiss him on the head. "Yes, we should have a dance party." Grabbing the remote, I flick on the music and then find an upbeat pop song. He jumps on the couch and I set the letter down on the table before standing on the hearth and shaking my booty. "Neil?" I call out. "Come dance with us."

I turn up the music just as he peeks his head around the corner. With a smile on his face, he comes in and jumps up on the hearth with me and starts dancing too.

Later that night in bed, I reread the letter and wonder if I should write back or call or do nothing. I'm not sure, but maybe he's telling me what he can't say to me in person. Maybe that's why I don't see him much these days. He's struggling to respect the boundaries I put in place. And now it's my turn to respect him and to protect him. I tuck the letter in my nightstand and go to bed with a smile beaming from my heart.

THE FOLLOWING DAY, around 10 a.m. my gate buzzer sounds. I get up from the kitchen table where I have a bunch of files spread out and answer it. Depressing the button, I say, "Who is it?"

"FedEx. I've got a package for Rochelle Floros."

I look through the camera and see the delivery guy standing there with a small box in his hands. Buzzing him in, I watch as he sets it on the front step and knocks. I open the door and sign for the package before closing it and locking it behind me.

I never have packages delivered to my home, so the whole thing is odd until I see the sender's name—Caggiano. I hurry into the kitchen and reach for the scissors to open it. When the flaps are released, I see a Disney hat with mouse ears on top. My name is stitched on the back and the note attached reads: *Wear Me.*

Following directions I put the hat on and then dig out the card. A Magic Kingdom ticket falls to the counter. The card says: ***Please meet me at 8:30 tonight, the front gates of Disneyland. Ask for Bob Hervine.***

Disney at eight-thirty? What is he up to? I'm too intrigued to not go. Looking at the time, I have hours before the kids are home. I pick up my phone and call Beth. She answers after the first ring every time, which I love. "Hello?"

"Hi, It's Rochelle."

"Hi, how's it going?"

"Good. I wanted to see if you were free tonight, around seven?"

"Sure," she replies. "You got a hot date?"

I pause to think about it, then reply with a laugh, "I'm not really sure."

"I'm happy to come over. I don't have any classes until ten in the morning, so feel free to stay out as long as you like."

"Thank you. I'll see you tonight."

I walk into the bedroom and start rummaging through my clothes to figure out what I should wear. When I go into the bathroom, I burst out laughing that I'm still wearing the mouse ears. I set the hat on my bed along with a sweater just in case it's chilly and sneakers on the floor since it's Disney and I'll be walking a lot. I'd prefer sexy, but for an amusement park, I'm going practical.

I RIDE the tram from the parking lot to the park. Walking up to the front gates, I'm wondering how I'm ever going to find a Bob Hervine at this hour when it's dark. As my ticket is taken, a Disney Cast Member says, "Wait right over here please. Bob will be with you momentarily."

Well, there you go.

"Ms. Floros?"

I turn around to see a stocky man with a rotund belly coming toward me and a huge smile on his face.

"Yes," I respond. "I'm Rochelle."

"I'm Bob. Nice to meet you," he says.

I shake his hand. "Nice to meet you as well."

He starts walking, but stops, and says, "C'mon. We're on a tight schedule."

"Oh." I hurry to catch up with him. "Sorry."

"No need to apologize, but Mr. Caggiano has planned something very unique and timing is everything." He's walking very fast, so I double my pace. "Mr. Disney built Main Street…"

I get a guided tour, although told very fast, of each main structure we pass and then through the castle. "The fireworks are about to begin." He smiles. "So we have to hurry. Magic is in the air."

"Magic?"

On the other side of the castle, the first fireworks shoot into the sky, lighting it up. I watch in awe of the grandeur of the huge display. Bob taps me on the shoulder, and says, "Don't look there. The real show is over here."

I follow the direction he gestures in and see Dex standing under the sign, Peter Pan's Flight. His smile is coy, a bit nervous looking, which is so unlike his usual confidence. I walk over, taking my time, letting him sweat it out a bit. "Hi," I say.

When he greets me, his smile grows. "Hi."

"This is a surprise, Dex?"

"Everyone can use a little magic in their life."

With an elbow nudge, I say, "You, sir, are a charmer."

"Thank you for coming on such short notice."

While he adjusts the mouse ears hat on my head, I reply, "How could I resist. I got a hat. I needed to show it off."

His laugh is contagious, or maybe it's because we're at the Happiest Place on Earth... or maybe it's because I'm happy to be here with him. He nods toward the entrance, and asks, "Wanna go for a ride?"

"Absolutely."

Taking my hand, he leads me through the winding railings that shape the line, miraculously empty, and I'm having a feeling this was also planned. We walk inside and are greeted by more happy cast members working the ride. Dex guides me onto the little pirate boat and we're off, through Wendy and her siblings' bedroom window, starting our own adventure.

It doesn't dawn on me until we're in the dark, immersed in the magic. Turning to Dex, I ask, "You brought me to Neverland?" Memories of our Neverland fantasies of the past squeeze my heart. It's a safe place for us, a place where our pasts don't matter and the rest of the world disappears just for a little while. A lump forms in my throat as I hold back the heavy emotions wanting to be heard while holding onto the safety bar in front of me. "I don't know what to say."

"It's not about what to say. Here in Neverland, I'm Peter and you're Wendy, remember? All that other stuff doesn't matter."

"I do remember," I say with a small smile. "In Neverland, no one can touch us."

"In Neverland, we work."

The pressures I feel when we're apart are gone, happiness taking over. Knowing we don't have much time in such a perfect place, I ask, "Why did you bring me to Neverland tonight?"

We cruise along in our flying pirate ship, past the ticking alligator before stopping over London. While staring out over the city below, he says, "How we left it at the beach that day... I make mistakes. A lot of fucking mistakes, bad decisions, and sometimes have poor judgment."

Tilting toward me, he adds, "But I'm getting better every day." He pauses and by his expression, I get worried, gripping the bar even tighter. "I used to wish you and Cory would break up. I had convinced myself that if you did, I would tell you how I felt about you. But you guys never did, and I'm glad. What used to be selfish wishes turned into something else. I liked you two together. You guys had the kind of relationship I wanted, one I envied. I need you to know that because of you and the boys, I would have traded places with him on that plane if I could. I loved him, Rochelle."

Looking down, I can't bear to hear him say that. "I know you loved him, but no, Dex, don't say that. He didn't have a choice and neither do we, so there's no point in thinking like that."

"It's the truth. Cory taught me to treat the ones we love with respect and to love them deeply." He shifts in the seat. "So even though I'm breaking our rule and bringing the past into Neverland, I need you to know that I understand how much you loved him. I'm not trying to replace him. I can't, but I want..." Dex looks away.

My voice is lower, just above a whisper when I ask, "What do you want?"

"I don't want to lose you."

Just as our ship begins to move again, I slide my hand across the hard plastic seat and find his. "You won't. I promise."

Our ship comes safely back into harbor and I hope our relationship follows the same path. I'm about to say something, but the attendants are excited to see him. He thanks everyone, shaking their hands and posing for three photos before we walk out.

Bob is waiting for us when we step outside. He claps his hands together once and asks, "How was Peter Pan's Flight?"

Dex looks over at me and answers, "Perfect."

"Are we ready for the magic to continue?" Bob asks.

I nod, excited to see what else is in store for us.

Bob starts walking quickly. "Stay close and follow me back this way. To the castle we go." I love the adventure he takes us on. We find our way to a secret entrance on the side and go up an elevator. Dex is smiling and in this most unique and fun situation, I see the guy I met down on Sunset again. I've started to treasure these little moments that take us back to a time when life was so much easier.

When the elevator doors open, my breath is taken away. A fire is roaring in the fireplace and a table for two is set up in front of it with a bottle of champagne chilling on ice. Bob pulls out a chair for me and I sit just as Dex does.

"Cinderella and Prince Charming?" I say, "You're pulling out all the stops, Mr. Caggiano."

"Not all of them. I'm saving some for another day."

The champagne is poured and Bob disappears, leaving us inside the private suite of Cinderella's Castle.

I take a sip, then ask, "I thought this place existing was just a rumor."

"Nope, it's real."

"It's beautiful. Ornate and over the top. Exactly how it should be."

A waiter walks in with two pieces of chocolate cake and sets them in front of us. When he leaves, I lean on my elbow and smile. "I think I'm in Heaven."

"You deserve Heaven for the Hell you've been through."

I stare into his eyes astounded by his ability to say such perfect things at the right time. We clink our glasses, toasting to that. The first glass of champagne is gone and after eating my cake, I ask, "Dex, are you wooing me or trying to win me? Because either way, you're doing an excellent job."

"Good to know. But really, I'm just trying to make up for everything."

I sit up straight, and say, "You keep saying you make all of these bad decisions and screw up, but I don't see you that way. Maybe I should." I think of Firenza. "I really should after finding you…" I don't bother since I don't want to drag up the past right now and ruin the evening.

He's silent as he stands. Leaning his hand against the mantle, he stares into the fire below. "The madness of love is the greatest of heaven's blessings"

"The madness of love feels fitting."

"Plato has a way with words. I have that tattooed."

"Where?"

"It's the inscription inside the shield on my heart."

Slowly, I stand up and walk to him. Touching his shoulder, he turns. His fingers unbutton his grey shirt while keeping his eyes on mine. The shield of armor, his family crest is revealed. Dex takes my hand and presses it flat against his skin that's been heated by the fire, and whispers, "It's been too long since you've touched me."

The silence of the room exaggerates every swallow and breath I take. I drop my gaze from his eyes down to his chest and see the quote printed on the arched top of the tattoo. "Does this shield represent your family name or protect your heart?"

He cups my face, and says, "Both," then kisses me.

22

ROCHELLE

GOING against everything I've said, Dex affects me like no other. He's gotten under my skin. Inside of Cinderella's Castle, I back up, pulling Dex with me toward one of the beds behind us. I take his shirt off and kiss the warm skin of his shoulder. When I look up, he kisses me as his hands slide up from my waist to my ribs, his thumbs running along the sides of my breasts. Slipping my arms around his neck, I pull myself against him. "Make love to me, Dex."

His breath covers my mouth as he pulls away. "No, it's not time."

"Time is irrelevant. We're living our own fairytale. I want to feel you again."

"I want more than just a physical connection to you, sweetheart. I want to own your soul the way you've taken possession of mine. It won't be quick and it won't be easy, but I'm gonna win you heart *and* soul, so much so that you'll be begging me to fuck you."

As much as his words hit that soft spot in my heart, they also make me want him even more. "I'm already begging."

He chuckles. "Nope, you're not quite there yet." Backing away from me, he picks his shirt up off the ground. "And sadly, our time is up." The grandfather clock in the other room chimes the hour as if on cue. "We have to go." He buttons his shirt while I'm left dumb-founded, confused, and downright horny.

Disgruntled, I huff as I walk past him and head for the stairs, needing to burn off the rage I'm feeling over being abandoned in this state.

Bob is downstairs with the same big grin he's been wearing all night. "Did you have a nice time?"

"I did, until the end," I reply without thinking.

"Oh, my apologies. Was something not to your liking?" he asks while Dex laughs.

I quickly clarify, "No, no, no. You were all wonderful and the service was impeccable. My date on the other hand seems to think teasing a woman is the way to her heart."

Bob nods, understanding without me having to go into the details. He clears his throat as he looks over at Dex. "Well, I'm glad Disney could be of service tonight. Mr. Caggiano, is there anything else we can do for you or Ms. Floros?"

"No, as Ms. Floros mentioned, it was perfect—"

"Perfect," I scoff, still frustrated... sexually.

Bob smiles. "Wonderful. Follow me then and I'll walk you out."

We follow, side by side, but behind Bob. The stragglers from the park are making their way out as well. I feel Dex's hand tap against me and then he loops his little finger with mine. I'm not really mad at him, but definitely confused, so I whisper, "What does tonight mean?"

"It means when the time is right, we're gonna be together."

"The timing isn't right?" I know it's a dumb question, but I guess I feel that maybe the timing *is* right, finally. *What am I missing?*

"We rushed into it the first time *and* the second time. This time, I'm not rushing, I'm changing so when we're together, I can savor and appreciate you."

"So you won't appreciate me if we get together now?"

"No. Because I still have to work on sorting my life out first. But I want you to know there's no one else for me. There never was."

His sweet words hit me like an arrow straight to the heart. His gentle side is so unexpected from the tough armor he wears for the public on a daily basis. "I don't know what to say to that."

"I don't need you to say anything. I just need you to know I may not ever be perfect, but once we're together, I'll always be true to you."

"And in the meantime?" I find myself chanting quietly, hoping he says what I want to hear. *Please say you won't date anyone. Please say you won't date anyone.*

He stops, pulling me to a bench, and sits. I do as well and I notice Bob stops up ahead, giving us a moment of privacy. Dex takes both my hands in his, then brings one to his lips and kisses the inside of my wrist. "I'm not gonna ask you to put your life on hold, Rochelle. I think you've done that for too many years already. But I will ask that you keep me in your heart."

My mouth drops open. "You're letting me go?"

"No, I'm letting expectations that are impossible for me to live up to go."

"So while you're sorting things out, you won't wait for me?"

"I'd love to make you a million promises, but right now I can't."

Disappointment settles in. "That's why you wouldn't be with me at the castle?"

He nods, releasing one of my hands. "It would have been so easy to make love to you and then tell you I need space." Dex presses his hand to my cheek and I find my eyes closing to the touch I missed so much, relishing it. He says, "I remember how it feels to be with you, to be inside you. But my life is a mess and I don't want to drag you and the boys into it."

I open my eyes, no tears to cry this time. My sentimental side touched by his thoughtfulness as my rational side agrees with his decision. "It's like we always knew, we can only be together in Neverland."

"It's learning how to make Neverland reality. One day I'll figure it out. You deserve it, Rochelle. You deserve magic and more."

"You say that I deserve so much, but so do you, so much more than you know."

Standing, he offers me a hand up. "Maybe one day I'll believe you. Until then," he says, signaling toward Bob who has stepped forward, unsubtly tapping his watch.

After taking a deep breath, I exhale long and slow. "Until then..." As soon as I say it, I start to worry how long 'Until then' will be and don't bother finishing.

Dex and my goodbye at the main gate of Disneyland doesn't last long enough, but it's sweet and when I lay my head on his chest, he embraces me with love.

I drive home replaying every part, every word, and every minute of our time together. Dex has grown, but he still has issues to deal with, addictions, and his family. He thinks he'll be whole, be better, be deserving if everything comes all tied up with a bow and wrapped up in a neat package. Life doesn't work that way. I know this firsthand.

But who needs tidy or pretty, bows, or happy ever afters? Romance is about the journey, the good, the bad, ugly and pretty, the highs, the lows. I don't need perfect and I don't want it. I want to be happy and enjoy this life I've been given. I want my kids happy and to be surrounded by love. I want that for Dex too and if that means he needs time to figure his life out, then I'll give that to him.

Strength and understanding guide my direction over the next week until finally, late one night, I realize how saying goodbye to Dex was like giving a piece of my heart away and hoping it finds its way home again.

23

ROCHELLE

THE STARS SEEM to sparkle tonight, so unlike most LA nights. Where are the clouds and the smog? I prefer when the weather suits my moods. My mood didn't seem to faze Mother Nature, which kind of bothered me.

I pull a handful of grass blades, hold it up in the air, and let them fall to the ground. There's no breeze to carry them, so they land on my stomach as does my youngest when he comes and flops down.

Grunting, I say, "Careful, buddy. You're getting big." CJ stands and I lift my legs, then bend at the knees. "Let's do airplane."

He moves quickly, always loving when we do this. I brace myself as he adjusts his belly onto my shins. When I lift, he squeals in happiness. "Look at me," he says.

"Look at you. You look like Superman."

His arms go wide and his legs straight out, and he says, "Superman needs to go potty."

"Eeps." I set him down and he runs inside.

Neil comes running from the swing set and stops next to me. "My turn. My turn."

"Yep, your turn." Neil rests on my legs and I lift. His smile is so sweet, so happy that I smile too. His arms automatically go out and his legs straighten.

Straightening my legs even more, I say, "Great Superman, Neil."

"My turn next." I turn to see Dex standing there.

My legs wobble when I hear his voice, but I steady them along with my heart. Glancing over at him, I smile, not able to hide my happiness.

"Dex!" Neil says, "Look at me."

"I'm looking, bud. Good job. How's the drumming?"

Neil shrugs, throwing himself off-balance, so I lower my legs quickly so he lands on his feet safely. With a smile meant just for me, Dex eyes me. "Hi."

"Hi," I reply. It's not hot out, but I feel hotter all of the sudden.

"Beth let me in. Hope it's okay." He licks his lips and it's hard to take my eyes off of his mouth, making me gulp.

Neil stands there, glancing between us.

Lifting up on my elbows, I say, "I'm free."

Dex questions, "Free?"

"You said it was your turn next." I signal to my legs.

Neil laughs. "Mom is strong, Dex. She never drops us."

"That's good to hear. I think I'd rather be base though." He comes and lies next to me in the grass. "Airplane?" he offers with a wry grin and slips his shoes off.

I nod as I get up. Positioning myself with his feet against my stomach, I reach down and our fingers entwine as our hands come together. The heat between us sparks fading embers back to life. He lifts up, surprising me, and we both laugh.

"Do Superman, Mom," CJ says, running outside, delighted by the sight.

"I'm Wonder Woman." I release Dex's hands and put my arms out and straighten my legs behind me. The boys start chasing each other, running around us in circles.

Beth calls the boys inside for homework. She gives me a knowing wink. "I'll just stay a little longer so you guys can talk."

"Thanks," I reply before turning back to him.

Dex stares into my eyes and says, "I never thanked you."

"Thanked me for what?" I ask, reaching down until our hands are connected once again.

"What you did for me that day. Coming to Barstow with Tommy and then... rehab."

Remembering what Johnny said to me years earlier, I say, "You don't have to thank me. The Resistance is a family. We take care of one another."

He nods a little before lowering me back to the ground. When he sits up, I sit down across from him. Lowering his gaze to the ground, he pauses. Just from his body language I brace myself. When his eyes meet mine again, I see the remorse in his entire expression. "I wanted to die."

Much like I was doing before he showed up, I grab a handful of grass, ripping it from its roots. This time from anxiety over the topic. "Why?"

"I couldn't see the big picture."

"You were blinded by the details."

"I was cursed by the memories."

I glance down needing a second, then say, "Memories of me?"

His fingers run over my knee, then his hand stills. "I hadn't done drugs since Cory's death, but I did them that night. I took everything I could find and then called friends who gave me more."

"They're not friends if they gave you drugs, Dex. They're enemies."

"Drugs are good about keeping your perspective skewed away from reality. Let's just say my perspective was skewed."

I don't mean to snap at him, but it slips out. "Where'd you meet those girls?"

He clears his throat. "I don't know." His tone then changes, lowers, just like his hand does as he replies, "I don't know how I got to Barstow either. I just remember that ride to rehab."

"That was a hard ride to take."

"God, that day sucked. But yeah, I never thanked you. I wouldn't be here if you hadn't been there for me."

"Tommy was there too."

"Tommy..." He shifts his weight and stands up. "...He's been a good friend to me." When he looks down, I see the words he's going to say in his expression. The embarrassment he feels coloring his words. "I was ashamed you saw me like that. But you should know that you were the only reason I walked out of that motel room."

"Dex," I say, feeling the pressure on my chest, making it harder to swallow. I take his hand and lead him to the tire swing.

"I wouldn't have left for Tommy. I know it. But then you were there... I hated myself for letting you see me like that. I hated myself in general. But I only got up because I couldn't do that to you. I couldn't put you through anymore pain with the pain you had already been through."

We sit opposite from each other and I cover his hand with mine on the chain. "You always say you're not a good guy, but a bad guy wouldn't have thought twice about my feelings in a time like that."

He doesn't blush but I see that the compliment embarrasses him in a good way. "Do you remember that night at my party?" he asks.

"I could never forget."

He rubs his chin. "I shouldn't admit this, but I watched you down by the pool."

"How long were you up there?"

"Most of the party."

"Why?" I ask.

"I was sitting there in the middle of this party full of people there to celebrate my birthday and I realized I didn't like half of them. Most of the others I didn't even know. Then there was you." He spins us by kicking off from the ground.

I lean my head back toward the sky and smile watching the world spin out around us. Closing my eyes, I enjoy the cool breeze as he pushes off again. "What about me?" I laugh, loving the lightness of my body and the conversation.

"You're a tease, Rochelle."

I open my eyes and waggle my eyebrows at him. As he pushes off again, my body sways to the left and I go with it, letting my arms straighten. "I wasn't teasing that night. I felt lost, but when I think back, I wasn't." I lock eyes with him. "I was there for you."

"You were Eve in a garden of evil that night. An angel appearing out of nowhere." He plants his foot and we come to an abrupt stop. "You didn't come looking for me, but you found me all the same. Tell me it meant something."

"It meant everything to me." He releases his intense gaze on me and smiles. I hop off the swing and walk to him. Placing my hands on his shoulders, I touch him gently. "I'm not trying to inflate your ego. I'm just telling you the truth."

He playfully pokes me in the side. "Too late. My ego is already inflated."

Laughing, I surprise him and spin the tire, sending him spinning. "Well in that case, I'll have to try harder."

I walk away, leaving him whirling. To my surprise, I'm grabbed from behind just seconds later. His lips touch the shell of my ear, his arms holding me tight, and he says, "I like the sound of that."

My body is instantly covered in goosebumps as I take a staggered breath and lean my head into the nook of his neck.

One kiss. One sweet kiss to that most hidden place behind my ear. He makes me want to ravage him, his touch always filling me with temptation and desire. One day I'm going to torture him just as sweetly. When the heat of his body leaves mine, I realize today isn't that day. But soon.

Very soon.

24

ROCHELLE

THE FUNNY THING about revelations are that they hit you when you least expect it. I'd been sitting here the last week thinking Dex was choosing to work on his life, which means we get put on hold. What I hadn't thought about is how I play into his plans, his life, or his future. I also hadn't thought about what I want for my kids and myself. It was easy when we were together. Everything with him feels so right.

But when we're not together, I wonder if he falls apart like I do. I wonder if this is why he doubts himself. More importantly, am I in any position to help him? He hasn't committed some great sin that can't be forgiven. I think he's just caught in a cycle of destruction, one where he's more comfortable dealing with than the change ahead.

After texting him a few times and leaving a few messages for him after calling him and getting no answer, I did exactly the opposite of what I wanted to do and I backed away. *It was a hard month.* He stopped calling, the letters didn't continue, and unless I had business with him, I didn't hear from Dex at all. It made me wonder if he'd always be damaged enough to not see the good through the bad. For his sake, I hope not.

Sometime in early November something arrived at the house, a letter of a different sort. The letterhead was labeled The Roosevelt Hotel in Hollywood. I opened it and read:

ROCHELLE,

I'm lost without you. I needed time, thinking it would get easier, but it hasn't. My life is worse. I've done things I regret and I don't know how to repent.

How do you save an unsalvageable soul that doesn't want to be saved? I want to drown in things that will make me lose my mind, so I can live in the numbness, even if only temporarily.

There's a void that music can't fill, that other women won't fix, that drugs won't blur, and that time won't relent.

My drug of choice these days is you...

Can you heal a damaged soul?

Love,

Dex

HE'S GOTTEN good at dropping these bombshells. But what he's written concerns me—Barstow coming to mind. The envelope is post-dated two days ago. Today is Friday and I have three hours before the kids get out of school. I grab my keys and head out, my mission—The Roosevelt.

Walking up to the front desk, I introduce myself. "Hi, I'm Rochelle Floros, and I need to see if one of my business partners is still staying here."

The young man, mid-twenties, blonde, brown eyes, smiling. "Good afternoon. I'm Bruce. Hey, you're with The Resistance, right?"

"Yes."

"I'm sorry about Cory Dean. He was the most amazing guitar player."

I should be used to his name being spoken in conversation by others and hearing Cory spoken about in the past tense, but some days are easier for me than others. Today, I'm walking a fine line. "Thank you. I appreciate that. I know he would have too."

Bruce's smile tightens and he leans forward to whisper, "Are you here to see Dex Caggiano?"

"I am. Is he still here?"

"He hasn't left his room in four days."

I sigh. "I know it's against policy, but I need to see him, so is there any way you'll share his room number with me?"

"Actually, you're the only one he has on his guest list, so it's not a problem at all. He also left a key for you. Let me get it."

Trying to remain calm, like that's not a huge surprise is hard, but I manage to act as normal as possible. "Thank you."

After I get the key, I'm directed to the elevators. Though dread fills my stomach, feeling like an ulcer is forming, I don't hesitate when I exit onto his floor. I anxiously walk down the hall until I reach his suite. I'd knock, but something tells me he left a key for a reason, so I use it and walk inside.

Dex is lying on the couch, facing the window. The curtains are open with a perfect view of the Hollywood sign outside it. I set my purse and the key down on the table before sitting down in a chair next to him.

He asks, "Do you know what it's like to have your soul stolen?" His voice is rough, like he's been partying and smoking all night. I have a feeling he hasn't been out, but doing that holed up inside this room.

Keeping my gaze out the window like him, I reply, "Yes, I do." I know all too well.

Our eyes meet and he says, "Sometimes I say the stupidest shit. Ignore me."

"I don't want to ignore you. I want to hear everything you have to say."

"That could take days."

"I have a few to give if you want them."

He smiles. It's lazy and utterly charming. "I'd take them all if I could."

"How long have you been staying here?"

"A week. Maybe more. I've lost count."

"Why aren't you at home?"

He chuckles to himself. "That's a tricky question."

"I didn't mean it to be. Why's it so complicated?"

"It's strange when you're touring. You start getting used to living in hotels. At the same time, you can't wait to get home. But then you get home and it doesn't always feel like it once did. So I checked in here."

"To fill the space between?"

"To transition back."

I nod, going to my purse. I pull the envelope out and ask, "Do you want to talk to me about the letter?"

"Sure. Shoot."

I move to the couch, lifting his legs, sitting down, and then returning them to lie across my lap. Looking at him, he appears worn down. That makes all the wrong questions surface, but I feel I need to ask anyway. "Have you been doing drugs?"

Staring out the window again, he says, "No."

"Have you slept with any women?"

His eyes flash back to mine. "No, I've not had sex with anyone or slept with anyone."

"When's the last time you talked to your family, Dex?"

"A week. Maybe more."

"So they're the reason you're here?"

"No, I told you why I'm here."

"Then why the correlation in timing?" I ask, rubbing the top of his leg over his jeans.

"Everything I'm going through, you've been through with Cory. It's fucked up."

"Your feelings are your own. They're unique. I've been through more than I thought I could handle, but I'm here and I'm living my life the best I can. It doesn't mean that my heart doesn't ache when yours does or that I don't feel lonely or miss you. I do, all of the above."

"Cory was your soulmate."

"I used to be so sure," I say, pausing to gulp. "I'm not as positive these days."

"Don't discount his importance for me. I know I'll always be second best. It's a position my family trained me for. I think I'll be okay playing that role in your life."

"First of all, I would never discount Cory for anyone. Secondly, I'm starting to think that maybe..." I sigh, not sure if saying the words will make them real.

"Maybe some people are like stars in the sky. They burn so much brighter than everyone else that they—"

"Burn out sooner." I stop, resting my head on the back of the couch. Turning so I can see the blue sky outside, I add, "He'll always be better than the rest of us. It sucks he left us behind to fumble through the world making mistakes—"

"And bad decisions."

"Not knowing how to move on."

"Or if you even should."

Looking at him, I ask, "Have you ever thought about death?"

"All the time."

"But you go on. You always go on. That's the gift of a new day."

"It's not the day I live for."

"What do you live for?" I hold my breath waiting for the answer.

"You, Rochelle."

Arrow right to my heart. He wins with his swoony lines and broken rock star image. He's not too far gone though. I have faith in him to pull himself out of this cycle he's found himself in.

He lifts his legs and I stand up. Scooting over, he makes room and I slide onto the leather next to him. As I rest my cheek against his chest, I close my eyes. His arm comes over, holding me tight. His scent draws me in, making my insides twist in such an amorous way as well as calming my other senses, feeling much like home to me. I want to argue with my own logic, but he needs to know the harsh reality. Whispering, I say, "You can't live only for me, Dex."

"I'm leaving tomorrow."

Wrapping my arm around him, I ask, "Where are you going?" I know he can hear my fears, the loss of him already felt deep within.

"I'm going to my grandfather's house for a week. My mother called a meeting. My brother will be there."

"Would you like me to go with you?"

He kisses my forehead, then says, "I wouldn't wish that kind of trip on an enemy. Definitely never on someone I love."

Love. My head swims in the undertow of his words. "You say things like that so easily, like you think I won't notice."

That makes him laugh, which is something *I* love. He replies, "I'm tired of hiding my feelings, but that doesn't mean I'm gonna shout it from the rooftops just yet. I have a lot of shit to deal with that I don't think you should be dragged into."

"I think we're both tired of hiding. That's why I came over."

Maneuvering over me, with an eyebrow wiggle, he asks, "So you've finally fallen for my charms, huh?"

I smile. "Your charms have been working a lot longer than you know."

Hovering over me and with a cocky head nod, he says, "I knew I'd wear you down."

"Oh, Mr. Caggiano, you've worn me out... I mean down, several times."

Pressing his hips and his very apparent erection between my legs, he says, "And I look forward to doing it again."

"Who knew the wild, bad boy drummer of The Resistance had the willpower of a saint? Not me."

With a deep laugh, he says, "Me either. Just know when we're together again, it won't be just sex. It'll be an unwritten contract. A promise from my heart to yours."

My heart starts thudding in my chest and I pull him down, bringing his lips to mine and kiss him, making my own promise to him. When I fall back on the cushion, I open my eyes and smile when I see the happiness in his. "Go do what you need to do," I say, rubbing his back. "I'll be here waiting for you when you get back."

"I'm gonna hold you to that."

"I like when you hold me." Dex smirks and I return the favor before pushing up against him and adding, "Also, I want you to check out and go home. If it's not feeling like home these days, let me know, and I'll help you find what you're looking for."

"Bossy *and* sexy. You're turning me on. You should probably leave before I pillage your body for the remainder of the day."

"I like pillaging and plundering."

"Yep, plundering is good too."

Reluctantly, I stand and look at my watch. After taking LA traffic into account, I say, "As tempting as plundering sounds, I should go." He stands up as well and I can see his mood has changed for the better. "Walk me to the door."

I tug him by the end of his belt until my back is pressed against the door and he's pressed against me. He says, "Thank you for coming."

"Thank you for the letter."

His eyes steady on mine, our mouths just a few mere inches apart. Leaning in, he says, "You're my constant. My north. The only compass worth following."

Taking his face in my hands, the scruff is rough against my skin, his temperament gentle as I caress him. "I know you, the real you, Dex. You don't ever have to hide from me."

He leans his forehead against mine and closes his eyes. As soon as I close mine, he whispers, "I love you, Rochelle Floros." Then he backs away, releasing me and adds, "Go before this turns embarrassing and I start telling you everything else you make me feel."

Gah! This man. I just want him in so many ways... Smiling, I open the door and step over the threshold. But I stop, turn around and run into his arms, hugging him tightly. With my cheek against his chest, I say, "One day, I want to hear about them. Every side, every emotion, every thought you have." And like before at Disney, I leave him with, "Until then," but as I walk away, I add, "You have my number if you need me. Use it sometime."

He nods, taking hold of the door before it swings shut. "Until then..."

25

DEX

I VOWED NEVER to come back to Diablo. At thirty, it finally seemed like the right time to sort my family life out once and for all. I sit in the Challenger for a good five minutes staring at the mansion before me and listening to Alice in Chains. "Rooster" somehow fitting right now.

I had so many good times and so many bad times here. It was where I learned my grandfather was not the overbearing monster my mom had sold him as, but later discovered he was worse.

My life seemed to develop and fall apart inside that stucco exterior. I was going one direction and then... and then everything changed. I sucked as a son and everything that my mother had wanted. I excelled at rebellion, so that's what I did to save my sanity. Now I'm back sixteen years later to face the demons that plague me.

Gage walks out, his head down as if he's already disappointed in me. Leaning his hand against the door of my car, I hear his wedding ring scrape against the metal, messing up my paint job. *No fucking respect at all.*

"Dexter. You're two hours late."

I pop the door open, hitting him, and step out. "I was given a day, not a time, so fuck off about some schedule you created in your head."

"Nice attitude," he says sarcastically. "And here I thought this week was about making amends."

Walking to my trunk, I open it and grab my leather duffle bag out. "So did I, so why are you out here busting my balls?"

Following a heavy sigh, he says, "There's an additional will that is to be read when the youngest Caggiano hits his thirties."

"I've been thirty for months."

My brother shrugs. "We've been busy."

Busy stealing I assume, but keep the thought to myself, figuring it's less confrontational that way. I walk past him and into the house. "Same room?"

Overtaking me, he goes to the bar. "Yep, same room you always had." I hear the ice dropping into the crystal glass. "Dinner's in twenty. Dress for it."

I stop on the stairs wanting to say something, wanting to give him a piece of my mind, but I keep my eyes forward and start back up. This week's gonna be hell.

I dump my bag on the bed and take a minute to look around. The room is exactly the same, like I never left. Being inside these four walls again makes me feel fourteen in the worst ways. I was abandoned here in the summer, feeling like I'd been forgotten. Anger builds inside.

Unzipping my bag, I choose a long sleeve, button up, but refuse to give in fully to their whims on decorum. Not wearing a tie is the only ammo they have on me when I have a luggage set of issues with them. After washing my face and brushing my teeth, I put on the clean shirt then head downstairs.

My mother is standing in front of the wrought iron doors that lead to the large lawn. Croquet is set up and I can only assume per my mom's request. She turns just as I enter the sitting room. With her token martini in hand, she smiles. It's small, rigid, but it's good to see she can form an emotion on her overly botoxed face. She was once a beauty queen. Sometimes I can see the girl who resides inside the bitterness of the woman. Sometimes I can't.

She stares at me. She always did say I was the spitting image of my father. I took it as a compliment to spite her inference. When she doesn't say anything, I tend to think she's lost in a memory of him. Finally, she relaxes and says, "Antonio, it's so good to see you."

I go to her and give her a hug because no matter what hurt she's caused me, I like to think her embraces are genuine. She hugs me back, careful not to spill her drink. "Hi, Mom." I take the spot next to her, looking out the window. "How are you?"

"You didn't wear a tie. Will you put one on?"

"No. Is dinner almost ready?"

"Always my non-conformist."

"Eh," I say, "It's working for me."

Her hand touches my cheek and I see a real smile form. "Don't ever change," she whispers, "You're perfect just how you are."

My eyes narrow, her unexpected compliment catching me off-guard. "What's going on?"

"So cynical, Son."

A loud clap disturbs us and Gage walks in bellowing. "Are they finally done with dinner? I'm starved."

At the sound, my mom's hand falls to her side and she sips her cocktail while turning back to look outside again. Bad timing on the interruption. It's been a long time since I've seen this side of my mother and I was enjoying it. A woman walks in and tells us dinner is ready in the main dining room.

"Good," Gage says as if he's been waiting all day for food. He rushes past us and takes the seat at the head of the table like he somehow earned it.

"You're an ass, Gage."

"I may be an ass, but I'm also rightfully head of the family as the oldest male."

My mother sits next to him quietly as if she doesn't hear the argument or she just doesn't care. Wine is poured and I thank the server. She's pretty, not flirty. Just tending to her job.

Dinner is tense with so many egos trapped in one room. I try to bring up the reason we're here several times, but nothing sticks. "Explain the situation with the additional will."

Gage uses all these hand gestures like he's lecturing a child in timeout. "The lawyer was held in strict confidence until your birthday or if you didn't live, your funeral." I glare at him. "What?" He shrugs. "I think we all know it was hit or miss with you."

"I'd call you an asshole, but I'm starting to think you like playing that part too much and you'll take it as a good thing."

My mom leans her elbows on the table, exasperated. "Boys, let's put all this animosity behind us and focus on the future."

Seeing her lose her manners in such an easy way makes me double take in her direction. Something's going on with her and I think Gage is too angry and too drunk to notice. The server comes in with our dessert plates. She serves Gage last. I'm thinking on purpose. He grabs her ass just as she sets his plate down.

"Excuse you!" she says, her face one of horror.

I stand abruptly. "I apologize for him. We'll not need anything else tonight."

She looks from him to me, her expression one of relief when our eyes meet. "Thank you."

When she leaves the room, I remain standing, tossing my napkin down. "I think we're finished here. I'm going to bed." I walk out, needing to clear my mind from the head trip laid on me tonight. The door is pushed open and I move quickly across the yard, stepping over a few wickets on the way. I go toward the shadows where I used to hide when I was a kid, but I break the pattern and pull my phone from my back pocket, dialing instead of drinking.

Rochelle answers right away and damn if I don't love that. "Hello?"

"Hi, it's me."

"It's good to hear from you," she says, "Everything okay?"

"Everything is complicated like always."

"Are you alright?"

I lie down in the grass and look up at the night sky. I can see a million or more stars out here, unlike in LA. "Go outside, Rochelle."

Without question, she goes. I hear her shuffling and the creak of a door. Then she says, "I'm outside."

"Can you see any stars?"

"Not as many as I'd like."

I smile. "I can see forever from here."

"Can you see to LA? I'm waving just for you."

"I can see you in my heart."

"I miss you, Dex."

"I miss you, too. It's good to hear your voice."

"You too, but you don't sound well."

"I'm okay. Tell me about your day."

"My day was boring," she says.

"Not to me."

I'm content listening to her talk, her voice soothing me. What she thinks is mundane, I find peaceful. It's a life I can only hope to have one day.

"...The boys still talk about you. They remember everything you taught them."

"Thank you for not making me the bad guy in their eyes."

"Dex, you're not a bad guy."

Taking a deep breath, I say, "They're reading another will of my grandfather's. You know how you found out I was from a wealthy family?"

"Yes."

"My grandfather was even wealthier. He was my idol once. He was a drummer."

"Ah."

"But when my mom was raped by my uncle, he blamed her."

I hear her sharp intake of air. It's a bombshell and no matter how it's dropped, it's gonna blow up, so there's no point in tiptoeing around the monsters in the family.

"Dex—"

"You don't have to say anything."

"You can talk to me."

I hear my mom calling for me, but I don't move. "I should go. It's getting late. I'm sure you need some rest and I need to escape."

"You're not in this alone. Call me anytime."

"Goodnight."

"Sweet dreams, Dex."

When I hang up, I start back for the house. Fortunately my mom is nowhere in sight. I've had enough of my family for one day and head to bed.

MY NIGHT IS restless and I get up as the sun starts to rise. I don't bother with formalities. Boxers, jeans, and a T-shirt are good enough to go downstairs to get coffee. When I'm walking down the hall, the door to Gage's room opens and a familiar looking brunette is sneaking out—*the server from dinner.*

Her shoes in hand as she turns and then jumps, startled by me. "Morning," I say.

"Good morning, Sir. I was just, uhhh, getting Mr. Caggiano his morning coffee." I wonder if lying makes her feel better and if she actually thinks I believe her? She continues, "I need to go."

She starts to dash off, but I say, "He's married with two small kids."

She doesn't look back again as she leaves the house. In the kitchen I find a Keurig with a variety of coffee pods to choose from. Popping one in, I wait as it brews. Gage walks in without a shirt and scratching under his arm. "Morn," he says, reaching for a mug from the hooks under the cabinet.

"What the fuck? You're married, Gage."

"I haven't even had my coffee yet. Can we hold this conversation until after we're caffeinated or better yet, never?"

"Britney loves you."

"And I love her, so what's the problem?"

I turn my back to him, leaning my hands against the marble

countertops, trying to control the rage he brings out in me. As a teenager I used to smoke pot with my friends. We'd trespass and go up to Griffith observatory to escape. When the band became famous, we'd trespass onto the Hollywood Sign and do coke or X.

I thought the night Cory died would be the last night I ever did drugs. I think I did everything I could get my hands on that night in Paris and my body paid the price. But Cory saved me. Now I carry guilt for falling in love with his woman, or falling *more* in love, I mentally correct myself. I loved her since the day I met her. Then add dealing with my asshole of a brother on top of that guilt and all I want to do is go break some shit, smoke some weed, and escape.

I won't do it because of her and the kids. Good must be hereditary and those boys scored. It sure doesn't run in my family.

Grabbing the coffee before the last drop falls, I return to my room. Gage was smart not to continue talking to me. I stay in my room and work on a song I've been writing, the lyrics coming in waves as I write them down. The band returns to the studio in eight days to record and I want this song to be perfect before they hear it. I've never written one for them before so I know they'll be more critical.

A knock on the door causes me to look up. With a guitar in my arms, I say, "Come in."

My mom walks in with two drinks in hand. "I brought you an iced tea."

"Thank you."

"Can we talk or am I interrupting?"

"We can talk." I set the guitar down, then say, "I could use some fresh air. Would you like to go for a walk?"

THE SKY IS blue and there's a nice breeze outside as we follow the gravel path around the outside of the gardens. "I have cancer." I had the glass to my lips when she tells me. I bring it down and stop in my spot. She looks back and says, "I don't want to make a big deal of it. Let's keep walking."

"Cancer is a big deal."

"Yes," she says, "But we must die from something. Dying is a side effect of life."

"You're downplaying it. Death seems like a really bad fucking side effect."

She wraps her arm around my elbow and we start walking again. "It's inoperable and too far along to bother treating. I'm good with this."

My mind can't seem to grasp onto anything tangible, her words make no sense to me. Questions fill my brain as her justifications don't provide the answers I need. "I'm not good with it. What did Gage say?"

"He doesn't know yet. I wanted to tell you first."

"Why?"

She pulls me tighter to her, leaning her head on my shoulder. "Because you're a better man than I ever gave you credit for. And, I knew you'd be more rational with this kind of news."

I want to be anything but rational. Feeling aggravated to have this laid upon me like this makes me mad. I'm trying to hold that in because she seems to crave peace and after years of craving her attention, she's finally giving it to me. I don't want to blow it now. "Why are you not fighting?"

"Because the doctors said weeks. Not months or years. Weeks. And I don't want to spend my remaining time fighting a battle that clearly cannot be won." She lifts her head and releases my arm. "I know what they will say and I'm worried about Gage and his troubled situation."

"Troubled?"

"Britney has left him and taken the children. He's blown through a lot of his inheritance and has asked for loans against future deposits." We come to a bench and she sits, her body sinking down only a bit as she does. Always a woman of pride and propriety, her posture is not reflective of her condition. I sit beside her, and she says, "Gage is not a Caggiano. He was conceived out of wedlock thus negating his claim to any of your grandfather's money or estates. The first will covered him. This second one will eliminate him from receiving anything more."

My head goes back in disbelief. "Holy shit."

"Please don't swear. Anyway, I know this is a lot to take in, but I need your help now. I'm not sure what to tell him. I think he'll be more upset about the loss of funds than finding out that he's the son of a poet passing through town. Or that I have cancer."

"He'll care. You two were always very close."

"We haven't been in a few years."

"Since the situation with me."

"Yes. I think it needs to be revisited. He needs to come to terms with the damage he did. You need to find it in your heart to forgive him, for me. You'll only have each other soon. As for me, please don't worry. I don't feel any pain. That's much different than I imagined when I was told. I'm just tired." She's calm, so calm as if she's come to peace with her past, present, and future all in one day. "I want to die at home if you don't mind forgoing the hospice the doctors will insist upon."

"Of course," I say, no hesitation to help her find that peace. "I'll get you whatever you need."

"Antonio, continue to shine like the star you are. I'm so proud of you and your accomplishments." She looks at me, and says, "I used to be a star, the belle of the ball."

Her confessions have me intrigued. Leaning forward, I rest my elbows on my knees and look at her. She speaks as if she's worlds away, maybe living in the memory she's recalling. "Your father, Joseph, was a wonderful man when I met him. I was sitting at a restaurant in downtown Diablo with Gage and he was having lunch next to me. He commented how I was a good mother to my baby, giving the baby all of my attention. One thing led to the next and he joined us for lunch."

"Was it love at first sight?"

"Most definitely." She sits back and raises her chin up while closing her eyes. "So handsome. So much like you," she says, glancing at me. "I don't think you have any of the Dexter features, except maybe my sparkling personality."

And here I thought she didn't know me at all.

"I've seen you on TV so many times. You're captivating and charming. I see why young women fall for you. But tell me, has anyone mattered? Is there anyone special? That woman you brought around to the country club perhaps?"

"Rochelle." I stop there, contemplating how much I want to share versus how much I should share. I decide there might not be another chance, so I say, "I fell in love with Rochelle the first time I ever laid eyes on her."

My mom smiles and asks, "When was that?"

"Eleven years ago. When I was nineteen."

Her eyes widen. "Well, that's a long time to be in love with someone. Why have you not been together?"

Sitting back, I sigh. "Life is complicated. Even when you think it falls at your feet, there's always something more, something just out of reach."

"Is Rochelle within reach?"

"Now she is." Smiling at her, I say, "She has two kids. Sons."

"Oh. And the father?"

"He's passed." I don't go into details. It still hurts me to think of Cory and face the fact that he's gone forever.

"You were close?"

"He was one of my best friends. He was in the band." I should be offended that she seems so careless in regards to knowing about my life. But I didn't share with her either and it's not worth the argument now. "They're great kids too. I'm teaching them to play drums. The older one, Neil, he's good. Natural talent. The younger one is four. CJ can charm the socks off anyone with his smile."

"You love them." A statement.

I shift, then smile. "Yeah," I say, "I do. I love Rochelle too."

26

DEX

IT'S ten at night when I call Rochelle. I'm hoping to catch her in bed before she falls asleep so she can talk. She answered after the first ring. "Hi there."

"Hi there yourself."

With a chuckle, she asks, "How's Diablo?"

"Umm..." I scratch my head, then look at the TV, which was keeping me company before I called her. "I'm not sure."

"Interesting. Are you doing okay?"

"I'm not sure."

"Do I need to be worried because you're totally worrying me right now."

"I'm not sure."

"Stop saying that, Dex." Her voice gets pitchy. "You're freaking me out."

I close my eyes, draping my arm across my forehead. "I'm kind of freaking out myself."

Her words are rushed and demanding. It feels good to know that she cares so much. "Tell me what's going on."

But scaring her was not my intention. I'm just unsure how to tell her everything or if I should. "I called because I need to ask a favor."

She's patient and lets me speak. "Is there any way you can fly up here tomorrow and spend the night? I'll drive you home the next day."

"You want me to be there with you and your family?" Her tone is now light, unbelieving.

"You're my family." It sounds so matter of fact, but she's right. We're family. "Will you come?"

There's a long pause before I hear her, her voice wavering with emotion. "Dex..." She sucks in a shaky breath and I can tell she's trying to stop from crying. "If you need me, I'm there. Always." Tapping is heard. "I'm looking up flights now."

"I'll buy your ticket," I say.

"I can afford the ticket. No worries."

"I know you can, but I want to buy it."

"Okay," she relents. "There's a flight into Oakland that leaves at one I can make."

"I'll send the confirmation to you."

"Thank you."

I yawn, worn out. "You're welcome, but really I should be thanking you."

"You'd do it for me... You've done it for me. You were there when I needed you most." She yawns.

"I'll let you get some rest and I'll pick you up from the airport. I'll be in the Challenger outside of baggage claim."

"I'll see you tomorrow."

"Until then..."

"Until then..."

As soon as I see Rochelle walking out of the terminal the following day, I pull to the curb, throw the car in park, and run around to greet her. She's beautiful as always, her long hair flowing over her shoulders. Her eyes bright and her smile big—just for me, so I kiss her, savoring the feel of her skin, her lips, the way her tongue caresses mine.

Leaving her breathless was my single motivation. I think it worked because she sighs, then whispers, "It's good to see you too."

After opening her door for her, I take her bag and put it in the trunk. I slide into the driver's seat and say, "Welcome to hell."

Fastening her seatbelt, she looks up and says, "And here I thought Diablo just meant devil."

It doesn't take long to get to the estate, less than an hour's drive with traffic. Rochelle's mouth opens when we pull up the long driveway. "This looks like what I imagine Hearst Castle looking like."

"My grandfather hated the Hearst Castle. I wish he was here just to hear the comparison."

"Do you want to talk about him?"

I park the car and look at her, the air vents blowing her hair wildly behind her. "I used to think he was this stuffy old man, then I found he was worse."

"What happened?"

"I found out he called my mom a liar and a whore after she was raped." I get out not wanting to see Rochelle's face or tears, her sympathies. I need to be strong and right now, I don't have enough strength for both of us. Grabbing her suitcase from the trunk, I set it down as she joins me. "Let's not talk about it. Okay?"

"Sure. Okay." She nods.

"Oh and ignore Gage. He'll offend you in some way, so it's just best not to pay any attention to him."

She takes a wavering breath and says, "I'm here for you, Dex. Only you."

Taking her hand in one and her case in the other, I lead her inside. At the top of the stairs, I say, "There's a guest room across the hall from mine..." I wait to see what she wants to do, hoping it's the same as what I want.

"I'm not staying with you?" If I'm not mistaken, her lashes flutter, reminding me of a butterfly.

My thoughts momentarily drift back to her mentioning her love of fireflies. "I want you to stay with me," I whisper, giving her hand a little squeeze.

A pink covers her cheeks, making me want to do so much to her right now. She says, "I'd like that."

Leading her into the bedroom, I set her bag down and she walks to the window, not giving the king size bed a second thought. "Your window overlooks a garden. It's beautiful."

"Nothing like your beauty."

She smiles at me, then turns back. "Roses are beautiful but dangerous. I've always been fascinated by them. What grows in the greenhouse?"

"I'm not sure. I haven't been back there since I've been here." Standing near the door, I ask, "Would you like to freshen up or for me to give you a tour of the house?"

Turning, she jumps onto the bed and falls back. "You're so formal here. It reminds me of when I lived in Boston."

"There were very strict rules when I visited here. Old habits die hard."

With her arm outstretched, she summons me to her. Pausing, I stare down at her, the image of Eve and all her mortal sins corrupting me to my core. But like Adam, I can't resist the temptation. Crawling onto the bed, I move on top of her. My weight balanced above her until her hands travel from my neck down to my waist. I drop down lightly, balancing just above. "What are you doing to me?"

Her eyes look into mine, our connection always present. Pushing me gently up, she giggles and says, "You're right. I'll take the tour."

She squirms her way to the side, but I grab her by the waist before she escapes and say, "We'll pick up where we left off later."

Her eyes give her desires away. She's not playing hard with such a sexually mischievous look in her soulful browns. "I look forward to it."

Following her out the door, we head back downstairs to the sitting room where I saw my mom last. Gage is near the door at the bar when we enter. He stops and eyes Rochelle blatantly, top to bottom and back up, and I want to punch him in the fucking face for it. Instead, I possessively take her hand and lead her to the couch across from the chair where my mother sits. She smiles at me and then to Rochelle before speaking. "It's so good to see you again, Rochelle."

"You too, Mrs. Caggiano."

My mom looks down and smiles while toiling with the throw on her lap. "We only had nine years together, but those years seem to have shaped my entire life."

Rochelle looks to me for further explanation when it's clear my mom is not going to give one. I lean back, getting comfortable. "My father and mother were married for nine years before he died."

My mom looks at Rochelle, new blood in the mix to share her stories to. But this time, I don't mind. This time, I make the time to listen. "He was the most handsome man I had ever see—"

"Nine years?" Gage asks, staring at us from across the room. "That's not right, Mother. You're forgetting in your old age."

"Shut-up," I say to him before turning back.

"What? You need to show off for you girlfriend here? Like she'll find a 'shut-up' impressive. I'll show her impress—"

I stand and cut him off. "Shut the fuck up, Gage, or I'll shut you up."

Gage cackles and swallows more of his drink. Looks like Scotch. "There's the fighter we all love to hate. Doesn't take much to provoke the lower class."

"You don't even know what you're talking about, man. Just stop, Gage. Okay?"

"Speaking of lower class, how's that band thing working out for you ever since that guy died?"

Rochelle stiffens beside me, her breath stopping altogether.

My mother says, "Gage, find something useful to do, like finding a job."

"After this meeting, I won't need a job." He walks into the other room, slamming his glass down on the cherry wood of the sideboard before exiting.

"I'm sorry." Both Rochelle and I look at my mother as she apologizes. "I'm sorry for your loss."

"Thank you," Rochelle says with a nod and a taut smile in place.

Squeezing her knee, I ask, "Are you okay?"

"I am. Your brother's an asshole though."

"Yep." I laugh. "He majored in it at Brown." I stand up and help my mom up. "We need to go or we'll be late."

In the garden, I hadn't noticed how frail my mom has become. Out there she fooled me by the way she held my arm. The change in her is more obvious now just a few short hours later.

"Would you like to come, Rochelle?" she asks.

Rochelle's eyes target me, asking the question again, silently between us this time. "I think you should stay. I'm not sure how long this will take. You can rest up for tonight."

"What's tonight?"

"I have big plans in store for us."

"In that case, I'll take a nap, so I can enjoy these *big* plans."

My mother clears her throat as she passes us. "Save that kind of talk to when your mother is out of the room." She laughs, but stops and turns toward me. "Follow your heart…" Her eyes land on Rochelle, and she says, "I'm very glad to have seen you again."

Rochelle smiles. "It was really nice to see you again as well."

"My apologies, Mr. Caggiano," the lawyer speaks directly to Gage. "I can't proceed with you in the room since the will is confidential and only allowed to be read to the beneficiaries."

Gage's mouth is hanging open. The shock of being told our father was not his makes his face go red with anger.

I reach over toward him, but he stands up. "What the fuck?" Staring at my mom, he says, "You were a whore and I'm the bastard who has to suffer for it."

I stand abruptly, at the ready if I need to kick his ass. One more comment like that and he's going down.

"Gage," my mom starts.

He pulls the door open. "I don't want to hear it." The wall takes the brunt of the impact when the door hits it.

The time seemed to pass in an orderly reading of a list, one item at a time. When it was all said and done, the car ride was silent as my mother and I returned to the house. After settling my plans for later with a few phone calls and staff help, I awoke my sleeping beauty with a kiss. Her eyes slowly blinking open and happy to see me. "How did it go?"

"Well."

"That's good," she whispers.

"I want to take you somewhere."

She nods and then sits up, rubbing her eyes. "Are jeans okay or do I need to change?"

"Never change. You're gorgeous just how you are."

27

DEX

We walk from the back of the house down the large steps to the crushed granite path. Rochelle smiles, which causes my own. I veer to the left, off the path, and through a grouping of pink flowers, taking her on a short cut. We're both careful not to crush any as we hop over the bushes. Her laughter draws me to look her way, her beauty captivating my heart entirely.

I'm nervous for some reason, but I keep guiding her. A few more steps and she'll see it. She stops, another smile gracing her stunning face. The greenhouse is ahead, trees and tall bushes making for a dramatic presentation. The front is covered in a vine of Purple flowers and the entrance is lit by the setting sun, making it more magical, even to me.

"Dex, it's even prettier in person than from the window upstairs."

"I'm glad you like it." I walk forward and open the door for her. Following her inside, I let the door close on its own. Moving to the other side of the center row of plants, I copy her slow, but steady pace as she admires the flowers blooming all around. I don't bother with the flowers and admire her instead.

She says, "This is one of the most beautiful places I've ever seen."

"My grandfather let the gardener do whatever he wanted. This was the gardener's private sanctuary."

"It's where he kept the good stuff."

"Yeah, it's where he kept the good stuff."

I hear a small gasp and look over at her. She says, "Dex, did you do this?"

The table for two is draped in linens and set with the finest china and crystal. A vase of pink flowers is in the center. "I arranged it. Does that count?"

"Yes," she says, nodding. "That totally counts. It's beautiful. Are we having dinner out here?"

"I thought you might like it."

"I do. So much." She comes to me, wrapping her arms around my middle and resting her cheek on my chest as we both look at the display before us.

It wasn't meant to be a big deal, but somehow I realize at the same moment Rochelle does, this is a very big deal. And I'm not talking about the dinner or the little touches, or the surprises I still have in store for her. Being here with her, like this, is a big deal.

"Champagne?" I ask. I feel her nod against me and when she holds me a little tighter, I embrace her fully. "You okay?"

"More than okay. Thank you for doing this. I'm really touched."

"C'mon before you get me all sentimental too." I grab the champagne and pop the cork. After pouring her a glass, I set it on the table and pull her chair out, wanting to impress her. When I sit across from her, we toast, "To good times and even better company. Cheers."

Dinner is served in three courses. I want us satisfied but not stuffed. There's more planned for the evening ahead. After dessert, the table is cleared by the staff and the champagne bottle is replaced with a bottle of wine. With our glasses in hand, I escort her to the back part of the greenhouse where the heat sensitive and specialty plants are kept. I open the door and as we walk under the arbor, I spin her around, keeping her back to the surprise. "I wanted to thank you for coming here." Before she can say anything, I kiss her, then slide my tongue down her neck, stopping to suck just enough to taste, but not enough to leave a mark. "You taste edible."

A small moan escapes her before she whispers, "Are you wooing me, Mr. Caggiano?" I can tell she's succumbing as her hands glide roughly over my shirt and stomach. She has a thing for my abs I've discovered. I do extra sit-ups just for her.

"Trying my hardest."

"You don't have to try that hard. I'm already pretty smitten."

"I like you smitten," I whisper. "Turn around."

The queen size bed is on a platform angled in the corner. The sheets a pale green, the comforter white. Mosquito netting is draped around with flowers hanging down. Cynthia did a great job making this happen.

With a hand covering her mouth that's dropped open in awe, Rochelle quickly closes it and says, "Do we get to sleep out here tonight?"

"If you want."

"I definitely want to. It's like a fairytale come to life. Dex," she says, her excitement getting the best of her. "I can't believe you did this. You gave me Neverland, again." She takes my hand and does this little sway of her hips. "I'm liking this romancing business." Signaling toward the bed, she adds, "I'm feeling like going to bed early. Wanna join—Oh my God! Are those butterflies?" Rochelle chases an orange and black butterfly until it lands and a yellow one flutters by, grabbing her attention. "Dex! They're everywhere. Look around on the plants. Butterflies."

I smile, enjoying seeing her so happy, flirtatious, and excited. Running up to me, she grabs me hard, her arms tight around my neck. "You did this. You did all of this for me?"

"I did. It's all for you."

"I'm going to spend all night showing you how grateful I am to have you in my life." She kisses me and it's not gentle.

"Ms. Floros, I could get used to this kind of gratitude on a regular basis."

"You haven't seen anything yet."

"Neither have you," I say, holding her steady in my sights.

"You don't even know what you do to me." Another kiss lands on my lips as she holds me by my shirt to her. "Make love to me, Dex. I want you."

The darkness outside and the plants along the walls protect us from outside prying eyes. "Take your clothes off and show me how much you want me."

Her eyes are sultry, the challenge tempting her. Moving across the room, I turn the lights down, the glow of the candles adding to the mood. The shadowed butterflies still fly about and I lie on the bed, getting comfortable.

Keeping her eyes on me, she takes her shirt over her head and drops it on a chair nearby. Her fingers toy with her jeans like she's toying with me. My cock is hard and getting harder from watching her before she even takes her shoes off. She turns around and bends over, giving me a full view of her fantastic ass as she takes her jeans down. The lace thong is a tease just like her. My palm rubs over my dick and I decide to give myself some more room to grow by unfastening my jeans.

Her arms reach around her back and she undoes the clasp of her bra with ease, letting it hang while she takes one strap and then the other down her arms. She turns back around, not hiding, but smirking and confident. Lifting the netting, she joins me on the bed by crawling up my body and pushing my shirt up as she goes. "Take *your* clothes off, Dex. Show me how much you want *me*," she says, repeating my earlier demand.

Like her, I strip my clothes off, but without the production, then kneel down in front of her. Slowly, I run my hands up her soft skin. When my fingertips reach her panties, I start to descend, taking them with me. I press my lips to the inside of her thigh. This time sucking hard, wanting her marked as mine. Her fingers find the top of my head and she rubs them through my hair. Moving to her pussy, I mimic her by moving my tongue around her clit, her back arching as her body lowers, bringing her closer. I slide my hands under her ass, gripping her hips and licking, taunting, and fucking harder, eliciting the sexiest moans I've ever heard.

My hair is tugged and I inhale her while driving her mad with pleasure. She squirms and I hold on tighter until I hear her breathing stagger and her body starts to tighten. With her head tilted back, her mouth wide open, she comes with desperate moans as her body is overwhelmed and tremors.

"Dex!" Her back falls flat against the mattress and her breath returns, her thighs easing around my head. I place one more kiss on her pussy before I slide up next to her. Her lids are heavy and a smile resides on her face. "It's been a while," she says, as if I'm judging her.

"It's been a while for both of us." I roll over so I'm resting on her bare chest, our bodies aligned. She kisses me, then I whisper, "I haven't been with anyone except you in almost a year."

She kisses me again this time lingering on my lips. "I've not been with anyone else in the last three."

My heart starts racing as I take in her words, her confession, and her commitment. Hovering over her, I feel the need to release my own confession, but this time not running away from fear of rejection. I say, "I love you."

Her eyes stay locked on mine and she says, "I love you too."

Pushing inside, her eyes close as her warmth engulfs me. I close my eyes and begin moving. The soft skin of her hand finds the rough surface of my face and she caresses. "Open your eyes, Dex." Her words are uneven like our breathing.

When I lift my lids, I finally see the love I've waited for what feels like a lifetime. It lies in the depths of her amber eyes. A jolt of reality restarts my heart to make every beat count from this moment on. Her nails scrape lightly up my back setting every nerve on fire and I start thrusting, all my energy put into the act.

Rochelle squirms, taking all I give and giving all she has, her desire a turn on and her confidence sexy. "God, Dex. You feel so good."

"You feel better." My words are slurred from the haze I'm under. My body moves of its own accord, sensations and frustrations building deep inside. Her body drives me for more, making me want to steal her soul like she's stolen mine. "Fuck. I'm gonna come soon."

"Come with me. Harder. Faster." Her words just escaping breaths. Her mouth tantalizes me, flipping my world upside down, and making me want to fuck her into oblivion. I fuck. I fuck hard as her groans of pleasure instigate. My eyes shut tight as I overcome desires that turn into bonfires, my body burning in her ecstasy as we come. I pulse and she squeezes, our bodies working as one with no end and no beginning, just us together.

I collapse, exhausted with no will or inclination to move. Rochelle's fingers weave into my hair holding my head to hers. "I love you," she whispers in my ear, making me smile.

With my eyes closed, I say, "I really could get used to this."

"I hope you never tire of me."

Lifting up, I push her dark hair away from her face and kiss her chin, her cheek, then the side of her mouth. "I could never tire of you. I've loved you my whole life."

She smiles, soft and more beautiful than ever before. "You keep saying things like that and I might start believing you."

With a chuckle, I lean my head against her chest. "Deal." When I hear a soft sigh of contentment, I ask, "Are you tired?"

"I am." She moves to get up. "Is the nearest bathroom in the house?"

"Just through the office in the corner over there. Sorry, it's small."

"No worries. I'll be right back."

I lay there, my chest burning. Putting my arm across my forehead, I stare up past the netting and through the glass, the moon seeming bigger and brighter than usual. My mind drifts to the woman I just made love to, curious if we can move beyond this night. The door opens and I look over, watching her, wanting us to be more than tonight, wanting it more than I have ever wanted anything else.

When she returns, she crawls under the covers and I take my turn in the bathroom. I come back and start turning out the candles.

She takes one and looks at it. "It's battery-operated. That's cool."

"Can't have the greenhouse filling with smoke."

"Clever."

"Not my idea, but I'll let Cynthia know."

She laughs lightly, then says, "Let's go to bed."

After I turn off the last candle, we lay in the dark, letting our eyes adjust. Lying on our backs, we look up as moonlight fills the greenhouse. "We should have made love with just the moon above." Cuddling into my side, she closes her eyes.

Whispering, I say, "Keep your eyes open just a few minutes longer."

She readjusts and looks up. As if on command, the first one lights up on her side of the bed. Sitting up abruptly, she says, "Are those fireflies?"

"They are. Lay back with me."

Slowly, she lays back down and smiles. "It's magic. Butterflies and fireflies. You gave me magic, Dex. It's the most romantic thing I've ever seen."

"You deserve romance and more. I'll give you everything I can because you gave me a reason to live. You gave me life." Rolling onto my side, I run my hand over her arm. "I never thanked you properly for saving me."

"I didn't save you, Dex. I think you might have saved me though. You fill my heart where a hole used to exist. Expecting more would be greedy."

Caressing her cheek, I lean forward. "I like you greedy... and horny." I slide my hand between her legs and her eyes look up to meet mine as a small, devious expression appears.

"Let's be greedy and horny together."

Under the moon, in a house made of glass, we make love slow and gentle, taking our time, frivolous in the knowledge of having a forever together.

WHEN I WAKE up in the morning, I open my eyes, and see the love of my life asleep next to me. An orange, black, and white butterfly sits on her temple, slowly opening and closing its wings. Both of them true beauty personified. I take a mental picture since I know it will fly away if I move.

Cautiously, I put my finger to her temple and the butterfly moves onto my finger. When I lift it up, it flies around the enclosure of the mosquito netting before finally settling on the sheer fabric.

"A fairytale," she whispers and I look over before following her gaze up. The outside of the netting is covered in butterflies of all different sizes and colors. Rochelle kisses me on the cheek and says, "Enchanting."

I kiss her hand, letting my tongue taste her sweetness. "Like you, my love. Good morning."

"Good morning."

"We should go soon. We have a long drive back."

"Can't we stay forever?" Although I know it's rhetorical, the way she asks makes me want to make her dreams come true.

"I promise you, I'll fill your life with magic."

"I don't need magic, Dex. I just need you."

28

ROCHELLE

Dex has been quiet for a large portion of the trip. "What's on your mind?" I risk breaking the silence just to hear his voice again.

He glances over while sliding his hand from my thigh to my knee and giving it a little squeeze. "Sorry." He smiles. It's small, but thoughtful. "I didn't mean to be so quiet. Just lost in my head. The will stuff and Gage. My mom."

"Do you want to talk about it?"

Dex has a way of confessing with such honesty. He's direct and sometimes it catches me by surprise. With his eyes back on the road, he says, "Gage isn't my brother by blood. My mom told me the night before the will was read. Gage found out during the reading and they made him leave the room."

Not sure what to say, I blurt, "I'm sorry." I have no idea if that's appropriate in this situation or not.

"He's an asshole for sure, but he's kind of always been my asshole of a brother. Know what I mean?"

I nod.

He continues, "I'm just not sure where this leaves us. He screwed me over before and now he's just lecherous since his wife left him.

His life is unraveling and he's the one pulling the string. I'm not sure what to think about things."

"It's a lot to take in. You need time to process."

"Yeah maybe." He nods this time, then exhales heavily. "Thanks for being here."

"Thanks again for inviting me."

Changing the subject, he smiles and an excitement comes over him. "So there's this spot I want to take you to. It's a little off the beaten path, but we'll only lose a few minutes in drive time. Is it okay if we go?"

I can't deny him this happiness. "I'd like that."

We veer from the highway and travel about ten minutes, then down a secluded road near a house perched on the hillside. He stops the car and parks on the dirt shoulder just in case any traffic comes. He takes the top of the car down and I sit up on the edge of the door and look out at the ocean that stretches the entire expanse of the horizon before us. The sun is still high since it's before noon, but I imagine the sunsets here are incredible. "It's amazing here."

Moving around the car, Dex comes to my side and faces me. "You're more amazing."

"Charmer."

"I'm not charming you. I'm just telling the truth." He leans forward and kisses me.

I pull him closer, loving the freedom I feel here in the open to love him.

With an eager expression, he asks, "Wanna do it?"

I burst out laughing. "Sure. Let's do it," I say, teasing him while poking him in the ribs. When I see he's not joking, surprise takes over my face. "You're serious right now?"

"Dead."

"Don't say dead."

His expression softens. "Yes, I'm serious. I want you." He slides his hands up my thighs, stopping on my hips.

Looking around, expecting to find an audience, I say, "We can't.

This is like someone's property or something. We could get busted and arrested. I can't be arrested, Dex."

"It's mine."

"What's yours?"

"It's my property. All the way from the main road down this private street, which is technically a drive." He points to the house. "I own that house too. And right down there," he says, pointing further down the drive. "I'm going to build a house with a wall of windows overlooking the ocean. Right there on the side of that cliff."

My mouth must be hanging open because he adds, "Nobody other than my lawyer knows I own this property, but I wanted you to know. I've imagined bringing you here many times, an escape from the rest of the world. The boys can hike the cliffs with me and explore the beach. I don't know, just seems kind of idyllic."

Moving my fingers through his hair, I kiss the side of his lips, lingering a moment before I say, "It is idyllic."

With a mischievous look in his eyes, he asks, "So we can do it then?"

Wrapping my arms around his neck, I whisper, "C'mon, handsome. No time like the present." I slip back into the seat and he hops the door and falls into the backseat.

His hands go behind his head and he smirks. "I want you on top."

"God, you're so demanding."

"Say that again."

I laugh as I'm climbing into the backseat. "You're so demanding."

"No, the other part."

Tilting my head, it's my turn to smirk. "God?"

His smile widens and he nods so arrogantly and so fucking sexily. "You're so bad."

"I think you should punish me over and over again by sitting right about... are you wearing underwear?"

Adjusting on top of him, I sit, looking down. "Yeeeesss, of course."

"I don't approve of that at all."

I roll my eyes. "I think you'll survive. After all, it is me wearing them, not you."

"I want them off." He lifts up and I stand the best I can, allowing him room. He undoes his pants and slides his jeans down... he has no worries of underwear since he's not wearing any.

Lifting my flowy skirt, I reach under and slip off my panties...

Dex is fast with the condom, but slow with his kisses and caresses. At one point, he sits up with me on his lap, our bodies joined together. His gentle rocks and thrusts are not hurried, but slow and languid, building my inner desire, twisting my insides until I come, squeezing him in the process.

With his lips pressed to my neck, he opens his mouth and his teeth scrape lightly while he holds me tight. A couple more thrusts and his body tenses as moans fill the open air around us—his and mine together.

When normally our bodies are allowed to go slack, relaxing in the aftermath of the euphoria, Dex holds me closer and kisses me with the passion most give before sex. I relish it, taking his passion and absorbing his heat. The moment is intense like he is and though our declarations have been spoken aloud, I feel his love filling my soul.

I pull back, wanting to see his eyes. When he opens them, he looks at me just as curiously as I look at him. "What?" he asks.

"You love me," I respond.

"Yes, I do, but you know that."

"No. I've heard you say it, but..." I know I must sound insane right now, but I say it anyway. "It's different. I feel it."

"Good." He smiles—gentle and satisfied. "Love is not for the ears, but for the heart."

I shouldn't cry. I really shouldn't, but I feel his love. I feel amazingly lucky and happy. The tears come from a place of joy and I don't bother to hide them. He readjusts back down and I come with him, resting on his chest. "I'm sorry," I whisper.

His hand slides under the back of my shirt and rubs, the touch is warming and comforting. "Why are you sorry?"

"Because I heard you say it and I've seen it in your eyes, but I never allowed myself to feel it until now."

With my ear pressed to his chest, I hear his breathing and heart beating just as he whispers, "I love you, Rochelle."

"I love you too."

WE GET BACK to LA just after the kids arrive home from school. When we walk in, my boys run to me. It was only one night away, but I missed them just as much. In a three person hug huddle, I rest on my knees so I can fully embrace my sweet boys. But then I feel a nudging. Out of the corner of my eye, I spy CJ's arm around Dex's leg, including him in our group hug. I wrap my arm around his leg too until my hand holds my youngest as well. Dex takes all of us in when he spans his arms around our small family. And there we stay for a minute or two.

When we stand up, I give my boys more kisses, then meet Beth's eyes. She has a wide grin on her face and I realize she's a witness to the start of something new, the start of something that feels like it could become a constant, something permanent. "Welcome home," she says. "Did you have a nice time?"

"I did. Thank you for coming on such short notice."

Her eyes glance to Dex before coming back to me. "No problem. I love spending extra time with the boys. They were great. Right, guys?"

Neil laughs, obviously not telling the whole truth. "Yep, we were super good for Beth."

CJ's face is serious when he says, "I only got sent to time-out two times, Mama. Only two."

Trying to stifle my own laugh, I say, "Well done, buddy. Maybe next time, you won't go at all."

"I try harder."

"That's my boy."

Neil asks Dex, "I've been working on some new beats. Can I show you?"

Dex seems surprised. "Yeah, absolutely."

Neil takes his hand and drags him through the living room and down the hall to his room. CJ announces that he's hungry and disappears into the kitchen looking for a snack. Beth remains, smiling at me. That smile that says she knows that I not only had sex but that I'm obviously head over heels for Dex. I don't even have a chance to say anything before she says, "Wow, that must have been some night."

Sitting down on the couch, I play dumb. "What?" I shrug. "He needed a friend to talk to. I'm glad I could be there for him."

"You mean in the friends with benefit kind of way?"

"Not everything has to end in sex, you know."

She crosses her arms and looks at me incredulously. "Really? You're gonna pretend like nothing happened between you two?"

"Who says I'm pretending anything?"

Pointing at me, her finger swirls in the air. "Then explain that hickey that's forming on the right side of your neck?"

"Uh!" I gasp, jumping up to see in the mirror.

"You totally just gave yourself away. There's no hickey."

"You play dirty, Beth."

"Eh, it's a gift really." She walks to the kitchen door and says, "But I want you to stop trying to hide the obvious and accept whatever you've got going on with Dex. It's making you all sunshiny and shit and you look good happy."

I roll my eyes, but smile after. "Sunshiny and shit? Nice."

"I'm just telling you the truth."

"I'm really liking all the truths I've been getting lately."

With a loud laugh, she goes into the kitchen leaving me there with my own thoughts on the matter. A hand touches my shoulder making me jump a few moments later. Beth says, "I'm gonna go." She takes her purse and backpack from the floor near my feet and adds, "Call me if you need me."

"Thank you for being here. I know the boys love spending time with you." I stand and walk her to the door. "So tomorrow after school?"

"I'll be here," she replies walking down the steps and to the gate.

I close the door and lean my back on it, wondering how long Dex and I can really hide our relationship from the outside world when apparently everything about me is oozing it. But just thinking about the word 'oozing' makes the smile disappear and makes me want to take a shower.

CJ walks out with a PB & J and we join Neil and Dex in his room. Sitting on the floor, CJ makes himself at home on my lap and I wrap my arms around him, holding him close. Neil and Dex have an interesting dynamic. There's a mutual respect for each other that is heard through the way they talk to each other and their patience. Maybe I'm witnessing the beginning of a friendship, the start of a bond that can last. I hope so.

Dex shows Neil one more beat that he's been working on then says, "I'll send you a demo of it. I want you to practice it until you've nailed it. Then you're gonna play it for me on my drums. Okay?"

Neil excitedly agrees.

CJ gets up when he's done eating and says, "I want to learn too."

Dex, who's on his knees bends down until he's eye-level with him and smiles. "You still have the sticks I gave you?"

"Yep."

"Then how about I get you a drum pad too? Would you like that, CJ?"

CJ turns to me and says, "I gonna be like Dex and Neil, Mama."

I nod, but in that moment, the walls waver around me. Using the wall to help steady myself, I feel my way up and hurry out. I tug the back door open abruptly and run outside. My lungs feel lighter the second I inhale the fresh air. Closing my eyes, I raise my chin to the sky and breathe slowly.

"I know how hard it is to ask for help," Dex says, his voice quieter than normal, controlled. Turning to look over my shoulder, I see him standing in the doorway. He continues, "I think you need to talk to someone, Rochelle. Someone who can help with these attacks."

"I just wanted fresh air. That's all." I shrug, but I can tell he doesn't believe me.

"You're in denial."

Turning my whole body around now, I feel my defenses growing. "About what?" I ask, crossing my arms.

"That back there with your sons, with Cory's sons." He steps closer and his voice gets even quieter. I assume so the boys don't hear. "I'm not gonna replace him."

"They want to be drummers."

"They aren't him."

I raise my voice though I don't mean to yell. "They'd be playing guitar if he was here."

Despite my emotions, his voice is soothing. "They still can because you're here to teach them."

A lump forms in my throat making it hard to swallow.

I'm face to face with him now, his hands holding my arms gently as they slide down until my hands are taken by his. He says, "Every time I see the excitement for music in Neil's eyes, I see Cory again. When I look at CJ's face, I see Cory. And they both have this kindness about them that they get from you. You both made them who they are, shaped them in features and personality. I won't let them forget who their father was, but if I can help them, I want to, if you'll let me."

Looking down between us, I sniffle. When I look into his caring eyes, I say, "You're a good man, Dex Caggiano. Not many men would want to take on two crazy kids and their even crazier mom."

"You're not crazy, Rochelle, but I do think you've never allowed yourself to grieve the way you should. Let your friends and family be here for *you* now."

I hug him and when his arms wrap around me, I close my eyes and take in his scent. Just like always with him, I feel my body calming.

"Hello." We move apart quickly when we hear Janice.

Pushing the hair out of my face, I say, "Hi, how are you?" I'm too rushed, feeling guilty. "I wasn't expecting you."

"Hi Dex," she says, her smile not quite tight, but not welcoming either. She holds out a casserole dish. "I brought homemade spinach lasagna. I made an extra for you and the boys."

Walking over, I take it from her. "Thank you. We'll have this tonight."

She follows me into the kitchen and says, "I hope I wasn't interrupting anything."

I see Dex over her shoulder. "Um, it's fine. Are you staying to eat with us?"

"No, just stopping by. Where are Neil and CJ?"

"In Neil's room practicing a beat Dex just showed him."

She comes to me and says, "Are you alright? You look a little pale."

"I'm dating Dex." *Oops.* There goes our secret.

She looks stunned by my confessional outburst and like a faucet, I can't seem to stop the words from coming. "I don't care if you think it's a bad idea or you think he's bad for me and the boys. He's not. He's a good man and despite all that he's gone through, even though a lot of it he caused, he's in a good place and he loves us. He loves me, Janice. And you know what? I love him. I may have to hide this from the public, the paparazzi, and the band for a while, but I'm willing to do that. For him, I'm willing to keep this private until everyone else can learn to deal with it. But here, in my house, I will not. If you plan to be around us you will have to accept my relationship with him."

I peek over at Dex. His smile is not cocky or showy, but shows how proud he is of me. I step around her and go to him, hugging him tight.

When I look back at Janice, she doesn't seem upset or even disappointed. A small smile graces her features and with a slight nod, she says, "Okay."

"Just like that?"

"No. I've given it tremendous thought over the last few months. I've also Googled Dex a few times." There's a sparkle in her eyes when she looks up at him. "Seems maybe he has changed and considering the scum that's out there, I'm going to trust my gut and say okay."

As he rubs my back, Dex speaks before I do. "Thank you, Janice. I appreciate that."

"Just don't go breaking my trust or Rochelle's heart. I can be a bitch when I need to be."

"Janice," I say on the verge of a gasp. "You never swear."

"Well, I'm loosening up in my old age."

"You're not that old," I add.

"Well, it's time I lived a little."

I go to hug her and I can feel the sincerity of her words in her arms. "Thank you."

"You're welcome. Nothing would make me happier than seeing you and the boys living a happy life."

"Thank you."

She turns and says to Dex, "Take care of my family and yourself." Walking past him she stops. "I'm gonna go kiss my grandkids. Dex, you might like the lasagna. You should stay. I'll see myself out."

He sits down at the table and replies, "I think I will stay if it's alright with you, Rochelle."

"I wouldn't have it any other way."

29

—————

ROCHELLE

WE DECIDED our relationship was best kept a secret—our secret for now, an intimacy that bonded us even more. Our bubble felt protected from outside opinions and judgment. But maybe it was the darkness that allowed us to believe in the illusion. The reality is, we knew we couldn't hide for long, but neither of us wanted to talk about it either.

So we continued over the course of a month, sneaking around in dives to grab a late night drink or sticking to the security of each other's house.

"How's your mother doing?" I ask, lying in bed with him. Glancing at the clock it's 5:30 in the morning.

When he turns to me, his brow is furrowed. "Really? We're talking about my mother right now? What happened to lying here recovering after sex?"

"Recovering? Do you really want to recover from sex with me?"

Rolling over, he rests on top of me. "You wear me out, woman!"

"With all of my sex demands?" I tease.

"Yes," he says, a short chuckle following. "You're a very demanding lover."

"Lover sounds so naughty and sexual."

He gets off of me, sits up, and turns on the lamp. "Aren't all lovers sexual? Like doesn't the word itself say sexual?"

I blush, my eyelids growing heavy. "I'm tired. I can't think straight at this hour."

He starts to stand, but I take his hand and hold him. "Don't leave."

Settling back down next to me, he tucks his arm under my neck and holds me to him. "The boys will be up soon."

Whispering, I say, "I know."

He reaches for the lamp to turn it off and I smile knowing today is the day, we become real, real to the world, facing the world together. When he stops, I look over at him and see him holding the small framed photo of me and Cory. My heart clenches. I quickly reach for him, not wanting to lose everything we worked so hard for. But he stands suddenly and the frame is abandoned in the spot he found it. The playfulness is gone as he walks to the bench at the end of the bed where he left his clothes. He starts getting dressed, so I ask, "You're going?"

"I should. I have some stuff to take care of."

When he sits on the edge of the bed to put his shoes on, I sense the change in his mood. I sit up and rub his arm. "Hey, what's going on?"

"Nothing," he replies too quick and a little snappy. Lying back, I watch him silently. His gaze is focused down and I watch the man I fell in love with disappear before my eyes. He looks back when the silence reaches him, our gazes connecting. He rubs my leg over the blanket. "I'm sorry."

Needing him to fill me in on what he's thinking, I ask, "For what?" My voice is meek and quieter than intended, but I can't handle my heart being broken again. And by the thickened tension, I'm feeling like that's close to happening.

His eyes leave mine before his hand does. "There's so much shit, so much to think about."

"What about the last month?"

He turns, slow and hesitant, his face one of regret. When he looks at me, I know what's coming before he even says it. I close my eyes to hide the tears I know will appear. "Rochelle," he starts, then pauses with a heavy sigh before continuing. "I need to sort through everything. I have legal appointments tomorrow..." He glances at his watch. "...later today technically. I'm seeing my mother for dinner. It's a miracle she's still here. And I still have to talk to Gage." When he stands, he keeps his back to me. He walks to the door and stops with his hand on the knob. Keeping his eyes focused on anything but me, he says, "I'll call you later." Then he leaves.

Our 'Until then...' isn't said. That's the moment I know we're over.

I roll to my side and pull the covers over my head. I thought I would cry, but the conflicting emotions I have surfacing are too confusing. Disappointment trumps anger, love, and the sadness I'm feeling. Dex is running. He's running from me, from everything despite how he's convinced himself he's not.

He's not used to being accountable to anyone, although I know he wishes he could be to me and the boys. He's just not there yet. Maybe the pressures of the new will and his mother's illness has stolen something from him that keeps him from being here for me. Maybe we were only as permanent as his surroundings are. Maybe our secret kept him only invested as much as he had to. What we thought was a way to protect something that was strong and growing has revealed the cracks instead. Like a side effect, the secrecy kept us fragile, something more delicate than we thought.

I look over at the frame that I know I should have put away long before now. Cory and I were only twenty-one and thought we had a lifetime to look forward to. I start to reach for the photo, thinking I can actually pack it away inside the drawer below. But I stop.

Dex leaving isn't because of a photo.

Dex will crumble with his family and unlike the last time, I can't save him. This would have happened if I had that photo out or not. I pull the blankets tighter around me and remember when I visited him the last time he was at rehab...

.   .   .

ONE OF THE *nurses told me I could find him out back near the cliffs, so I walk through the open doors that lead to a large patio and expansive view of the ocean. In any other setting, this would take my breath away. But I remember where I'm at, so I avert my eyes to the surroundings—other patients reading, chatting, and or staring at me. I keep walking down a small curved set of stairs and over some gravel before I reach the grass and see Dex sitting and another patient on a bench across the lawn.*

The woman laughs and I hear Dex return with his own laughter. It's good to hear. It's been too long. I just wish it had been under different circumstances. When I approach, I suddenly hesitate, suddenly questioning if I'm interrupting. She sees me first, then nods to him to give him a heads up regarding my presence. When Dex turns, I see the lightness in his eyes, a happiness he shows me before his expression changes and a look of betrayal crosses his face.

"Hi," I say, hoping he doesn't hate me.

The woman stands, her hand rubbing across the top of his. "I'll see you inside."

He nods and she leaves. When we're alone, he rests forward, his elbows on his knees and scrubs his unshaven face a few times with his hands. Our eyes meet again and he asks, "What are you doing here?"

"Can I sit?" His hand swings out over the bench as an invitation. I sit down and look ahead at the ocean, seeing white caps in the distance. I feel his gaze on me, but when I turn, he looks away. His jaw is tense, so I ask, "Am I interrupting?"

"Jealousy isn't flattering on you, Rochelle."

I laugh, though I don't find his tone or words funny at all. "Jealousy? You think I'm jealous. Of what? Your friend there?"

"Why are you here?"

"I wanted to see you, to check on you."

He stands and walks ahead a few feet away. "I'm here," he says, turning around.

"How are you feeling?"

"How do you think I'm feeling? I want a hit of anything and I can't have it. But I stay because I want to stay in the band and if doing two

weeks time in here will keep me doing the only thing I care about, then I'll stay."

"Why are you so angry with me? Because I brought you here?"

His eyes meet mine and he replies, "This shit is expected from Tommy, from Johnny. Hell, everyone, but you. I needed you, Rochelle."

"You had me. You have me now. I've always been here for you when you needed me."

"You sided with them against me. I could have worked through this at home. I had time before the tour. Instead you stabbed me in the back."

"You had seizures, Dex, just like you did in Paris. How many times are you willing to put your life on the line for a 'hit of anything'?"

"Fuck this. I don't need your lecture. You know shit about what I've been going through." He starts to walk away.

I stand and shout, "You're right! I know shit because I've been dealing with my own shit, like Cory dying and raising kids—"

"Don't drag him into this."

"Drag? I didn't drag him into this. Some days I can't even breathe to save myself much less you. I've been dragged into something that's bigger than you needing to get high to escape a life of privilege."

I see the change in him before the hate is heard in his words. "Yes, Rochelle, my life of privilege has solved all my problems," he says sarcastically. "Doesn't money buy you happiness?" I can tell he wants to leave, but holds himself in place. "What we had... what we did, one day you'll see, it was everything to me."

"I don't know what to believe anymore when it comes to you. You're not the man I expected to see today."

He huffs and kicks the grass beneath his feet. When he looks back up, he says, "You're seeing the real me for once. Oh, and yes, you were interrupting, so excuse me I have an appointment in her room in five." Dex walks back not in any hurry, but walking away from me holding his head down and his shoulders tight.

THE CAR DOOR slams behind me, causing me to jump. Neil and CJ run ahead as if they're at the park. They know exactly where to go since we've been here so many times before.

Thirty minutes later, Holli jogs to keep up, taking the boys by the hands and walking back to the car. Johnny stays silent, but I feel his heavy heart, like mine, weighing down the air around us. I move forward stepping directly on top of the grass. My heels dig in and I let them sink a bit into the ground. It doesn't matter. Not really. It gets mowed and tidied, cleaned up regularly. My shoes don't affect the dead.

But for some reason I step out of them. Maybe it's the grass I need to feel. The cool blades against my skin. Or maybe it puts me just a little closer to what used to be Cory. I don't know. I've lost my ability to reason in these types of situations. Nothing makes sense, so I don't bother trying.

I sit down and my skirt goes out around me. Cory never wanted to be buried. I did it for Janice, giving her a 'place' to visit. I get it now. I realize how important this is not just for me, but for my kids. And for the fans. The anniversary of his death always brings more flowers and memorabilia, tokens of appreciation of what he gave the world surrounds the tombstone. They sneak in to pay homage and respect to the man that has become a legend before his time. But maybe that's how legends are made.

The cemetery is private and has security, but they get in somehow without notice and leave their gifts to be found by... I'm not sure who collects all the stuff actually. One day I should ask, wondering what happens to everything they find here.

I slide guitar picks, photos, flowers, and other odds and ends to the side, and lay my head on the base of the tombstone. I close my eyes and in the serenity I hear his voice, his laugh, the last melody I ever heard him play for me.

"They're memories, Rochelle," Johnny says, his voice sounding as heavy as his heart. "You'll always have them, but live in the present."

"I want to be strong, but I'm struggling."

"We all struggle. That's life. But what's the fun in easy?"

"I wouldn't know."

"Yeah, neither would I." He sits down.

Lifting up, I sit up next to him as he rests his back against the tombstone. Flicking blades of grass, he says, "I miss him every day. Some days, I wake up and I've forgotten he's died. I pick up my phone to call him..."

I relax back too and lean my head on his shoulder. "I used to cry every night, but never in the daylight."

"That sounds like a song that needs to be written."

"Maybe we're all just lyrics waiting to happen."

He looks over at me and one side of his mouth goes up. "Maybe."

"I don't want to be sad anymore." I close my eyes.

"I don't want you to be sad anymore either." He sighs. "Tell me. Who are you when no one is watching?"

His question makes my heart ache for him. I straighten up again, wanting him to tell me so much more, to share with me the thoughts he's not. "What do you mean?"

"If you could be anyone without judgment who would you be?"

Reaching my hand down I grab a handful of grass. "I don't want to be someone else. I just want to be happy again."

"When was the last time that happened?"

"My kids make me happy. It might sound strange but I'm still amazed I have them. I'm so fortunate."

"Your kids are amazing, like their parents." In another bout of quiet between us, there's no reprieve from the obvious elephant. "Have you talked to Dex?"

"No."

"Do you want to?"

"Our situation is in his hands, not mine. I tried to be there and he pushed me out."

"What would you say if you had the chance?" he asks.

"I'm not sure. Why do you ask?"

The wind picks up, my hair covering my eyes.

"Look over there," Johnny says.

I tuck my hair back and follow in the direction where Johnny points to the car.

Dex is hugging the boys and then one quick one to Holli before Tommy brings him in for a squeeze. Dex looks over at us and down, says something, then starts coming our way.

Johnny gets up. "I think I'll go help Holliday with Neil and CJ."

"You don't have to go."

"Yeah, but something tells me Dex is here to see you, so I should."

I silently agree, thinking he's probably right. Watching as he walks away, they greet each other and talk. They both look at me, then away again. Something else is said and Dex nods. One more handshake and a hug, then Dex heads my way.

He stops a few feet away from me and squats. "Hi."

"Hi."

After a quick glance over his shoulder, he looks at me again and says, "Is I'm sorry even going to work anymore?"

I keep my head down, but can't resist peeking up at him. "I don't know. Try it."

"I'm sorry, Rochelle. I'm so damn sorry."

"Why? Why are you sorry?"

"Because I pushed the good in my life away again."

"It's a bad pattern, Dex"

Sitting down, he stretches his legs out and taps my shoes with his. "Has it really been four years?"

I take in a deep breath and slowly exhale. "It has." Looking into his eyes to see if I still know the man before me, I ask, "Why are you here?"

"Because I miss him and I needed to make things right with him before I tried to make them right with you."

"Looks like you get two for one today."

"I'm sorry."

"I'm tired of apologies. I'm just tired, Dex. You know nothing goes as planned when it comes to emotions. We can't control our feelings. We can only try to control our reactions. So as much as I want to open my arms and kiss you again," I say, "I can't right now."

He pulls something from his shirt pocket. When he turns it over, he shows me. It's the photo from his bedroom and the one I packed in his duffle before shipping it to him. "You've seen the photo, but I should explain."

"Is now the time?"

"I took it from Cory's stuff years ago. I shouldn't have. I always felt bad for stealing it, for betraying our friendship like that, for being in love with his woman. I didn't care when it came down to it. I couldn't give it back. I even helped him search the hotel room for it."

"Dex—" His name comes with a warning. He's getting too close to territory I can't have him enter or I'll lose it entirely.

"I came here to return it to him. I was a shitty friend to him and he never gave up on me. You never gave up on me either, so I can at least return the damn picture."

"The picture doesn't matter. Your honesty does. He'd understand."

He laughs. "He'd understand that his friend and the drummer in his band is in love with the same woman as him?"

"No," I say with a laugh. "Maybe not, but none of that matters now. Just say your peace and don't worry about the rest."

"Maybe one day I'll forgive myself and you'll find a way to forgive me again, to see the man I was when we were together."

"Maybe," I say, not to be cruel, but to let him know I can see he's not ready yet. I stand up next to him, dusting off my skirt. When I'm done, I remain there without looking at him, my arm touching his. "It all starts with seeing the errors of your way. Stop punishing yourself over the petty stuff that doesn't matter. There's a lot of pain that comes with life. Focus on the good you've been given." With my fingers grazing over his shoulders, I walk back to the car.

"Rochelle," he calls.

I turn around and stop, wanting to hear what he says... and maybe steal one last glance at him before leaving. "Yeah?"

"Do you think you can forgive me?"

"Try me sometime."

With a gentle smile and a nod, he says, "Until then..."

"Until then..."

30

ROCHELLE

STANDING THERE in front of the mail basket, I didn't know what to make of the invitation in my hand. I'd read it three times already, but decided I need to read it again hoping it would clarify things for me.

Dear Ms. Floros,: You are cordially invited to the home of

Katherine Dexter Caggiano
High Tea
Friday at 3:30 p.m.

Nope, it makes no more sense to why Dex's mother is inviting me over than it did the first three times I read it. I pull up the planner on my phone and clear it. If she's asking me over, I feel I should go despite the absence of her son in my life.

I start to wonder if Dex will be there or does he even know I've been invited?

I miss him so much.

Lara stops by with lunch.

"I missed you. Stop traveling so much," I joke. "I kid, kind of. Okay, I mean it. I've missed you."

"I've missed you too. I brought us sushi."

"Excellent. I'm starved. Let's eat outside." We walk to the back patio and sit down at the table I've set. White wine is poured and we dig into the food and fall back into all the latest gossip. "How was New York?"

"It's New York. It never changes, yet, it's always changing. That makes no sense, but I'm just not a New Yorker. I need sunshine and the ocean to inspire me and my designs."

"I'm glad you're back. I've needed someone to take my mind off things."

"So Dex hasn't called?"

"No." I drag my salmon roll through the wasabi, then say, "I've seen so much tragedy come to those who got too much in life too soon. But slowly we're all working through it, sometimes together, sometimes apart. Dex seems to be caught in a mixture of emotions. He's happy when he's with me. I can tell he's at peace. But something inside of him wants to destroy us, to destroy that peace as if he's undeserving of it. He's gonna have to figure this out or we'll never be together."

"So you're willing to wait and see?"

"I am for him, but he doesn't know that yet."

"You're a wonderful person. Better than most." Lara holds her glass up and we toast. Though I'm not sure what we're toasting to.

I'm prompt, as everyone should be when invited to afternoon tea. I've never had high tea, but I understand there are rules and etiquette that accompany it. Being on time is probably one of them.

The door is opened by Charles. I remember him from the first time we stopped by. "Right this way," he directs.

I'm quickly intercepted by Judith and her wide smile. "It's so good to see you again, Ms. Floros."

"You too, Judith. Please call me Rochelle."

She nods, and says, "Right this way, Rochelle. Mrs. Caggiano is waiting for you."

With my hand, I stop her when I touch her forearm. "Should I be worried?"

Her smile eases into reassurance. Her hand covers mine, and she replies, "No, Mrs. Caggiano likes you. I've heard only good things from your visit to Diablo. But I will warn you that she's weak, weaker than she lets on."

"Thank you."

I walk into the conservatory. Dex's mother is seated in the far corner in a plush, floral fabric covered chair as she stares through the glass outside.

"Ms. Floros," Charles announces.

Mrs. Caggiano turns and smiles when her eyes land on me. "Come in," she says, starting to stand.

I rush over. "No, don't get up for me." Standing before her, she sits back down and reaches a hand out. I take it, and say, "Thank you for having me here for tea today."

"I'm glad you could join me. Please. Sit," she says, signaling to a chair next to hers that also faces out toward the gardens.

"I must admit, the invitation was unexpected."

"Yes, but I'm glad you accepted. We didn't have enough time to chat in Diablo."

"Was there something in particular you wanted to chat about?" I ask.

"My youngest son."

"I should tell you that I care about Dex, but we currently aren't seeing each other."

She leans back in her chair and an understanding grin appears. "I know. I don't mean to pry. I've been hands off with him for many years, too many. I've failed him in so many ways. I've tried to reconcile that with him, but some scars are too deep to heal overnight." The tea and tray of finger foods arrive on a large silver tray, interrupting her. She waits until everything is set up on the table before us, then continues when we're alone again. "Antonio and I may not be able to heal all of our old wounds, but I hope he can carry on with less pain weighing on his heart."

"He's a good man."

"You love him though he's left you... in a way."

"In a way?" I question, curious to what exactly she knows about our situation.

"He loves you. He's being a silly man and hoping to spare you his burdens to bear. What he doesn't understand is that women are built to share our partners' troubles. Wouldn't you say?" She leans forward and pours the tea. "Please eat something."

"I would help him if I knew how, Mrs. Caggiano." I drink my tea straight and take a bite of a small chicken salad sandwich.

His mother says, "I've jumped ahead of myself and forgotten my manners. Please call me Katherine."

Setting the sandwich down, I dab the side of my mouth with the white cloth napkin. "Thank you."

After sipping her tea, she says, "I'll be gone soon. My expiration date, according to the doctors, has come and gone. Yet, I'm not really feeling inspired. I worry. Antonio has been left with a huge responsibility not only with my father's estate, but his company as well since I won't be around. I did the best I could to get things in order. I left an internal board to run things for years. I never had a knack for those types of dealings."

I touch her wrist that is resting on the arm of the chair. "I'm sorry."

"Thank you. Cancer is not how I expected to go... I wonder about my sons and if they'll make up. They disagree about," she says, with a light laugh, looking at the floral pattern of the chair, her finger tracing a violet peony. "Pretty much everything. Gage is troubled a lot like my father was. Anto... Dex is like his father. Troubled in other ways." She looks up. "I need to ask you a favor, Rochelle."

I want to readily agree, but my heart begins to race and without warrant I start to hold my breath in anticipation of what's coming next.

She smiles. "Take care of my son when he finds his way back to you."

A slow exhale is followed by me asking, "How do you know he will?"

"You're the love of his life. He didn't have to tell me that, though he did. I could tell the first time I ever saw you with him. Diablo confirmed my suspicions."

"What if he never comes back?"

"Then he'll miss out on his own love story."

I smile. "In Diablo, you told us to follow our hearts."

"Follow your heart. It will lead you home."

ON THE DRIVE HOME, I ponder her words and my thoughts drift to Dex and the mess he must feel his life is. It makes me want to call him, but I don't. Even Tommy told me to give him time.

So I do. I also wonder about my future and what role am I willing to let Dex play in my life and in the boys' lives. As much as I love starting this new chapter with Dex, hoping he follow his heart back to me, the reality is, I need to close other chapters, fully opening my heart to him.

The kids go through our nightly routine until I crawl into bed. My entries haven't been as regular recently, so I pull my journal out of my nightstand and write:

DEAR CORY,

I've been working on the tour that starts in five months and closed two deals for Kaz and Derrick. Johnny seems content with the music—writing and recording in his home studio to care about marketing. Tommy's been working with the tour designers and stadiums. We all seem to be caught up in our own thing, but Dex is lost to us all.

I'm worried.

He sends the boys videos, so they can keep learning. They miss him, but understand that sometimes grownups are busy. They seem satisfied for now with the videos and packages he's sent them though they ask about him a lot.

I shouldn't bore you with this stuff. I'm sure you see right through me. You always could. So I'm just going to get this off my chest now.

I still hold onto the notion that time will heal all wounds. My heart wants to believe what my head logically knows is an impossibility. You will never be replaced in my heart. But maybe, just maybe, there's a little room inside for someone else too.

I know you wouldn't want me to spend my life alone. Nor I you, but it's easier said than done, like most things. I've been closed off for so many years that I've come to realize that I will be alone forever if I continue to live like this. You, my love, will always be a part of me. But now I'm asking you to loosen the reigns around my heart and let me live in love again.

MY TEARS DROP down onto the paper, smearing the ink a bit, but I continue writing.

PLEASE DON'T HATE ME, *Cory.*

I don't want to lie to you or hide my feelings any longer. Hoping you find contentment in me finding happiness again would be amazing and freeing in so many ways. I'm not sure if that will ever happen, but like Holli always says, Dare to Dream.

So I'm not sure where this leaves us—you and me, Mr. Journal. But I think this might be my last entry. Before I go, I must say this one more time—I Love You, Cory.

Goodbye.

XO

31

ROCHELLE

THIS IS NOT how I planned for us to see each other. I didn't have any real plans, but this was never a thought until now. I see the gravesite up ahead and the gathering of people circled around. Despite my deep-seeded desire to run away, I walk forward. I go because Dex needs me.

I don't quite make it to the grave when I spot him off on the other side of a tree sitting down. His sunglasses are on and I'm thinking they might be hiding more than his eyes. He sees me walking across the groomed lawn when I veer toward him, breaking away from the crowd. He doesn't say anything when I reach him, so I sit down despite that I'm wearing a dress. I decide not to say anything for the moment, not sure that anything I say is wanted. But I do lean my head on his shoulder, selfishly wanting to be close. Dex doesn't move or say anything until Gage spots us, sending a glare our way. "I'm now the head of an empire I never wanted."

I lift my head and look at him, seeing behind the dark lenses to the eyes that have cried over the death of his mother and maybe more today. "You only have to be what you want to be."

He looks my way. "How'd you hear?"

"Tommy. Why didn't *you* call me?"

Turning back to watch the last of the cars unload and the mourners joining the funeral, he says, "When we left Diablo, I thought we finally had our chance. I didn't count on the impact my mom's illness and the new will, Gage, all of it would put on me."

"I was there for you."

"I know you were." The left side of his mouth goes up quickly before disappearing again. "But I was being buried alive with responsibilities I never asked for. The company is generations old and I own it. All. What do I know about manufacturing?"

"You have a strong team of lawyers and other managers to help you figure this out. It doesn't have to be the same week your mom passed away."

I catch his eyes on me again and he doesn't turn away this time. "I missed you. Do you know that?"

I exhale, my heart starting to beat faster, then say, "I missed you so much."

"You know, Rochelle, we've been through a lot. You've been through more. I didn't want to put you through anything else."

"That's why you left?" I ask.

He nods. "One of the reasons."

"You can put on this big show for everyone else, but I know who you really are, Dex, and you're not gonna scare me that easily. I didn't stop caring about you because you stopped calling."

I see the corners of his mouth go up. "I didn't stop caring either." He wraps his arm around my shoulders and says, "You're pretty damn strong, sweetheart."

"I'm here to share the burden. Just let me in."

Dex stands and helps me to my feet. "C'mon. The sooner we do this the sooner we can leave."

Just as he turns to join the others, I stop him by taking hold of his arm. "Hey Dex?"

"Yeah?"

"Don't rush through the funeral. I understand the desire to get through this and to be anywhere but here, but this is important, not just for others, but for you. Stay present in the moment, for your mother."

I see the emotion he's held back start to show as he looks down, lifting his sunglasses to wipe at his eyes, then lets them fall back into place. "I don't want to sit in those chairs. That makes it real."

His denial is familiar. I remember thinking the same thing years ago, but I didn't want to upset Cory's family by not sitting next to them. "You don't have to. Stand where you want. I'll stand by you."

Shifting, he swallows hard. "I didn't do the same for you at Cory's."

"You didn't have to. I understood. All that mattered is that you were there."

"I didn't know you saw me," he says, reaching for my hand.

When our fingers entwine, I reply, "You were leaning against a tree. You wore a black shirt and sunglasses. You were holding something shiny. I remembered it catching my eye as it reflected in the sun."

He releases my hand and pulls out his wallet. Digging inside, he produces an oval coin. I recognize it before he says anything, my heart beginning to throb out of my chest. "Cory gave this to me in Paris. It's St. Christopher." My breaths shorten as he continues. "He said he's the patron saint of travelers."

"I know." I take it from him, holding it in the palm of my hand. A tear joins it. "I gave this to him the first time he left to tour without me. He didn't want to go alone." I look up at Dex. His sunglasses in his hand, his tear-filled eyes on me. "I told him he was never alone. He had you, Johnny, and Tommy. And you guys would always be there for him when I couldn't." I fold my fingers around it.

"He told me this coin would help me find my way home." His hand wraps around my fisted one. "It was the last thing he said to me before he left Paris."

The sob I was trying to hide from him breaks free. I sniffle, then ask, "Did you?"

"It led me to you, Rochelle." He puts his sunglasses over his eyes again and releases my hand. His voice shakes when he says, "I just wish it didn't come at the expense of him."

Adjusting my sunglasses down over my eyes, I say, "We didn't come at the expense of Cory. The universe doesn't work in such cruel ways. This is how it was always meant to be."

Taking my hand again, he asks, "Were we always meant to be?"

"We may have taken the scenic route to get here, but we're here now, baggage and a few cute kids along for the ride."

"Dex," Gage calls from behind us.

Dex turns to look. When he turns back, he says, "Guess we should go over there, but before we do, I want you to know that having you share the journey has made the road less traveled worth the risk."

"Dex!" Gage yells, ending the conversation.

Dex turns and with me by his side, we stand behind the chairs, two people mixed in with the large crowd and watch as his mother is put into her final resting place.

I STAND BACK in a corner of his mother's living room with Johnny and Holli, Tommy, Kaz, and Derrick. None of us are talking much. I'm not surprised. Funerals suck.

Holli nudges me. "Maybe you should go hang out with him."

"I don't want to add to his obligations today. Everyone wants a piece of him to help them find peace with his mother's death."

She touches my arm. "I understand, but you being there isn't a burden to him."

"Everyone knows about us, don't they?"

Nodding, she says with a reassuring smile, "And supports you. He's a good man. It just took a while to get to know the man underneath the façade. You're good for him."

"He's good for me."

Johnny takes Holli's hand and moves closer. "Holliday's right. I remember Dex being pretty cool back in the day. He just lost himself along the way. Fame does that to some people... to most. You reminded him of who he really is. I think he might have done the same for you, you know, reminding you of who you always were." He steps forward. "We're gonna go talk to him and take off unless you want us to stay, Rochelle."

"No," I reply, "it's fine. You can go. I might help him escape soon anyway."

Johnny and Holli leave after a hug and Derrick and Kaz follow closely behind, leaving me and Tommy there. When I lean against the wall next to Tommy, he says, "You know that time we went to Barstow?"

"How can I forget it?"

He rubs his chin in a thoughtful manner. "When Dex called me. He told me two things. One was the motel's name. The other thing... he said and I quote, "If I die, tell Rochelle I'm sorry."

I look at him in shock. "Sorry for what?"

"He didn't say, but something inside me thinks he really was close to death that day. Something made him want to apologize to you and I'm guessing he wanted to go with a clear conscience."

"I'm guessing it was the drugs," I remark dryly.

Tommy pushes off the wall, and says, "I'm gonna go. We should talk about the tour soon. Call me next week."

"I will," I say, nodding.

I watch as he goes over to Dex and Gage, shaking their hands. Dex's eyes meet mine across the crowded room before he looks back at Tommy. Once Tommy leaves, a few other mourners talk to them as I make my way over, weaving between small groups of people. I veer to the back door and nod toward it when Dex looks at me. He smiles though I can tell he feels guilty for the small act of happiness when he's supposed to be sad. I remember battling the same contrasting emotions.

Outside, he finds me smelling the roses. While I'm bent down, his hand slides over the curve of my hip. I turn to him and smile. "Frisky?"

"I couldn't resist."

"You've been resisting for a while now. What gives?"

"The company is in the capable hands of my cousin and Gage has reconciled with his wife."

"What about you?"

"I have a tour to prepare for, the album releases soon, and there's this girl I've been meaning to talk to you about. Is now a good time?"

My heart drops to the pit of my stomach. But I'm not surprised. It's Dex—handsome, funny, so sexy, and famous. He has his pick of women and I guess over the last month or so, he decided not to pick me. I raise my chin a bit, hoping I'm come off as strong, something he said he always admired about me. "Sure," I say while looking away from his brown eyes that hold me captive every time I look into them. *Stay strong.*

His fingers grace my cheek. "Rochelle, look at me."

When I finally look up, daring to meet his intense gaze, he says, "I'm in love with you. I always have been. But, I'm no good for you right now."

"I don't understand. Why are you the judge and jury when it comes to me?"

"Because you have responsibilities that I can screw up. I've got to get my life together. But I'll make you a promise right here. I won't be with anyone else. I don't want to be. I only want you. I'm just hoping you can hang on a little longer and wait for me as well."

"How long, Dex? My heart can't take this back and forth."

"I want to give you answers. I do, but all I can say is that we'll know when it's right. I need to deal with my family first... Gage will always be my brother whether we share the same blood or not. He's the only family I have left."

"You've got me and the band, the boys, and Tommy. Dex, you have so much goodness. Don't lose it to the troubles of today."

"I have to get my mom's estate settled. I've had a lot of time to think. It's been good for me. I don't know the last time I really blocked out the noise of my life, but I liked it. I also thought a lot about us. About you. Nothing new there, but I just want you to know that I love you. I keep saying it hoping you'll believe me."

I touch him, my fingers around his hand. "I believe you. I just want to be with you. I shouldn't. Not with how you've left me in the past, but I love you too much to let this fade away as if it never happened."

"You're so damn beautiful." He laughs and looks around. "The old me would take you upstairs in the middle of this depressing party and fuck you."

He makes me smile with his confession and I ask, "And the new you?"

"The new me wants to take you upstairs and make love to you."

Laughing, I squeeze his hand. "You know, you don't have to change on my account. I like all your sides."

"You're the best reason for all the changes in my life. I don't do drugs anymore. I don't have seizures anymore. I wake up with a clear head though sometimes my heart is cloudy."

"Sounds like a song."

With a grin, he says, "It is. I want to play it for you soon."

"Dex?" Gage calls from the back door. He doesn't see us and Dex doesn't make a move to respond either.

He finally says, "I should get back. You were right."

"About what?"

"Being here. You once told me that you never had a chance to be weak because you were so busy being strong for everyone else." He signals over his shoulder toward the house. "That's what this is. It's about helping everyone else through the loss they're experiencing."

"What about you?"

He smirks. "I could ask you the same."

"I've mourned. It may have taken me a long time to do, but I've done it. I'm choosing to live my life now."

Leaning down, really close to my ear, he whispers, "You're incredibly sexy. Go home. I'm gonna kick everyone out shortly. I'll give you a call."

"I hope you do. Oh, and why are you sorry?"

"Sorry?"

"Back in Barstow. You told Tommy to tell me you were sorry. Sorry about what?"

"Dex?" his brother yells outside again.

Dex says, "That's my cue. We'll talk soon."

32

ROCHELLE

I WATCH the drapes blow in the breeze slipping in through the cracked open French doors. Rolling onto my side, I grab the other pillow, cuddling it to me. I know it won't satisfy, though I'm hoping it does, like it can somehow fill the void that Dex has left. I wish we could go back to those times where it was just the two of us, happy. I wish I could take away his pain and heal him. Thinking about the last four years and the roller coaster of our relationship, I smile. Ridiculous I know, but Dex makes me smile... still.

Maybe I can heal him, slowly. Maybe I'm what he needs. Pushing down my doubts, I pick up my phone wanting to get past all the hurt and I text him: *You make me so mad sometimes.*

A minute later, my phone pings with a message from *Dex: **When you're mad, you have this fire that burns on the inside and sparkles in your eyes.***

Awwww. That's so sexy of him to say. I don't let him win though. I need to get this out. My fingers begin flying over the letters as I type: **When you push me away, it hurts my feelings.**

I stare at the phone for a minute before the next message pops up: ***I envy your ability to stay strong when everyone else is weak.***

*Me: **Your long hair used to annoy me.***

Dex: Good thing I cut it off then. You can do better than that, Lovely Rochelle.

Me: You use sunglasses on stage like a shield to protect your heart.

Dex: I never wear them around you.

Me: Your arrogance is not as charming as you think.

Dex: So you admit it is charming though...

Me: I admit nothing.

Dex: You're stubbornness is sexy.

Me: You're always horny.

Dex: Only for you.

Me: I'm sorry for any pain I've caused you.

Dex: Rochelle, you only bring me happiness.

Me: I'm sorry for dropping you off at rehab like I did.

Dex: It was worth it in the end. I'm sorry for hurting you when you visited. You were the only one who visited btw.

Me: I visited two other times, but never got out of the car.

Dex: I know. I saw you.

Me: I missed you.

I gulp and go for it, putting my heart on the line again for this sweet, vulnerable, mess of a man. I type: *I miss you now.*

There's a pause and my heart starts to beat a little faster from waiting. When my phone dings again, it reads: *I miss you between every sunrise.*

I take in his words like a word problem, then it dawns on me and I reply: *You miss me every day?*

Dex: Every day, all night long.

I stop, holding my breath as I read his message over and over again. I finally press the key I should have pushed long before now. When he answers, I say, "Come over."

"If I come over, this is it for us. There's no more late night or early morning goodbyes—"

"Only good mornings and goodnights."

"So we're on the same page?" he asks.

"We're on the same everything, Dex. Come over."

"I'm on my way."

The phone goes silent and I finally understand that giving into him doesn't mean giving up on other things. He makes my life more vibrant and brings a steady rhythm to my days. Dex makes me feel and crave, reach and strive for more. More that I didn't know was possible before.

He gave that to me. So when he shows up just after midnight, I let him not only into my house, but into my life. Open arms. Open heart. Wholeheartedly. "Come in."

With a soft smirk playing on his lips, he says, "I love you, Rochelle. And I want you to know that I've waited a lifetime for this day, for you. I would have waited another if I had to."

"This was all about my life too, right? Me not mourning how I should have?"

"Yes. You weren't ready before. I know you think you were, but you weren't."

"So, I had to lose it all again to see what I missed?"

"Did you mean what you texted me? Did you miss me?"

"So much." I step forward and lift up. Just before my lips press against his, I say, "I love you, Dex."

Dex

SHE PULLS me by the belt into the bedroom and shuts the door. After locking it and with a fucking sexy smile on her face, she asks, "Why are you wearing so many clothes?"

With a chuckle, I reply, "You stole my line. You seem to have a knack for stealing things of mine." She knows what I mean without me having to say it. I slide my hands under her old Nirvana t-shirt. "Sleeping with the competition I see."

"They were never competition," she says and takes the shirt off abruptly.

Her hair covers her, so I push it behind her shoulders and look her over. Her tits are perfection—pert and begging to be touched, fucked. Reaching up, I take them in hand and squeeze, watching as her eyes struggle to stay open. "Make love to me, Dex." Her voice is raspy, exposed, and completely sexy.

She unbuttons my shirt, then pulls it down over my shoulders and arms until it falls to the floor. Her lips are wet when they press against the skin of my chest as her hands undo my belt and pants. She moves around, her hands caressing my shoulders as she kisses my back. I feel her fingertips outlining the tattoo she's never seen before. I say, "The Phoenix rising."

She doesn't question, just responds, "I like it. It suits you."

Even more turned on by her approval, I help her along by flipping off my shoes, spinning her around, and moving her toward the bed. Her legs hit the mattress and she falls back. My pants drop. I take off my socks as she removes her underwear. Both of us naked brings back all the good that we've always been together. Like a predator, I hunger for her, to taste her, to feel her all over again.

Her hands go from my neck up into my hair, her body leaning until I'm on my back and she sits atop of me. Moving until I'm positioned, she looks up at me.

"You're stunning," I say, her body taking me in and causing my eyes to close briefly.

Seated with me fully inside her, Rochelle whispers, "You once told me your soul is damaged. We're all damaged inside. It's how we carry on that changes the outcome."

Grabbing a hold of her hips, I want to move, the sensation of her tightness around me makes me want to fuck, but her words feel like a remedy to my burned heart. "Do you think it's too late for me to change?"

She begins to rock, resting her palms on my chest for leverage. "I think you have perfect timing. It's everything we've lived through that brought us here together."

Hesitant to ask, to ruin how damn fucking good this feels, I do it anyway because I need to know. "Do you have any regrets?"

Stopping, she leans down and kisses me, then whispers, "Only one."

"What is it?"

With a wicked sexy smile, she replies confidently, "Not being with you sooner."

Looking into her gorgeous brown eyes, I see all the possibilities of a life worth living. "You were the new start I always wanted. You're my second chance." I kiss her like I've never kissed, giving in and giving her everything I can as I flip her under me and make love to her, making up for wasting so much time.

My hips thrust causing her to moan, her chest pushing against me. "More," she calls to me.

I move faster, not able to continue the steady pace, our making love morphing, scorching and carefree. Enjoying this too much, I take her body over and over again until she quietly calls out my name and I call out hers like a profanity slipping out.

Later, we're lying in bed together and I have my arm wrapped around her, holding her to me. The silence that surrounds us isn't tension filled or filled with questions. It's light, airy and filled with a future we're finally both sure we want, making me feel sentimental in my attachment to her. "I'm sorry for letting you walk out of my life the first night we were together."

She lays there, still and quiet, then whispers, "I'm sorry for walking out."

"Don't be. Please know that it was never just about sex with you. You hurt my ego, but *you* were hurting more and I failed to notice. I'm sorry."

"It wasn't your job to save me, Dex," she says, looking down. Dropping her forehead against my cheek, she wraps her arms around me and pulls me closer, making me smile. Sitting up suddenly, she looks at me with a big smile of her own on her face. "You always knew we'd be together, didn't you?"

"We were written in the stars long before now. I love you."

"I love you more," she says.

"Not possible," I tease, "you just don't understand the depth of my love."

"What I am going to do with you, Dex?"

"You're gonna marry me." I watch her face, not sure what to expect in reaction. But she just smiles.

"You're a romantic, Antonio Dexter Caggiano."

"Only when it comes to you."

"You know how to make a girl swoon." She looks up at me. "And maybe on the days it gets rough," she says, snuggling closer, "we can escape to Neverland again, even if just for a few hours."

"I don't need Neverland," I say. "Reality with you is better than any make believe world ever could be."

I rub her back, living in this moment, and she asks me, "You're here for good, right?"

Leaning down to kiss her, I say, "I'm here for good. Our destinies were always bound together."

She sits up and says, "I'm giving you my heart, Dex."

Sliding my hands up her arms and over her shoulders, I stop when I slip my fingers into her hair. Bringing her down until we're so close, I can almost taste her, I whisper, "You've had mine since the moment I laid eyes on you."

EPILOGUE
ROCHELLE

One year later…

I OPEN my eyes and exhale slowly. I can do this. It's just like at home. No different. I readjust on the stool just as Johnny takes to microphone. The spotlight hits him and the crowd starts screaming so loud that it's hard to hear him at first.

I feel Dex's hand on my lower back. "Play from the heart," he says, positioned on a stool next to mine with his guitar in his hands.

"What if I screw up?"

"You won't. Only us, sweetheart. Just like at home. Block out the noise."

"…most talented guitarists out there. She taught the great Cory Dean how to play and has written many of our best songs. It's time for her to show the world what she can do. Give it up for Rochelle Floros." I hear Johnny just as he looks back, his eyes locking with mine, a huge smile on his face as his hand swings out in our direction and the spotlight follows.

When the bright light hits us, I freeze, my mind going completely blank. I miss my cue altogether, but then I hear Dex, his soothing voice, full of enough confidence for both of us. "Only us. Play with me."

We were two people following our own melodies who discovered the music we create together is the sweetest song of all. My fingers start moving, knowing the notes without the mental reminder. I close my eyes and keep playing. I lean forward and the words come just like we practiced, just like they were supposed to.

Songs that had been written apart became a song together that we sit on stage singing for the world to hear today. Every note gets easier and easier and when I hear Dex join in, hitting his own cue, I open my eyes and smile, looking over at him. I'm given a smile in return as he sings into the shared mic.

We lean back, strumming to a song we wrote together. The violins sound out behind us as does a slow and steady drum beat, Kaz filling in for Dex. Johnny walks back to a microphone setup in the shadows across the stage just as his part kicks in. I continue singing and when the chorus starts, Dex leans in again, our cheeks almost touching and sings.

Three minutes of our love put out there for the world to hear. Just as the song ends, Dex moves from his chair and gives me a standing ovation. Exhilarated that I just played in front of eighteen thousand people, when I stand, I laugh, then take a bow. The stage goes dark, but the crowd is still cheering.

Dex says, "You nailed it." He kisses me, our guitars clanging between us. When we part, he adds, "It's time the world sees you for the star you are. It's your turn to shine."

He wraps his arm around my shoulders as we walk to exit the stage. I wrap mine around his back. "Thank you for believing in me."

"Believing in you has always come easy, but you were there when I needed you most. I owe you my life more than a few times over." His guitar is taken by a roadie and he takes his sticks, shoving them into his back pocket.

"Two minutes. Get to your kit, Dex," Tommy yells from behind us.

I start to step off to the side, but Dex grabs my hand. "Hey," he says, gently moving my guitar to my back, the strap keeping it safe back there.

Surprised by how relaxed he is while everyone else is rushing around us. "You conquered your fears, Rochelle. You're still the strongest person I know."

"You are too, Dex. Don't ever believe otherwise." I touch his cheek. "You gotta go, your fans are waiting."

"I've got time."

Slowly, he moves forward as if he has all the time in the world. His hand slides into my hair and he lowers down to kiss me. I lift up, our lips meeting in the middle. His other hand caresses the side of my face. As soon as he moves it, I realize the spotlight is on us. I gasp as the realization that we are on display hits me. All of that is forgotten entirely when Dex drops to one knee in front of me. He reaches into his back pocket and pulls one of the sticks out, handing it to me. Wrapped around the middle of the wood, a diamond and platinum ring sparkles under the intense lights.

I gasp again, at a loss for any other rational response.

"Rochelle, I was everything you never wanted or expected. But you saw who I always wanted to be, you saw the potential when I thought I was a lost cause. You gave my soul the pulse I've spent my life looking for and in return, I'll give you a life filled with the beauty you deserve. You took a chance on me and trusted me with your heart. Now, I'm here before you asking you to take the biggest chance of all. Will you marry me?"

From behind me, I hear CJ when he says, "Marry Dex, Mama."

Tears fall when I spot my sweet boys behind me, Lara holding each of their hands off stage with tears of her own in her eyes. She nods and smiles. When I turn back, I reply, "I believe we were written in the stars long before now. We're a chance I'm willing to take, so the answer is yes, Dex. I want to spend the rest of my life with you."

I'm grabbed as he stands, his arms encompassing me, and our lips meet in a fit of passion. In that kiss, I don't hear the crowd, or the crew and the applause around us. The band waits patiently for us to have our moment together. But none of it matters. What matters most are the little arms that encircle our legs. When our lips part, I look at him, the man who stole my heart when I least expected to find love again. And I realize that sometimes we find love in the most unlikely of places... and sometimes it was there all along.

The End

THE REVOLUTION

My world was rock solid.

Until I saw her.

Lara Kessler showed up as if heaven sent her to me, and suddenly my priorities changed. Love is funny like that. One minute you're living the dream, then BAM! Half my soul shows up backstage wearing a purple shirt and sexy skin-tight jeans, making me realize what I've been missing all along. Loving her means exposing a life I've tried to bury.

My heart had lost its beat.

Until I saw him.

Kaz Fabian caught my attention the moment I laid eyes on him. Love is funny like that. The famous guitarist was every woman's fantasy-- great face, chiseled jaw, cut biceps. The rock star was pure sex on and off stage, but his charm and charisma won me over. Loving him means burdening him with a life I've tried to leave behind.

With her future dim and his past in the spotlight, can they overcome their fate or will they just be another tragic love story?

PROLOGUE

The woman I've fantasized about is finally in my bed. The one who's starred in my dreams and I've imagined when fucking others. She's here, lying next to me and I can't sleep.

My chest hurts while watching her. She's the most beautiful woman I've ever seen and equally the most fascinating. She teases and jokes, flirts... and she trusts me. She trusts me with her life. That's what brought her here tonight. I would do anything for her and she knows it.

I sit up and scrub my hands over the way-too-long scruff that covers my face. She stirs beside me, making me want to stay. I really should, but I just can't stay here any longer...

A promise is a promise and all that. But some promises are worth breaking. *This is one of them.*

1

LARA KESSLER

STUPID MUSICIANS!

Stupid, sexy guitarists in fitted shirts that highlight muscles and accentuate abs that should not be hidden behind cotton nor confined under it. But when muscles become eight-packs that's what happens. Score one for him. He's got my complete attention and it's so annoying.

"Lara?"

I look back over my shoulder. Rochelle smiles while adding an accusing lifted eyebrow. Damn her and her all-knowing self.

"What?" I reply as innocently as I can.

"Really?" Crossing her arms over her chest and the stagnant stare tells me I'm not fooling her. "You ready or do you need a few more minutes to stare at the band?"

Caught.

Did Rochelle really think bringing me backstage to The Resistance sound check would be a quick in and out? I want to see the guys. Johnny Outlaw, the lead singer, may be the one most clamor to see, but not me. Everything about him oozes sex appeal, but despite that, my attention tends to go elsewhere. Dex, the drummer, is hot, but he and Rochelle... I'm not sure what's going on there. The other guitarist,

Derrick, is cute, but definitely not my type. Kaz on the other hand... I let my gaze linger on his ass in those tight jeans, the holes at the knees formed naturally, literally torn from wear. *So freaking hot.* "A few minutes," I joke. Kind of.

She laughs, pulling the band around my topknot out before I can stop her. My long brown hair comes tumbling down over my shoulders and she says, "Fine, I'll meet you at the car." Teasing as she walks away popping the band she just stole from me, she adds while pointing at my hair, "That's much better too."

"Hey there." And there it is, the voice I was longing to hear.

Before I have a chance to mess with my hair, I run my hand down the front of my purple silk shirt hoping it's not a wrinkled mess. Not like guys care about that. Not that I should care about that. But I do when it comes to *him.* When I turn back around, Kaz is standing in front of me. His smile is sweet, one I haven't seen him reveal in months, maybe since our beach encounter. I don't kid myself though. I'm more practical than that. I'm probably one of many he's actually shown it to, but I like to think it's just for me. "Hi."

"You coming to the show tomorrow?"

"I wouldn't miss it."

Tommy, the band's manager, calls him from the dressing room and waves him over.

When Kaz's caramel-colored eyes are back on me, the corners dip down along with his smile. He looks frustrated. "Guess I should I go. We've got some stuff to do before the show. I'll see you tomorrow?"

I'm honestly not sure what the game plan is, but I won't miss this opportunity either. Nodding, I reply, "For sure." I give a little wave and turn with a big smile on my face. I push through the double doors and am instantly blinded by the sunlight. When my eyes adjust, I see Rochelle's SUV and walk to it. I've just closed the door when she says, "You're gonna get yourself into trouble if you're not careful. You need to be very clear with Mark, and do it today."

Exasperated I'm still dealing with this mess, I lean my head against the seat. "I have several times. He refuses to listen."

Her annoyance is clear, even though I can't see her eyes behind the large designer sunglasses hiding them. Her head tilts and her smile flattens into a straight line. Rochelle is stunning even when she has no patience for things like her friends' terrible relationships. "Make him listen. It's not fair for you to live like this—"

"This? I don't want to hurt him, Ro."

"You know how I feel about everything that's happened. You also know what's happened to me. Don't waste time on things, or people, who don't make you happy." She shifts the Escalade into drive, and turns her focus forward.

I've felt many emotions over the last few months, but the one that stands out is fear. I've felt it deep inside, yet it's one I've not spoken of before, so I whisper, "I'm scared."

Smiling sympathetically, she reaches over and squeezes my hand before returning it to the steering wheel. "It won't be easy, but you've wanted this for a while. It's time to move on with your life, Lara."

"I know. I'll do it soon."

She drives through the parking lot toward the guarded gate while circling back topic-wise to where we began. "In the meantime," she starts as a security guard presses a button and the gate lifts for us to leave the arena, "Tomorrow, we party. It's been forever for me. I need a night out."

"Me too." Kaz crosses my mind and I wonder if how I'm feeling about tonight, about seeing him, is wrong. Flipping down the visor, I open the mirror to see how much I really embarrassed myself with Kaz. My hair is a wild mess of waves I can live with, and the charcoal gray eyeliner that rims my blue eyes is still in place, thank goodness. I push the mirror closed and lean back just as we pass a billboard advertising season tickets for the local major league baseball team. "It will be fun." When I glance her way, I add, "Don't let me drink too much."

"I won't. Or I might. I'm thinking you need a night out just as badly as I do." She's my friend through and through. She may freely give her opinion, but she won't hold it against me if we differ. Following a laugh, she says, "I like Kaz. I'm just worried what your boyfriend might think about this friendship forming with him.

Mark's known for two things: homeruns *and* his temper. He wasn't happy the last time you brought him around the band."

Mark flipped out on the band manager for talking to me a four months back. I haven't brought him around since. "I'm allowed to have friends. Separate friends from him. Besides, Mark and I haven't been coupling since the playoffs began."

"Coupling?"

I shouldn't share my sexual secrets but it's one of the reasons I'm leaving Mark, and I trust her with the information. "There's no intimacy."

"You don't have sex?" The shock is heard through the higher octave of her voice. "Lara Kessler, please tell me that's not the case."

"Did you just full-name me?"

"I did. Now tell me you haven't gone without sex."

I shake my head. "I've had sex, though it's been longer than I'd like to admit, and there's no intimacy. It's about him getting off and getting his body in tune to play. Sex is something he does for himself. Not me. It's all about the sport—baseball and sex."

"But I thought players went at it like rabbits in the off-season?"

"Everything in Mark's life revolves around pre-season, the baseball season, and the playoffs. All else is considered a distraction to his routine, including me."

"I'm sorry. I had no idea."

"It's sort of embarrassing to admit, so I don't talk about it."

"When was the last time you... you know?"

"Speaking of rabbits," I laugh, "can we stop at the store? I'm out of batteries."

Rochelle doesn't laugh, but her grin shows her amusement. "Definitely. I'll even buy the bulk pack for you." Traffic in LA sucks so she takes advantage of the time. "Mark has a competitive streak when it comes to pro baseball, but his jealous streak rivals it when it comes to you. Again, not to hound, but make a clean break before you flirt with disaster."

She's right. He's very protective of me because he believes we're meant to be, but the feeling isn't mutual. "Is flirting with disaster a reference to Kaz?"

It's too hot today, so I pull an elastic from my purse, and twist my hair back into a knot on top of my head. Her lack of answer causes me to say, "I was afraid of that."

"Your friendship with Kaz is not wrong."

She's right. *Of course.* So for myself, I say, "We're only friends. He's a great guy, but we're *only* friends. I'm not looking to jump from one relationship into another."

"What if Mr. Right shows up?"

"I don't need Mr. Right. I'm just looking for that damn elusive O. No matter how many batteries I go through, I'm not able to find him. *It.*" I correct. "I mean it, not him."

She laughs along with me, but it lulls as we both realize what I mean. Then I just feel sad. "My mind is a mess these days."

"We need our minds romanced as much as our bodies. The O will come. But not until your mind is free. You need to get yourself in a good place mentally." Touching my hand again, she says, "Things work out how they're supposed to, Lara."

"Is that how you feel about Cory?" I shouldn't have said that and I know it, but I'm curious and usually too afraid to ask. My defenses lower as regret sets in. "I'm sorry."

"It's okay." Her fingers tighten around the leather wheel, but her face remains neutral. "Things work out how they're supposed to," she repeats, her shoulders and tone much more stoic than her façade of calm.

2

LARA

MARK'S DRIVEWAY IS LONG. I've often thought it was a source of pride for him, as if he believes we are judged by the entrance to our homes instead of our hearts. He chose the former to highlight in life. I chose the latter. Another reason in a long list that we were never meant to be more than one hot night on Mulholland.

Stars are hidden behind clouds, or smog, making my night even more ominous than it already felt. The gate closes behind me and I'm left pulling up to a house that is grand and over the top with hideous Greek columns and an ostentatious Roman fountain with pissing cherubs. This house has a Hollywood legacy of a famous showman from before films existed through famous actresses who held huge society parties in the 1950s. More recently it was a porn producer's home until he went to jail for tax evasion. The mansion was put on the market and Mark scooped it up below value. He transformed the place and made it grand again. It's a symbol of his success and makes him feel important in a town full of players. I get it. He's known for his homeruns and ego. After meeting some of his teammates, it's clear he's not unique in this way.

But this house sets him apart. It's a status symbol that many other players can't afford. Mark's marketability affords him luxuries most will never experience.

Sometime in the last month I realized I was another status symbol like this house. I was a pretty package he could display in front of cameras as the doting girlfriend. I'd foolishly fallen for the charade and had played my part. The role of trophy without the wife title never sat well with me.

I may not be wealthy, but I make a good living and am recognized in my industry. Mark's never appreciated my achievements. He's paraded me up and down red carpets, World Series, and parties. It was fun, at first. In time, the real Mark Renner was exposed and his dark side wasn't pretty. We weren't real. I know that now. Sadly, I had changed to become what he wanted, what he demanded not so subtly. I barely recognize myself anymore.

And for what? *Fame?* I don't need fame. *Money?* I don't need money at this level. *Happiness?* I don't even remember when I gave that up. *Integrity? That's* what I most long for, what I desire to recapture. I may have lost my soul to the darkness of Hollywood, but I believe I can get back to a place where I feel proud of myself again, where I sleep at night without the help from a glass of wine to relax. Where tears and exhaustive arguments are no longer part of my daily routine. Where dreams replace the nightmares I've had longer than I remember.

We're not meant to be.

I didn't see the differences soon enough to stop this train from wrecking. He parties too much and I don't like the changes I've seen in him. From tabloid photos of him with other women while on the road to drunken fights on nights out with his buddies—he's a disaster and he's dragging me down with him.

Now that I've been investing into *my* life, and me, my friendships have strengthened again and hope is on the horizon. He may have been able to talk himself out of any situation before, but my instincts tell me not to believe him anymore. And I'm good with this.

Tonight I will walk away from his world, out from his shadow, and start living my life again.

After parking, I walk toward the house. Rap music penetrates the glass and iron front door. It's locked so I use my key and let myself in. The music is louder when I enter, the bass bouncing off the marble entryway. "Mark?" I call, shutting the door. "Mark?"

I leave my purse on the foyer table and make my way into the large living room with ornate and gaudy framed paintings. I don't have the heart to tell him he was had in Vegas when he bought what he thought were original masterpieces. They're knock-offs. Any fool can tell with one glance, except Mark.

When I round the corner to the kitchen, Mark is rapping at the top of his lungs. His back is to me as the blender runs giving me this last look at how handsome he used to be to me—broad shoulders and dark hair, golden skin from hours of practice outside. He's not the same man I met. The brightness that used to fill his eyes—joy from the game, excitement from being with me—has dulled. Now, online images show eyes that spark from alcohol and easy women. Even the way he stands is different to me now. He's weaker in my eyes, and I'm convinced I need to end this relationship. "Hi," I say loud enough for him to hear, but not startle him. He's not someone you want to surprise or sneak up on. Lately, he has been edgy. His size alone is intimidating, but his speedy reactions would land me in the hospital if he were startled.

He looks over his shoulder. "Hey, babe." Pointing at the stuff in the blender, he offers, "Protein shake?"

I soften under the endearment and the offer, and shake my head. "No, I'm good. Is that dinner?"

His bright white smile is engaging as he stops what he's doing and comes to hug me. "We can order a pizza if you're hungry."

"I ate earlier."

"Without me?" He looks hurt just from the thought.

"You weren't around earlier when I called."

"Coach started two-a-days today. I needed the extra cage time so I stayed later." He lifts my chin and the gesture is so caring that I almost forget why I'm here. "You okay? You look troubled."

This.

This is the Mark who charmed me into bed that first night. This is the Mark who had waffles and crispy bacon ready for me when I woke the next morning. This is the man I fell for never thinking twice that it was a side I'd rarely see. Seeing this man before me now, I feel sentimental as I forget the bad and warm from the good we have had.

SOMETIMES I SABOTAGE MYSELF. I've been working on it for a while, and when I gave in after he guilted me into staying, I realize I'll be working on it a lot longer. To his dismay, we didn't have sex. He wanted to break our streak, but I didn't. Sex isn't only physical for me. It's in my head and my body. Hence no orgasms in longer than I care to think about.

I'm having trouble sleeping. Again. Being awake in the middle of the night is no joyride, so I pick up my phone from the nightstand, careful not to wake Mark, and scroll through Instagram. As a decorator who's established a name and reputation in this town, I have many celebrity clients who have become friends. Their posts are exactly what people expect from them—parties, schmoozing, exotic vacations, and everything else most consider glamorous. Although I'm not rich, I have lived among the uber-wealthy long enough that I'm used to seeing the most amazing photos of incredible adventures. I used to get envious, but I see beyond the bright selfie lights. Their lives are, for the most part, superficial and highly coordinated. They don't order takeout without their manager's approval and their publicist's press release. It's suffocating, even to me as an outsider looking in on their lives.

As I scroll, I come across a photo posted by Mark. It's a pic of him working out with no shirt on. His body is amazing. He works hard for it and it shows. I just wish he didn't have to show it all the time. He has over three-thousand likes on the photo and at least one hundred comments, most from women—some vulgar, some flattering. All annoying.

Scrolling past Mark's, I don't bother liking it. I don't want to encourage more shirtless shots. His ego is big enough already, and he wouldn't notice my like anyway. Next is a photo of Rochelle's boys and I smile. Then I spy a photo of Kaz. It's a photo Rochelle posted. By the look of their clothes and the background, it was taken backstage earlier today. Their arms are around each other and their smiles are genuine. The lighting sparks in their eyes, revealing their happiness. I understand why Rochelle posted it. It's real. They're real. So different from the world I'm engulfed in right now.

"Turn off your phone and go to sleep," Mark snaps. His voice is gruff, short-tempered. He's warned me before about it, so I deserve it since I woke him.

I set the phone on the nightstand and slide down under the covers. "Sorry," I whisper, sad to see the sweet Mark gone so quickly.

He turns his back to me and within minutes he's snoring loudly. Half a year into our relationship and I don't feel the love I should for him. The spark was gone too soon for my liking. I was supposed to come over and break up, but I hate hurting people. *Even if it means hurting me in the process.*

I'll have to do it tomorrow.

"I'VE GOT A crazy day today, so I'm gonna head out," I say with the shower curtain between us.

"Okay," he says from the other side before burying his face under the spray. "I'll see you tonight."

I pause. "I'm not sure about tonight. I have the concert with Rochelle."

Just as I turn to leave my wrist is grabbed. "Hey, what's up?" His hand is wet, the tendons in his forearms bulging from his grip.

I turn my arm and try to wiggle free. Fear doesn't enter my psyche from the way he's holding on to me until his eyes narrow and his grip tightens. My mind wars with itself as I struggle internally to decide if it's fear I'm feeling or something else. I can't pinpoint the other emotions running rampant so I settle on fear and say, "Nothing. I have a long day ahead with a job in Malibu."

"I want to have dinner with you. Come by the gym." His fingers loosen around my wrist.

"I can't. I have the concert afterward. I'm already going to be late for it."

"Come over after."

"Maybe. I'll text you."

Bunched eyebrows. A disdainful snort. *He's irritated.* "Don't make this a habit."

My hair rises from his authoritarian tone. "Don't make what a habit?"

"This. Last night. This morning. Tonight. I barely see you these days and you haven't blown me in months."

My head jolts back from the slap of his words. "Blown you? I'm sorry. I must've been under the impression that I was more than a mouth for your pleasure."

"God, Lara. Don't be such a bitch all the time. You know I'll fuck you if you want me to, but you don't seem to want that. Maybe we should be talking about that."

Checking my watch, I say, "I've tried." Looking back at him, he stands naked before me, half in the shower, half out. "You had no interest in talking to me and last night I wasn't in the mood."

"Is this what last night was about? You're so uptight lately, I'm afraid you'll bite my head off if I touch you."

"I highly doubt you're afraid of much, much less me."

"Fine, let's do it. I wanted to last night."

Offended, I say, "I don't want to *do it*. I want you to realize I'm more than this hole or this one." My hand goes from my mouth and then points below my belly. "You used to—"

"Fuck *used to*. I don't want to hear it." He ducks back into the shower stall and allows the water to drown me out. He shouts over the water, "Go be a cunt with your friends."

What the hell?

There are times in our lives that someone pushes you too far.

There's an imaginary line that's been drawn in the sand of your mind that you're not even aware of until you're pushed over it. I just discovered my line.

With my fists balled at my sides, I yell, "We're done." I turn quickly, fear and excitement coursing through me, and escape the house. I finally did it. Not the way I planned, but the only way he would hear it. I mentally blur the line, hoping never to return to the other side again.

I'm done with him.

We're done.

The deed is done, and as I watch the gate close behind me, I release a long-held breath. My hands begin to shake in disbelief. I finally did it. It's done. A smile filters its way onto my face as I drive away.

I'm finally free.

3

———————

LARA

"Guess what I just found out?"

I don't even have time to say hello when I answer, so I take the opportunity now. "Good morning, Ro. And how are you?"

"Fabulous. Good Morning," she says, laughing. "And how are you?"

"Excellent. Thank you for asking." I laugh too, life feeling lighter by the minute. "So, what did you find out?"

"A mutual friend of ours just bought a house. You know what that means."

"I do know what that means. They might need a decorator."

"Ding. Ding. Ding."

"Who's the mutual friend?"

"Kaz Fabian."

An involuntary smile sneaks onto my face. "Oh really? Are we supposed to know about the house yet or is it still a secret?"

"I read about it online. I knew he was looking and had bids in on two properties. I guess the deal was finalized between the lawyers last night at Spago. A blogger overheard and leaked it overnight."

"That sucks on the leak. I know he was sharing a house in West

Hollywood with Derrick and wanted his own space, so it's good news on buying."

"Want me to ask about the house and see what he plans to do with it?"

Rochelle is someone I've always been able to rely on, a friend of a friend who became my friend. We just clicked and two years later, here she is thinking of job opportunities for me. "That would be awesome. Thanks."

"No worries. Where are you going this morning?"

"I just left Mark's. I'm driving home. I have a job in Malibu today."

Her voice lowers, the subject calling for it. "Did you do it?"

"We'll talk about it tonight. I need to get my head out of that space or I'll be crying and I just don't want to cry over that asshole."

Her silence is telling, so I let it stay, speaking for us.

She finally asks, "New client in Malibu? And anyone I've heard of?"

"You might have. Calliope Mathers."

"Wow. Hot actress of the moment. That's a good job to have. Maybe you'll get some press out of it. We all know how much she loves the attention."

"She's not that bad once you get past the fur-lined robes and teased bleach-blond hair. She's actually sweet sometimes."

CALLIOPE STAMPS HER high heel on the marble flooring, the tantrum proving her point. "See? There's an echo. I don't like that."

"But you'll get that with any flooring other than carpet and you said you thought carpet was, and I quote, 'Gross.'"

"I never said that," she protests with a toss of her highly hair-sprayed hair. It doesn't move though her hand continues the motion.

"You did when I brought the samples. You said you didn't want a 'beach-themed' house. You wanted expensive and over the top. That's what the whole design was based on."

She walks past me into the kitchen where a uniformed maid

hands her an espresso. "Latte?" she asks me, holding her cup to her lips.

"That's an espresso, and no, I'm good. Thanks."

"I thought the tiny cups of coffee were lattes?"

"Lattes have milk—" I stop myself from continuing on this ridiculous path. "The marble is stunning and it's custom. It was imported from Europe. If you want to dampen the sound, we have rugs on order that will do that. Don't stress. Let's stick with our original plan and then decide once everything is in place."

She comes closer and hugs me unexpectedly. "Fine. You're right. You're always right, Lara. What would I do without you?"

I'm starting to question her sanity, but in this city, I'm considered the odd one out. I return her hug, thinking she just might need one. She leans back and looks me in the eyes with a small smile on her face. "You know, because you're my friend, I'll totally get you an appointment with Stanz, my fab hairdresser. He could knock the dull right out of your brown hair. It does wonders for the self-esteem and all the guys in LA would be after you. Well, all the guys who aren't coming after me that is."

My grin is tight, but my annoyance is kept buried. "Thanks, but I'm swearing off men for a while."

"What about your soccer player?"

I don't bother correcting her. "I'd rather not talk about him right now."

"Soccer just isn't that popular though. You could really land someone bigger. You have such a pretty face." In other words, my ass is big, but thank goodness my face is pretty. *Ugh.*

I can't deal with her today. Taking a step back from her, I grab my purse, and say, "He's a *major* league baseball player, and I'm all set on the hair, but thanks anyway." Totally irritated, I head for the door. "The rugs should be in next week. I'll see you then."

"Tootles."

Clueless.

I cringe when I see the time. *Damn it.* I'll be sitting in rush-hour traffic for the next two hours. I settle into my Range Rover and turn on Vivaldi to keep me company on the trek back to Hollywood Hills. I've moved so much of my stuff into Mark's that I forgot the small detail of removing things before I broke it off with him. Now I'm stuck with my clothes in his closet. My saving grace is that I know he's at practice so I'll be able to slip in and out with a few armloads of clothes before he returns later tonight.

Like an LA miracle, I get to his house sooner than expected. I walk in and dump the keys and my bag on the table in the dining room before being startled by Mark in the living room. "Hey," I say, grabbing my chest. "I didn't think I'd see you."

"But we had plans," he says. His fingers are steepled and he's glaring at me. His look is intense, his tone tight. The rigidness of his body makes me nervous.

His brusque behavior gives me pause, and I worry if honesty is not the best policy for my safety. I venture there first though, testing the waters. Keeping my voice calm, I ask, "I have the concert tonight. Remember?"

"Oh right," he says, playing it off as he sits back and lowers his hands to his thighs. "But you can skip it. Some of the team are getting together with their girlfriends down at O'Malley's to watch the Red Sox preseason opener."

His ease causes irritation as he discounts not only my plans, but dismisses what I told him this morning. "What are their wives doing?"

"I'm not going to argue with you, Lara." Mark's not amused by the snarky joke. He can't argue it, though, since a few of his teammates actually do have girlfriends on the side, if not most. I used to wonder if he did too. Now I just want to move on from him. "Get dressed."

"Don't tell me what to do. We are no longer a couple. I'll collect a few things tonight and be out of your way shortly." He's on his feet before I have a chance to turn away. My wrist is grabbed, the tips of his fingers like spears to my skin as he digs in. "Mark!"

Pulling me close, he holds me tight against his side. "I will not be embarrassed. You will come with me tonight." With one strong shove, my knees hit the hard floor and the palms of my hands slap down roughly. The smart is instant as pain shoots through me, breaking through the shock of what just happened. My eyes well, but my anger rules. I swing my head around and my hair flies to the side when he reaches for me. "Get away from me."

"I'm sorry," he says, but there's no feeling behind the words. His tone is the same as before he pushed me. He stands and says, "We're not broken up. No one breaks up with me."

Despite the pain, I get to my feet, stand tall, and face him. "I just did." Pushing past him, I head for the door. Forget the clothes and everything else. I need to get out of here before something worse happens.

He steps back and to the side to block my way. I look up, straight into his eyes. "Move out of my way, Mark."

A cocky smile that had come easily to him is replaced with a scowl. "Look, I'm sorry if I hurt you." He comes closer. "I care about you. I don't want us to be over."

"Too late," I say, keeping my expression straight and my tone firm. "This isn't working out. You can go out with your friends and meet all the women you want. They'll be thrilled to hear you're single."

"No."

"What do you mean, no?" I back away from him toward the door. Quickly, I turn and unlock it, holding it wide open, something in my gut telling me to just in case I need to scream.

But whatever made his demeanor confrontational before is gone, the nice guy that wooed me months earlier has returned. "Lara," he says, his voice soft. "Don't do this. Give me another chance. I don't want to lose you. Please. One more chance."

I gulp, debating if I should make a run for it or stay and try to leave on good terms. "I think it's best we go our separate ways. I'm never going to be what you need. Trust me, you'll meet the girl of your dreams, but I'm not her."

Disappointment settles into his features. "We can work this out. Please be open-minded. We are everything together and nothing apart."

Starting to feel bad, I acquiesce. "I'm not going to change my mind."

He stops in front of me and rubs my wrists where he grabbed me earlier. I'm not scared, but I recoil involuntarily. When he sees me flinch, he frowns. "I'm sorry. I'll make it up to you. I promise. We'll talk tomorrow."

We're done. So done. There's no way I'm changing my mind, but to keep him calm, I nod before walking out.

As soon as I shut the door to my car, I lock it, and breathe for what feels like the first time in minutes. Inhaling slowly, my lungs burn. *No one breaks up with me.* Trying to regulate my pounding heart, I exhale even slower to release the tension in my body. *I will not be embarrassed. You will come with me tonight.* I start the car with shaking hands. *No, Mark, I won't.* Even though the signs have been there since before the playoffs, I shouldn't have ignored them; I've never seen him that aggressive. I'm not sure why he's become more aggressive, but I can't stick around to find out either. At six five, he's a big guy. I cover my wrist with my hand and rub. It hurts. *He* hurt me. I need to leave, so I ignore the pain and back down the driveway.

4

LARA

AFTER GETTING PAST three different bouncers, verifying my name, and flashing my badge, I'm finally backstage. My stomach is still upset from earlier, my head still spinning, but I try to shake it off and enjoy the night.

Lifting up on my toes, I search for Rochelle amongst the chaos. A familiar face pops up in the crowd when she jumps, then waves her arm. Holli comes over and hugs me, the smile on her face welcome. "Good to see you, Lara," she says warmly. "Glad you could make it."

Holliday Hughes—gorgeous, smart, and down to earth. She's the most put together woman I know. She's definitely someone to look up to. And as if she didn't have everything already, she also owns the heart of the one and only Johnny Outlaw—the front man and lead singer of *The Resistance*. I've always liked her, but everyone does. She makes it easy and is the kind of person people gravitate toward. "Good to see you," I reply, embracing her while protecting my wrist. "I'm excited to see the show. I love the new CD."

"God, so do I. I know I'm partial," she says, smiling, "but I think it's their best album yet. Are you looking for Rochelle?"

"Yes, I'm late. Have you seen her?"

"I think she's with the guys. I'm not sure if we should disturb the preshow routine, but we can get a drink at the bar and wait for her, if you like."

"Sounds good."

"How's business?" she asks, weaving through the crowd.

"Busy. I've been working on a job in Malibu that has me pulling my hair out some days, but it's finally coming together beautifully. How about you?"

We reach the table set up outside their dressing room. It has bottles of liquor and mixers, cups, and ice. We start making our drinks as we continue to chat. "I flew to New York and Chicago recently. I'm supposed to head to Miami next week." She stops pouring the vodka and looks up at me, and whispers, "Dalton is not happy about it."

"Dalton?"

"Johnny. I call him Dalton." She carries on making her vodka tonic. "My marketing director is pushing another campaign. More photo shoots and models. I'm not sure, but I'm testing the waters by exploring more of the ideas and locations."

"Sounds exciting."

She shrugs. "Sometimes. I'm not convinced I need to be in the ads to sell Limelight products."

"You're beautiful, so I see why they'd want you."

I'm sure it's something she hears often, but she smiles genuinely. "Thanks. Guess we'll see." She laughs, looking down, and then sips her drink.

Tommy opens the dressing room door and looks out. When he sees Holli, he nods toward the door. "C'mon in."

Holli touches my hand, and says, "Let's go in for a minute. I want to talk to Dalton real quick."

I follow her inside and watch as she heads straight into his arms. The way he looks at her is the same look I dream about, hoping one day a man looks at me like that. It makes my heart ache with envy. *Did Mark ever look at me like that?* I fell for his attention because he was so different from anyone I had previously dated. What I realize now is he didn't want *me*, he wanted to own me. I still have no idea why he chose me. I learned a hard lesson though: desire to me was power to him.

Johnny kisses her as she wraps her arms around his neck, then she whispers into his ear. I turn away, feeling like I'm intruding on their intimacy.

I'm grabbed from behind and turned quickly, flinching in the process. Rochelle is all smiles to my startled expression. "You're here," she says, fortunately not noticing. "You're late, but I'm glad you came."

"Me too. It wasn't easy, but we can talk about it later. I just want to enjoy the show."

She nods, understanding my need to keep the heavy at bay. She starts to tug me toward the door, when Dex stands with his sticks in hand, he says, "Good to see you, Lara."

"You too. I'm excited to see the show."

"Thanks." He maneuvers next to Rochelle, and whispers, "Stay close to Lara and Holli."

"I will," she says. Warmth softens her expression as she looks into his eyes. "Break a leg."

Rochelle opens the door and turns back. "Let's wait for Holli."

I lean against the wall by the door, taking in my surroundings and this unprecedented opportunity I've been given. This band is a legend in their own time. Through hits and tragedy they have fallen and risen to the top again. Biographies have been written about them, and a movie has been made. They are the reigning kings of rock 'n' roll and I'm standing in the same room as them as if I belong.

Kaz comes out from a back room. When he sees me, he doesn't smile but I see something in his expression that draws out mine. "Hey," he says, adding in a singular tilt of his head.

"Hey," I reply quietly.

He walks over and everything goes quiet in my world. Or that's just my world grinding to a silent stop. My heart is racing watching his body move like he knows how to use it. He's a beautiful man, the word handsome insufficient to describe his dark features: hair like midnight at the beach, eyes like caramel candies melting from the heat of the sun, and skin tinted by the southern California weather. Then the door next to me opens and he says, "See you after," as he passes.

I want to die. Die of embarrassment. I mentally facepalm that he just caught me daydreaming about him while staring at him.

"Yeah, okay," is all I manage to squeak out before Derrick passes, then Dex and Johnny. Tommy follows them and I'm left with Holli and Rochelle, both of whom are shaking their heads at me, and then start laughing.

I'm so busted.

Holli heads for the door, and states, "He is really cute."

I roll my eyes, my face heating from humiliation. Rochelle adds, "Super cute." She wraps her arm around mine and turns me so we walk out together. "Don't worry. I don't think he caught the sexual fantasy playing out all over your face when he walked by."

"Ugh. Was it that obvious?"

She answers with a laugh.

"Just kill me now."

Tapping my drink, she says, "Drink up, Buttercup. You need it."

"And about five more to erase this embarrassment." *And the situation with Mark earlier tonight.* I rub my wrists and look down, making sure the leather bands hide the redness. It should be gone by tomorrow. Hopefully. Now, I just need to settle my nerves.

"Ah, good ole alcohol. The great eraser. I've used it before, but it only relieves temporarily. Trust me on that." Her arm drops and she hurries to catch up with Holli. Looking back over her shoulder, she says, "C'mon. I don't want to miss Dex's opening. It's my favorite part."

I have to get over what just happened and decide to laugh it off. What does it matter? Millions of women have fantasies about him. I'm sure Kaz Fabian is used to it. One more won't make a difference to him. I join the girls and we go down the stairs and around a gathered group of men in suits. After bypassing them, we cross through a red velvet curtain and out a door. A large bodyguard takes to Holli's side and leads us to a section in the front. The lights go down and the crowd goes quiet.

Rochelle grabs my hand and squeezes. I can tell she's nervous. When I look over, she's biting her bottom lip and staring at the stage. The first hit on the drum kit gets my attention and I search the darkness on stage until a spotlight hits Dex, who is pounding his intro solo to his own beat. Rochelle screams and so do I; the beat is contagious. The excitement is invigorating.

As soon as Johnny starts singing, a spotlight hits him and the crowd goes wild. The lights flicker to the chorus and the stage lights up revealing Kaz and Derrick flanking Johnny.

Kaz is on the opposite side from us, too far for my liking, but I enjoy the song and move to the beat anyway. Drinks are delivered to us three songs in and the girls and I toast to the night. I'm swaying my hips and closing my eyes, letting the rhythm dictate my moves. Rochelle hip bumps me to get my attention. "Look up."

When I do, Kaz and Derrick have switched sides. He has his eyes focused on the guitar as he plays but then glances in our direction. When his eyes meet mine, he smirks with a little head nod before leaning back and getting back into the music. The muscles in his arms are buff and the veins strain from the intensity as he strums. He's passionate about playing which is incredibly sexy and intoxicating, making me want to discover what else he's passionate about.

During the next song, Derrick and Kaz swap sides again and my view is partially blocked by Johnny. Not that it's not a great view, but he's taken. Another forty-five minutes pass and I continue to watch Kaz, captivated by the way he moves his fingers over the strings and holds the guitar pressed against his body. He's sweaty and sexy and—

"Let's get another round before the encore," Holli says, taking our hands.

Probably best. I'm getting too hot anyway.

Rochelle and I follow her backstage to the bar set up on the table outside their dressing room. She pours a large glass of water just as the guys, surrounded by bodyguards, start walking toward us. She hands Johnny the water and he takes her by the hand with him into the room. Rochelle makes a drink for herself and I refill my glass, giving the band their space. Just as I look up, Kaz winks at me and follows the other guys into the room.

Rochelle leans against the wall and says, "Sometimes I like to stay out here."

She gets reflective, her thoughts changing her expression. While she looks down at the floor, I start to wonder so many things about when she's back in this environment and if she's okay or not. I worry about her, but do I need to? "Do you still think of Cory?"

Her reaction is a smile and bright eyes. "All the time. He was such a great songwriter and guitarist. It's hard not to think of him when they play one of his songs." She pushes off the wall. "But the band has lived on long after he did." After taking a sip of her drink, she adds, "Dex has really helped me." Her smile grows and she blushes. "There's just something about that bad-boy drummer..."

Kaz and Derrick replaced Cory, who was one of the founding band members. I just thought it would always be Cory and Rochelle and their sons. But things change, things outside of our control. I've thought a lot about them over the last month. Knowing I couldn't waste my life being unhappy, I knew I had to breakup with Mark. We're not in so deep that we can't crawl back out with only minor damage. I believe in love, which means I'm open to finding the real thing. My heart and head know it's not going to be found with Mark.

I take a long gulp, the stress of a "talk" with Mark still weighing me down. Turning to Rochelle for support, I whisper, "I did it."

"Did what?" she asks.

"I broke up with Mark."

Her eyebrows go up and her eyes go wide in shock. "You did it? Like finality, *finito* did it?"

"This morning and then again tonight. That's why I was late. I went to get some clothes and he was there." I look away. "I thought he'd be at practice, but he was there as if nothing had changed, demanding I go out with him."

"Oh honey, are you okay?" She moves over to the side of the table where I'm standing and sets her drink down to hug me.

"It was a long time coming, but doing it was hard." A memory from earlier still haunting me—*my wrist is grabbed, the tips of his fingers like spears to my skin as he digs in.*

"I'm sure it wasn't easy, but you're so much better off. I didn't want to say anything, but I saw an Instagram photo of him and some woman the other night. If I was with him, that would have been it for me."

"He tried to explain that photo, but she was on his lap and her hand was touching his inner thigh, so yeah, I didn't believe him. We had a huge fight over it. That's why I don't know why he's fighting so hard to stay together."

"What do you mean? He wants to keep dating?"

"Yeah. He wants to talk again. Tomorrow. He didn't seem right tonight. It was odd."

She looks surprised. "No, that's not a good idea. You broke up. It's done."

"It's not that easy, Ro. He has some of my things and I want us to end this amicably."

"How will it end amicably if he doesn't want to breakup?"

The door opens near us and Tommy walks out. The bodyguards come over and the band walks back toward the stage. Holli follows them out, but stops to make a cocktail. "You girls ready?"

"Yep," I reply.

She waggles her eyebrows once and says, "This should be good. Dalton's all fired up."

Rochelle laughs. "You always have a way with him." She dashes off suddenly and slaps Dex's ass as she passes. Holli and I trail behind laughing.

HOLLI AND JOHNNY rarely come to the after parties from what I hear and Dex and Rochelle do some of the time. Tonight Rochelle said she wants to party, so she grabs me, and Dex is right there with her. He's got it so bad for her. He has for a while, but it's new for them. It will be interesting to watch how they maneuver through their relationship. I'm in a Suburban with them, Derrick, Tommy, and Kaz. Kaz is sitting in the front and I'm sitting next to Rochelle who is whispering to Dex. His hand is rubbing her shoulder as he listens intently. Tommy and Derrick are in the third row discussing some ancient artifacts exhibit in Washington, D.C. that they want to see when they fly out there for the tour.

It's weird being in a situation like this, knowing I'm fresh from a breakup. I'm left feeling caught between being a fifth or sixth wheel and awkwardly wondering what I should be doing or if I should just be sitting here quietly. From my position I have a full view of Kaz. He's showered and changed. His hair is still damp and I don't know if he washed it or it's from sweat but I'm intrigued enough to want to find out. Guilt overrides the fun. Mark has a way of inserting himself in all aspects of my life, even when he doesn't have the right any longer.

When Kaz turns, he catches me watching him, so I turn to look out the window instead. The lights outside are suddenly the most fascinating things in the world. I shouldn't be thinking about him the way I do... the way I have for a while now, if I'm honest with myself. Nobody wants to be a *rebound*. *Is that what Kaz will be?* I haven't had sex in so long that he just might be a bound at this point.

It's amazing to think I even have the option. I glance back at him. Our eyes meet and he stretches his arm and rubs the back of my jeans-covered calf. "I'm glad you came."

My whole body warms from his touch. "Me too."

He turns back and I sit there melting in all the swoons for the rest of the ride. I had no idea he'd even noticed me before the other day or even in the last year. Sure, we've been around each other more than a few times, but the only time we talked was during group settings, parties and such, or backstage with other stuff going on. Except this one party Rochelle took me out at Carillo Beach, the night before I met Mark...

Everyone was dancing on the beach, drinking, roasting marshmallows. A few were even skinny-dipping. If the rest of LA only knew how many celebrities were out here right now, this state beach would be overrun with groupies. Tonight, the band, the actors, and the models, they were just people out for a bonfire with their friends.

Rochelle went back to the house to get another round of drinks for us. I remained outside because the music was too loud in the house to enjoy any kind of real conversation, and I liked the sound of the ocean. The group thinned when Derrick went looking for weed and the Brazilian model hanging on his arm accompanied him. Kaz stayed.

He always seemed preoccupied with others when I was around or with the band. I've seen women flirt with him. I've seen him flirt in return, but when I really think about those times, they were more on the courteous side than returning their interest.

That night it got chilly as soon as the sun set, and I shivered. He moved closer and set his beer down in the sand. Taking his leather jacket off, he wrapped it around my shoulders. Surprised by his gesture, I said, "You'll get cold."

Kaz shoved his hands in his pockets. "I'll be okay."

"Thank you." I set my Solo cup down and slipped my arms into the sleeves. The worn leather smelled like warmth if warm had a scent—comfort and musky, cognac, and sunsets. I then looked at Kaz differently. I watched as he stared into the fire, the flames' reflection flickering in his irises.

He glanced my way and a small smile made its way across his mouth. I'm sure he's used to people staring at him because of his fame and because he's gorgeous. I looked away after holding the connection a few seconds. I didn't know what to say, the loss of words coming with a loss of breath from his nearness.

"This is the first time we've had a chance to talk," he starts. After pausing, he turns back to the fire. "So you're a deco—"

"Dude! Kaz, c'mere!" is shouted from a group nearby. Derrick. "Kaaaazzzzz! Get the fuck over here."

Kaz stares into my eyes. "I'm sorry."

"It's okay."

He nods, appearing as disappointed as I feel. I start to take the jacket off, but he moves in front of me, fists the front and tightens it closed again. "It looks good on you. You should hold on to it. You can return it next week after the show."

"I'll be there." I still don't know how I was able to speak with him so close, his warmth filling my lungs.

Rochelle returns laughing and handing me a drink. "God, the line was insane." She begins telling me a story about some guy hitting on her and Dex almost getting in a fight, but I don't hear it. I just watch Kaz walk away. He turns back once with a sexy smirk and then joins the guys in the band.

I never made that concert. Mark had a game and he wanted me to be there to watch him play. Rochelle returned the jacket for me.

This is our second chance. Remembering that time at the beach and how he's looking at me now, it's not the same as he looked at the women frequenting the parties or the after-parties. There's more in his smile for me. The tilt of the right side of his lips is more suggestive. There's more emotion behind his brown eyes. There's more in the way he touches me, as if *he* might be the one to get burned.

Inside the bar, the lights are so dim that it's hard to see beyond the table we're sitting around. We have a corner to ourselves and the table seats at least twelve. Other celebrities have stopped by to talk to the guys and tell them how great the concert was. Women have tried to talk their way into the VIP area and failed, so they linger near the bouncer, hoping they get spotted and invited in. I don't blame them. All the guys are good-looking and they're rock stars, so what's not to be attracted to? I feel fortunate to have inside connections to get to hang with them, and really lucky I get to hang out with my friends. Speaking of, I elbow Rochelle. "Hey, talk to me."

"Sorry." She laughs.

I look at my glass that's empty. "I need another drink. Wanna come with me?"

"I'll come with you." We both look across the table following the offer to find Kaz smiling. He holds his glass up and adds, "I need another and the waitress hasn't restocked the bottles yet."

Rochelle practically pushes me out of my seat. "Yeah, go. And order me a white wine while you're at it."

Kaz stands and offers me his hand, helping me up. He holds my hand high in the air as we move over everyone's heads until we're standing together at the end of the table. "What are you drinking?" he asks.

"A greyhound with a dash of orange juice and a twist of lime."

"Sounds complicated." We reach the edge of the bar and he leans on it, looking right at me. "Are you complicated, Lara?"

I answer honestly. "I'm not sure anymore."

That makes him chuckle. "Okay."

I lean on the bar next to him and ask, "What about you?"

"I try not to be, but shit happens."

Nodding, I agree. "Yep, it sure does." We place our orders. "I heard you bought a home."

"I think everyone has heard that. For some reason the press finds every move I make very interesting."

"Well," I start, but suddenly feel awkward, and I never feel awkward talking about my business. I'm successful because I have a great eye for making generic spaces unique and comforting, modern and homey. *So why am I now hesitant, almost shy?*

"You decorate houses, right?"

Feeling relieved by his lead in question, I reply, "Yes. And other spaces, some offices, but mainly homes."

"I could use your help. Do you have time in your schedule to look at it?"

"I'd love to."

"I have no idea what I'm doing and I don't want to just throw inflatable mattresses everywhere."

Laughing, I tease, "Yeah, don't do that. Anyway, they're bad for your back. Just let me know what your schedule looks like and we'll set up a date... I mean, time."

I'm not sure if he caught my flub, but if he did, he lets it slide. "The owners are getting the rest of their stuff out today. I have a show in Indiana on Sunday and then we're back. How does Tuesday night look for you?"

"I usually don't work nights, but I know you're busy, so I'll make an exception."

The drinks are set before us and he tells the bartender to add it to the tab. Turning back to me, he clinks his glass against mine. "Sometimes the exceptions are what the journey is all about."

I swear my heart flutters from his words, or maybe it's just his proximity to me thinking he might make an exception for me too. "Are we still talking about decorating appointments?" I ask coyly, my cheeks flaming hot.

Full of confidence, he leans down until he's eye level with me. "Not at all."

And just like that, I have a date... I mean a *meeting* with Kaz Fabian.

5

LARA

"COME SIT BY ME," Kaz says. "We won't have to yell to talk."

My cheeks heat again and I'm starting to think this might be how it always is when I'm around him. I should use less blush, if this is the case. I'm also not sure why I'm so goofy over this guy. I mean, sure, he's hot with his longish hair and soulful eyes that seem to be from another time. His body is rock hard, and he's a musician, which speaks my body's language, seeping under my skin. But it's the way he looks at me. His eyes speak to me without him saying one single word.

I'm breathless as I slip into the seat next to him. My heart pulsing in time with the music, my thoughts releasing the guilt I was carrying earlier. I'm free. Free to do whatever I want, and right now, that's Kaz. Leaning in so close his lips touch the shell of my ear, he whispers, "I hear you have a boyfriend."

Not really a question, so I let it lie there between us long enough to take a sip. I know he's recently single, but I don't know the details of the breakup. Kaz's phone lights up on the table in front of him, but he ignores it. "You can answer it if you need to," I say.

He doesn't look at the screen to see who's calling before replying, "It's not important."

"You didn't even look."

When his eyes hit mine, they penetrate deeper than the surface of the conversation we're having. "Nothing's more important than living in the moment. And this moment is worth being present."

His words momentarily stun me, then I ask, "You sure you're only twenty-six?"

With a laugh under his breath, he looks around again. "I'm pretty sure and I like that you know my age." Leaning closer, he adds, "As for me *only* being twenty-six, I've lived a lifetime or two in those years."

"I don't know much about you," I say, pushing my fingers through my hair and hoping I don't come off like a groupie. But the way he listens to me puts me at ease. "I've learned a few details over the last year from being around you, but I'd like to know more."

His smile falters as he sits back. "I'd rather hear about you."

"Nice role reversal. Are you shy?"

A wry grin pops into place. "Do I seem shy to you?"

I shake my head. "Why are you so mysterious?"

"Am I?" His brow furrows. "I find it hard to be mysterious in LA or when you're in a band as big as *The Resistance*. My face is in the tabloids. Paparazzi seem to be everywhere. And my private life has been used for entertainment purposes by the media. So mysterious isn't really a word that comes to mind when thinking about my life." Resting his arms on the table, he adds, "But I have a few skeletons I'd like to keep in the closet. Now you on the other hand…"

Looking down, I turn the glass in my hand. "There's nothing special going on here."

"You don't see what I see." My gaze darts up, and I see his eyes set on mine. "Tell me about your relationship with the baseball player."

"Why do you want to know about that?"

"I like to know about my competition. It's easier to assess the opportunities."

Competition? Opportunity? Is he really interested in me? I laugh, liking his attention. "I've been warned about boys like you."

He leans in really close, so close that the scruff blanketing his jaw tickles the skin behind my ear when he whispers, "I'm no boy, babe." His words are drawn out and husky, his dulcet tone making me tingle all over.

When I turn, our lips are so close to touching that I start to move, but his hand captures the back of my head, and he asks, "Want to get out of here?"

I suck in an uneven breath, but manage to nod without fainting from swooning. Quick to his feet, he takes my hand, taking me to my feet with him. Rochelle looks between us. "Leaving?"

"We're gonna go."

She smiles and sits back. I trust Kaz, but I know Rochelle, and if she approves, it's okay to go with him.

As we work our way toward the exit, Kaz looks back at me as if making sure I'm still there. He flashes a smile that is somewhere between pure sex and the sincerest of grins. I have no idea how he does that, but it must get him laid a lot. I'm not sure which one I prefer, but I really like the way his hand wraps around mine—gentle and secure, possessive and with purpose. With the smile and that hand holding together, I'd follow him anywhere he wants to go. How is that even possible? I'm not frivolous with my emotions, but here I am, eager to follow.

I tried carefree with Mark. That didn't turn out well for either of us. Nothing about the way Kaz touches, speaks, or looks at me feels careless. It's all ground, just like Kaz, with meaning, a depth that goes beyond good looks and talent. I'd venture to say by how our skin feels pressed together that it's heart deep.

I hold on to him even tighter, knowing I have started to slip, maybe even begun to fall for him.

Out front, we get a cab, leaving the Suburban for the rest of the band to have when they're ready to leave. We slide in and he looks at me. "Your place?"

I tell the driver my address and lean back. Kaz puts his arm around me and we ride in silence. I have so many thoughts rushing through my head, so many feelings running through my chest. I'm free, I remind myself. Free to do as I please, *like Mark has done when he wasn't free.*

Kaz traces figure eights up my thigh, building the anticipation of what's to come. Hopefully that will be me. My breathing deepens. It feels good to be touched—*desired*—the sensations sparking every nerve to life. This cab ride has got to be the longest fifteen minutes of my life.

After hitting what seems like every red light between the club and my place, we finally arrive. I practically trip out of the car to get him inside.

Kaz gives the driver a wad of bills and tells him to keep the change and we hurry to the door. He grabs me by the hand and spins me around until I'm pressed against him. His lips meet mine, his other hand rubbing my cheek gently. We're out of breath when our lips part, our eyes bright from excitement. He says, "You never answered my question."

"About?"

"The boyfriend."

"We're not togethe—"

My words are cut off by caressing lips and a tempting tongue. My back falls against the wood of the door, and the shattering of glass fills my ears.

We jump apart and look down. "Shit," he says. "Sorry about that. I'll clean it up."

I'm still confused to what it is until I see a note amongst the red roses. "What is it?"

"A vase of flowers. My bad. I didn't see them."

"Me either." I reach for the note and Kaz guides me over the broken glass. All I need to see is the one name for me to want to avoid this altogether—Mark. I drop the note back down and unlock the door. "Let's get inside."

As soon as we step inside, my purse is dropped and I'm grabbed, then pinned to the wall before the door even shuts. His mouth is on mine. He tastes of whiskey and the faintest of mint, and I can't get enough. My nails run gently through his hair as his hands lift me up. I wrap my legs around his middle and kiss him hard while holding on to him tightly. I come up for air and open my eyes. Looking at him, I feel reckless, wild and crazy, *free*. There's that word again and it feels so good. "The bedroom," I mumble. "Down the hall."

Kaz turns quickly, holding me to him, but I straighten my legs and he sets me down. I turn and this time I lead him, taking his hand, and walk to the bedroom. He grabs me right before I enter the room and spins me around. With my back to the doorframe and my breath coming out harshly, I look up at him wondering why he stopped us. "Hey," he says, searching my eyes. "You sure? Once we go in there—"

I don't need to think twice, I'm sure. "Yes. Are you?"

"More than sure."

He picks me up and I scream as he tosses me over his shoulder. He's about to toss me onto the bed, but he stops and holds me there. I'm squirming and squealing, but then I stop and hang upside down laughing. "Are you going to put me down?"

His hand runs over my ass. "I'm liking the view from this angle."

I slap his ass as hard as I can. "Wait until you see it naked—"

I'm tossed to the mattress in one quick motion and he falls with me, landing over me, and looking down. "I don't think I can wait much longer."

The lamp on the nightstand is on, and something about what I'm sharing with Kaz makes me want to leave it on, to see everything, to watch him as he fucks me. With my eyes locked on his, I whisper, "Then don't."

He falls to the side. In a frenzy of flying clothes, we undress ourselves. Within seconds we're naked and back in our original position. Our breathing is fast, our hearts beating harder, and our desire mutual by the way his expression is reflecting how I feel. "Scoot up," he says. His voice is huskier than before, lust occupying some of the deeper notes.

I move until my head is on the pillow and knees bent with my feet on the mattress. He comes closer, tapping his fingers on the underside of my thigh. "Do you have condoms?"

"Yes. Nightstand."

He reaches over and pulls a few foil packets out and rips one off. I watch as he rolls it down his cock—smooth and long, thick, and if I wasn't so turned on, I might be worried by the size. He continues to fit the stereotype of rock stars quite well. My bottom lip is pressed between my teeth as I gaze down. He peeks up and smirks. "You ready for me?"

The question seems more loaded than the simplicity of the physical connection and I start to wonder if an emotional connection is possible between two people who share an intense attraction. Mark wounded more than my pride. He made me doubt if a deeper bond between two people is even possible.

Kaz moves to his knees and touches my chin. "Hey, you here with me?"

I push all else aside and focus on the feeling tightening in my belly when I look at him. "I'm here with you." And I am. I feel wanted. Desired. *His.* And I realize I need this. I need this attention, even if it's only for one night.

His hands spread my legs apart enough for him to settle between them. His tongue runs over his bottom lip as he looks at my breasts. He kisses each and then reaches up for my mouth and kisses the corners. His breath is hot, his body heated like mine. We're infernos. Our bodies become combustible together as the sparks fly between us. We tried for gentle, but quickly work our way into shameless and wanton. I move beneath him, my body reaching its own desired accord. I want to feel him, all of him. I want his cock pressed between my legs, deep inside. I want to come and then I want him to fuck me until I come again. *God, what is this man doing to me?*

Kaz Fabian makes shameless feel refined. His body presses between my legs as calloused fingertips slide down the curve of my breast, dipping in at my waistline and out over my hips. Pulling back, he looks down between us. "You're so fucking sexy."

Two fingers slide into my most intimate of places, making me want him even more. Heaving beneath him, I plead, "Kaz, don't tease."

"I'm not teasing. I'm appreciating."

As if all the other stuff wasn't enough, for that alone I'd kiss him again, and I do. His fingers rub and splay until I'm weak to him. I'm so close. His touch... the intensity in his expression... It's all for me. *For my pleasure.* My body starts throbbing inside, my mouth falling open, and a moan escapes as long-sought-after waves rolls through me. "Oh God."

I want to thank him, thank him for putting me first and making me feel so much that I've become grateful for an orgasm like it's a present from the gods. Instead, I try to show him how appreciative I am. I push lightly on his chest until he rolls to his back, and I say, "I want on top."

"You can have me however you want me, babe."

I straddle and position him, his cock so hard just for me. My tongue rolls over my bottom lip before leaning down and sliding it over his. He cups my breasts, kneading them while admiring them. This is it. There's no going back and I don't want to. I'm feeling something real for the first time in forever and I need more. Sliding down his length, I go slow, enjoying the fullness as he fills and stretches me, making me realize how empty I've been until now. His eyes close and he mutters, "You feel amazing." *And so does he. So amazing.*

Rocking back and forth a few times, I start slow, not wanting my body to tear like my soul has been torn. We start moving together, his hands sliding down my back and grabbing hold of my hips. My head drops back as our passion picks up. A moan and then another escapes as each breath is thrust out. I move my hips while holding his thighs. "You feel so good," I say between jagged breaths. He starts to move faster and I drop my hands forward on his chest, using his body as leverage as I join his rhythm, rocking hard on top of him. My eyes meet his and this time with my hair hanging all around me, the tips touching his chest, I smile. "You really do feel amazing, Kaz."

He bites his bottom lip and sits up quickly, his hands going around to my back. "C'mere," he says, and my lips meet his. Our tongues entwine as our bodies gyrate together.

Rolling us over, he licks my neck before sucking. I don't think there will be a mark, but I start wishing there was so I'd have something tangible tomorrow to hold on to. I moan loudly as he thrusts harder and harder. "Fuck!" he exclaims loud enough for me to know he's close.

I start moving, exhilaration blooming throughout my body. Holding on to his strong arms, I open my eyes and see the beauty in the pleasurable pain he's experiencing. I'm right there.

Right. There. With. Him.

He drops down on top of me and bites my shoulder, this time leaving a mark as he comes. It hurts too good to stop him and it'll be something I'll savor in the daylight, a memory that remains from tonight.

IT'S JUST PAST four in the morning. Kaz fell asleep less than an hour ago, but he's already sleeping soundly, his breaths regulated and deep, his face handsome and at peace with the world. My heart feels full as much as my body feels worn out in the *best* of ways.

I'm not experienced in one-night stands. The only other one I've done ended up in a long-term relationship I ended yesterday. So I need to contain the emotions that blanket my heart in something that feels like more than a friendly fast fuck.

I don't even know what he thinks of me, especially now after I slept with him so quickly. Am I now categorized as an easy fuck or a groupie? Mark thought I was easy when I had been sincere in my interest in the beginning.

Strings weren't discussed but it was clear neither of us wanted any attachment. But talking about it and preventing it are two different things when the heart is involved. I'm sure I'm another number on his bedpost, but tonight I'll snuggle into his side and enjoy the time we do have together.

Tomorrow I won't pressure him or make it awkward. I'll let him figure out what he wants and I'll move on either way. *Even though it was so good. Even though he said I felt amazing.*

I've been on my own since I was eighteen. I created a life that most would call lavish. I call it earned. I break hearts before they break mine. So I'll lie here against the warmth of his body and enjoy this night whether it leads to more or leads to another lesson learned.

6

LARA

THE SUNLIGHT MAKES its way across the room until it hits my face, then stops and decides to stay there until I can't deny it's morning. The inside of my eyelids are red from the brightness and I silently grumble. When I reluctantly open them, I look down and see two well-defined arms cocooning me. The heat from Kaz's body warms my backside, and his large endowment is pressed against my ass. This is more than spooning. He's holding me like he never wants to let me go. I relish the comfort.

"Let's stay in bed all day." His voice is deep, rough from sleep, his hold tightening even more. He drags the bridge of his nose along my neck, then kisses me. "You smell good."

"I probably smell like sweat from the concert, beer, and sex."

With a soft chuckle against my neck, he says, "Like I said, you smell good."

I laugh softly, closing my eyes again and enjoying his arms around me. I wake up two hours later. I open my eyes and see him beside me. The blinds are closed this time, I assume by Kaz, and he's asleep next to me. I watch how he sleeps, how he breathes, each breath powerful in the rise of his chest. I wonder if he always sleeps this well or if last night wore him out because of the show. Performing like they do must be exhausting.

He stirs, rolling toward me, and slowly opens his eyes. "Good morning."

"Good afternoon," I whisper.

"I'm working on evening with you."

I giggle and reach over to stroke his cheek, dragging my nails lightly down his neck. I like the feel of his scruff. Mark is always super clean-shaven. I shouldn't compare, but I always was a little weak to a bad boy. I smile, thinking about how special he's made me feel. Kaz may not be that bad of a boy. He matches the image, but has a heart of gold. If I'm not careful like Rochelle keeps warning, I just might fall a little in love with the man. It would be so easy to do. "Any plans today?" I ask to distract myself before my heartfelt thoughts get away from me.

Taking my hand in his, he kisses my fingers one by one, and replies, "I have lots of plans. All of them include you, this bed, maybe a little nourishment, this bed, and you."

"Do you treat all your one-nighters this well?" I look down, his attention making me blush.

His fingers gently pinch my chin and he lifts it until my gaze meets his. "Is that what you think?"

"I don't know what to think."

His hand dips under the covers and finds my hip. "Look, Lara, I know you had a boyfriend. I've asked around. We've been flirting and whatever, but I knew you were in a relationship. Last night you said you weren't taken, and I'd apologize for taking advantage of a recent breakup, but I'm not sorry. With that said, I've still been expecting your boyfriend to barge in here all night long and well into this morning. It's the afternoon and he isn't around, you're not calling him, and I'm still naked in bed with you. I'm not sure what's going on and I'm not that eager to leave, but if you want me to, I will, but know it's because you asked me, not because I want to."

"Why are you so nice? Don't you have a rep to uphold?"

He shakes his head. "No, no rep. Just me. You get what you see."

"I like what I see."

"I like you more and have for a while."

Annnnd I die a slow swooning death. His honesty affects me. How does he confess his true feelings so easily? "I don't know what to say to that."

He turns onto his stomach and buries his face into the pillow. When he peeks over at me, he says, "You don't have to say anything." *God, the man is cute.*

"I told you last night that I don't have a boyfriend. We broke up."

"I heard otherwise, so I wasn't sure."

"If you weren't sure, why'd you sleep with me?"

"Like I said, I've liked you for a while." He sits up and leans forward. With his eyes on me, he runs his fingers over the open palm of my hand.

His touch sends shivers through my body. The attraction is more than skin deep and I'm starting to want to see that cute little dent in his chin more often. I sit up and lean against the headboard, taking my hand away from his.

"What's wrong?" he asks. "Did I upset you? I don't like to lie, but maybe I said too much."

"You didn't. What you said was... I liked it, Kaz."

"Then what's wrong?"

"You're dangerous to my heart."

"I don't want to hurt your heart and I won't hurt you."

"I know. That's what makes you so dangerous."

His tongue dips out and slowly slides over his lower lip before he bites that same lip and looks away. He repeats what I said earlier, "Now *I* don't know what to say."

"Don't say anything at all," I say trying to recapture the ease of a few minutes earlier. "Just kiss me."

A smile runs across his face as he turns and takes me in his arms. "My pleasure." He makes love to me again and then I bring him to his knees with some of my own tender loving care before we fall back asleep.

The best conversations happen on lazy days.

There's a spark in his eye, a fire from within that drives his soul. I could listen to him talk all day and night. Every once in a while I hear a slight twist on a word, an accent that doesn't seem to fit. But he's entirely too captivating to stop to ask. "You probably understand the high you get when something you created from your thoughts, your time, you own abilities comes together."

Bringing my knees up, I snuggle into the covers a little more while facing him in bed. "I didn't know you were a songwriter."

"I'm a musician who likes to create."

"I call it blood love. You do something you love so much that you bleed your passion to life."

"Very visual," he jokes. "But true. I bleed for music. I do every time I perform." *That's exactly what I saw when he played last night.*

"It shows. You're amazing to watch."

"So are you," he says, dragging his hand over my shoulder. I love the way it feels, like he can't keep his hands off me. It's as if he has to find ways to touch me.

"You never told me what you did before you joined the band."

"You never asked."

"I asked you to tell me about you."

He rubs his eyes as if the topic is either boring or annoying. I can't tell.

"My life before *The Resistance* was a life not worth living nor mentioning." Rolling onto his back he takes some of the covers with him so I cuddle against him and rest my head on his chest. "I was living in an excuse. Saying and doing anything to avoid the expectations placed on me."

"I think most of us spend our teen years rebelling. What were you rebelling against?"

"My parents."

"Did they want you to become a doctor or a lawyer or something?" I laugh.

"No, worse—a professional musician." He smiles this grin that borders on cocky, but fully embraces sexy.

"You suck at rebelling, you know that?"

"Ha!"

"So you failed." It's fun to tease one of the most famous musicians in the world.

He sighs heavily as if there's more to the story. "If you only knew." He looks at me again and says, "Lie with me. I leave tomorrow and want to remember this."

I nod, letting the topic of his past go... for now, but hoping I get another chance to ask him about it later. I snuggle with him, wanting to remember this too.

I SHUT THE door and lock it behind me, smiling as I walk into the kitchen for another cup of coffee. Kaz and I had our first cup this morning and now after having a too-long-to-be-appropriate goodbye to him, I'm left lingering in my kitchen not sure what to do. He's only been here once, but his presence has taken over the whole space. And I like it. I like him.

Damn him and his enticing ways.

My phone rings. *Kaz.* "Hello," I answer aloud while swooning inside.

"I was thinking we should do it again." His voice is free-spirited and I'm reminded of his sexy smile.

"I'm up for *it* again."

His chuckles fill my ear. "Yes, that too, but I meant I want to see you again."

"I thought we were, on Tuesday?"

"Oh, yes. I'd almost forgotten the business at hand, too side-tracked by the business of you."

"I hope I'm not too distracting." He's too much fun to flirt with. "I could send my assistant over instead?"

"No. You're just the kind of distraction I've been looking for."

"Are distractions really a good thing?" I ask, smiling.

"In your case, most definitely."

"You can be very charming, you know that, Mr. Fabian?"

"I do, Ms. Kessler."

"And so humble," I tease. "It's a good combination."

His laugh initiates my own. "I should go before we end up taking this conversation a whole other route and the driver overhears what I plan to do to you next time.."

"Yes, I wouldn't want that." Oh my God, so much. I want to know what he wants to do to me so much. I'm looking forward to seeing you on Tuesday. Drive safe and talk soon. Bye, Kaz."

"Goodbye, Lara."

He's cute all right... yep, dangerously so.

***

LATER THAT EVENING, I sink into a tub full of hot water and bubbles. I sip my wine and lie back. Closing my eyes, my head fills with naughty thoughts of the rock star too delicious to not think about.

The serenity in my bathroom is ruined when my phone rings. When I see the screen and Mark's name, I try to hide my cringe. I hadn't really thought of him in the last twenty-four hours, which seems like a lifetime considering he used to try to control every minute of my day. He's trained me well and I push the answer button before I have time to think twice. *Shit.* "Hello?"

"Lara, where are you?" he asks.

"At home."

"You're coming over, right?"

"Why would I come over?"

"You didn't call me yesterday. I left messages. You promised we'd talk."

"Oh. Um. I'm sorry. I had my phone off so I could sleep. I guess I forgot to turn it back on." More like I was too caught up in bed to even think about my phone.

"Practice sucked. I want you to come over."

I let out a heavy breath. "I'm sorry."

"You're sorry? That's it?" he asks, his voice wavering between aggravation and hurt. "You're not coming?"

"I just want to take a bath, go to bed early, and read tonight. I have a busy Monday."

"You were never here for me when I needed you."

"I was there for you every night, even when you weren't. This weekend was the first time in a long time I was home for me."

"You must be starting your period. You're acting bitchy."

"I am not. You're just being an asshole." I hang up the phone, fuming from his remarks.

I finish my wine, then dry off, and trek into the kitchen for more. There isn't a bottle big enough to tamper my hot-temper tonight. Working my way back to the bathroom, my anger hasn't ceased, but increased. Mark better be damn glad he hasn't called back.

I have absolutely no doubt that I made the right decision in ending us. This is the ugly side of relationships, the ones that don't work out. I slip back into the hot, sudsy water, lean back, and close my eyes again. My exceptional time with Kaz is at the forefront of my thoughts, taking over completely.

When the water cools, I get out, and dry off again. After pulling on some cotton underwear and a tank top, I crawl under the bed covers. I can smell Kaz's cologne and take a deep breath, inhaling his scent from the pillow, and then smile. Giddy from the thrill of this new relationship and excited to see where it leads, I lie there with a smirky grin on my face and anticipate *our* next time.

My phone rings again. *Mark*. Nope. Sending to voicemail. I refuse to let him ruin my good mood. It's sad to see what had so much potential early on deteriorate so quickly, but it's obvious we were never meant to be.

We used to be fun... Mark Renner was coming off a winning season, voted MVP for his team, and had just been re-signed with a big pay raise. We met at a party in The Hills. The attraction was instant and mutual, but I'm thinking it might have been more physical than mental. Emotionally, we're very different, want different things in life, and expect different things from a partner.

Partner—that's the problem. He never wanted a partner. He wanted a shiny trophy for his arm, a prize to add to his collection. I'm more than my looks. I'm not unaware that I get attention for the superficial stuff, but I've worked hard to build my business. I've earned every accolade I've won.

I take a gulp of wine and lean back against the headboard, fuming. How dare he call me bitchy just because I didn't cater to his whim? *Spoiled!* He's spoiled and believes his own hype. I roll my eyes.

My phone rings, startling me. Moving to see the screen, the sheets bunch at my feet, sheets that Kaz and I were tangled in all night. Seeing Mark's name on the screen ruins my memory. No way am I answering it. I'm already too riled up to deal with his shit again. Then the banging on my front door begins.

Grabbing my robe, I wrap it around me as I make my way to the front door. I peek through the peephole. *What the hell? When has he ever come after me like this?* Never. Possibly because I always turned up when he beckoned. My mistake. Another lesson learned. I take a deep breath, steadying myself and my thoughts, then exhale and open the door. "What are you doing here?" I ask, no patience for this man.

He pushes past me. "Is someone here? Is that why you've been ignoring me?" He walks around the living room and then into the kitchen searching for suspects while I remain at the front door with it held wide open.

"You have no right to be here. I want you to leave."

His eyes narrow, a vein exposing itself in his forehead. It's one I only see when I've seen him in playbacks of his losing games. It means he's pissed. This time though he's pissed at me. That bulging vein is aimed in my direction. "What the fuck, Lara? Who's here?"

I close the door not wanting the neighbors to hear the fight I can feel brewing. "You need to leave. Now." He takes off down the hall and kicks my bedroom door all the way open. Running after him I yell, "Stop searching my house and leave. I mean it, Mark."

He turns in an instant and pins me by my shoulders. My breath escapes me as my back slams against the hallway wall. "Are you cheating on me?" There's a rage running rampant in his eyes that turns my blood cold. I was scared before, but now I'm terrified. My hands fly up to push him away. My wrists are grabbed and ground against the stucco wall, the rough surface scratching my skin as his thumbs rub harshly over the veins on the underside. "You're so... breakable. Perfect and small."

"Mark," I start, my voice trembling. I clear it, needing to gain my composure, concerned for my safety if I don't calm him down. I've seen him mad, but now it's channeled completely at me. "You're hurting me. I know you don't want to hurt me." I wiggle my wrists until his grip loosens.

His breathing is jagged, but in his eyes I see the moment the man I cared about returns. A slow intake of air calms him enough to reason what he's just done. "Lara..." He backs away, his own back hitting the other wall, as if invisibly pushed off me. "I'm sorry. I don't know what came over me. I'm sorry."

I look down and rub my wrists one at a time. They're scratched and raw. When I look back up, my voice no longer shakes. It's firm and direct, "You should go."

"I'm sorry." He shakes his head like he hopes his better judgment comes back. "I didn't mean it."

Shaken, I fight the tears wanting to appear and walk back to the living room and straight for the front door. With the door held open, I see the roses. "I want you to leave and take your damn flowers."

When he walks to me, I back away with my eyes lowered. My hand is gripping the doorknob so tightly that it's starting to hurt.

"Please let me—"

"Please, Mark. I don't know what just happened. I don't want to make things worse by arguing."

"I had this crazy thought that you were blowing me off because you were cheating."

I look into his eyes, scared to say the words I know will upset him, but I need to make myself clear. "We're not together anymore."

He nods, his head down, his shoulders slumped forward. All six five of him crumbling in shame right before my eyes.

He deserves to live in that shame for the night. The nerves in my wrists lick with fire as they pulse with pain. Just as I look down at my right wrist, he says, "I love you."

The shock of hearing him say this after months of holding back, throws me, sending my heart and head into a tailspin. "Please go, Mark." That's all I can muster while holding back the tears desperate to fall in protest. I can't believe he would say those three words because of duress from the situation instead from love and happiness.

Finally, he walks out the door, but stops on the mat, and says, "Call me when you wake up. Okay?" When I don't respond, he insists, "Okay? Promise me."

"Okay," I quickly agree, but only to end this. I shut the door, locking the three locks, and activate the alarm system. I go to the kitchen and run my wrists under cool water. I'm gentle as I run my fingers over them. There are a few scratches and there might be a little bruising added to the other ones, so I dry them and pull two icepacks from the freezer.

I wish I could call Rochelle or talk about what just happened, seek another opinion, or find reasoning in his behavior. But no one can know about this. One leak and this would be bad for him. *Don't embarrass me, Lara. It's bad for my career.* His career...

Did I do something wrong? Am I missing something?

Although my mind is blurring with emotions, I'm willing to chalk it up to a moment of insanity on his part. My tears finally fall.

I angered him.

He acted from fear of losing me when he was already feeling rejected. He's an athlete, used to being physical, so he got a little rough. I know he didn't mean to hurt me.

"You're so... breakable. Perfect and small."

I know in my heart he didn't mean to. I'm just... small. Easily hurt.

He didn't mean to hurt me.

7

LARA

A GRANDE COFFEE is set down on my desk, and Lane, my lead designer slash assistant, says, "You were late. How is that possible when you live here?"

"Good morning to you too, Lane. I needed a coffee that I didn't have to make." I needed to get tested for STDs because of Mark's philandering, and thankfully, my doctor's office squeezed me in. That's the truth I'll lie about this morning. "Thank you."

"You're welcome. Hey. What's with the throwback to Madonna "Like a Virgin" and bangle days?" He leans against the desk while I finish attaching a swatch to the board, my bracelets jingling. "Are we not talking about it?"

"About what?" I look up at him, hoping my wide-eyed innocent expression will throw him off the scent.

He walks around behind me and hovers over my shoulder, judging the board with a silent chin rub. "New client?"

It worked. "Yep."

Moving back to the chair in front of my desk, he sits.

"Fine, I'll drop harping on the '80s wardrobe throwback so you can fill me on the client."

"Kaz Fabian."

"*Ooohhh*, Kaz Fabian. I like the name. *So sexy.* Now where have I heard it before?"

Taking the coffee in hand, I sit back in my chair and sip the hot brew, then smile. "Kaz Fabian is a guitarist in the band *The Resistance.*"

"*Ahhh*, the boys in the band. How are they doing these days?"

"They're busy, but getting a break soon. Kaz just closed on a house and he wants us to start immediately."

Lane takes the electronic tablet from my desk and starts taking notes. "I'll need the address, his phone number, any house regulations, limitations, expectations. Remodel or only design decorating? Timeline? Deadline? Rush or standard? When can I see the house? What's the code to get in if gated? Does he have any pets I need to be aware of, and, last but certainly not least, is he cute, single?"

I burst out laughing, and am so glad I wasn't drinking at the time or it would surely be spewed all over the visual board I just created. "Wow, and frisky too."

"Frisky, caffeinated, and happy."

"It's working for you. Direct that energy into design and we'll have a kickass week. As for the other information, I've seen online photos from the realty site, but I won't see the property until tomorrow night when he's back in LA. Also, he's very cute." I can't hide the smile I get just thinking of Kaz, so I start gathering the papers spread out on my desk as a deterrent.

He does an over-the-top eye-roll, then starts typing again. When he looks up from the tablet, I busy myself with the crap on my desk again. "That desk hasn't been cleaned in months."

"I know. That's why I'm cleaning it."

"You only clean when you're hiding something or you're avoiding a topic because you're not ready to share. Which is it?" He leans forward conspiratorially. There's a giddiness to his tone when he says, "So how'd you land the Fabian account? Did you have to sleep with him?"

I about choke on my own spit, and start hacking. Lane jumps up and hits me on the back until I manage to say, "Okay. Okay. Stop."

Walking around the desk back to the chair, he mumbles, "Just trying to help."

My hands feel cool against my heated cheeks as I try to regain my breath again. I clear my throat and look away from his suspicious eyes. "Thanks for the vote of confidence by the way."

"Oh, come on. Two hot singles in the City of Lost Angels—"

"I never said he was single."

"You didn't have to. I think the choking, cleaning of the desk, red face, and avoidance techniques kind of say it all, don't you think?"

I slip my fingertips around the bangles, silencing them. "You know when it comes to business I keep it professional."

He turns the tablet toward me, showing me a large photo of Kaz. "Dammmnnnn."

I look at the photo and let myself smile in front of him, knowing he'll always protect any secrets.

"Let's face it, Mark Renner, hot player extraordinaire, is the luckiest of them all to have snagged you, my dear."

My wrists begin pulsing from the mere mention of his name. My heart starts thumping in my chest as I look down at the bangles.

I feel something on my shoulder and scream. The back of my chair hits the windowsill as I grab my wrists protectively.

"Lara?" My eyes bolt up to see Lane. "What happened? Are you okay?"

Snapping out of the memory from last night that held me captive seconds earlier, I try to smile for him, to ease the worry written on his face. "I'm sorry. I forgot something in my bedroom." I stand and rush to the stairs. "I'll be back in a minute."

He lets me leave in silence, which is so unlike him. I'm relieved as I turn at the top of the staircase and head up to the main floor of my place, and run for my bedroom. As I pass the spot where I was pinned in fear, my hands start shaking, so I fist them to steady myself and hurry away. I head straight to the medicine cabinet in my bathroom. The Xanax aren't hard to find, but I don't use them much. Once I needed a few after a car accident I was involved in. I couldn't sleep or eat, reliving the accident over and over in my head. This feels a lot like that same post-traumatic reaction.

I down a pill and follow it with water I have cupped in my hand over the sink. I don't want to think about last night, and attempt to blow off my overreaction by the lack of sleep getting the better of me. I lean toward the mirror, palms flat on the marble, wrists aching from the pressure, but I push through it. "I will be fine. I will be fine." I say it one more time, hoping to believe it if said again. "I will be fine."

Swallowing hard, I raise my chin and lift my hands, my wrists aching from the memory more than his grasp. There's minor bruising that can be easily hidden by makeup or bracelets. As for my emotional state, it's a little more damaged, but easier to hide. My heart steadies and I close my eyes, then exhale. A light knock on the door draws my attention. I look up and straighten my hair quickly, and exhale.

Lane pokes his head inside, just as I turn around. "Hey there. Just checking on you. You okay?"

"Fine. Fine," I reply, "Sorry. I'm tired. I didn't get much sleep over the weekend. We're too busy for me to be tired though. I'm fine now."

He nods as if he believes me. "I'm heading over to Calliope's. Her end tables, the two large entryway mirrors, and dining room set have arrived. I want to inspect each piece before the delivery guys leave."

"Thanks." I nod to ease his concern for me. "Touch base with me. I'm scheduled to go over later for the bedroom furniture. Can you confirm the appointment for that delivery while you're out there?"

The concern never leaves his face as his eyes glance to my wrists and back up. "No problem. Talk later." He leaves, but comes right back, and says, "If you ever want or need to talk without the usual witty remarks, you know you can talk to me, right?"

I smile, for him, to put him at ease. "I do. Thanks." *And I do.*

"Okay. Catch ya later, Chica-bee."

"WHAT ARE YOU DOING?"

Kaz's voice fills me with joy. "Thinking about your house and tracking down a rug for a very demanding actress. What are you doing?"

"I like that you're thinking about my house, but I can't help but want you to be thinking about other things of mine."

"Is this you flirting, Kaz?" I sit back in my chair and start a slow spin, loving that he called me.

"I suck at it, don't I? Maybe that's why I don't have a girlfriend."

"You don't suck... well, sometimes you do, but I liked it." I bite the end of the pen in my hand, grinning.

"I do suck better at some things than others."

"As a firsthand witness to your sucking, your sucking does not suck at all, just so you know. And I like your flirting. Go on..."

"I'll go on and on when I'm back tomorrow. I want to see you."

My heart eats up his deep voice and playful words. "Is this a professional call or personal?"

"Can't it be both?"

"I don't normally mix business and pleasure."

He chuckles. "I thought we already had this talk about exceptions."

"Ahhh yes, you are definitely one worth making an exception for."

"You're not too sucky at this flirting thing either, Ms. Kessler."

"Thanks. I've had many years of experience."

"And here I thought I was special." He sounds pouty on the other end of the line. "How much experience are we talking about anyway? Girl-next-door innocent or Call Girl?"

"Those are my choices? Wow, you don't leave much gray area. How about Catholic school girl?"

"I'm impressed. You were wild then."

"I'm wild now," I joke, spinning around again in the chair.

"You're beautiful too." I bite my lip, not sure how to follow such sweetness. He lowers his voice. "Too soon?"

I'm shaking my head though he can't see me. "No, you've got perfect timing."

He lightens the conversation back up and says, "I am a musician. Timing is everything."

"Yep, timing is everything. As for the house, I'd love to see it."

"Oh yeah, the house. Dinner at the new place around seven?"

"That works for me. I'll need to take measurements and pictures for reference."

"Are we still talking about my house?"

I burst out laughing. Repeating what he once told me, I say, "Not at all."

"Good because we have all night."

"Perfect. I'll see you then."

His tone gets husky, an element of appeal that conjures naughty thoughts of the last time we were together. "Goodbye, Lara."

As I type the appointment into my planner and sync my phone with the program, my stomach fills with fluttering butterflies of the most wonderful kind.

I still have so much to process with my love life. The butterflies for Kaz have definitely jaded my thoughts toward Mark. I stare out the large window overlooking my backyard and realize Mark jaded my thoughts when he hurt me, not Kaz. Surely Mark can't think we'll get back together after what happened or with how bad things were before we talked. Everything happens for a reason and thinking back on what Kaz said, timing is everything, and maybe *our* timing is perfect.

8

———————

LARA

MY TEST RESULTS came back clean and I can finally relax. Or so I thought...

Flowers start arriving around two o'clock and don't stop until nine when the final bunch is hand delivered by Mark himself.

"I'm sorry," he says, shoving the bouquet at me.

With flowers against my chest, I wrap one arm around them and keep one hand on the door. I stand there in shock that he has the nerve to show up like this. "What are you doing here?" I hold the flowers out, not wanting them. "And take these. I don't want them."

"You said we could talk."

"I did say that, but I don't see the point."

He walks past me without my permission and I step back, intimidated by his stature. Holding the flowers out to him again, he sees the change in my expression. He must see the fear I wear so obviously as my hands shake. His eyes set on mine, and he says, "You know I didn't mean to hurt you. You know that, Lara. I wouldn't hurt you. Not ever. I love you. You believe me, right? Right?"

"Mark—"

"Don't say my name like that. I can hear the change in your tone." He quickly grabs hold of my arms and the bouquet falls to the ground. His grip is firm as I cower down. "I love you," he pleads, shadowing me. "My love for you is real, Lara. You have to believe me. I've never felt like this for anyone."

Fear snowballs in the pit of my stomach. "I believe you," I whisper, not sure if I even hear my voice. His hold on me loosens just enough for me to slip out and back away toward the couch. I'm hoping to make it to the other side, to have something large and solid between us. "We can talk. All right?"

"Sit," he commands.

I sit down knowing I can't get to my phone in the office downstairs without him catching me and doing who knows what to me.

"Thank you," he says, sounding calmer as he sits in the chair across from me. This is the Mark I know, but I'm guarded by the sudden turn. "I don't know what happened last night, but I promise it won't happen again."

"Or after the other incident? How can you promise that when you don't know what happened?"

"Lara, please. Just trust me. You know I would never hurt you on purpose—"

"You hurt me last night and it seemed like it was on purpose. I have bruises to prove it." I push up the sleeves of my robe and show him the scratches on the top and bruises where his thumbs dug into me. "You hurt me just now."

He sucks in a breath. It stutters in his throat as he stares at the bruising. His head shakes. "I didn't do that."

Confused by his reaction, I reason, "You did, Mark."

Standing up, he looks down at me. "I'll make this up to you. Flowers won't heal this mess."

I hold the arm of the couch, bracing myself. "You don't have to heal this mess. We're not together anymore."

"No." He stands there looking strong, his chest appearing bigger than a moment earlier. "What happened last night won't happen again. I promise you. I had a rough day and you weren't there. I was upset. Practice sucked. I was benched half the day. I just want us together." Kneeling down in front of me, I see the desperation in his eyes. Seeing this strong man breaking before me is hard to watch despite the incident from the night before. "Please, Lara. I need you." His head drops to my knees and I hear him sniffle.

"Mark—"

"Please don't say my name like that. Say it like you used to, like when you loved me."

"I can't. I'm here, but only as a friend." *Friend* is being generous, but I'll say what I need to right now. *I just need him to leave.*

He wails in distress and I'm not sure if I should try to comfort him or not. "Please don't do this. I'll be good."

Refusing to kick someone when they're down, my defenses crumble. "Maybe you can be better. Maybe you won't hurt me again, but my heart is not in this, Mark. Please. You have to let me go and move on."

"I can't. We're so good together. I screwed up and I'm sorry. I promise I'll be better."

My heart's not racing from fear, and my hands aren't shaking anymore. Seeing a man of his size—of his demeanor—break is heartbreaking in itself. I do what I know I shouldn't, but can't help. I stroke his hair as his head lies in my lap.

THE NEXT DAY I walk into the restaurant and hang my purse by the strap on the back of the chair. Exasperated, I say to Rochelle, "I have so much to talk about."

She laughs. "I have so much to talk about too, but you go first."

I slide into my chair and scoot up to the table. "Did you order wine?"

"I did. Of course. This isn't my first rodeo." I laugh just as two glasses of wine arrive along with the bottle in an ice bucket. "You go first," she says.

"I spent the night with Kaz and then I spent another."

"That was fast," she says, relaxing back with the menu in hand as if she expected it all along. Maybe she did. "How do you feel about that?"

I reach for my glass of wine, needing someone else's perspective on the situation. Rochelle will never utter a word to anyone about it, so I know I can trust her. "I like him, Ro. Is it too soon? Am I just confused because of the breakup with Mark?"

She leans forward. "Not too soon if you don't regret it."

"I don't, but I feel like I should."

"Why? You're both recently single, young, hot. You're both creative types. Sounds like a match made in Hollywood Heaven."

The waitress arrives, takes our orders, and tops up our glasses. When she leaves, Rochelle says, "You've dated someone famous and understand the baggage that comes with that fame. Be upfront with him and demand the same from him. Secrets destroy happiness."

"That's why they're secrets."

Our salads are delivered, but my stomach is in knots. She adds, "You've worked hard to build your reputation and career. It's very admirable."

"Thank you." Thinking of Kaz, I ask, "Are we moving too quickly?"

"You both just broke up with your others, but that doesn't mean it should dictate your future relationships. Do what feels right."

I nod in agreement because she's right. "Maybe we should slow down." I'm starved and start eating like it's going to be stolen from me.

"So what if you didn't. We're adults and if it felt good and no one was hurt, just keep doing what you're doing. Anyway, I like you two together. And Mark is on the same page now?"

"I think he understands we're done."

"You think?" she asks, her fork clanging against the porcelain plate.

"We are. We're done."

Her eyes are set, her complete attention on me. "What is going on, Lara?"

"Nothing," I lie, not wanting to expose the dirty details with Mark. "I told you. I slept with Kaz, and it was great."

"You actually didn't tell me the sex was great, so good to know, and ick. He's like a brother to me."

I laugh, and roll my eyes. "One minute you're pushing me on him and the next you're grossed out."

"Yeah, I want you together, but I don't want the details." Now she's laughing.

"Good, because I don't want to share them."

The laughter stops and a wave of heaviness rolls in. When I look up she asks, "Are you sure you're okay?"

"I'm sure." I'm lying. I'm shaken and a little wounded on the outside and a lot on the inside, but my shame feels more powerful at the moment. I never thought I'd find myself in this situation. It's embarrassing to admit, so I put on a smile for her, and say, "I'm fine."

"It's good to see you happy again. You deserve it. You deserve someone who treats you with respect. As for the details, maybe a few. I need to live vicariously for a few minutes before I return to mommyhood."

In minutes, spending time with my friend has turned around my whole day. I feel so much better than I did after saying I would be Mark's friend last night. My relationship with him is thick with deceit. It's nice to have the reprieve.

I PARK JUST inside the gate. There are no other cars at Kaz's new house, so I'm not sure if I should wait in my car or see if the door is open for me. I decide to get out and walk up. The house is great, a beautiful Mediterranean. From the outside, it's one I'd be interested in if I was in the market to buy a new house. Deep green vines cover the walls on either side of the entrance that are anchored by large planters and that house large black wooden doors that look old from time instead of design.

After being on Calliope's project for months, it's a nice break to work on a man's house. The lines and design tend to be less over the top, even with the history of the home coming into play.

I check the front door and it opens, so I go inside. I cross through the foyer and enter the main room; large dark wood beams highlight a vaulted ceiling that gives the space an airy, but impressive feel. There's a back wall of what appears to be glass pocket doors showing off the beauty of the landscaping. I love the warmth and see why he bought it.

The only piece of furniture in the room is not furniture at all. A beautiful black baby grand piano is tucked in the corner. No guitar like I expected, but he's not moved in yet. The bench is protected between the wall and the instrument. Drawn to it, I admire the shiny lacquer and the scale. It's perfect in this room.

"The house has been well maintained," Kaz's voice greets my backside.

I turn with a smile, my back against the piano. "It has been. It's beautiful."

"So are you." He comes closer. "It's good to see you."

I can't help feeling coy, and I know I'm blushing just from his smile. "It's good to see you, too."

Leaning in, he kisses me on the cheek, then whispers, "I can't stop thinking about you."

Just as he's about to move away, I hold him and kiss under his jaw. "You've been on my mind since you left."

We stand in the middle of the room. His body is relaxed under my hands and his scent is masculine and calming. His hands are on my hips and our bodies close the distance. I can feel his heart beating steady and mine steadies in sync.

The back of my head is stroked and the gesture is so loving that I close my eyes, wanting to stay in this moment for as long as I can.

A sharp inhale is heard and his breath covers my neck followed by a sweet peck. He whispers, "Would you like to eat or have a tour first?"

"Give me the tour and start with this," I reply lowly, weak to this man.

A smile plays on his lips, tempting me to kiss him. He says, "The piano is one of the few items I own. It's a Steinway. Other than the house, it's my biggest splurge."

"Do you play?"

"I play."

"Will you play for me now?"

"I doubt it's in tune after being moved in yesterday."

"Maybe another time?"

"Definitely another time." He starts toward the stairs. "Ready to see the rest?"

"Lead the way." It's still daylight and our voices echo in the empty house, but there's an intimacy he maintains when he takes my hand. I grab my measuring tape from my purse and leave the bag on the floor.

Signaling to the stairs, he says, "We can start in the bedroom... or mix it up and hit the kitchen first. Where do you like it?"

I love a good double entendre but this man is well versed in the language of seduction, so as much as I want to react just like my body is, I stick to the business at hand. "Kitchens are the heart of the home. Let's start there."

He laughs under his breath, turns, and takes me into the kitchen. He pats the wall, and says, "It opens somewhat to the living room, but I'm wondering if we take down part of this wall if the kitchen, this breakfast area, and the living room can flow even better."

Standing in the middle of the breakfast area, I look behind me and into the kitchen. "I see what you mean. The breakfast area is really another living space and we can treat it as such. We can easily fit a table for ten in here. If we go smaller, then there's still enough room for a couch and chair, a coffee table and barstools at the bar. From the photos online, the space wasn't used effectively by the previous owners." I'm about to continue as I walk into the kitchen, stopping near the island, but I feel the weight of his gaze on me, coating my insides in ways that feel new and exciting. Slowly I glance over my shoulder and find his eyes directed on me, an indiscernible expression on his handsome features.

His phone rings, shattering the building intensity and I start breathing again. When he looks at the phone, he says, "I need to take this. Feel free to walk around. I'll catch up." He walks to the back door and answers his phone. "Hey, what's up?"

I take the opportunity to check out the rest of the first floor. The house really is stunning. It doesn't shout showy or celebrity. It's not a home most twenty-six-year-olds would choose when coming into a lot of money. It's large, but the perfect size to raise a family and have room to grow. I can see a lifetime spent in this home, changing with the different stages of life. *It's not just for show or to flaunt his wealth. Unlike some...* I'm impressed with his refined taste.

When I go upstairs, I start in the master bedroom. It's the most important room on this level and will need the most attention to detail. There are several large windows facing the backyard, which appears to be at least two acres, if not more. The view is spectacular. Downtown visible in the distance. Prime old Hollywood real estate.

"The house feels good, right?"

Staring out the window, I agree. "Very good. It's warm." I turn around and find him leaning against the doorframe. "It's a great home. I'm getting house envy."

He chuckles. "You're welcome here anytime." Moving to the ensuite, he asks, "Have you gotten the measurements you need?"

I haven't gotten any. I've been way too distracted. "Actually, I'll send Lane out to do that tomorrow if that's all right. He's my right-hand designer."

"That's fine." Running his hand through his hair, he questions, "What are you thinking construction wise? Much to remodel or do you like what you see?"

Looking him in the eyes, I reply, "I like what I see, and I also like the house." A perfectly imperfect smirk resides on his face. It's startling how disarming it is. I make a move to leave and pat his chest. "See? Two can play that flirtation game." I leave him in the bedroom with the sound of his laughter bouncing off the barren walls.

When the tour is complete, we end up in the living room. It's all good until my stomach decides to let the world know I'm hungry.

"How about we eat?" he asks. "I brought salads and sandwiches, soups, crackers, some cheese and sausage, grapes, strawberries, and dessert."

"That's a lot of food."

"I didn't know what you'd want so I bought most of the menu." He takes my hand and leads me into the kitchen where the bags cover one of the countertops.

"You're very thoughtful. Thank you."

Kaz hops up on the counter and reaches into a bag. He pulls out a handful of grapes and pops one in his mouth. "Tell me how this works."

I hand him a strawberry while I hold on to another. "Usually you take it and touch it to your lips like this." The strawberry glides over my bottom lip. "Then you bite it." I take a bite, then lick the juice that's about to drip from my lip.

His mouth is hanging open before he says, "I meant working with a designer, but I like this a lot more. Continue…"

I laugh out loud. "Ohhhh. Well, since you know how to eat a strawberry, let's talk business. My designs depend on what the client wants. You have a Mediterranean home style wise but maybe you want a modern interior or maybe you want to match the home and bring out the home's unique features. Or maybe we can highlight what makes you so unique. Personalizing a space is always the best. You'll feel more comfortable when you're home. What do you want?"

"I want you."

"You've got me. I'm here. We're talking about the house just like we planned. I've already talked to Lane about the project and done a preliminary design board."

He hops off the counter and comes closer, trapping me between his arms. When he leans, he bends forward until he's eye level. "I meant what I said earlier. I couldn't get you off my mind."

"You didn't try hard enough." I gulp from the intensity as I drag my finger down the front of his shirt.

"I didn't want to try. I rather liked the memories, but seeing you here now…" he sucks in a rough breath, "I don't want to talk about the house." His lips meet mine and the two-day absence feels like a year when enjoying the bliss of this sweet pressure. I'm picked up and set on the counter. The surface is cold, the granite slick and expansive. A hard bulge teases between my legs as he pulls me to the edge, harder against him.

I lie back, my arms draped over my head. The top button of my jeans is opened, but he leaves that area, distracted by my exposed stomach. My shirt is pushed up as he slides his hands over my skin. Then I'm left alone. My head pops up and I anchor myself on my elbows to stare at him. "What happened?"

With an arrogance written across his face I know he can back up, he leans against the opposite counter, and says, "I think we should eat first."

My gaze darts to the erection in his jeans. "Really? 'Cause it looks to me like you'd rather do other things first." Then it hits me as I glance around. "Is this about respect? You know, you don't want to treat me bad and do it here on the counter or whatever?"

He scoffs. "Fuck, no. I have no problem disrespecting you on the counter, or anywhere else for that matter." His hand rubs over his cock. "I just thought I should at least feed you once before fucking you." He comes over and grabs my ankles. One swift pull and I'm face to face with him again with my feet on the ground. When I wrap my arms around his neck, he kisses me once on the lips and again on the neck. "Let's eat and then I'll be more than happy to disrespect you several times over."

He's addicting.

Body.

Mind.

Voice.

I'm head over feet completely addicted to him.

9

____

LARA

Kaz properly disrespected me twice before I drove home. I considered staying after being invited, but since he had no furniture we would have to go back to the place he shared with Derrick. If I had to see Derrick like that I'd feel like one of many and that's just not a self-esteem issue I was ready to deal with after leaving his house on a high.

The next day I'm back out at his house with Lane. Kaz and Tommy show up after we have measured the three rooms we're starting on first.

I try to remain professional, but why does Kaz have to have that dimple in his chin? Those eyes that seem to darken when his gaze lands on me? That damn shirt that fits like it was tailored to show off all his hard work in the gym? And I can't ignore the jeans that highlight his awesome ass. He makes it so hard to resist and resisting is exactly what I should be doing on a client call.

Tommy is asking questions, curious about my creative process. "Do designers have visions or is that something I got from TV?"

I lean down and drop the measuring tape into my bag. "Sometimes I get visions and see a space's finished design in my head."

Kaz steps forward and with his hand pressed gently to my lower back, he says, "I can take you out back and show you the pool and hot tub."

"I love hot tubs." I admonish myself the second the words come from my mouth. "Sorry. That sounds so pervy." I shrug. "But I do despite the germ reports."

Smiling, his eyes light with laughter. "No worries. I'll have it thoroughly cleaned for you. Unless you want to live dangerously and take a dip."

I should almost feel ashamed for acting this way in front of Lane and Tommy. *Almost.* But I don't. I'm happy on the inside and that kind of happiness can't be contained on the outside. "I don't have a suit with me anyway and I'm not sure if I should be getting naked with a client." I wink as we open the pocket doors. They stick a bit. "I'll have someone check on these doors. They should glide smoother."

"Will they have to be replaced?"

"No, they're great quality. Just in need of an oil." I step outside and follow a path that leads to the pool. Just beyond the pool I see a cave-like area hidden by the waterfall feature. "What's back there?"

"The grotto with the hot tub."

"You have a grotto?" I ask, insinuating everything. "How very Hugh Hefner of you."

"The man is ninety and he's still got game—"

"So you're thinking the secret to his sexual success is his grotto?"

"Figure it won't hurt."

I can't help but smile, peeking back at him as I walk up the path. "Nope, it can't hurt. Have you ever been to the Playboy Mansion?"

"I've partied there a time or two."

"I went a few months ago. Apparently some of the Playmates are fans of my ex."

"I heard he plays pro baseball." He sits on a large rock near the grotto while I look inside. "How long did you date?"

"Six months or so."

"Not serious then?"

I'm flattered he's so interested in getting to know me better. Inside the grotto, I lean back on a short wall made of rock. Reflecting on that state of affairs. "I'm not sure what it was anymore."

Kaz sits down on the opposite side, the hot tub dividing us. His voice goes quieter when he asks, "Did you love him?"

I finally look up. "I think this conversation is too heavy for a Wednesday."

He nods, not saying anything else. Slowly he gets up and I watch him go inside. I stay a few minutes longer liking the solitude of the cave. No wonder Hefner always scored. Grottos are the way to go. Beyond the sex appeal of the intimate space, it's peaceful. I go inside to find Lane talking to Kaz and Tommy. They're getting along, which is good, but I know I'm going to hear more than an earful once we leave. I'm just wondering if that earful will be good or bad.

I grab my phone out of my bag to check emails and find I've missed two calls from Mark. *Ugh!* I really don't want to deal with him anymore, but I'm going to have to get my things sometime, and sooner is probably better than dragging it out and getting it later.

"Did you get the measurements, Lane?" I ask, joining the group in the kitchen.

"I did. And I got the two other spaces. Kaz said he wants to go ahead and get those done at the same time."

Kaz adds, "Makes sense to get it all done from the beginning." With his eyes on me, he leans against the counter, looking relaxed. "When do you think you'll have the preliminary designs Lane mentioned?"

"I sent you an email this morning with the questions. Once you fill it out, we can meet and go over your answers. The design part will begin after that."

"I'll work on it tonight. Unless, of course, I get caught up in something else."

Not subtle. *To anyone.*

I swear my body reacts to his voice. "Caught up happens sometimes."

Lane whispers so everyone can hear him, "I think he means you, Lara. I think he means caught up in you."

My eyes dart to Lane's, and I scowl. With a bop to his arm, my sarcasm drips with laughter. "Yeah, got it. Thanks."

Tommy rolls his eyes and heads for the door. "I'm gonna go. Your sexual innuendoes to each other aren't really innuendoes. I got the hint."

Kaz follows him. "Yeah, okay. We'll talk later."

Talking to me, Kaz asks, "Can you stay?"

Lane answers before I can reply, "Yes, we both can."

Kaz and I shoot Lane a surprised glare. He huffs. "Fine. I'll leave so you guys can get it on."

"Lane! We're not going to 'get it on.' We're discussing business." I'm not sure he believes me since my arms are waving around wildly. "And decorating stuff."

"Stuff?" Lane asks, his face contorting. "You never call it decorating *or stuff*." When he looks at Kaz, he says, "You've done good, Fabian. You're the first man I've ever seen make her go loopy."

"There's always a first time. Glad I could be it," he says all suave and full of himself. He's hot like that. "Did you need any more measurements?"

Lane looks at Kaz's crotch and taps his chin. "Maybe your insea—"

"Okay. Okay," I interrupt before this goes even further south— literally and conversationally. I grab Lane's arm and start pulling him toward the door. "I'll see you back at the office later."

He smacks my hand on his arm. "Hands off my Vincent Vittori shirt. You know how protective I am."

Rubbing the fabric, I add, "It is very soft."

He leans in and whispers, "It's the material and the hand-sewn seams."

I can't stop from laughing and hit his backside. "It's fabulous. Now get your fabu-ass out of here."

With a hair flip that doesn't flip because it's styled to perfection on top of his head, he says, "I have to go out to Malibu. Calliope is having a dinner party and wants my input."

"With your help, I know it will be amazing." Just before he walks out the door, I bring him in for a hug. "Thanks for the help out here today."

"Always a pleasure."

The door shuts and I turn to face Kaz who's standing too far away for my liking. I start walking to him, but my phone rings and we both look at my bag, the moment slipping away just a bit. "I should get that. I like to be available to my clients during business hours."

"It's okay." He walks to the back and steps outside.

I reach for my phone, but see it's Mark, again, and hesitate. He can wait, but I have a feeling he won't, so I suck it up and take the call. "Mark, I'm with a client."

"I need to see you."

"You need to stop this."

"I can't."

With my patience gone, I speak directly and clearly into the phone. "I'm hanging up."

"Don't. *Please.* Just hear me out."

Kaz catches my eye when he walks back inside. Trying to act as professional as I can in front of him, I say, "I'll call you later."

"Okay. I love you."

I hang up and tuck my phone into my pocket. "I have a board in the car I can show you and get your initial thoughts on."

"I'd like to see it."

Leaving him, I go to my car and take it from the back of my Rover, wondering again why Mark is so insistent. *Why?*

When I'm back in the kitchen, I set the board on the counter and back away to give Kaz space and to watch for his initial reaction.

He leans over the board on the counter, the muscles in his arm flexing as he rests his hands on the countertop, showing the gorgeous definition. I want to trace over them, but I look away instead, resisting the urges he brings out in me.

Because of the lack of furniture, I hop up on the other counter and wait.

Kaz turns, leaning against the cabinet. "I like what you've done."

"I made this from the photos I saw online."

"What about now, now that you've been in the house?"

"I want to bring emotion into play."

"What does that mean?"

"I want it to feel like you, like how you make me feel, how you want your guests to feel."

"How do I make you feel, Lara?" His words stroke my heart, coming in purrs when he says my name.

"I'm better with visuals than words."

"I'm better expressing myself through music."

"Seems we're both at a loss for what we want to say."

He smirks while crossing his arms over his chest. "How about we do what we know best and reconvene? Can I hang on to this for a few days?"

"It's yours." I get my bag in the living room and throw the strap over my shoulder. "Fill out the questionnaire when you have time."

"Okay."

"We can meet. We can go to dinner and discuss the direction of the project. My treat," I add with a goofy smile hoping to get the chance to have more time with him.

"I'm gonna hold you to that."

"I keep my promises."

"Good to hear," he says, following me to the door. "I was hoping you'd stay a while, but I know you're busy." *If only he knew how much I wish I could stay too.*

Turning around, I take him by the front of the shirt and pull him closer. "I want to, but I need to tie up some loose ends."

Wrapping his arms around me, he rubs my back. "Go take care of whatever it is you need to take care of and give me a call when you're free."

"Free is a frivolous notion."

"Free is what we all should be."

"How do relationships come into play if we're all free?"

He runs his index finger over my lips, then kisses me. "That topic feels too heavy for a Wednesday."

I laugh having my words used against me. "Very true. We should save all this heaviness for a Sunday or a Monday."

"How about Saturday? Dex is having a party."

"You want to take me on a date?"

"I do, but if your loose ends are tied up sooner, I'm free on Friday."

"Good to know." I lift up and kiss him quickly. "Very good to know." I twirl in his arms and head out the door. "See you soon."

"Goodbye, Lara," he says, admiring me with that look in his eyes that makes me want to stay. *And I want to stay. I want to feel. I want him.*

Sadly I can't. It's time. Time to tend to those loose ends...

10

LARA

This relationship with Mark has got to end once and for all. Not because of Kaz, but for me.

I find a Starbucks needing the energy to be on my toes for this confrontation. I want my things and a final conversation so we can end this once and for all. While waiting on my grande, I step off to the side and check Instagram. I scroll past the landscapes and beach pics, over the celebs puckering for the camera, but stop when I see a photo of Mark from last night. *You've got to be kidding me.* He has a girl in a bikini on his lap who's kissing him on the cheek while he's taking a selfie of them. Last. Night. The hot tub is his. I recognize it instantly. *The bastard.*

Anger takes over. I can't believe I fell for his lines. He doesn't care about me. These aren't the first pics to show up with him like this. It's the third or fourth in the last few months. *Does he think I'm a blind fool? He says he loves me, but how can snuggling up—and probably more —with other women indicate love? What's his game?* I don't understand the fake tears and begging me to stay. What part of *"We're so good together. I screwed up and I'm sorry. I promise I'll be better"* does he believe to be true?

My name is called and I grab my drink and rush out, furious.

While I drive over to his place, I know some could say I'm doing the same thing, but I haven't been begging him to stay in a relationship with me. This seals the deal... well, the deal was already sealed, but now it's super-glued.

When I arrive at his house, I punch the code to the gate in, but it doesn't open. I push it in again and still nothing. I call him on the phone, but there's no answer. "Damn it." *What the hell?*

"This is ridiculous." I'm not waiting. I am so done. Frustrated, I drive away, getting angrier each mile.

A PIERCING NOISE interrupts the bad dreams I'm having. It's louder and louder until it can't be ignored anymore. I peel apart the swollen lids of one eye with my fingers. Turning toward the noise, it's my landline. I forgot I even had that phone. I mentally add to my forever-growing checklist to cancel that service. In the meantime, I must change that annoying tone when I'm more awake.

My other eye finally opens though the sun coming in through the window is blinding and painful, making my eyes water. I grab my phone quickly and head under the covers where it's dark, just like my mood.

I answer, "What?"

A frantic voice says, "I need your help."

"Rochelle, why are you calling me so early and help with what?"

"The party. I need more liquor. And it's not that early. I can't believe you're sleeping in. You never do that."

I reach over and turn on my cell phone, hoping I don't regret that decision. "What time is it?"

"What's going on, Lara? First you don't answer your cell and now you don't sound like yourself."

"I've fallen behind on some projects so I worked 'til three in the morning. I'm just tired. And I turned my phone off to avoid any calls from Mark."

"Oh. I'm sorry. I feel bad for waking you."

"No. Don't worry about it."

"What's the deal with Mark?"

"I'm just stuck in this mess with him and I don't know how to get out. I went over last night to get my stuff but I was locked out of the gate. I called, but no one answered, so I came home and worked to take my mind off it."

"How about I bring you a coffee and something to eat and we can chat for a few. I have to run out for more food. I didn't buy enough."

"You'd do that for me?"

"Of course. I'll be over in twenty. I'll let myself in. Go back to sleep and I'll see you soon."

After we hang up, I roll over, twisting myself into the covers and try for some more shuteye.

Footsteps coming down the wood-floored hallway wake me. I open my eyes and push the covers away from my face. "I need you," I whine, holding my arms open for Rochelle.

The weight of a truck lands on top of me. "I need you too. I'm sorry."

I scream, scuttling out from under Mark. "What the hell? Get off me!"

"What's wrong?" Genuine shock is written on his face.

Jumping out of bed, I hurry to my bathroom and stand in the doorway for protection, similar to what I do when we have earthquakes. *He's* a force to be reckoned with and has caused me more damage than the threat of a natural disaster.

"What's wrong?"

"You're kidding me, right?" My voice sounds pitchy, but I don't care.

With his hands up as if he's the voice of reason now, he sits up and eyes me. "Calm down, Lara. I love you. Can't you see that?" When he stands, I back inside the bathroom. "Are you scared of me?" His eyes narrow as if he's approaching a wild and wounded animal. He is. "I don't deserve that. After all these months, you know I would never hurt you."

"You did hurt me. Look at my wrists." I hold up my arms for him to see the bruising, though it's fading fast.

"I didn't do that."

My gaze lands on him with a harsh scowl. "You did do this to me, again. You keep hurting me and you've been hurting me all along by your cheating."

"I didn—"

"Don't lie to me! I've seen so many pictures. They're all over the Internet. Even one from two nights ago. I trusted you, but I don't anymore. I was a fool for thinking you cared for me."

His tall frame is overbearing even in the best of situations, but he's flat-out intimidating and scary when we're fighting. I swallow hard, trying to stand my ground when all I want to do is lock myself in this bathroom until he leaves. He nods his head and lowers his voice as if he can convince me to change my mind. "We're not over. We're far from over, Lara. You're mine. You were always meant to be mine." I see his hands fist at his sides and the breath is knocked out of me, fear replacing it. "We're so good together."

I hate that my voice shakes, making me sound weak when I should feel strong. "We're over, Mark. I've been very clear and from the photos online from last night and every other night, you've moved on."

"You're not innocent, but I'm not throwing it in your face."

"You just did, but what did I do?" I challenge him. I know deep down that even if I had wanted to do something, I would have never cheated on him.

I see the change as something occurs to him. His eyes widen as some great revelation sets in. "It's two in the afternoon. Why were you in bed? You... you weren't expecting me, but you *were* expecting someone. Who is it, Lara? Who were you waiting in bed for?" His fists loosen and he reaches out and grabs me.

Just as I'm about to scream and fight my way to escape, we both hear a large gasp followed by, "What's going on?"

Behind Mark stands Rochelle. *Oh thank God.* "Rochelle—"

He yells, his voice both menacing and booming. "Leave us alone."

Her eyes meet mine as she scans me, making sure I'm okay. "No," she says to him with no fear in her voice. "You need to leave now, Mark, or I'll call the cops." Dialing 9-1-1, she holds her phone up in the air. "All I have to do is push one more button."

"And tell them what? Lara's boyfriend used the key she gave him to come in and climb into bed with his *girlfriend*? Call them. They'll find no case, so run along and play house with that loser. We all know he needs the supervision."

"Shut up, Mark," I say, gathering strength from my friend. I push past him into the bedroom. "I'm only going to tell you one more time. Leave." He stares at Rochelle, then turns to me and returns the same glare as I'm giving him. I have no patience for his bullshit anymore. "Get out of my place. Now!"

"You don't mean that," he says, but by the confusion written on his face, perhaps reality is hitting him square in the head.

"I do. I want you gone for good."

"Whatever," he says, walking toward the door. When he passes Rochelle, he hits the wall above the door. "Fuck this."

Rochelle looks worried, but she stands strong until he's gone. Eyeing me, she says, "You're shaking. Stay here and I'll make sure he leaves."

I nod, wrapping my arms around my body, then take my robe from the hook in the bathroom, I slip it on and sit on the edge of the bed, and wait. When she comes back, she sits next to me. "He's gone." My breath stutters as I inhale. I drop my head into my hands and cry. A comforting arm embraces me. "It's okay. You're okay."

Leaning my head on her shoulder, I continue to cry, the last few days finally overwhelming me. "What if you wouldn't have shown up when you did?" My voice trembles even more now I know it's safe to show my emotion. *What would he have done?*

"Why didn't you tell me? I could've helped you."

"It's not him. He's not been like thi—"

"Lara, wake up. You're making excuses for him. Why?"

I drop my head again. "I'm ashamed."

"You did nothing wrong. There's nothing to be ashamed of. Has he hurt you before?" *I can't tell her the truth.*

"No," I continue to lie, not even understanding why anymore. "I've seen a change in him. I've seen moments of his temper, but ignored my gut feeling that something was really wrong."

"I'm sorry this happened. I had no idea."

"It was only two times. I'm not trying to justify it, but it's since we broke up. He's always had mood swings. He says it's natural for pro-athletes. But the last few months they've gotten worse."

"Maybe he's taking drugs."

I shake my head. "He wouldn't. They test regularly and he works closely with a kids' foundation against drugs."

She hugs me tight. "I'm glad you're safe and I'm even more glad you're not with him. You need to steer clear."

"Yeah, good riddance." I flop back on the bed. "But I still need to get my stuff." *And get my locks changed.*

"Send someone to collect it. You don't go, okay?" She lies back next to me.

Wanting to change the subject, I nod. "You said something about liquor for the party?"

"Don't worry about it. You have enough to deal with."

"I'm happy to help. Anyway, I'll need the distraction. Tell me what you need and I'll bring it tonight."

We lie there—me trying to forget what happened—Rochelle showing her concern by taking my hand and holding it. "I'm here for you."

I give her hand a little squeeze. "I know you are. Thank you."

After many reassurances I'm fine, Rochelle leaves. She's planned a party because she's happy the guys are home, even if only for a short time. There's still a lot to do she says as she walks out the door with only a few hours left until show time.

I promise her I'm up to the task, then shut the door, making sure all the locks and the alarm are set. I make a cup of tea and heat up a bowl of soup from a can. Settling down on the couch, I set my food and drink on the coffee table and reach for my favorite swatch binder. It's my go-to binder for male clients. The colors, textures, and patterns tend to draw their eye. I flip through it this time with Kaz in mind, finding comfort in my work—my happy place.

Kaz exudes warmth, making everyone feel at home around him. It's not something he tries to do. It just comes naturally to him. He's open. His heart is welcoming. Maybe he's too trusting. I guess we share that trait.

A few swatches are pulled, then leather samples are set aside that coordinate. Picking up my phone, I text Kaz: *What time can you meet at the house on Monday? I want to lay some paper down to look at paint colors and arrangements.*

His response is quick: *What time do you need me to be there?*

I smile, then type: *How's ten?*

Kaz: *How about noon?*

He has a knack for mealtime. I type: *Noon works too.*

Kaz: *It's a date, but I'll still see you tonight?*

I'm quick to reply: *I'll see you tonight.*

I hold the phone to my chest, a huge smile on my face with hope in my heart. Then I realize how ridiculous I'm being and get back to work. I spend the next hour saving images on my iPad of furniture pieces I think will look amazing in his house before I start getting ready for the night.

My shower doesn't take long, but picking out the perfect outfit does, especially since I have a date with a hot rock star. I want him to find me as irresistible as I find him. I want to bring him home. I want to make love all night and sleep all day with him again. He seems to make me want so much. *Is it too early in our relationship to want the world?*

Do we have a relationship? Or am I just swept up in the moment?

I finally settle on black fitted jeans and a black blouse that has a gold pinstripe. It flows over the curves of my shoulders and breasts, but is tailored at the waist and gets tucked in. I leave the top two buttons open and add three dainty gold necklaces, a few bracelets though the sleeves are long, and gold stud earrings. With my gold strappy shoes, the outfit is chic, but sexy. Just the way I like to look and feel. And after the week I've had, I deserve to feel good and have an even better night.

11

LARA

THE ORDER WAS ready at the liquor store and the employees loaded the boxes into my car for me. The gate to Dex's drive is open already when I pull in and park next to him. He gets out of his car and comes around to my door just as I cut the engine. "Hey," he says to me. "What'd she send you to do?"

"Liquor pick up."

"Nice."

"You?"

"Haircut." He chuckles. "She likes it shaggy but not long."

He does look good with shorter hair. "Looking good there."

"Thanks. Go on inside. I'll carry the bottles in." He joins me at the back of the vehicle. When I open it, he smiles. "She ordered a lot."

"I think she knows her audience."

"Guess she does."

When I go inside, Rochelle is frantic, holding one open bottle of champagne in one hand and her phone in the other up to her ear. Her back is to me, her long brown hair enviously wavy, and her figure in her shirt and jeans makes it easy to see why Dex is drawn to her. With all she's been through, I hope she can find happiness again.

"Hellooooo," I call out as to not startle her.

She spins around and sees me, a wide smile appearing. "Maybe around midnight," she says into the phone and nods for me to follow her. As soon as we reach the kitchen, Dex enters with the first box trailed by two valets carrying the others. "Thank you."

She hangs up and turns to the guys. "Make sure he tips well for doing his job for him."

Her teasing earns her a hug—Dex swoops in and grabs her. "Speaking of tips—"

"Not now," she says, laughing. She blushes and I turn away, the intimacy between them incredibly sweet.

Pushing the valets out, I tell them, "He'll be out shortly. Thank you for the help."

Rochelle catches me in the living room. "Thank you."

"You're welcome."

Her arm slips around mine and we walk to the guest room together. "How are you?"

"I'm fine. No need to worry." I set my purse down on the floor in the corner, and reassure her again. "Really. I'm fine."

"Okay." She doesn't push. "I'm glad you're here. Want to help get this party started?"

"I do indeed."

The first few guests arrive right after me. Rochelle is setting out the platters of food and I'm snacking on mini carrots she left in a bowl on the counter. I watch her and consider how much she's changed over the last few years. She's become herself again, but different in a way. She's a better version of the woman and friend she's always been. I envy her determination to be happy after the tragedy of losing herself along with her first love.

Breaking up with Mark hasn't been a tragedy by any means, but his turn is worrisome. Shaking it off, I decide to forget him for the night and have fun. It's the only thing that will help me forget the fear I felt earlier. "Did you make all of this?"

She smiles proudly with a tray of brownies in her hand. "I did. I started early this morning."

"Why not use a caterer? That would have been a lot easier."

After setting the tray down, she says, "I once had it all and it was taken away. I'm not afraid of hard work, so I don't need easy. If I did, I wouldn't be starting a relationship with Dex."

"I didn't mean—"

"No, no. It's okay. It's just being here—throwing this party—feels like a statement of sorts and I just want to show everyone that I care."

"You don't have to throw a party to do that. Everyone loves you and cares about you. You have the biggest heart of anyone I know." I look around at the table and at the bar being set up outside, and look back to Rochelle. "You are amazing in many ways. Make sure to enjoy the party."

"I will. And thanks."

"Can I do anything to help?"

Rochelle smiles. "Just have a good time."

"How about I get us a couple cocktails. Champagne?"

"I just opened one. Do you mind taking it to the bartender? It's a sparkling rosé, my fave."

She goes back to organizing the buffet and I head to the bar. The bartender leans forward on the marble top and asks, "What can I get you?"

"Rochelle said there's a bottle with her name on it. Two please."

"Coming right up," he replies with a wink. He removes the stopper and fills the glasses before setting them on the bar between us. "Friend of the hostess?"

"Yes."

He nods. "You gonna hang out awhile?"

"I'll be here all night."

He comes off as a cocky frat boy. Maybe he is. What he's not, is my type. "That's a coincidence. So am I."

"Thanks for the drinks. I should let you get back to your job."

"You're very welcome. Come see me again."

"I'm sure I will. You are the keeper of the liquor after all." I return to the kitchen, handing Rochelle her glass. "Cheers." We tap glasses and sip. Dex walks in, his eyes seeming to light up when he sees her.

It's amazing to see a man look at a woman like that. They went from hiding their love away to sharing it with the world.

It makes me realize no one has ever looked at me like that. Envy fills my belly, mixing with the wine bubbles. "I'm gonna walk around." I slip off to the living room.

Sitting in a chair near the fireplace, I watch the orange and yellow flames as my thoughts drift back to Mark. It's a bad habit I need to break, but the stress of everything with him makes it hard. With imperfect timing, my phone buzzes in my pocket. I look down at the message on the screen: *I'm sorry. I miss you. I love you. I'll do anything to make this up to you. Anything.*

I won't reply. He doesn't deserve it and I don't know what to say anyway. What I do know is I *don't* want him back. But now I'm scared… scared *of* him. Deep down. I know he's hurting. Breakups are hard. He needs to move on. He needs to find his passion again and I'm not it. We're over and it's best if I remember the bad like today as a reminder when I'm feeling sorry for him.

Some of the band is gathered in the corner, but not Kaz. I look toward the back when I hear, "Who you looking for?"

His voice makes me smile, my body instantly on alert. I turn around, captivated by expressive eyes. My insides curl in on themselves. I'm well aware that an emotional attachment has already bridged the gap between us. "You."

He rubs his thumb over his bottom lip while looking at me with a wicked glint in the pupils of his eyes. "If it makes a difference, I was looking for you."

I touch him because I struggle not to, so I indulge my needs for this man, and give in. With my hand on his chest, I say, "It makes all the difference in the world."

Coming even closer, he whispers, "It makes all the difference to me too." A kiss follows, being placed so effortlessly on my cheek. I love his confidence and comfort in expressing how he feels. I love his openness to the world and his gentleness with me.

Giving in to my other needs, I lean in and close my eyes, ready to kiss him all night. My phone rings in my pocket, jolting us from the moment. *Damn it.* I pull it out and look down at the screen. *Mark.*

Kaz sees it. "I'm gonna get a drink and let you take that call." He walks away, taking all the ease and joy we were sharing with him.

Left standing in a bog of mixed emotions, I send the call to voicemail. My heart's not broken. He already destroyed that possibility. But I feel as though I should feel guilty. *Should I feel bad that I don't feel worse? That I don't feel heartbroken?* When I walked away from him, it was the best thing for me. *I know that's true.* Walking into the kitchen I find Rochelle refilling a tray of food. "You should have had it catered," I say, setting my glass down and helping her.

"I like to cook. It allows me to enjoy the process of planning for the party. Slows things down and I get to focus on the task at hand." She looks up with a smile. "This is the last tray anyway, so if you're hungry, you should eat now. As soon as the guys start eating, there will be nothing left." She laughs.

I sigh. "I've lost my appetite. I just sent Mark's call to voicemail."

"C'mon," she says, taking the tray and setting it on the table. She walks straight to the bar and grabs two more glasses of champagne and then makes her way outside. We stop just outside the door and she hands me one of the glasses. "Let's go over there." She points to two chairs at the other end of the pool.

We sit and she leans back, looking up at the stars starting to appear. It's that perfect part of the whole day, when day meets night, and twilight appears for a brief time. "A lot has changed over the years. Some for the worse. A lot for the better." When she looks at me, she says, "I've never had a man treat me how Mark has treated you. But I also understand how pliable, how resilient and strong the heart is. Forget what you're supposed to say, and tell me the truth. Do you still have feelings for him?"

"I have feelings but love isn't one of them."

"You and Mark were a whirlwind. It all happened so fast that I think you got caught up in the hurricane of his life."

"I often compare him to bad weather ironically."

"Maybe not so ironic. At the end of the day, it doesn't matter what I think, Lara. It's not my life. But from what I know, what I've seen the last couple of months, and seeing your happiness disappear, I think you're now heading toward a better emotional place." She looks beyond me, then back. "I like Kaz, but maybe you're heart needs some time to heal."

"I'm fine, Rochelle. I understand you're worried, but I really am fine."

"You have unfinished business with Mark. Wrap up the mess you're in the middle of and give yourself and Kaz the respect you deserve. He's a good guy. Don't make him a rebound."

I pause before I speak, surprised by the ferocity in her voice. "I won't. We're just getting to know each other, but I like him."

"I can tell. He likes you too. I've not seen him like this. His last girlfriend," she starts, "was a drama queen. He hated that. We all hated it."

"I can imagine. I know you and the band are very private. You mentioned respect. Respect seems to be a running theme lately when it comes to timing. Thinking about you and Dex, you took years, out of respect, to be together. I'm sure looking back you wish you could have some of that time back."

"I do in a way, but I wouldn't change the journey we took to be where we are now. We wouldn't be the same people if we skipped some of the steps along the way. Take your time now so no one gets hurt later."

"I hear what you're saying." Glancing over my shoulder, I see Kaz through the open doors. He's talking to Derrick, but his eyes are on us. "I don't want him to be a rebound."

"Then don't put him in that position. Get your crap from Mark and end the phone calls and texts. End all contact. Finalize it." Leaning closer, she touches my arm, and adds, "You are a strong woman. Don't let him destroy who you are because he's weak." She stands and starts walking back toward the house, but stops and turns back to say, "Oh and I said nothing about sex. You should totally have all the sex you can get."

"God, I love you."

"Love you too," she says, smirking.

When she walks in, Derrick and Kaz walk out. They stop and talk to her a moment. All three look at me. She smiles, saying something else to them before she departs.

Derrick takes her chair, making himself at home in front of me. Kaz grabs a chair nearby, carries it over, and joins us. When he sits down, he leans forward on his knees. "I think I need a smoke."

"I've got weed," Derrick offers.

"Nah," he responds.

I watch their interaction. You can see how comfortable they are in their friendship. Derrick asks me, "You smoke?"

"No," I say, shaking my head.

"Do you care if I do?" Derrick waits for my response.

"No." I stand, locking eyes with Kaz. "I need to make a call anyway." Moving farther away from the guests, I try to figure out what I'm going to say.

"Hey, Lara?" Kaz calls me quietly, just the two of us around.

"Yeah?" When I turn back, he's close.

He's nervous by the way he shifts, turning us around so my back is to the party. "I came on too strong the other night. I know you said you aren't together, but it's new and considering he's sending you flowers and still calling you, I feel like I took advantage of the situation and it was selfish of me. I wasn't thinking about you. Well, I was thinking about you." He grins mischievously. "But I wasn't putting your needs first. I'm sorry about your breakup."

Reaching out, I touch his hand with my fingertips. "You don't have to apologize. I did what I wanted to do and don't regret anything if that's what you're worried about."

"I'm worried about you."

"I know you are, but you don't have to be." Then I tell him the first lie, "I'm fine. Everything's fine." To lighten things up, I prod for my own enjoyment. "Are you sorry for the flirting?"

"I said I felt bad and I shouldn't have done it." He leans closer, his hand taking hold of my arm gently. He's so close that I can smell the

Jack and Coke on his breath. My eyes close, relaxing in the comfort of his touch. "But I'm not sorry."

When his lips touch my cheek, I lean into the kiss he's giving.

"Lara!"

My lids fly open, my body tense and shaken when I hear Mark over the music. Kaz's hand drops and he steps forward, shielding me with his body. His jaw is tense, contracting and tightening, his eyes set as he glares at the intruder to our conversation.

Hurrying around Kaz, I try to diffuse the scene that's building, and ask, "Mark, what are you doing here?"

Mark's eyes are locked on Kaz, his attention determined as he stares at him. I touch his chest, but he doesn't look at me until I tap him. "Weren't we both invited to this party?" I drop my hands to my side and I take a small step back, weary of his anxious demeanor. He's domineering and intimidating, his tone harsh, but threateningly low. "What are you doing with him?"

"Mark," I whisper. "I was invited. These are my friends. Why are *you* here?"

His pupils are small, little pinpoints, but like little daggers aimed at me. "No, no. We need to talk. You need to give me a second chance. I deserve that much. I deserve you."

My wrists prickle with pain, a harsh reminder of what he actually deserves, and that's not me. "Go home and we'll talk tomorrow. Now is not the time and you are not welcome here."

"Because of him?" he asks, pointing over my shoulder at Kaz.

"This has nothing to do with him. Go home. You're making a scene in the middle of Rochelle's party."

He grabs my arm. "If I'm leaving you're leaving."

Kaz is suddenly there, his hand on Mark's arm. "Let go of her." He's not yelling, he's calm and in control. His gaze is a glare, solid and unblinking.

Mark's grip tightens, marking me as his property instead of allowing me to be my own person. I try to free myself, but if he holds me any harder, I'll be bruised. "Mark, you're hurting me."

Kaz grits, "This is your last warning."

His hand falls away instantly and his attention is back on me. "I'm sorry. I just want to talk to you, to sort through everything."

"Not here. Not now," I say, trying to stay calm, which is the exact opposite of how I feel. Kaz stands tall next to me, his arm pressed to mine. A lump forms in my throat, leaving me unable to speak as my eyes fill with tears.

"Please," Mark pleads, "talk to me. This is torture. I'm going out of my mind without you."

His eyes water, tears depicting the inconceivable emotion he wears on the inside for the rest of us to witness. Even I have a heart. When looking up at a six-foot-five professional baseball player with tears of desperation settling in, my stance on the matter falters and he takes advantage. "Please, Lara. Let's talk out front and I'll bring you right back to the party. Twenty minutes. That's all I'm asking for."

I don't even realize I've moved, my mind fogging from humiliation, until Kaz calls me, "Lara?" When I look back at him he's shaking his head. "Don't go."

"Please. Ten minutes," Mark bargains.

Knowing the relief I'll gain if I settle this tonight, I agree. "Ten minutes."

"Yes. Thank you." He takes my hand in his and turns for the door.

Just as I tear my hand free, I hear, "Lara?" and am pulled in another direction by Kaz's concerned voice. "Can I speak with you?"

Mark answers before I can. "I'll bring her right back."

"I'll be okay."

Kaz stands there with his arms crossed. "You sure?"

No. But I go anyway desperately needing this closure for Mark and me. I pass Rochelle. "I'll be back."

She eyes the two of us, worry creasing her forehead. "Are you okay?"

I nod while tucking my phone into my back pocket just as we reach the door. "Ten minutes, Mark. Not a second more."

He looks at me with a shit-eating grin on his face. "Nope, not a second more."

The door closes behind us and we walk to his large Hummer. As soon as we get in and the doors lock, I know I've made a fatal error.

12

KAZ FABIAN

I SHOULD HAVE STOPPED Lara from leaving. My instincts told me to, but I didn't act on my instincts. I trust her even though I don't trust him. "I'll be back," I tell Derrick. He's sidetracked with the girl who's made herself at home on his lap anyway.

Working my way through the crowd, I look for Rochelle. I spy her in the kitchen with Dex, Johnny, and Holli. Dex has his arm around Rochelle's shoulders. Johnny and Holli are holding hands. I feel as though I'm intruding, but I need to speak with Ro. When I approach, everyone says hi in good spirits, but by the expression on Ro's face, something is weighing heavily on her, and I have a feeling it's the same thing weighing me down. Signaling over to an empty space nearby, I look at Rochelle. "Can I speak with you in private?"

She nods. "Sure."

Clearing my throat as we walk a few feet away from the others, I don't hide my feelings. "We shouldn't have let her go."

"I know. I was feeling uncomfortable about it, but they need to end this."

When she won't look at me, I ask, "What's going on?"

"I'm worried. I don't know why I didn't stop her."

"It's not your fault."

"She was so insistent and I know she wants this ended once and for all, but..." She looks up at me, but doesn't finish that sentence. "They left. I messaged her, but haven't heard back."

"I didn't know they were leaving. I thought they would talk outside."

"I didn't either. That's why I messaged. I don't know what to do." I see something change in her eyes. "If she's not back in ten like he promised, I'll text again."

Dex joins us. "What's up?"

Rochelle leans against him, her head falling back on his shoulder. "Nothing. Just chatting."

"About Lara?" he asks, wrapping his arm around her.

We both nod, but neither of us says anything. "Okay, can you guys be acting any weirder?"

Rochelle looks up at him and smiles. "C'mon, let's get a cupcake." She takes his hand and pulls him back toward the crowd, but when she glances back at me briefly, her eyes are sad, worrying me even more. Looking at my watch, it's been four minutes. Six more to go.

Ten minutes turns into twenty, and then I'm done waiting. I find Rochelle. "I can't sit here any longer. I've got to do something."

"We can't call the police. She went willingly."

"Do you know that for a fact?"

"She walked out of the house willingly."

Tommy knows everyone in this town. "I found out where Mark lives."

"I'll go with you."

She's feisty, and always been so strong, but she needs to be here. "Stay. Try to enjoy your party. I'll call you."

"Please, Kaz. I'm worried."

"I know you are. Stay here with Dex. I'll keep in contact."

She lifts up and kisses me on the cheek. "Call me."

"I'll have her call you."

Smiling, she says, "Thank you."

Slipping out of the party without saying goodbye to everyone isn't easy, but I'm swift enough to do it. I drive straight over to the baseball player's house, but it's gated. I should have had a plan, but the fucking security guard isn't budging and doesn't recognize me.

None of my texts or calls are returned, so I drive by her place. No lights are on and I don't hear any movement inside to make me stay. I call Rochelle on the way home and tell her, hoping she'll tell me Lara is back at the party, but she doesn't. I can hear the worry in her voice. She's gone from patiently waiting to shaking. "I should have told you, Kaz, but I know Lara doesn't want anyone to know."

"Know what? Tell me."

"He's gotten rough with he—"

"What the hell? Why didn't you tell me earlier? Why would she leave with him? We should have stopped—"

"I know her. She would have done it whether we wanted her to or not. She still feels she can get through to him and end this."

"Fuck." I rub my temple, a headache flaring on the right side. "What do we do?"

"We wait. I don't want to, but have to at this point."

My hands fly up and slam back down on the steering wheel. I'm frustrated and pissed the fuck off. "Call me if you hear from her."

"I will," she says, "I promise."

I cruise back to my new house. I can't be around Derrick as he fucks some girls in the other room while I'm worried about the one girl I care about. I had a mattress delivered with some things from the apartment. My wishful thinking that I might end up back here with Lara was a misplaced notion. Rochelle's right. She went willingly. I don't think she would have started something with me if she was still in love with him, but maybe she is. Maybe I'm so busy thinking the worst and she's fucking—No, that's not Lara. She knew what she was doing when she left. *She said she was fine, but now I'm thinking it was a front. Was she too scared to say anything? Shit.* I need to wait and allow her to tell her side of the story.

There's a brand new bottle of Jack Daniels waiting for me when I walk in. Unfortunately there's no mixer or glasses, so I unscrew the top and tip it back, taking two good shots before releasing it from my lips. The burn feels good. The first half of the night was good, watching Lara mingling, seeing her in all her beautiful, sexy glory. The second half? Not so good. Not one I'm keen to remember. *Have I lost her before I really had the chance to have her?* I tip it back once more but lose interest in the idea of getting drunk and set it on the floor. I empty my front pockets and keys next to it, and then go into the bedroom and lie down on the mattress that's taking up space in the middle of the room.

MY PHONE RINGS, waking me. I look for the clock on the nightstand, but there's no nightstand or clock or furniture. Momentarily I'm stunned into confusion. *Where the fuck am I?*

The phone keeps ringing until I grab it from my back pocket, finally remembering I'm at my new place. "Hello?" My voice is gruff as I roll to my back and drape my free arm over my eyes. My ear is met with crying, causing me to sit up. "Hello?"

"Kaz, it's, it's... it's Lara. Can you... come? Get me?"

I'm on my feet heading for the keys. "I'm on my way. Where are you?"

"I screwed up, Kaz." Her sobs are getting the best of her and it's hard for me to understand her.

"Where are you, Lara? Tell me. I'm coming to get you."

"I... I'm not sure. I think I'm near the golf course in Calabasas."

"What do you mean you're not sure? Are you okay?"

Her breathing is broken, gasps between cries. "No. I... I... I stole his Hummer. He'll kill me. I have to leave it. I need to get out of here. I need a ride."

The area comes to mind. I've been there. I've been to that golf course. "There's a shopping strip near the country club. I'll pick you up in the parking lot in front of the market." I'm about to hang up, but add, "Keep your phone handy and call the police if he shows up."

The phone goes dead and my heart follows as anger courses through me, imagining the worst. It takes me too long to get to her. I lost track, her cries circulating in my head the entire time. I see the center on the right and pick up speed. At three thirty in the morning the parking lot is vacant except for a silver Hummer. I drive by slowly and see the driver's seat is empty. Looking around for any sight of her, I come to a stop and park. A woman comes from the shadows and makes her way toward me. I know it's her and jump out to meet her. "Lara?"

The light from a tall lamppost shines down as she hurries to me. Her head is down, her shirt ripped. Her body hits mine and her arms go around me. She buries her face into the crook of my arm and her body is trembling. I'm not sure if it's from sadness or fear, but I need to get her out of here and safe.

"We need to leave," she says. "Please. Can we leave?"

"Come on."

As soon as we get into my car, she slides down while locking the doors. Her seatbelt is fastened, but she turns away from me. I fasten my seatbelt and take off as soon as I can. I want to give her time, but I need to know what's going on and what to do, how I can help her. "Do you need to go to the hospital?"

"No."

"Do you want me to take you home?"

"No."

The darkness of her tone twists my insides, an unfamiliar fear coating each of her harsh breaths. I try to keep it cool and not push her to tell me what the fuck is going on, but I want answers. My shortness comes through breaths and I grip my steering wheel tighter. Steadying myself, I ask, "Do you want to come back to my house? The new one so we can be alone?"

I'm answered with only a nod, which is good enough for now in the confines of the car. Moments later, her voice is weak and quiet, when she says, "Can you stop by the store? I think I need ice."

My heart starts pounding as I pull into a store parking lot. "What do you need ice for?"

I park and there's enough light shining in from a Ralph's sign that when she turns, I stop breathing altogether.

"Please don't look at me, Kaz." Her voice is barely a whisper, her tears reflecting the light, her face swelling with red and purple coloring.

"Lara..." My words choke in my throat looking at what he did to her. Dried blood rims the right side of her mouth and her left nostril. It's light pink under her right eye and her cheekbone is starting to swell. He knew what he was doing to get away with this. Hard enough to hurt her, but just shy of long-term damage. "You need a hospital, and I need a fucking baseball bat."

"Don't. Please. Can we just get icepacks and go? I don't want this all over the news. I don't want to be all over the news like this." She reaches to touch me, but hesitates. As if warring with herself, her eyes close and she touches my arm with such care. It's the same care she deserves in return, so I cover hers with my hand.

"He deserves to go to jail for what he did. You need to think about pressing charges."

"We can take pictures if we need to, but I can't go tonight." Tears streak down her cheeks. "I can't. I'm sorry. I'm ashamed. Weak. I thought I was strong, but he showed me I'm not."

Anger forms, fueling me forward, wanting to kick his ass. "Lara, whatever he said to you, whatever he did to you, it's not because you're weak. It's because he is. You need to remember that." For her sake, I'll go get the ice, but I hate leaving her here. "Will you be all right by yourself?" She nods. "Hold on to your phone in case I need to call you. Don't answer any calls from him."

"I won't."

I get out, but duck back in, and say, "Lock the doors and don't open them for anybody but me."

She nods again and does as I say. I hurry into the store to the medical aisle. I grab several icepacks and some I can bend to make it go cold on the spot. The others I'll put in my freezer when I get home. I rush to the frozen aisle and grab some bags of peas and to the meat department for a small steak. At the register I get four bottles of water, grab a Vitamin Water for her, and take a small bottle of Ibuprofen next to the register. Tempted by the candy, I also buy some chocolate in hopes to see her smile.

When I get back to the car, the door is unlocked and I squeeze the bag behind my seat. I take a bag of peas out before getting in. "Put this on your face."

Leaning back in the seat, she closes her eyes, the bag of peas being held to her cheek. When I pull out onto the main street again, she whispers, "Thank you."

"I'm sorry this happened to you."

"I am too." She laughs lightly, but it's followed by an, "Ouch."

"Do you want to talk about it?"

Inhaling deeply, she then exhales slowly, bringing the peas down and holding them in her hand. "I know you probably have questions and rightly so since I dragged you into this whole mess, but can we talk later? I'm really tired."

"I have a mattress at the house now. Not much else, but at least you can get some rest."

"I'll feel safer than being at mine tonight."

How the fuck is she so calm when I'm shaking on the inside I'm so furious?

Once we get into my house, she heads for the bathroom and I unload the grocery bag. The last owners left the fridge and now I'm grateful as I place the icepacks in the freezer with the other bag of frozen peas. Noises echo around the empty house and I hear her nearing. When I turn, she's there, and that's when I get a good look at her. Oh, shit. With watering eyes and messed-up hair, she looks down, embarrassed in way a woman should never be. Her shirt is ripped more than I first noticed and her feet are bare.

"What did you do with his keys?" I ask, wanting to take them and destroy that motherfucking, gas-guzzling, piece-of-shit vehicle. Just like I want to destroy him. I'll make him pay for what he's done.

"I left them in the Hummer and locked the doors."

"Do you have shoes?" I ask, wondering if she took them off or I missed that detail earlier.

"I took them off upstairs."

I find some relief in her answer. The blood on her face is gone and she's cleaned up. Hating to have to ask this, I ask anyway because we need to have the evidence. I step forward wanting to be close but scared to touch her, to hurt her. "We should take photos. Just in case. Okay?"

"I don't want to take any photos." She wraps her arms around herself protectively.

"What can I do to make this better?"

"You're here. That's enough. Thank you for picking me up."

"Don't thank me when I feel I've failed you."

"You didn't. You helped. So much more than you know." Delicate fingers touch her cheek.

"Are you in pain?"

"My whole body hurts."

"We need pictures. You need them. We can call Rochelle or Lane if you'll feel more comfortable with them."

"No, I don't want anyone else to see me like this." Looking down, she says, "Just you. Is this too much? I know it's a lot to take on when we're just getting to know each other."

"No. It's not too much." I cover her with my body. It's easy to do when she's so much smaller, but my anger surges again, knowing she's even smaller compared to *him*. "You need photos." I lean back and look at her, the top of her head as she keeps her eyes lowered. "I'm not letting this go and you shouldn't either. We can take them with your phone so you have control of them, and no one else, just in case you need them."

Contemplating the options, she finally looks up and says, "With my phone only, right?"

"Yes."

"Okay."

Each mark, each bruise, for every hit he put on her, he'll get three. I will kill Mark Renner. Trying to focus on getting the photos is doing my head in. Seeing her shame, watching the tears trail down her face, breaks one of mine free. I shake it off, making sure she doesn't see how my heart is breaking for her. Just take the pic. Just do this, for her. We spend the next five minutes taking photos of her body and close-ups of her face.

When I give the phone back to her, I say, "Back these up and protect them."

"I will. Thank you," she replies shyly.

I raise her chin up, but it's still not any easier to see her like this. I tamp down the anger raging inside that could bury me knee-deep in my own pain and tears for her. I have to be strong. For her. "Don't let him touch your soul. No matter how he tries, he can't steal your beauty, who you are, or what makes you special. Protect yourself. Protect your soul." I kiss her cheek. "And go easy on yourself. There's nothing you could have done differently. This is on him. Promise me you'll keep the blame where it needs to stay—on him."

It's just a murmur, but I hear it. "I will."

I kiss her mouth gently. "Good girl. I bought a steak for your eye. The enzymes are good for healing."

That evokes an unexpected smile. "I think I'll pass on the raw meat for now and stick with the peas."

"I have whiskey."

"I definitely need a shot or two of that."

"No glasses, but a bottle."

"Perfect."

I retrieve the bottle, unscrew the cap, and offer it to her.

She comes to me, taking the bottle in hand. "I know I shouldn't drown my miseries in liquor, but I think tonight will be an exception." Putting the bottle to her lips, she keeps her eyes on me and takes a few large gulps of the liquid. "Ah! That burns."

"You're gonna need Ibuprofen and water before you go to sleep." She takes another gulp before handing the bottle back to me. I take a few gulps of my own before capping it. "I can get some for you now."

"Thank you."

With the bag in hand, we head to the bedroom together and stop just inside the door. "I can sleep out there." I hand her the bag.

"No. Please, Kaz, can you stay?"

"Are you sure?"

Looking me in the eyes, she says, "I want you to."

"What side do you like to sleep on?"

A smile is hidden in her expression. "Whichever. I don't mind. I usually end up in the middle."

Seeing her smile makes me glad she trusted me enough to call me. "Rochelle was worried about you."

"I'll text her." She picks her phone up from the floor next to her shoes and starts typing. "I'm going to tell her I'm all right so she doesn't worry." She looks to me for the promise she's seeking.

"I won't tell her tonight, but you need tell her tomorrow."

"I will." After setting her phone back down, she comes back and stands in front of me. "Is it okay if I take these clothes off? I don't want to make you uncomfortable or anything."

Make me uncomfortable? How could she think that? "You're safe here." That's a promise I can easily make. "I'm here however you need me."

"I knew I could trust you." While taking down her jeans, she says, "He's on steroids."

"Your ex?"

"Yes. I don't know how he passed the drug tests, but he did." She looks up at me and says, "I can almost pinpoint when he started. It was about three months ago. I left the party with him because I thought I could give us closure. He thought we were getting back together... or he hoped." I watch as she pulls her shirt overhead not bothering with the buttons. After all, it is ripped.

The bruising on her chest is worse when she's fully exposed. "He hit you here more than once..." Reaching forward she doesn't flinch or move when I touch her, which makes me realize how much she trusts me. I run my fingertips over her chest, right above her breasts. She bites her lip and closes her eyes. Stepping closer, I embrace her, stroking her back gently. And her tears start falling.

She must sense the change in me as anger fills every muscle of my being because she whispers, "Forget about him. Stay with me." Her hands touch my face and our eyes meet. "Stay for me. Please."

"I want to pummel him for what he's done. I want to obliterate him, but for you, only you, I'll stay."

"Promise not to leave me?"

"I promise," I say, leaning forward and kissing her forehead. "Come on, sleeping helps the body heal."

"And a bag of half-thawed peas," she says, taking the bag from the floor onto the bed with her. She settles under the covers, takes two Ibuprofen with a water chaser, and turns on her side to face away from me. "Hold me, Kaz?"

I hate hearing doubt in her voice. There is no way I wouldn't hold her. I take off my jeans and slip under the covers next to her. Leaving no space between us, I caress her hip as I slide my arm around her middle. Her breath catches, but settles. She puts the peas on her cheek as I move her hair away, letting it slide down her back. I place one kiss just at the curve of her neck, and then lean back. Neither of us says anything more. We don't need words. We'll speak through actions, caresses. This feels good... right. I just wish it were under different circumstances.

Lying in the dark with her, I listen intently to each of her breaths, hoping she finds sleep and knowing she needs the rest. Minutes later, the peas fall to the bed, letting me know she's asleep. I stay still a while longer, then release her, rolling to my back. So many thoughts are running through my mind, rage in my veins, my heart weakened to the woman next to me.

The woman I've been dreaming about is finally in my bed. The one I've fantasized about for over a year and I've imagined when fucking others. She's here, lying next to me and I can't sleep.

Watching her, my chest hurts. She's the most beautiful woman I've ever seen and equally the most fascinating. She's so smart, teases, jokes, and flirts. And... trusts me. She trusts me with her life. That's what brought her here tonight. I would do anything for her and I think she knows it.

I sit up and scrub my face with my hands. She stirs beside me, making me want to stay. I really should, but I just can't stay here any longer...

A promise is a promise and all that. But some promises are worth breaking. *This is one of them.*

13

LARA

I WAKE UP to an empty bed and a wet spot where the peas have defrosted on the mattress in front of me. I'm not happy about either. My body aches in ways it never has before and I'm hoping never does again. *This is not good.*

After a few minutes, I force myself up, my neck just as stiff as my body. "Kaz?" I call, but no one answers. I slowly walk to the living room and call again, "Kaz? Are you here?" My heart starts racing from nerves and fear. It's barely dawn outside and he should be here. Looking out the front window, his car is in the driveway. He's in the driver's seat with his head down.

I run for the door and straight out to his side of the car and knock. He jumps when he hears me. Seeing the door is unlocked, I open it, but he just stares at me, a haze of emotions built up inside his normally happier eyes. His silence is frightening, so I shatter it with worried questions, "What are you doing? Why are you out here?"

"I couldn't sit by and do nothing."

My hand covers my mouth as I suck in a jagged breath. "What did you do?"

"I went to see him—"

"Kaz, no." I lean into the vehicle and hug him. "Are you okay?"

When I stand back up, he says, "I couldn't get to him. I tried. I almost rammed the damn guard gate down."

I reach for his hand on the steering wheel. Resistant at first, he finally loosens his grip and allows me to tug gently. "Come inside." I'm hoping to coax him from the car. "Please. Come with me."

His eyes meet mine and our gazes hold an aching few seconds before he slowly unfolds from the car to stand in front me on the driveway. The moon is hidden behind clouds, the dark still fading away despite the pain evident in the lines carved across his forehead, marring his handsome face. He cups my face and holds my chin up. One kiss, and then another on the lips before he leans his forehead against mine. "I couldn't protect you or help you. Please forgive me."

There's intensity held between us as another kiss is placed on my forehead and his arms wrap around me, holding me as if I'll disappear if he lets me go. I slide my hands around him and hold him just as tight, until it starts to hurt my ribs. "Going after him doesn't help me, Kaz. Being here like you have does." I lift up until I'm looking into his eyes. "Thank you. Thank you for caring, but I'm relieved you didn't see him. He's…" I tuck my head against his chest and look down, shame filling my chest. "He's not himself right now."

"I know you want to see the good in him. I know you struggle inside against what you thought you knew and what he's revealed himself to be. But you don't have to fight this war. He doesn't fight fair anyway. A man should never hit a woman. *Ever*. A coward does." His soft strokes are comforting, his words firm in his belief. "You're stronger than him and he knows it. He's trying to intimidate you to get you back. You can't fall for it, Lara. Promise me you won't."

"I won't." The reply comes easily as the truth resides inside my heart. And then I confess too much. "I don't want to be with him. I want you."

"I know," he repeats as if reaffirming the first part, but not responding to the latter. Releasing me, he shuts the car door and then takes my hand. As we walk to the house, his body is stiff, the muscles in his arms tense. "My father hit my mother and my sister."

"What?" My heart pauses before picking up at the news he's just dropped. For a lack of anything else to say, I go with my gut. "I'm sorry."

"Don't be. No one should make apologies for him. He should own the damage he's caused. It's squarely on him." He waits at the door for me to pass and shuts it behind us.

"Do you mind if I ask what happened?" I have an idea, but I want to know everything about Kaz, even the darker side.

"Which time?"

My eyes go wide.

Kaz's chuckle is low, not like the lighthearted laugh I'm used to. He says, "It became the norm for them. I couldn't adapt."

"No one should adapt to abuse," I say shocked as we walk into the bedroom.

"I tried to tell them that. They wouldn't listen to me. I was a kid."

"Oh my God, Kaz. That's awful. Who broke it up?"

"His bodyguar—" He stops just as he seems to catch himself.

I climb into bed, but look at him before pulling the covers over me. His shirt comes off and his pants are removed. He slides in next to me and lies down, staring up at the ceiling. Turning to my side, I lay my head down on the pillow gently and watch him. "I've never heard you talk about your family. I don't know anything about you."

"My family is complicated."

"You said that last time."

"It's the truth every time. Nothing's changed."

"Do you see them?"

A wry grin spreads slowly across his face and he looks at me. "It's almost six in the morning, get some rest."

I move my hand so it's on his chest and I can feel his heart pumping beneath. "Why won't you talk to me?"

"I do talk to you. I've already said way more than I intended to."

"You don't trust me."

Kissing my hand, he says, "This isn't about trust. I trust you, Lara. You wouldn't be here if I didn't."

"Then what is it? Why do you hold so tight to some things and are so open with others?"

Most guys would be irritated by now—all this talk about feelings and family—but not Kaz. His smile returns, the one that's most genuine. The backs of his fingers glide lightly over my cheek bringing me back to the reality of how I must look. "Go to sleep," he whispers. "We have plenty of daylight hours to learn every last thing about each other."

"Do we?" I ask, moving closer to him and placing a kiss on his shoulder.

He kisses the top of my head and slips his arm under me, holding me close. "We do." His body gives me peace, his words settle my mind, and I drift off... *hoping he won't leave me again.*

THE SUN HAS RISEN, his body silhouetted by the rays streaming in from the windows highlighting the strength of his muscles, his broad shoulders, and strong back. He's whole under the night sky, but the sunlight shines through his broken pieces. I move quietly from the bed and touch his back, gentle not to startle him.

The hardness of his body softens when he turns around and looks at me. Really looks at me, as if he's counting my bruises. "You're so damn beautiful and he tried to destroy that. What he didn't count on is your beauty goes deeper than your skin." His hand caresses my cheek. His touch is gentle, a caring gesture I wish could heal my outsides. He does in more ways than he knows for my insides. "No more swelling. That's good."

"Magic peas, I guess." I shrug unsure what to do in the light of day.

When I laugh with a softened tone, he leans in and kisses my cheek, moves to the edge of my lips and places another. His hand holds the curve of my neck, his touch more careful than I like. My eyes close, letting him cover me in his caring affection. "I've wanted to do that to you longer than you know." He stops the kisses and rests his forehead on my shoulder.

"You've kissed me before," I whisper.

"Not like this. Not with all the barriers gone and the obstacles out of our way. Free and easy like we have all day." His lips find mine and a passion ignites between us as our mouths open. My fingers weave into his hair, holding him to me. I want to enjoy this before the moment is burst by reality.

Our mouths part and he takes my hand. "Come with me."

We need to talk, but whether that is now or later, I'm game for either, weak to the man leading me back to bed. Kaz goes to shut the bedroom door though we both know no one will disturb us. I like the privacy, but I really like his thoughtfulness, or maybe it's a protectiveness he feels.

When he returns, he sits on the mattress and kisses me again. This kiss is not a solitary act, but one that leads to more. Our bodies fall back, entwining and sharing each breath we take and exhale. His knee parts my legs and he moves to position himself over me. The pressure elicits heavy breaths and quick whispers from him, "I want you... so much."

"Don't stop."

We lift and he takes my shirt over my head. I move forward to kiss him again, but when our lips meet, his are still. Kaz sits back and I look up at him, leaning back on my elbows. "What?" Following his gaze, I look down. The bruising has transformed into darkened abstract shapes. And my breath is taken away in the worst of ways. My hands fly to cover myself, heat swarming my cheeks.

But before I can run, he covers my hands, gentle to the touch. "I won't hurt you."

"I don't want you to see me like this. I'd forgotten," I say, looking away, every little detail of plaster easier to stare at instead of the eyes that made me feel beautiful. *I don't want to close my eyes or I'll see Mark's disdain again as his punches landed on my skin.* Kaz's silence twists my insides, knotting my emotions, tears replacing the strength I thought I possessed.

He traces the bruising over my breast. The touch of his fingertips is cooling, and I look up when he asks, "What did he hit you with?"

His eyes stay focused on my body, when I reply, "I don't want to talk about that and ruin this, what we were doing."

"It's not ruined. I just don't understand how someone could hurt another person like he did you. *Until now.* Now I want to hurt him in ways that will destroy his career and rearrange his face for-fucking-ever."

"You're better than him, Kaz." I touch his chest, rubbing over his heart, that deep throb calming me. "I know you are. I see the good in you even when you pretend to be so bad."

"I have..." He turns away, but then leans down again and kisses me. "I don't want to talk about me." When he kisses me this time, it all changes from sweet caresses to a pressure that tells me his darkest desires. In a low voice that teeters on midnight, he asks, "Do you want to be with me?"

My lips feel abandoned, so I lift up, and press mine to his this time. "I do. So much. Make love to me, Kaz."

Running his hands over my shoulders, he says, "I don't want to hurt you."

"We'll take it slow."

With his mouth on my neck, his hot breath blankets my body in ways that make me want him more. "I don't know if I can with you."

I adjust beneath him until his eyes are over mine and our bodies are aligned. The feel of his erection through our underwear makes me squirm. The dreams I've had of being with him are becoming reality. Pushing my thoughts away, I go with feelings and act on instinct, succumbing to the fantasy, to the sensations, to the man himself.

His body taut, but gentle as he moves against me, pressing himself between my legs. Our kisses become a language spoken to each other, the words not needed. His body slides to the side, his breathing coming in pants like mine. Lying back, he covers his eyes with his arms, blocking the brightness of the room, blocking me out. "I don't know if I can do this."

My hands cover my chest as rejection trickles in. "What?" I ask, my voice weak, protecting my heart. "You don't want me?"

He turns to me, taking my hand and squeezing. "No, I'm sorry. That's not what I meant. I just don't know that I can be what you need right now."

"What do I need?"

"You need to be cared for and all I want to do is fuck you." He lies back with a groan. "See? I'm a fucking Neanderthal."

"Maybe I don't want care right now. Maybe I want to fuck too."

Levity invades the heavy space when an all-knowing grin appears. "I was afraid of that."

"Are you really afraid?" I tease.

"No, but it makes me so fucking hot for you."

My mouth drops open. "All I have to do is tell you I want to fuck and bam, just like that, we get to fuck?"

He nods with raised eyebrows. "I'm tired of us dancing around this," he says, waving between us. "This attraction, our chemistry. Whatever you want to call it. I want more than just sex with you. I..." His gaze lowers from my eyes to my hip where he traces over it with his hand. "I like you, Lara. I have since Rochelle started bringing you around a year ago. I thought that night at the beach might be our time, but our timing's been off. It's not now, and I'm not going to miss this opportunity. So if you want me to make love to you, I will. But if you'd rather take this slow and go out for breakfast, we can do that too."

My heart flutters to life, breaking free from the cocoon it's been sheltered in for months. I don't want breakfast. I just want him. "You won't break me, Kaz."

Deft fingers hook the sides of my undies and take them down, painfully slow as his eyes take me in. I want to squirm, to move from his view, but I stay still trying to fight against the humiliation Mark's attack has caused me. I liked my body and now I feel shame. I hate him for making me feel unworthy of affection.

"Open your eyes." His voice is low, but firm. I hadn't realized my eyes were closed, much less squeezed tight. When I see him, his are set on me. "Don't close your eyes when I'm touching you like that. I'll stop if you want me to, but if I'm hurting you, tell me."

"I'm sorry. You weren't hurting me. I like you touching me." I muster the courage to reveal my inner thoughts. "I feel embarrassed for you to see me like this. *He's* made me feel embarrassed to show my body."

"You have a beautiful body. These bruises will go away, but I'm worried he's scarred your beautiful mind."

"Me too. But I don't want you to stop. Help me through this. I want you to touch me, to feel me, to hold me, and to fuck me. Make me feel you, only you, Kaz." *Make me feel less battered and bruised.*

He kisses my chest, healing my soul as his hands caress my body. His fingers dig deeper into my hips, then his hand slides up and squeezes my breasts. "Tell me you want me to fuck you again."

I trail the tips of my fingers down his chest and lower until I'm holding his erection firmly in my hand. "Fuck me, Kaz."

As he licks his lips, his hands go to my waist. "*Fuuuck.* Are you sure?"

"I want you to make me forget. Replace all the bad with this. I want you." Just as he leans down to kiss me, my hands fly up to his chest to stop him. "Do you have a condom?"

"Shit!" He falls back heavily, his hands scrubbing over his face. Then he jumps up abruptly, surprising me. "I don't have anything here. Maybe in my car?"

Sitting up quickly, I grab his arm before he takes off running naked out of the house. "I've got one."

He looks back at me, an impressed expression on his face. "You do?"

"I do," I reply with a little waggle of my eyebrows. "Ouch. Remind me not to do that again."

"You're not allowed to hurt yourself either. Where's the condom?"

"In the bathroom drawer. I left it there the other day, just in case." He's gone only a few seconds before he returns with the packet between his teeth and a smirk that could light up LA. Lying back on my elbows, I watch him and anticipation builds.

Kaz is just as hard as he was a minute ago and I take that as a compliment. He crawls up the bed. If crawling can be done with swag, he owns it. Cocky, confident, and totally hot. He rips the package open, sits back, and rolls it on. With a nod of his head, he asks, "You ready for me?"

"I don't know."

His smile falters. "You don't know?"

"No." Spreading my legs, I add, "I think you should take a closer look and find out for yourself... with your mouth."

His eyes go wide. "Damn, Lara."

I shrug. "I know what I like."

"You're fucking sexy as hell." Lowering down onto his stomach, he rests his upper body on his elbows. When his mouth is level with my vagina, he doesn't wait for permission. He's not gentle and doesn't ease into it. Kaz just plants his mouth on me, causing my breath to flee momentarily, and kisses me much like he kissed me earlier, and the fire deep inside is reignited.

I collapse onto the mattress, my body sinking into it as his tongue teases and his lips embrace. A moan too breathy for my liking escapes and I open my eyes and stare at the ceiling. I can't hold them open for long. His tongue swirls and I'm lost to the feeling again. My back arches until I grab the sheets on either side of my body to anchor me. A tornado forms, gathering strength on the inside and building into so much more until I can't hold back any longer. I hold his head, my fingers woven into his hair, as I fall apart beneath him.

Loud moans and soft sighs are given to the man who makes me feel everything too much. Heat covers my chest and he slips up my body and peppers kisses across it. When he reaches my mouth, his eyes meet mine just as he presses down, our lips parting and our tongues finding each other again.

I feel a different pressure as he pushes up to look down at me. "You lied."

"I did?"

"You're ready for me." A rough thrust forward and my head tilts back. I'm so full as a healthy stretch burns me in ecstasy.

When his chest meets mine, his head drops to my shoulder, and his body stops moving. His breath is heavy as if the whole world has weighed him down. I reach around and hold him, stroking the back of his hair, and whisper, "Hey there."

Turning his head into the nook of my neck, he replies, "One sec."

"Are you okay?"

He nods and starts moving again, slowly at first, then picks up the pace. Our bodies grind in love as we maneuver and relish each other. Pushing gently against his shoulders, I say, "I want to be on top."

Rolling us over, I'm situated and moving, using his chest as leverage. He struggles to hold his composure, and my hips are grabbed as he slams into me, grunting in a way that is sexual and such a turn on that I can't remain quiet. Sensations like these have to be expressed. "God, Kaz."

My body gives in just as he calls my name, "Lara, fuck!" His enunciation is dirty and the ending a hard K to go with the orgasm.

I lie forward, my own body depleted and worn out in the best of ways. With our bodies pressed together, I give him three kisses. He whispers lyrics in my ear while strumming along my spine, leaving goose bumps in the melody's wake. "He'll never hurt you again. I promise."

14

LARA

REGRET FILLS ME as I watch Kaz sleeping. I shouldn't have involved him in this mess that is my life, but he is just so damn irresistible.

It's early in the afternoon, the day not shot. I get up quietly and tiptoe to the bathroom, taking my clothes from the floor with me. I shut the door and get dressed. When I'm done, I peek out. Kaz is still sleeping and I feel guilty for leaving.

I should stay.

I want to stay, but I know Mark and this will be bad if I don't leave now. I walk out the door, then stop, tears filling my eyes. Everything about this moment. Everything I'm doing. It's all wrong. Entirely wrong. Every bone in my body tells me to stay with him. I take another step, but my heart remains behind.

His phone is nearby. I need to call a cab. There's cash in my jar at home. I can pay the driver when we get there. Taking another step, I stop again and look back at the door that divides me from something that feels like it could be more than just a few-night stands.

Kaz feels more like a forever. *Am I willing to walk away from my forever?*

Can I walk away?

Turning around, I go back into the bedroom and undress again. I slip under the covers and into his arms as he curls around me. "You okay?" he asks, his voice husky from sleep. *More than okay. This feels right.*

"I am now."

"WHAT ARE YOU GONNA DO?" Kaz asks.

The grass under my body tickles my hands. I sit up, looking around the backyard. "Go about life the best I can." Feeling like this conversation is going to need more than I can give at this time, I stand up. "I should get going."

He gets up, and with his hand on my lower back, he guides me inside. "I meant what I said. I want you to stay. At least for a few days."

My heart listens as I'm reminded that he wants me, as I do him. My head wages a war against the possibility. "I know, but I need to go to mine. I can't just disappear from my life as much as I want to right now." I reach to grab my purse out of habit, but I don't have anything here. "Do you mind driving me home?"

"Yes," he says, looking irritated. "Why are you going home alone?"

"Because I live alone."

"Does he have a key?"

He does. "He won't use it."

"How do you know?"

"I don't know. I don't think he meant—"

"What the fuck, Lara?" His voice is raised, but the anger isn't directed at me. "Come home with me. Or let me get you a hotel for a few days, a week, enough time until you're safe and have changed the locks."

"I don't want to live in fear."

"Look where your bravery got you."

"Stop," I warn, my head starting to hurt again as I climb into the car. "I'm going home." Then tears start to come again. When he gets in the car, I look at him, letting them fall. "I need to do this. I need to prove to myself, and to you, that I can be strong. I'm not this person. He's made me into someone I don't want to be."

"You don't have to prove anything. You don't have to change for me. You don't have to be anything but who you are with me. But you do need to be safe and I'm not as confident as you when it comes to that."

"I can't just stay away forever, Kaz."

"Stay away another night."

Looking down at my lap, I wish I could, but I don't want us to be about him. Our time is precious. It matters in ways I can't tell him yet. I won't taint it any longer with my burdens. "I have to work."

He watches me. Kaz sees everything and he knows I'm not giving in, so he shifts the car into gear and nods. "Okay." Reaching over he rubs my leg. "I'll buy you a coffee on the way."

"Deal."

After getting a large cafe mocha, I'm anxious to get home and shower. I'm sure Kaz is as well since the new house doesn't have towels, soap, or clean clothes. After texting Lane to stop by and leave his key for me under the mat, I sit back. Kaz's hand finds its way between mine and our fingers intertwine. His eyes are focused forward, the air in the car changing with the emotion that burdens us. "When will I see you again?" he asks.

"I'm not sure." I glance out the window before saying, "I'm not sure about anything right now. I don't know how to feel. I'm sorry. I know *what* I feel, but that seems to be all." I take a deep breath and release it before finishing. "Obviously I have some stuff to sort out. But I can't even think clearly until I clean up and assess the damage."

"How does your face feel?"

"Tender to the touch, but I'm okay. A lot of it I can hide with heavy makeup. But I'll work from home for a few days to make sure all the swelling is down. I don't want this getting out."

His words aren't harsh, but there's an underlying fury hiding in the question. "Why are you protecting him?"

"I'm protecting myself. I don't want to answer questions about what happened. I just want it to go away."

"Will *he* go away that easily?

Resting my arm under the window, I whisper, "I hope so."

"I'm struggling not to go over and kick his ass for what he did. I need you to be angry as well."

"I am. My head's just crazed, my thoughts scattered. I can't believe he did this to me, to be honest. I need time to think, to process what's happened, and to make sure nothing else does."

"Okay." He pulls up to the front of my townhome. Before I can stop him, he's out of the car and headed to my side. When the door opens, he says, "I'll walk you up." I won't argue with him. He needs to do this and I like that he wants to.

My front porch is filled with vases of roses in the deepest shades of red. I pause when I see them. *Oh God. What will Kaz think?* There are at least ten vases with a dozen or more roses in each. My hold of the railing tightens and I look back, catching a glimpse of Kaz's troubled face.

I try to pretend I'm not scared, try to pretend that my heart hasn't dropped to the pit of my stomach, try to fool Kaz into believing that I'm fine. Moving forward, I step through the vases, leaving them there to rot outside. I don't have to guess who they're from. I know, and I want them gone, out of my sight, but I don't want to worry Kaz though I have a feeling from his expression it's too late for that. When we reach the door, I turn, put on a wide smile, and say, "Thank you."

With his brows cinched together, he looks past me to the door. "Do you mind if I have a look around before I go?"

"You don't have to do that," I say nonchalantly.

"Lara."

His tone is enough to cause me to step aside. He opens the door with the key we find just where Lane left it, and walks in, looking around. His gaze darts around the room and I follow him inside. Maybe he's pretending like me because he asks, "You'll call or text me?"

Each door is opened, but he's not intrusive, just glancing around each room quickly.

"I will."

He seems satisfied and heads for the door. "The offer still stands. You can stay with me or I'll get you a hotel."

"As you can see, I'll be fine. But thank you. That doesn't feel adequate for all you did for me last night, but it's sincere."

"Anytime. If you ever need me, I'll be here for you."

I nod, then lean closer to kiss him. I whisper against his lips, "Thank you," then step back again. Neither of us says goodbye and I'm glad. I can't handle the permanency of that, not with what I still have to face. He does say, "Change the locks right away."

"I will."

He shuts the door behind him and I lock it, then lean against it and take a deep breath. When I exhale, I push off and go into my bedroom.

I'm not home even ten minutes when a ring of the doorbell sounds throughout the townhome. I look through the peephole, but it's the flower guy. Well aware of the routine at this stage, he sets them down and leaves.

I go into my bedroom and straight for the bathroom to start the shower. While taking off my clothes, I get a glimpse of myself in the mirror, something I'd been avoiding. My mouth drops open, breath catching, and the color in my face drains away in an instant as reality sets in. Kaz had taken my mind off things, allowed me the time to forget. But here it is in all its purplish glory, now perhaps Mark's bragging rights to his steroid-using buddies. He's not the first pro-athlete to hit a woman. In time, his paychecks will rise even higher and I'll become locker-room fodder.

Covering my cheeks with my hands, I step closer. I'm hideous in blues, purples, grays, and hints of yellow. A little scab has formed at the corner of my mouth and my eye still has a little swelling around the lid, but I never would have known around Kaz. He treated me like he always does—like I'm beautiful.

I'm not. Mark took that away. He stole it without so much as an apology.

He's not going to let me ride off into the sunset with Kaz. He won't be happy until I'm as miserable as he is, and he's come close already. I just don't understand why. A knot in my stomach tightens, pulling my heartstrings attached to Kaz in with it.

I don't want Kaz dragged under in the process of settling things with Mark.

In the shower, the water flows over my body, drowning the negative away and leaving me clean with the memories of being with Kaz. There's something about him that exposes my heart in ways I've been so careful to protect in the past, an openness that I trust, and an honesty I need. He doesn't have a hidden agenda or want something from me. And he wants me.

Once I'm out and dressed, I go into the kitchen. With a hot mug of tea in my hands, my subconscious braces for what lies ahead. My hands begin to shake, my thoughts well aware of the inevitable confrontation with Mark. He said I was his. *Only his.* He said I will stay willingly or he'll make me. All the things he said come flashing back like the ringing in my ear. Hot liquid and shards of glass hit my feet making me jump, my scream deafening on the inside, but outwardly silent. I teeter on shaky legs as I slide down the cabinetry. The shattered mug and tea-covered floor beneath my feet. A throbbing draws me to look down and blood swirls with the dark liquid.

A lump forms in my throat stifling the need to call for help. There's no one to help even if I could vocalize my need. Grappling for the edge of the counter, I secure my hand on the side, and pull myself up, careful not to press down on the balls of my feet.

I step out from the mess and hobble to the sink. Hopping up on the counter, I inspect the bottom of my foot. The cut is small, but the shard remains. The irony of Mark and the broken glass not lost on me. I pull the glass out and run it under water a second to clean it. Getting back down, I look at the mess as I pull a roll of paper towel from the holder. I kneel down on my hands and knees and with a huge wad of towels, clean the mess. This chaos of browns and reds on the paper, purples, blues, blacks on me, this is my life. Somehow in the span of a couple months, my better senses turned against me allowing me to let the little signs slide. This is what happens when you lose sight of the reason you started in the first place. This is what happens when you witness horrible things and brush them under the rug, or worse, don't do anything at all.

Mark Renner was a ticking time bomb in our relationship. It started out good and somewhere during the fun, he twisted it into a game of control, obsession, and possession. *How did I not see that?*

I shouldn't have confronted him about the drugs. Not alone anyway. I had no choice. I was just turning a blind eye to what deep down I already knew, as the changes in him were evident. I grew up in LA. I know the signs. I've dated guys who did drugs. But Mark was different. He was a master of disguise. *Don't the major leagues drug test?* I know they do, but they didn't catch him. Or they turned a blind eye in exchange for a title win. Maybe I relied on what I assumed instead of what I knew.

My doorbell rings. *Again.* I know it's more flowers, as it seems that's his "thing" when he's done something wrong. By the onslaught of deliveries, he knows it's bad between us. I've told him. He knows. Why is he so desperate to hold on to something that he can't? I heat my kettle to make another tea, not bothering with the door, but then I hear it open and freeze. *Damn it!* The deadbolt. *Shit.* I forgot to latch it. I reach into a drawer and pull out a knife.

"Lara?" Mark calls.

My hold on the knife tightens, my legs shaking as much as my hands. I stay still and silent, hoping he doesn't find me.

When he rounds the corner a smile covers his face. "Hey there."

The knife shivers in my hands as I hold it up. Despite wanting to drop into a ball on the floor, I steady myself, and force myself to speak. "Get out of here."

The smirk on his face sends anger shooting through my veins. He shrugs. "Babe, c'mon. I came over to apologize." With his hands up in surrender, he looks at me like I'm the crazy one, and chuckles. "No need for violence."

I choke on his words. "No need for violence? Look what you did to me."

"No. No." Now that asshole grin disappears. "I didn't do that."

My eyebrows shoot to the ceiling in astonishment. "What are you talking about? Look at me." My phone is nowhere near and my land-line closer to him, but I square my shoulders. "Leave or I'll call the police."

He steps closer and my breath catches in terror. I swing the knife in front of me, my thoughts unclear if I am strong enough to take him on if it comes to it. "Don't come any closer, Mark. I mean it."

"You don't look that bad. You're always beautiful. You'll always be my pretty woman. I screwed up, but I did not do that to you. You must have fallen and hurt yourself. You're clumsy."

"No, I'm not. I'm not weak and I'm not clumsy. I did not fall. You hurt me," I spew through gritted teeth. "Leave. Now!" I step forward, stomping down the fear that leaves tremors along with my words. With my life on the line, my grip firms, and the knife is solid in front of me as my body steels itself for a fight.

"I can leave, babe. But we're not over."

"You're a delusional drug addict. Get out!"

He pulls something from his pocket and I flinch. When he opens his hand, I see a flash drive. He sets it on the counter and backs up, giving me space.

My gaze flickers between it and him. "What is that?"

"It's us, babe."

My brow furrows, causing pain to shoot across my battered fore-head. "What do you mean?"

"I screwed up. I apologize. But despite everything, I still want to be with you. You're successful and smart. You're not a gold digger, and I can bring you home to my parents. Basically, you look good on my arm and I look better for it. You're what every successful athlete needs standing behind him: a woman who believes in him; a woman who can take care of him. That's you. You're that woman for me."

I'm dumbstruck by his audacity to plead his case as if he has a chance in hell with me. "You're lucky I don't press charges, Mark."

"Just watch this," he says, pointing to the flash drive on the counter. "I'll give you tonight alone. I expect you back at mine by tomorrow night."

"You're fucking crazy. I will never return to you or your house. Now get out!"

He leaves without another word and I follow him with the knife held in front of me until he's out the front door. I bolt the locks this time. His key doesn't work on the bolt, so I'm safe for the time being.

My heart races as I lean against the door, exhausted from the unexpected confrontation. I'll call to have the locks changed tomorrow. That's easier than trying to get my key back from him. I go back into the kitchen and grab the flash drive. My curiosity has gotten the best of me. When my computer comes to life, I plug it in, and wait to see what pops up. There's only one file—a video.

I pause as dread fills my limbs. With the knife set next to the mouse, I click play.

My heart stops.

My breath stops.

My world stops.

Both hands cover my mouth just as a loud gasp startles me. Then I realize that sound came from me. I stare at the screen in horror. Mark is naked on top of me as he grunts my name for the camera. *My body is exposed.*

Mortified, I turn it off, not able to watch anymore. I run to grab my phone and dial his number.

"Hello?" he answers from his car, sounding so fucking full of himself.

"What have you done?"

"Nothing yet, babe."

"Why do you have this?"

"Originally, because I liked watching it, but now I've found a new use."

The fight leaves my body as dread sets in, knowing what he's going to say next. "And what is that?"

"That's up to you, Lara."

"Just say it, Mark," I cry. "What do you want?"

He sighs, and if I know him at all, he's shaking his head. "Have I not made myself clear?"

"You're as clear as mud." I wrap my arm around my stomach, worried of losing its contents. "What do you want?"

"You. It's that simple."

"You can't have me. I don't want to be with you."

"I've been nice—"

My anger battles with fear and my words and accusations come barreling out. "You beat the shit out of me and then say you didn't. Are you psycho?"

"Lara, I remember us fighting, but I don't believe I did that to you. I love you. I wouldn't do that. I've never hit a girl before." He pauses, then says, "Maybe I blacked out—"

"You knew exactly what you were doing." I look down in disgust while readjusting the phone in my trembling hand. I want to throw it across the room, but I don't, knowing this has to be finished. "You make me sick. I will never be with you again."

"That video says otherwise. It's my insurance policy. It's awards season and I want you by my side."

"No."

"Yes, or I'll send a copy of that video to every publication in California. And then I'll send the other twenty-six videos I've made over the months to all the tabloids in the world, as well as hire the most successful porn directors to release it as my compilation."

"You wouldn't." I hit him where I know it will hurt his ego. "You would lose sponsors."

"When was the last time an athlete looked bad while having sex with his girlfriend? And," he says, and I can tell by his tone, he's smirking, "I look damn good in them. But as you know, the public doesn't look well upon the women in sex tapes. This would destroy your career and make you the talk of the town in the worst of ways. God, I love public opinion."

"You're sick and need help."

"But I'm also right. And you're smart enough to know it."

I'm too angry to cry, the hate I feel for him comes in a wave of venom.

"I'll go to the police and show them what you did to me. No one likes an out-of-control steroid-using athlete. You'll be ruined."

"You know what people don't like?"

He pauses, toying with me. The words held hostage until I play his sick game. "What?"

"A druggy rocker who beat up a groupie after a sex-filled rager."

"What are you talking about?" My words barely make it out, my heart sinking to the pit of my stomach.

"Your boy on the side. What do you think is more believable? An all-American hometown hero or a replacement guitarist who can't handle his drugs and liquor? The more likely conclusion isn't me, sweetheart."

Kaz.

I can't be with Kaz. Not with Mark like this. I can't. The tears finally fall over the lids and down my cheeks. "I won't," I whisper. "I won't hurt him. I won't let you either."

"You sound so convincing right now, babe. I'm almost tempted to turn around and make sure you understand what choice you're making." My head jolts back as I listen to his threat, his tone menacing. "Maybe it was a blackout. Or maybe it wasn't."

He's going to kill me. I can feel it in my bones. Resolve is starting to fill my veins. He's never going to let me walk away, not without a fight for my life.

"Why are you so quiet, babe? Reconsidering?" His tone is back to normal as if he's just asked if I want kung pao chicken or beef and broccoli for dinner. *He's not delusional. He's dangerous. But why me?* He could and does get any bimbo he wants.

"Why do you want a girlfriend? You were cheating on me. Be single. Play the dating field. It's what you do best."

"How about this? We go out a few more times when your face looks pretty again and I catch you hitting on another guy at a bar. I kick his ass. Of course. And then you and I have a big fight in front of the paparazzi. We break up and I hit the talk show circuit to talk about how heartbroken I am and win the sympathy of America, which in turn, makes me look good going into mid-season."

"And makes me look bad, right?"

"All's fair in love—"

"And war. You'd be wise to remember that."

"You'd be wise to look like the arm candy you are and remember your place."

"Fuck you!"

"Fuck you, babe. I'll see you tomorrow with a smile on your face, or else. And bring dinner. It might be a long night while we plan the big event." He hangs up and just like the mug that broke, I'm left with shards, destroyed in an instant by the man I once thought I had a future with. *It's not love.*

KAZ CALLS AROUND nine that night. I had fallen asleep on my couch watching an old black and white movie. I answer, but I shouldn't have. Not in the state I'm in and not when I know what I have to do, and how it will hurt him. It's a domino effect of the tragedy that has become my life. Better now than later before love is involved. *Because he is a man I could love.*

"Hi," I whisper into the receiver.

"Sorry for disturbing you. Were you sleeping?" he asks.

"I was, but it's okay."

"I wanted to check on you, see how you're doing."

I hide under the throw, wanting to disappear wholly. But reality keeps me grounded right here in heartbreak. "Kaz, we need to talk."

"That doesn't sound good."

"It's not," I say, my true emotions bleeding through. "I like you so much, but there's this stuff I have to deal with that you shouldn't have to suffer through."

"I like you too, Lara, that's why I'll be here for you, however you need. Just name it and I'll be it, for you."

"Be my friend. Be my client. But we can't be more. Not right now."

"What's going on? Don't shut me out. Be honest with me. What has changed?"

"Kaz, I'm sorry. I am. More than you know. You're good. You're amazing, but I can't do this with you. I can't be anything for you right now. My life is just full of complications that I can't drag you into any deeper." I hate the hitch in my voice, but I need to get this out. He needs to be free of me, and any threat to his career... his life. I take a deep breath. "I'm not even sure we should work together."

"I'm not the groveling type, so if you don't want to be with me, we won't do this. But what the fuck happened in the last five hours?" His words are short. His voice is tight and controlled.

"Kaz—"

"Stop saying my name like that! *Fuck.* I thought you were different."

And there it is. There is my out, and even though my heart will splinter into a thousand pieces, I take it. "No," I say, barely getting the single syllable out. "I'm not." Save him the trouble of getting involved with me. Save him from this disaster. He's silent for a moment, and I hold back the sob so desperate to escape. I add, "I don't think it's wise for us to work together either."

"Fine. We won't work together. Then it's okay? Right?"

"I can't—"

"Did last night mean so little to you?"

"No, last night meant everything to me. But today, I have to live in reality."

"Don't do this, Lara. I can come over. We can talk."

"I can't. I can't talk to you anymore. It's too hard. Please don't try to convince me. This is just no good for either of us."

"We're good. We're so good, Lara. Don't do this. Whatever has happened, we can talk through this, we can—"

"Kaz, stop." I close my eyes, but I lower my voice until I'm whispering, "It was good while it las—"

"You're giving up."

"I have no choice. It's too much, too complicated right now. You need to be happy and that can't be with me."

"I don't know why you're doing this, but I really hate you for it."

The word hate is a dagger to the heart and I start to cry. He says,

"I've dragged this out long enough, I guess." He stops and I hear his rough breath before he steadies his tone. "Have a good life, Lara." Then he hangs up on me before I have a chance to say goodbye. I don't know if I could anyway, but this time, I wanted the chance.

I'll trade my heart to protect his. The pain now is far less than it will be down the road. He'll see I saved him the trouble. *I just hope one day he forgives me and knows I only did this for the best.*

Even if my heart died in the process.

15

LARA

I ANSWER MY phone on the third ring. "Hello?"

"Open the door, Lara." Rochelle sounds irritated.

Dragging myself out of bed, I don't bother with my robe, and go. When I crack the door open, I keep my head down, not wanting her to see my face. She stands on the other side of the field of delivered roses, all still looking beautiful despite the intention behind them. "What is this?" she asks.

"Flowers."

"Obviously. Who are they from and why are they still out here?"

"One guess."

"Mark?"

"You got it."

"Man, he spent thousands on these. Guess you've talked then." I hear the glass vases grinding against the cement as she rearranges. I peek out, but she catches me. "Can I come in?"

"I'm sleeping. I was—"

"Sorry about that. Since you're up, wanna brunch?"

"I can't." I fake yawn, hoping to convince her how tired I am with my bad acting. "I'm just gonna lie in bed all day."

"What's going on? Why aren't you opening the door? And since when do you do nothing all day? You don't know how to relax."

"I'm tired."

Her hand reaches the door and she presses, but I hold firm, only one eye still revealed to her. But she's onto me, and I'm a shitty liar. I've got to get her to leave. After everything she's been through, I don't want to be another burden when she's finally found peace, so I say, "Thanks for stopping by. I'll call you later." I shut the door and lean against it, guilt covering me from head to toe. I run to my phone and call her, trying to assuage my emotional turmoil. When she answers, the words come rushing out. "I'm sorry. I just, I can't do this today, Ro. I want to tell you everything, but I need some time."

"You're scaring me, Lara. Open the door."

"Don't worry about me. I'll be fine. I'm just dealing with stuff I can't talk about right now."

"What is going on?"

"Please trust me. I'm fine."

Her frustration is heard. "Are you sure? I'm seriously worried by this conversation."

"I'm sure. I'm gonna go back to bed and rest. We'll talk soon."

"I'm going to trust you, but if you ever need anything, call me."

"I will. Thank you again."

I don't like to lie, especially to my friends, so keeping it vague keeps us all safe for now. I look down at the time on my phone. Seven hours to figure out what I'm going to do or show up at Mark's with a smile and dinner ready.

THE STREET IS QUIET. If all the people only knew what I was about to do; if they only knew how far their neighbor has fallen from his shiny pedestal. If they only knew what he was making me do.

I know. And I feel worthless for doing it.

I feel despicable.

Disgust.

Shame.

I hate myself for doing this, but it's a necessary evil. The man is unstable, so this is for the greater good. Until I figure out a way to end this forever, I'll do what I have to, to survive, and to protect Kaz, who I already miss so much.

The gate code has been restored to the one I know and I'm let in. Once inside, the large bag of takeout is set on the kitchen counter and I start unpacking the food. After pulling the plates from the cabinet, I serve the food and set the table just the way I know he likes it. Stupidly, I once thought we were just getting to know each other when he'd comment on domestic things I did around his home, like setting the table, doing his laundry, and straightening up despite him having a maid once a week. Now I realize I was the one set-up. He wanted me barefoot and pregnant, his little stereotypical Stepford wife.

I stop my inner tirade and my fingers begin to shake.

He's home.

I can sense him near, my emotions curling in on themselves out of fear. He's chosen to torture me, to use this "insurance" to his complete advantage, and here I am a pawn in his sick game.

Satan himself enters the room. I move quickly behind my chair, hoping he just sits and eats, and doesn't expect more from me. But I'm foolish to think he'd want any less.

"Sit down, Lara," he says from the head of the table. "You know I don't like to eat alone."

"I thought that was why you pay the hookers," I reply, inwardly berating myself for speaking out.

"Silly woman." He laughs, but there's no amusement in his eyes, sinking fear right back into me. "I pay hookers for deviant sexual acts that you wouldn't do. Oh, but maybe you'll reconsider now." The smarmy smile that crosses his lips makes me lose my appetite, as if I had one. "Now sit down."

I sit and take my napkin, folding it across my lap. After a few sips of wine, I gather my thoughts together before raising my chin. "What are you doing?"

"What do you mean?" He sets his fork down, as if my very voice annoys him.

"You don't have to do this. You can have a million women. You're famous, rich, and Mark Renner for crying out loud. Why are you doing this?"

"I told you. But I also told my parents about you. I said you were the one."

"If I was the one, you wouldn't have been fucking all the others."

His hand slams down on the table. "Are you dense?"

I jump and the saltshaker tips over. My breathing picks up, so rough in my chest that I reach for my water to quench my throat that's gone dry. "Do not touch that glass," he warns. I look up, our eyes meeting across the table. "You were supposed to be different." He makes it sound so easy, so obvious. "And now you know too much. You could destroy me in one leak to the press. I can't have that. I'd lose everything. Now eat."

"I won't say anything. I promise," I beg. "I'll sign anything you want and be silent, never speak a word of it to anyone."

He stands so abruptly that his chair falls back, causing me to jump. His plate hits the kitchen cabinets, making me scream. All the visions of him hitting me come flashing back as he yells, "Clean that mess up!" His heavy footsteps are heard as he walks out of the room, leaving me in the middle of his disaster.

I swallow hard, wiping away the tears that flood my eyes. My body ceases to rock and I stand up, holding on to the table for support. I don't understand how life can change so dramatically in a few days. I don't know if I should clean up or leave or try some other tactic. Fighting against everything I want to do, I take a deep breath, a large gulp of wine, and go into the game room. He practically lives in there when he's home.

When I open the door, the projector is on, the reel from last season playing on the large screen. Any other time, this would be normal for him. He watches playbacks regularly, but this isn't a playback reel to see what went wrong and to correct it. This is a highlights reel. He sits in the center recliner and stares at the player like he doesn't recognize him.

I don't anymore. Scanning the room for a laptop, I don't see one, so I say, "Please erase the videos, Mark." He doesn't move, not even an inch. "Please."

"I feel like you haven't been listening to me, Lara."

"I have." My voice quivers. Damn it.

"Bring me that black box on the bar and make me a drink."

Since dinner didn't go as I planned, I do as I'm told, trying a new angle. "Mark, it doesn't need to be like this. Women love you. Men envy you. You should be with someone who celebrates you, not fears you." After dropping the ice in the glass, I fill it to the halfway mark with Scotch. I grab the box and take both to him.

"Do you fear me?" There's sincerity in his tone that brings me to look his way. The handsome man I was first attracted to gazes back at me in curiosity. Then confusion clouds his eyes, as if he genuinely doesn't understand why I would be afraid of him.

"Yes." The ugly truth—plain and simple.

He closes his eyes and I stand there waiting. Waiting on a reaction, realization of what he's done, for him to do anything to make this right and hoping it doesn't get worse.

When he opens his eyes again, he takes the drink and downs it, and then hands the glass back to me. Looking right into my eyes, he says, "Fear is a strange emotion. We fear love sometimes or the act of falling in love. We fear death. We fear losing. Sometimes we fear winning. Winning isn't always easy to accept because we start to fear never winning again after tasting victory." Taking the black box from me, he opens it on the wide arm of the leather chair.

I thought I knew fear.

I didn't.

I don't move a muscle, not even to breathe when I see the needles and vials inside the dark blue velvet-lined box. "So fear," he says, preparing the needle, "is not always a bad thing." He loads a vial and I watch though I should probably be running for my life. Tapping the needle twice, he looks up at me and squirts a little, testing it. "Fear drives us to do things we wouldn't normally do."

"So do drugs," I add, wishing I had my phone to record this so I have my own insurance policy.

He nods, and then slowly repeats, "So do drugs."

He injects himself right in front of me, my body tensing even more as if that was possible. Acting calm, cool, collected, I can tell by the intensity of his tone that this isn't just a casual conversation. This is a confession and I'm going to be held liable to keep the secret. "We pay a lot of hush money to keep this secret, but I'm not paid millions for fun. I have to perform and my team looks the other way. Do you think I'm the only one? They love to win as much as I do. You don't get to our level by playing fair. This isn't little league. This is the Majors."

Leaning back in the plush chair, he asks, "What else do you fear, Lara?"

His lids blink, the action not smooth, then he hits me with his gaze again. "Do you really fear those videos being leaked? You fear that people will find out that you have sex, that you enjoy sex? Most people have sex. It's nothing to fear for them to find out, so I'm thinking it's not the videos that you worry about." His hands are balled, fisted until the knuckles are white. "What do you really fear?"

When I don't answer, he stands, grabs the back of my hair and twists down. I scream. My defenses kick in and I slam my fist into his stomach. His hand tightens until I'm bended on my knees in pain, sobbing for his mercy.

His hold on me stays firm while he sits back down. Hatred fills his eyes, his lips contorted in disgust. "You *should* fear me. I can end you. I can end him."

Him—Kaz.

End both of us. My heart lurches into my throat.

"I can make it so he never plays that fucking guitar again. So I'll ask you again. What do you fear, Lara?"

Through pained breaths, I answer, "You."

I'm released and pushed to the ground. "Good."

He clicks play on the remote, and with his eyes glued to the screen, he says, "The Entertainers of the Year Awards are in ten days. I'm nominated in two categories—MVP and Homerun Hottie. Be ready. You're going."

Scrambling to my feet, I trip and land on my hands and knees just behind his chair. Pain shoots through my kneecaps and up my thighs and that's when I realize there is no escaping this. He doesn't hurt me where it can be seen this time because of next week. *Bastard.* There is no escaping him, much less time to search his computer for the videos.

Nice doesn't work.

Fighting back doesn't work.

He's right. The sex tapes don't matter at the end of the day. I might lose clients, and I'd definitely lose respect. One day though, someone else's scandal will bury mine.

But Kaz... I don't know that I can save him when I can't even save myself, but I'm willing to do anything to try.

I don't run this time. I get to my feet and look at the screen. There's a man running bases with a huge smile on his face and the taste of victory on his tongue. That's not the same man sitting in the La-Z-Boy.

No, they're not the same at all.

The man on the screen used to be charming with an award-winning smile. He had a contagious laugh and caring touch.

The man in the chair would hurt someone just because he feels threatened, because he feels little inside. The man who used to play the game because it made him smile is lost. He traded his soul for a paycheck and his greed may kill me in the process.

My heart goes numb, the beats quiet to the slight ringing in my ears. Walking out of the room, I grab my car keys and leave. The night air is thin and I shiver from the chill.

I'm not the woman I was in that house. I'm not weak. *Normally.* He wants me to be. He wants me weak and under his thumb. What length is he willing to go to make that happen? What length will he go to not just control me, but to hurt Kaz?

Mark is a drug addict. That much is clear. Will it be an intervention or a drug test that takes him down? I'm willing to stage both. This is not about my safety or me.

I have to do something to end this once and for all.

16

LARA

I MANAGE TO avoid most everyone the next week, especially Kaz. He had two out-of-town shows, which helped me to stay away. But his words have played over and over in my mind. *There's no point dragging this out then. Have a good life, Lara.* I have almost texted him so many times, wishing I could replay our last conversation and tell him how I wish things were different. My life is in shambles though. I can't—won't—drag him down with me, so I try to remain strong most of the time. Despite what we decided, my heart hasn't gotten the memo.

My office down the hall is busy this morning. Lane comes into my bathroom while I'm putting makeup on and sets a coffee down in front of me. "Late start?" he asks.

"Tired." I've covered the remains of the bruising, which is light at worst and gone for the most part. Hopefully no one can tell.

"Oh God, me too. This guy at the club was a mess last night. I had to rescue a friend, dragging his ass home, after they got in a kerfuffle." Kerfuffle makes me smile. Lane makes me smile. He's resilient, troubles rolling right off his back. It's a quality I've always admired in him. I take things to heart and carry my troubles around like a mass that can't be amputated.

He sits on a bench near the tub and starts scrolling on his iPad. "I have Calliope's this morning. The samples came in from France for the toile we ordered. You need to approve two before we can take them to show her. You have Kaz's this afternoon and," he says, smiling to himself, "maybe into dinner, if all goes well. Hubba hubba."

"The Fabian project has been cancelled. Take it off the books please. What time do you leave for Calliope's?" I ask while swiping on mascara. "I'll work from the studio today and I have four ca—"

"Whoa. Whoa. Whoa! Hold up. I know he's been traveling, but what do you mean the Fabian project has been cancelled?"

I dig through my makeup tray, keeping my eyes lowered. "It's been cancelled. No big deal. Just changed his mind is all."

"No."

My eyes meet his in the reflection of the mirror. "What do you mean, no?"

"I mean that no one cancels on us and especially not someone I know for a fact, after much pressuring from Rochelle, admitted that he likes you. So try again. What's the real story?"

"Don't go all Sherlock on me. Sometimes it is what it is. There's no hidden conspiracy here, so move along, Watson."

"Oooh, nice work in with the Sherlock reference. Gives me an idea for Halloween." He comes over and leans his ass against the counter next to me. "That's another conversation though. Now tell me the truth, woman."

I drop the mascara into the tray. "We decided to stay friends and with that, not work together. It would put undue stress on our friendship that neither of us wants right now."

His eyes search mine, his happiness showing in the smoothness of skin around his eyes. "Why are you wearing so much makeup? That's not like you. Special client?"

"No, just got some freebies and trying them out."

His non-response grabs my attention. When I look at him, he asks, "What did you do to your eye?"

My hand flies up in response and I cover it and turn away.

"Nicked myself with the damn flat iron. Don't you have work to do?" I sidetrack him and walk into the closet.

"Going. Going."

The quiet of the room signals it's safe to exit. Lane's gone, but he leaves a message written on the mirror in red lipstick. There's a heart and the word "you." Although he can't hear me, I smile and say, "Heart you too, my friend." And I do. Especially. On a daily basis, he provides color in my very dark world.

Today I will try to avoid everyone as much as I can. I'll either be caught or a pro by the end of the day. Burying myself in my work will be nothing new. My team understands my passion and supports it, so I become a professional by the time six o'clock rolls around.

TWO HOURS OF lying in bed with a raw steak on my face, three different creams promising to reduce bruising, and a day later, I'm almost ready for the awards. They've been working. Thank goodness. I couldn't have a makeup artist do my makeup for the awards or they would see. So I spend the afternoon doing it myself. By the time I'm done, nothing is visible.

The strapless blue dress I choose to wear is fitted with a mermaid bottom. I wear a single strand of diamonds around my neck. Simple, but beautiful.

I dread tonight. The cameras. The attention. Mark. *The Resistance.* Kaz. I dread it all. I will go only because I have to. Sleep was replaced with thoughts whirling like a dervish last night. I know what I have to do to get the much-needed leverage back, but I also need to earn Mark's trust back in the process.

Mark shows up on time. When I open the door, he looks me over disapprovingly. "I want you in black and something short. Go change."

"This is a designer dress, Mark. It's perfect for the red carpet."

"I said go change. Make it fast or we'll be late."

Closing my eyes, I try to calm the anger that's awakened inside, and take a deep breath while turning to go upstairs. To my back, he says, "Snap. Snap. Chop. Chop."

"Don't talk to me like that," I snap before I think. The glare I send over my shoulder is instantly reduced by the fury burning in his eyes. My knees weaken, but I reach for the railing to steady myself in front of him.

The change in him is physical, all his anger dissipating before my eyes. His shoulders ease and a small smile appears. "Please change. Black always looks good on you."

I'm not sure how to handle him, or his mood swings. Wordlessly I go to my bedroom and walk into the closet. I have at least five little black dresses and three of them are formal enough to work for the night, so I pick the prettiest since I'll be photographed, and slip it on. My shoes are exchanged for Louboutins, and my handbag is a black beaded clutch. I spend a few extra minutes putting concealer on my knees. It will hold for a while, hiding the damage, but I bring it with me when I hurry back out. Surprisingly, I'm greeted with a big smile. "You look beautiful, Lara."

Ignoring him and his worthless compliments, I walk past him and out the door. When he comes out, I lock it and follow him to the car waiting to drive us. The ride is quiet. Mark plays on his phone. At one point he gets engrossed in a text conversation that I notice he purposely hides from me. A stupid grin is on his face as he reads the messages. He's definitely still fucking someone else or plans to soon. Another reason why I'm so confused that he wants me by his side. It's humiliating. *She* knows about me, but is happy to fuck him anyway. It's the first time I've ever regretted making an effort when it came to becoming who I am. I had convinced myself otherwise, but he's proved I'm weak. I'm practically a bull's eye for his target practice. I can't live like this. I won't. He has to be stopped. Somehow. Some way. I will play along until I have enough information to bury him. One opportunity is all I need to destroy his computer and back-up Cloud.

On the red carpet, I wait in the wings while he has his photo taken over and over. Some photos are taken of us together. I have a hard time smiling when my emotions are getting the better of me, but I manage for the most part.

The fans in the stands scream loudly letting us know someone big has arrived. Mark turns to see over the crowded red carpet. I know he loves being famous and just below the surface his jealousy bubbles. He hates when others steal his thunder. When he turns back, he says, "Your little friends are here."

I don't have to see above the sea of bodies to know who he's talking about. My heart races and I lift up to catch a glimpse of *The Resistance*. Even in platforms I'm not tall enough to see over everyone. Sharpness slices through my side and I grab hold with both my hands. Mark places his hand on my back. "What's wrong?"

"I don't know. I need to sit down. You finish here and I'll meet you inside."

Before he can weigh in with his thoughts, I hurry toward the hotel where the awards are being held. Once I'm inside, I frantically search for a bathroom. When I spot a restroom sign across the busy lobby, I walk fast, hoping no one notices me beelining it. The door is pushed open and I'm leaning against the sinks heaving for breath by the time I'm alone. My heart hurts so badly that I wonder if I'm experiencing the early signs of a heart attack.

The door opens again and an older woman walks in. "Are you all right?" she asks when she sees me.

I stand up, trying to appear as normal as I can. "I'm fine. I just overheated out there."

She smiles kindly. "I hate these events and crowds, but my husband is nominated, so I come for him."

"Congratulations to him. That's quite an honor."

She touches up her lipstick, then turns to me. "Thank you." She smiles. "You're looking much better now. You've got some color in your face again."

I turn toward the mirror, something I'd been avoiding as much as I could. If it didn't involve applying makeup, I wanted no part in seeing myself. "Yes. That's good," I reply, humoring her as I walk out, but stop to say, "Thank you and good luck to your husband."

"Good luck to you," she replies as if she sees right through me, sees the bruising on the inside.

Back in the lobby, the crowd has grown as more celebrities have made their way inside. I stand off to the side and look around. Mark is tall with broad shoulders and stands out in a crowd, but I don't see him. He must be on the red carpet still doing interviews. I head to the bar and take a glass of champagne. I finish half before I lean against the wood bar top.

"Hi." *That voice.* My heart begins to ache in ways it only does for one man.

I peek to my right and see Kaz's eyes with their comforting warmth. Kaleidoscopes of chocolate make up their uniqueness, and as he looks at me, I feel his comfort, as though he's wrapping me in his leather jacket like he did once before, warming me with his nearness. *He shouldn't show me such gentleness, not after our phone call.* As if I hadn't cruelly pushed him away, he reaches up and strokes his finger down my cheek. I wish I could lean into his touch, but I can't. "You shouldn't be here." *I don't deserve your kindness any more.*

"The band was nominated."

Daring to look at him though I know I'll struggle to leave once I do, I correct myself. "I don't mean at the event. I mean talking to me."

His eyes narrow, so I turn away quickly. I look for Mark, making sure he doesn't see us.

Kaz states, "I'm not scared of him."

"I am." I walk away, easily slipping through groups of people and escaping before I'm caught by Kaz again. I can't have him involved in this mess.

I'm grabbed from behind and abruptly taken aback. Mark nods to the doors to the ballroom, and says, "Let's go in."

I nod and follow. His hand is wrapped tightly around mine until I'm at his side. He keeps his arm stiff so I can't stray until we reach our table. Pulling my chair out for me, he's the appearance of the perfect gentleman, but I know the monster lurking beneath. If only I'd seen the real him sooner.

Glasses of champagne are served and more drink orders placed. I don't allow myself to look around the large room though it's all I really want to do. I want to see him again. Breathe him in. Touch him. Be with Kaz. But there's no use indulging in what can never be.

The lights go down just as the first course is served. The comedian should be funny, but this charade is drowning me. Mark touches my arm, and normally I would consider it gentle, but I don't like him touching me at all so my skin crawls beneath his fingertips.

"My first award is up next. Wish me luck."

I look at him, hating the man before me. If only the daggers I want to shoot him in my glare were lethal. "Good luck." My reply is dry and as heartless as I can manage, the champagne letting my real emotions loose in the moment. But I calm, saving the stronger emotions for when I need the physical strength to handle him.

Over Mark's shoulder, I see Kaz, the band, Rochelle, and Holli two tables away from ours. Kaz's eyes are fixed on me. I want to look away. I really should, but I'm captivated by the man, entranced by the emotions he wears for me on his sleeve.

I shake my head and look away. At this point, Mark is winning his game, and until I can end this, I'm stuck. *I know too much. He could destroy me in one leak to the press.* Would Kaz be there after the fallout, after leaked tapes spread?

Mark wins his category and like a doting girlfriend, I play my part. There should really be an Oscar for this performance—showing my support while controlling my gag reflex. As soon as Mark's on stage, I glance toward Kaz, but he's gone from his seat. I see Rochelle instead. Her expression shows her sadness, which is understandable. In her eyes, I've returned to Mark. I wish I could tell her more, tell her the whole truth. I look away, not able to handle that right now. When Mark leaves the stage, I escape to the bathroom. Once inside, I stare at the reflection, staring at someone I barely recognize, someone I'm ashamed to be.

"You can't say things like that then disappear on me."

My eyes meet Kaz's in the mirror. "Please go, Kaz."

"What if I say no?"

I turn around just as he leans forward, trapping me between his arms. "I know you're scared of him, but you don't have to be scared of what you're feeling for me, what I feel for you, or of us." His lips almost touch mine, teasing me in ways I won't be able to resist for long. "I see how you look at me. I see that same desire I feel inside for you in your eyes for me. You're conflicted and guarded, but you don't have to be. You can always trust me."

"But you said—"

"Forget what I said the other day. I want you, Lara."

17

———————

LARA

"I WANT YOU any way I can have you. I want you in my bed. I want to make love to you and then fuck you so you never forget me."

I sigh, dropping my gaze to his chest. "I could never forget you."

"Why are you doing this then? Why are you with him?"

"Because I have to be."

"That makes no sense. I want you. You want me. I can tell."

With his fingertip, he raises my chin until I look into his eyes again. My knees weaken just by the sincerity I find there. He whispers, "Whatever you need, I'll be. Just give me a chance to show you, to prove to you how much I care about you."

A tear teeters on the edge of my bottom lid before falling, which reveals to him my true feelings. I push him away and leave the confines of his arms. I start to run, but I can't, my traitorous feet remaining planted near him. I turn back and say, "Kaz, you can't. You don't understand—"

"I'm trying to, but you won't tell me anything. I know he beat the shit out of you and for some reason you feel the need to stay with him. I don't get why. Leave with me."

"It's not that simple."

"Fuck, Lara." He turns his back to me, his hand running over his head, agitated. "You make this so goddamn difficult." When he faces me again, his frustration is heard. "Is he threatening you? This makes no sense. If you don't want to be with me, just say so, but I can't promise to leave you alone."

My mouth remains empty of what I know I need to say. I bring my lower lip under my teeth and scrape. This was awful over the phone, but saying these words to him in person, where I can see his gorgeous face, is torture. "We're done, Kaz."

I repeat the lies—the heartless words—but there's no passion in them, no truth to be found.

Thunderous applause from the ballroom fills the doorway when a woman enters the bathroom. Her eyes go wide, but then she smiles, recognizing Kaz instantly. "You just won."

He glances to me. "Not even close, baby." Then he rushes past her. I'm left unsure what to say, so I start to leave, but she practically swoons in front of me. "You're so lucky you got to talk to him. He's so hot."

"Yes, he's amazing." I walk out and back to the ballroom, entering in time to see the band on stage accepting their award. I know he can't see me from up there, but deep down, I wish he could. He would see the smile I save for him, the one only he can evoke.

When Mark's large paw of a hand rests on my thigh, I'm glad Kaz can't see me. He won't have to bear witness to my weakness, my waning strength.

Sitting through the rest of the show, I barely touch my food. Mark doesn't win the second award, and he's been restless since. My mind starts to wonder what that means for me later. I peek at Kaz several times throughout the show, but make sure to look away before he sees me. The lights brighten the room and we get up to leave. Kaz is already long gone. Mark takes my hand and kisses the top. "You ready to go to the after-party?"

I've resolved not to bother with speaking to him. It's pointless. My anger can't be contained and I don't want to make a scene in public. I tried that once and I was shown who is more powerful between us...

"You act like six months is six years, Mark. Don't be ridiculous."

"Don't call me ridiculous."

"Then stop acting like—" My arm is grabbed hard, jerking me to a standstill, and cutting off my words.

"Ow!"

I try to pull away, but his fingers tighten around my upper arm, and I'm yanked against him. "Shut your mouth," he warns, his voice gruesome and terrifying.

The shock of it stiffens my body. Every red flag flies up, putting my muscles on alert.

Fight or flight?

He's my boyfriend... was my boyfriend. He won't hurt me. Until his nails dig into my skin. Then I reminded he will.

Fight or flight?

"Mark, please. Let go of me."

"No. You won't embarrass me like this."

"I don't love you. You can't possibly love me when you can't even be faithful to me."

"I do. I love you."

"If you love me, let me go."

"I can't. Don't you see?" he asks, shaking me. "I need you."

Fight or Flight?

Trying to remain calm, to not show weakness to this hulking figure of a man, I ask, "For what?"

"To love me." Darkness is etched into the soul of his eyes, something I never noticed before. It's not sadness. Disdain? Power? Desperation?

Fight or flight?

My gut knows. No good is going to come of this. He's not the man I dated.

And I can't trust him.

Fight!

Swinging with all my might, my hand goes for his face. He blocks my arm, grabs, and twists it behind my back. An excruciating pain heats my shoulder and I cry out, "Stop. Stop. Stop!"

"Will you stop?" He tightens, my shoulder feeling close to broken. Pain overpowers my thoughts.

From the corner of my eyes, I see them. Strangers in the distance, but close enough to see what is happening. And they do nothing. So I do what I have to. "Yes," I reply through tears running down my face.

Fight!

As soon as I'm released, I kick him in the balls as hard as I can. Mark keels over and I run...

We begin walking up the aisle toward the ballroom doors. I'm pulled aside and in the dark of the corner near the exit, he asks, "Can you not muster any enthusiasm, Lara? Tonight has not exactly been torture. Do you know how many women would like to be you tonight?"

"I assume many were willing to fuck you knowing you had a girlfriend."

"You're always so fucking sarcastic." He gives up his energy on me. "And *had*?"

"Had," I reply definitively.

"Try *have*. And I'm being nice. Can you be nice?"

"Nice? Why would I be nice to you?"

"Because I've asked one favor. We can plan the breakup for our next date, but give me tonight."

"Are you psychotic? You do realize you forced me to come here tonight, right?"

"I didn't force you. You freely got in the car. So when did I force you?"

"You beat me, Mark. When you accept that responsibility, I'll be nice." I walk past him and out the door to where our car is waiting.

He joins my side, and opens the back door. "Get in the fucking car."

Every ounce of my sanity tells me to run, but I can't. My feet feel like lead, heavy, making it impossible to move. I know the outcome. I've been here before. So I make a choice that I'll be judged for later, but that saves me now.

I get in the car.

The after-party is at a popular restaurant nearby. We walk the shorter red carpet, smiling for the cameras, then I make my way toward the head of the line like I'm directed and give Mark his shining moment. A man with a clipboard hurries Mark along, announcing *The Resistance's* arrival.

Perking up, I look past Mark just as he grabs my upper arm and squeezes. My eyes catch Kaz's gaze locked on me and I watch it play out before I have a chance to react.

The rest is a blur of commotion.

Kaz closes the gap in a few long strides, his arm raising as he closes in on his target. One perfectly executed right hook lands squarely across Mark's jaw, sending the giant to his ass and me wobbling. And the feeding frenzy begins.

The photographers raid the red carpet, encircling the two. Kaz is pumped, light on his feet, fists up in defense. "Motherfucker! If you ever come near her again, I will kill you."

I was already running, but I'm grabbed by a security guard and held back. "No, Kaz. No! Don't."

Struggling to break free, I bear witness to the horror before me. Mark is on his feet and lands a straight hit to Kaz, and I scream, "No, Mark! Please. Don't hurt him."

Kaz is swinging again, but is grabbed, each arm restrained. Johnny and Dex pull Kaz back. Mark with his huge ego smiles as if he's won. Blood covers his teeth and he laughs, but a fist to the face stops him cold.

"Don't fuck with my friends!" Derrick stands proud to have ended the fight.

Security takes hold of Mark, trying their best to hold him back.

Kaz's arms are behind him as he lunges forward, fighting through what must be pain from the expression on his face. But is he in pain from the guys or because of me? He shouts, "I will hurt you five times worse than you hurt her, asshole." His eyes remain focused on Mark as he struggles to get free, adrenaline coursing through him. "Let me go. You don't know what he's done."

Bodyguards surround the band members, but Kaz still fights for his freedom. Chaos surrounds us. Johnny's yelling for Kaz to stop and walk away. Derrick is fully invested in the fight. Dex is working with the bodyguards to pull Kaz from the scene. Paparazzi engulf us, making it hard to move anywhere.

Their security detail gets them to safety at the beginning of the carpet and whisks them to their black SUVs. A strong hand embraces my arm, guiding me through the cameras. Tommy is in front of me, protecting my space while we walk. "Get in the car. We need to get you out of here." The door to one of the vehicles is opened and he lifts me up to the running-board.

"Lara!" Mark's voice booms from behind me, rattling my insides, but I don't look back.

My world lights up when I see Kaz inside the car. His fists hit the seat and he yells, "Fuck!"

Tommy gets in behind me as I slide across the leather and cling to Kaz. "Oh my God, Kaz! Are you okay?"

The Suburban starts moving. Kaz's arms come around me, his breath heavy in his chest under my cheek. When I look up, he says, "That's what I should have done the other night. I'm sorry I didn't."

"No. No. You don't need to do this for me. I'm not worth the trouble."

"He hurt you."

Tommy sits next to me and leans forward to stare at Kaz. "What the fuck? You realize you just attacked Mark Renner, *the* Mark Renner, in front of fifty journalists?"

"Paparazzi aren't journalists," Kaz says sarcastically.

"You know what I mean." Tommy shakes his head. "I don't understand what just went through your head."

Kaz warns, "Tommy, stop."

"He's a fucking major league baseball player. You play guitar for a living." He glances down at Kaz's hands, which causes me to do the same. *Oh no.*

His knuckles are bloodied, the skin ripped apart across the top. I shield them from view, careful not to hurt him more by touching them. "I'll take care of you when we get home." The word home rolls off my tongue so naturally with him.

Kaz directs his eyes back to Tommy. "I have my reasons." Then he takes my hand and brings it to his lips and kisses.

"Leave it to a woman," Tommy says with an eye-roll. "This is a PR fucking nightmare." Tommy leans away from us, his arm against the window.

"I'll take the heat, Tommy. Don't worry. I'll make sure the band isn't dragged into this mess."

He sits up abruptly, anger getting the better of him. "Too late, Kaz. What were you thinking?"

I remain quiet, the side effects of my actions sinking in. "I left him."

"Good," Kaz adds.

"You don't understand. I left him. *I* left *him*. In front of the press."

My hand starts shaking. Kaz now covers mine with his and gently squeezes. "It will be okay. I'll take care of you. I promise."

"I don't want you to take care of me. I want to take care of myself." The rage in Mark's voice. I feel sick hearing him call my name over and over on a loop in my mind. Grabbing my head, I close my eyes. "What have I done?" I turn to Tommy as desperation sets in. "I need to go home. Please take me home."

"Lara—" Kaz starts but I whip to my other side to face him and beg. I'm not above it for him. "Please. Please, Kaz. You have to take me home."

After a long hard look at me, he doesn't argue. He turns to the driver and gives him my address. The next fifteen minutes of listening to Tommy tap away on his phone are painful. The lack of a kind touch, the absence of his comforting words, the tension that never existed before wedges between us like a tangible emotion, hurts—my heart, my head, and my soul. I feel the wound caused by Mark's scheme gaping open. *I know what he is going to do next.* My blood runs cold from the thought of the violation I will endure. No one wants what was sanctioned in the bedroom thrust into the limelight for all to see. And of course, there is no way I can be with Kaz. Any way I look at it, there's no winner in this nasty game.

Only pain.

The car stops and Tommy's door swings open. He gets out first and as I'm maneuvering to exit, Kaz catches me. "Tell me," he says, coming to terms with our situation. "Tell me why you can't be with me. Give me something, Lara, I've got nothing left to lose."

"Kaz," I start, feeling horrible, the door that leads to my heart already closing. I can dance around the truth all I want but that's not going to fix this mess. It's not going to heal his heart. Not when I have to put distance between us now more than ever. Mark will seek his revenge. I just need him to take it out on me and not Kaz. "Please understand this is for the best." I lean back over and kiss him. Surprisingly he lets me and kisses me back. My mind swirls with all the feelings he evokes, sensations I want to grab hold of and keep. But I know to keep him safe I must give him up. I reach up and move the hair that's fallen over his eyes to the side and kiss him gently on the cheek. I don't know what possesses me, or what inspires me, but with my lips lingering on his skin, I don't say goodbye. "Live a great story. And share it. Share it through your music, your lyrics, your notes." Turning away, I slip my feet to the ground, landing solidly on my high heels. I glance back just long enough to see his eyes, to see something wild blooming inside... wild with possibility.

With my head down, I close the door, and walk away. Like his eyes, my heart beats wildly in my chest. Terror of what's to come, or what could be ahead: if he's in my home, or *if if if* rumbles through my body and I swallow hard, pretending everything is A-okay as I leave Kaz. With my finger on a lit-up phone, I'm ready to call the cops if needed. While knowing I need to fear what's right in front of me, my thoughts are on all the different outcomes when I walk inside my home. The *what ifs* run free.

What if I choose Kaz?

What if I take the chance?

What if Mark releases a video or more?

What if Mark hits me again for leaving him or... kills me?

What if I die on my terms instead of his?

What if I choose love?

What if Kaz ignores my pleas and comes after me?

I've got to form a solid plan that can succeed this time. How do I do that? What do I do? What if—A knock breaks the vicious what-if cycle and I swing open the door before common sense kicks in. Kaz is standing there. Like too often lately, tears fill my eyes. "What are you doing?"

"Choosing to live my story with you."

My body crashes into his and we kiss as if *what ifs* never existed.

The threat of Mark's retribution.

The ominous knowledge of broad-spectrum humiliation.

The fear I've lived in, the fear of Mark, the fear of losing Kaz forever.

It's all replaced with warmth, hope, and love.

Kaz's warm lips feel like heaven compared to the hell I've been living. I pull back and look him in his glorious, loving eyes. "I'm going to pay for this, but I need and want you so much." I kiss him again, wanting to wipe away all thoughts of Mark and his threats, to live a new story.

18

LARA

THE SUV DRIVES off just as Kaz pulls back from me this time. "What do you mean, you're going to pay for this?"

"It's about Mark. You must know—"

He stops me. "Let's go inside."

After we're safely in and the door is locked, I lead him to the kitchen. "Drink?"

"Yes, but tell me what you mean?"

"You're gonna need peas too. Fortunately, I have a few bags in the freezer." I grab a bag and go to him. Holding it to his cheek, I place my other hand on his chest. "Stay calm. I need you to know what might happen if you're choosing to be with me."

"I'm here and I plan to stay."

"Kaz, the other day I wanted to see you. It was all I wanted, but he turned up here. He's made videos of us." Hoping he understands without me going into great detail, I leave it open-ended.

"Videos? Of you having sex?"

"Yes." I turn my back to him, feeling ashamed as if I did something wrong, as if I should be embarrassed. *Again.* Another moment Mark has tainted.

"You knew, or you didn't know he was filming?"

When I turn, I plead, wanting him to know I wouldn't have made them with him. "I didn't know. I didn't know about any of them, but he says he has a lot and he'll release them if I leave him."

"He's blackmailing you into dating him?"

"Only until he can break up with me. Publicly. He wants to win the hearts of America by playing the *Poor Me* role of the heartbroken golden boy to the media."

His brow furrows. "Why?"

"Ego," I reply, the only word needed to explain. "I couldn't let those videos get out. I couldn't let him drag you through the media."

Fingers flex at his side. "What do you mean *me*?"

"We should clean and bandage your hand." I reach out offering mine, relieved when he takes it. I lead him down the hall and into my master bathroom. He sits down on the bench while I dig out the first-aid kit.

When I sit next to him, I start cleaning his wounds with hydrogen peroxide. He never flinches, but asks, "How can he drag me through the media?"

"He said he would." I take a closer look to make sure the blood is gone and his knuckles are ready to be bandaged.

"And?" He chuckles, seemingly amused by what I'm saying when my heart is still firmly planted at the bottom of my stomach.

"What do you mean *and*?" I start wrapping the bandage tape around his hand. "I don't want to hurt your image, the band, your brand. I know how Hollywood works."

He laughs, a laugh that's hardy and deep. "A sex tape being released of my girlfriend and her ex doesn't hurt my image." He caresses my cheek. "You can't hurt my image. You can only make me look better, baby."

A bunch of words are coming from his mouth, but I only hear one. "Your girlfriend?"

"Yeah," he says. "I'm not letting you go this time. We've been playing at this tug of war for too long." The caress of his hand soothes my soul and he leans in to kiss me. "I don't want to be one of those couples who loses sight of what's important because of bad communication or misunderstandings. Like I told you before, I want you. I want to be with you. What do you want?"

"I want you." There's no hesitation in my voice.

"I'm so damn glad you said that." Nose to nose, he breathes me in, closing his eyes, and licking his lips. My own breathing deepens and I close my eyes as his hands hold my face to his. "I'm going to kiss you again. And again."

I move his now-bandaged hand to my lips and kiss, hoping to heal it quicker. "I want more than a kiss." My voice is breathy and desperate, but that's how I feel whenever he is near.

Turning my hand in his so he's holding me, he says, "Come with me." We only make it as far as the door. "Take off your dress, though I'd like to add that you look amazing in it."

My eyes go wide from surprise because his are deviating from polite to determined to demanding in an instant. "Thank you. You look amazing yourself."

I lift my leg up to take off my heel, but he kneels down in front of me and takes my ankle between his hands. Looking up at me, he rubs his hands up the back of my legs and under the hem of my dress. "You wanna play truth?"

"Not dare?"

"No dare needed. Just truths."

It's so easy to forget the world outside these walls when we're together. So easy. And wonderful. "Tell me all your truths, Kaz."

Encouraging me, he guides me closer, pressing his face against the fabric at the apex of my thighs, and he inhales. Hot breath strikes and I inhale sharply. I stand before him, watching him, allowing my fingertips to rest on his shoulders. He inhales me again, moaning from pleasure. The sound is vulgar and raw, his voice husky when he looks up. "I'll tell you a secret if you tell me one."

"You go first." His lust-filled expression engages the very core of my being and gives me confidence.

Hiking the bottom of my dress higher, he takes one of my legs and lifts it over his shoulder, and confesses, "I've gotten off more than a few times imagining your legs wrapped around my neck, and your heels digging into my back while I fuck you with my mouth."

Just take me now.

But he asked if I wanted to play along, and I intend to. Feeling sassy and very flirty, I set both my feet back on the ground and take a step back. With his eyes glued to me, I bend over, sliding my hands down the front of my legs until I reach my ankles. All those years of yoga have paid off when it comes to my flexibility. While bent over, I look up and ask, "Shoes like these?"

"Shoes exactly fucking like those."

I lift up, curving my back in the most seductive way I know how. "Then I'll leave them on for you." I turn my back to him and move my hair to one side, and over my shoulder. But I look back while I do. "Maybe you can help me with this dress."

"I've wanted to do that all night." His fingers take to the top of the gold zipper and he slides it down slowly as his breath blankets the back of my neck.

I drop my head forward and close my eyes. The troubles of the day drift away. Kaz's touch consumes me. His lips against my skin cause me to sigh in pleasure, his sentiments intoxicating. "I missed you." The sweetest of kisses is placed along my spine, followed by another even lower.

"I missed you." His hands slip into the open back of the dress and around to my chest. He takes my breasts in hand, taking what he wants, making me feel sexy and desired. His erection is steel against my back, and my body reacts, molding my softness against his hardness.

He kisses the curve of my neck and my head rolls to the side as he lets the dress fall to the floor. "Lara," he whispers, then kisses my shoulder while caressing my breasts. "You pushed me away, wanting me to hate you, to feel used by you. But I know you. I know you would never do that. It's not in you. That's why I came for you. It's why I can't leave. You're the most beautiful woman, the only woman I've ever dreamed about. I want to be yours. And I want you to be mine. *Mine.* Promise me you'll be mine."

Turning around in his arms, I look up. It doesn't matter that my body is bare, or that he's fully clothed. We're equals together. *I want you to be mine. I want to be yours.* It's not a demand. It's a request. This is not about ownership but a relationship. It's about us. "Yes, with all my heart."

Kaz makes me feel special, sexy, and intelligent. I don't need to hear a promise in return. I can feel what I mean to him and that's a heady combination. "Kaz," is all I manage to say before he takes me quickly, backing us onto the bed behind me.

His belt is undone. His jacket comes off. The buttons on the front of his shirt are popped off as he pulls it open across his chest. After settling between my legs, he hovers over me, his words a bond. "All I need is you. Only you."

"You say that as if you can predict the future," I whisper, searching his eyes for his truth.

"I say that knowing that what I feel for you has never been felt before. Our love is unique, Lara. Our love is a world of undiscovered prisms fighting to be seen for the first time. Together, there is only good."

"I need to know all of you. Your good. Your bad. What I feel for you is new and different. It scares me, exposing me as a fraud in every relationship before now. How is that possible after such a short time?" *What bad have you known, Kaz?*

"We can't see the future, but we can change it. Your past doesn't matter just as mine doesn't. Right now I need to kiss you, and I want to make love to you."

"I want to make love to you." I whisper, "Just us. Nothing between us. Just us."

"Are you on the pil—"

"Yes."

Divine lips take mine as if he's owned them all along. He enters me, my mouth falling open with a light gasp from the delicious pressure. Tilting my head back, I leave my neck exposed. Kaz sucks gently, moving along my throat, and down lower. I tighten my legs around him and run my fingers through his hair. His movements have a purpose, a mission to please me. He does, feeling so good. Our bodies heat as our breaths pick up. "I want on top," I say, my desires getting the best of me, wanting any control I can muster to help take my mind to otherworldly places only Kaz takes me to.

The bed feels too small for something that feels so amazing, so explosive in my chest. The blinds are open and the moonlight streaks across the bed. Messed dark hair, alluring eyes, and hands that know my body—he's magnetic.

I climb over him and sink down, take a deep breath, and embrace the fullness that could easily overwhelm if I let it. My head lulls back as I begin to rock forward, the sounds of our sex slick as moans fill the air.

When I look down, his eyes are open and fixed where our bodies are joined together. My hands land on his chest and I gather the control to slow things down. I want to remember everything—everything between us—about him, and this moment when ecstasy overrides everything else.

I'm flipped in a drastic turn of events, and he says, "You're teasing. Turn over."

With a devilish smile, I admit, "I might have been, but I was enjoying you."

When I roll over, he takes my hips and lifts them up, angling me before he touches me between my legs and thrusts his cock deep inside. With each push, my breath is forced out and I close my eyes, loving his strength. I drop my head forward just as my orgasm hits, taking over.

His chest covers my back as his body falls into the same blazing bliss. Kisses are placed on the back of my neck and down my spine, bringing the romance back full circle. He falls to the side. My body is stiff, betraying me after such an amazing high. I straighten my legs, falling flat on my chest. When I turn to look at him, my hair sticks to my face, but Kaz carefully pushes it away until I can see him. He watches my mouth, then leans down and kisses me. "You're worth the trouble."

"You say that now, when everything feels good, when we feel invincible."

"No, I say that always. So I gotta warn you now, you might be stuck with me."

I kiss him, then with my eyes closed, I lean my forehead against his, appreciating the peace I feel with him. "That sounds like an offer I can't refuse."

19

LARA

I TOLD MYSELF I would never rush into another relationship ever again, but that was before I was with Kaz. He makes me want to free-fall from the clouds, like that is an actual possibility. He gave me hope when I was at my lowest, swooping in and giving me strength when I struggled to find it.

But as I watch him in the hours just before dawn, Mark's threats replay in my mind. Good and evil. Kaz and Mark. Kaz is reliable and caring, everything Mark is not. Mark is unpredictable, and the drugs are making him rage. How he'll react to the red carpet incident is worrisome. I know him too well. He won't let this go. His plan didn't play out how he wanted and he'll make us pay. How? When? Where? I feel edgy from the questions that linger in the air.

I kiss Kaz on the cheek. I don't want to give him up. My like... my *love* for him runs too deep. Our relationship has been on a fast track and reckless, but it's true and wild, and free. Mark can't destroy us. He may hinder, but he won't win in the end. My faith in the man next to me is too strong.

Slipping out of bed, I tiptoe into the bathroom, wanting to freshen up. I turn on the shower and brush my teeth while the water warms. Removing my makeup will show the little bruising that remains, but

I'm not worried about exposing my flaws to Kaz. He's seen me at my worst physically and emotionally, and been at the receiving end when I pushed him away. I don't have a fear of him leaving me now. He's done more than he ever needed for me to believe he plans on sticking around. I just hope he'll see I'm willing to do the same for him.

The water is the perfect temperature when I walk into the shower. I close my eyes and let it rain down over me. It feels good to wash away the night, especially knowing I get a fresh start with the man in the next room.

The door is opened, and cool hands caress my breasts from behind. The bridge of his nose glides behind the shell of my ear before he whispers in it, "You snuck off."

"I wanted to get clean for you."

His hands go lower, one moving between my legs. "I like you dirty."

Curious, I ask, "How dirty do you like it?"

"However dirty you're willing to go?"

"Can I be honest with you?"

My body is left bare and he moves in front of me. His voice remains relatively calm when he replies, "Always be honest with me." Despite looking into Kaz's open and warm eyes, I hear Mark's bitter and snide remarks as if he was here in the room. *I pay hookers for deviant sexual acts that you wouldn't do.*

"I'm boring. I've not really done anything sexually adventurous."

"I like that."

"But you're a rock star. You'll get bored." *I don't want to see photos of him with other women too. I think that would break me.*

"Hey," he says, his tone changing as worry creases his brow. "We're not just sex, Lara. We're more than that."

"Are we?"

"Yes." He taps my chin. "It's you, Lara. Only you."

"I feel the same for you, Kaz."

"There's shit to sort out and consequences. I may be a rock star, but I'm also just a man. With us, it's not just about who has been more sexually adventurous. Sex between us is amazing because it's you and me. Okay?"

My smile for him is soft as I touch his cheek with one hand and hold his hand with the other. "Okay." Words can be toxic when spewed from a narcissistic, controlling drugged asshole. But Kaz's words heal, a soothing balm to my battered and bruised heart.

"I still need to know that you're okay."

"I might have some bad times, but right here with you, I'm more than okay."

"Since we're opening up—"

I grab the shampoo and pour some in both of our hands. "Are we opening up? I don't seem to know much about you. Still."

Instead of scrubbing his own hair, his hands come to my head and he rubs the shampoo on top before massaging my scalp. "I'm weak to a head massage."

"I'm hoping you're weak to me in general."

I look up at him. "I am. Can't you tell?"

"We're on equal footing then."

I love that he considers us partners, both all in with the same stakes on the line. I reach for his head and say, "Bend a little." He cocks an eyebrow and bends. I clean his hair, rubbing it together to make it stand in a sudsy Mohawk. "Tell me the craziest thing you've ever done."

Laughter echoes in the space as a smile appears, fond memories surfacing in his eyes. "The craziest *and* stupidest thing I ever did was standing on the hood of a car on the Autobahn while it was going forty miles an hour. I lost to a guy who made it up to fifty."

Slowly blinking in disbelief, I ask, "You mean you fell at forty miles an hour?"

"No. I stomped, which meant stop the car."

"That is crazy stupid."

"That was the last time I did molly. That drug made me brave in ways that would eventually kill me if I kept doing it."

"It made me feel sexual the one time I did it in college."

He dips his head under the water and rinses, his gaze firmly on me. "I like you sexual."

"I don't need drugs with you."

Spinning me around so I'm under the water, he kisses my neck as I rinse my hair. "You could very much make me do crazy and stupid things."

"Like a drug."

"I'm already addicted to you."

I kiss his lips, and then say, "Me too. And I think enough happened yesterday to satisfy those checkboxes. How about we try happy and calm things?"

"Right after this." He lifts me until his hard cock is between my legs. With my back to the cold marble wall, I hold tight around his neck, my body wrapped around his, and I slowly slide down until he's inside me. The feel of his slick erection feels too good, but I don't stop him. I trust him and what he's told me.

I don't close my eyes this time, wanting to see his face, his reactions, his pleasure while embracing our connection.

Kaz's head is tilted back, his lids heavy, a reflection of how I feel. His lips are parted and I get a glimpse of his tongue when the tip touches the front of his teeth. His hips move making my body slippery against the wall. With a quick adjustment, I'm pinned in place as he thrusts. Wet kisses fall away as he leans down to tackle my neck with sweetness and lust combined. He doesn't whisper. He states his needs, the words emblazing themselves like a tattoo on my skin. "I want you so fucking badly."

My fingers tangle into his hair. "You've got me."

"I want more. So much more. Give me everything, baby. You feel so good. So, so good."

I understand his needs. "You make me want to rush because this feels so good."

"More. And faster."

"Faster. And harder."

He pumps in and out of me harder, listening to my cravings. "Fuck!" he yells against my chest as he comes, his body erratic. A deep inhale of breath, then exhaled in frustration as his fist slams to the wall. "I'm sorry. That was too fast."

"It's okay. I like when you lose control because it feels too good."

"I wanted you to come first, but you felt too good."

"I'll come next," I say, running my hands over his shoulders.

He sets my legs down and steadies me. "I'll make you feel so good, baby." He lowers to his knees and leans forward kissing up the length of my thigh before making me come twice with his hands and mouth. I can get used to coming last if it's this good every time.

I sleep another three hours before I feel stirring next to me and hear Kaz's groggy voice. "Your phone."

Rolling onto my back, I open one eye and look up at the ceiling. "Huh?" I ask half asleep.

"Your phone is ringing."

As I come to, his words start to make sense. "Oh." I look around, but it's nowhere to be found. I can hear it though. I hurry from bed and into the living room where I find my purse on the chair. I dig in and pull the phone out. Mark's name flashes once before it goes to voicemail. Reality pops my peaceful bubble. I know I have to face my problems but I was hoping to do it after lunch.

Quietly padding back into the bedroom, I slip under the covers and close my eyes pretending that call never happened and trying for sweet dreams with Kaz again. He asks, "Was it him?"

I roll onto my side to face his direction and sigh. "Yes."

"Did you want to answer?"

I'm not going to lie anymore. "It went to voicemail."

"I don't want you to see him again. I shouldn't say things like that, but it's how I feel and I'm not going to hide how I feel. I have to hide enough in my life, so I don't want to do it with you."

"I like that you told me how you feel." I scoot closer to him. "If it makes a difference, I don't want to see him again either. Everything I need to say can be said over the phone."

"What is left to say?"

"He will get revenge. He's not going to let yesterday just go. Neither will the press. He believes he holds the power by having those videos. But maybe there's something I can say that will convince him not to release them."

"Maybe there's not. Then you're just wasting your breath."

I nod with my hands on his chest. "Kaz, I need you to trust me and let me do what I think is best."

"I do trust you, but I don't trust him. I don't want you to see him again. He's not safe." He gets out of bed and walks into the bathroom. His shoulders are tense, his body agitated.

Sitting up, I wait with my back to the headboard and the sheet held over my chest. When he comes out, he leans against the doorframe, looking a little tired, but still so sexy. He's not shy or embarrassed being naked like that. He's just comfortable and all Kaz. "This situation could get nasty in the press. I don't want to pull the band into a tabloid mess, but I'll stand by you. I care about you and that's what we do for people we care about."

"It's just that easy? You'll risk being annihilated by the paparazzi because you care about me?" I look down, feeling terrible. "I don't want that for you or the band. I don't want that for us. That's why I tried to push you away."

His phone rings interrupting us. "That's Tommy's ringtone, so I should answer it. He doesn't call before two if it's not important."

I wait on the bed as he runs to the living room to retrieve it. I hear him talking, a muffled voice that becomes louder and clearer. "What do you mean?" *Silence.* "No." *Silence.* "Fuck!"

As much as I want to rush to his side, I know he'll tell me when he hangs up, so I give him time and wait. He comes in and grabs his clothes. "I've got to go."

"What's happening?"

Dressed in jeans and a tee, he sits on the bed and starts to put on his socks and shoes. "I fucked up." I stare at the back of his head, and he turns, our eyes catching. "And I'm about to pay the price for it."

When he stands, he comes around the bed and sits down next to me. I take his hand, not wanting him to go. "Stay. Please." I hate the wobble in my voice. It makes me feel weak.

Touching my cheek, his voice is not his own, but one that seems to carry burdens beyond since I've known him. "I can't." His smile is not big, but it makes me smile. "You're so fucking beautiful, Lara." His hand falls from my cheek and he says, "I'll call you later."

Sitting back, I watch him leave the room, eventually hearing the front door open and close. I go to lock it behind him and peek out the side window. Tommy is parked at the curb and Kaz is sitting in the passenger's seat. He looks upset. Tommy looks like he's in shock. I start to worry about what's happening and am about to go out the door, the sheet wrapped around me be damned. But they drive away before I have the chance.

My phone rings and I go to turn it off, but it's a number I don't recognize. It might be a client, so I answer it. "Hello?"

"Lara Kessler?"

"Yes."

"I'm David with *Caught Magazine*." My heart starts to race as he continues, "The great missing prodigy has been discovered fighting for your honor. Do you have a comment?"

Great missing prodigy? *What?* "I think you have the wrong Lara Kessler."

"You're the right one. Designer to the stars. Mark Renner's girlfriend. Oh, I'll need to correct that. Are you and Kaz Fabian dating? Did you leave Mark for Kaz?"

"I don't know what you're talking about."

"So no comment on leaving Mark Renner for Kazimir Petrowski?"

"No comment," I mumble and quickly hang up.

Kazimir Petrowski.

Missing.

Kazimir Petrowski.

Prodigy.

Kazimir.

Kaz.

I run to my laptop and type the name into the search box. An image of Kaz hitting Mark at the awards banquet pops up as the most recent results. I scan down the page to a link to Kazimir Petrowski and click.

Kazimir Fabian Petrowski—world famous pianist. A prodigy at age fourteen who won the world over with his talent and playful, but dramatic style. At fifteen, Petrowski, descended from Russian royalty, was touring Europe and playing for sold-out crowds that included royalty anxious to see a legend in the making.

In shock, I stare at a picture of a youthful Kaz. I've heard of the mysterious missing Petrowski, but I never put two and two together. No one did. Until now. *Oh no.* I did this. I'm responsible for this getting out. Kaz held this secret so tight that even his closest friends didn't know and now because of me, the world knows who and where he is. *But how? How did this get out?* Surely Mark didn't know about Kaz? The damn paparazzi. The punch that took him from the back of the stage to front and center spotlight is the downfall for my mysterious rocker. The paps are better than the CIA when it comes to digging up dirt.

Looking at the ceiling, I feel terrible for being the cause of this exposé, and exhale. When I look down again, I continue to read the article. *Petrowski skipped two concerts from reports of him being ill, but he finally showed in Luxembourg to another sold-out venue. The audience waited forty-five minutes for him to begin before the show was cancelled. He did his last interview after that performance in the dressing room. He reportedly said, "I played the entire show in my head. I just couldn't get my fingers to cooperate."*

He left that night and disappeared. At age sixteen, his career was over. The greatest pianist of his time walked away from that stage determined to disappear into anonymity and he succeeded.

Rumors have spread with alleged sightings over the years, but with no photographic proof, the rumors have remained just that—rumors.

One of the greatest pianists of our time was hiding in plain sight, right under a spotlight. With the incident on the...

I take a minute to absorb the information before picking up my phone and calling him.

20

KAZ

Fuck!

It was one punch.

Fine, two.

And then Derrick's. But what a pussy for filing restraining orders against us. What a fucking coward.

My life is so fucked. My life was coming together. Finally. Did I really think no one would discover my secrets? No. I'm not naïve. But I had hoped. Life had been going great for the last ten years, and even better in the last few weeks.

Two punches.

That's all it took to take down a baseball legend. Technically the first landed him on his ass. But now, I'm a wanted man—by the press. Correction: wanted even *more* by the paps and fans. My life took center stage overnight. Everything I've worked so hard to hide is now headline news because of the interest in the man who took down the baseball All-Star. Literally. It's a lead topic on the news channel.

Missing Pianist Prodigy Found!

As I scroll through the headlines on my phone, Tommy cuts into my racing thoughts, "Why did you have to go after Renner's girl? Lara

Kessler is a hot piece of ass and sweet as pie, but, man, she wasn't just taken, she was off limits."

I shoot him a look. "Don't call her that."

"You're awful touchy over a girl you barely know."

"I know her."

"Fuck me, Kaz. What are you talking about? Rochelle brought her around a few times and you're acting like a love-sick groupie."

The reference makes me smile. "I would be a groupie for her."

He takes a turn sharply, jerking me to the side, and pulls over, stopping in front of a house. Shifting the car into park, Tommy's eyes narrow in disbelief. "You're knee-deep in a whole lot of media mess all because of a girl. You hitting Renner drew all the attention to you. Did you think they wouldn't dig into your past?"

"I wasn't thinking about me when I hit him."

Sighing loudly, he says, "Truth. I need it. I need you to tell me everything, Kaz. I can help. I'll cover. I'll lie for you guys, but tell me what I'm dealing with."

I rest my elbow on the door and lean against it, debating with myself. How much do I want the world to know? Tommy won't tell, but I'm not sure I'm ready to share.

"With one blow to Renner's face you became the target of the media. Once they show interest, they'll dig every dark secret out of your past. So how the hell did we not know you were a pianist? By the way, that's really fucking close to penis. What jerkoff thought that was a good name? And if you're this so-called prodigy, why the fuck aren't you on keys?"

Chuckling lightly, I sit up. I know he means well and is trying to make me feel better the only way he knows how. But I'm not in a good mood and his humor is lost right now. "You need to know I don't like to talk about it, so I don't. This isn't easy having my skeletons scattered across gossip sites like there are no victims. There are. A whole slew of them. Myself included. I hide my life for a reason and now it is dragged out for entertainment purposes." I would still hit that asshole even at the expense of my past being exposed.

"Is it worth it? This thing with Lara?"

"I don't regret hitting him. Maybe I'm supposed to because of where it's landed me, but I don't. And I'd do it again."

"You said he hurt her."

"He beat the shit out of her two weeks ago. He's six foot five. I don't know if she reaches five foot four. He could've killed her. That sick fuck knew what he was doing. He slapped her across the face, but hurt her the most on her body so no one would see."

"Shit." His eyes close tight and he rubs the bridge of his nose. He finally looks back at me and asks, "Did you see?"

"She called me to pick her up after it happened."

"And why would she call you, Kaz?" *Because she knew I would be there for her. Because she trusted me. Because I had given her my heart. Because she wanted to give me hers.*

After a hard long stare, I just say it, "Because we love each other."

The back of his head hits the headrest. "I was afraid of that." He shifts the car into drive and says, "I'll help take care of this, but you need to let me know what you want out there and what you don't."

"I want that fucker to pay for what he did, but I don't want to hurt her in the process."

"Are you willing to sacrifice yourself to save her?"

"Yes," I reply instantly.

"Don't answer me now. Think about this. Really think about it. Everything you've kept hidden for a reason is about to be exposed and on a large scale. If the information about Renner gets out, it will take the heat off you. No one's going to attack her in the media. She's the victim, but to be on the safe side, does she have proof?"

"There are photos."

"She needs to file against him immediately." He pulls up to Johnny Outlaw's estate gate and punches in a code. We drive up the long driveway and park. Tommy looks over the hood at me when I get out. "This isn't just about you. It's about the band."

"It's about Lara. She's the victim here. Everything I did I'll own, but I won't throw her under the bus to protect myself. I won't."

"Okay. Then I'll stand by you. A band meeting has been called. Let's go inside and figure out what to do next."

"Thanks, man," I say following him to the door.

"Don't thank me yet. I'm good, but I can't work miracles."

Grabbing his shoulder and giving it a squeeze, I say, "You've been known to pull off a few, so I rest my faith in you, Tommy."

"*Fuuuck.* We're going down with this ship then."

I laugh and open the door. Inside the band isn't around. Holli peeks around the corner from the kitchen and says, "They're in the studio."

"Thanks," I reply. "All good with you?"

Tommy smiles and waves. "Hi, Holli, I'm heading downstairs."

She smiles at him. "Okay." When she looks at me the smile remains. "I'm good. How are you holding up?"

I lie. "Like I have no problems in the world."

That makes her laugh as she comes around and leans on the corner of the wall and crosses her arms. "Hold on to that feeling, Mr. Petrowski."

"Not you, too?"

"I can't let the boys have all the fun."

"Well, you could, but it's fine. There are worse things to be called than your birth name."

"Very true."

"How's Lara?"

"Worried about me."

"Women tend to do that."

"I'm worried about her."

"Do you need to be?"

Such a simple question. I should be able to answer it easily, but when asked, I pause. "I want to protect her."

Her smile is soft, sympathy seen in her eyes. "I have no doubt you will." She takes a step forward and hugs me. We've known each other for a while, and Holli's always treated me like I belong. She whispers, "Take care of yourself too. The band needs you."

"I will."

We part and she says, "The guys are waiting for you. I'll bring some snacks down later."

"Thanks, Holli."

"You're welcome."

WHEN I ENTER the recording studio, everyone is in their prospective places: Derrick on the far side, Dex on drums, Johnny in a chair up front, and Tommy off to the side. This is where we rehearse and record. Each section of the large soundproof room has designated space that we've taken over, staked claim as our area. "Hey," I say dropping down into a large beanbag near my amp.

Johnny's expression is tense, his eyes holding a million questions that his tongue holds on to. Tommy starts, "The label's publicist is handling the media, but she wants to know if you're willing to go on record with your story—the family drama."

"Do I have to?"

"I think it will settle the rumors quicker and quiet a lot of the press," Tommy answers.

I look to Johnny. He's had to deal with a shit-ton of press—good and bad. "What do you think?"

"I don't know your story, man." He sits back. "We're a band. That makes us family. We'll do whatever you need us to do."

I was on my own for years. This band saved me in many ways and here they are saving me again. They're my family and it feels good to be a part of theirs. They're my brothers, Rochelle and Holli sisters to me. "My name's out there. It's only a matter of time before my family is found."

Dex cuts in, "If they haven't already. Russian royalty? Really?"

I nod and shift, never comfortable with my title.

"Shit," Derrick says, "this whole time I've been rooming with Russian royalty. You were late with rent a couple times. What the hell, dude?"

Knowing he's teasing me, I say, "I lost all my inheritance when I didn't walk out on that stage in Luxembourg."

Rochelle appears in the doorway, and asks, "Why'd you leave?"

"Because my mother and sister chose to stay."

Tommy says, "Less riddles. We don't have much time to make a decision."

"My dad was violent and hit them. Everyone respected him because of his name, his family, his job. He ran a successful investment firm out of Moscow. I was the pride of his eye, the boy he bragged about, the one who would inherit the legacy. The only problem was that he drank too much and he liked to take out his problems with his fists. He particularly liked if they were weaker— my mom and eventually my sister. Anyone who crossed him was fired. Anyone who tried to stop him never came back to work. He didn't scare me. I saw who he really was underneath his suits and furs, and his money."

Rochelle sits on a stool nearby and says, "You were sixteen?"

"Yes."

"Your quote said you couldn't get your fingers to cooperate." And with that comment, she leads me back into a time I want to forget.

"I hit him. And then I hit him again and again until his bull of a body hit me again and again. My mother screamed and my sister cried. But he was finally taking his disappointment in his life out on someone closer to his size. I sprained my wrist, which caused damage to the tendons running down two fingers." I drag my finger over my right hand. "I couldn't play, so the family counsel lied, saying I was sick. Then continued to lie because I wasn't healing fast enough to keep the concert dates."

"That's when you left?" asks Tommy.

"No, I left two months later when I got in a fight with him while touring. He backhanded my mother when she asked if I wanted tea. Her mistake? She didn't ask him if he wanted one first. So fucked up. I lost it. Saw red. Her knees hit the floor and I was on my feet to stand between them. He pushed me. I pushed him. He punched me. I punched him. That's when I realized my injuries hadn't healed. Something in my wrist snapped and he laughed. My mother and sister ran to help me, but he gave them an ultimatum. *Yesli vy vybirayete Kazimira, vy vybirayete golodatz.* They had to choose either me and starvation or him. In the middle of a palace in Luxembourg, I stood with an injured wrist and bloody knuckles and they chose him." I can still see their faces, their broken, desolate faces. But in the end, their inexplicable loyalty made my decision easy. *I don't even know where they are. How they are. If they're still alive. How did I let so much time go by without checking on them? I used to do it, secretly, every couple months, but once I joined the band life got hectic.*

Comforting arms wrap around my neck from behind. Rochelle cradles against my back like the sister I should have had, comforting me in that familial way I've missed. My hands cover her forearms when she whispers, "You have us. We're your family."

"Thanks."

Johnny looks as troubled as I feel. "Where did you go? What did you do about your wrist?"

Rochelle sits down and then looks up. I follow her gaze and see Lara in the doorway. Standing, I go to her. Tears glistens in her blue eyes, her hair a beautiful mess, a wrinkled plaid shirt over ripped jeans. Fuck, she's stunning.

"I had twenty-four hours before they cut off access to my credit cards," I answer him, so I can talk to my girl in private. "I went to the hospital, got my wrist wrapped, and then took out two thousand dollars and flew to Amsterdam."

The guys laugh. Derrick says, "I would have done the same, but probably skipped the hospital. Just get me to the hashish."

"Of course you would," I joke.

Lara's not joking though when she asks, "What happened after that?"

I touch her cheek to ease the lines that show her concern. "Got odd jobs and bought an instrument I could take anywhere I went. Pianos are a real bitch to carry around." I turn my wrist several times. "I'm all healed. Don't worry about me."

"Of course I worry."

Taking her by the waist, I turn her around. "Come with me." Over her shoulder, I tell the band, "I'll be right back."

Around the corner, the door shuts, giving us privacy in the dark hall. Before she has a chance to speak, I bring her chin up until our lips meet. *This.* This is what I need. All I need. *Her.*

Her heels lower her back down and she leans her forehead against my lips. I happily kiss her head. Looking back at me, a tear falls down her cheek. "You're a guardian angel on earth. You're built from strength and compassion, goodness. I'll be here for you like you were there for me. But I need to ask you something first."

"Okay." My heart braces from the unknown.

"Do you love me because of this situation we've found ourselves in?"

The strength of this woman astounds me. *With all she is going through, she came here. She came to find me, to see if I was okay.* "I love you because my heart bleeds for you. I love you because the sun rises in the east and sets in the west. I love you, Lara, because without you breathing becomes useless. I'm in love with you because you're as beautiful on the inside as you are on outside."

She wraps around me, holding me tight. I close my eyes holding her tighter. "I love you, Kaz Fabian. Petrowski, Kazimir. Whatever you want me to call you, I will, because I love your soul."

I kiss the top of her head. "Kaz Fabian is good. I left Petrowski behind a long time ago."

"Why didn't you tell me about your family? About the abuse?"

"Because my world ended that night. I no longer had a family to talk about. As for the abuse, it started when I was younger and when I was old enough to know it would never change, I left."

Derrick opens the door and says, "Come back in."

We walk in hand and hand and take a seat on the couch along the closest wall.

Tommy asks, "Where do we go from here? Do you apologize to the fucker to make it right in the media? To get them to back off?"

"I won't. I told you. I don't regret hitting him, so I'm not going to back down. I'll take the consequences that come along with it."

He leans forward resting his arms on his legs. His brow is creased, his mouth twisted. "What about your family?"

"I stand by what I did. I wouldn't change it. I know in my heart what I did was right. They chose him for money, for worldly comforts. They chose to live in fear instead of stand by me and fight. That was *their* choice. I couldn't stay and watch the destruction he was causing, so I left."

"And now the great pianist is back," Johnny says with a smile. "Why the fuck do we not have you on keys? Get to work on some melodies. We need new material."

Relieved by the support, I joke, "Happily, but don't kick me off guitar yet."

Dex says, "We can't. Derrick still screws up too much."

"Fuck you," Derrick snaps, laughing while nailing Dex in the head with a pillow.

While the guys sling cheap shots at each other, I chuckle. Lara's hand squeezes mine, and she smiles. "So what are you going to do?"

"Guess it's time to face my demons."

21

LARA

I HEARD IT takes twenty-one days to break a habit or replace it with a different behavior. I wish I had reached that goal already, but some things take time to heal.

It's only been a few weeks, but Rochelle referred me to her therapist who helps patients who have gone through traumatic events. I've been seeing her four days a week and with her help, I already know Mark was never a habit. The sessions have shown me that he was a distraction, someone I once had fun with. That I didn't spend every night with him, or even see him every day during our relationship, nor miss him during our times apart, should have been a clue. He was fun. All those memories reveal who he really was. I was too blind to see, but I see clearly now.

Walking out of my therapist's office, Kaz is leaning against the car, head down, looking at his phone. His gaze lifts to mine and my heart speeds up, my steps lighten, my burdens lift.

His smile makes me weak in the knees and the way he looks at me —I'm gone to this man. He didn't take twenty-one days to takeover my heart. He's a habit I've happily taken on. I even talk about him to my therapist. She tells me to take it slow.

But I know.

There's no slow when it comes to *Kaz*. And there's no in-between when it comes to *us*.

He pushes off the car and meets me in the middle of the parking lot. With his hands cradling my jaw, I lift up and kiss him. Heat-sweltering, heart-singeing passion ignites my whole body, an inferno in my chest that only burns for him.

"My therapist confirmed it. You're dangerous for my heart."

A smirk quickly takes over—the cocky one that often appears alongside his ego. "And what do you think?"

"I *know* you are."

He kisses me again.

LANE IS BACK on the Fabian project, helping me, much to his delight today.

Tonight, I'm back on Kaz, much to mine. "Oh God! Yes!"

Kaz rolls me off him. "From behind." His eyes are alight with a fiery lust as he looks into mine.

Coming down from that blissful space between heaven and hell, I roll onto my hands and knees and brace myself. Large hands take hold of my hips as he taunts with his cock between my legs. "You're teasing."

"Just making sure you're ready."

"I'm ready." The words are more a plea than statement. *He always makes me so hot, so ready for him.*

One of his hands disappears and I'm surprised when rough fingers dip deep inside between my legs. "You're so wet. You're so ready, baby."

My fingers fist the sheets when the tip of his cock presses against me. His chest covers my back, our bodies covered in sweat. Lifting up, his tongue glides over my shoulder blade as he pushes into me. My head falls forward, the top of it pushed into a pillow as he fucks another orgasm right out of me. I rest my cheek against the mattress until his fitful movements cease, his bliss captured.

Both of us are sated after the second round tonight. I'm lucky to have this man in my life, both physically and emotionally. With his forearm over his eyes, his breathing is hard as he exhales, exhaustion taking hold of him. I know he is burdened, but in the last week he's only told me portions of his history. I want more. I want him to feel free. Lying on my side facing him, I reach over and rest my hand on his chest as it rises. I whisper, "Talk to me."

"I can't."

"Please."

His voice is low, eerily so despite the intimacy of our bodies. "I've been thinking about my family. I'm all over headlines here and in Russia. They're gonna know where I am and who I am. What if they try to contact me? Am I a bad person if I don't want to see my family?"

I rub my hand softly over the shield of his body that protects his beating heart. "No. You did nothing wrong. They forced your hand and you took the offer. You made a life, Kaz. Now that life has been spun around. But you don't owe them anything. Nothing. Not even another chance if you don't want to give them one."

"But you said it—my life has been spun upside down. Things were easier, more black and white. The feelings I held for them were buried. On purpose. Now the lines are gray and I'm expected to push my pain away like it never happened. Just open my arms as if we're the same people we once were."

Moving, I mold against his side. His arm comes around and holds me close. "The world's not gray, black, or white. It's whatever color you want it to be."

"Red, for how I feel about you." He kisses my head. "I worry."

"About?" I whisper.

"Us."

"Why?"

"Because you're dangerous for my heart too."

"Red seems fitting then."

"I love you, Lara."

"I love you too, Kaz."

My eyes grow heavy, and I'm lulled to sleep from the sound of his heartbeat.

I awake to the sound of dishes clanging around in the kitchen. A smile makes its way quickly across my face. *Kaz.* The night was too fleeting. My time with Kaz feels much the same. Only a few weeks together and then our world has crumbled again. I want more time. I want easy and relaxed. I want Kaz in the morning just as the sun rises playing his guitar at the edge of the bed. Coffee in hand and the scent of us all around. I want late-night chats on the patio and grilling outside as if we're a normal couple, as if we didn't overcome huge obstacles to be together, or have more to face. I get up and walk down the hall, thrill to see him again coursing through me.

When I enter the living room, I'm not sure who screams first, but Lane's is louder. Jumping back, my arms go to cover my body. My knees knock together. "Oh my God." I turn and run back to the bedroom.

His voice trails behind me though I can hear the distance growing between. "Oh my God, is right."

I grab my robe from the bathroom and swing it around my shoulders. My heart is still racing when I return to the kitchen. Laughter greets me first and then Lane says, "Good morning, sunshine."

"Oh good Lord, let's pretend that never happened. Okay?"

"It will be hard to forget. I may not be attracted to women, but your perky boobies are so cute."

"Ugh." I roll my eyes, wishing this morning could start over. My head drops down. "Please don't talk about my boobs. My humiliation level is already at an all-time high after that incident in there."

Kaz grabs the belt of my robe and pulls me to him where he stands in front of the stove. "I like your perky boobies if that makes a difference." *My sweet, man.*

"It does indeed make a difference. A huge one," I say, rubbing up against the front of him.

He leans down and whispers into my ear, "They're the best tits I've ever seen, tasted, touched, licked, and I plan to do that again later. Do you want me to do that to you, Lara?"

Kaz's words are aphrodisiacs and my body reacts, pressing against him, and closing my eyes.

"I'm still here, just in case you forgot," Lane says from behind me.

I smile, and then open my eyes. "I could never forget about you, Lane. Why are you here so early though?" Kaz hands me a mug of coffee, just the way I like it—two sugars, two creamers—and I take a hot sip. "Thank you."

He smiles. "You're welcome. Hungry?"

"Starved." Kaz turns back to the eggs he's scrambling while I steal a piece of bacon cooling on the paper towels on the counter. "So hungry."

Lane takes two pieces and goes to the barstools at the counter and sits. "Are we really doing this whole love-bird thing? I'm not griping. It's good to see this lady so happy. She's practically floating. Whatever you're doing, Kaz, keep it up."

"I'll keep it up. No worries there," he replies so casually, so comfortable in the kitchen. I love it.

Lane's palms land down on the marble. "Okay, on that note, I've got work to do."

Kaz turns and asks, "Not staying for breakfast?"

Walking into the living room, he replies, "I'm not sure I can handle the ooey-gooey sexy sweetness. You know what they say. If you can't handle the heat, get out of the kitchen. I'll see you in the office in a bit."

"I'll be in shortly."

Kaz yells, "Maybe an hour or so. I have plans."

"I don't need to hear about those plans," Lane calls over his shoulder, "or any screaming from the bedroom, so keep it down. Or better yet, I'll go visit Calliope today."

Laughing, I say, "Probably best."

When the office door closes, Kaz puts the eggs onto a platter, then turns to me and says, "C'mere."

"It might be safer to keep this bar between us."

"It definitely is, but c'mere anyway." Then he gives me that look. The one that says all the things we don't say out loud, one that communicates the hunger inside that craves me in ways I'm willing to give in to. I walk into his arms and we stand there wrapped in each other's arms. "I fly out for a few shows on the East Coast tomorrow." I try to lean back and look at him, but his arms tighten around me. "I don't want you here alone. Will you come with me?"

"Only because you don't want me here alone?"

"No, because I'm a selfish bastard and want you with me."

"And?"

"And yes, I don't want to worry about your safety."

Closing my eyes and with my cheek pressed to him, I take in his shower-fresh skin mixed with his musky cologne. The depth of the musical notes make me take in another inhale, wanting to take him all in and hold him close to my heart. "I can't."

"You can't or won't?"

This time I lean back and he lets me until our eyes connect. His hands lower down my back while still holding on to me. "I can't. I would if I could. I have three projects in the final phase of completion, so I need to be here for them. How long will you be gone?"

"A week. I can fly back between shows. It's just tiring to do that."

I run the tip of my finger over his bottom lip and then lift up and kiss the dip in his chin. "Don't do that. I need you rested when you come back." I follow the kiss with a gentle little bite.

Grabbing hold of my ass, he lifts me until we're eye level. "Don't you worry about me, baby. I'll have plenty of energy for you." We kiss good and hard.

The tips of my toes touch the ground and my feet roll the rest of the way down. "I'm still starved, but now I'm not sure if it's for the food or you."

"Not sure, huh? I think I need to swing things in my favor." Scooping me up, he says, "The eggs can wait. You're all I want to eat for breakfast."

"What about the bacon?"

"You're right." He bends us down and I grab the bacon. "We definitely need to bacon in bed."

I burst out laughing. "I love that bacon has become a verb." Taking a piece, I feed it to him as he takes us back into the bedroom.

With the door shut and locked, he sets me on the bed. "Question."

"Okay," I answer.

"Lane is working. Are you going to be able to keep it down?"

"Pfft. Me? *You* are the problem." My robe falls open on one side.

"Oh really?" His gaze is otherwise occupied when my chest is exposed.

I like his eyes on me, so I don't move. "Yeah, really, noisy pants. I can be quiet, but I have a feeling you're going to be yelling the f-word before I even get off."

"God, you're so fucking cute with your f-word and perky tits."

"Perky. Perky. Perky. One day they won't be so perky. What then?"

His gaze slides up to mine. Maneuvering over me, his hips dip down to meet mine. "Then we live happily ever after."

My breath quietly catches in my chest and my heart stops. "Kaz," I say half warning, half worried, "don't say things like that."

"I can say how I feel. You should too."

"I don't want to be hurt."

"I will never hurt you."

"How do you know? How can you say that when we've been together a month."

His weight settles on top of me when he kisses my cheek. Then my mouth. And then my nose. "I can say that because I knew the minute I saw you that everything I've been through, the life I've lived, has led me straight to you."

I want to live in his words, his confidence, and that world. But my life has been shaken, my once strong beliefs turned inside out. Finding faith has been hard, but I've been doing it every day. Some days I need a little more reassurance. I rub over his shoulders and up his neck. "How can you be so sure?"

"I was born from royalty and destined for greatness." He speaks with such confidence and I'm completely captivated. "My family raised me to believe in destiny. I thought it was playing piano. I thought it was coming to America and planting roots. I thought it was when I joined the band. It wasn't."

"When was it?"

"It's been almost a year to the day since we first met. You didn't notice me—"

"I noticed."

He smiles gentle like his expression. "You were in and out of my life for too long, our timing off. Six weeks ago, you were wearing a purple shirt and tight dark blue jeans. Your sunglasses were on your head and Rochelle had told you she'd be in the car." He whispers the rest. "Tell me, Lara, why didn't you leave with her that day at sound check? Why were you still standing there as if waiting for your own destiny to arrive?"

"Because I was." The admission sends my thoughts to relive every stolen moment we shared before I knew that my soul mate was right in front of me all along.

22

LARA

I HATED EVERY minute of our goodbye. I'd prefer a *see ya around* much better. But after the death of a band member, goodbyes are always said just in case there's not another chance.

Sitting across from Rochelle and Holli with an empty pitcher of Sangria between us, I wait for someone to say something. They've been too quiet for too long. "We should do something," I suggest. "To take our minds off the guys."

Holli smiles and holds up her glass. "I thought we were."

"It's not working," I reply.

"You've got it bad."

"No worse than you, my friend." Rochelle elbows her playfully.

She sits up and sighs. "We've been spoiled by them being home."

Rochelle says, "I have the night. Why don't we go dancing or somewhere else with some atmosphere?"

Holli replies, "Somewhere not so paparazzi ridden."

Rochelle agrees.

I say, "Somewhere where we can have fun but still talk."

THIRTY MINUTES LATER we're sitting at a table in the back of The Hotel Café, a singer is on stage playing guitar with two band mates—a drummer and a guitarist. The music varies from Frank Sinatra to *The Church*. They're good and not so loud we can't talk.

"They're halfway through the set. They should be on the seventh song," Holli says, her eyes on the band, her fingers tapping the table lightly.

Rochelle adds, "*Beautiful Deathly*."

I ask, "How do you guys know that? I've never heard this band before."

Two sets of eyes land on me and then they burst out laughing. Holli says, "*The Resistance*. We've got the set schedule down. It's weird, but I like to know when they have their break before the encore and be ready. Johnny calls me, even if it's a quick call."

"That's so sweet," I say, wondering if Kaz and I will be *that* kind of couple, the kind that sneaks time together when apart or if we'll have a family. Wow, a family. My mind struggles to wrap my head around having a family. I take a quick gulp of my cosmopolitan.

Holli adds, "Dex does the same. It's so sweet."

If there was more light I might be able to prove it, but I swear Rochelle is blushing. She's also waving her hand frantically in front of her as if that will brush us off so easily. "Uh-uh. Let's talk about anything, anything but me. How about Kaz being of royal descent?"

Leaning forward, I rest my elbows on the table and move in closer to whisper. "He hasn't told me the details. He hates talking about it because of how it all played out with his family. The few things he has told me break my heart for him. He basically left that night of the concert and disappeared. I don't know how he survived, but I know it hurts to see the pain in his eyes when he thinks back on that time."

Rochelle looks around to make sure no one's listening to our conversation. "He's agreed to an interview next week when they're back. I've been working on the details. It will be at a secret location so there's no chance of leaks before it airs. But he agrees that this is the only way it's going to be put to rest. He's been thrust even more into the spotlight that he didn't ask for. He has a fascinating story to tell though, so the media's going to hound him until they get it."

"It's good he has this opportunity," Holli adds. "Some of us aren't so lucky. He has a better chance of keeping it contained this way, making sure the truth is out instead of the blatant lies."

The thought still weighs on my heart. "I worry about him. He's a private person."

Rochelle asks, "Would you like to come with us? You can be there for him. It might help. When you agree to these types of interviews, you can dictate what is off limits, but that doesn't mean they stick to the script. Reporters have a way of working in a curveball or two. He might like the extra support."

I love the thought of being there for him how he needs, but I worry about being intrusive. "I should wait to talk to him. Make sure it's something he wants."

She smiles. "I can ask him so it's not awkward."

"Thank you."

We watch the band play a few songs and I let my mind wander to last night and how good, how natural, how at peace I feel with him.

"How's the house coming along?" Holli asks, breaking into my thoughts.

"I love it there. It has such a great energy about it. It's actually been a dream to work on. It has a style that defines the structure, but with Kaz, everything is lighter. Lots of light streaming in. Whites, soft beige, blues, and navy are playing a strong role in the design."

"Sounds beautiful," Holli says. "Can't wait to see."

Rochelle smiles. "Sounds like Kaz is finally becoming an adult. First he gave up the hard partying, then he bought a house. You're having a great effect on him."

"He did that before I was in the picture."

"You were in the picture, Lara. You just didn't know the role you were already playing in his life. I knew you were good for him."

The thought of Kaz putting the stepping-stones in place for a relationship is romantic, but then I remember the hard time Rochelle gave me for showing interest in him and laugh. "Then why did you tease me relentlessly?" The answer pops into my head as soon as I ask her the question, and our smiles and good times are gone. She doesn't answer. She doesn't have to.

My stomach twists as the name taunts my mind.

Mark.

Mark.

Mark.

I stand. "I'll be back."

Rochelle grabs my hand before I can escape to the bathroom. "Do you want me to go with you?"

"I'm fine." I put on a fake smile and leave the table. Fortunately there's no line when I reach the restroom. I go to the mirror and check for blood, swelling, and bruises. They went away weeks ago, but they're still there on the inside. With my hands on my cheeks I stare at the woman reflected back at me. She's not who I want to be. She deserves happiness and love.

I've not taken any of Mark's calls and not opened any of his emails. The threat of filing a restraining order against him has kept him at a distance, but I wonder for how long. Forever? For another few months, weeks, or days? Hours?

Kaz's story has overshadowed Mark and my relationship troubles. Royalty is intriguing to everyone, especially when it's a member of a popular band.

My heart starts to race and I wish Kaz were here to help calm it. I reach for my phone but remember I left it at the table. *Shit.* He's doing a show. Panic starts to rise, the pit of my stomach reaches my chest, and each breath becomes harder to grasp until I'm gasping. My head drops down as I press my palms into the cold, tile countertop.

"Lara?" Rochelle calls, but I can't open my eyes. I can't speak. "Lara, breathe. In through the nose. Out through the mouth. Do you hear me?"

A jagged breath works its way in my mouth, but I lose it when she tells me, "Nose. Breathe in through the nose. Listen to my voice, Lara. In the nose, out the mouth."

I focus on her words and take a slow breath into my nose, my grip on the counter loosening. When I exhale, I open my eyes, the tightening in my chest, the viselike squeeze on my lungs releases, and I look up.

"It's okay, honey. You're safe."

I take in another deep breath and release slowly. "I'm safe," I repeat. "I'm safe."

"Come here." She hugs me lightly. "You're safe, Lara."

Wrapping my arms around her, I rest my head down on her shoulder. "I'm safe. I'm okay."

Her arms tighten around me. "You are." She leans back. "Are you really okay?"

Rubbing my hands through the ends of my hair, I manage a small smile. "I am. Thanks." I release another breath feeling the heaviness lighten under my ribcage. "I don't know what happened."

"You had a panic attack."

My head goes back in disbelief. "No, I don't have panic attacks." Rochelle remains quiet as my mind starts to process this information. "I'm happy." But as much as I try to convince myself, it's clear I'm not convincing her. "You have panic attacks when..." I can't seem to finish the sentence and feel a different kind of panic take over. "When does someone have panic attacks?"

Rochelle takes my hand. "It's okay. All kinds of people have panic attacks, even happy ones. It's your body feeling overwhelmed with emotions, sensory overload, or other stimulus. I used to get them."

"What? But..." *Cory.* "But why would I get one? I'm in a good place."

"You weren't when you left the table. It's okay though. Now you know what you need to do when that—"

"It's not going to happen again," I state defiantly. I take a step back, pulling my hand away in the process.

If I've hurt her feelings, she doesn't show it. Her kind soul is exceptional, and I'm lucky to count her as one of my dear friends. "Okay, but if it does, remind yourself to breathe through it." Reaching for the door, she says, "There's nothing to be ashamed of."

"Rochelle?"

"Yeah?"

"Thank you."

Her expression lifts. "You're welcome. Come out when you're ready."

"I'm ready now." I follow her back not wanting to be alone, still so confused by what happened. *What did happen exactly?*

When we reach the table, Holli announces excitedly, "It's almost time."

Rochelle checks her watch. "The break before the encore." Her phone is placed next to Holli's on the table, and they stare in anticipation.

When mine rings, all eyes land on me. Looking down, Kaz's photo is on the screen and I smile, like a seriously goofy big grin. When I meet their eyes both of them are smiling too. With a twinkle in Holli's, she says, "I think it's more serious than you thought."

Rochelle excitedly says, "Answer it."

I grab the phone. "Hello?"

"Hey there." Kaz's smooth dulcet tone comforts me and I release a breath that felt like it was trapped in my throat. *Until now.*

"Hi. How's it going?"

Both Rochelle's and Holli's phones ring.

I plug my free ear so I can hear him better. "Good," Kaz says. "We're taking a quick break and then heading back out."

"I heard it was sold out."

"I'm not sure. I miss you. How are you doing?"

This time I smile, but I want to hide it away and keep it safe for his eyes alone. "I'm doing okay," I reply, not worrying him with small details like panic attacks in bar bathrooms. He has enough to worry about without me adding more to the load than I already have. "I miss you, too. Six days."

"Six days." He pauses and the quiet makes me nervous. "So, I've been thinking."

"About what?"

"You and me."

Fluttering emotions swarm my belly. "Yes?"

"I was thinking maybe since you have a key and all, you might be at mine when I get home." How am I meant to resist that? *Resist him?*

"You want me to wait for you at yours?"

"Yeah, like I've said, I've been thinking about you and me. When I do, it's at my place."

Smiling ear to ear, his sweet nervousness entirely charms me. "I'll be there."

"We get back late."

"I'll wait up."

There's a commotion on the other end of the phone. "I have to go."

"Yeah, there are about thirty thousand people waiting for you."

"You're the only one I care about waiting on me."

I lower my head for a bit more privacy. "Kaz?"

"Yeah?"

"Thank you for calling me."

"I love you."

And there it is without any obligations or requirements, without anything expected in return. Love. *True love.* "I love you, too."

"I'll call you later."

"All right. Break a leg."

"Goodbye, Lara."

"Goodbye, Kaz," I singsong, and then we hang up.

Rochelle stands with her glass in the air. "I love *love.*"

Holli stands. "To being in love and to being loved."

When I join them, I raise my glass. "To love and all the happy side effects that come along with it."

"To love," we say in unison. *And I realize I feel happy. Content, something I haven't felt for a long time. How did I get so lucky?*

We all finish our drinks. I head to the bathroom to use it this time and they stay to order another round.

When I'm finished washing and drying my hands, I open the door and practically walk into a wall.

My feet stop and I look up and right into my biggest fear.

23

KAZ

"Hey, it's me. Give me a call back when you can." I hang up the phone after leaving a message for Lara.

My back is slapped and I'm dragged forward under Derrick's arm. "Man, we fucking rock. It's pussy time."

Wrangling out from under him, I say, "Yeah, you go do that."

With his arms out wide, he stops walking. "What happened to my boy? I need my wingman back, brah."

I laugh him off and keep walking. "I'm off the market, brah."

"For now."

"Might be for good."

"Ugh! You're killin' me. Not you too."

Walking backward, I shrug. "What can I say? I've got feelings for the woman."

"Fuck," Derrick replies just as Tommy walks by. Derrick grabs him by the neck. "Come out with me. You're not fuckin' ball and chainin' it up yet, are you?"

"Not yet, but I'm not going out with you. I'm tired."

"C'mon guys."

Jimmy, one of the roadies, says, "I'll go."

"Fuck, man. I'll take whatever I can get."

"Never mind," Jimmy says and walks off.

Tommy and I laugh at Derrick. We turn and go to the dressing room. Taking a seat on the opposite end to Dex, I settle in for our usual after-gig wrap-up. Dex is banging his sticks on the arm of the couch. Johnny tosses his tee that's been ripped from fans and grabs a clean shirt from a hanger when he says, "Good show." He glances at me. "What do you think?"

I look behind me and then realize he's asking my opinion. Wow, this is new. "It was good. We missed the bass kick in during the encore and one of the left amps blew during *Beautiful Deathly*."

Dex stops his drumming and stares at me. "Awe, our little boy is all grown up."

Johnny stands there with his arms crossed over his chest and nods. "Holy shit, you're like a real member of this band now." Sticking out his hand, he says, "Welcome to *The Resistance*."

I shake it, but I also roll my eyes and laugh at my expense. "What the fuck ever. I won't mention shit next time."

"You're supposed to so it doesn't happen again," Johnny says, laying down the law. He grabs a bottle of water, downs half of it, and then looks right at me. "You did good, Fabian."

Here's the thing. When one of the greatest singers and musicians of our time gives you a compliment, you take it. He doesn't dole them out freely and he's not one for idle chitchat. He says what he means and getting his respect is not easy. I've done several things in my life that I'm proud of: played piano for kings and queens, performed in front of sold-out shows before I was fourteen, got hired to join one of the greatest rock bands that ever existed, and now earned Johnny Outlaw's respect. Yep, it ranks right up there for me. "Thanks, man."

Dex stands, tucks his sticks in the back of his jeans, and holds his hand out to me. "You did good. 'Bout time."

When I shake his, Derrick pipes in. "What about me?"

Dex laughs. "You're lazy as fuck. A damn good bassist, but lazy. Now fix the bass kick in. I never heard it either."

As the teasing continues, I check my phone, wondering why I

haven't heard back from Lara. The guys go about their business, but Tommy yells, "Pack your shit and get on the bus. We hit the road in thirty."

"How long is the drive?" Derrick asks.

"Four or five hours. You'll get to the hotel around three, but sound check isn't until five, so you'll be able to get some sleep."

I grab my jacket from the couch and walk to the door with my phone in hand. Looking back, I ask, "Is security in place? I want to go to the bus." I want to find somewhere quiet I can call her again.

Tommy answers, "They're outside the door. Take two with you. The crowds are huge out back. We'll wait until they return."

Nodding, I open the door and make eye contact with a guy twice my weight with a good five inches on me. I'm not a small guy, but this guy is a monster. When I start walking, he and another guy flank my sides. I hate this part. The attention sucks. Everyone stares. Everyone. Most are looking for Johnny or Dex, some for Derrick. I've got my fair share of fans and more attention than I care for or ever need. I'm called sexy, hot. My name is shouted like a thunderstorms heartbeat —throbbing all around, a pulse that puts your body on alert. They shout things at me—*number-one fan, pick me, fuck me, take me home.* It gets vulgar from there.

My phone vibrates just as we reach the doors. The double doors are swung open and I'm squeezed between the bodyguards—one in front, one in back. I keep my head down, watching their steps as they lead me to the bus. The phone buzzes again, but I can't answer until I'm on the bus. Lara's pretty face graces the screen.

I push forward and take the steps by two. The bus door closes tight behind me and I rush to the back, pressing the answer button as I walk. "Hey."

She doesn't respond.

"Lara, can you hear me?"

Nothing. *Fuck.*

I call her right back, but am sent right to voicemail. *Shit.* I scroll contacts and call Rochelle. She answers on the second ring. "Hey, it's Kaz."

"Hey," she shouts.

"Damn." I hold the phone away from my ear. Bar. She's out. But is she out with Lara? "Is Lara with you?"

"Yes. She's in the bathroom."

"Can you tell her to call me right away?"

"Sure." Just before I hang up, she says, "Shit."

"Ro?"

"I should have checked on her. I think she's been gone a while.

"What do you mean a while? How long?"

"Let me call you back."

"No, Rochelle. Don't hang—" Fuck. Fuck. Fuck. I immediately call Lara again.

"Hi," she answers. The background is quiet and she sounds normal. *Too normal.*

"Where are you?"

"Home."

"Home?" I ask, baffled. "Aren't you supposed to be with Rochelle and Holli?" There's a pause that drags. "Where are you?"

"Home, Kaz. I'm home." Her voice trembles on home.

"Are you okay?"

"I'm fine. I'll call you soon."

"Soon? What is going on?"

"I'm tired," she says. "I'm going to bed. We'll talk tomorrow. Okay? Later gator."

Later gator? Something's wrong. "You're home, right?"

"Don't worry about me. Later gator."

No goodbye... "Later gator."

We hang up and I call Rochelle back. "Kaz, I can't find her. She's gone."

"Find her right now. Go to her home. I'm calling nine-one-one."

"What's happening?"

"I don't know but I could tell she was trying to get me off that call. I think that sick fuck is there."

Rochelle sounds out of breath and the noise from the bar is going in and out of the background. "Holli and I will go right over. Do you think she'll be there?"

"I don't know. She kept saying she was there. You've got to get over there as fast as you can. I'll call the police."

"Kaz?"

"What?"

"Her purse is still with us. I thought she was going to the bathroom. Are you sure she's at home?"

"No. I'm not." I admit the thing I was trying to avoid, feeling sicker by the second. "I'm across the country, Ro. I can't help her. I can't save her. I can't even fucking protect her from here. You've got to find her."

"We will. I'm sure she just went home. Didn't want to deal with the crowds here. The place is packed."

"How would she get home without her purse?"

She can't answer that, so she says, "We're catching a cab now."

"Call me back."

"I will."

The call only rings once. "Nine-one-one. What's the emergency?"

"I need the police. I think my girlfriend has been kidnapped."

"Sir, slow down. How long has she been missing?"

"I don't know. Twenty, thirty minutes. She was with her friends at a club. She went to the bathroom and never returned. Her purse was left behind."

"I'll need more information to move this case forward."

"I don't have to wait?" My fear.

"Not in California. Some departments may choose to wait twenty-four hours, but you can file if you want to go down to the department."

"I can't. I'm in Georgia right now."

"Okay, can you answer a few questions for me?"

"Yes."

"When did you last speak to the missing person?"

"Maybe ten minutes or fifteen minutes ago."

"Sirrr," this time the operator sounds sympathetic, but I can tell this isn't going to go anywhere. "Do you know it's illegal to file a false report?"

I hate the way my fear turns to panic. It summons memories I had successfully buried. "It's her ex. He's hurt her. I'm afraid he's got her right now, taken her against her will."

"And why do think that if you just spoke to her?"

"She left her friends at the club. She left her purse there. How'd she get home? And she said 'Later gator' to me. She never says that."

"Later gator? That's not compounding evidence even added together. Sir, if you want to file a report you will need to go to a local police station. I can't file a missing report or send police to a home when you just spoke to the missing person or because they used a term she doesn't normally say."

"Please."

"Sir, would she have gone home with someone she met, someone you're not familiar with, or someone she didn't want you to know about?"

Now my frustration turns to anger. "She wouldn't cheat on me if that's what you're implying."

"We have other calls, emergencies that need immediate attention. I'm sorry, sir. Please file a report at your local department for further assistance."

I'm hung up on.

I want to throw my fucking phone, but I can't because I need to call Lara and Rochelle. I try Lara, but get voicemail. Next is Rochelle. When she answers, I ask, "Are you there?"

"Not yet. I tried her phone, but she didn't answer."

"I'm telling you. I know something is wrong."

"Calm down, Kaz. We'll be there soon. Try to breathe. It may all be a misunderstanding."

"A misunderstanding that she took off and not only didn't tell you but left her purse?"

"I'm freaking out too, Kaz. Please just wait until I call you back to freak out. Okay?"

"Sorry."

"You don't have to be. I'm nervous like you, but I'm trying to stay calm."

"Call me back."

"I will."

The bus door opens at the front and the screaming infiltrates the quiet that was occupying the space. All four of the guys load on. The door shuts and Dex and Derrick flip onto the couch. Tommy tells the driver to take off. Johnny leans against the wall and looks at me. "What's up?"

There's a good possibility I could be freaking out for nothing. I hope that's the case. But I don't want to lay it on the guys without having more information. I stand and brush past him and climb onto a bunk. "Nothing."

"Okay," he replies. I know he won't delve into it. He's good at giving others their privacy.

Dex on the other hand… "Why is Rochelle upset?"

I poke my head out and his glare hits me. "Just give her a few. She's checking on Lara."

Johnny asks, "With Holliday?"

Nodding, I lie my head back down and close my eyes. I know he's not going to let it go when it involves her, but I'm about to lose my shit, and can't deal with his concern right now. "Call her. She's okay."

"She fucking better be." He takes his phone and calls her. "You okay?" While she talks to him, I wait with my phone in my hand.

When it rings, I sit up and hit my head. "Fuck." I manage to still answer it but I'm going to have a knot on my head. "Are you there?"

Rochelle says, "She's not here."

"Are you sure?"

"Positive. There are no sounds coming from inside and from the windows no lights are on. What do we do?"

"I don't know. I feel so helpless."

"Did you call the police?"

"Yes, after they practically laughed at me, they hung up." I stand up and pass the guys, and step down a step at the door. The world is moving at least sixty miles an hour outside and I have no fucking clue what to do. "Tell me what to do, Rochelle? I'll do it. I'll fly back."

"No. Don't worry yet. We'll find her. Get some rest. You'll need it for tomorrow night."

"I can't sleep. Not knowing, I can't."

"Unfortunately, I think you'll have to."

I can't lose her. She's my air. My sun. My light. I can't lose her.

24

LARA

THERE ARE TIMES when you sit and reflect on what went wrong and how to learn from your mistakes.

This is not one of those times.

I know exactly what went wrong and no matter how many times Mark says we're good together, he won't convince me. I can't forget what he's done, although he acts like he's forgotten, which makes it more disconcerting being here now. I'm the one who paid the price, and I continue to. I don't know if he was stalking me, but I don't believe it was a "happy accident" we ran into each other like he claims. As if the physical damage he caused wasn't enough, he is determined to destroy everything good that remains—like Kaz.

The threat has always been there. I just didn't know Mark could stoop lower than he already had. He showed me an email that had the photos Kaz took of me attached. Every bruise and bump in its full glory with implications of Kaz Fabian as the abuser from some anonymous account Mark created.

Mark Renner worked out a plan while I was stuck in this closet. I should have cleared my phone, but I thought I might need the evidence handy. Now the photos are in the wrong hands and Kaz and I will both pay the price for my carelessness.

Over and over again he's repeated his mantra: If he can't have me, neither will Kaz. Pacing in front of me like a caged animal, he holds all the cards, but seems close to losing it all. His anxiety rolls off him and right onto me when he asks, "Who took those pictures? Did he? Did you let another man look at you, touch you, be with you?"

When I don't respond, he slams his fist against the door, sending it to hit the wall. He's trying to break it like he wants to break me. He may have stolen the pictures off my phone, but he won't take anything else away from me. My hands haven't stopped shaking since I ran into him at the bar, but I refuse to go down without a fight though. "What are you doing, Mark?"

Bloodshot eyes hit me and my breath stops. His demeanor has become more crazed the longer we stay here. I was shoved into my closet and told to sit on the floor. All the lights are out, but the door is open and the blinds let a little light in from outside. He stops in front of the door, his fingers flexing, an action that should scare me, but doesn't. It's more concerning. Unpredictable. Something tells me he's looking for something other than to hurt me. He finally replies, "I don't know anymore."

I refuse to be afraid of him. "What happened?"

His head drops and he says, "My teammates turned me in. They got me hooked and then fingers started pointing when Coach was onto them."

"What does that mean?"

"It means I'm suspended indefinitely because I failed the drug test."

The gasp is caught in my chest, and silence is my only response. He lives for baseball. If that's taken away, what's left?

Me.

In his mind, it's only me left in his life.

"They'll have you back. They'll make it go away. You're their weapon, their strongest team member, the highest-paid first baseman in baseball. For a reason. They won't risk losing the season by losing you."

"They already have."

"Talk to them."

A fist slams against the closet door, causing me to jump. "I have. I have a failed drug test and that scene your boyfuck caused on the red carpet and they don't want the bad publicity. Do you know what this means to my contract?"

"Your contract should be safe. I heard—"

"There's a code of conduct clause, Lara. I've broken it under these allegations."

Allegations... *truth*. He's completely unhinged.

"What are you doing with me? You show up at the bar, threaten me and others, and you want me to what? Sympathize? Help you? I can't. Not with that threat still out there."

"Be with me. The coaches like you. The owner's wife likes you. America loves you, Lara. They love us together. Why can't you just pretend to like me?"

My glare should be enough. It's not as he looks at me so expectantly. I stand up, willing to take whatever he rages my way. I swallow down the quiver in my voice and speak firmly. "You're leaving, but before you go, you are going to delete that email. And then when you get home, you are going to delete the photos you stole from my phone. You're going to delete every video you have of us, and every image we ever took with or without consent. You are you going to walk to the front door and leave as if you were never here. Do you understand me?"

"Why would I do that when you're my only hope to come back from this?"

"Because you aren't going to mess your life up any further. You have damaged me in ways I will never recover from, but if you don't leave right now, you will have to kill me. I will never help you. I will never let you get away with hurting Kaz. I will never let you have another night of peace on this earth if you hurt either of us again. Do you understand, Mark? This is it. We are over and we will never be again."

"What am I supposed to do?"

"Fix your life. Stop using steroids. You didn't enter the major leagues a drug user. You didn't get MVP for three seasons doing drugs. You didn't become Mark Renner, the great baseball player, because of the drugs. You had talent. You still do. Be the person you know you can be. Make your parents proud again. Prove the naysayers wrong and win their hearts all over again."

Standing before me, in all his height, his hands twitch at his sides and inside I flinch. My phone rings and I look back at the floor.

Kaz.

For a very brief second, I feel hope. And then I hear Mark's angry roar.

Kaz

NO UPDATES.

No calls.

No Lara.

I push the curtain to my bunk to the side and get up. The bus is quiet, the lights out as the guys sleep, and we rumble our way to the next city. I can't remember where we're going as I make my way to the small galley kitchen. Pulling a beer from the fridge I need something to help me sleep. This won't help, but since I have no idea what's happening with Lara, I don't mind if my thoughts are numbed until I do.

Sitting down in the co-captains seat, I ask, "Where are we?"

Doug, our driver, has a smile in place, appearing happy to have some company in the middle of the night. "Somewhere in South Carolina. We've got about two hundred miles or so to go." His eyes return to the road and he asks, "Can't sleep?"

"No."

"Great show earlier."

"Thanks." I take another long pull from the can, set it in the cup holder, and rest back. The monotony of the dark road, the soft road noise as we drive, does a good job of relaxing me. I don't know how long my eyes dip closed, but I'm startled awake by a hand on my shoulder. "What?" I ask, looking up.

Dex is there, lit by the little light coming in from the dashboard. "Rochelle just called me."

I stand, wiping the sleep from one of my eyes. My phone is in my other hand and I flip it up to see the screen. No call. "What'd she say?"

"Come on. The guys are up."

I glance to Doug whose grin is gone. Patting him on the shoulder, I walk back. Derrick is leaning his head out the top bunk bed. Johnny's leaning against the wall near the sink. Tommy has moved to the table, and Dex takes a seat on the couch. Bent forward resting his arms on his knees, Dex looks up at me. His usual bravado and charisma not seen, so I ask again, "What did she say?"

"Lara was in an accident."

What the fuck? "What do you mean?"

"She's alive, but she's in the hospital."

I didn't need a beer to numb myself. Those words do a damn good job all on their own. Not a heartbeat to be felt. No breath leaves my mouth. No words escape my lips.

But my thoughts are thrown into chaos.

I look to Derrick. We've been through a lot together over the years and I need to know what he thinks. This is a big decision. If I leave the band and go to her, I'm potentially cancelling two shows. He hops down and says, "You need to go to her."

"Can you go on without me?"

"No. We don't go on without you. She's important to you, she's important to us. We're a band. That means we band together." Johnny stands with his feet planted firmly in place, and says, "We're going back to LA. Tommy will have a plane waiting for us at the nearest airport."

Tommy stands and moves toward the front of the bus. "On it."

Lara

WARMTH KISSES MY SHOULDER, fingers strumming down my spine. I shiver from the delicious chill that follows as a hand cups my ass, and whispers fill my ear, "You're safe, baby."

I want to burst with flowers and hearts, love songs, and romance. The emotion is strong inside, cradling me in its depth. Rolling over onto my back, his fingertips dance across my chest, his lips kiss mine, and an audible hum awakens me.

"Lara?"

I try to open my eyes, but they're heavy.

"Lara?" A familiar voice calls my name. "She's awake."

Bright lights and shadows come into view. I close my eyes tight searching for the man that keeps me safe—protects me from the bad —in the back of the orange-red of my lids.

"Wake up, baby." The warmth of a hand holds mine and that voice draws me to lean to the right. "Lara, can you hear me?"

My lids flutter open and I see a man. My body, faster than my sluggish thoughts, moves instinctually against the far side of the bed, a cold railing digging into my back. My throat is rough, and gasps and coughs replace the words I want to scream.

"She's awake." I'm startled by Rochelle. "I'll get a nurse."

As my vision clears, I jump again, sitting up in the process. "Stay away," I work out, my voice scratchy while tears flood my eyes. I scream, "Help!"

"Lara?" He reaches forward to touch me and I scream again.

I run from the bed, the IV ripping from my arm and causing more pain. Holding my wrist, I run for the door just as it opens. A nurse and Rochelle are there and I drop to my knees and plead, "Help me."

As I sob at their feet, the nurse calls for help and Rochelle kneels down next to me. "Honey, you're safe. Kaz and I will take care of you."

I look into her eyes. "No. No. No. No. No. Please. Please. Help me."

"We will." She looks over her shoulder. "Kaz and I are here for you."

My gaze slides up the white linoleum, higher up his jeans, and into that bastard's eyes. A pain reflects into mine, but I know what happened. *I know how he hurt me.*

I'm on my feet as fast as I can scramble up and run out the door. I only glance back once to see him fast on my heels. I'm grabbed before I reach the turn. His hand covers my mouth just as I scream. Two orderlies grab me and the nurse starts saying, "Calm down. You're safe, Ms. Kessler."

The man holding me contradicts that. *I'm not safe. Why doesn't anyone realize that?*

My thoughts run wild.

Dreams.

Reality.

Which is which?

Rochelle is sitting bedside when I float into daylight. My body is numb, my desire to fight escaping me. I give up and roll my head to the side. "Where am I?"

"You're in the hospital."

"Why?"

"You were hurt in a car accident."

"What? I don't remember."

There's no smile on her face, not even a comforting one. "The doctor said that would probably be the case. Your parents are getting coffee. They'll be right back."

"Are my injuries that bad?"

"No," she replies sadly.

I don't understand her reaction to me. "Then what's wrong?"

"We should wait for the nurse. I'll go get her."

She reaches the door quickly. "Rochelle?" With her hand on the doorknob, she wordlessly looks back. I ask, "Is everything all right?"

One nod. That's all she gives me before she disappears and I'm left alone in this hospital room.

Where the IV is attached stings, and I have bruising up and down my arm. My wrist looks swollen. I see the marks on my chest and a flash of light hits behind my eyes and I close them. Headlights.

The door is opening and I look up. My parents rush to my side and smile. "Hi," I whisper, tears forming just from the sight of them.

"Sweetie," my mom coos. "You're awake. How do you feel?"

"Groggy."

My dad says, "That's to be expected. The nurse said she can give you something if you're in pain."

"My legs are stiff," I tell my dad.

"They say that's normal. You've been in the same position for hours and your body has been through a lot."

"What happened?"

"You were in a car accident," my mom says. "We're lucky you're alive." *A car accident? Why can't I remember that?*

"So it was bad?"

Dad shoves his hands in pockets, clearly uncomfortable. It must be hard to see your only child in a hospital surviving a car crash. "It was. Do you remember anything?"

"Headlights."

"Do you remember who you were with?"

"Michael? The nurses said not to interrogate her right when she wakes up."

I laugh at the admonishment. "It's fine. I don't remember anything. Who was I with?"

"Mark. Mark Renner."

Sitting up, alarmed, I ask, "Is he okay?"

They glance to each other before looking back at me. "He's in a coma."

"Oh my God. I need to see him."

"What?" my dad asks. "No. You can't."

"Dad, I need to. He needs me."

My mom says, "Get a nurse, Michael." She sits on the side of the bed. "Honey, why do you want to see him?"

"Because he was trying to protect me."

"From what?"

"From Kaz."

25

KAZ

THE REFLECTION IN the window stares back at me. Night had come crawling back before I had a chance to appreciate the day. I don't know the time, but my body's tired. My mind is worse. I lower my head and rub my temples as if this nightmare is just that and I can wake up from it.

As if Lara running to escape me, screaming in terror because of *me*, wasn't enough, her words shattered my heart. The nurses say this is a normal side effect from a traumatic event, but I'm calling bullshit. *How could she think I would hurt her? Does she not know I did everything I could to protect her?*

How does she not see me? The one who loved her through the worst thing to happen to her? How does she not see the man who made love, real love, with her, to her?

"Kaz?"

I look back at Rochelle. "Is she asleep?"

"She is. It's not peaceful, even under sedation. I don't know what happened to her, but she's struggling."

"I want to help her."

"But you can't."

"She remembers me as a monster. Why?"

Rochelle sits in a chair. The waiting area is busy, but it's large, so we have privacy in the corner. "I don't know. Whatever happened before the accident is what has messed with her mind, but she doesn't have amnesia, so this will pass. The doctor even thinks it will be soon."

Glancing at the guys, I stand and go over. "You guys can go home. She's safe and the media presence will rise with the sun."

Dex steps forward and shakes my hand. When I take it, I'm pulled in for a hug. "She's going to be okay."

Nodding, I step back. Johnny shakes my hand next and brings me in again. These guys are softer on the inside than they let on. With a pat on the back, he says, "We're family. Remember that."

"I will." I return a few pats before we part. Holli slips between us and hugs me tight. I wrap my arms around her waist, but Johnny stands there watching us, so I loosen my hold. "Thank you for checking on her last night."

"I'm sorry. The lights were out. We knocked and didn't hear—"

"You're not to blame. You did what you could."

"I'm sorry," she replies, sniffling. "I'd like to stay."

"Go home. Get some rest. You've had a long night."

When we separate, she says, "So have you. I'll stay if you want to go home."

"I can't leave her." She nods. "Go home with Johnny. Rochelle will keep you updated."

"Okay. I'll be back in a few hours too. I want to shower and change clothes. Maybe a few hours sleep."

When she moves under Johnny's arm, I slap hands together with Derrick and we bring it in for a chest bump. I say, "Brother."

"I'm sorry, man."

"So am I."

"You want me to stay? Keep you company? Get some real food or coffee?"

"Nah, go home. We'll keep in touch."

"Call if you need anything."

"Why?" I ask with a grin. "Your lazy ass won't leave that bed once you hit it."

He laughs. "True. Call Holli or Tommy."

"Ha!"

They start walking toward the garage where they can avoid the paps that have been waiting outside basically since we arrived. Tommy offers, "I'll stay. For real. You go home and get some Z's."

"I can't leave her."

"I'm gonna head to the coffee shop next door and grab a cup. I'll bring you one."

I could try to convince him to go home, but I know Tommy. He's a giver. He sees us as the family he needs to protect. I know he's not going anywhere. Maybe he will in a few hours. I'll try then. For now, I reply, "Thanks."

Rochelle walks Dex down the hall. They stop at the far end and hug. He touches her cheek, lifting her chin. Her long hair hangs down her back, and then he says something that brings a small smile to her face before they kiss.

I want that.

Back.

I want that *back*.

With Lara.

I want that back with Lara.

Sitting down in the hard chair, Lara's dad sits across from me. "She's asleep."

"Rochelle told me."

"Tell me something, son."

Looking up, I stare into his face. I see Lara in some of his features, but she resembles her mom more. Worry creases across his forehead. "What do you want to know?"

"You love my daughter."

"Are you asking?"

"No. I can see you do." I watch him as he stands and walks to the window. "Why was she with Mark if he had done what Rochelle told us?"

"That's a good question. I'm not sure I have the right answer."

He tucks his hands in his pockets. "What answers do you have, Mr. Fabian?"

"I don't think she was with him willingly. And I know she loves me... loved. Maybe I don't have the answer to that anymore."

"Rochelle said she loves you. Lara's mother says she does. Lara told her. She's been more secretive with me. I think she knows I wouldn't have reacted well to the news of what Mark did to her."

"I didn't."

The right side of his mouth rises and he looks back at me. "I know. Thank you."

"It was actually my pleasure."

"So the bastard is in a coma."

"Seems that way."

"The police think he was trying to kill them, that he purposely crashed the car. What do you think?"

I rub my temples, tired and angry and tired of being angry. My stomach twists thinking that he tried to kill her. The thought has crossed my mind more than a dozen times. "I think they might be right."

"He tried to kill my daughter."

"Twice."

"He's right down that hall."

"In room thirteen sixty-four and unguarded."

Our eyes meet and we nod. There's no sympathy when Mark Renner is the topic of conversation.

"For the time being." He exhales and walks to the waiting area. "I should get back to Lara's mother."

"Good talking to you."

"Good talking you." With a nod, he walks back to Lara's room.

I'm tempted to follow, but since the last incident, I stay. Leaning back, I try to get more comfortable in the chair. Eyes are on me, so I can't relax. I get up. Rochelle comes toward me and gestures. "Come on." I enter Lara's room quietly, following Rochelle inside. "Wait in here with us."

Lara's mom says, "We're going back to her townhouse for a few hours. She's stable so we'll come back in the morning. Will you be staying or would you like a ride home?"

"I'll stay."

Coming straight up to me, she hugs me. "Thank you for taking care of our daughter."

I hug her back, dropping my head to her shoulder. "I love her," I whisper.

"I can see how much." We part, but her kind yet tired eyes, so much like Lara's, stay on me. "Maybe in the morning we can sit down and you can tell me about it. Lara confided in me. She said you were the one."

She said I was the one? If my heart didn't ache so much, I think I'd be overjoyed by that. I just hope she feels the same when she wakes, because I'm not sure I'll cope if she doesn't. "She's afraid of me now."

She reaches up and touches my cheek. With a soft smile, she says, "Her heart knows you. It will work out." Walking to the door, her husband joins her. "Good night."

Rochelle and I both answer, "Good night."

When we're alone, I go to Lara's side and take her hand. Raising it to my lips, I kiss it, letting my lips linger against her skin.

Rochelle says, "Maybe I should get some sleep."

"I'll stay up."

"All right. Wake me up if she wakes up."

"I will."

Rochelle lies down on the small sofa against the far wall and closes her eyes. I pull up a chair and sit, resting my head so her hand is under my cheek. The quiet room insists on sleep and I reluctantly close my eyes. After being up for a day and flying across the country, I give in.

Comfort caresses me, fingers weaving into my hair. All the love I've ever felt for her is there and I see it in her eyes. She rests her head on my shoulder and I hold on to her, not wanting to lose her again. My arms come up empty and I cry out for Lara. But the darkness falls away, replaced by light when I open my eyes. I look up. Lara is looking at me. Her eyes aren't wide with fear like before, the corners easy with concern. *For me?* She whispers, "You don't scare me."

I sit all the way up, hating that her hand falls to the bed when I prefer her touching me. I don't push her, although all I want to do is hold it. "I hope not."

"I know what we had. I just don't know what happened last." Her voice is too steady, and distant, her emotions held firmly at bay.

"You will. You have to give yourself time to heal."

"I'm sorry."

"For what? You have nothing to be sorry for."

She exhales and looks up at the ceiling. "For earlier. I don't know why I reacted like that." When her eyes meet mine, she adds, "Well, I do, but I don't at the same time. It makes no sense. I know I loved you."

Loved.

Her gaze leaves mine and she pulls at a loose thread on the hospital blanket. "What happened at the end?"

"There are only two people who can answer that: you and him."

"He's in a coma. Is he going to live?"

I'm afraid so. "Yes."

"Maybe I should visit him."

We turn to the far side of the room when Rochelle speaks, "I don't think that's a good idea, Lara." She stands and comes to the other side of her bed, opposite of me. Briefly glancing to me, she tells her, "He's responsible for the car crash."

"The accident hurt us—"

Rochelle's voice raises just a notch. "It wasn't an accident."

Lara turns back to me, then closes her eyes. "How do you know?"

When she looks back to Rochelle, Rochelle replies, "Because the evidence suggests otherwise."

"Ro."

She looks at me. "I know the doctor said to wait, but I won't sit here and let her believe that psycho wasn't trying to kill her."

A gasp draws our eyes to Lara. Her hand is over her mouth and her eyes wide. "He tried to kill me?" she stutters as the heart rate monitor blips faster.

Shit.

"He didn't," I say.

"He didn't try to kill me?" she asks with the innocence of a child.

"No, he tried, but he didn't succeed. You lived with no permanent damage."

Rochelle says, "You've got to remember something, Lara. The police need to know any detail you can remember."

"I only remember being at my place. Kaz was there. I took him to the airport to meet the band."

"That was four days ago," I say. "Do you remember anything after that?"

"Lane. We were at your house. Two chairs arrived and a buffet, your dining table, but only three of the eight chairs. Don't worry though. I called the manufacturer. They're going to rush the chairs."

I smile. "It's okay."

"No, it's not. I wanted those two rooms finished before you got home."

Rochelle's mood has lightened like Lara's and mine. She asks, "Do you remember going to dinner with Holli and me?"

Lara shakes her head and looks down.

When Rochelle covers her hands, she says, "You will. Just give it time."

"Why have I forgotten?"

Sitting down next to her, I take her other hand gently, but she pulls it away. I try not to let her reaction hurt me, and stay strong in the belief that she'll come back to me. I try. "Because it was that bad."

"My mind's blocked it out." Her bottom lip wobbles. "I don't want to remember then."

"You must," I insist, my heartbeat lurches into panic mode. *I can't lose her.* "Just give it time."

"Take it easy," Rochelle tells her.

Lara turns her back to me, pulls her hand from Rochelle, and closes her eyes. "I'm tired."

"We'll let you rest," Rochelle says and walks to the end of the bed. Taking me by the arm, she gestures toward the door, knowing my heart's just been ripped out. "Come on. We'll get coffee."

When we walk out, I look back once. Lara's eyes—the beautiful blues I fell in love with—stare back into mine just over her shoulder. But there's no love seen in hers, only curiosity.

And then the door closes.

26

LARA

My mind is playing tricks on me, but I see the truth.

Sort of.

Kind of.

I sigh, frustrated that I've lost days somewhere in the back of my mind. The memories are there, they're just locked away, so I just have to find the key.

When I woke up, I was quiet, wanting the time to think, but Rochelle walks in with a nurse, both wanting to check on me. I've slept for hours. The nurse smiles and greets me, but goes about her business checking the monitor and my IV. "Are you in any pain?"

"A little on my left side."

"You're bruised, but your ribs aren't broken. It's a miracle you walked away." Her eyes land on mine. "Well, not walked, but you're in one piece and you'll be good as new. That's what counts. You have a concussion but we're monitoring things. If you need anything, just call for me. I'll be here all day. Shift change and you're stuck with me." A kind smile appears.

"Thank you. How long do you think I'll stay in the hospital?"

She takes the chart and starts writing. "The doctor will check you out later. If all goes well today, I bet they discharge you tomorrow." Looking to Rochelle, she asks, "You'll arrange transportation?"

"Yes."

"Good." The nurse walks to the door and says, "Buzz me if you need me."

"Thanks again."

When the door closes, Rochelle asks, "How are you feeling?"

"Tired. Some pain."

Sitting on the edge of the bed, she rests her hand on my leg. "He's in a lot of pain too. It may not be obvious, but he's hurting out there."

I look away, not able to bear the accusations in her eyes. "I'm sorry. I don't mean to hurt him."

"You remember him. You remember how much you love him, but you're scared of him. What happened?"

"I don't know." The pressure to find that key in my thoughts weighs on me and tears fill my eyes. "Why don't I know?"

"Your brain is protecting you from something horrific. You've got to realize that you're not alone. I'm here. Kaz is here."

"My parents are here."

She smiles. "Yes, they're here." When the smile fades, she rubs my leg to comfort me. "Your parents know what Mark did to you."

"I figured. Has my dad killed him yet?" I cover my mouth and shake my head. "I shouldn't have said that when he's in a coma."

She snaps, "Stop worrying about him. He's going to live."

"I just meant—"

"I know what you meant, but you need to hear me. Whatever Mark did to turn you against Kaz is wrong. You shouldn't feel anything but hate for Mark. He tried to kill you, Lara. I know it. The police know it. You know it. You just can't remember. You will though. And then you're going to need that man out there in the waiting room who has stayed despite the pain he's feeling from your rejection."

"Don't yell at me, Rochelle. I'm trying—"

"Try harder." She stands. "I won't sit by and let you defend that psycho while pushing away the guy who took care of you when you were abused by Mark Renner. Kaz was the one drying your tears. He was the one who had us check on you. He was the one that called the police. It was him that had everyone searching for you." Walking to the door, she says, "I need fresh air and you need rest."

"I'm sorry."

"Don't apologize to me. It's Kaz who's been hurt."

The door closes and I turn to the window. The sun is rising, the sky getting brighter. The start of a new day should bring hope. Not today. The door opens and I sit up when I see two female officers walk in. A dark-haired officer takes the lead. "Hi, I'm Officer Rodriguez and this is Officer Caprusso. Is it all right if we ask you a few questions? We need to fill in some blanks on our report."

"Sure. I already told the other officers what I remember, but I'm happy to help if I can."

After pulling out a small notepad from her shirt pocket, she reads, "We don't have much information on Mr. Fabian. We do know he's been living under the alias of Fabian, but his last name is Petrowski."

Petrowski, I repeat in my head. *Petrowski.*

Officer Rodriguez says, "He called nine-one-one. Would you recognize his voice if we played you the call? Can you identify it?"

"Yes."

"Do you mind verifying it for us?"

"No. As I said, if I can help, I will."

Officer Caprusso holds out her phone. "Just press play."

The other officer presses play and the operator begins talking. When Kaz speaks, panic is heard in his voice, *"I need the police. I think my girlfriend has been kidnapped."*

The monitor speeds up along with my heart while I listen. I recall snippets of a conversation I had with him.

"When did you last speak to the missing person?"

"Maybe ten or fifteen minutes ago."

"Sir, do you know it's illegal to file a false report?"

"It's her ex. He's hurt her. I'm afraid he's got her right now, taken her against her will."

"And why do think that if you just spoke to her?"

"She left her friends at the club. She left her purse there. How'd she get home? And she said 'Later gator' to me. She never says that."

Later gator? Do I really say that? When it's over, I close my eyes.

Later gator.

Later gator...

Later gator!

"He knew!" I say, popping up in the bed.

"Who knew what?"

"Kaz," I tell the officer. "He knew I was in trouble."

"How?"

"The code words. Later gator. We don't say that. We always say goodbye. Just in case."

"Just in case of what?"

"Just in case someone dies."

Both of their gazes hit me. I wave my arm. "Morbid, I know, but we say it."

"One other question. You said you don't remember that night. Have you remembered anything? Any detail, even small, can really help fill in the blanks."

Later gator.

"I remember talking to Kaz." I close my eyes, the key to unlocking the events of that night within reach. I stretch my mind and take hold of it. "I remember. I talked to Kaz. I was in my closet and Mark was blocking the door."

"Of your closet or his?"

"Mine. Kaz had a show in Atlanta and kept calling to check on me, so Mark told me to call him to get him to stop."

"Did it work?"

"He knew." My heart starts inflating again, filling with the love I held on to when my head couldn't. "He knew I was in trouble and that's why he called nine-one-one."

Officer Rodriguez leans against the end of the bed, watching me intently. "Anything else?"

Looking off to the side, I try to focus internally. A shiver runs the length of my spine and I squeeze my eyes shut. The bruises. The pain in my side. My throbbing eye. Kaz. My hands start to tremble, but I fight the urge to close my mind off. I fist the sheet and persevere...

The phone rings and I look back. Kaz. I knew he wouldn't give up on me.

"That's him?"

I turn back to Mark, and reply, "Yes. He won't stop until he believes I'm safe."

"Safe from me?"

"Safe, in general."

When his phone rings, he looks down at it. He turns his back to me and answers it, "Tell me good news, Coach."

I back away and grab my phone from the floor. I've missed his call, but I can text.

A thunderous, "No," scares me. It's more like a roar. Mark punches the wood frame of the door. His death glare is latched on to me. There's no escaping. I know it. He knows it. "No pay and they're dropping my contract effective immediately."

I'm trapped in here, so I try a different route. "I'm sorry." All the moxie I had mustered a minute earlier is gone, like the fight from my body.

"I'll lose my sponsors, my titles. They want my World Series ring back."

Panic was understandable earlier. It was a reactionary emotion that could be dispelled by asking the right questions. What I see in Mark's eyes is wild and untamed. There's no going back for him. This is the moment where logic needs to win out.

"It's just a ring. You'll have the memories and the record."

An anarchist fire burns in his eyes. He rubs his temple, then says, "Let's go."

Fear has returned, and knows no bounds. "Where?"

I thought the "No" earlier was stormy. He's a hurricane brewing out in the wide-open ocean, looking to destroy our peace on earth. "Get in the fucking car."

The voicemail on my phone chimes. I look back once wishing I could grab it but I'm yanked by the nape of the neck. We walk while I cry out, "Please. Stop, Mark. You're hurting me."

"Not for long."

Not for long? He's going to let me go.

I was a fool thinking he was going to let me go. He has no plans to do that. That much is crystal clear. We've been driving for twenty minutes. He's mumbling in the driver's seat, buried so deep in his head. "It will be okay. You'll play somewhere else."

"No, I won't. No one will touch me now. My ball career is over."

He tosses the phone to me and I look at the screen. The email he threatened to send earlier is up. "I'll never take your side, but if you blame him—"

"Don't tell me what I can and can't do. I can end you."

Looking at the phone in front of me, I say, "You can, but you'll never end my love for him."

"I will."

I'm confused. One minute I'm holding the phone, the next it's flying into the windshield. I reach up to stabilize myself, but my seatbelt cuts into me.

Opening my eyes, the nurse rushes in the door and past the officers to the machine. "Help me up," I plead. "Please." I struggle to sit up, but once the nurse assists me, I move my feet over the side of the bed. "Agh." My ribs. I cradle my taped middle and use the steel stand of the IV to level me to my feet.

The nurse protests, "You need to get back in bed, Ms. Kessler."

"I need to see him." I head for the door to her dismay.

"You won't catch him. He's just left after I updated him on your condition. I told him to go home to get some rest. Anyway, you're going to hurt yourself if you're not careful."

"Please help me. Please," I cry. "I love him. I don't want to lose him."

She shakes her head, and then says, "I can't help you. I'll get in trouble." My hope deflates until she adds, "But I'll look away. You've got five minutes and then I'm coming for you."

"That's all I need." I manage the door and she holds it with her foot, keeping her back to me. "Thank you."

"Go."

I tell the security guards, "I'll be right back." They don't listen and step forward to follow. Looking down the corridor, I don't have time to waste with them and pick a direction, going with the one that leads to the parking garage. I move slowly but steadily hoping he stopped to talk to anyone, maybe Rochelle, someone that could slow him down. I round the corner and that's when I see him. Kaz is standing at the elevator doors waiting for them to open. I keep moving, but the doors open and he steps inside. "Kaz? Wait." Right when I reach the silver steel doors they are closing. It's too late. Our eyes meet and the doors close.

The stairwell is to my left, but I can't take the stairs in this condition, so I remain in the last spot where he left me. Dropping my head down just as tears start to fall, I cry. "Please don't leave me. Please don't."

Ding.

When I look up, he's standing there. His arms go wide, holding the offending doors open, and he says, "I would never leave you."

My tears are still falling but now in happiness, each filled with hope. "I know. I remember everything."

27

KAZ

THE ELEVATOR BUZZES in protest as I hold the doors wide open. The most beautiful woman I've ever seen, the one who holds my heart, controls my emotions, stands before me in an ugly hospital gown somehow even making that look incredible.

Lara's eyes are wide with anticipation, tears filling them, hope written into her soft smile. Pride swarms the blue of her eyes as if she's solved the world's problems, not knowing she's solved mine with three simple words: *I remember everything.*

"You do?" I ask.

"I do." She takes a step closer and quietly says, "I love you. I think I loved you before I even knew I loved you, Kaz."

I drop my arms to my sides and step out of the elevator. She takes one more step and the distance between us closes. Taking her by the back of her head and her waist, I kiss her like I've wanted to kiss her for the hours, days, and years that existed but were never complete without her in it.

When we part, I close my eyes and our foreheads come together. I whisper, "I love you, Lara. I love you. I love you. I love you." The words are a chant so her heart never forgets our love again, even if her mind can't remember.

Her breath warms my chest as I hold her close, so close, never wanting to let her go. "You saved me."

I'd confess that I feel at fault I couldn't be there, that I left when she needed me, that I couldn't stop him from taking her. The confession lumps in my throat. I'm so grateful I can hold her now and that she's here, she's alive, she remembers. I take her hand carefully from my arm and bring it to my lips, kissing near where the IV pricks her skin. "Let's get you back to bed. You need rest. You need to heal."

"Stay with me," she says, looking up into my eyes. A halo of light is reflected in them, brightening her plea.

I smile. "I'm not going anywhere, baby."

We walk back to her room together. My arm stays wrapped around her waist but I'm cautious. I don't want her in any more pain than she already is.

The nurse is standing outside the door, tapping her foot. Her smile gives her away though. "Ms. Kessler, you need to get right back in bed. They won't discharge you if you're not better."

"I had important business—"

"Mr. Fabian *may* be important business, no doubt, but healing is more important." Stepping inside, she holds the door wide open for us. "I'm sure he understands. Right, Mr. Fabian?"

Spying her nametag, I smile to get us on her good side. "Yes, Nurse Martin."

She cracks a wider smile as she takes Lara's side and helps her back into bed. "Food will be brought around soon. I suggest you eat. You must be starved. Can I get you anything else in the meantime?"

Lara glances to me. "I'm good. Thank you."

Nurse Martin scolds playfully, "Mr. Fabian, let her rest please."

"I'll make sure she does." As soon as the nurse shuts the door, I tell her, "Scoot over. I'm coming in." Lara wriggles to her right and I slip off my jacket and then my shoes. When I climb in, I wrap my arm under her and she turns on her side, snuggling against me. "I love you."

"I love you, too. I'm sorry for last night."

"Do you know why?" I don't finish the question. It hurts me to even say it, but I need to know why she was so scared of me.

"There's an email. He wrote an email that included the photos you took of me."

Anger sweeps through my veins, but I try to remain calm so I don't worry her. "What did it say?"

She's still, so still that I tighten my arm around her.

"He was going to send it to the press saying you did that to me. I remember reading it, seeing the photos, trying to convince him not to when we crashed."

"It was the last thing you saw." *The bastard. Sick, fucking bastard.*

"I'm sorry."

"Don't apologize. Your mind played tricks on you. It was the last image you had, the words that said I hurt you. You knew, deep down, you know I wouldn't."

"I know you won't."

I kiss the top of her head. "Get some rest. I'll wake you when the food is delivered."

She nods wordlessly, closing her eyes. It doesn't take but a few minutes in my arms for her to fall asleep, her slumber even and her breathing steady. If she gets real rest so she can heal, I'd stay like this forever.

It wasn't food that woke Lara from her sleep. It was a doctor. He knocked lightly disturbing my sleeping beauty. We turned and although I know I should trust doctors, I still kept my hold around her firm enough to protect her and light enough not to hurt her.

"I'm Dr. Herman. I'm sorry to interrupt but I needed to speak with you."

Lara readjusts and sits up, my body remaining her support. "Hello."

"I'm Mr. Renner's doctor."

She shudders. Our peaceful space invaded by the name alone. "We want nothing to do with him."

"I understand that, Mr. Fabian, but like we ask our patients to follow doctor's orders, we try to follow our patients requests if we can."

Lara clears her throat. "He has a request? I thought he was in a coma?"

"He's woken up."

Our sanctity—that Mark Renner was unconscious—is broken. Violated by the news, I can feel it in my girl, the way she's shaking. Her heart monitor beeping.

I'm firm. There is no room for any misunderstanding. "We don't want anything to do with him. You do realize that he not only kidnapped her, but tried to kill her, right?"

"I'm not here to judge. I'm here to heal. I won't be put in a position to be judge nor jury on this issue."

"I will. I will be judge, jury, and executioner if he even utters her name."

The doctor shifts and puts his hands in his pockets. "I will pretend I didn't hear that—"

"You don't have to pretend. I'll say it to his fucking face."

He looks at the chart in his hands, then back to up. "I'm only here to let you know he's woken up and he would like to see Ms. Kessler."

"No way!" I state, unflinching in my stance.

The doctor turns to Lara. "Ms. Kessler, the decision is ultimately yours. I understand the situation is heated, but I do need to tell you that he's not in great condition."

She replies, "Because he tried to kill us. I don't owe him anything despite his health. I won't be seeing him ever again if I have my way."

The doctor goes to the door. "Very well." He leaves, but Rochelle shows up before the door closes.

"Hey, you two. I heard there was good news in here and seeing you together like this—this is very good news." She walks around to Lara's side of the bed and they hug. "How are you feeling?"

"Better. Much better. Memories intact."

"Your parents will be so happy. I'll let them get a few more hours sleep before contacting them."

"Thank you. Do you know when the doctor will be around to check me out? I don't want to stay here any longer."

She replies, "I'll check for you. What's going on?"

I say, "Renner's awake."

Rochelle's eyes widen. "How do you know?"

Lara says, "That was his doctor. Mark has requested to see me."

"No," Rochelle responds adamantly.

I always liked Rochelle.

Looking down at her hands, Lara speaks low, but we hear when she says, "I can't rest knowing he's down the hall from me. I just can't."

"You don't have to," I say. "We're getting you released today." I ease up to my feet.

Rochelle looks at me. "We need to talk about the two shows that were cancelled and the interview."

"Shoot."

"Tommy and I thought it was best to flip things around since the shows were pushed to next week. The interview will be postponed, but I don't know how long. Do you think you're up for it?"

"I can't think about that. We need to push it until Lara's better."

Lara sits up. "You should do it. If you don't, the speculation will get worse and they'll start digging deeper. This is your chance to put the rumors to rest." Turning to Rochelle, she adds, "I still want to be there."

"You're not going to be there. You're going to rest. The interview can wait."

"I don't want you to have to wait on me. The paparazzi are hounding you as it is."

"I can handle them. You focus on healing. We'll get you home and settled, so you can recover in comfort."

"I don't want to go to my townhouse."

I'm not even sure if it's showing, but I feel that damn cocky smirk on the inside. "Who said anything about your place, beautiful?"

A squeal erupts but not from Lara. We both look at Rochelle who is smiling ear to ear with excitement oozing as she bounces. "Oh my God. You want Lara at your house?" Turning to Lara, she says, "Say yes, Lara. Yes to love."

Lara looks to me. I nod. "Say yes to love, Lara."

There's a pause as she looks between us. Her eyes settle on mine, and with the first unburdened smile I've seen on her in a while, she says, "Yes. Yes to love. Yes to you, Kaz." *Best four words I've heard in a long time.*

THERE ARE TIMES you should go with your gut. Correction: always go with your gut. It will never lie to you. It may trick you. It may even be wrong sometimes. But it won't lie.

I trusted the wrong thing. The bodyguards said they were "On it." They weren't. One small slip in their judgment and Lara was put at risk again. I was only gone an hour, details of the upcoming shows organized, the interview questions approved, a call to Lara's parents placed.

Nodding to the bodyguards, I open the door. Lara gasps, then relaxes when she realizes it's me. I rush to her bedside. "What's wrong?"

"He was here."

"What? Who was?"

"Mark. He was here." *What the fuck?*

"What do you mean he was here? How?"

"I don't know. He was wheeled in by some man, and we were left alone despite me telling him no." Her strength caves and she starts to cry.

I hold her. "Did he hurt you? What happened? What did he say?"

"I'm fine. I am. It was just so unexpected. He took me by surprise."

My teeth grind together. "Lara, what did he say?"

"That he's sorry. He said sorry."

"What else?" I hold her tighter, trying not to lose my shit. *That fucker was in here.* "I know there's more. Just tell me."

"He wants something I'll never do for him. He asked me to lie to protect him."

"Lie about what?"

"You."

"What did he say?"

"That we had broken up after a bad fight. You were irrational and hit me. I ran to Mark for help. He was driving me home and a deer ran in front of the vehicle causing us to crash."

"What? That's not plausible on any level. What did you say?"

She takes my hand, removing the pressure from my knuckles as I grip the railing of her bed. "I will never lie for him and I will never betray you."

Hugging her, I try to comfort her as best I can. "I know. You sure you're okay?"

"I am," she replies while I rub her back.

"Rochelle will be in to pack up your stuff. I'm going to get you discharged. You're not staying here any longer."

I start for the door, but she calls me, "Kaz?" When I look back, her gorgeous eyes are on me. "You can't protect me from everything. I know you're trying to, but I'm okay. We're okay. Please stop worrying."

"I'll never stop worrying. Not while he breathes."

"All of this, this isn't how we're going to live. I can't live like this. You can't put your life on hold to helicopter around me."

"I'll feel better when we're home."

"I like when you call it home." *It's only home because of her.*

"It was never home without you."

With a shy smile, she asks, "Just so I'm clear, are you wanting me to stay or live there?"

"What would you like to do?"

"I want to be with you, and I want what you want."

"I love you, Lara. Live with me then. Let's just do this. Let's be together."

If only I could capture the smile on her face and keep it forever. She's so incredibly lovely. She's also giggling in giddiness. "You love me enough to make that offer so freely?"

"I do. What about you?"

"I do. I do, too."

I'm hoping it's only a matter of time before she's saying I do to me forever.

28

———————

LARA

Spending time in bed with Kaz is the best medicine. We talk, we cuddle, we watch movies, and we sleep entangled in each other—our bodies and emotions. He's healed my soul as much as my wounds.

It's only been a few days since being discharged from the hospital, but so much has happened that I've decided to stay disconnected from the world a little bit longer. Kaz had my townhouse packed up and my stuff brought here. Two of the spare bedrooms are filled with boxes and my furniture. My clothes have taken over his closet, and both bedroom closets. And he has not complained once. Though I have. I feel bad, but then he makes me feel so much better with his kisses, and hugs, and afternoon delights. That's when he talked me into staying and two days later, my townhome was on the market.

It's just after midnight. Kaz met with the band for a few hours earlier in the evening, but he's been home since. And score one for me—he made me a Russian dish called Pelmeni. I'd like to say it was good, but it wasn't just good, it was amazing. He's quite the chef. "Where did you learn to cook?"

"My mother. She said it would drive the girls wild."

Smiling, I lean my head on his shoulder. "She's right."

"That was a big motivator, but I also found it relaxing. It's a process to follow. You can get creative or get lost in the process. It's nice to be lost in your thoughts sometimes. I get that when I play guitar too."

"What about the piano? You never talk about playing, you never play, but yet, a beautiful piano is the centerpiece of your home. The whole house revolves around it."

"It's a ghost that haunts me."

"Will you play for me?" I ask nervously. I don't want him to feel uncomfortable, but I want to help him like he's helped me.

He leans his head to the side, far enough over to look me in the eyes. "I'll play for you, but not right now." His lids are heavy with sleep, worry and the world weighing them down. "Let's go to sleep."

"Okay." I lift up just enough for my lips to reach his and kiss him goodnight, hoping to kiss away his troubles. But I have a feeling his troubles run deeper than he lets on. "I love you."

"I love you, Lara."

ANOTHER DAY PASSES and no piano. Another night arrives and we're cuddled on the couch in the bedroom, an old movie is on the TV, but I don't think either of us is really watching.

I say, "I got a call that his computers were taken as evidence and the videos found. They asked me what to do with them once they were done."

"What did you say?"

"I told them to destroy them. I just hope they didn't watch them. I can't worry if they did though. It is what it is. As long as they don't go public..."

"And the photos?"

"They'll be gone with the videos, the computers destroyed."

"Are you okay?"

I lean my head on his shoulder. "I'm fine." I entwine my fingers with his and ask, "Why did you walk away that day in Luxembourg?"

"I knew I wasn't living the life I wanted to. I was convinced at one time it was, but I knew. I woke up. I showered. Got dressed and went to the concert hall. I was watching the symphony warming up. Just stared at them, thinking."

"About?"

"About my life and how I saw it going. My hand was injured and I was struggling with the slow healing and the intense touring sched-ule. I thought *what if I didn't play*? What if I walked away? What would happen?"

"You injured your hand protecting your mom and sister."

"I've never thought for one second it was a mistake."

"But you lost everything—your piano career and your family because of it."

"I didn't lose it. I left it behind to discover what was ahead. I'd do it again. It was never about them choosing me over him. It was about stopping someone from hurting others. Unfortunately, it didn't work."

"Kaz?" He keeps his eyes on me when I say, "Thank you."

"You don't have to thank me."

"I want to, for me and for them. Your heart is so big, right and wrong, so clear to you when it's a fuzzy line to everyone else."

"It's not to you, but your soft heart might cause you problems sometimes. Here's the thing though—stay soft, vulnerable, open. Don't let anyone harden you against what matters."

"What matters?" I ask, whispering.

"Love."

THE LIGHTS HAVE BEEN out for an hour or more. I've been tracing the design on his T-shirt with my finger and thinking a lot about his life before he walked away. I have so many questions, but I start with some obvious ones. "If you didn't want to perform, why are you in one of the biggest bands in the world?"

"I never said I didn't want to perform. I just didn't want to do what

I was doing anymore. I wasn't happy under that spotlight and public interest was growing in the press back home."

"But you're in the spotlight now."

"It's different now. Johnny Outlaw is the frontman. Dex gets his own fair share of attention. I'm a guitarist in the shadows of their spotlights and I'm good with that. I don't need the attention. I just want to play music that people enjoy." He smiles, then winks. "And being in *The Resistance* pays damn well." He slides farther down under the covers and ends my questions for the night.

The notes are heavy, the melody trickling into my dreams and gently coaxing me awake. My eyes are tired, but I turn to check the time anyway. 2:47 a.m.

Lying there in the dark, I hear him. For the first time. And I know he wants me to, so I get up and pad across the floor, dragging the sheet with me as I go. I tighten the corner into a knot above my chest and continue down the hall until I see him. I had full intentions of going closer, but seeing him stops me still. Moonlight lights the room, but Kaz is a shadow in its night. His head is lowered as his fingers play from a memory that captures the vividness of a life once lived.

The familiar music gets darker hitting a crescendo of emotion, and I call to him. "Kaz."

His fingers stop moving, his head rises, and his eyes land on me, and a smile that weakens my knees appears. "The piano was a spontaneous purchase. I haven't played it before."

Leaning against the wall, I watch him as his fingers run along the top of the keys. "Tell me about it."

"I'd just bought the house, but we had flown to New York for a show. It was late, maybe around midnight and I was with some friends, Derrick was there. We passed a piano store and a guy was playing it. Only one light on, but the music could be heard from the street. I stopped and watched, missing that feeling of getting lost in it."

"Do you not get lost when you play guitar?"

He looks up with a smile that's so sincere it's hard to believe so much weighs him down. "I do. I love the guitar. I couldn't choose if I had to, but I missed playing piano. I knocked on the door knowing the store was closed. When he answered, I told him I'd buy it, but I wanted that one. The richness of the timbre was what I'd been missing." He taps a black key. "But I've not touched it since it's arrival."

"Why?"

"I was worried I'd forgotten the music."

"You didn't. I heard you play by heart."

His smile grows, pride seen in his expression. "Since it was moved cross country, I didn't even know if it was in tune."

Standing next to him, I run my fingers through his hair. "I had it tuned while you were on the road."

"Thanks," he replies shyly. "I woke you. I'm sorry."

"Wake me anytime you need me." His arms come around my waist and he rests his cheek to my stomach. I cradle his head to me.

"I wanted to play something more romantic for you the first time, maybe Tchaikovsky? But Beethoven has a way of capturing the music that plays inside me tonight."

"You played the music inside you that needs to be heard."

His arms tighten around me. "You've saved me in ways I didn't know I needed saving, filling the holes where pieces escaped, and the light exposed me for the fraud I am."

"You're not a fraud. You've lived two lives. Those lives don't have to be separate. You can be whole again."

"I don't want this attention, for people to see the gravity of my old life."

"We all have skeletons we want left buried. You have nothing to be ashamed of. You have nothing you need to hide."

"What if..." He doesn't say anymore. He just closes his eyes and holds me.

"It's going to be okay," I whisper, the hour growing longer, my body wearing down, not recovered yet. "You're going to be okay."

"You'll be there tomorrow? You'll come with me to the interview?"

Despite how I feel physically, I will be there for him like he's been there for me. "I will be there however you need me to be."

THIS. IS. *INSANITY.*

Word got out, though no one accepts responsibility for the press leak.

The doors can't open because of the crush of people surrounding our vehicle. When I look around I expect to see *The Resistance* fans. What I don't expect to see are the Kazimir Petrowsky fans out in force. Russia's great prodigy has returned and they are here in droves of support. Tommy tells the driver to go around to the parking garage.

Once we're safely inside, three bodyguards wait just outside our door. Rochelle stands by the door waiting, another woman with a harsh black haircut and deep red lips is beside her on the phone. Tommy hops out and I unlatch my seatbelt. Kaz remains still, the same debate I saw in his eyes earlier playing in the intense expression. I squeeze his hand and the door opens.

The driver says, "*S'vasrasheniyem,* Petrowski."

Looking back over my shoulder, I watch his mouth form the words, his lips speak the language. Before my very eyes, I watch Kaz Fabian become Kazimir Petrowski.

Two Hours Earlier...

So tense.

"You're tense." I rub his shoulders, but they don't ease under my touch.

"I'm nervous and I don't get nervous." Kaz sets his coffee mug in the sink and fills it with water to soak. *He's so damn neat.* He puts me to shame.

I follow him into the bedroom and farther into the en-suite bathroom. He turns on the shower and I sit on the edge of the tub. "Opening up about my life... I've hid it for so long that it feels foreign to me now."

"You don't have a Russian accent, not even traces of one. I thought I heard something a few times, but nothing to make me think twice."

"I let it go and watched a lot of American movies. I binged on Christopher Walken for a while, but I was told that was not typical. It was just easy to mimic. I watched Ryan Gosling movies, listened to *The Resistance* ironically, and went to a voice coach a few times. It was really just being here, blending into the culture that helped. I met Derrick and focused on his. That might have been a mistake. He's got a laid-back Southern California dialect going on." He laughs and it's good to hear the sound. "Come in with me."

"And make you feel better?"

An eyebrow is cocked and he smiles. "You always make me feel better."

We undress and go into the shower together. The hot water washes away the worry that plagues me and I move in hopes that it does the same for him. His head falls back as the water covers him and his broad shoulders. He moans and I get dirty ideas just from the sight of him.

His heart is all giving. His kindness to me can never be repaid to the extent he deserves. I'll do my best to show him how I care through love and devotion, through actions and words. I kiss his chest and he lifts to look at me and kisses my temple. I place another just a bit lower and his breathing picks up and I start to go down.

Strong hands stop my descent. "Wait." When I look up at him, he says, "You don't have to do this."

"I want to do this for you. Do you want me?"

"I want you, so much." He squeezes his eyes tight when he says the last part. Looking back into my eyes, he says, "But I don't want you to think that I can't wait for you to feel better. I can. I will. For you, I'll wait until you're ready."

"I'm ready. I want this."

His mouth opens but no words follow, just the sound of his breath as it deepens. I take him into my mouth slowly, enough to tease, enough to keep him on edge, to maintain control so he loses himself for a few seconds at the end. The same hands that held my arms rest on the back of my head as I take him deeper. Soon our movements are synchronized, his pleasure at the tip of my tongue and then engulfed until I'm swallowing around him. It doesn't take long for him to let go, to release himself and his burdens, letting me carry them for a while.

Taking me by my elbows, Kaz helps me to my feet. The water rains down over us and I close my eyes letting it drench me completely. I don't know how long we stand there, two bodies melded together as one.

Hearts beating together.

Breaths short and quick until long and even.

Tender strokes of fingertips and palms soothe our souls.

It could have been seconds, but I wish it could be hours. I wish we could stay cocooned in this sanctuary, protected within these walls for just a few more days. The world outside is deceivingly pretty with its blue skies and fluffy clouds. Birds can be heard chirping. Despite the beauty of the moment, tears still come.

"Why are you crying, baby?" he asks so softly it almost breaks my heart.

"I cry for you."

"You don't need to cry for me. Hiding who you are can never be hidden forever. The truth always comes out."

"But it came because of me."

"My hitting him brought the attention on me, not you." My chin is lifted. I never hide from him. He's seen me at my worst and loved me through it, healing me from the inside out. "But you need to know what you mean to me. Everything I do is because of you now and I have no regrets. This life is worth living because of you. The air crackles in excitement because you dared to enter the room inside my heart. The blood that flows through my veins flows because of you. Can't you see, Lara? I'll take any bad because I've tasted and savored the good. I feel alive again." He kisses me wholeheartedly. "Because of you."

29

LARA

"*S'vasrasheniyem*, Petrowski."

Kaz replies in Russian, "*Spasibo tebe, moy drug.*" He follows me out of the large SUV and wraps his arm around me, holding me against his side. I'm not sure if the closeness is for him or me, but I feel the same, so I slip my arm under his jacket and around his taut middle. Rochelle leads, Tommy by Kaz's side, the woman with the harsh hair behind us. She's still on the phone, her smoky voice matching her hair.

"I don't give a fuck. Make sure it's done or you're fired."

As we're whisked through an employee's corridor of a hotel in downtown LA, I ask, "What did the driver say?"

"Welcome back."

"And you?"

This time he looks down at me, and smiles. "I told him thank you."

"That sounded like a lot of words for thank you."

"We called each other friend. *Drug* means friend in Russian."

"Really? That's interesting. I guess that's where our culture got the word from."

He laughs. "Yes, probably."

Tommy halts us and the entire group stops, waiting to move forward. The bodyguards are on full alert and block us from view. We're given the all clear and collectively start moving again.

Thinking back on the crowds and the driver, I ask, "You were more than a prodigy, weren't you?"

"A prodigy isn't enough?"

"It is, but the crowd outside. They weren't Resistance fans. They were Petrowski fans."

"The name carries the weight of a blue bloodline. Russians are very loyal. As a people, we've ruled the world and been at the mercy of it. We are strong through and through and when one does well, it's a reflection of the people themselves. Even if that person was born into royal society. Petrowski an extension of a great time in history, but in today's society it just means we were born into wealth."

Ms. Harsh Hair starts to talk to Kaz and Rochelle steps to my side. "We'll be in the room, but across it. I'm told it's a large suite where many interviews are held. You cannot say anything when they're filming."

"I won't."

She looks at me. "Nothing. Not even if you know it makes him uncomfortable to answer." When I don't reply, she adds, "We've gone over the questions several times, had some marked off, and others replaced, but we are bystanders only from this point on."

Kaz's hand finds mine and though we're looking in opposite directions, our fingers mingle together. Together. We're together in this. And we'll get through it together.

A service elevator is waiting with doors wide open. Kaz has to get up to the suite and get mic'd. Unfortunately only half of us fit, so Ms. Harsh Hair asks me to wait for the second one along with Rochelle, a hotel manager, hotel security, and one of Kaz's bodyguards. When the elevator door opens for us, I wait knowing the security guard is probably anxious to get to Kaz and do his job, but he holds out his hand and says, "After you."

"Thanks."

Rochelle and I step on and he walks on before the manager. The button is pushed and we're off. Once we're off, I whisper, "I need the restroom," to Rochelle.

The manager answers, "Right this way. There's one down the hall you can use."

We start walking and the bodyguard follows behind us. I glance over my shoulder surprised to see him with us. The manager opens a suite and we all go inside. I offer, "You can go first since you need to get back to Kaz."

"I'm assigned to you, Ms. Kessler."

"Me? What do you mean?"

"My job is to cover you, to protect you. I'm part of your security detail."

"You are? Who hired you?"

"Mr. Fabian."

"Oh. Well, thank you. I feel much safer with you here." What am I saying? I inwardly roll my eyes at myself. Do bodyguards like to hear that or was that creepy? I bet it was creepy. Ugh. I just go to the bathroom and try to block out my embarrassment.

The three of us head back to the other suite and enter quietly. It's just about to start when I find Rochelle off in the wings watching. Kaz looks handsome in his button-up shirt and jeans. His hair is a damn sexy mess of dark that looks like he just rolled out bed.

The female reporter seems to think so too. She has the nerve to stand from her chair and touch his hair that's hanging down over his eyes at one point.

And I want to break her fingers for it.

Taking a deep breath, I try to relax. I'm definitely more nervous about this than he is. With his legs spread wide, he owns the space around him, sitting calm on the outside. I wonder how he's doing on the inside.

The signal is given and the interview begins. Misti Roberts introduces herself and the segment before introducing him as Kaz Fabian, member of the rock band, *The Resistance*, and missing pianist child prodigy, Kazimir Petrowski. He doesn't react to the names, but smiles and greets her. Always the gentleman.

She starts in rapid fire. "Do you prefer to be called Kaz Fabian or Kazimir Petrowski?"

"Kaz is fine."

"Let's go back to your days in Russia."

He interrupts, "I was born in Russia, but I spent most of my life traveling to different countries."

"So Russia is not home for Kaz Fabian?"

"Russia is my birth country. I love Russia, but it's not been my home in a very long time."

"Where do you call home?"

He glances my way. *Home.* Then he answers, "Los Angeles. I've lived here almost nine years." I know he can't see me in the dark back here, but he knows I'm here. He knows I'm his home as he's mine.

"Are you here on a visa?"

"No. I got my citizenship three years ago."

"Before you were a member of *The Resistance*?"

"Yes."

"So Johnny Outlaw, the band, and management never knew that you weren't an American?"

"I am in all ways except by birth. As I said, I'm an American citizen."

She leans in as if the conversation is between friends, intimate, just the two of them. "So tell us, a star by fourteen, talent that was unmatched by others who had studied and performed for years, and you walked away."

He stays the course and remains how he's sitting, not responding to the leading statement, but waiting for the questions as instructed prior to coming here.

Misti continues as if repeating his life back to him will be news to him. "You attended Julliard at age twelve, living in New York City that year with your parents and sister. The Petrowskis have managed to maintain wealth and status for hundreds of years, through wars, and transitional times in your birth country. How does your family make their money?"

"That would be a question to ask them."

"You're not close with them?"

"When I left, I knew what I was walking away from—"

"A life of luxury from what our research has determined. You walked away with nothing. Why would you do that? Why would a boy of sixteen walk away from a burgeoning musical career, his family, status, and wealth, Kazimir?"

He stares at her. Unblinking.

I don't realize I'm holding my breath until Rochelle releases the one she was holding. He replies, "I am part of one of the greatest bands to ever play music. I would have played guitar for them even if I had to do it free. That's success. I didn't have success when I was fourteen, fifteen, or sixteen. I had fame. I don't need fame, Misti. I need purpose. I started a journey that brought me around the world and set me in the middle of the land of opportunity. So I don't think of myself as leaving wealth, status, or a career behind. I didn't leave those things. I found them right here."

"You didn't mention family."

"The band is my family. My girlfriend is my family. I have everything, so it's not what I left behind. It's what I have now and that's all I'll ever need."

Misti shoots a look my way. "About your girlfriend—"

Rochelle nudges me, and whispers, "You were off limits."

"Seems I'm back on."

Kaz is firm when he states, "I don't talk about my private life now. I'll answer the questions we agreed to about me and the speculation surrounding my disappearance, but my girlfriend is not something I'll discuss publicly."

"Since you brought her up, I thought we could clarify a few things. Mark Renner, for example. When his rep was called, they released a statement to us. Would you like to know what it says?"

"No," Kaz replies coolly.

She reads it anyway, "Mr. Renner is deeply saddened by the turn of events that has caused Ms. Kessler any pain. He apologized to her in person recently and wants to take this opportunity to apologize publicly."

"I don't want to hear anymore."

"It's not that lon—"

"I don't. Want. To. Hear. It."

"Maybe Lara Kessler does," she insists, turning to me.

Kaz's fingers start moving along his hip. What appears to be a meaningless motion to some is noticeably a nervous habit to me. Rochelle grabs my arm and pulls me farther back. Ms. Harsh Hair intervenes and flips off the reporter. Offense is heard in Misti's gasp and seen in a forehead that I would have bet money couldn't wrinkle. It is though, causing me to smile.

Clearing the silence, Kaz asserts, "This interview is about me, not the ones I love."

"Love, Mr. Petrowski? Lara Kessler is embroiled in a bizarre event with Mark Renner. How does love factor into this situation?"

She's poking. *Poking. Poking.* He'll only remain cool for so long before he loses his patience with her questions. Whispering to Rochelle, I ask, "Is she allowed to ask him these kind of questions?"

"There's no law. It's a guide. We've seen a lot of reporters pull this bullshit. We can stop the interview."

Tommy's hand rises. "One moment, let's see how he does."

Kaz shifts in his seat. "I thought we established that Fabian is my last name?"

She falters under his glare. "My apologies."

"As for Ms. Kessler, you can contact her PR rep after our interview and ask the question I don't have a right to answer."

The reporter stands. "I have a surprise for you."

Rochelle and Tommy are on alert. The three bodyguards are focused.

Tommy rushes forward. "He was set up."

The double doors to the suite open wide and just as I look from Kaz to the people walking in, it clicks.

He's been ambushed.

The bodyguards are in motion. Rochelle jumps over cables to get to Kaz, and I do the only thing I know to help. I hurry to the producer, and say, "She can interview me. Anything. She can ask me anything."

Kaz stands. "No."

Misti is beaming. "Join us."

"No, Kaz goes if I do this."

She seems to debate so I spell it out for her, "Kaz Fabian, Kazimir Petrowski. Mystery solved. Me and Mark Renner, the famous baseball player-turned killer. What will sell more commercial spots?"

"Your story."

"There's your answer."

Kaz shakes his head. "No. You're not doing this."

"*Zdravstvuyte*, Kazimir."

We turn toward the thick accent of an older woman. I know who it is. Her hair is lighter, her eyes darker, but the love for her child is evident. Spinning to face him, I place my hands on Kaz's chest. "I'm here for you, Kaz. Whatever you need. Remember, I'm here for you."

His gaze is fixed over my shoulder, a deep line forming between his eyes. Confusion is the heaviest dose of reality and I know anger or pain is next. "What are you doing here?"

With her hands holding a large leather purse, his mother speaks to him in English, "We are invited guests."

Misti smiles proudly. "We organized a reunion. The camera is still on by the way, so we've captured it all."

"Stop recording. We've revoked all rights to do anything with this footage." Ms. Harsh Hair is my hero. I need to find out his publicist's real name, this one not fitting anymore.

Misti's shoulders square and she glares at her. "You can't. We already own the interview. He's already been paid."

His publicist wins the battle when she retorts, "Read the fine print, princess. A stunt like this terminates the contract and we retain the fee, so bye, Misti."

Rochelle jumps in between Misti and Kaz and tells him to go. Her voice rises as she talks to the bodyguards. "Get them out of here."

Kaz takes my hand. "We're leaving."

Walking wide around the camera equipment, I'm well aware that we're avoiding his mother. Debating if it's best to leave or to face his mother, a woman who looks sad watching her son leave without the reunion she hoped for, I ask, "Your mom, Kaz?"

"My parents want their prize back. They don't care about me or they wouldn't have shown back up like this. It's all for show. Playing it up for the cameras."

His mother cries, her words slipping between Russian and English. One phrase is clear: "I love you."

"Kaz?" I hesitate.

He doesn't. "No, I won't give them this. If they want to speak with me, they can do it privately."

I don't argue because he's right. I don't know what they want or why they're here, but it's not a good place for him to be—emotionally or physically. We make it down the elevator to the bottom floor and down the corridor that leads out the employee entrance when Kaz jerks us to a stop.

Before us stands a woman a few years older, not by much, maybe five, with a lifetime of sorrow written on her face. Taking what life has given her out of the equation, the resemblance is remarkable. Her eyes match the unique color I've fallen in love with. Her hair is the same dark shade as his that recalls midnight over the Mediterranean. "Hi," she says.

Looking to Kaz, I wait to see what he wants to do.

"Hi," he replies. His hand tightens on mine as they stare at each other.

"Please don't leave," she pleads. "We need to talk."

"I have nothing to say to you." His tone slips into an accent that hits the letters more intensely.

We start walking again, sidestepping around her. The door is pushed open, the SUV waiting for us just beyond it. But before we can leave, his sister says, "*Otets* is dead."

30

LARA

Kaz stops.

Standing beside him, I wait, letting him make the final decision. The door in front of us is wide open. We can leave, forget all this, and try to live the life we had this morning. Or we can turn back and fill the holes that make up the emptiness in his heart.

Will we keep walking, leaving his sister behind, or do we stop and face the ghosts of his past life?

"Father is dead. You don't have to run any longer."

Kaz turns his head toward me, but speaks to her, "I haven't run in years."

"We couldn't find you."

"Because you weren't looking." Our eyes stay locked on each other's.

Even with my back to her, I can hear her say, "I'm looking now."

"Maybe it's too late," he replies, looking down, away from me. I miss his eyes already. The pain filling them makes me want to hug him until it's gone again, but I don't dare move. Not an inch.

Her voice sounds closer when she says, "Maybe it's not. I miss you."

His head lowers forward and he closes his eyes, his emotions seeming to overwhelm him. Our hands separate and he turns around, staring straight at the woman he once tried to protect. "What do you want from me, Katerina?"

"I want my brother back?"

"Why? Because father's dead?"

"No, because I love you. I miss my younger brother."

I take a step back, feeling intrusive standing so close to the two of them as they try to find peace between them.

Rochelle, Kaz's mother, and a few other people come off the elevator. Tommy taps Kaz's arm. "Time to go."

Kaz turns to leave, but I stop him this time. "You'll regret leaving them behind. Maybe not now, but one day."

The back of his hand runs over my cheek. "You're too forgiving."

"You might benefit from that one day."

A smile appears. "True." He takes a step, but stops again. Looking back at Tommy, he says, "Make sure they arrive at my house safely."

"Will do."

I take hold of his arm and we head for the SUV. The door is open and we settle in quickly before Misti comes after us with a cameraman in tow. The door is slammed closed and the vehicle takes off. Kaz looks out the window as we pass the fans on the sidewalk. "Well that went to shit fast."

"Did it?"

He looks at me surprised. "You think that went well?"

"I think there's an opportunity for it to turn out well."

"Jesus, Lara, have we not been through enough?"

"More than our fair share. That doesn't change that your mother and sister are here to see you."

"For the publicity. If they wanted to see me before, they could have. My dad is dead and they need someone else to take care of them. Don't let that soft heart of yours blind you to the facts."

"You walked away. You said that. Now you want to punish them again for it. What if they made a mistake? What if they are here to make up for it?"

"Don't turn this on me." His hand fists at his side. The other fist goes up tapping against his closed eyes. "I felt the loss for years. I finally don't and look who shows up." He lowers his hand and his fingers flex. Looking at me with eyes that plead for mercy, he says, "I know you want to see the good in everyone, much to your detriment, but there are not two sides to this story. There's one and the facts remain. They chose the man who hit them over the kid who would have fought to the end for them."

Reaching forward, I hold his right hand in mine. "Fight for them now, Kaz. This is your chance to do what you didn't get to do before. You may call my heart soft, but you fought for me. Before you loved me, you fought for me. That's who you are. That's the man you are. Your family is back and this is your chance to find your way back."

"What if I don't want them back in my life?"

Covering his hand that rests on my thigh, I feel safe talking to him about this. Someone has to and he's open to hearing my thoughts. "I think you do more than you let on."

Turning to look out the window again, he says, "Maybe."

My phone rings. My lawyer. I hired a business lawyer while in the hospital. I knew there would be "stuff" to deal with that I needed to have handled for me. "Hello."

"Lara, I've got news."

Grabbing hold of the door handle, I brace myself and turn my back to Kaz. He has enough problems of his own to continue to take on mine. "And?"

"He confessed to the police."

"Mark did?"

"Yes. He's now being held in county until a judge can make a ruling in his case."

Stunned. I blink several times. "What did he confess?"

"To taking you against your wil—"

"Kidnapping?"

"Sort of."

"Sort of?" I close my eyes and focus on my breathing.

"You walked out of the club willingly, Lar—"

"Because he threatened to hurt Kaz."

The sound of disappointment fills the line. "He's going to fight. You know that."

"What else?" I snap.

"He admitted that he tried to commit suicide."

Correcting him, I ask, "You mean homicide?"

"He's arguing temporary insanity and that he gets treatment instead of prison time. There are still a few outstanding issues with his case."

"He's going to win. I know it."

"We can hold out hope, present the evidence and your testimony from the hospital." There's a pause. "He has very good lawyers."

"If he's found guilty on the charges, how long will he serve?"

"That's for the judge to decide based on the state laws, his confession, and the charges filed against him. Your statement will be used, but with his confession on the record, you shouldn't have to testify. I have good news though."

"I need good news right now."

"The restraining orders against Kaz and Derrick have been dropped. Yours remains in place against Mark."

"Okay. I'll tell him."

"Look, Lara, we've presented a file backing our recommendation for a longer sentence. I would recommend putting this behind you and moving forward the best you can at this stage. It's out of your hands. I'll keep in touch with details as things move forward, and I suspect they will fairly quickly now. Lie low. The media will hear of the confession within hours and they'll be looking for a statement from you. Don't say anything. Direct them to me."

"Okay."

"Take care of yourself and we'll be in touch soon."

"Thank you." When I hang up, I peek back at Kaz.

His gaze is burdened, his shoulders stiff. "What's going on?"

That is the million-dollar question. I have no idea what is going on. How do I put this behind me when it still stands squarely in front of me? I can't talk to Kaz about it now. He doesn't need extra worry. Just give him the basics. "Mark confessed."

"Really?"

I release a deep breath and relax for the first time in months. "I can finally move on." Reaching over, I wrap my hand with his. "We can finally move on."

Kaz moves across the leather seat and puts his arm around me. I rest my head on his shoulder and he kisses me. "Finally."

I hope.

———

KAZ PACES.

Anxiety courses through him, his fingers tapping at his side, his jaw tensing, his eyes focused on the floor but his mind so obviously on something else.

I sit in the middle of the couch in the living room and watch, giving him peace before the storm arrives. The gate buzzer rings his phone. He stops and looks at me before punching in the code. I see his lips purse and he blows out. Then he comes and sits next to me. "So this is it," he remarks and looks down at his shoes.

"What do you want, Kaz?"

"I want to believe that we can be a family again."

I kiss his shoulder. "It's not about believing. It's about knowing. You know deep down they love you. They were put in an impossible situation. I don't think they chose him over you. They chose to survive the best they knew how."

"I feel betrayed."

Putting my arm around him, I whisper, "I know. You have every right to feel that too. Just don't let that feeling make decisions for you. This is a new opportunity. You can take or leave it, but at least listen —openly—with your heart and head."

A knock on the door pulls us back to the moment. He pats my legs and we kiss quickly. I stand when he goes to answer the door.

It's not a boisterous reunion in the entryway, but quiet and cautious on both sides. Kaz hugs his mother and then his sister bringing tears to everyone in the room. He leads them into the living room and introduces me, "This is Lara Kessler, my girlfriend. My mother, Vera Petrowski, and my sister, Katerina Petrowski."

I reach forward to shake their hands. Despite their smiles, they don't accept right away, but then I realize the mistake I've made. Oh my God. They're royalty. Maybe I insulted them by not curtsying. So I try my best to recall every Disney movie I ever saw with a princess in it, and curtsy.

Kaz chuckles and reaches down to take my arm. "No, you don't have to do that."

His mother and sister are giggling. Rochelle is laughing.

Shit.

"I wasn't sure."

Kaz rubs my lower back. "It's okay." He signals to the sofas and chairs. "Let's sit."

His mother eyes the piano and asks him something in Russian.

Kaz says, "English."

Tension sucks the air out of the room with that one word. I feel I should go, that I've become an obstacle for them to climb their way back into each other's lives. His mother glances to me, and smiles when she looks at him. "Do you still play?"

"Occasionally," he responds not missing a beat. I've gotten to know Kaz well enough to read the emotions he tries to bury. His expressive eyes always reveal his true feelings.

He's trying so hard to keep them out, to keep them at a distance, to protect himself. His mother's interest is natural though he's fighting receiving it. His reluctance to pretend he's not hurt is also natural. Was it only his talent that held them together? If that's all that bound them together, it's also what tore them apart. If they only understood how fighting for them effectively sabotaged his ability to play. And he lost them anyway. With a shattered hand, he left, but the true shattering was in his heart.

When he looks at me, I see more pain. Conflict.

Perhaps sensing his unease, Kaz's mother asks me where the restroom is, and I direct her to the guest bathroom. She says nothing until she comes out, and then I see steel in her expression, one so similar to her son.

"You love my son."

"With all my heart," I answer. She closes her eyes and then a wistful smile overtakes her beautiful face.

"I've never forgiven myself for letting him leave. I've never stopped loving him, praying he was safe and happy. Seeing him... happy..."

I want nothing more than to reassure her, but I can't make it about her when I need to protect him. "I think he wants you back in his life, but he needs answers. He feels abandoned. But he also needs honesty. Don't lie to him to get back in his good graces. You need to apologize."

"I failed him for so many reasons he has never known." She whispers, "I'm so incredibly proud of him for what he did. So proud of him for the man he has become."

"Tell him."

My gaze lifts over her shoulder and I can tell from Kaz's expression that he heard her. As we slowly walk toward him, I see him take a deep breath, possibly for courage to attempt reconciliation.

"I haven't played much over the years, *Mamasha*." He takes one of his guitars from the corner and wraps the strap around his neck. "I taught myself to play guitar. It was more portable." Shrugging while he strums, he says, "I think I'm a better guitarist these days and my work keeps me on the road. I've seen the world with the band."

His sister perks up. "You are friends with Johnny Outlaw?"

All eyes in the room turn toward her, then a small backing of laughter replaces the heavy. Kaz nods while smiling. He rubs the back of his neck and says, "Yes, but I'm not sure how I feel about my sister asking about him."

She's about to say something, a smile appearing and then disappearing just as quick and she hesitates as if she isn't sure she can joke with him. But a determination I've seen set in his eyes flashes in hers and she slips into a typical girl. "He's dreamy."

"He's married," Kaz counters.

She shrugs. "Still nice to look at."

"Let's make sure he never finds out you said that."

I tease, "Kaz has many admirers himself."

Katerina laughs but makes a sour face. "I can never see my baby brother as a what do you call them—heartbeat?"

I jump in again. "Heartthrob. And that he is indeed."

Kaz frowns. "Hey! I'm right here." He may be griping from the teasing but I can tell he enjoys the back and forth with his sister. It's apparent he missed the camaraderie that comes so naturally between siblings.

His mother smiles. "They always fought. It's good to hear it again." She hiccups a small sob, and I can see how much this has broken her. Losing her child. Losing her family.

Katerina pats her arm lovingly. "We went through a lot with *Otets*. His death and funeral seemed easy in comparison." She looks at Kaz. "I hope you understand why we stayed."

"I don't," Kaz replies, his pain finally cracking in his voice. "I've never understood why you would stay under those conditions."

His mother says, "We would have been penniless. We would have had to leave Russia. Where would we go?"

"Anywhere. We would have survived together." He stands and walks to the piano. Tapping one key twice, he looks back at them, and adds, "I've done well?"

I don't know why he's asking the question. It's obvious he's done well on his own. Maybe... my heart starts to ache for him. Maybe he still needs acceptance from them, reassurance for the little boy inside him that he has made them proud.

His mother stands and walks to him. Leaning against the other side, she says, "You've done well, my son. You were meant for greatness. It's who you are. You have a good life?"

"I've had a good life."

"I was living the fate life gave me. I was too old to survive without any comfort. Your sister..." She looks down, shame breaching her soft features. "I told her to stay. I promised to find her a good husband and that she'd live a good life." When she looks to her daughter, they both have tears in their eyes. "I should have sent her away. She should have gone with you. She's had a life, but not an easy one. With the Petrowski last name, there's always interest in our family. Katerina is single and beautiful. The media hounds her. They call her cold as ice. She's not. Her father..."

"I'm fine," Katerina demands, standing this time. "It doesn't matter what has happened. It's time we heal what we can." She walks to Kaz and cups his face. "You were right to leave. You got out. Look at you and the beautiful life you've created for yourself. I'm so proud of you, Kazimir."

Holding her upper arms, Kaz softens before us. "You have money, right?"

"We have more money than we can spend."

The insecurity in his voice is heartbreaking. "You're here for me?"

She nods. "We don't expect miracles. Healing takes time. But we don't want to live without you any longer. We had no idea where you were until we were contacted by the press. And then suddenly, there you were. Right there in plain sight. My brother, the amazing musician." She hugs him and when he embraces her, she says, "It's okay if you're not ready to be part of this family again, but please don't close the door."

His mother comes to them and wraps her arms wide around them. "This is what I've yearned for."

Healing does take time, and together, I think they'll be fine. Seeing them makes me miss my parents. I take my phone out and send them a text to come over.

The gate buzzer sounds again and Tommy says, "I'll handle it." He gets up and goes to the security camera and phone near the door. I hear him say, "Come on up."

Tommy joins Rochelle in the kitchen. They're talking in low voices and settle at the table. I turn my attention to Kaz and his family. His sister is looking me over. When she smiles, it's kind, so I return one.

Somewhere in the conversation, his sister and mother apologize. He doesn't need to hear the words, but I know he likes that they took responsibility. I like hearing them laugh and seeing the tears shed between them. Joy and love. No tension lives here.

Tommy goes to the door and when it's opened, we all turn toward the voice I know instantly. "I refuse to stay away any longer. She's my girl too."

Signaling toward us, Tommy rolls his eyes.

"I've missed you too," I say to Lane, walking around the couch to greet him properly with a big hug.

With his arms around me, Lane says, "Damn, he's so good-looking, but he makes me so mad."

"Why?" I ask, leaning back.

"He stole my friend."

I hug him again. "He didn't steal me. He's healed me. I'm right here, better than ever."

Lane smiles, flashing his pearly whites. "That's wonderful to hear because Calliope is driving me mad."

"Wait, what? We finished her project already."

"Nope. We're starting on her boudoir and let me tell you, the woman is divine. We've never decorated a playroom before."

Surprisingly, Kaz speaks up, "I've got a friend who would be happy to help her out."

Lane's eyebrows go up. "You do?"

"My best friend in the band."

I laugh. "Derrick?"

He smiles. "Yup. I think he just might be what that princess needs."

Katerina whacks him in the chest. "Forget about Hollywood princesses. You have a sister with a royal title who wants to meet your friends. Especially friends in the band."

I nudge his sister. "Trust me on this. Let Derrick go for the actress. They are complete opposites and perfect for each other."

Tommy comes back into the room. "Why can't I date a kinky actress?"

Rochelle pats his arm. "Because you have too much heart for

someone so shallow. Your girl is out there. Don't worry. You'll find her right when you need her most."

He huffs. "I'm getting a drink. Anyone else?"

In unison the whole room says, "Me," then erupts in laughter again.

Within the hour, my parents have joined the party. BBQ is delivered and the kitchen table is covered. Friends and family are spread around the living room, the kitchen, and outside. Everyone is eating and drinking, talking and laughing.

I like Kaz's sister. She's good people. A tad star struck by the mention of the band, but I've been there so I let her giggle and burst with excitement. It's not every day you find out that your brother is part of such an amazing band.

When I come inside the house from the backyard, Kaz is standing in the kitchen showing my mother how to make Pelmeni. My father is watching a game on the TV and I take the seat next to him at the bar. He smiles when he sees me. "He confessed."

"Yes, he did."

"I didn't protect you. I think... You know what? I didn't think. I would have never guessed that someone so well known would hurt my daughter. I'm sorry."

I lean my head on my dad's shoulder. "No one did. I didn't either. I'm here though and I want to focus on the good things in my life."

"I suspect this is your life now."

Sitting up, I watch Kaz. "He's the man my soul belongs with."

"Love is funny like that. We think we know better, but it has a plan of its own. You were in one place and he in another—worlds apart. Love changed everything, brought you to where you were meant to be, brought you together."

"You and mom weren't worlds apart and you're still happily married twenty-eight years later."

He chuckles as if remembering a secret that amuses him. "Her father said I was a rotten, no-good kid who wouldn't amount to anything."

My mouth drops open. "What? I've never heard this before."

"Yep. I was the man her mother warned her about."

"A bad boy? Mom fell for the bad boy?"

"She sure did." He winks.

I look over at my mom—my cute little homemaker mom—and suddenly I see her in a whole new light. My dad runs a successful business. They have a beautiful home in the suburbs where they raised me. I was never spoiled but I never went without. I always felt safe in their love growing up, so to say I'm shocked is an understatement. "So how do you feel about me being with a bad boy?"

Nodding his head toward the back of Kaz, he replies, "He's not as bad as his rock-star reputation would lead you to believe."

"So you approve?"

"He was there for you when you felt you had no one else you could turn to. He is helping you heal, not just your bruises, but also your heart. I see how you look at him, but I also see how he looks at you. Love. It's a funny thing."

Smiling just from looking at Kaz, my heart is filled with happiness. "It sure is."

EPILOGUE
KAZ

Three months later…

FUCKER.

Six months.

Mark Renner only got sentenced for six months in county jail and six in a treatment facility. No actual prison time. It was deemed an unsafe environment for him after taking his fame into consideration. He didn't take Lara's life into consideration. *Asshole.*

"Attempted" means he wanted her dead. The judge saw things differently. I assume he's a baseball fan. I suspect we'll see him with some primo box seats next season. Fucker.

Renner's just fucking lucky he didn't succeed.

So am I.

I look over at my sleeping beauty, not knowing where I'd be if she hadn't survived. She thinks I saved her, that I healed… that I'm healing her. She doesn't see the truth.

She saved *me*.

When I walked away from what everyone called a life of privilege, I knew where I was heading. Not physically but I knew I had to leave, that something better was calling me. I thought it was *The Resistance*.

I can't lie. It's a sweet gig, but finding your soul mate, even in the middle of chaos, is sweeter.

I'd sacrifice my soul for this woman. She knows she has me wrapped around her little finger, but I think I have her all wrapped up too, so all's fair.

Leaning over, I kiss her, and then slip out of bed. I leave the bedroom and walk down the hall. The house is finished. Lara decorated every last room. It's exactly her taste and it's perfect. She captured the two of us in the details. I see her pride when she looks around at what she's accomplished. She doesn't see my pride when I look at her.

When I reach the living room, I struggle to shake off the breaking news of her ex getting off so easy. She did though. She went straight to sleep and has slept soundly. She tells me I give her peace. Maybe I do. I hope I do.

I lift up the piano bench, grab the small box inside, then sit down. When I reach for my guitar in the corner, I stop and turn, deciding to play piano instead. I've been working on a song. It's lighter than I used to compose. I happily blame her for my changing mood. I take the box out and open it, then set it on top of the shiny black surface.

It only takes a few notes before she appears from the hall. Naked in the moonlight as it shines in her eyes. Hair hanging down, messy from sleep. A smile graces her face.

My gorgeous girl.

"C'mere," I say and pat the bench next to me.

She does. A moonbeam follows, as she comes toward me, a guardian angel to save my soul. "Can't sleep…" Her gaze falls on the ring. Her eyes flash to mine.

"What do you think about that?" I ask, trying to sound casual. My stomach is twisted in knots, waiting, hoping she loves it.

Swallowing hard enough for me to see her struggle, her eyes fill with tears. I always hate seeing her cry, but I'll take her happy tears any day. "It's beautiful."

I take the box in hand and get down on one knee, kneeling before her. With her delicate hand in mine, so small and soft against my large and calloused hand, I see our differences. Yet, we fit together so well, perfection found in the details of our past and present. "I want a future with you. I want late-night talks, early morning sex, a soft place to land in a hard world, a wife to come home to, and if we're fortunate enough, a family with you. Lara," I say, and then kiss her hand, "I love you, baby. So much. I want you in my life. I need you. Will you marry me?"

Nodding, she says, "Yes. Yes, I love you so much, Kaz."

Her arms come around me. I stand, lifting her into the air with me. Our lips come together and we kiss, our destinies sealed as one. I set her down on the top of the piano. Taking a blanket from the couch, I cover the flat surface. "I'm going to make love to you on this piano. I've dreamed about it since I walked into this house and saw you bent over it."

The tips of her nails drag lightly down the back of my neck. "I've dreamed about it too. So many times."

"Lie back."

When she does, I lift her legs by the ankles and rest her feet on the top. They part for me and I lean forward, running my hands up her stomach and over her breasts to her shoulders. Taking hold of her, I move down and kiss her pretty pussy, using my tongue to taste her inside and out. She squirms but I hold her in place.

It doesn't take long before she's calling my name on the peak of an orgasm. When she's wholly mine, limber under my touch, I angle her body toward the keys, then yank her closer. She slides easily across the slick surface while on the blanket.

Her pretty blues are trapped in desire. "I want you inside me."

Lifting her just enough to bring her down lower, the keys ring in retaliation as she lands softly down.

"Kaz?"

I place my forehead against hers and whisper, "Shhh." Maneuvering between her legs, I kiss along her temple down to her ear. "I love you. I love you." Her body clings to mine as her warmth takes me into its soft embrace.

Deeper.

Deeper.

Pressing deeper until we're connected in ways that feel too good to ever leave. Lara leans back, her head on the top of the piano. I grab her hips and thrust faster and harder. Our breaths combat the music we're making, fighting to be heard, to be felt, to be freed.

"Ty vladeyesh menya. Serdtse. Telo. Dusha."

This is freedom.

With her I can be who I am completely. She loves me as I love her —deeper than physical, stronger than emotional, longer than this life will allow.

"Tell me what that means," she says. Her eyes are closed, our bodies slick with sex and sweat.

I kiss her neck and drag myself out of my head. "You own me. Heart. Body. Soul."

A smile appears and I kiss the corner. She holds on to my shoulders and moves, fucking me. "I love that. Say it again."

"Ty vladeyesh menya. Serdtse. Telo. Dusha."

"God, that's so sexy, Kaz."

Moving faster, I warn her, "Hold on."

Her hands go to her side, the tips of her fingers on the keys. I lose myself in her love, her body, her scent, her moans, until I can't hold on any longer. Grabbing her hips, I fuck her until nails dig into my shoulders and her pussy tremors from another orgasm. I fuck her until I find my own release, blinded by the brightness of ecstasy.

With a chest full of heavy breaths, I exhale, and sit down on the bench. I bring her down with me holding her body across mine as we both try to catch our breath. Reaching forward, I tap a few of the ivories.

"Look at that. We made music together."

She giggles and it's the best sound in the world. Then she looks up at me with love in her eyes and says, "Play for me."

"Anytime." I reach my other arm around her and start playing the song I know so well as if I've known it my whole life, even though I wrote it for her recently.

Kissing my cheek, she says, "It's beautiful."

"Like you."

"I already said yes, charmer."

"Better get used to the compliments because you're gonna get a lot of them."

"I can get used to it." She wraps her arm around my neck while I continue play. "Kaz?"

"Hmm?"

"Do you think we got together because of what we went through? I kind of dragged you into my mess."

I stop playing and rest my hands on her lower back, holding her to me. Looking into her eyes, it's easy to see why I fell in love with her, but it was more than her beauty that drew her to me. I saw her soul that night—vulnerable and exposed. In her weakest moment she showed me her strength. She fought back. She survived. She came to me at her worst and gave me her best. "No. I think we came together because we connected on a level we knew was unique. But I think we'll stay together because of what we went through. We fought for this. We fought for love."

"Love is funny like that." She rests her head on my shoulder and I finish playing the song for her.

I've not felt this content, this peaceful, this happy in years. The notes flow from fingers to keys with ease. Having Lara here has made all the difference. She's helped ease the transition with my family as we try to fit the pieces of our puzzle back together. I was never responsible for their choices, but I feel better from this outcome. Having them back has meant more to me than I expected. Lara even helped them find a house in Beverly Hills. Temporary, but it's nice to have them here. Maybe one day, they'll leave Russia and stay. I think they like being out of the public's eye here and by how much my mother has doted on me, I think they like having me around.

I finally introduced Katerina to Johnny. Shaking my head at the memory, I have to realize she's not just my sister, but a woman now.

Derrick asked me about her the other day... I breathe out. That fucker is not going anywhere near my sister.

When I play the last note, I wrap my arms around her and hold her. Lara whispers, "I have a surprise for you in the grotto. A little housewarming gift now that it's decorated."

Getting up, we walk into the bathroom and clean up. After slipping on some boxer briefs, we hold hands and go outside. "You didn't have to do anything. It's your home too."

"I wanted to."

When we reach the grotto, I see a box and peek over at her confused. "Why is it out here?"

"Just open the box," she replies slyly.

I lift the lid and there inside is the best gift I've ever received... next to her, of course. "You bought me a smoking jacket?"

She shrugs. "Figured you can't have a grotto unless the image is complete. A young Hugh Hefner in the making."

Chuckling, I remark, "I'm thinking I'm not going to get away with his lifestyle."

"You get the jacket and the grotto. That's the most similar to Hugh I want for you."

I take her by the waist and pull her to me. "I don't need anything or anyone else. You're all I need, baby." I plant a firm one on her lips until she's weak in the knees. When she holds on to me, I know I've done a good job of kiss-vincing her.

Twenty minutes later, I'm lying next to her under a sky full of stars. I turn in the lounge chair just to admire her. I can't believe she's my girl. She's more stunning than the stars could ever be. "Thank you for saying yes."

She touches the lapel of the jacket. "Thank you for asking," she says, amusement in her eyes and playing out in her smile. "You know people will say it's too soon."

"I don't care what people say."

Her body stretches next to mine and she moves against me. "I don't care either. We've lived a lifetime in a few months, more life than most live in years. I was so lost until I found you."

"I was found until I thought I lost you. I knew then and there that I would do whatever it took to give you the life you deserve."

Cuddling with my girl, I say, "How about we take the next sixty years easy?"

"Make it seventy and you've got yourself a deal."

I kiss her nose. "How about I give you life?"

"Plus eternity and you've got yourself a deal."

"Done. Now let's fuck on it."

Giggling, she says, "I love you, Kaz."

"I love you, Lara."

The End

THE REBELLION

I got over Jaymes Grenier no problem. I never think about that little bow at the top of her pink lips, or the way her green eyes admired mine. Nope, I barely recall the way she fit so perfectly in my arms when I held her at night. The sweet way she would whisper she loved me has long faded from memory.

These are the lies I regularly tell myself in hopes of believing them one day. Yeah, I was told I'd get over my first love.

I didn't.

Derrick Masters marked me the moment we met back in ninth grade. He called me over--all bravado and bad boy mystery wrapped in a James Dean-esque package. Dark hair, blue eyes and a rebel without a cause charisma. He was everything I was warned about, but I couldn't resist. I was his from that moment on.

His career took off almost as soon as he did. I knew it would. I just thought I would be by his side as his partner in crime, best friend, and forever.

These days, I don't have the luxury of letting my head live in the lure of La La Land. His dreams may have come true, but mine were extinguished. It's not just about me anymore, but something bigger, better than we were ever meant to be.

When Derrick's dreams come crashing back into my reality, I start to wonder if this is our second chance at a fairy tale ending or another heartbreak in the making?

PROLOGUE

Climbing in the back of the SUV with the rest of the band, I slam the door shut behind me. "Go."

The vehicle makes it around the corner before the fans even realize we left through a different exit. Somewhere along this tour, we've developed a drive-away habit with Johnny in the third row, Kaz and Dex in the middle, I'm in the first row, and Tommy is upfront with the driver. The best thing about this arrangement is that I can spread out and lie down, which is exactly what I do. Scrubbing my hands over my face, I close my eyes and remember when this used to be fun.

Running from rabid fans builds an ego fast. But after two years of sneaking away through back exits, finding groupies in hotel bathrooms, and getting mail with locks of hair and proclamations of eternal devotion, the illusion I once lived in has been destroyed. *All hail the life of a rock star.* My rose-colored glasses have been traded for scratched designer shades that shield me from the normalcies of everyday life. The lap of luxury has replaced simple pleasures. The lifestyle of the rich and famous is *and was* intoxicating for a while. Now I just wish I could walk down the street without being harassed for an autograph or a picture.

The ride from the arena to the hotel doesn't take long, but the adrenaline from the concert is draining, leaving me lifeless on this seat, and a little annoyed. "Did you see that couple in the front row?"

Johnny asks, "What couple?"

"The one face-fucking the entire fucking concert."

He laughs. Once. "What about them?"

"They should be coming for the music."

Kaz says, "They were."

"If they were, they should be listening to it."

Now Dex is laughing. "What the fuck's gotten into you, Derrick? What do you care if some couple is getting off to our music?"

I sound like a lunatic, and a prude at that. Why do I care? They paid their thousands for those seats. If they want to strip naked and fuck for real it shouldn't bother me. But it does and I don't know why.

Maybe it's because I haven't kissed a woman like that in a long fucking time. Not a real kiss—one with more meaning behind it than getting laid for the night. The last time I kissed someone like that . . . I stop myself from going there because every time I do, it's a downward spiral from there. But when I think of a kiss, she's the only woman who comes to mind, the only woman that when our lips embraced, a part of our souls were exchanged.

Did she keep all the pieces I'm missing? The holes I'm still searching to fill that she left behind?

The door slides open and I sit up to get out. The guys pile out behind me and we go in the back entrance to the private elevators. One helluva good-looking brunette catches my eye while the guys brush by quietly. It's always quiet after a show. We're exhausted and tired of being "on" for everyone.

She hands me a card key and her business card, and says, "We've upgraded you to one of our suites. I'd be happy to give you a private tour, Mr. Masters."

Tempting. *So damn tempting.* I could fuck all night, but it's not going to change the fact that my head's already fucked up over a girl I can't seem to stop thinking about lately. There's no reason for me to give her a second thought. She *should* be nothing but a ghost from my past—part of a past I left behind.

I just wish I hadn't left her behind with it. I slip my shades back on as flashes from the lobby start going off in the distance. "Thank you for the upgrade. I'll take a rain check on the tour."

"My pleasure, and my number's on the card if you need anything at all."

Funny how life works.

The one thing I need is the only thing I can't have. *The only person I can't have.*

"Get the fuck in here." My shirt is grabbed and I'm yanked into the elevator by Dex.

The brass doors close behind me and I stand there facing the band, this band of dreamers who live their dream every day. "I should have taken her up on the tour."

Kaz leans against the corner. "I'm surprised you didn't."

Music is piped in and it takes a second, but we all hear it. With our heads tilted toward the speaker, one of our most popular songs has been turned into classical elevator music. Johnny shakes his head. "Fuck me." Turning his attention down, he starts texting.

Dex is drumming his fingers beside him on the railing. "Now I feel fucking old."

Kaz is laughing and hits me in the chest. "Can't blame us. It's classic Resistance. A song put out before our time."

Tommy asks, "Anyone up for drinks later?"

Everyone ignores him. Kicking my shoe, he says, "Derrick?"

"Going out? Nah."

"Staying in?" Tommy asks in disbelief.

"Yeah."

"Don't leave me going solo. What's gotten into you, Moody?"

"We've played six cities in six days," I complain, catching a glimpse of myself in the metal doors. I look exhausted, my dark hair a mess and my eyes bloodshot. "I need sleep."

"You're twenty-three. These are the best years of your life. Don't waste them sleeping. Right, Johnny?"

Johnny's phone rings, and a wide smile cuts across his world-famous face. The elevator doors open just as he says, "Hey baby," and walks off.

Dex and I follow suit and get off. Holding my key in the air, I wave to Tommy and Kaz who remain on the elevator. "It's good to be me," I tease.

Kaz flips me off and Tommy is cut off by the doors closing, "Fucke—"

Dex walks past me and says, "At twenty-three, I would have taken the tour."

"Maybe I still will."

I slip my key card into the door and enter the suite. My luggage is in the middle of the living room. A bottle of Jack Daniels and a fruit tray are on the table by the window. I toss the business and key cards down next to the bottle and open it. I don't bother with the glasses or the fruit tray. I drink straight from the bottle, stand at the window, and stare at the neon lights of the street below. The room is too quiet, the lingering buzz from performing live still rings in my ears. Another sold out show for The Resistance is behind us and I'm left with the silence of a hotel room. Sometimes I love it, when I'm at home, but the road gets lonely. I pick up the phone and call downstairs. When the pretty brunette answers, I say, "About that tour ..."

1

DERRICK MASTERS

Sitting up in bed, I watch the back of her bent forward while she clasps the straps of her heels around her ankles. She looks back, and says, "If you need any—"

"Yeah, I'll call you."

A sleek smile slides into place and suddenly I don't feel like my "tour" was a one-time thing for her. She stands and straightens her skirt. "You've got my number."

I reach for the card on the nightstand, and hold it up. "I do. Thanks for—"

"My pleasure."

I'm relieved she cut me off. This is the awkward part I dislike the most. Thanking her for sex would up the weirdness factor. She grabs her hotel manager's jacket and slips it on over her shirt. One last wave, and she says, "It was great meeting you."

"Yeah, you too."

When she disappears, I take her business card in hand again and read out loudly, "Brenda." The door to the suite shuts and I hear the distinct sound of the lock clicking into place.

Another city, another—*meaningless*—distraction. Physically I'm sated, but now what? I pick up my phone and text Tommy Rhodes, the band's manager and my wingman since Kaz abandoned his post: *When do we leave?*

A return text comes fast: *One hour.*

I text again: *Where are we going?*

Tommy: *Nashville.*

Me: *Where are we now?*

Tommy: *Miami.*

Nashville. Miami. East Coast. We're a damn long way from home in LA. It shouldn't bother me. It's not like I've got anything or anyone back home waiting.

I slide my sunglasses over my eyes and lie back down. I'm a rock star, damn it. This is probably why I used to do drugs in the first place. I could leave my own mind for a while and live in the euphoria of fame. But being in the band means being clean. Sure, they don't give a shit about marijuana or booze, but with the history of the band, anything harder breaks my contract. That contract is all I ever fucking dreamed about so I'm not going to screw it up for a temporary high. Anyway, I may not have anyone back home that gives a shit about me, but on the road I can have a Brenda in every city.

Life can be pretty damn sweet if I look at the bright side.

The only problem with my bright side these days is that my head is overrun with memories of a girl I left with a broken heart and out of tune guitar. I meant to fix that before I left—the guitar. There was no fixing the heart unless I stayed, and I couldn't. Good reasons at the time, but hell if I can remember what they are now.

I TOSS my carry-on in the seat next to me and open the shade. Sunny Miami. I'm leaving before I even had time to experience the city. Other than the arena we played last night, I didn't see anything beyond the inside of the hotel and an SUV. Releasing a hard breath, I slam the shade back down and close my eyes.

"Rough night?"

I don't have to open my eyes to recognize the voice—Kaz. My best friend, my former roommate, and the bassist for The Resistance aka the best band in the world, moved on. I know I'm lucky. I was chosen from guitarists vying for this spot from around the world to join this band, along with Kaz. It was a quick and easy fix to a spot they had open. At the time, it was a two-for-one kind of deal.

It took the man behind the brand, Johnny Outlaw—lead singer, former rock star bad boy, and the face of the band—two minutes to decide. As a guitarist himself, he knew what he was looking for. We continued to play through three more songs for the other surviving band member, Dex Caggiano—drummer extraordinaire—to decide. He said he actually didn't need to hear more, but liked watching us sweat our hearts out through every chord we played. It was an asshole move. So basically he's my idol now.

The trial period ended a long time ago and we've been officially part of the band for years now. Our dreams came true. Dreams and goals, bucket lists and accomplishments, but once those goals are reached, *what then?*

Before I can say anything to Kaz, Johnny sits across from me and buckles in. Fuck. This can only mean one of two things—I fucked up something in the show last night or he's firing me. The dude never sits by me. He actually sleeps in the bedroom of the private plane most flights. Or is stuck in interviews and doing PR shit. Having him sitting across from me right now is worrisome to say the least. He's not talking at me. He's talking to me. I like this shift in our relationship, this new dynamic.

He stares at me until I remove my sunglasses, then he says, "We all burn out at some point or another. Some take longer to get there. Some sooner. It's how you handle it that determines your future. How do you plan to handle it?"

Sitting back, my leg begins to bounce and I scoff defensively. "I'm not burned out."

"Bullshit."

"There's nothing to handle. I'm happy as a clam."

His jaw tics. That usually only happens when he's pissed, but his eyes don't show any anger. Blowing out a deep breath, he looks out the window as the plane starts down the tarmac. He says, "Mine was Germany."

"Your what?"

"My bottom." When he turns back to me he says, "The fallout from partying, drugs, booze, women, the whole fucking cliché was a year earlier. Sure, I still did a lot of shit after, but no more hard drugs. As for the women, it was entertaining for a while, but there was no substance. No one I wanted to call the next day or even get their number. Some of the time . . . a lot of the time I didn't even bother with their names."

Brenda comes to mind. I caught that one as she was walking out the door this morning.

"Look," he says, leaning forward and resting his elbows on his knees. "It happens to all of us. Not many relate, or ever will understand this life on the road, the demands of being in a band that's as successful as The Resistance. But we do. All five of us do. Tommy's given up his life to put us first without the fame or notoriety we have. The rest of us, we're doing the best we can in an extraordinary situation. But I'm telling you. I see the signs. I see it destroying you. Slowly. Meticulously, almost to where you don't notice you're not you anymore." We haven't reached altitude yet, but Johnny stands. "It's great to be a rock star, but not at the expense of having a life. Two tours in two years wears on you. When we get back to LA, find a life again, Derrick. It's the only way you'll survive when you're on the road." I watch as he walks down the aisle to the bedroom and disappears inside. *What the hell?*

As soon as the door shuts, Kaz pops into the chair Johnny vacated. "Shit, man. What'd he say?"

Find a life.

Get a life.

Live my life.

"Find myself again."

"I didn't know you were lost."

"Neither did I. Until now."

WE LAND a few hours later to fans screaming behind the metal fence at the private airport. I wave while coming down the stairs and then slide into the first SUV. Dex slides in after me and shuts the door. Tommy, Kaz, and Johnny take up the next black SUV parked beside the plane.

My head pivots in Dex's direction. "What up?"

He nods while staring at his phone, reading something on the screen.

I look out the window next to me already forgetting which city we're in.

"I'm not going to lecture you," he starts. "I leave that to Tommy and Johnny. This band is their baby, hence why we're still hitting the road so hard with each new album."

I'm actually surprised he's talking to me about this. Dex is reserved. Most would say he's not, but over time I've learned he rarely instigates trouble despite his bad reputation. He's more of a reactionary man. "It's fine." I'm not sure what to say. "It's smart to support the record."

"I heard what Outlaw said on the plane. He's right. We see the signs."

"What are they?"

"You're fucking up, not on stage. You're incredible on stage. But you don't have anything keeping you grounded."

"I'm not gonna float away."

"We've had that happen. I fucking did it. You know my story. I think you're a lot like me, Derrick."

"And this is a bad thing?"

"Nah." He chuckles humorlessly. "I just liked to party. There's nothing wrong with that, but the thrill is fading for you. After the show tonight we're home for a few weeks. Take it off. *Really off*, like out of the limelight, and regroup if you can. Well, don't take off from the band sessions, but the other stuff. Hang out with your friends, get laid by a girl you want to have breakfast with, and get some fucking sun. You're pale as a ghost these days."

If only I could have breakfast with the only girl that I'd want to. "What are you gonna do when you get back?"

"See my woman, play with the family. Just live a real life." He drops his head back on the seat and closes his eyes. "I've been given a damn good life, but it comes with sacrifices. That I'm here today, has been no easy feat, and I bow down at the feet of those who got me here. That's who I'll be spending time with. The people who make it possible for me to do this. The people who are there for me when I fall, which as you know, I still do. But these days, I don't fall as far."

"Am I in that bad of shape that everyone is concerned?" I chuckle.

"No." He looks at me. "Just that, I know sometimes it feels like you and Kaz versus me and Johnny. It's not." He holds his hand out to me. "Johnny once told me that being bandmates makes us brothers. I'm always here for you, brother."

We do our handshake that the band adopted soon after we joined. There's comfort in knowing what I'm feeling is normal . . . as normal as a rock star can be. A new perspective is loaded, the trigger cocked, and hits me right on target.

Another day. Another hotel. Another back entrance. We're shuffled through quickly and into our rooms before the fans realize where we're staying. Or so I thought. Five stories below, "Johnny" is chanted, the hum of fans outside penetrating not just the walls, but my head. I peek out the window before swallowing ibuprofen and lying down. Six hours before sound check. Time to settle my mind and try to get some sleep.

2

DERRICK

I'm woken up by Tom Petty singing about his girl. It's been my ringtone for years and never gets old. 'Cuz Tom Petty rocks.

Grabbing my phone, I answer, "Yeah?"

"Hi, dear, it' s Mom."

"Hi, Mom." My voice is gruff and I rub my eyes before checking the time.

"You're sleeping?"

"Yeah, I'm tired. We have a show tonight, so I want to rest while I can."

"I'm sorry. Do you want to call me back?"

I push the button on the remote and the curtains begin to open, letting the setting sun in. "No, I need to get up. How are you?"

"I'm good. It's been a little chaotic today. I finally had someone come fix the cracked window in the kitchen. They had to replace it in the end."

"That's good. It will keep your electric bill down. Did you have them send me the bill?"

"No, son. I took care of it. You do too much as it is."

"I want to and I can afford it. You did more than you should have when I was younger. I've got money now, Mom, let me repay you."

I hear the sigh. The one that reveals the battle between not wanting to accept money from her son and that strong independent woman who raised me when she had nothing but love to give. Even though she worked three jobs, she made sure there was dinner on the table every night. She only missed one of my soccer games because her boss refused her the time off. She had another parent record the entire game and watched it that night with me, cheering like it was live. We lost, even though I scored twice. She treated me to ice cream and a consoling hug while praising what a great job I did. She is literally the best woman I know.

Bringing me back to the present conversation, my mom says, "Having a kid isn't a debt owed to me. I chose to have you because I wanted you. I love you, but keep your money this time."

"I love you."

"I love you too, Derrick. You don't sound good. Talk to me."

"I'm just tired." I scrub my free hand over my face.

"Where are you?"

I know. This time I know. "Nashville. I'm sorry I need to cut this short, Mom, but I need to hop in the shower. Everything else good?"

"Yes. Great. Will you come over for dinner when you get back?"

"Of course. We come home tomorrow, I think. How's the day after that?"

"Perfect. Have fun."

It cracks me up that she said the same thing to me when I was eight years old and going outside to play, when I was sixteen and hanging out with the guys, and now as a twenty-three-year-old who performs in front of twenty thousand people. I hope she never stops. I kind of like that I'm her baby boy.

Fuck. What is going on with me? Baby boy?

I need to pull it together.

"I will. See you Thursday."

"Bye, son."

I hang up and toss the phone on the bed, lying prone a few minutes before I finally drag my lazy ass into the bathroom and shower the tiredness away.

If only showering was a cure that would last.

SITTING on the couch in Kaz's room, I scarf the last of the pizza, and finish a can of energy drink that tastes awful, but it's necessary.

Kaz leans back, rubbing his stomach. "I'm stuffed. The rest is yours."

"I'm good." I sit back and kick my feet up. "Remember eating pizza at three a.m. and passing out on the floor?"

"That sucked so hard, but five years ago isn't as long ago as it feels."

"We did what we had to, to survive. If that meant eating pizza about to be thrown out and sleeping on the floor until we got mattresses, we did it."

He's quiet, so I go quiet too. Looking around the suite, he comes back around and I know what he's thinking.

Keeping my voice low, I say, "I think about it all the time."

"We're damn lucky."

"Nah, we made our luck. We wouldn't be here if we hadn't played clubs every night and restaurants during happy hour. We gave up our lives in pursuit of our dreams."

"And it paid off. Are you happy?"

I shake my head and sigh. "Not you, too." I stand up, ready to grab my stuff and go.

"I wasn't talking about you."

Stopping in front of the door, I turn back. "Are *you* happy?"

"I'm happy we're going home in the morning. Playing the shows are great, but I might be ready to have *more*."

"Luxuries a few years ago wouldn't have afforded us. Well, maybe you, Prince Kaz."

He laughs, but it fades and he eyes me. "I worry about you."

"Don't. We're not chicks."

"As your bandmate, I can say that. As your best friend, I can admit that the guys are right. You look like shit."

What the hell? I open the door. "I'm going to sleep for a week when we get back, let my liver dry out, and do nothing."

"Sounds like a good plan." Grabbing his phone, he gets up and follows me out.

"What about you?"

"I think I'll move up the wedding and start working on that *more* I mentioned."

The old me would have ragged on him so bad for even mentioning a future with a wife and kids, teasing him relentlessly for giving up his manhood.

The *new* me, if he actually exists? Having watched Outlaw and Kaz lately, how they have a stillness about them that's linked to the women at their sides, I am starting to want the same thing. The *same* thing I'd been so set against in my youth. What's more confusing is that it seems to have happened overnight. And having just spoken to my mom, who I love more than life itself, I'm reminded of the girl I let go. The one who has owned my heart for years, but until recently had been pushed to the periphery of my brain. Why can't I stop thinking about her now though? Why does she own so many of my thoughts lately? *It's torture if I'm honest.*

Walking into the bright lights of the parking garage a few minutes later, I realize I miss the sun, and fresh air. I miss my freedom. I climb to the back of the SUV and kick my legs up on the seat. It's too small to stretch out, but it's good to have the space. Now I see why Johnny likes sitting back here. It's less crowded. More room to think.

The guys pile into the van. Johnny stops when he sees me, but then gives me a nod and an understanding grin before he takes the seat closest to the door.

I should have known better. Living in my head for twenty minutes isn't really an option before a concert. Pre-gaming for a show is much louder than after. We're pumped, keeping the energy high. By the time we reach Vanderbilt Stadium, we're wired. We tour the stage for sound check and I pluck a few chords, tighten some strings, and test them again. I'm not feeling it. Last minute, I decide to change out guitars altogether. "Tommy, get me Jaymes."

He returns with my most treasured guitar. I usually don't bring her on the road with me, but I found myself carrying her on to the plane when we left LA. Maybe that's why the woman behind the guitar has been monopolizing my thoughts. I strum and tune and then sit on the edge at the front of the stage and let my fingers play the song they can play in their sleep. *She* used to say I did.

Our song, the one we wrote together sitting by a fire pit made from old bricks we stole from a construction site, runs through my fingers onto the guitar. The nights were chilly, but that fire felt just right. Just like the girl. She would play along with me and sing like a little songbird, hitting all the right notes, hitting me in the heart. I remember the night I gave Jaymes her first guitar ...

"Two hundred. I can't take a dollar less."

"I've got one seventy-six. C'mon, Tank, cut me the deal. It's Jaymes's birthday present."

Tank doesn't usually negotiate. Given his size, there was no need to explain his name, but under the wall of muscle and bad attitude, he is a softie at heart. He sold my mom my first guitar five years earlier. He claims he got the full hundred out of her. She once told me she paid fifty. I don't blow his cover. I think he just wants to help us local kids find something better to do with our time than sell drugs or pretend to be badasses with real guns.

"I'll do the deal for Jamie, but on one condition."

"Name it," I reply with a wide, winner's grin.

"You both play my grandmother's ninetieth next weekend."

"What?" I'm offended to even be offered the gig, much less be told I'm playing at a grandmother's birthday party. "Fuck, man, really?" He grabs the neck of the guitar roughly and lifts it from the pawnshop counter. "No. No, that's cool. We'll be there. Just tell me the time and place."

The guitar is set back down and his open palm waits as I slap every dollar I have left after buying groceries, paying some bills, and passing some cash to my mom. Six months of savings and my goal of saving to fix up the truck went out the window. My girl is worth it. Every penny. Every minute of hard labor on that construction site. All worth it. If I can't follow my dream, I'll sure as hell do everything to help her achieve hers.

Three hours later, I've picked Jaymes up from her job at the sandwich shop. Our dinner wrapped neatly in the wax paper between us. Two Cokes in the cup holders clipped to the window sill. Tom Petty playing on the CD player. A sky full of stars and a truck cab full of dreams. We make our way to what feels like another land, a land where wishes come true. Through the Los Feliz neighborhood, we drive to Griffith Park, and closer to the Observatory.

Parking off by a trail entrance, we hop out. I don't have much time. She'll spot her present when we climb in the back. So I say, "Close your eyes."

On the other side of the truck, she smiles, knowing she can trust me. Always trust me. Her hair is the color of night. Her eyes sparkle under the moonlight—looking more gray than green in the dark. "What are you up to, Derrick?"

"No good. Just the way you like me."

"I like you good. You're good through and through, Masters, and you're so good to me."

Leaning on the opposite side of the truck from her, I reach out until she follows my lead and reaches for me. The tips of our fingers touch and I say, "I'm good because of you."

She's emotional, always wearing her heart on her sleeve for the whole world to see. I tell her people will notice and take advantage of her kind heart if she's not careful. Deep down, it's one of the things that drew me to her. She's soft when the world we live in is hard. She loves openly and had somehow reached in even though I had closed myself off. My songbird sings of hope and impossible things when the rest of us struggle to keep faith. "Close your eyes," I whisper again.

This time she does, our hands falling away. I remove the blanket and pick up the guitar with the deep pink bow. Her favorite color. Coming around the back of the truck, I hold the guitar and say, "Happy birthday, baby."

Her mouth falls open, but her hand is quick to cover it as her eyes go wide. "You did not."

"I did." I move closer. "Do you like it?"

"*Derrick.*" *She says my name like it's a warning, which makes me laugh.*

"*Don't worry about the money.*"

"*How can I not worry about the money?*"

I move until she has the guitar in hand and I have mine wrapped around the back of her as she strums. "*Just promise me you'll always sing.*"

"*I do.*" *Her vow echoes through my soul and I hold her closer.* "*Thank you. It's the most beautiful gift I've ever been given.*"

"*I feel the same about you.*"

. . . Damn, I loved her.

Last I heard, she had shacked up with my *ex*-friend. I moved my mom out of that dump of an area and told her to never speak of her again. Curiosity is starting to get the best of me.

What does she look like now?

How has time changed her? Age? Life?

Me leaving?

Does she still hate me or can she forgive me?

Does she still like The Resistance, still listen to the songs, listen to me playing them?

They used to be her favorite band.

What does she think of me being a part of the band? Is she happy for me? Or does she hate that I got out and she didn't?

Maybe I should look her up when I get back home? Or maybe it was good I left. Maybe we were never meant to be. Or maybe—Nah, no use dragging old feelings into my current life. If there's one thing I've learned, it's that leaving that life behind is the only reason I have the life I lead now. It may be lonely, but I don't wake up ready to hit the floor and hide from cops. I don't worry about being pulled over and the police finding a gun under the seat or drugs in the trunk. I don't go to bed thanking God for letting me survive another day, but maybe I should.

I push up off the stage and walk to Tommy. Handing him the guitar, I say, "Save her for another day. I'll use the Stratocaster."

"You got it."

He hands it off to a roadie, and I add, "Careful."

Another roadie runs on stage with Old Faithful. I stroke the sleek design when I take it in hand, plug in the cord, and tap my effects pedal when Kaz and Johnny walk on stage with their guitars. We work as a well-oiled machine, so sound check never takes long. Two songs for the crew to work out the kinks and we're done.

Backstage I spy some hotties lingering around near the exit doors. I smile. They wave. I wink. They giggle. I head their way. They stand straighter, their lips are licked, and whispers exchanged between them.

"Hey."

Tommy's hand anchors my shoulder. "Hello, ladies."

"Hi," they reply in unison with an expression that is more than a little friendly. The redhead holds her hand out. "I'm Cherry."

"Did you know my favorite pie is cherry?" I take her hand and kiss it.

"I'm glad to hear you like pie."

The euphemism isn't lost.

Tommy's already scoring a phone number when I hear Dex down by the dressing room yell, "Get down here, fuckers."

The girls look anxious, their opportunity slipping away. I take a step back. Cherry steps forward. "Let's hook up after the show."

Her phone is out and I glance down to it, then back up to her. "I'll find you."

As I'm heading to the dressing room, she says, "Promise?"

I look back, give her my best *sure, sweetheart* smile, but keep going. How is it that girls willingly beg a stranger for a random hookup? To promise they'll bang them later. *I hate that I've never been good at keeping promises.* I sure as fuck ain't keeping one to a stranger looking to score with any celeb that glances her way.

The door to the dressing room closes behind Tommy and I head for the couch next to Kaz who's fixing a broken guitar string. I grab the yo-yo from the table on the way and sit down. The toy is spinning down and back up before my ass hits the vinyl. It's a substitute, a distraction from a craving that hits me every now and again. It's not the drugs I want. I was in deep, but got out before I went deeper, before they controlled me. It's the habit. The smoking. Jaymes. The nerves I try to suppress. The habit of having something in my hand to occupy it when I'm not playing my guitar. In my old life, I'd raise hell to burn off this restlessness. In my new life, I do tricks with a yo-yo while hanging out with my best friend. My how times change.

When Dex, Johnny, and Tommy leave to eat dinner, Kaz and I hang back, still full from the pizza we ate before leaving the hotel. I work on a new song, fleshing out the second stanza while he plays Word Wobble on his phone. He gruffs out loud, "Damn it."

I look over.

"Ignore me."

"It's hard to ignore you when you're shouting about a word puzzle game on your damn phone."

"I missed an easy one."

Trying to block him out, I strum the next chord, but he pipes in again, "How's your mom? My mom wanted to invite her over soon."

Not able to concentrate, I toss the pencil down and lean back with my guitar over my lap. Strumming softly, I reply, "She's good. Hey, I've been meaning to ask you about Lara and if maybe she'd consider helping my mom finish decorating her place."

Kaz smiles, that goofy grin he sports anytime his fiancée's name is mentioned. "I'm sure she wouldn't mind."

"I'll pay her. I don't want my mom spending a dime."

"I'll make sure she charges you double," he replies, going back to his game.

That sixth sense kicks in and a text comes through from my mom as if she knows we're talking about her. I tap the screen and read: *Having lunch on Thursday with Nita. She's picking me up since my car is going into the shop. Can you pick me up from her house?*

What? Nita?

I reply: *Nita Grenier? Jaymes's mom?*

The dots are flashing and I'm losing patience, along with my shit. Finally her text arrives: *Yes.*

Damn. Coincidence or irony?

She hasn't seen Nita Grenier in years. Fuck, it's been, what, three years? Nita had once been someone special to me, someone, who like my mom, had wanted more for me. *More for us.* Why is Mom going to have lunch with her now? They went through a lot together, as did most moms of that neighborhood. But few emerged from its smothering darkness. My mom being one of the few. Not everyone was so lucky. Some of her friends lost kids to gunfire. Some to drugs. A few escaped. Mom and I are the lucky ones.

I was given a second chance, a new beginning, but not everyone was that lucky. *Jaymes.* Whether she chose to stay for her mother, or chose to let me leave alone, she remained behind. From the rumors I heard before I forbid her name mentioned, she has paid the price.

I type: *No problem. Why is your car going into the shop?*

Mom: *It has a recall and now they need it in to fix it.*

Oh. Me: *Let me know what they say.*

Mom: *Okay, dear. Love you.*

Me: *Love you.*

A lump forms in my throat. Jaymes doesn't live with her mother, Nita, like she once did, but if I happen to run into her while picking Mom up, do I really want to take that risk of seeing her again? *Stupid question, Masters.* You know you *need* to see her again. To somehow put all these memories to bed once and for all.

Or reopen old wounds.

Hell, they've already reopened.

Maybe this time they'll heal.

3

———————

JAYMES GRENIER

I DON'T THINK I've ever bolted from bed so fast. That's what bad memories do to you. All it takes is one riff from "Here Comes My Girl" by Tom Petty to send me flying toward my alarm. Everything about that song reminds me of one person, and *that* person is the last one I intend to ever give any of my time to again. He just stole my usual five-minute bonus snooze.

Damn him.

The alarm clock is whacked and the song that reminds me of a life I let go of years ago is silenced. *Tried* to let go of . . .

Sometimes thoughts of that life still linger along with my girlhood dreams of marrying someone who loves me unconditionally, reminding me of what has become a fantasy. Disappointment sets in for like the billionth time. I know with all my heart that I'd never trade Ace for fulfilled dreams. Often I just wish fulfilled dreams *and* Ace could have gone together.

I flick my bedroom light as I walk into the hall and pad quietly past his room. Sneaking into the bathroom, I turn the light on and squint as I work my way to the shower and start the water. Stripping my pajamas off, I step in before the water heats up. The reality is it's never going to get hot enough to make that much of a difference. I'm just hoping for lukewarm this morning. I tilt my head under the spray, keeping my body angled away. I'd rather deal with cold air than ice-cold water.

Five minutes later I'm out and drying off. Cold showers have taught me to be quick. It's funny what we get used to when we're out of options. While scrubbing the towel over my head I realize this applies to more than cold showers. I don't dwell. It's a trait I embraced wholeheartedly when I decided I would—*and could*—face whatever life threw my way. I'm not making lemonade out of my lemons quite yet, but I strive for it every day. For Ace. *He* deserves better than this life has given us.

A soft knock pushes the door open. As a single mom, I never use locks inside the house, but the bathroom one is broken anyway, so any pressure opens the door. I pull it open the rest of the way and smile when I see my sleepy little baby. "Good morning," I say, leaning down and kissing the top of his head.

My sweet five-year-old rubs his eyes, the light from the bathroom blinding compared to the dark room he came from—*from the darkness he came from.* He's good. So good. My light. My purpose. I would trade my dreams any day for him. No matter the circumstances, I've been blessed to be given this purpose, blessed to be his mom.

"Good morning, Mommy."

The best name I've ever been called. "Good morning, buddy. You hungry?"

"Yes. Pancakes?" He looks up with all the hope I used to have. It's contagious. Big brown eyes that don't match mine, but I can't help loving. Bright. Happy. I put that there. I'd give him everything if I could.

"I think we have just enough mix to make some."

He jumps up with excitement. "Yay!"

"Go get dressed and I'll start making breakfast."

He runs off just as I bring our small apartment to life, switching lights on as I make my way to the kitchen. With a towel wrapped around my body, I start making the pancakes. I see the TV flick on a few minutes later and Ace sitting on the loveseat with the remote in his hand. The news is on, and he looks frustrated the way he's handling the remote. The pancakes aren't bubbling yet, so I take a piece of tape from the drawer and go to sit down next to him. Taking the remote, I flip it over and tape down the battery door. When it's loose, it won't work. I hand it back and he smiles when it works as if I just performed a magic trick.

Running back into the kitchen, I flip the pancakes and a few minutes later, I mentally add syrup to the shopping list in my head while serving the pancakes and the last of the syrup. It's the simple things kids love and appreciate. I've become the hero of my son's world just for making pancakes. Like being his mother, pancake hero is another title I adore. I relish. It's good to feel loved without conditions, loved for just *being*. I treat him the same. This world will do its job and cause enough damage, so I'll work hard to do mine and try to protect him from it.

With my hair dried and my skirt on, but unzipped, I pull my blouse on and give the warning, "Five minutes, buddy. Brush your teeth and hair and get your shoes on."

"'K, Mommy."

Ten minutes later, we're heading out the door. I've learned to build in extra time. With a kid, it's inevitable we're going to be late. I don't have that luxury though. I can't be late to work or I'll be fired.

The car starts with a gruff and a puff of black smoke kicked out the back, but it starts and that feels like a victory in and of itself. After dropping Ace off at kindergarten with a kiss and a lunchbox, I drive the twenty minutes to work. My backpack is slung over my shoulder and I head inside.

Leah, the office manager and one of my closest friends, greets me, "Good Morning, Jamie."

"Morning." I drop my pack to the floor behind the reception desk and take the chair.

She leans against the wall with a cup of coffee in her hands. "How are you? You look tired."

My head tilts. "Geez, thanks."

Shrugging, she laughs. "Sorry. I've seen you look better."

I push my hair back away from my face and sigh. "I am tired. My classes are tough this semester. I'm not getting much sleep. I was up until three studying for a test I have tonight. Six a.m. was painful."

"Oh no. You should have told me. I could have talked to David."

"You know he doesn't allow anybody to be late, so it wasn't even an option to ask."

She sighs, standing back up. After glancing at the clock on the wall, she says, "True. Well, if I can help out this weekend with Ace, let me know. Roger's on the road through Wednesday. So I'll be around."

"Thanks. I might take you up on that offer. I have to go to the library at some point and do some research. It would be easier not having to keep one eye on Ace the whole time."

"You got it."

Through the windows to the side, we both spot the king of used cars—at least in a two-mile radius—also known as our boss, parking his very shiny new car. "Off to work we go."

She hurries to her desk, both of us at our stations for the day, exactly how he likes us. The door swings wide and he grumbles until he sees me. It's only eight in the morning, but his balding head is already beading with sweat. Traffic is hell when you drive in from a fancy neighborhood like Brentwood each day to slum it with us on the south side. Five graying hairs cling to his brow before he brushes them to the side. The only thing he's missing is the beer belly. He may not have a lot of hair, but he's relatively fit, so he can catch a woman's eye. It's his personality where he falls flat. Recently divorced, he has become a man on the prowl for his next ex-wife. I've managed to say no despite the very attractive drunken proposals I've received. I mean, I'm still surprised I was able to resist his lecherous hands cupping my ass when I was changing the toner on the printer last week. He told me I was missing the opportunity of a lifetime. I kept my eye-rolls in check until he left the room. I also added another shot of bourbon to his coffee the way he likes it. The thought of his hands on me still makes me cringe. With the smile I know he expects to see on my face, I say, "Good morning, David."

"Mornin', Jamie. Any calls?"

I covertly click the after-hours voicemail system off, and reply, "None so far."

"Good. I'll be busy most of the day." When he says this, it means he'll be playing poker online. He has a nasty gambling habit. "So only disturb me if it's absolutely necessary or to close a deal."

"Gotcha."

He stops in front of my desk, and his eyes seem to have problems focusing on mine. He talks to my breasts regularly. Even though I'm buttoned practically to my chin, he still stares, and then disappointingly sighs. "You're very dressed up. You're not interviewing somewhere else, are you?"

No. I'm keeping your eyes from molesting my chest. With a plastered smile still on my face, I don't say what I really think because I need this job. "Nope. Just thought I'd look nice."

"Well, you do," he replies somewhere between giving a compliment and feeling left out of the party. The phone rings. *Thank God.* "I'll leave you to it."

Turning away to start my day, I answer with fake enthusiasm, "It's a wonderful day to buy a Calvert Car. How may I direct your call?"

And so it begins ...

I'M startled awake and turn to the window. Jose, our top salesman this month, is just outside my car. I wipe the drool from the side of my mouth and check my watch. *Shoot.* The door flies open and I'm already dreading going inside. "Gracias, Jose."

"Mr. Calvert's looking for you," he replies in a thick accent. His smile is gentle, leaning toward sympathetic. He knows David can be an asshole.

"Thanks," I say, dashing for the door. I undo my top two buttons, needing to use any ammunition I have, before reaching the door. It swings open and I step into the air conditioning. It feels good against my heated skin. My lunchtime nap in the car wasn't long, but I can't afford to leave it running. The afternoon sun is strong through the cracked windshield, so I feel a little sweaty, the cotton sticking to my back.

David is sitting at my desk. "The phone rang."

"I'm sorry," I say, rushing toward him to take my place. "I fell as—"

His hand goes up, stopping me before I can finish. "I'll let it slide this time, but you can stay late on Thursday to make up for it."

Not a question, though he likes to hide behind the ambiguity of it. "Sure." I have no choice. I've tried to argue before, but to no avail. I'll just be reminded how he's done me a favor and if I don't appreciate it, I can find work elsewhere.

He stands. I sit, and then ask, "Did the call get taken care of?"

"No. I can't be answering my own phone. How would that look to customers? Small time." He knocks on my desk. "That's how."

Small time. That's how I feel. *Small.*

I'm left to do my small job, in my small life, and my even smaller future. "I've got to graduate next semester," I mumble under my breath. So much hinges on that one thing. Graduation. With my degree, I'll finally dictate where and who I work for. I'm not wishing for the stars. I'm not dreaming above who I am. But I will be more than a glorified customer service operator working for someone who hired me in hopes of sleeping with me.

I'll never be anything more than someone else's employee, but at least I'll be respected. *At least I'll have that.*

4

———

JAYMES

FIVE MINUTES over on my lunch the other day and I'm stuck doing an extra hour in penance. I'm well aware that David does this on purpose to ensure I'll be alone. It's the only way I'll *voluntarily* spend time with him—forced atonement.

Leah did me another favor and picked Ace up since my mom is working until six. I owe her a mountain of favors in return. Another debt I'll never be able to pay off. At least my mom feeds her. She loves that, and Ace.

David saunters in after the last employee has left. I smell the bourbon before he even gets near the desk. I keep my headset on as a deterrent. I'm a great actress when I need to be. My mom says I missed my calling, but really it wasn't the big screen calling. It was the stage. That call just never came through like I once dreamed it would.

With papers shaking in the air, he says, "Jamie, I need you to—"

With my hand pressed to my headset, I hold my finger up, and mouth, "Hold on."

Looking impatient, he waits, standing closer to me than I like. He won't dare interrupt a potential customer or sale though, so I know I'm good for a minute or so, hoping he gets bored and goes back to his office. The problem is, ever since his divorce last year he spends a lot more time hanging around here, and especially around me. Beyond the inappropriate proposals, he has asked me out more than a dozen times, offered to make my life easier, and to, and I quote "help take care of that kid of yours. He needs a father in his life." After swallowing down the bile that filled my mouth after that offer, I politely told him to fuck off. Though my exact words escape me, they were more along the lines of me wanting to do this on my own.

What a lie.

This was never how I planned to live my life. Having a kid out of wedlock wasn't a big deal. Not in this day and age, or any other. I can defend my decision if need be. What I can't defend are the actions of Ace's father.

David leaves in a huff and I stop jabbering like someone is actually at the other end of this fake call.

By seven, I'm out the door and driving to my mom's house. I park out front and am welcomed with open arms from Ace. "Hey, you," I say, cupping his face and smiling. "How's it going?"

"Missed you, Mommy."

Bringing him to me, I hold his small body in my arms, close my eyes, and breathe easier now that I'm here. "Missed you too, buddy." I stand and take his hand, walking to the house. "Did you eat all your dinner?"

"Yes, Grandma said I did good and made me brownies."

My smile grows. "She's the best like that."

Leah is on the front porch, waiting. "We need to talk." If she said that to me without the big smile on her face, I would have been worried.

"Now or in a few?"

"It can wait, but not long."

Laughing from her mysterious, but excited secret holding reaction, I ask, "Do I need wine for this?"

"Most definitely."

We go inside just as my mom calls from the kitchen, "Brownies are ready."

"Hey, Mom. I'm here."

Her head pops around the corner, and a smile that has seen more than its fair share of tragedy to dampen it, still shines bright for Ace and me. "Jamie, you're here. I saved you a plate. You hungry?"

"Always for your cooking."

When we enter the kitchen she's pouring three glasses of white wine from the box spout. Not the expensive stuff, but it gets the job done and I can't complain. I also like the taste. "Did Leah already tell you?"

"No, but she's bursting at the seams. What happened?"

"C'mon, you. The grown-ups are going to talk." My mom ushers Ace out and sets him up in the living room with a cartoon, a brownie, and a glass of milk. She returns and picks up her cup and takes a sip. A plate of food is set down at the table and we sit around it. "I had lunch with an old friend today."

"Oh? That's nice. Who was it?" I take my first bite of broccoli.

"Diane Masters."

I start to choke, coughing furiously until the food dislodges from my throat.

Before I can react with more than the wide eyes and a sore throat, Leah says, "Derrick came by to pick her up."

Derrick.

Derrick Masters.

How can she say his name so casually? His name rolls off her tongue in a way that reminds me of many nights confiding in her through tears and wine and support. My heart even now, fracturing inside.

The fork slips from my hand and clatters off the side of the plate. I watch the metal as it bounces across the table. I shake my head as the name Masters makes my heart start aching. My mom picks up the fork and hands it to me. Softly, she asks, "Are you okay?"

"Yeah, I um." Two sips of wine and then a big gulp to empty the glass follows.

Leah takes my empty glass and stands. "Let me get you another."

"No, it's okay. I have to drive home, and I have studying to do." This time I stand, push back from the table, hoping my legs will hold me. The metal feet of the chair grind against the linoleum. Somehow the screech of the chair feels like the noise of hearing *his* name. Later I'll try to get my head around the fact that my mom had lunch with Diane. *Much later.*

"I'll get Ace."

My mom grabs the plate. "I'll wrap this up for you." I hear the nervous tone. "You can eat later."

"Mom." I reach for her before she turns her back. "I'm fine. I am."

"You don't seem it."

"I." Swallowing down the lump in my throat, I close my eyes. I'm about to speak, but I'm struggling to share my real feelings. *Or rather, I'm terrified to share my real feelings.* "I think I'm just tired."

My mom carries on and grabs the foil to cover the plate, but Leah is living the high life on this whole mess. "He sure is cute. I can't believe you once date—"

"Leah!" My mom and I stop her from going further in unison.

Her mouth closes quickly. I shake my head. "No, please not tonight."

"Okay," she replies gently. "Sorry."

"You don't have to be. Just . . . I'll tell you everything soon. Just not tonight. Ace? Come on. We need to get home."

Ace runs into the kitchen with chocolate all over his face. "Did any make it to your belly?" I tease, reaching for the wet wipes.

"I want another."

"I'm sure you do, but that's enough for tonight." When I stand my mother hands me two plates. My dinner on one. Brownies on the other. I kiss her cheek. "Thank you."

"You're welcome. I know you have to study, but I don't want you up all night. I see the dark circles under your eyes. You're not getting enough sleep."

"I'm doing the best I can."

"You're doing a great job. Just be kind to yourself too. You're everything to everyone else, Jamie. Be good to *you* every once in a while."

We walk out the front door and I'm about to walk down the steps, but I stop and turn back. "I'll try." Her brown hair is pulled back with a few strands flying free. The lines she earned worrying about me, but maybe they were destined to be there from living. I like to think I contributed more to the lines that create her smile. If you were to ask her, I did. She's always been there for me, even when I had no one else. Hugging my mom, I whisper, "How did he look?"

Her arms wrap around me and I feel enveloped by her love. *I needed this hug.* "Disappointed."

My smile comes easy. "Thank you."

"I'm only speaking the truth."

I step back and turn to hug Leah. "Thank you for picking Ace up and bringing him over here."

"No problem. You know I love hanging out with him. And your mom."

"She loves it too." I look between the two of them and point my finger. "You two are trouble together."

Wiggling her hips with her hands on them, my mom replies, "I think I'm due a little trouble."

"Oh, good grief. Ace and I are leaving before you get any sassier. Love you both. Thanks again."

We load in and I turn back and look at my son as he buckles into his car seat. "All ready to go?"

"Yep."

Ace tells me every detail of his day, including who got yellows and notes sent home to their parents in their folders, and who got an extra turn to read from the book during their story time. I got a whole earful about Francisco stealing grapes from the cafeteria line and getting caught. I gave my usual response of knowing what's right and wrong and stealing is wrong. It's a hard lesson to teach in an environment that encourages it. The other kids in the apartment complex where we live have already approached Ace several times. His father's reputation protects him, but for how long? They're scared of what might happen now, but shortly those kids will be turning eleven, twelve, and thirteen and recruited by gangs sooner than they know. The cycle will repeat itself, as it so often does.

Six months. That's all I need until I'll have the tools to move us out of here to somewhere safe, somewhere my child won't be the target of rival hate. I'll get him out, just like Derrick got out.

It's possible.

Derrick.

I go through the motions of getting Ace to bed and spreading my books across the coffee table, preparing for another long night. I have a test tomorrow and I'm behind two chapters. I start the coffeepot, but don't worry with heating my dinner. It's good cold. So I eat, and read, take notes, but my mind still wanders back to what my mother said.

Disappointed.

Derrick Masters looked disappointed.

Of all the things she could have said about him, I hadn't expected that. *Who would?*

What could he possibly be disappointed about? He has everything he ever dreamed of. Everything he ever wanted. Easy Street came so easy to him, practically dragging him away from me without a second glance.

Seeing him this many years later and the only word my mom chose to describe him with is disappointed.

Fascinating.

I click over and open a new search tab on my clunker of a laptop. It's slow. I think dial up back in the day was faster. But as soon as it pops open, I type in Derrick Masters. I pause before pressing enter though. It's not like I've not searched him before. My browser history would be the first to bust me. This time is different though. This time I'm trying to figure out why he looked disappointed. Is it because I wasn't there? That's a flattering thought, but I hardly think after all this time, he'd be disappointed not to see me. Relieved was probably more like it when it comes to me.

My mom has great intuition though, so what if he was disappointed he didn't see me? Or worse? What if he saw Ace? Oh God. Disappointment wouldn't be the only thought he'd have. I quickly press enter and watch my screen suddenly fill like lightning struck it.

"Oh now, you're in a hurry." I roll my eyes. Even my computer is a traitor when it comes to Derrick.

Scanning the news page, I read that The Resistance just wrapped the East Coast leg of The Rebellion World Tour. Livin' the life. I smile. Even my residual anger and pain can't keep a little pride from seeping in. He did what he set out to do. I click on the top article.

The band arrived back in Burbank on their private plane to a crowd of cheering fans ... Johnny ... Dex ... band manager ... I scan farther down the page until I see Derrick's name. *Derrick Masters, the band's lead guitarist didn't have a comment at this time.* His head is down in the photo next to the text, and I find my fingertips tracing along his jaw and my heart beating for him, just like years ago. "Oh Derrick. What has become of you?"

That's when I see it. The truth is found in a video.

I click the video of the reporter hounding him as he cuts through the crowd of paparazzi. "We've been hitting the road pretty hard. It was great to be out there, but I'm happy to be home for a while. I think I'll sleep for the next week."

My mom had it all wrong. He wasn't disappointed.

He was exhausted.

A lot like me these days.

Just for *very* different reasons.

Unlike me, he still looks damn good. Square jaw that I used to caress. Broad shoulders that have widened with age. He looks taller, if that's possible. Darker hair than I remember. Familiar in so many ways and foreign in others.

Damn him.

Damn me and this stupid lovesick heart. And there it is. The splintering in my heart. I close the window. That's enough of that for one night. Because when it comes down to it, it doesn't matter if he's tired or disappointed. It's only momentary. He's not mine to worry about. My heart doesn't matter.

Hopefully, these feelings will subside one day. All I need to worry about is asleep in the back bedroom. I don't need anyone else or anything. All I need is my son. We'll get by just like we have the last five years. Just the two of us.

"We've been hitting the road pretty hard. It was great to be out there, but I'm happy to be home for a while."

Lucky him. Home for him is respite, rest, and parties, whereas home for me is constant responsibility, studying, and fatigue.

You have all you need, Jamie.

You have all you need.

5

JAYMES

Sitting on the bench, I watch Ace run around with a girl playing tag. The park isn't busy considering it's a Sunday. I like it. It's peaceful. Looking down at the textbook next to me, I feel instant guilt. I should be studying, but I don't want to. I'd rather be distracted by birds singing in the trees above or the sound of giggles from happy children playing. Even the cars driving by on the other side of the playground seem to garner my attention.

I think I'll give myself the morning. It's too beautiful a day to waste not appreciating it. Anyway, I always have this evening to bury my nose back in the books.

The sound of a thumping bass interrupts the tranquility of the park a few minutes later. I watch the shiny royal-blue car with sparkling silver rims roll by and know it's going slow to keep an eye on me, and Ace.

My heart thuds in my chest louder than the music could ever be blared. A guy I don't recognize hangs out of the window of the vehicle just far enough for me to worry. When he falls back into the shadows of the interior and the car drives off, I feel the breath I refused to breathe release. And just like that, the little peace I had found is gone.

I toss my textbook back into my backpack and shove our water bottles into the side pockets. I'm ready to flee this park, wishing we were in another part of the city altogether. When Ace comes running up with his new friend, the mother of the other child looks over concerned. I wave. "It's okay," I reassure her. I'm sure she lives with the same fears I feel. The same fears our mothers once held for our futures. Maybe they still do since we're still here. Since we haven't gotten out yet. I'm going to change that. I'm going to make good on everything I swore I would. I'll show Mom a better life. I'll make sure that Ace doesn't have to fight the same battles I fight. I'll sleep at night knowing we're safe, instead of living in perpetual fear.

One day I'll even get the puppy Ace so desperately wants. I may not be able to afford an extra mouth to feed now, but one day I will.

Ace asks, "Can we stay longer, Mommy? Tegan wants to play on the swing. I said I would push her first if she pushed me second."

My smile grows. This is the biggest concern I wish my son to ever have. "Of course. It's good you're taking turns and helping each other out."

Ace shrugs. "That's what friends do."

They run off and I repeat, "Yeah, that's what friends do." Maybe not loves of your life, but friends.

I decide I should study before my mind drifts to a sexy guitarist that looks disappointed when I'm not around . . . I mean *tired*.

NOT SURE HOW long I've pushed my peas around my plate, but Mom is. She says, "Just put the poor things out of their misery and stop toying with their emotions."

I start laughing and set my fork down. "Dinner was good, Mom. Thank you." Ace jumps up, but I correct, "Sit down please."

"Can I go?"

"Not *can I go*. You need to ask, 'May I please be excused?' "

"May I please be 'scused?"

"Yes." He's running before I can ask where he's going. The back door squeaks from its rusty hinges and then slams closed. He's safe in the backyard, one of the few places I never have to worry about him. It's small and tidy with just enough room for a growing boy to burn off some excess energy. "He starts soccer next week. Will you still be able to help out?"

My mom sits her elbow on the table and I know a heart-to-heart is coming. "I'm always here for you and Ace. My job, not so much. I just had my hours cut back—"

"Again?"

Resting her chin in the palm of her hand, she nods. "I was thinking maybe you and Ace could move in. I know you like your independence and I like mine—we're similar in that way, but I love you two more. With less money, I'm not sure I can keep the house, and I know it would help ease some of your expenses by splitting the bills."

"Mom—"

"Just hear me out, Jamie. You're busy. He's over here all the time already—"

I reach over and take her hand. She sits up and I hold tight. "You don't have to sell me on it. I think this is a good idea."

"You do?" she asks, surprised.

"I do." I breathe out and it feels like some of my load has lightened. "I'm tired of fighting this war, trying to prove to God only knows, that I can be super mom. I'm exhausted—mentally, physically, and financially. You're right. This way we can keep the house and help ease some of the financial burdens. Then next year, we're moving away anyway."

"Jamie, you work so hard. It will pay off for you and Ace."

"And you. We're all going to get out of this part of the city. I promise you. No more worrying about *him*, or his guys."

I try to never say *his* name. Not ever unless I'm being forced to, which has happened before. Once to the police who sent me right back to face him on my own. Once when he forced his name on Ace's birth certificate just like he forced himself on me.

That pain in my chest comes back with a vengeance, the tears that blur my vision come quicker. I hate feeling weak. I hate being weak. My mom is up and her arms are wrapped around me before I have time to turn away. I close my eyes and the tears are squeezed and fall to the table. "It's okay, honey. Everything you said, we'll do."

Nodding against her, I'm too choked up to speak. I finally pull myself together and she sits back down. "I promise you. I'll get us all out of here. If I give my notice by morning, I won't have to pay another month. The sooner I'm out of that place the better."

The tightness of her lips would indicate otherwise, but the look of determination in her eyes matches mine. "I know." She stands and smiles, her sunshine smothering the heavy, and bringing back the light. "Can I get my pretty daughter a bowl of ice cream? Oops, I mean *may* I?"

We laugh while I stand. "I'm good, but I could bet my paycheck that the little guy out back wants some."

"That's a sucker's bet. You go out and I'll bring the ice cream."

Sitting under the stars, I look up. They're hard to see in the city, but I manage to make a few out. Ace has finished his ice cream and had another burst of energy from the sugar rush. My mom has a glass of wine and is in the chair next to me. "Diane says hello."

I turn her way. *Diane Masters.* "We never did get to talk about your visit. How was it?"

A thoughtful smile appears. "It was so much fun. We talked for hours. Just like old times."

"It has been a few years since you've seen each other, right? Why is that?"

She sips her wine and then watches Ace make a divot into her lawn with his play shovel—an imaginary game of Whack-A-Mole happening. "I guess we just drifted apart after she moved a few years ago."

"I'm sorry."

"For what?"

"You guys were good friends and the breakup—"

"You and Derrick had nothing to do with Diane and me not seeing each other. We are grown women. We let life get in the way of our friendship, but we're going to change that. Lunch last Thursday was a renewal. We're actually going to see each other again this week."

"Really?"

"Really. So if you want to come a few minutes early on Wednesday we might get to see something other than disappointment on a certain someone's face."

"No, don't even go there. That ship has long sailed."

"Maybe there's a port nearby?"

I give her the look, the one that warns her not to even contemplate whatever she's already plotting.

"He sure is handsome."

"Mom. No."

"I'm just saying."

Tilting my head back, I look for the stars Derrick used to say only shined for us. In my darkest hours, I would search for the fated couple, wondering if Derrick was searching for them wherever he was in the world. The stars seem to align better when we were together, the memories from back then still too vivid . . .

The tailgate was pulled down and a blanket was spread out. I stood by waiting until it was ready. Derrick had gone to so much trouble that I didn't want to ruin it by taking over, but the giggles still came.

"Fuck it," he says, then looks back at me. His expression responds to mine, and he smiles. "I tried."

"It's perfect."

"It's not. I want it to be for you, but it will have to do."

"It doesn't matter. We're together."

He nods and then lifts me by the waist and sets me on the tailgate. I scoot to the back and take my guitar before settling on the pillows and stretching my legs out.

With ease, he jumps into the back of the truck bed. Grabbing his guitar, he sits across from me and starts strumming. His fingers move from memory as he looks up. "Perseus." I follow his line of sight to the dark night above. "Perseus. Poor but determined to live a better life."

"Is life so bad with me?" I tease, but like the tides, Derrick's mood has shifted.

"I'm moving to Hollywood."

My hand stops, the chords crashing together in an unsoundly catastrophe. "You're leaving?" Me?

"I want us to leave. It's time. Six more months max. I've already started looking for places. I found a cheap—"

"I can't leave my mother. My father died not even a year ago. I can't leave her now."

"We'll leave. We'll pack our moms and just go."

"Derrick, you're talking crazy."

"No, I'm not." His voice falters to anger. "I can't keep Reggie off my back much longer. You know what that means?" I do. He continues, "I've been busted for possession once. Reggie twice. He's not going to go down. He'll pin it all on me. And then what happens to you? What happens to my mom if I go to jail?" His fingers run through his hair. "What happens to me?"

I set the guitar down and crawl over next to him. The cool air chills my legs exposed by the short skirt, but I settle on his lap, his guitar discarded to the side. With his strong, warm arms around me, I lean against his chest. "Tell me about Perseus again." I know the story of the boy who became a man when he cut off Medusa's head and fulfilled a destiny predicted long before his birth, but I like hearing him tell the ending.

Derrick's hand rubs over my thigh, the veins more prominent as he grows bigger and stronger, becoming a man. "Jaymes, my beautiful Andromeda," he whispers against my neck. "Together we'll forever live in the heavens."

I tighten my arms around his neck. "Forever in the heavens together."

. . . I was naïve enough at seventeen to believe we could be together forever here on Earth. Seventeen feels like a long way from twenty-three these days. So much life has happened I don't think he'd recognize me now. I barely recognize myself. "Hey Mom?"

"Yes?"

"Don't get your hopes up, okay? Sometimes we've got to let the ones we love the most go so *they* can live their dreams."

She doesn't say anything, but I can feel her sadness through the air between us. Or maybe it's mine I feel. Either way, hope isn't a luxury I can have these days. I deal in reality. Always reality. I peek back up at the sky and there they are shining brightly despite the haze of the surrounding lights. Perseus and Andromeda.

Together forever.

But only in the stars.

6

DERRICK

THE CAN I toss hits the side of the bucket and bounces onto Kaz's stone patio. My heels press against the fire pit and I lean back, balancing on the back two legs of the chair. "The stars betrayed the raven night. Two lovers caught in the shining light. Each held a dream to believe. Their love, like their hope, stolen by thieves. Winter now shuddered and spring lay nigh. What was once forever became a dreadful goodbye."

"We should record that with the band."

I don't move anything but my eyes when I swing my gaze to Kaz. "It's written in a past that pulls me back too often to admit."

"You used to sing it. One of our more popular songs. We played it every night whether we had a gig or not. It's when we lived in that first apartment down on Sunset. Remember? The one with the broken air conditioner and no fridge."

"We lived out of a cooler for drinks and leftovers foraged from the great wild hills of Hollywood."

Kaz laughs. "How many couches do you think we slept on?"

"Too many to recall." I look at him. Really look at him. He's different these days. Still my same friend always looking to the sunny side of life. Talented. So damn good with a guitar, and any instrument you put in front of him. But in the last year he's had his own form of evolution. He's changed. He's at peace with the war he was waging inside. "How's Lara?" There's that damn smile again, just from the mention of her name. I roll my eyes, but find myself smiling too. "I want that."

He tosses his empty beer can and makes it into the bucket, his arms flying up in victory. "What do you want?"

"That feeling."

Kaz rarely shows all of his cards, but we know each other well enough for him to lay down his weapons. "We don't have just one shot. The beauty of living is that we get better. Every day is a new start. But nothing is gonna change if you don't. Toss me another."

I reach into the cooler, like old times, and toss him a cold one. He takes a long drag before belching operatic style.

"Like I was saying, tomorrow's a new day. You going to live the same as today?"

My gut twists as disappointment sets in. "I was hoping to see her. Was that an asshole move to show up like that?"

"Not when your mom asked you to. The asshole move was waiting all these years to see her, and then *only* go because your mother wanted you to."

After popping the top on another for me, I swig and swallow. I grab my guitar and he grabs his. We start a song we've played in front of thousands, but keep it acoustic and just for us tonight. I stop halfway through and add, "The guy I trusted with my life growing up is the same one who stabbed me in the back the second I was out of sight. She's been with him ever since."

His hand stills and he turns his baseball cap around, bill backward. "You sure about that?"

"It took a lot to get out of that shithole. I owe him. He won't forget or let it slide."

"You owe him what? Your girl? He got her. There. Done deal. What else do you think you owe him that keeps you from getting the life you deserve?"

I'm still not sure I deserve what I have now, or ever will. "Why do I deserve *this* life, Kaz?"

"Because you worked for it. Your fingers bled for this job. It's not about being hired players. We're part of the band. A permanent part. We're not gonna get fired. We're contributors. The band is where they are now because of us. Own it. You deserve that recognition. So whatever the fuck those guys back home think you owe them, you don't owe them shit. But you do owe a lot to yourself." He shrugs. "Some people are just born into greatness. Others work their asses off for it."

Jaymes was born with the most perfect voice I'd ever heard. Add in her guitar-playing brilliance, and she was also meant for more than the life she's living. Choosing to stay for the right reasons killed her chance of getting out. She should be reaping the rewards in a music career. She is *that* talented. *She* deserves the recognition. But there was no talking her into leaving . . .

"Come with me, baby. Just pack and leave."

Her tears cover her lap, her head hanging low. "I can't. I can't leave her."

"I'll come back for your mom. I promise, but I have to go tonight."

As if I've injected hope straight into her veins, she looks up—bright, but pleading eyes on me. "Okay. Tonight. That means we have a few hours to figure things out. We can go inside and talk to my mom." She reaches for the truck door to open it, but I stop her.

"No. I don't have hours." I take her face between my hands, my anxiety making them shake when I touch her. "You've got to listen to me, Jaymes. They'll come here—"

"Who? Reggie?"

"Yes."

"Good. He can help us."

"No. He won't help us. Please. Just pack—"

Her hands wrap around my wrist. "I need more time. I can't just leave because you want me to." The air thins in the cab of the truck, our eyes lock together, until I blink, realizing this is it. The feel of her skin becomes a memory keeping my palms warm as I pull away.

"I love you."

Tears flood her eyes as her hands still hold tight like a vise around my wrists. "Don't leave me," she whispers.

My voice matches hers; so quiet I can't hear it in my heart. "Please. Come with me."

"I ca—"

"I'm begging you. Please come with me."

I once swore I'd never beg anyone for anything again. That sick feeling that settled in the back of my mind at ten telling me I was less, not worthy of even food some days comes back like a bolt of lightning. For her. For Jaymes. For love, I'll beg. "I'm begging you."

She sits back and looks away from me, solidifying that emotion in my gut. "I love you."

I reach for her again, touching her hand and bringing it to my lips. As soon as I kiss her delicate skin, she looks my way. The tears overcome the barrier of her lower lids and fall in streams down her cheeks. "I will always love you."

"Come back for me. Don't leave me here forever. Promise you'll come back for me."

My heart hurts, so much that I struggle to look beyond the pain. I say the words, although I'm not sure I can back them. Not right now. Not under the circumstances that have driven me to make this rash decision. I understand she can't leave her mom. I really do. I'm leaving mine too. But I want her with me. Need her with me. But I won't force her. I love her too much to do that. "I promise."

The door opens and I close my eyes. I can't watch her leave me. She steps out, but looks in. "Derrick?" I loosen my hold on the steering wheel and look her way. The quiver in her tone is heard when she says, "I know I just made you promise, but I changed my mind."

Confusion sets in quickening like the beat of my heart. "Don't come back. Not for me. Not for anything. Go do great things and don't let anyone stand in your way. Not even me." The door slams closed and she turns and runs inside her house.

She meant every word. There were no tears in her eyes. All I saw was the strong determination of the stubborn girl I love more than life. "Don't come back. Not even for me." Oh, Jaymes . . .

But my time's run out. Reggie's probably already left my house. He'll come here next, so I can't be here when he arrives.

He'll stay away from Jaymes as long as I stay away.

The only way to protect her is to stay as far away.

Until I can *come back for her.*

That's a promise I can keep.

Shifting the truck into drive, I pull away from the curb and head into the heart of LA.

. . . "I didn't know it was goodbye for good."

"It doesn't have to be. You don't know what's going on in her life. Maybe you should put some feelers out."

"My mom knows, but I told her not to tell me."

"So she won't? Even if you want to know now?"

Sitting up, I say, "I need Lara."

Kaz's head jerks back. "Whoa. Whoa. Slow up there."

Shaking my head and rolling my eyes, I say, "Not in that way."

———

MY MOM NUDGES ME. "I don't need a professional to help me."

"You've talked about having friends and family over for meals and parties. You need a table to do that. You hate shopping, so let Lara help you out."

"Have you seen the prices? That's why I hate shopping."

"Stop worrying about money and let Lara and me worry about that. You just pick out stuff you like. Then you can start hosting your friends over here."

She stops and turns toward me. "Friends like Nita?"

"Exactly," I reply with a smirk that gives it all away because she's onto me.

"Maybe this *is* a good idea." She pats me on the arm and walks away. "Lara?"

I sit on the couch and open the photos on my phone. Scrolling back to the first few I ever uploaded to this phone dated back to the night Jaymes and I celebrated four years of dating. On a whim, we drove down to the Hollywood Bowl. Her favorite band was playing and I wanted to surprise her. I didn't have tickets, but I planned to get us in any way I could. I scored two tickets in the parking lot thirty minutes after it started, but we got them for a discount. I brought binoculars. We needed them, but she loved every minute and sang every song. She danced, her skirt blowing in the wind as her legs swayed to every note of the greatest band in the world's music. All three original members of The Resistance were on fire that night. That's when I knew what I had to do.

I'd get us out. I would be the one that took dreams and made it happen. Watching the band on stage, I knew that's what I wanted to do and nothing would stop me.

I flip to the next photo. Jaymes's hair was wild that night, a flurry of dark hair flying around in the wind. Pink lips puckered for a kiss that was just blown my way. God, she was so gorgeous. I'm reminded of what Kaz said the other night. *Feelers.* "Hey Ma?" She and Lara are looking at an iPad on the kitchen counter. They both stop and look my way. "When are you seeing Nita next?" There's no point pretending. The woman always could see right through me.

"Wednesday. Maybe you can pick me up again? Say a half hour later?"

"That works." I look back at the phone. *Feelers.* That's all it is. Just a quick *hi, how are you?* Nothing more.

Unless there's a chance for more and maybe feelers can turn into a conversation. I turn off my phone. My imagination is getting the best of me, but I can't help feel that I might finally get the chance to keep the most important promise I once made.

7

———————

JAYMES

THREE TEXT MESSAGES LATER, it's confirmed. Diane Masters is at my mom's house. This wasn't anything but good news last week. I was simply happy my mother had reconnected with her long-time friend. Diane got out. Derrick fulfilled that promise. He never owed me anything, but when Diane moved it felt like that last remnant of the glue was gone. There would never be any reason left for Derrick to come back.

I didn't just miss him. I envied him.

He did it.

He chased his dreams. Made them happen. I was both proud he made it and sad that I didn't. When we were together, I never thought it had to be one or the other. I have no ill will that he found fame, or has made money. It's quite the opposite. I still care. I still cheer. I still smile if I see him on a billboard or hear him on the radio. He was always confident, so damn confident. The irony from the night we went to the Hollywood Bowl still plays in my mind sometimes . . .

"I'm going to play that stage one day. Just you wait, baby." His arm wraps around my shoulders and he pulls me to his side, one of my most favorite places to be. His six-foot-one frame towers over my five-foot-three body so I fit snuggly against him. I feel loved. I feel safe. His smile is conta-

gious when he looks down at me. "You and me and the whole wide world will be ours to see. To own. Hollywood won't know what hit them."

"You think—"

"I don't think, Jaymes. I know. That's gonna be me. And you, my song-bird, are going to sing for the world. Every station is going to be playing your songs. Maybe even our songs."

"You dream big."

"As big as the universe. What's the point if any schmuck can do it?"

He's got a point. I close my eyes and lean my head against him. We sway to a ballad that breaks my heart and heals me again. The lyrics of this song remind me of Derrick's. There's a haunting quality that rolls through my soul like a fog creeping out to sea.

. . . A few years later, Derrick Masters joined *The Resistance*. The announcement spread like wildfire; he was now lead guitarist. The news was received on shaky grounds. Some were thrilled and proud of a local making good. Others, like Reggie, were wound so tight I thought he might go after Derrick just to bring him down again. It took a lot of convincing, calming, and negotiating to keep him from pursuing the vendetta he had, but I did it for Derrick, and for Ace's safety.

I listened to him complain. A man with a wounded ego is dangerous and nobody hurt him more than being betrayed by Derrick. It's the only time Reggie ever treated me like a human with feelings. Might have been my face of disgust when he touched me or that he knew deep down what I was really up to—trading myself for Derrick—but either way, mercy was shown. Now I carry the debt Derrick once owed Reggie. I just wish I knew what that debt was.

When I pull up and park, I pack my memories away and look over at the house. My headlights shine on a shiny blue Lincoln. I cut the engine and take a deep breath. That's not my mom's car. Diane is driving nice wheels these days. Inside my rusting Corolla, that David gave me a *great* deal on, I stare into the front window of the house for signs of life. If I thought my hands were shaking before, that was nothing. Even my lip is trembling, so I bite down on it to keep it steady.

Leah picked up Ace from his after-school program and was supposed to drop him off here while I went to night school. But her car is still in the driveway. I was so tempted to ask David if he needed me to come back and work late. "What am I doing?" I whisper, leaning my head against the steering wheel. My stomach has been full of butterflies all day. Over what? He's probably not even here. She obviously drove herself this time.

I always adored Diane. She was like a second mother to me and that our moms were best friends, it just made our lives so much easier to spend time together. But now, years later, I'm a nervous wreck over seeing her again. I know damn well it's not just her I'm nervous to see. Taking my gloss from my purse, I swipe over my lips quickly and rub them together. Flipping my visor down, I look in the mirror. I pull my hair from the messy topknot and then twist it back up when I see it looks worse down. "Shoot." He might not be here, I remind myself.

A knock on the window startles me and I jump a mile, my heart beating right out of my chest. When I look over through the passenger door window, I see Ace. "Oh, thank God."

"Hi, Mommy."

My world calms when I look at his face. "Hi, baby." I get out and walk around the front of the car. "How was your day, buddy?" I ask, just as I catch something out of the corner of my eyes.

On the front porch, leaning against the wood column in all his newfound glory, stands the most breathtaking man I've ever seen. As a teenager, I thought he was the best-looking *boy* I'd ever seen, and based on how I'm struggling to breathe just from looking at him now, I think he still holds the title. *But now he's a man.*

Ace is talking about what some kid named Shiloh got in trouble for today at school, but I'm still staring at Derrick Masters.

Derrick Masters.

My very own Perseus, though right now I'm thinking he was more my Achilles heel in the grand scheme of things.

Derrick Masters is standing on my mother's front porch like he belongs there. A smile that shines like the star he's become appears and he waves. Not sure if it was the grin on his face or the wave that sends me tripping flat on my face into the grassy lawn, but I'm cursing the curb when I lift up and look right into the dark blue eyes I've tried to despise.

"Are you okay?" he asks, trying to help me up. His voice is deep, the timbre the same one that always made my heart beat a little faster. It's not that thought that runs through my mind. It's his hands on me, grappling to help me to my feet.

He's touching me.

Derrick Masters is touching me and I consider lying there longer just to savor the feel of his calloused fingers again. Ace tugs at my ankle like that will help me up. "Mommy, you fell."

Mommy.

Mommy.

Derrick knows I'm a mommy.

Oh my God. *What does he think?*

Does he hate me? Disappointed in me? Happy for me? Or not care at all?

I would care if I found out he has kids.

Maybe he already knew . . .

Maybe I'll just lie here as long as I can until he goes away.

Ace lies down next to me and rests his face on my hand. Looking at me with wide eyes, he asks, "Are we playing a game? This is fun."

"Yes, I quite like it here."

I hear Derrick chuckling just above me, enough to feel his warmth covering my body like sunshine as I lie in the cool grass. I might be mistaken but it sounds like he's behind me now. On the ground with me.

Ace's eyes look over my head. "My friend is here too." He giggles. "See? Right there."

Lying like a dead fish, I smile at my cute son not quite ready to face Derrick Masters. "What's your new friend's name?"

"Derrick. He plays a guitar like you, Mommy."

After a tap on the back, Ace's new friend speaks, "Hi."

I miss Derrick's hands on me, even if it was just helping me up.

Ace is a ball of laughter and gets up. I watch until he runs behind me. "I'm here now. We're all here. This is fun. Oh look, the moon."

I can't avoid him forever and the grass is grounding, literally, and settles my anxiety over just this kind of thing happening. I've embarrassed myself and he's found out I'm a mother in the course of one sexy smile and a wave. I shake my head and close my eyes annoyed with myself for acting so foolishly in front of him. *He was once my everything.* When I roll onto my back, the top of our hands meet in an innocent touch that neither of us bothers to retreat. Finally building enough nerve, I turn my head and look straight into his eyes again. "Hi," I whisper.

That devastatingly charming smile reappears, and he says, "It's good to see you, Jaymes."

Lying on the other side of Derrick, Ace pipes in, "Everyone calls my mom Jamie."

"It's okay, buddy. He can call me Jaymes." Just like old times. My gaze goes to the evening sky. I can't see our fated lovers, but I can feel them, their presence mingled with ours.

My mom's voice slices through the feelings threatening to arise. "What are you guys doing out here?"

Tilting my head, I catch another glimpse of Derrick on my way to looking at the three women who have congregated on the porch. All three with wry grins that will eventually mortify me with their teasing and taunting. "We were just coming in."

Ace runs to the house and I look at Derrick, not sure why I'm feeling so emotional. Fortunately, joy overrides the rest. "It's good to see you, too."

He sits up and then he's on his feet offering me a hand up. "That was quite a trip you took."

"I didn't even bring a carry-on."

"No," he says, chuckling, "but you played the whole thing off really well if that makes a difference."

I take his hand and he pulls me to my feet. In one fell swoop, my body is against his. The questions will come. I'll answer. His piqued curiosity will be sated and then he'll be off for good this time. I like this quiet before the storm I know is coming. Taking the few extra seconds I have before this bubble is burst, I let my gaze wander over his broad shoulders and higher. His chiseled jaw is shadowed in light stubble. His hair messed in ways that remind me of the mornings after we spent all night making love. Is it possible for him to be even more handsome than when we were younger? Because he is. He so is. It's unnerving. I feel I've aged thirty years in the time we've been apart. He's aged just right.

Standing in front of him, pressed to him like this, and looking into those dazzling eyes that match the LA night skies, I feel myself melt. It's not just that he's even more gorgeous. It's his eyes. His warm, caring eyes haven't changed, and I'm a little in awe.

"I have pie," my mom says, receiving cheers from Ace. "Come on inside."

Seconds later the screen door slams closed and I know we're alone. I mean, the whole city is revolving around us, but none of that matters.

It's us.

The emerging stars above.

And the man I once thought I would be with forever. We're now standing in the same place where he left me. I don't know what to say to him, except, "Rebel finally returns."

8

JAYMES

DERRICK TAKES A STEP, his hands falling to his side, and his tongue running over his bottom lip. I think he's unsure what to say, so I fill in the silence, "Come on. You always did like her pie." The first steps I take are the hardest, but I keep going and it gets easier this time to walk away.

His footsteps are heard behind me with each step up the stairs and across the porch. With the door in my hand, wide open, I turn back. "Don't say anything about us in front of Ace. Okay?"

"Nothing's been said yet."

"Thank you." I slip inside and walk into the kitchen where everyone's gathered.

Leah hands me a plate. Her eyes dart between me and the man I know is standing probably too close.

I sit at the table as he's handed a plate and fork. He sits down across from me and even though I'm doing everything not to look at him, I know he's looking at me. The kitchen is too quiet. Ace is the only one oblivious to what's really happening. He's just thrilled to be eating dessert. If only my life were that simple. These days it takes a lot more than blueberry pie to make things better, though I can admit as I take another delectable bite, it's helping.

My gaze finally works its way across the lightwood tabletop and higher when Derrick says, "I've missed your pie, Mrs. Grenier."

I think he catches it as soon as I do, my mouth falling open. As my mom revels under the spotlight of compliments, I stare at him with wide eyes. He looks down and I see his chest puff with a hard breath. When he looks up, we share the silent joke together and smile. For a brief second it almost feels natural.

I'm quickly reminded that we aren't those people anymore. "Mommy?" Ace bumps into me and wriggles onto my lap, causing me to scoot the chair back to make room.

"Yeah?"

"May I leave the table? I want to go." I smile. He is just the cutest little person.

"Are you tired?"

"I want to see my show."

Leaning my forehead against the side of his, I nod. "Okay, buddy. Go pack up your stuff."

He dashes off and that's when I realize the room had gone quiet watching us, including the man across me. My knee begins to bounce and I tap the table twice. "Well, I should go. He's going through a Curious George stage. I don't know if I should be worried that he loves a troublemaking monkey or that the man only wears yellow."

"The yellow."

All of us look at Derrick when he speaks, but Ace walks in with his backpack and says, "I like yellow."

Derrick smiles, breaking whatever tension was building. "Me too, buddy."

My heart clenches hearing him call Ace by that name, but when he rubs the top of his head, I rush from the room. "Come on, Ace." It wasn't tension that was building. It was pain, regret, shattered dreams, and lost love. That's what Derrick is to me now, and to see him be so sweet to my son breaks me.

I don't know if Ace has ever seen me move so fast. I'm halfway to the door before my arm is caught and I'm brought to a stop. "Hey." I rip my arm away when I turn back. "Don't touch me."

His hands fly up in surrender. "I'm sorry. Don't leave, bab— Don't go. I'll go. You stay." He corrects himself, but some habits die hard. I should know.

"Don't tell me what to do. I've got to get my son home."

Slowly lowering his hands, Ace comes up next to him. Right there before me is the future I thought I'd once have. Blueberry pie isn't going to fix the tangled mess my life became. Taking Ace by the back-pack strap, I pull him closer until he's in front of me with my arms protectively around his shoulders. And maybe I'm reading too much into Derrick's expression, but it looks a lot like how mine felt moments earlier. He nods and steps around me as the ladies enter the living room. The door is opened and slams closed and my heart deflates when he leaves.

Their three fallen faces kind of express everything. I swallow and say, "Thanks, Leah, for everything with Ace."

"No problem. Do you need me on Friday?"

"No, class is online that night. My professor is out of town. Thanks though." She hugs my mom and tells her she'll see her next week. I'm given a sympathetic side hug. I'm sure I'll hear more in the morning at the dealership, but she's kind enough to let it go tonight. The door opens and I hear their muffled voices on the porch.

Ace says, "I'm going to see Derrick." I let him, too tired to worry about the *what could have beens*.

"It's good to see you, Diane." Her whole face brightens and I'm instantly soothed by the smile I used to find comfort in. She comes to me and takes me by the hands. "Your mother has bragged about all of your accomplishments with school and Ace, your work. I'm so proud of you, Jamie."

The tears I denied in the kitchen come this time. Just two. I only allow two, but I let them fall. I've had an exhausting day and my emotions are paying the price. "Thank you. That means a lot to me." It does. Her approval and support mean so much more than I ever thought they would.

"You've grown from a beautiful girl into a stunning woman."

I look down from her gaze, feeling self-conscious. I don't feel stunning. I feel harried and exhausted. "Thank you," I reply tugging at the loose strands of hair hanging down over my neck.

When I look back up, she says, "Well, you have a sweet little boy to get home and . . ." She stops to laugh. "I do too."

Now we all laugh. *Sweet little boy? He hasn't been that for a long time.* She was always a role model when it came to parenting. The man out front is a testament to her efforts. I hope my son will see me the same way one day. Diane and I walk outside and she gives me a warm hug. "I would love to see you again and spend some time catching up. Maybe you and your mother can meet me out for brunch this weekend?"

Mom mode kicks in automatically. "I'd love that, but I have Ace. It's only mom and me. Leah helps when she can, but I hate to ask too much of her." It's not until I stop talking that I remember Derrick is standing nearby, listening to everything I've just said. I dare look his way. Like the day I met him, I'm drawn into the ocean-blue of his eyes as the storm brews inside.

Diane draws my attention back, and says, "You can bring Ace. He's so delightful. It will be good to have a kid around. I'll call your mom with details. Bye, Nita. Thank you for the tea and pie, and the company." She squeezes my hand and walks down the steps to the sidewalk. "Are you ready to go, son, or do you need a few minutes?"

Derrick looks from his mother to me. When I give him the smallest of head shakes, he replies, "No, I'm ready." He steps past me and my mom embraces him. "Thank you, Mrs. Grenier."

"Please call me Nita. I think you're old enough now." When they part, she says, "Maybe you can join us again—"

I interrupt in a flash, "Mom."

She smiles and shrugs. "I want to hear about the band. You're not the only one who listens to them, you know."

My huff of annoyance comes louder than I intend, but Derrick ignores it, and says, "Next time then."

He doesn't stop to hug me or even say goodbye. He's quick to turn and rush down the steps, but he gets about halfway to the car and stops. I follow his line of sight. Ace comes running to him and

Derrick kneels down so he's eye level. I can't hear what he says, but Ace bumps knuckles with him and giggles, making me smile.

Before he stands, his eyes meet mine, and he waves. "Good seeing you, Jaymes."

"You too," I reply with no regard to my crushing heart because it is. It's so good to see him again, even though I'm fairly sure it will be the last time.

I hug my mom and she then walks me to my car just as Derrick is turning his car around. His mom waves to us with a broad smile on her face, but Derrick doesn't and just that little lack of acknowledgement feels a lot like rejection. I hate it. I swore I would never let a man control my emotions again. I fought for it. I fought for my sanity. I had to so I could be everything my baby needed me to be. But I guess when it comes to first love, emotions don't play by the rules.

I get in the car, make sure Ace is buckled in the back. When I roll the side window down, my mom leans in, and says, "You are an astonishing young woman and an even better mother."

Wanting to wipe the tears that have surfaced, I reply, "What brought that on?"

"Sometimes when we're caught in the crazy that is life it's good to hear something positive, something we're doing right. I don't tell you enough. Tonight was a good reminder. You make me proud every day, Jamie." She reaches into the back and tickles Ace. In a kid tone, she teases him, "You do too, big guy. Take care of your mommy. All right?"

"I've got it covered."

My heads turns to the side as laughter boils up from his surprise comment. "I don't even know what that means."

He winks, and says, "I've got your back, Mommy."

I'm not sure how much time he and Derrick actually spent together, but it's apparent that it was enough to rub off on him. "And I've got yours, buddy. Say goodbye to Grandma."

When we get home, Ace is bathed and is now watching his show. He's curled on the loveseat while I sit on the floor with my legs under the coffee table. A toy guitar was dragged out of the hall closet the minute we got home and he sat plucking the strings until his show started. The guitar was discarded, but for minutes after, I stared at the empty stand in the corner that used to hold mine. The pain over having it stolen still hurts. Even with the out-of-tune sounds of Ace's toy, the room feels warmer with music filling it.

Now I find myself with my laptop open, and although I do have my test material open in Word, I've also got a new browser open with four words sitting in the box ready to search as soon as I hit enter.

Is Derrick Masters single?

Right when I'm about to push enter, worry filling every second that ticks by, I hear the soft slumber of my little boy and look behind me.

Smiling, I lean back and kiss his head, stand up, and then lift him into my arms. He's growing fast. I'm not sure I'll be able to carry him much longer, but while I can, I savor holding my baby in my arms. Before I take him to his room, I click the X and close the tab.

It doesn't matter what Derrick's dating status is. My life is full of everything from raising my kid to work to school to finding a way to a better life at the end of the day. I don't have time for love, or lust, or whatever that little ball of messy feelings is that's growing. I just need to stop feeding it so it goes away. Just like Derrick did. *Our* dreams died the day he left. But I will achieve my dreams. My new dreams.

He got the life he deserved, the rewards he'd worked so hard for. I never regretted the tactic I used. He would have stayed otherwise. I know it. He'd have driven off but he would have been back the next day. Breaking his heart meant breaking mine, but I'd do it again if it had the same outcome. Better to save his life than for both of us to suffer and eventually blame each other. Our love would have turned to hate, dreams stomped out like a cigarette. Hating the only man I ever loved wasn't an option. It wasn't the ending either of us deserved. It wouldn't be living. That would be hell.

It didn't feel like a sacrifice despite the pain that consumed me. It was the only option we had. He just didn't know it at the time. Hopefully he never will.

Derrick looked good tonight. Healthy. That's what telling him to never look back that day did—gave him a chance at a happy life.

9

DERRICK

What just happened?

Jaymes Grenier.

That's what just happened.

"... pie recipe. What do you think?"

Taking my mom's exit, I brake when we come to a light and look at her. "Huh?"

"I can't put my finger on it and it's driving me nuts. Cinnamon makes no sense with blueberries."

What the fuck is she talking about? "What?"

"The pie." She looks annoyed. "Nita's pie. The secret ingredient. Have you not been listening at all, Derrick?" Her annoyance quickly turns into an all-knowing smile. "*Ahhh.* You haven't been listening. Got something on your mind, or should I say *someone*?"

"No."

"I say yes."

I glower. "I'm not ready."

A hand reaches over to comfort. "It was a lot to take in."

And Ace . . . *Grenier? Rogers?* Damn, she has a kid. "Did you know she had a kid?"

Mom sits up properly in her seat as if she's just taken the stand. "I did. I'm sorry, but you told me not to say anything about her."

My betrayed heart speaks for me, "A kid kind of overrules that, don't you think?"

"Don't be mad, Derrick—"

"I'm not mad at you. I just . . . I don't know." I deserved to know that she started a family with that asshole. But I'm not sure it's the anger that I was betrayed by her, lied to by my mother, or the jealousy that she has a family with another man that gets me more upset. "Deep down I thought maybe we'd find a way back."

"You still can. She has a child. She's not married."

"Why isn't she married to Rogers? That's Reggie's kid, right?" Some friend he was. *Fucker.* Moved right in the second I moved out. They wasted no time. I don't fully blame him for it. I knew he always had a boner for my girl. I guess screwing him over gave him the right to screw me over. She fell for it. She didn't have to go there, but she did anyway and it felt like everything we had been through together, everything we were to each other meant nothing. *She'd told me she loved me.* The timeline is obvious. Did they even wait a day? Fuck me. The years apart were a waste of regret, making me regret every time I ever thought of her and for coming back.

When my mom doesn't respond, I check on her. "What's up?"

"You don't want to hear it."

"One minute you're going on about pie, the next I'm having to drag information out of you. I want to know. Tell me. What's on your mind?" I turn down her street.

"He's a cute kid."

He is, kind of ridiculously so and I'm not a kid guy. He's also cool for a five-year-old. The kind I could probably tell a secret to and he wouldn't tell anyone. None of this surprises me though. Jaymes is his mom.

Jaymes.

Damn.

Just as I pull up to the gate of her complex, she says, "She's had a hard time, Derrick. I know you're upset and hurt right now. It was a lot to take in, which is why I thought it better for you to experience it more than just hear things and let your mind wander. She's a good mother who is working so hard to give not just Ace a better life, but her mom."

I pull into a spot in front of her townhome and park. "Mom—"

"No, I want you to listen to me. You're caught in your emotions. I get it. I do, but you need to cut her some slack." The car door opens and she gets out. When I get out, I glance her way over the roof. "She's not married to him. She's single. I think you should know that, but from my perspective, it wasn't easy for me either. You know I loved you two together. Maybe your soul mate is still out there, or maybe she's right where you left her. I don't know, Derrick. I know I look at that little boy and think of you. You were such a sweet and innocent kid before . . ." She doesn't have to say more than that. You either survive this part of the city or it destroys you. There is no in-between. "I look at them both and think of what could have been. How he could be my grandson."

Dropping my head down on my arm, I lean against the car. When I lift up, I try to hide the anger. What is usually an emptiness inside me fills with rage. I love her, but I can't be buried by what she needs when I'm barely holding on these days. "I can't do this. I can't live with both my regrets and your disappointments."

"I'm not disappointed, son. I'm so proud of you. Look at what you've accomplished. You've made something from nothing. You did that." She walks to the sidewalk and waits for me. When I hand her the keys, she adds, "You have both changed. I'm not saying you should give it a second chance, but I'm not saying you shouldn't either." I roll my eyes, but give in and give her the smile she's earned for all her efforts. I receive a poke in the stomach in return. "Are you staying or going?"

She's given me a lot to think about. Jaymes even more. "I should get going."

"Thank you for driving me. I know Nita was so happy to see you again." I walk her to her door. With her key in the lock, and her back to me, she says, "I'll text you the details for Sunday."

"What's Sunday?"

"The brunch." She steps inside. "Love you," comes rushing out of her mouth as the door starts to close.

My hand slams against the wood of the door stopping it from closing. She peeks out the crack all wide-eyed and innocent. "Nice try, Mom."

"What?" She shrugs, willing to keep the act going.

"Brunch with Jaymes."

"Oh, yes, she'll be there, but you can come with me."

"I know what you're doing."

She opens the door back up and puts her hand on her hip. "What am I doing?"

"Jaymes is off limits. She has a life. You said it yourself. She made that very clear to me too. She's got no time for any of the bullshit that distracts her from her kid." I roll my eyes, knowing the romantic soul that is my mother.

"I want you to be happy. Why do you think it can't be with Jamie?"

"She made it clear she didn't want to see me again."

"She told you that?" she asks, suspiciously.

"She didn't have to. She has a life now, one without me and doesn't need me intruding on her life."

A self-satisfied smile appears. "If she didn't say it, you shouldn't assume it." The door starts to close again, but she stops to say, "You're leaving on the tour again soon, so you're coming to brunch and I'm not hearing otherwise. Be safe on your drive home."

This time I let the door close. I don't know what's worse—an encounter with your ex-girlfriend that knocks your life out of its regular rotation or a mother determined to nag you to death over said girlfriend. I mean ex-girlfriend. Either way, I know I'm not getting out of brunch on Sunday, and I'm not so sure I want to.

Jaymes Anne-Marie Grenier.

She once told me her mother named her Anne-Marie to go with

the traditional French last name she acquired once she married Jimmy Grenier, James. He moved her here once they got married and promptly left her when she became pregnant. Upon hearing of Nita going into labor, he sobered up enough to make an appearance just as his daughter was born into the world. Nita saw the man she fell in love with that night as he made promises to take care of them. With tears in his eyes, he apologized for leaving her and said he'd never make that mistake again.

To honor her husband's commitment to their family she signed the birth certificate—Jaymes Anne-Marie Grenier—after her husband.

They made it a month before his gambling and alcohol addiction kicked back in and they ran out of money. He was gone the next day, leaving Nita with no savings and a newborn to raise on her own. Jaymes said she only saw her mother cry once when it came to her father. I never told her I saw her cry too, or that I had also met her father.

Jaymes was scheduled to close the sandwich shop that night, but needed to study for a biology test the next day. She had forgotten her book at home because she'd been running late. I went by her house to grab it so I could bring it up to her. Her house was like my second home. I had a key and all. So when I was about to leave, and saw a man walking up the path, I didn't think much of it. He did.

He wailed into me about this being his wife's house and asked if I was fucking her. I was seventeen at the time. It was as if he wasn't even aware that he had a daughter a few months younger than me. I was not as big as I am now, but I was growing. I'd already been hazed into Reggie's gang, got the tat and all to prove it, so he didn't scare me. But he did cross a line. Especially when he spit on me.

With poor timing, Nita came outside, and defended me. I didn't need her to. I don't even know why she did other than maybe it was her mama bear protective instincts kicking in. When he shoved her to the ground, I beat him to damn near death.

Sometimes I think about him, and wonder what happened. Is he dead or alive? I didn't kill him. He walked away that day, but he never came back either. He wasn't a man bent on changing his ways, so he was smart enough to stay gone for good.

Sometimes I think about Nita, and wonder why she never told Jaymes what happened. Was she protecting Jaymes or me? I'm not sure. I never thought it right to question her decisions when it came to how she ran her family. I wouldn't want my family questioned. Things are the way they are now because choices were made along the way that set things in motion. Good or bad, things were set in motion that day. A pact was made with her mom. I vowed I would always protect Nita and Jaymes.

Yet, I drove away, leaving both of them a year later.

Another promise I didn't deliver on.

Sometimes I think about Jaymes, and wonder how she looked at me like I made the sun shine just for her. When I brought the book to her that night, she sat next to me and smiled like she didn't have the shittiest misfortune to have James Grenier as a father and a mom who was fighting a battle her daughter never knew about. As I stretched and fisted my fingers under the table, she never saw the pain I was in or how sad I felt for her. She never saw because when I looked into her green eyes, I did what her mother did. I put on a smile and gave her enough love to make her feel whole, to keep that smile on her face, and to give her hope. She may share a name with that fucker, but she would never suffer again because of him, or any other man.

Except me.

"Fuck, Derrick. Get your shit together." Tommy's voice floods my internal thoughts. Tilting my head up, Tommy is flipping me off from the sound booth.

Kaz kicks a leg on the stool where I'm propped with my guitar. "You need a break, or what?"

"No, I'm good."

Johnny doesn't look convinced when I catch of glimpse of his reflection in the glass, but he lets it slide. "That was too fucked up to fix. Let's go from the top."

This time I don't think about James or Nita. I push away all thoughts of Jaymes and Ace, and play the damn song perfectly. This is my life. My future. My focus. *This.*

It's not until I leave the studio that night that I realize how much I've hidden behind the bright lights of stardom. Yes, The Resistance is my life, my future. But in my heart of hearts, I know it's Jaymes I've been thinking about for all these years. *The biggest regret. The most important dream I've yet to fulfill.*

I slip into the custom leather seat of my refurbed 1972 Gran Torino Sport and wait for my Bluetooth to connect.

"Well to what do I owe the pleasure?" My mom sounds chipper.

"I'll come to brunch on Sunday." I hear her giggles of excitement and shake my head. "Happy?"

"Very," she says. "It will be fun."

"Yeah, guess we'll see."

10

JAYMES

I WALK into the kitchen and my mom's mouth falls open. Holding my finger up, I think I catch her in time. "Don't say a word." Her mouth closes and swerves into a smile, so I call her out, "I can see right through you."

"And yet, you still came."

Shrugging, I reapply my gloss. "Call me curious."

"Curious."

Ace skips through the kitchen and out the other door. I don't think I've ever welcomed an interruption so much. "We should go or we'll be late. You know how bad traffic gets with the Sunday brunch crowd."

"Californians brunch like it's their business." She grabs her purse just as Ace runs by. "Go potty and we're leaving."

In the car, my mom tells me how she picked a small restaurant that was out of the way to avoid paparazzi. That is something I never thought would be a concern, but here we are at a quaint café.

"I'll pay for valet, Jamie."

"No, don't waste your money. I'll drop you guys off and park down the street. It's fine." I pull to the curb and they get out. I can't stop from doing a quick scan for any sign of Derrick or Diane. The place looks fancy though. As soon as I find a spot two blocks down and around the corner, I apply my gloss one more time. I think it's a nervous tic I'm developing because of a certain hot ex-boyfriend. I grab my bag and head back to the restaurant. I start to get nervous as I approach the little café, tugging at the hem of my shirt. My flats are scuffed at the toe and my jeans are old, but they fit. I drag a large section of my hair around to the front of my shoulder and play with the ends nervously. I reach the door just as it opens. Derrick is there and smiles. "Hi."

"Hi."

He holds his phone up and says, "I've got to take this. I'll be right back."

The door is open wide so I move around him, but my arm brushes against his middle. I just keep walking hoping he didn't mind the bonus of my bony elbow to his abs. "Sorry."

"It's okay. They're out back." The phone is to his ear and he walks outside and down the sidewalk.

I survived. In the courtyard out back, I sit in one of the two open seats that are conveniently together at one end of the table. The moms dote on Ace as he scribbles on the kids' menu. Diane looks my way and says, "You always had such pretty hair, Jamie."

Looking down, I grab at it again. "It's a mess," I lie. I spent over an hour styling it and putting it up only to let it come down at the last minute.

I'm alerted to his presence just from his proximity, the heat of his body warming my whole soul. "It always looked lovely any way she wore it, but particularly down and loose around her shoulders."

Lovely. He just said my hair is lovely. I look up as he sits down next to me and my cheeks actually heat. "Thank you . . . Diane." I turn my attention to her, but she's pretending to be engrossed in Ace's art. When I look into the eyes that once only shined for me, I reply, "Thank you. That is very sweet of you to say."

"I struggled picking my favorite way you wear your hair. You had it up on your head in a rubber band the other day and that looked good too."

Resting my chin on my hand, I lean in. "Was this a difficult struggle, thinking about how I wear it? One that kept you up nights or just a passing fancy?"

"Up all night thinking about you."

Our eyes lock, and I'm unaware of the magic that must be happening to have me here. I'm surely in fantasyland in my best blouse sitting next to a world-famous musician who's insisting on complimenting me as if I can live up to the celebrities he's used to dating. I sit up and take my napkin, the perfect distraction, and place it across my lap. "What are you doing, Derrick?"

"I'm drinking coffee and making small talk."

"Your small talk feels awfully large in the scheme of things."

"I don't need to lie to you and I don't want to hide behind some charade like we're supposed to be on a blind date or something. That's not us." He stops and says, "Look at me, Jaymes." When I do, he lowers his voice and whispers, "I would really like to spend some time with you alone and catch up, instead of brunch under the watchful eye of our moms."

The moms are up and scooping Ace from his seat. The crayons roll off the table and flustered, Diane says, "We forgot our . . . our . . . um—"

"Bicycles," my mom shouts.

Diane nods. "Yes, our um bicycles?" Turning to Nita, she asks, "Right?"

Ace looks between them. "What are umbicycles? Can I have one?"

"Yes, let's go get you one. You two stay and talk. We'll be back in a few minutes."

Derrick and I watch them weave through the tables like they've actually got somewhere better to go. When I turn to the man who once owned my heart, I sigh. "That was subtle."

"Not at all."

"Nope. Not at all."

Picking up where he left off, he says, "I don't even know if you want to talk to me, but I would love a second chance."

"Dating?" I ask, stunned.

"No, talking. Well, um . . . what?"

He takes a large gulp of water and I cut him some slack. "Sorry. I don't know why my mind went there. You meant a chance to talk. We can do that. We're here. Apparently alone. What do you want to talk about?"

"Should we start with Ace?"

Tension fills my shoulders as my defenses go up. I twist the napkin in my lap and look down at the splintering wood of the table. "Sure." I hate how meek I sound, but when it comes to my son, I shouldn't have to explain anything to anyone.

"He's great, Jaymes."

Surprised, I look back up. "What?"

"He's a great kid. I haven't been around either of you much, but I can tell what a great mom you are just by the little time I've spent with him."

My smile grows. "Thank you. That means a lot to me."

Taking my hand, another surprise on his part, he says, "I'm not going to pretend I know what's gone on in your life, but I'd like to know. Even more so, I'd like to know what's happening in your life now."

"What do you want to know?"

"I want to know if anyone's going to be upset about you having brunch with me."

Reggie. My heart quickens like any other time I think of him. Fear does that to you. I'm not sure it will ever change. Not until I know Ace and I are safe from him forever. I pull my hand back slowly despite how much I like Derrick holding it. "I can't answer that. I'm sorry." This time I don't look away.

His disappointment is seen and he lowers his hands to his lap. "That seems like an odd question to dodge."

"I'm not dodging. I just can't give you the answer you want to hear."

"So you're seeing someone?" He's annoyingly handsome even when his brow furrows.

Despite his good looks, I have to look deeper because of the complicated situation I'm in. "Please, Derrick. Let's not do this. It's too—"

"Too what? Soon? Invasive? Close for comfort? Backstabbing?"

"Backstabbing? What? No. Me?"

"Yeah." He moves away from me by leaning back in his chair. His gaze casts down and his arms cross over his chest. He looks genuinely hurt.

By me? "You left, not me."

"Why didn't you, Jaymes? Tell me. You've got to tell me why you chose Reggie over me."

I'm standing, my bag in hand before he even finishes that question. Staring at him, I search his face for the guy I once knew. Instead I'm met with a man I don't recognize. I swing my bag over my shoulder and leave. Searching the inside for the moms and Ace, I don't find them, so I push through the door and walk out to the sidewalk. I look both directions with no luck.

I reach for my phone in my bag when Derrick comes barreling out of the café. "No. You don't get to walk away like that."

"You can't stop me like I'm one of your roadies."

His head goes back. "What are you talking about? First off, I don't control the roadies. They're there to do a job. Secondly, why are you talking to me like you don't know me?"

"Because I don't. I don't know you anymore. As much as I thought I should come today, I see I made a big mistake."

"Why?"

The moms and Ace come around the corner, but as soon as they see us they scurry back, disappearing again. Turning my attention back to Derrick, I take a breath. "Look," I start, then readjust the bag on my shoulder. Ace's books are starting to weigh me down. Or maybe it's my emotions. Either way, I'm ready to go. "This was a fun little attempt by our moms. I don't know why they thought this was a good idea, but it clearly wasn't. I'm in no position to offer you anything more than friendship—"

"I'll take it."

"I was going to say we used to be friends but now we're better off acquaintances. You don't want that."

"I want anything I can get with you."

Without realizing it, our voices have gone from strong-willed to barely above a whisper, our proximity closer, almost touching. "It's not just me not knowing you anymore. You don't know me either." Looking down the street, I say, "So much has changed. I've changed. I'm not the same girl you once knew."

He takes my hand in his, his fingers lightly manipulating mine as if I were strings on his guitar. My chin is touched, so delicately, but with enough pressure to turn me his way. Our eyes meet, and he whispers, "Then let me get to know the woman you are now."

"Why are you so insistent on this? You're as bad as the moms."

"If I tell you that you're more beautiful now than ever would it kill any chance we have of reconnecting? Or that when I look at you, my heart hurts just enough to remind me I'm still alive? What about that when I play certain songs I still think of you? What if I told you those things, opening myself up in a way that I never do? Will you walk away or will you stay?"

There's no logical reason for me to stay. Ace. Reggie. My job. School. My life. I can't fit another thing in without sacrificing more of myself, but here he is more open than he ever was when we were together. His heart is open and his words are an elixir, tasting sweeter the second time. I'm in dangerous territory that could cost me more than my heart. It could cost me Ace. "I'm sorry. So sorry."

I walk away. Inside, I am running. I can't lose Ace. *I won't lose the most precious gift I have.*

I hate myself for doing it, for hurting Derrick, but it's not just him I worry about anymore. Despite my desperate need to look back, to go back, to run into his arms and find the comfort I once felt in his arms, I can't. I can't think about anything but protecting my son. *Just keep walking. Don't look back. Just go.*

"Wait."

Pulling my emotions under control, I gnaw on my bottom lip before turning around. My heart is pounding. I know I should have listened to myself seconds earlier. When I see him running toward me, my better senses fall away and I force my arms to stay at my sides instead of opening wide.

He says, "I forgot something."

"What?"

"You."

I'm about to ask what he means, but then I don't have to because his hands are on me, holding my face, and angling me up as he bends down. My heart pounds against my chest and this time I don't have the strength to deny him.

Or me.

11

JAYMES

With his lips pressed to the side of my mouth, he kisses me so sweetly that I almost pressure him for more. I ease into the feeling of us again, but then he whispers, "You. God, Jaymes, I missed you."

My heart is racing, my emotions rampant as the consequences of feeling something, feeling everything for this man again pulses through me. I push him back, and stumble out of his grasp to get away. With a good ten feet distance keeping him safely away, I shake my head. "No. You don't get to say that."

"I did. I said it, Jaymes. I'm sorry if that upsets you, but I've missed you."

"No." I start pacing, my hands going into my hair. "No. You can't do this."

"I'm doing it."

Stopping, I look at him confused. "I don't understand. It's been a long time, Derrick. Nothing about what you're saying makes any sense."

"That's because you're trying to make sense of how I feel. Sometimes we just feel and that should be enough. Like love."

"Oh no, no. You don't get to drag love into this. You drove off that day. Were you thinking of love then? Were you thinking of me? For years I've had to live with the sound of your tires as you drove away like you couldn't get out of there fast enough."

"You know why you remember the tires instead of me? Because you ran away. A lot like you're doing now."

"Accusations are easy to throw around—"

"Two-way street, baby."

"Mommy?"

When Derrick turns his body to look behind him, Ace is there, our moms keeping their distance. I bend down and put on a smile for my son. "Hey, buddy. You ready to go?"

"I'm hungry."

"I'll make you pancakes at home." Holding my hand out, he takes it. I glance to Derrick who looks as gutted as I feel. "Goodbye."

"Bye," he says, tucking his hands in his pockets. "See ya, Ace."

"See you, Big D."

Squeezing his hand, I quickly correct him, "No, we aren't going to call him that."

"Why not?"

Good Lord. I need to get out of here. "Just no, Ace. Call him by his name Derrick, or Mr. Masters. It's more respectful."

"Okay, Mommy. Why are we walking so fast?"

I tap his nose. "'Cuz Mommy's hungry, too." I doubt I'll be able to eat anything by the way my stomach's twisted in knots, but I need to, just like I need to leave Derrick Masters in the past. Just before I turn the corner, I sneak one peek back. Damn him. Why did he come today? What was his agenda? To try and pick up where we left off? *"I want anything I can get with you."* Why?

Why does he have to look so damn good when I'm a complete mess?

Or maybe he's a mess inside just like me, but wrapped up in one hell of an enticing package. Either way that man's off limits. Not only for me, but there's no way I can let Reggie find out or I'll have hell to pay.

I start the car and make sure Ace is buckled in. My mom comes around the corner and gets in. When the door shuts, her mouth opens, but I'm getting quicker, "Not now. Not in front of Ace."

"What not in front of me?" he asks, pouting in the back seat.

"Don't worry about it," my mom and I say in unison and then turn to each other.

I break first and start laughing. The reprieve needed. Exhaling loudly, I grip the steering wheel and then look back. "In-N-Out Burger?"

Ace's arms fly into the air. "Yay!"

Shifting the car into drive, I avoid looking at my mother. I feel her thoughts spanning across the console. I don't need to see her disappointment too. When Ace is happily distracted naming the color of every car that drives past us, I say, "The boat can't be rocked."

"He has too much control."

Reggie.

"I have no choice."

"You do. You're just choosing not to use the power you have."

Glancing into the rearview mirror, I see my son and his smile. I will do anything that protects the light that shines bright for his future. "He'll take him. I can't let that happen."

She reaches over and rubs my arm. "Maybe Derrick can help."

"It's complicated."

Resolved, she breathes out. "It always is."

"I'm not having this fight with you. There are things you don't know that I can't tell you."

"Can't or won't? I don't understand his hold on you. I know you don't love him."

"Enough." I shoot her a look that this conversation is over. I hate being curt with her, but I cannot do this again.

Ace pipes in, "Love who?"

"Whom." Catching a glimpse of him in the mirror again, I say, "Nothing, sweetie. The big question is—animal style?"

"Yes please," he replies joyously.

When Ace and I get home, I drop my bag by the door and hang my keys on the hook. I'm anxious. My skin crawls from the thought of the depths Reggie is willing to go to hurt Derrick. He never loved me. I'm just a pawn in his game of revenge. I deserve some of the blame. I knew what I was doing when I made that deal, but Ace and his innocence are now and forever caught in the middle. Kids weren't part of the bargain. Why Reggie still shows such interest when he never wanted to be a father is beyond my rationale. My nightmares are based on the reality of his words, his threats, to take my son away. To turn him into the prince he wants him to be. His legacy.

I will die before I let that happen. I'll do anything it takes to make sure Ace gets out like Derrick did.

THE SUN HAS SET and Ace is snug in his bed when the banging begins as if his ears were burning today. Ace runs into the living room and grabs hold of my leg. "Who is it, Mommy?"

"Go back to bed and don't come out for anything, okay?" I shuffle him back to his room as the banging continues matching my heartbeats. "Get in bed. Now."

"I'm scared."

Steadying my voice, I say, "Don't be, buddy. I'm not." I put on a fake smile and blow him a kiss. "I love you."

"Love you," he replies with the covers up to his nose. I shut the door and grab my phone. Texting my mom, I hit the agreed upon letter and send. Setting my phone on the coffee table I rush to answer the door, knowing he won't go away when he knows I'm home.

One lock clicks open and the banging stops. I remove the chain and turn the knob lock before opening the door. Raising my chin, I come face to face with true evil—dark hair, eyes so light that they're hard to see at night. Just pupils black as his soul shine in the dark, like now as he stands under the porch light. I whisper, "It's late. Ace is sleeping."

Reggie's hand flattens against the dented metal door and he pushes it open. "Aren't you gonna invite me in?" He's slurring and those black as death pupils are pinpoints. Drunk and high. My fear builds and my mouth opens to deepen my breaths. I don't want him to sense how scared I am. He gets off on it.

"It's late." I try my best to wrangle even a fake smile, but can't seem to manage.

"Where've ya been lately?"

"I'm always here."

A dirty nail tipped finger runs along my jaw. I start to turn but he grabs my face and yanks me back to look at him. "Don't you ever turn away from me."

My neck aches, but the pain is overridden by the sounds of Ace's door creaking open. No. No. No. Please, God. Let him go back to bed. "I'm looking at you, Reggie," I say as calm as I can. My hand covers his and slowly lowers it back down. "I'm looking right at you."

Leaning against the doorframe, a smarmy self-pleased grin injects itself on his face. Touching his lips, he licks his finger, and then reaches for me. "So pretty. One taste will never be enough."

Blood rushes in my ears as the horror of him "tasting" me comes back. I flinch, my eyes closed tight. One. Two. Three. Four. One. Two. Three. Four. I reopen my eyes to find his, too lazy to notice, giving me an opportunity. "Shayna is a very jealous woman, Reggie. You know she doesn't share."

"Might be interesting to see what you can do—"

"Ace needs me. You know that."

Pushing me, he walks in. "Where's my boy?"

I hurry around him, a barricade he'll have to destroy to get to my son.

"He's sleeping. Remember? It's late, Reggie." My hands are against his chest. "You should go home to Shayna."

Moving me back, he demands, "I want to see my son. What's he like three now?"

"Yes, something like that. He needs his sleep. You should go home."

He stops, his gaze piercing mine. Locked in a silent standoff, neither of us moves. I don't even breathe. I've got five minutes left to call my mom back before she calls the police. I can't let this escalate.

I'm about to distract him with another threat of his girlfriend, but his body goes slack and he starts laughing. "Fuck, woman. You're tougher than you look. I like that."

Just as I pretend to smile and play along, I'm grabbed by the back of my hair and brought in, my body slamming into his. I fight to silence my terror but it slips out in the form of a weak cry caught in my throat. I hate myself for not being stronger.

The smell of rotting flesh burns my nostrils as he holds me so close I feel his breath against my cheek. "Don't you ever fucking tell me what to do or I'll fucking take my son and leave your ass for fucking dead. Do you understand me?"

Tears well in my eyes. Another tight pull and I know he's pulled some out this time. My head is angled up when he pushes his mouth against my ear. "You were *his*. Now you're *mine*. Or did you forget?"

"I didn't forget."

Inhaling me, he closes his eyes as his grip on me loosens. "I give you my patience. No one else, but you receive my mercy on a regular basis. Why do I do it?"

Remaining quiet, I let him play out the fantasy in his head. He's not someone I can reason with in this state. And honestly, I don't know why he's spared me. Often, I think it's leading to something bigger. He's a showman, a lot like Derrick—probably the only thing they have in common. He's waiting for his big finale, but hopefully I'll be gone before he gets to it.

Taking a deep breath, he rubs the back of my head with his grimy hands as if that will soothe the ache of my scalp. "Rebel tried to fuck me over. Payback's a bitch. Right, Jamie?"

"Yes." That I can agree on.

"Our Rebel has lived up to his name. Wonder how we can get a cut of all that dough he's making." He walks away, but makes sure to watch my face when he asks, "You ever hear from him?"

For someone so out of touch with reality, he seems to be in the dead center of mine. "Nope."

"Oh man," he says with his hands covering his heart. "That's gotta hurt. He burned you good." Finally, he walks to the door, but turns back. "But don't worry, I'll take care of you. It's the least a friend can do for another friend. We're friends, right?"

"Yeah. Sure. Friends." Disgust fills my stomach that I am stuck dealing with this disgusting excuse for a human. Sometimes I wonder where he went wrong, what happened to fill him with the hate that he breeds now. Sure he was stabbed in the back by a friend, but that wouldn't lead to this. He was well on his way to who he is now long before Derrick left. How did he turn out so bad? What led this kid who once won a ribbon for his poetry into the gang leader he's become now? Life means nothing to him, except for his own. Yet he fills his with nothing but hate, killing himself slowly.

Does it make me a horrible person that I've prayed for him to overdose? Looking at him now, threatening my son and me like our lives mean nothing, I want him dead.

"If you hear from our famous friend, you let me know. One step back in my hood and his ass is capped. If he even comes within two miles of you or my son, everyone will die."

A wadded-up twenty-dollar bill hits me on the chest. "You remember who lets you go to school. It's me who lets you have a job. You have this place because I allow it." Then he says what he always says, "Don't ever lie to me and don't go gettin' crazy ideas in that pretty head of yours about skipping town. You know what I do to people who betray me?"

I do, so I nod. People go missing, or get shot, or hurt. He destroys lives. Coming back over, he pats me on the head. "Good. Make sure to buy my kid some fuckin' toys." He leaves, slamming the door behind him. I scramble to my feet, lock the door, and grab my phone to text my mom: *Okay. I'm okay.*

If she only knew the full truth. Shame works its way in and I start to cry.

She's quick to reply: *I love you.*

Through blurry, tear-filled eyes, I type: *I love you too. Night.*

I rub the back of my head, strands tangling between my fingers, a clump. I don't know how long I stand there with the phone and my hair in my hand. Pulling them close to my chest, I realize I don't have anyone I can call. With my back to the wall, I slide down slowly, still holding on to the phone like I'm holding on for dear life. Maybe I am.

When my ass hits the carpet, I look down. What is this life I'm leading? How many lives do I have left before he kills me, or worse . . . I can't even think it. I'll do anything for Ace. I will do *anything* to protect him. And against my better judgment, I'll continue to protect the man I once gave my heart to, even if he did leave it behind for lights brighter than the ones that once shined in my eyes just for him.

I wasn't enough to keep him here and there wasn't enough time for me to go with him.

But I told him to go and never look back.

What was I thinking going today and seeing him?

The touch of his lips to my lips.

That can't happen again. No. It's not worth the risk.

Derrick Masters needs to stay in the past. That's the only way I can make sure I stay on track with my plan. *I will take Ace out of this hellhole and get him away from that dangerous, vile monster.*

The only plan that matters—saving my son from being taken.

That connection I felt stretching across the table, the one that once had me head over heels for that man, needs to go away. Five minutes more and my heart would have been his all over again. That can't happen. Not ever.

Ace. My sweet son. How will Derrick look at him, or treat him when he will always know that he's Reggie's. And my mom. I need to make sure they're safe. Love can wait. My heart will have to bear the brunt of more time.

Destiny sure does have a screwed up sense of humor.

12

DERRICK

Twenty minutes. I was granted twenty minutes with Jaymes and not only did I completely blow it, but she was even more amazing than I remember. "If I start writing fucking happy-go-lucky love songs like some sixties musical sitcom, shoot me."

The expression on Kaz's face is one of horror and confusion. "I don't even know what you're talking about."

"Never mind. I forgot you're not from around here." Resting my arms behind my head, I add, "If it gets to that point, it's bad. That's all you need to know."

He leans back on the lounge chair of my deck and drops his sunglasses over his eyes. "You named a guitar after her. That was already crossing a line if you were trying to get her off your mind, don't you think?"

"There was no other name for it. That guitar was created in her likeness—sleek, black wood to match her hair. The inlays on the face of the fretboard match the unique green of her eyes. The strings are taut and I've never seen such a well-crafted guitar. Jaymes."

"I think you've already crossed it." He pulls his fingers into a gun and shoots me. I don't tell him that shit is dangerous even in jest. He knows almost everything about my past. He knows my history with gangs, but he never judged me. Kaz is a stand-up guy. He took me at face value instead of nosing around the baggage I was carrying. I've left a lot of it behind, but that guitar, like the girl—there's no getting over her.

"...one week. Lara's not happy."

The tour. Like the rest of us, he's been bitching about the time we'll be gone. We got our new schedules yesterday. Instead of two weeks on and two off, we're filling in the gap and adding shows to our sold-out tour. "One month on the road. How many shows is that?"

"Twenty."

Joking, I say, "They're going easy on us."

"We have a few days off I guess, but I've never felt older than I have in the last two years."

"That shit will age you, but I don't know. These days I prefer the stage. For a show built on dramatics and performance there's less drama there than in real life."

He looks my way. "Brunch didn't go well?"

The mocking tone can be heard in the way he says brunch. I would have been mocking him for that shit, so it's only fair to get it in return. "No. Not well at all."

Sitting up, his body angles in my direction. "You haven't talked about her in a long time and now she seems to be back in play. What gives?"

I keep my shades over my eyes to hide what I'm feeling inside. When I don't respond, he stands. "Since you're not going to tell me why you're suddenly thinking about your ex again, beer?"

"Nah, but help yourself. Grab me a Topo Chico while you're in there though."

"Fuck you and your imported water."

"Let me enjoy the perks that I have enough money to splurge on mineral water." Flipping him off, I laugh. "Thanks, brah."

He laughs in response and goes inside.

My phone chirps with a text. Mom comes on the screen. Usually I'd be annoyed by all the extra texts I've been getting lately, but I'm not. Not when they involve a raven-haired beauty. I read what she's sent: *You didn't want to talk about what happened yesterday, but I'm here if you ever need me.*

I respond: *I know. Thanks.*

Mom: *Nita said Jamie was in a foul mood.*

Foul mood? Fascinating, and I need more information on this bad mood. Speed dialing my mom the next second, her phone rings. "Hello, son, how are you?"

"Tell me about the mood."

"I thought you might find that interesting."

Jaymes is never . . . I should say *was never* in a foul mood unless she was really bothered by something. She should have been pissed off at me more than she ever was, so to hear she was bothered yesterday, kind of inserts a little hope in my day.

"What happened? I know she told you, so spill it."

"She said you would have thought your name was Satan's himself." There goes that hope. She continues, "But I guess she mumbled something about not just how handsome you are, which you are—"

"Okay, Mom, just say it."

"Nita said she was drinking a strawberry shake and cursing some connection that has never gone away. And that seeing you has stirred up a whole slew of emotions that she doesn't have time for." Did my mom just giggle? "I think you should ask her out."

My lips curve up. She always did like anything strawberry. "Wait, what? No. She told me no." *Did she mean yes?*

"Derrick, listen to me. I didn't think I had to tell you about women. I mean, you seemed to know quite a bit too soon for your age, but Jamie Grenier is showing all the signs."

"Signs of what? That she hates me?"

"She doesn't hate you. Quite the opposite according to Nita."

Although I like that apparently Jaymes is thinking about me and might not hate me, I shouldn't encourage this route to her heart. "Mom, you and Nita are trouble together. Stop the matchmaking. It's not going to happen."

"We're not matchmaking. We're simply pointing out the obvious."

"No," I say, standing and walking to the edge of the deck. Staring out over LA, I run my hand through my hair. "You're so busy hoping for this to happen that you haven't heard what she's saying. Well, I did. It wasn't pleasant, neither was her reaction to me. That's not usually a good sign."

"It's because she likes you. Still."

"God, Mom. Listen, we're not ten and hitting each other on the playground because secretly we like each other. She has a kid, a kid who comes before me or any other guy. That's her priority and I don't blame her. I commend her for it."

"I do too, honey, but—"

"No buts. Not this time. You gave it a valiant effort, but I can't see Jaymes again unless it's on her terms." The silence on the other end of the phone starts to worry me. "Mom, you there?"

"I am. I'm just thinking about what you're saying."

"Good." Kaz comes out of the house with my water and his beer. "I've got to go. Kaz is hanging out."

"We'll talk later."

We'll talk about Jaymes some more and run this topic into the ground is what she really means. "Fine. Later, Mom."

"Bye, Mrs. Masters," Kaz yells just before I disconnect.

"Back off my mom."

An eyebrow lifts, along with a half smile. "She was a young mom. I hear the roadies talking about her."

"Fuck me, no. Just no on this."

"She's what? Forty-five?"

"Fuck you. She's my mom. And she's older than that."

He laughs. "What, forty-seven?"

"Maybe. Now shut up about it and if you ever hear anyone talking about my mom other than her being my mom, tell me so I can kick their ass."

Reclining back on the lounge chair, he goes on as if this is the funniest shit he's ever thought about, "Whoa. You said your ex has a son who's five. Damn, brah. Crazy thought, but what if you were his father. The cycle would have continued. You would have been a dad at like eighteen or something. Can you imagine that?"

Yeah, imagine that. "Drink your beer and let's play some music. I'm tired of talking." I don't know if it's sad or crazy, but I can imagine it. Ace is a good kid. As for Jaymes . . . fuck, she was right. I felt it too. That damn years-old "thing" that was always there is still intact like it had never gone away.

I park and get out, but then get back in the car. "What the fuck am I doing?" Knocking my head against the steering wheel a few times, I hope to knock some sense into myself. I can have any girl. Shit, I've got a phone full of numbers and texts full of tits. I can have anyone.

But I'm sitting outside a used-car dealership with sandwiches from the same place where she once worked in one hand and a melting strawberry shake in the other. "What the fuck am I doing?" Just go, I force myself out of the car.

Stop thinking. Just go.

A guy in a tie, which means I already don't trust him, fast approaches. "Good day, sir." He eyes the food in my hands. "Are you stopping by shopping for a car on your lunch break?"

My pace never slows as I head for the door. "No. Is Jaymes here?"

He hurries next to me and opens the door. "We don't have a James here."

Shit. "Jamie. Jamie Grenier?"

"Oh. Yes," he replies with a *too happy to be thinking about my girl* grin. Narrowing my eyes at this guy, I cross my arms to intimidate. He better not be thinking about my girl, or worse, have his eyes on her. I remind myself that she's not mine. Yet. So I attempt to tamp down the emotions that rhyme with hellousy. The ones I have no right to be having much less acting on. I take a deep breath and walk inside. I recognize Leah from Nita's house. She stands, her mouth open. Her eyes wide. I can see her tapping the desk next to her. My gaze shifts right and there she is—*my girl.* I keep going until I'm right in front of them. Jaymes has her back to me as she types away on the ancient desktop computer anchored on her desk.

I smile at Leah and she stutters, "Ja-Ja-mie."

"Hold on," Jaymes replies making me smile even wider.

"No," Leah says, "You need to see this."

In pure annoyance she swivels around in her chair. "What?"

When her eyes land on me, her mouth hangs open, and I say, "Hi."

She's standing. Straight up. Her palms run down the front of her gray skirt. I've never seen her dress like a "professional" but she makes that skirt look damn sexy. "What are you doing here?"

Holding the food out for her, I say, "I thought you might be hungry." Her mouth opens. Her sweet pink lips part and I'm tempted to toss the food and devour her instead. When she doesn't seem to find any words, I stretch my arms toward her. "I brought sandwiches."

"From Ernie's?"

"Yeah."

"We should go to the back for more privacy." She scoots around her desk, glances at Leah, and has completely managed to avoid any eye contact with me. Her skills are impressive. She's honed them over the years. I follow her to the back break room that has no window, a large vending machine with dusty candy bars, and smells of rotten cheese, or a guy's locker room. Kind of the same smell.

"What are you doing here, Derrick?"

"Like I said, I brought food."

Her hands go to her hips. "No, for real." She finally looks directly into my eyes. "Why are you here?"

"We didn't get a chance to break bread the other day. I wanted a second chance."

"You keep talking about second chances like I'll change my mind."

I set the food on the table and sit down in the metal chair. "Why are you so adamant about hating me? Can't we lower our weapons and just eat a sandwich together?"

"Hating you? Is that what you think?" Her voice raises like her anger by looking at the red flooding her cheeks. "You think I hate you?"

"Sure feels like it."

"Then why would you come around? Why would you bring food for someone you think hates you?"

"To make amends."

Her fingers entwine behind her head and she takes a deep breath as if to calm herself. When she opens her eyes, she says, "No amends need to be made." She maneuvers around the table, heading for the door, but I catch her by the wrist.

Her breath catches and it's quick, but I also see the terror that crosses her face. My hands are off her and I'm standing. "I'm sorry."

Her eyes snap back to me, but she seems to be focused on her breathing. In the quiet of the room, both of us stand there motionless, but I hear the faintest, "... three. Four," from her.

Holy shit. What the fuck? "Are you counting?"

"I um," she says, shifting back, away from me. "It's just something I do. Sorry."

"Why are you sorry?"

"You looked worried. I'm sorry for worrying you."

"What?" I move closer, but her back hits the wall, causing me to freeze to the spot. "Are you afraid of me? Did I scare you?"

"No," she whispers, looking at the door ready to escape. "You should go. Thank you for the food, but I don't have a break today."

I stare at her. Where's the feisty girl I once knew? Where's the fierce woman from Sunday? "What the fuck is going on here, Jaymes?"

The salesman from earlier comes to the door and peeks in. "Everything okay in here?"

When's it more than apparent that she's not going to say anything after a few seconds that feel like a time bomb's about to go off if she answers, I reply, "Fine. I should get going."

I move past him and walk through the car showroom. Pushing the door open, the sun is blinding, so I pull my sunglasses from the neck of my shirt and slip them on. They don't just shield the sun, but they're damn good at hiding the emotions I'm struggling to hide.

Angry.

Confused.

Defeated.

Hungry.

Hurt.

Concern.

Fuck.

Just seeing her—I feel everything all at once. Is there a name for that fucked-up emotion?

Yes. It's Jaymes Grenier.

13

JAYMES

MY HEART SINKS. I close my eyes and mentally beat myself up. How can I let him leave when he came here so sweetly searching for me? Damn it. I open my eyes and see Jose staring back at me. "You okay?" he asks.

He's not nearly as interesting to look at as Derrick. "I am. I'm good. Really good."

Jose shrugs. "Cool."

I run past him, through the showroom, and around a Hyundai. Shoving the entrance door open I run out into the daylight. Derrick is getting in his car when I shout, "Hey!"

When he looks my way I suddenly feel like one of those girls on the tarmac when The Beatles came to America for the first time. Another fan vying for the great musician's attention. My arms lower . . . ah, screw it. I run to him, wishing I were in sneakers instead of these high heels. Coming to a stop right in front of him, he stands still, door still open, sunglasses covering his eyes, hair lightened by the sun, and just enough stubble to make me wonder if he shaved for me today. "Hey," he says.

But I'm still caught up wondering if he was always this gloriously handsome. "You're tall."

"You're kind of short." He looks down, but takes his time working that gaze back up. "Even in those shoes."

"There are two sandwiches."

"Thought you might be hungry."

I can't stop my smile listening to him try to act like what he did was no big deal at all. "That's a lot of food. Maybe you might stay and eat one with me? And was that strawberry shake for me?"

Although he fills out the rock-star status nicely, I see the boy I once loved so easily when his shoulders shift down and he relaxes. "Yeah."

"Come back with me. Please?" I hold out my hand, needing to give him those few minutes he asked for. I owe him that. I owe him more, but I start with this peace offering, "I'm sorry."

The twitch in his neck isn't exaggerated, but I see it. I know him. I know this man before me, like no other. He always hated apologies, even more so when they were mine . . .

The pads of his thumbs wipe away my tears. His lips caress my cheek, and then he whispers, "Lovers. Soul mates. Friends. Those three words come with three others—trust, love, and forgiveness. They're not given. They already exist between us, baby."

Looking up into his indigo eyes I get lost in my love for him. It's deeper than the ocean and vaster than the universe, but it keeps me here, gravitationally pulled to him. I don't know when it happened or why we fell like we did, but I cling to it, to him. "I don't deserve you."

He chuckles. "You're right. You deserve better."

"Don't say that." I run my hands over his chest, underneath the leather jacket and around his middle until I'm fully pressed to him with my ear over his heart. The beat is strong like his arms around me.

"It's true, but guess what?"

"What?" I tilt my head up and wait.

"You're kind of stuck with me."

The smile on my lips feels good, like him. "Why do you love me, Derrick?"

Reaching down, he grabs my ass. "Because you're hot."

I giggle. "That's it? You like the way I look?"

He leans against the side of his truck and crosses his legs at the ankle. Scanning me down and then back up, he runs his thumb over his bottom lip. When he finally speaks, he says, "It's a nice package, but it's your heart I'm after."

"Such a charmer."

"Maybe that will be my next tattoo."

The glare is instant. "I can't believe you did that."

"It was inevitable."

"I know," I reply, the disappointment engulfed by the sadness I feel for our situation. "We're never getting out, are we?"

Taking my hands, he parts his feet and pulls me close. The warmth of his hands cradles my face. "I promise I'll get us out of here and I'll always take care you." The heavy breath tasting of peppermint fills my mouth as he kisses me. He's always so gentle, but not now. Desperation fills our kiss, but we part, panting and searching each other's eyes. "If anything ever happens to me—"

"Stop saying stuff like that. We'll leave before it gets worse."

Worse. He'll be killed and where will that leave me? A body without a soul? "You're marked for life, branded to them."

"Branded to me. It's only a tattoo."

"It's across your whole back."

"Good. We won't have to look at it much." Rubbing my arms, he asks, "What was your plan anyway?"

"I wanted to stop them. I wanted you to stay you."

Taking my hand to his lips, he kisses it and brings me back to him. "I'm me. As long as I'm with you, I'm me. No tattoo is gonna change that unless you hate Rebel."

"I don't hate Rebel. I hate what the nickname represents. I love you."

The questions are seen in his eyes when he asks, "You'd leave with me, right?"

"Any day. Anything to leave this hell behind."

"What if we never make it to heaven?"

"We'll always have each other."

"I love you, Jaymes."

Though the air is heavy with our circumstance, I manage to smile. "Why do you always call me Jaymes?"

"Because everyone else calls you Jamie."

"But I'll always be your baby." I spin away from him.

"That you will." I'm promptly pulled back in, dipped, and kissed like in the movies. Deep. Real. Raw. Passion. Love. Forever. He says it all without saying a word.

. . . He asks, "What are you sorry for?"

"Brunch and how abruptly it ended." Looking down, I whisper, "Us and how abruptly we ended."

"So, you do have a lunch break?

Glancing over my shoulder, I see David leaving out the side door. He'll be gone to lunch at least an hour if not more. "No, but I'm taking one anyway." My eyes meet his again.

"Look, we don't have to dwell on the past, not right now. How about we just enjoy your lunch break?"

"I'd like that." As we walk back in, I don't tell him I don't have an official lunch break today because I have to leave early for class. I also don't tell him that I've missed him so much that my heart still aches for him. Or that when I dream, I dream of him holding me again. We sit across from each other and I do tell him what I should have told him years earlier. "I'm sorry for embarrassing you in front of the guys when you got the Rebel tattoo."

"Why did you cry?"

"I think I was crying for our lost youth. Sounds silly to say that at twenty-three, but I feel much older than my years these days. Anyway, at the time, I thought I lost you to Reggie and the . . . guys."

"Call it what it is—a gang. But to be clear on one thing, you never lost me, Jaymes. I was across town, not across the country. I should've checked on you. I should have done more, but I was hurt. That's silly, not that you mourned for youth. I get it. I sucked it up that day because I had to. There was no more stalling and I wasn't ready to leave you. At eighteen, I knew you wouldn't come."

"I couldn't. I wish I would have though."

"You're doing so good, Jaymes. You really are. You don't have much school left either. You'll have a degree, something I never got. My smart girl. Always so damn smart."

Hearing him call me his girl is like an arrow to my heart. I take a deep breath, inhaling his words deep into my soul where only he's allowed to visit.

"You're making me blush, Derrick."

"I like you blushing. If you're blushing, you've lowered those walls that you carry like a fortress around you."

"I know you so well, but sometimes I forget that someone out there knows me just as well." Leaning in, I whisper, "Don't tell anyone I let you in or they'll all want in." I laugh.

"Your secret's safe with me."

"Can I ask you something?"

"You just did."

"Ha!"

"Ask away."

"You're not seeing anyone, are you?"

"No."

"Is that why you started coming around?"

"No." A playful smirk appears.

I take a sip of the shake when he seems to be intent on keeping his secret. "This is delish. Thank you."

"You're welcome."

"Are you going to eat?"

Unwrapping the sandwich, he laughs. "Sure." It's a carefree laugh, and one I remember from years ago. He was always easy to be with, and if the tension weren't here because of our past, or he wasn't a rock star and loved by the world, I know I'd feel just as comfortable now.

But things have changed.

Reggie.

His threat from last night comes racing back. Derrick takes his first bite, and I say what I have to say, "It's been good seeing you again—"

"It's been good seeing you again, too."

"Please. Stop being so nice."

That makes him gut chuckle. "Now I'm too nice? That might be a first, Jaymes."

"No," I say, sighing. "Just let me get this out."

His sandwich is discarded and I get his full attention. "It's good to see you again, but I can't keep seeing you."

"You said that the other day. Something about no time for any relationships."

"Unfortunately, that's where I am in life. I'm sorry. I don't mean to hurt you."

"I think that's like your fourth sorry in less than fifteen minutes."

Setting my sandwich down, I say, "I am though. So sorry for so many things."

"I don't want you to be sorry. I want to know what's going on."

"Life, Derrick."

"Life? Like I'm not living one?"

"You're living a big one and I'm just trying to survive while raising my son."

"It's not bigger than yours. You're a mother. God, Jaymes. You're a mother. That's amazing. *You* are amazing."

I turn away from him. His pride feels unwarranted. I've failed in so many ways. If only I could change the past. "I'm not. I'm barely getting by." My life feels so little compared to his.

"Don't believe the lies in your head. What you're doing, raising Ace, is the most important job ever."

Peeking back up at the attractive, passionate man across from me, I say, "It's not glamorous like yours."

"I can't lie. I love performing live. The energy. The excitement."

"You were born to be on that stage."

"You always believed in me, even when I didn't. I just want you to know that all the success you see, it's yin and yang. Life balances itself. With the good, you get the bad. I like recording in the studio. I dig the travel. But it's wearing me down. It's hard sometimes . . . or maybe it's just lonely."

"Why are you lonely? You're surrounded by thousands of people who adore you every day."

"But I'm only looking for one." He pauses and I think it's the first time I see him a little unsteady. I know I am from the turn this conversation has taken. He fills the seconds, breaking my heart a little more by saying, "Despite the house I own, I feel lost, homeless at times. My north star has moved and I can't seem to find it."

"You have a home—"

"No, I have a house." Leaning in, he glances to the door, then back to me. "I can't stop thinking about you."

I lean back, away from him. "You shouldn't think about me at all."

"I shouldn't?"

Standing up, I grab my sandwich, my appetite gone anyway, and toss it. "I have to get back to work."

"What are you doing?"

"I have to go before I get in trouble by my boss."

He meets me by the door, throwing his uneaten food away. "No. What. Are. You. Doing?"

I know what he means, but with last night's encounter too fresh in my mind, I know what I need to do. My heart be damned. "You've got to stop this. No more coming around. No more meet-ups with the moms." I look away from him, not wanting for him to see how hard this is for me. "No, nothing. Whatever this is between us can't turn into more." My eyes go wide and I point at his mouth. "No. No. Whatever you're thinking, stop. Whatever that smirky smirk thing you're doing, don't."

"What am I thinking?" His body presses to mine and my back hits the wall, knocking the light switch. The room is dark, but the light from the showroom reveals his every bad intention. Tempting my body, his lips entice when he leans down and whispers, "What am I doing?"

I know I shouldn't. Everything that matters is now at risk, but my soul misses him in ways that I can't let go. My fight weakens. I can almost remember the life I once shared with him. The beat of my heart quickens. "We shouldn't."

"We should."

"This is bad." My breath comes short.

"I'll make you feel so good." His counteroffer is so tempting.

My arms wrap around his neck. "Derrick?"

He takes me in his arms. "Jaymes?"

"One kiss and that's it."

"Or two or three," he replies, cutting a deal. His nose slides along the bridge of mine. "Then I'll go. I promise."

"Swear?"

Our lips come together and my body gives in, molding to his as if we were never apart. He speaks of performing on stage in the same way I feel about this kiss—the energy, the excitement. I was born to kiss this man and I wish I could spend my life doing it.

Large hands rub along my middle and soft moans escape him. I inhale him and his sweet sounds, loving this . . . *loving him* too much.

14

DERRICK

"Damn you and your seductive kisses," she says, pushing her hands against me to put distance between us. "We can't do this."

"We just did." Moving in again, I whisper, "Now let's do it again."

"No, Derrick."

But I see the smile that belies her words. She liked that kiss. I loved it. I lo—nope. Not going there. I steal another quick kiss and leave before she gets in trouble. The gasp is heard as I walk away. "Damn you," she whisper yells.

I can only imagine she's shaking her little fists me. Turning back, I have to see her. She was always incredibly sexy when she was mad. If she was mad at me that meant one thing—make-up sex. Fuck. She was a vixen in the sheets.

"You're impossible," she adds, full volume.

"See you around, babe."

I pass Leah, and cock a smirk with my nod. She says, "Byyye."

The salesman opens the door and says, "If you're ever in the market for a quality used car, Mr. Masters, let me know. My name's Jose."

"Thanks. I'll let you know."

My alarm chirps and I open the driver's door. Slipping into the sleek leather seat, I start the car, and back out before that ball of fucking sexy fire makes its way outside. I like her feisty. That means she won't give up. It also means I'll get another shot at wooing that woman. Yep, I said woo. Now that I know what I'm missing, I don't want to miss anymore. It's as if just from my lips touching hers, that I can forgive how quickly she was with Reggie. How quickly she *moved on*. How much I want her still.

This car dealership is a long way from the Hollywood Hills, but I don't even make it five minutes before I get a call. I don't recognize the number, but I'm glad I don't send it to voicemail once I hear Jayme's voice ring out through the speakers. "You're a bastard, you know that, Derrick?"

"I do. I also remember how much you loved it."

"Your rebel ways. You still got that tattoo?" She sounds mighty pleased with that zinger. Bringing up sore subjects is used like ammo for her defensiveness.

"Come over and find out."

She laughs, annoyance in every note. "Like I said, impossible."

"Let's make possible together."

"Do you ever give up?"

"You know me, right?"

"Right. Stupid me. I almost forgot who I was talking to."

"Speaking of me, come over."

A loud sigh punctuates the debate I know she's having, probably sitting at that messy desk of hers with the ancient computer sputtering shit she doesn't even care about in front of her. But the fun we were having seems to dissipate and her voice goes quieter, "I can't. I'm sorry."

"Again with the *sorrys*. When did our conversations just become a bunch of apologies? No, don't answer that. I have a feeling I don't want to know the truth."

"There's lots you don't want to know, so we need to make this goodbye for good."

"So a goodbye versus a *bad* bye. That's progress, I think."

"No, they both end the same with bye."

"Wait," the word rushes out. She doesn't hang up. Thank God. Her breath remains light as it dances through the line. "I leave in four days. Please. Come over. I just want to see you again. I won't even ask how you got my number . . . though I'm curious." She hmms. So I continue, "You said whatever this is between us can't turn into more. You, yourself, admitted not only is there something here, but it could be more. Come explore that more, baby."

"You shouldn't call me that."

"I know, but I can't seem to stop myself. I'm not giving up. One date."

"Now it's a date you want?"

"I want more," I say, chuckling. "But how about we start with a date."

"Your honesty is almost endearing."

I laugh. "The girls got jokes."

"Not many these days. Look—"

Taking a left, I'm already onto her emotional tides that change her mind. "I know what you're going to say. I'm asking you, Jaymes, for your time. Just a little. One-on-one without interruption. We'll walk away putting this, whatever it is between us, to bed, or maybe it will turn into seeing each other again. I don't know. I just know it feels good being around you again."

"It does," she admits, which feels like a victory of epic proportions.

"One meal. One date. One hour of your time?"

"Okay. But will you promise not to tell anyone?"

"Are you that ashamed of me?" I tease.

Finally a laugh, and it's the sweetest music to my ears. I'm tempted to record it and listen to it on replay or drop it into a song. "Not at all. It's complicated, like I said. I don't want anything affecting Ace in anyway."

"My lips are sealed unless you want to make out and then I'll totally give it up for ya."

"Like I said, you're impossible. I've got to get back to work before I'm fired."

"How's tomorrow night at seven?"

"You're not going to give up, are you?"

"You know it."

"So if I hang up now, you're gonna bug me about this, aren't you?"

"I'll text you my address and see you at seven."

The silence starts to extend. I can imagine her face, pursed lips, brows pushed toward the middle. Then resolve. "Eight works better."

Gotcha! "Eight it is."

"Fine. Oh, and my mother gave me the number. She programmed it into my phone after spending time with Diane. I think the moms are conspiring to get us together."

"There could be worse things."

"I'm not so sure about that."

It's probably best to hang up before she changes her mind. "See you tomorrow, baby."

"Stop calling me that, Derrick."

"Habit, baby." *Not sorry.* I know how she used to love when I called her that.

I don't have to see her to know she's rolling her eyes. "Tomorrow, Romeo."

WHAT CONSTITUTES OVERBOARD? When it comes to ordering food, I don't know what Jaymes likes anymore. She used to love Mexican food. What if she loves Chinese or Japanese or Italian? Thai? Mongolian? Fuck. American?

"It's too much," my mom says looking at the delivery bags.

"Help me," I reply.

A smile tickles her lips. "You like her."

"I used to love her. Of course I like her." I push the Chinese food down the kitchen counter. "I think we'll eliminate this one. Your turn."

She grabs the Italian. "I'll take this one with me."

"Dude. Not the Italian. I ordered the spinach manicotti. Do you know how amazing their manicotti is?"

"No," she says, shaking her head, "but I look forward to finding out."

"Take it. Take the Japanese too. I have a feeling the woman is similar to the girl. I'm going with the cheese enchiladas, rice, and beans."

"You can't go wrong with that."

"Fingers crossed. So, wine or beer?"

"Wine. I brought two bottles of white. Perfect for Mexican."

"I was thinking tequila."

Her glare hits hard. "No tequila."

"I reach for the bottle of Patron. "What's one shot?"

"Trouble, that's what. No tequila, Derrick. I want you on your best behavior."

"No one ever complains about my behavior when it comes to dating."

"I'm your mother. I don't want to hear about your so-called dating. And this is Jaymes. Remember that."

She puts the Chinese and Japanese food in the fridge and takes the Italian. "I'm going. You be good." Her finger goes up. "Don't reply to that."

I laugh. "Be safe driving home."

"I want some details tomorrow."

She knows me too well. Hearing about sex when it comes to her son's activities is not something she wants the gory details on, so I always edit, edit, edit for her. In the last two years though, nothing . . . or should I say no one has even been worth mentioning much less edit-worthy.

Maybe tonight will change all that.

<hr>

SHE'S LATE, but it's LA, so instead of giving her a hard time, I give her a pass. I also receive two texts when she enters the neighborhood that went a little like: *You're kidding me, right?* And then another that said, *Really?*

Hope she likes the house.

The doorbell chimes and I wipe my hands on a dishtowel and run to answer it while tucking the edge of the towel into my jeans. When I swing the door open, I about choke on the comment I had prepared to welcome her with, but I manage. "You take this *hot for the teacher* thing to a whole new level."

A quick roll of her eyes and she says, "I went from work to class. I didn't have time to go home and change."

"Glad you didn't. Come on in."

"Nice towel by the way."

"Thanks. My mom gave it to me as a housewarming present."

She's scanning the entryway and beyond into the living room. "This house is the most amazing house I've ever been in."

"It's not all that fancy, but I like it."

"You live in the Hollywood Hills. It's fancy, all right."

I take her bag and set it on the table in the entryway. Taking her hand this time, I lead her through the living room and into the kitchen. When we're well within the confines of the room, and time when it would be perfectly acceptable for her to release my hand or vice versa, neither of us does. We stand there in front of the oven, and she asks, "You cooked for me?"

"No. But I bought it and can reheat like nobody's business."

There's that smile that makes me want to commit a crime or at least a sin worth confessing every time I see it. I pour her a glass of wine and I toast, "To feeling like old times." One clink and we both drink.

She leans against the counter and asks, "What's it like to not worry about money? And to live in a place like this?"

It's hard not to feel guilty when you're living in a castle compared to the shacks you grew up in. "It feels like what we dreamed about."

Taking another sip, she says, "I bet it's wonderful."

"Where's Ace tonight?"

"With my mom. Sometimes he'll stay with her if I'm out late."

"Are you out late often?"

"I'm not seeing anyone if that's what you're asking. I have school, work, and Ace. That's enough." She walks around the bar and sits on a stool. "I'm not trying to ruin dinner but I need to be open with you. If you want me to go, I will without question. I understand that most men won't want to take on my mess."

"Do we need tequila for this?" I half-joke.

"We might." She swirls the wine around in her glass, then looks at me. "You know Reggie is Ace's father, right?"

"I didn't know for sure, but I assumed."

"It wasn't planned."

"I hope not since I had just left."

The wine settles in the glass and she closes her eyes briefly. When they reopen she says, "I've apologized for a lot of things, but I won't ever apologize for Ace."

"I would never want you to. Years ago I made the best and worst decisions of my life. I'm still paying the price for losing you."

"Reaping the rewards of leaving me."

"You told me to go."

"I lied. That was the worst decision *I* made and it's one I've had to live with for years."

"How about we clean our slates and start over?"

She smiles. "I'd like that, but I also think you might have questions. Hit me with them now."

"Do you love him?"

"No. I never did."

She never loved him but had sex with him. "Were you ever a couple?"

"Nope." She sips her wine. "You're circling around that night, so I might as well tell you that it was only one time. Ace was just determined to exist."

"Why was it only one time?"

"We're not on good terms. Tumultuous is the only word that comes to mind right now when I think of him."

"Does he help with Ace at all?"

I think my line of questioning is making her uncomfortable. I'm sure it is, so I stop. She shifts and finishes the wine in her glass. "I have a confession, Derrick."

Resting my hands on the counter in front of her, I ask, "Sure you want to share more?"

"Let's blame it on the wine."

"Okay."

Biting her lip, she inwardly debates, but when our eyes connect, she confesses, "You're the only man I've ever loved."

I reach out and take her hand, holding it in mine as I savor her admission. *"You're the only man I've ever loved."* I never knew how much I needed to hear those words. It had hurt when I found out she'd been with Reggie. I can tell I don't know all the details, and probably it's better I never do.

But those words? Knowing she's never loved anyone but me? It's as if a switch has been turned on. I know with absolute certainty that I'm the same. *She's* the only one I've ever loved. We used to complete each other, but having her in this house, knowing where she lives and the life she struggles in daily, I know she feels the disparity of all things material. But she has Ace, and I can tell the love she has for him sustains and pushes her. *You're the only girl I've ever loved, Jaymes.*

Maybe by the end of dinner, I'll confess my secret too.

15

JAYMES

THERE'S SO much familiarity wrapped in this man; so much that makes me feel content around him. I see the way he looks at me like love only exists for us. A longing found deep in his eyes that comforts, forcing my walls down with the simple act of a smile.

Our reality was never simple and it definitely wasn't easy. Two kids from a part of town stuck in the life the generation before ours couldn't escape. What made us think it would be any different? But here I am near the giant Hollywood sign that sparkles like a star, allowing average people to become one.

He did it.

Derrick said he would and he did. I may have sacrificed my own well-being to enable his escape, but I'm still envious of his outcome.

He tops off my wine.

"Is this glass made of crystal?" I ask, dabbing the very tip of my finger in the wine and then run it along the rim.

The beautiful sound rings just as he says, "I guess so. I didn't buy them."

"Who did?"

"I don't know. Maybe my friend's fiancée? She helped me find the place and decorated it."

My mouth falls open, but like a fish gulping for air, I say, "Huh? Um . . . Wow . . . I don't even know what to say to that."

"I know what you're thinking, Jaymes. Get out of your head and just be here with me. You know me. You know who I am inside. Don't let all this make you think otherwise. It's money. Nothing more." His words are as casual as his body language. His muscles never tense, the most relaxed I've ever seen him.

Is that what money does? Gives you peace? "It's money. Nothing more," I repeat, trying to see if the feeling can be transferred just by saying them out loud. Relief doesn't come. My body doesn't ease. My worries are too big for a simple solution. No magic is going to save us. Everything I know about my situation and his means this can't happen. I can't throw words out like that, like they have no repercussions. My son's life hangs on the basic thread of me working as much as I can to earn money. I won't ever earn money of this magnitude or live in a house in The Hills or drink from crystal wine glasses that a personal shopper bought for me without a second thought. But if I can get Ace and my mom out of that neighborhood, I'm winning in life. My perspective is way different from Derrick Masters' these days.

His life is actresses and stardom, fancy events, and fans falling at his feet.

My life is nine-hour days at a used-car lot and hours of night school, *triple*-checking my locks every night, and hoping I can pay the electricity bill each month.

The ache of a shattering heart throbs and I share another confession, "I'm here, but I can't stay." Derrick's eyes track mine for lies. He used to be able to see right through me. It's not a lie I'm telling, but it is a betrayal, even if just to myself. "I shouldn't have come. Call me curious. I wanted to see how the other half lives."

Coming around to my side of the counter, he comes just close enough to trap me, but stays far enough away to make me wish he were closer. "Why do you keep insisting you shouldn't be here, you can't see me again, this is all wrong?" He rests his hands on my thighs and leans in. I like his proximity. Too much. "What if this is all right? What if we're right?"

I turn away so he stops looking at me like . . . like time hasn't passed and we haven't changed. "It's different now."

"What are you scared of, Jaymes?"

"You." It's true, but I can't tell him the whole truth. I'm scared for him as well as well as scared of my feelings for him and how strong they are. But I'm really scared of Reggie.

"Bullshit. You're not scared of me. You never were. So tell me what keeps you running away from me when I can see how curious you are? And it's not just the house you're curious about. You're curious about me just like I am about you. So, what do you want to really know?"

"How many girlfriends have you had?"

"One."

"Since me, I mean."

"None."

One heartbeat.

Two.

Three heartbeats.

Four.

I whisper, "I've seen articles."

"But not the truth."

"How is that possible?"

"How many boyfriends have you had since me?"

"None."

That lady-killer smile is in full force and I can't deny the effects it has on me. "That's how it's possible. Riddle me this. How did two really fucking attractive, if I do say so myself, people not find love again in the last five years?"

"Because they never got over it the first time?"

"It's not a question, baby. That's the truth the articles don't tell you." Moving to the side of my chair, he's just about to kiss me. I'm just about to kiss him. The oven timer goes off.

Closing his eyes, he sighs. "Not sure about that timing. What do you think? Saved by the timer or unwanted interruption?"

A trick question that I could easily say in one answer, but that would encourage him in ways I shouldn't. "I just think it means the food is ready."

"Yeah," he says, chuckling. Turning away, he gets oven gloves and pulls the dish out, setting it on top of the stove. He takes the oven mitts off and tosses them on the opposite counter. "You staying?"

My stomach growls. I only had a granola bar at lunch. It's the end of the month and funds are low, so it was my lunch or Ace's that had to go and I'll never deprive my kid of something healthy to eat. It smells so good. I bite my lip, trying to resist, trying to tamp down the hunger pangs. I'm starving though. "One meal."

"At some point, I'm going to have to leave." I close my eyes while resting my head on the arm of his couch. Maybe just a quick catnap to help this food coma I'm slipping into.

"You can stay."

A lazy smile rolls over my lips. When I open my eyes, his are on me. "I think that's your answer for everything, but it's much too complicated to make it that easy."

With a foot on the coffee table, he leans back in the chair, settling in. "You sure do hold a lot of secrets. You know, I'm a good listener, and maybe I can help in some way."

I sit back up, well aware that this night shouldn't have happened at all much less continue so blissfully. We've talked about his touring, what it's like to sing with The Resistance, whether or not it's as good as he dreamed it would be. We've talked about Kaz, and how he quickly became such a good friend to Derrick. We've even laughed together about some of the funny backstage antics. Even how it's always been hard to juggle school, being a mom, and work, but I've enjoyed the challenge. *Sometimes. Well, rarely.* But talking with Derrick? Relaxing with him? It's been *easy.* "Is this what our life would have been like together?"

"Our life . . . Things weren't always good, but they weren't always bad."

"I hate that I'm part of your bad."

"You're always part of the good to me."

"I stayed away because I couldn't risk seeing you and being rejected again."

And there it is. My heart hurts, my soul sad from what could have been. "For two teenagers, life sure was complicated back then."

"I also thought Reggie would be gunning for me, but I was in LA. He knows I'm still here. He's never come after me. He's weak. He likes being a big dog in a small yard. More bark than bite." Sitting forward, he lowers his foot and rests his forearms on his knees. "I want to help you."

"With what?"

"Life. You and Ace."

I stand. "No." Still shaking my head I walk around the couch and repeat myself, "No."

He beats me to the doorway of the entry before I reach my purse. "No. I'm not letting you leave like this. We're just now getting somewhere and you want to walk away?"

"You're just going to have to trust me. It's best this way. We can't get attached again."

"Attached again? I think the problem is I never detached."

"You leaving was a pretty damn big detachment." I hate that I say it, but it's out there resting between us now. I dare look up, but find only hurt in his eyes. I hate that more.

Stepping aside, he lets me by. No arguing. No stopping me. No charming quips or slick compliments. I take my purse and move toward the door, but this time, I stop. When I turn around, his back is still to me. He's standing exactly how I left him. "Derrick?"

His head drops down. "Yeah?"

"Thank you for dinner."

"You're welcome."

This is for the best, even if he's hurt now. At least he won't be hurt in the long run. At least I'll know that I had more of a choice in closing the future from any possibilities with him. Yes, I told him to go years ago, but this time . . . This time I'm making the wisest decision for me. For my future. For my heart.

I open the door, but then I hear, "Jaymes?"

"Yeah?"

Turning around, he says, "I think you're right."

"About?" My knees are feeling weak. *Please don't tell me you agree. Please.* I don't want this dreadful goodbye.

"I don't think we should see each other."

Why does doing the right thing hurt so much? "Probably best," I whisper, trying desperately to be strong.

"When you leave here tonight, do you think you'll detach from me? Find love this time?"

I should go, but my feet, maybe my heart, keeps me there, standing in place. "Do you think that's really possible?"

"I'm starting to think not so much."

Whispering, I say, "Me too."

Our eyes stay connected, much like our love. We seem to be caught in a cycle that neither of us cares to break. "You know," he starts, the bravado gone, his vulnerable side revealed, "maybe we can make the impossible possible?"

I allow myself the one thing I hadn't—to feel everything with him again. Adrenaline fills my veins and for the first time in forever, hope grows. Want and need take precedence, my better judgment buried under a good meal. Just one more time with him to settle the reignited fascination I have with him. We will both be able to put us in the past for good. "It's a challenge I think I'm ready to take. Just one more kiss."

"Or more."

Taking a step back into the house, I ask, "What if I kissed you this time?"

One step closer for him, and he says, "What if I kissed you back?"

I know better, but all that *better* seems to fly out the window when I take two more steps. "Kiss me, Derrick."

The good thing about him is when it comes to making out I never had to ask him twice. One deep, love-filled impossible kiss later, and I can't hide my feelings. My body gives me away. It's just so easy to feel so much for him. In the second kiss, I realize everything we had before, still exists between us.

The third has me against the wall.

The fourth on the couch.

By the fifth kiss, I'm underneath him.

The sixth—my skirt is pushed high on my hips.

The seventh—he's situated between my legs.

His body has changed. Gone is the boy I fell in love with, replaced by the man I now lust for. *Lust.* Such a dirty word. Sinful. A sin I commit regularly just looking at him. But this time, he's here. This time, he's touching me. This time he's loving my body as if he never gave up.

The calloused fingertips remember my body, and he strikes a chord with the firm pressure at my hip. My breath is ripped away as soon as he touches me like he still knows my inner desires, the ones my body never expresses anymore. My nails press into his broad shoulders. The expanse of his muscles angle down to his carved waist and across his abdomen. I slide my hands over the hard muscles and into his hair, holding him close because I need that eighth, ninth, and tenth kiss.

Patience isn't a virtue either of us ever aspired to have. No, Derrick Masters was no angel and never took his time. He took everything he wanted from me, including my heart. Back then I never noticed it was gone until it was too late. I feel alive, my body awakened by his desire for me. *I've missed being touched. Being desired. Loved.*

I can't confuse what this is. This isn't about love, despite how careful, how caring he's handling me. It's about that other four-letter word that starts with L.

Lust.

But, God. It feels so good.

16

DERRICK

"Oh my God."

"What?" I ask, lifting up just enough to see Jaymes's face. Her stunningly beautiful face—flushed cheeks, ruby-red lips, emerald eyes alight with fire burning on the inside.

"Make me stop."

Surprised by the request, I ask, "Why would I ever do something so stupid?" Because there is nothing I'd rather be doing than this right here. I touch her over the lace fabric between her legs.

"Because I'm not strong enough to stop, especially when you're doin—Oh, good God, that feels amazing." I slow my pace and add a little pressure. "Don't stop that—"

Dropping her head back on the cushion, she runs her hands through her hair. "It's been so long. So good. You feel too good."

"Too good," I repeat, chuckling. "Never, but you feel damn amazing, woman."

I find her lips when I move up higher on her body, and kiss her. Our tongues meet in a heated embrace, and I'm transported back to a time when we would spend our free hours in bed. Love, we always made love like it was going to be taken away one day. We didn't know it would be, but damn I loved her. Being with her now, the pounding in my chest and the erection in my jeans, I'm going to struggle to keep it cool with her.

After untucking her shirt, I slide my hands under it, feeling her silky skin beneath. "Can I take this off?"

She nods and starts on the buttons. I'm about to fucking rip the rest off, but I don't want to upset her and I have a feeling ripping her shirt might do that. I slip it down her arms and toss it to the other end of the couch. "The skirt." I don't ask this time. I stand up and pull her to her feet as we both start stripping down.

Her eyes linger over my chest. When her skirt comes down, her hands are on my biceps. "You're hot, you know that?" She laughs. "I'm sure you're told that all the time."

I don't have to guess what she really means. She's probably seen the gossip all over from the tabloids to the shows to the online blogs who have nothing better to do than stalk the band and me and print whatever shit they dig up. I bring her warm body against mine. "Hey, I like that you think you I'm hot. I think you're gorgeous."

Her hands run over my chest and so quietly, she asks, "Can I see it?"

I know what she means and I suddenly feel self-conscious, but I turn anyway. The tips of her finger trace each letter of the ink. R. E. B. E. L. Her lips press to my back and her head leans against me momentarily. Coming around, she whispers, "I've missed you."

The air between us thickens and I kiss her. "I missed you so much." We lean our heads together, taking the seconds to slow things down. She's about to take off her bra, but I cover her hands. "Let me."

This time it's not just a part of the process, it's a fucking gift I've been given. "I can't believe Jaymes Anne-Marie Grenier is standing in front of me." I say it because fuck it all. I'm not sure why I expected her to be so different, and she is in ways, but all for the better, if that is even possible. But one thing is for sure. She still owns me.

With a soft smile resting on her lips, she tries to hide her eyes from me. I'm not having it. I tilt her chin up and say, "Watch me while I watch you." I tuck one finger under the left strap and another under the right before I pull them up and around her shoulders until they're hanging down.

She's not comfortable under my heavy gaze, but I want her to experience being cherished again, being loved, being treated like the goddamn queen she is. Reaching around her, I unclasp the bra at her back and let the pink lace fall between us.

Standing there, her arms start to move, start to reach up and cover herself. "No, you're beautiful. Don't hide from me."

The pink in her cheeks darkens and she nods. I pick her up and toss her over my shoulder. "You're mine now."

Through fits of giggles, I traverse the stairs and run down the hall to my room. She lifts her head up and says, "Nice room, playboy."

The name doesn't bother me. It motivates me to prove her wrong. When I lay her down, dark hair fans over the white sheets. My heart beats faster in awe that I have this woman in my bed again.

"You're staring at me," she says, pulling the sheets up to her nose.

I gulp, the weight of this very moment hitting me. "I can't believe you're here."

"Me either. Now join me before you make me regret staying. You're making me feel self-conscious."

Lying down next to her, I pull the sheet low enough to expose the perfection of her tits. Fuck me. "Every part of you is gorgeous. I'm just the lucky bastard that gets to appreciate it." I lower just enough to kiss her neck until she relaxes again. She molds to my body, every soft part of her fits to my hard ridges. "You feel that, baby?"

Her answer comes on the tail end of a heaving breath, "What?"

"This. How perfect our bodies fit together. We were made for each other." I run the tips of my fingers under the lace that keeps us apart. I slide down to take a nipple that matches the natural pink of her lips after I've kissed her for hours into my mouth. Lightly teasing with my teeth, her back arches, and a harsh intake of air fills her lungs. Slowly, I move her underwear to the side and slip my fingers through her lower lips. "You're so wet for me, baby. Just like you always were."

"Derrick?"

Running my tongue over her breast, I then move to the other and bite just hard enough to illicit another of her sweet gasps before looking up. For someone virtually naked under me right now, she looks shy all of a sudden. "Yeah?"

"It's been a while," she starts, then wraps her arms over my shoulders. "I'm nervous."

The frenzy that was twisting inside loosens just a little and I smile. Positioning myself between her legs, I make sure I'm eye level, and run my hands through her hair. "I want you to enjoy this. If we need to slow down, we can."

"I think I need that." She turns away from me and stares out the window.

I whisper, "Okay," then lean down and kiss her cheek because I feel her slipping away from me emotionally. Something in her gaze is leaving the here and now and disappearing into her thoughts. Taking her chin, I turn her back so she's looking at me. "Hey, you want to talk about it?"

Her head is shaking before she even replies, "No. I want to just feel. I don't want to think or talk at all. Kiss me. Make love to me. Just make me forget."

"I don't want you to forget this. I won't, that's for damn sure."

"Not *this*. *This* I want. I want you. I just don't want to think about anything but this right now, *us*."

"Okay." I kiss her. My desire to be everything this beautiful creature needs overwhelms any needs of my own. Our bodies tangle and soon our legs are twisted and moving together. "You're so beautiful." Her breath responds when she can't. "I've missed you." I'm rewarded with her nails digging into my skin, urging me for more. "I want you so fucking much."

"Take me, Derrick. Like you used to."

No way will I fuck this woman. We fucked a lot but we made love more. That's what she needs—love. That's what she has—all of mine. Going lower, I leave wet kisses down her body and blow on her skin creating goosebumps across her tan, smooth skin.

Toying with her underwear between my teeth, I finally decide *fuck it* and take the fuckers off. I'm keeping them though. I tuck them under the covers where I know I'll find them later. Returning back to her pretty pussy, I inhale. Her desire is intoxicating. Like a recovering Jaymes addict, being given a hit after so long makes me feel drunk. My thoughts are lucid as I devour her, and then tease, flicking her clit with my tongue until her hips buck. I hold her down and fuck her with my tongue. The way she pulls my hair sends the blood right to my cock. Hard as Fort Knox, I want to fuck, but I remind myself that it's love we're making tonight. Like I teased her nipples earlier, I tug lightly on her clit between my teeth and insert a finger just below. Speaking of Fort Knox. She's not lying. She's tight as fuck.

Holy shit.

The hold on one finger makes it damn hard to add another. And if I can't add another or more, there's no way my dick's going to fit. "Relax, baby. I'll go slow."

She nods and takes a deep breath. I feel her viselike grip on me loosen and I kiss her lips like I'd kiss her mouth—slowly, appreciatively. This is my chance to make things right. I'll do anything for her. Anything.

I carefully add another finger and pause. Her ribs expand and her breath is heard as she adjusts to the new size. "You okay?" I ask just to make sure.

"Fine. I want you in me."

"I will be, but I want it to feel good too."

Her body relaxes even more after that and I ease all the way in, spreading my fingers and pulling out and then pushing back in. With my lips still on her clit, I suck lightly and add pressure. I can hear her breathing change from air to soft mewls as her fingers twist in my hair. She's getting close so I pick up the speed and go deeper. I'm rewarded with tremors ripping through her body as she releases so hard that my fingers are squeezed tight. "Oh my . . . Derrick!" she cries and I continue to fuck her into her oblivion of ecstasy until her body calms and her eyes open. Emotions race across her face, but the bliss still sits on her lips and grows when she smiles. "Now, babe. I need you now. So badly."

Babe.

Finally. Fucking finally. I haven't heard it since the day I left and I've missed it every day since. To be rewarded with her orgasm and the moniker, I'm hard as a fucking rock. I almost sink into her, but remember protection. Fuck. I reach over into my nightstand drawer, causing her to watch me—reality setting back in. I don't want to lose this feeling between us so I'm fast with the condom and repositioned between her legs in seconds. And for good measure, I kiss her because that's all I want to do with her when I'm not making love to her.

Just as our tongues touch, I push in and she moans.

Pause.

Acclimate.

Pause.

Acclimate.

I lift up. She says, "I want you. All of you. You feel so good. Don't make me beg, babe."

"You're so fucking sexy." I'm buried to the hips with adept speed. I'm tempted to pause again but she starts wiggling for me to move, so I give the woman what she wants.

So fucking tight. Two fingers don't prepare her, but she takes me like she owns me.

She does.

The thought sends me on a high I haven't had in forever. I thrust and pull, fuck, and love her, making up for every goddamn minute I wasn't with her doing exactly this right here.

It doesn't take much—it's Jaymes. I'm in heaven again. Her body mine. Her mind mine. Her soul mine to keep forever. My orgasm hits hard and fast taking punches along the way. My body collapses, drained of years of the pent-up need and want I held in a locked box now set free again.

I love her.

I still love her so fucking much.

She was always meant to be in my arms. I roll over and settle her on top of me. She's mine. Only and always fucking mine. I wrap my arms around her and hold her tight to my chest.

"I've always been yours."

My body stills when I realize I said that out loud for her to hear. I relax back just as fast. I don't care if she knows. She should, but then I feel it. It's subtle at first; her body trembles. At first I think she's cold, so I grab the sheet and pull it over us. Even with it covering us completely, I feel it again. That's when I lean back to get a better look. "Hey?"

Not looking up, she answers on a shaky breath, "What?"

"Look at me."

"No, let me rest." She tries for lighthearted, but I can see through the quiver in her voice.

"Jaymes?" I hate how demanding I sound. When she finally looks up, I see it. Watery eyes blurring the bright green that had just been there. Sage and moss instead of brilliance and emeralds. When she blinks, tears slip down her cheeks and land on my chest. "Why are you crying?"

"I'm not," she replies, sitting up, and swiping under her eyes.

I can tell she's about to bolt, so I grab her wrist. "Talk to me."

"I need a minute. All right?" Her tone has turned, so I release her, and let her go. Rolling to my side, I watch as she disappears into the bathroom and shuts the door behind her.

Staring at the door, I debate if I should check on her not. I don't remember her having moods after we had sex. This is new territory. Maybe this is what happens when two pasts collide in the present. For me, it feels right. I feel that I've found the missing piece of my life. Of my heart. Of me. But for her? Even though my life has been going full throttle for years now, it's as though in reality I've stood still. Waiting for her. Waiting for us to be together again. But she's made a completely new life. *Literally.* Maybe I'm deluding myself that she could still love me. She didn't say *I'd loved* earlier, and I had heard that as a possible *I still love you.* Maybe we're only colliding momentarily.

Maybe this is what we are now—shifting tides under the evening sky.

No. That is not what I want.

Fuck it. I toss the sheet off and go to the bathroom. Knocking lightly, I call to her, "Jaymes, can I come in?"

"Yes."

Her response makes me glad I made the effort. If I can make her smile again, I'll do the best I fucking can. I open the door and see her small frame wrapped in my large black robe. Sitting on the edge of the whirlpool tub, her face contrasts the darkness that surrounds her from her hair to the robe to the dark night in the window behind her. I keep my tone low, the vibe feeling like I should, when I ask, "You okay?"

"Your bathroom is the same size as my bedroom."

Looking around, I smile. "Yeah. It's big."

"Who cleans it?"

"Not me."

"Thought as much."

"Can I sit?"

"Sure. It's your house." I might be wrong, but that sounded like there was a little disdain in the way she said it. Letting it slide, I don't worry about that shit. This is new. I once had to adjust too. I owe her more than just an expectation of acceptance. Grabbing the other robe from my closet, I put it on before sitting down on the tub next to her. "You have two of these robes? What are you the king of England these days?"

Chuckling, I reply, "Something like that. I actually didn't buy them, but I do dig them."

Running her fingers over the gold embroidered initials over her heart, she says, "I dig them too. This is the softest material. What is it?"

"I have no fucking clue."

"Thank God some things don't change. I'd be worried if you cared enough to know. That's never been who you are."

"Who am I, Jaymes? To you, who do you see when you look at me?"

"A dream I once had."

Nodding, I look down and pick at the soft threads. That's a lot of heavy considering what I just said in bed. "Why did you cry?"

"I have a feeling you're not going to let that one slide."

Putting my arm around her back, I hold her to my side. "Is that what you want?"

"For the time being I do."

As much as I want to know, I need to give her the space she needs or I'll lose her again. "I'll respect your wishes."

That brings a smile to her face. "Just like a great king would. Granting wishes." She stands up and moves between my legs. This time she takes my face in her hands. Runs the tip of her finger over my lips and then drags her gaze up to my eyes. "Thank you," she says and it sounds like she means more than not badgering her about the tears.

"You're welcome."

Her lips meet mine and just like we started, we end our night with a gentle kiss that feels like more than any casual caress. It feels like us. *Again.*

17

———

JAYMES

"Well, that didn't go as planned."

I roll my eyes while sitting at a stoplight. I haven't even hit the freeway and I'm already regretting what I just did. My phone rings, plucking me out of my head right before I tailspin. "Hello?"

"Hi, beautiful."

Smiling, I say, "I thought you'd be asleep by now. You wore me out. I was hoping I did the same for you."

"I've never felt better. I feel like I could conquer the world right now."

"You can. You even have the robes for it."

"Robe. Singular."

I run my hand over the plush material draped across my lap again, for like the two hundredth time since I left. "Thank you for giving me the robe."

"Promise me you'll wear it and think of me."

"I don't have to be wearing a robe to think of you. Tonight . . ." I pause. I want to say was perfect. Amazing. Incredible. I should be telling him that it can't happen again, but somehow, after saying the words and then going back on them physically, I feel like it would be a bitchy thing to tell him. Instead, I struggle for what I need to say over what I want to say. *I love you. I've never stopped loving you. I wish I could live in your dream.* "I'm—"

"Sorry. Yes, I know, although I was hoping you wouldn't go there again. I don't believe you're playing games with me, but I do wonder if you went with your feelings instead of your head if you'd arrive at the same outcome."

"Derrick, please."

"No, hear me out because I've been thinking about this. There is no good reason your head should be denying me either. We come together so easy, so quickly—"

"That's just sex." *I hate the lie. I hate that I just said that to the man I've loved forever.* The line goes quiet for several discomforting seconds, so I ask, "Are you still there?"

"Yeah. I'm here." His silence becomes deafening and I feel sick to my stomach. "Okay, Jaymes. Thanks for coming over."

"Derrick, wait—"

The call goes quiet and I know he's hung up. *Shoot.*

I immediately call him back, although it's probably best if he chooses not to answer. Just when I think I'm going to be sent to voice-mail, he answers, "Don't do that."

"What?" I ask.

"Don't destroy something that was good. Tonight was good. Tonight was fucking great. Let's not ruin it in the aftermath. Fine, you don't want to come over again. That I can work with, but you throwing a verbal grenade into our conversations does more than end them. It destroys them." *It destroys me too.*

I'm about to apologize because I feel like shit for being mean to him, but also because he's right. When it comes to him, I'm leaving a destructive path in my trail while trying to find a better life. He won't understand why, but that's still not an excuse.

"It doesn't matter how much you push me away, and yes, I know that's what you're doing. I don't know why, but I see it. I see the conflict in your eyes when you look at me and say words you don't mean. I let you walk out my door tonight without a fight. That is the only regret I have. If you have regrets, I hope when you look back they don't damage what we did, what we mean to each other, or what we are when we're together, because that would be a damn shame."

"I liked it." *No, I loved it.*

"What was that?"

I know he heard me, but repeating myself is the least I owe him. "I liked being with you again. Everything you said is true for me too. I didn't mean to sound otherwise." I have to choose my words carefully. If he gets any whiff of bad times, he'll feel the need to swoop in and save me. I know him well enough to know that. He already offered to help Ace and me, but I can't accept anything. Not from him. His death could come from the goodness of his heart. Reggie can never find out about him being in my life again and Derrick can't know what's really going on.

I have to keep him safe. He's another person I'm responsible for. "I'm drowning in all the things I have to do, the stuff I have to worry about, the lives that depend on me." Tonight I put my son and mom at risk, and for what? An emotional and physical attraction that could end us all? "I keep saying this, but I need you to hear me. There is nothing wrong with us. I agree. It's just so easy to slip into the old us that we almost forgot that there's a new us. An us that moved on from the other. You're leaving. I'm staying. We both just keep moving."

"Let me help you, Jaym—"

"It's not charity when it comes to you and me. You know that." His voice is deep, his tone as comforting as his words. And for a brief second I consider the offer—what if he could save us? Just one friend helping another. Maybe we could be more and live that happily ever after all . . .

Despite the hands around my throat, I can hear Ace crying for me in the back room. I don't think Reggie does. I pray he doesn't. He will have to kill me before I let him near my son.

At two years old, Ace can sense my distress when Reggie visits. He hides like I taught him to and usually is very quiet until I retrieve him. Reggie swears he will hunt me down like a dog, kill me, and take my son under his wing if I ever betray him. I don't have to lie when it comes to Derrick. I don't know anything about him these days. It makes me wonder if I ever did. Some days I wonder if our relationship was simply a part of my imagi-nation and less a part of my memories the more time passes between us.

I fear Reggie. I fear what he represents in my life. Control.

"We used to be friends, Jamie. Real friends. Friends who had fun together. Friends . . . friends . . . I don't think I have any friends anymore. Rebel fucking loved you. But I wanted you first."

I don't know why that popped into my head. Pieces that didn't make sense then, now do. Reggie liked me. And Derrick knew. So has my life really been controlled by his jealousy all this time? I've been thinking it was because Derrick sold Reggie out to the police over that deal. I think I've sorely underestimated Reggie's ego and how far he'll go for revenge. *Over me.*

At the end of all the days, he's still Ace's father. No matter how many times I cried for it not to be true, that fact is never going to change.

"What do you want me to do, Derrick? Take your money and what?"

"Get the fuck out of that part of the city. Buy a house—"

A house? I scoff. "You're going to give me enough to buy a house?"

"If you'd take it."

"I won't," I reply too quickly, the response automatic.

"Without thought, you answer. Without even considering the possibility, you respond so quickly." I've been on the freeway for a few minutes and the quiet hum of the road under the tires is the only sound heard until he adds, "I owe you so much. A house is one thank you I can give you."

"You owe me nothing. Don't let guilt override your better judg-ment. You've done so well for yourself. Get out on that stage and play your heart out. Music is in your blood and it's a gift you can share. Share it, Derrick. Then meet a girl who treats you well and have a family. Forget about me. Tonight wasn't a coming together. It was the goodbye we never got."

"It was the goodbye I never wanted."

Despite the verbal punch to the gut, I continue, not letting my pain show, or at least not all of it. It would be impossible to hide. "Circles. We're still spinning in circles, but I can't ride this merry-go-round with you. You might not know it, but I'm so happy for you and your success. I smile when I hear your songs on the radio and remember the good times when I see you perform on TV. It's time for you to let go of the past that's dragging you down and move into that light that shines brightly just for you."

"And for you." *No, there is no bright light for me. Not yet.*

"No," I say, "In another life, I'll live out that dream. In this one, I just need to keep moving. Goodbye."

"Good night works better for me."

"Good night? Fine. If that's what you have to tell yourself to sleep at night. Good night." I disconnect before he can talk me out of it and before he talks me into coming back to his fancy house. I arrive at my mom's just before midnight. She's waiting up for me and hugs me when she sees me. Getting a good look at me, she says, "Why didn't you stay?"

I close the door behind me and lock it. "Why would I stay?"

"Ace fell asleep at eight. He's not woken up." Relief is found that he sleeps so well over here. She walks to the kitchen and starts the coffeepot. "You're a grown woman, Jamie, but if you want to continue acting like a lovesick teenager, I'll play along a little longer." Staring at her, I can tell she knows. She says, "Well, at least you had a good time."

My eyes go wide. She really does know. "Mom."

"Don't *Mom* me. You look a mess, but you look happy, so I'm happy." Leaning against the counter, I watch as she gets two mugs from the cabinet and pours in creamer. She knows exactly how I like my coffee, even when we drink decaf at midnight. "How was his house?"

The most incredible place I've ever seen. I think about the robe I'm going to be sleeping in later and how even something so basic like a robe can be that luxurious. "I can't even imagine living in a place like that. Even the wine glasses were crystal." She smiles and pours the hot liquid into our mugs and stirs, mixing it up. The dark brown turns to a tawny and she hands me mine. I take a sip and goodness fills me. "I can't fall in love with him."

"But you want to?"

"I don't think there's ever been a choice when it comes to me and him."

Her happiness really does shine right through her smile and the creases around her eyes that only deepen when she's happy. "You're going to be moving in here in a week. Once you're under this roof, Reggie loses power. I won't allow him to continue his tyranny over you or Ace." She comes to me and sets my mug down. Holding my hands, she says, "I will protect you and Ace always, however I can. Together, we can figure out how to stop him."

Moving to the small rickety table, I drop my head in my heads. "He will never let Ace go, even if he let me and that seems unlikely. I'm stuck. He's holding all the cards. He doesn't care about him. He never sees him. He's just waiting for Ace to hit double digits, so he can step in and play a part in his life. Him not being around now works to my advantage. If I don't make some money, we're going to be stuck here forever."

She sits next to me and rubs my arm. "For now. Only stuck for now."

Instead of coffee, I opt for bed. Since Ace sleeps in my old room, I pull out the foldout couch and make it up with my mom. She tucks me in and kisses my head. "Things will get better. I promise you." *I hope so. I hate the despair I live with daily.*

"I love you."

"I love you too."

The lights are out, the curtains closed. I lie on the couch wide awake. Thinking about everything from the night I was raped to tonight. I hate that I can even have those thoughts in the same night. For every harsh and violent thing Reggie did to me, Derrick covered me in love and kisses, soothing the damage that was left behind.

One day I'll only have a highlights reel of memories to remind me of my life, and like he is now to the rest of the world, he'll always be one of the stars in mine.

18

DERRICK

THE BAND HAS BEEN JAMMING all afternoon. We stopped for food and then started up on a few of the new songs. We've been playing them on the tour, but there have been a few kinks we're still working out.

"Fucking hell, Derrick!" A drumstick flies by. When I look at Dex, he says, "If you fucking miss that lead-in one more time, I'm going to play my solo and then come fucking play your part right after."

I call them kinks. They call them screw-ups. Whatever. It's all the same. "I'm fixing it. Next time I'll nail it."

The other drumstick flies across the room and slams into the padded wall of the studio. He picks his stool up and raises it above his head. Right when he's about to slam it to the floor, he stops, and turns his back to us. The stool is set down again and he walks through the room toward the door. "I'm getting a Coke."

Johnny checks his watch, a watch that probably cost more than— well, that analogy doesn't work since my first and second cars were pieces of shit. He looks up and says, "I have forty-five minutes until I need to get home, dressed, and ready to take my wife out on a date I've been promising to do during this tour break. I can't be late. Holliday threatened me already."

"Why do you even want to go out?" I ask. "Aren't you just harassed the whole time?"

"I don't need it, but every couple of months she likes to see if we can go out and do regular stuff like shop for watermelon water at Whole Foods or see a movie at Grauman's and then walk around after seeing if my feet were as big as John Wayne's. Other times it's The Pier in Santa Monica or shopping at The Grove." He sets his guitar down and grabs his phone from a chair next to him.

"Does it work?" I ask.

"No, it doesn't work. It never works, but Holliday is determined to lead as normal a life as she can and she likes to think we can do that together. It's supposed to keep us grounded."

He's the most grounded person I know in the band. He could legit walk away from all the fame, the band, and everything and be happy living out his life in Ojai Valley. I've heard the stories, read the shit published about him, but he's changed. I think that's what is happening to me.

Change.

It can't be that fucking bad if Johnny Outlaw chose to do it. He's my idol. Everything he went through, where he came from, the work he puts into the music—he's a legend for a reason. "You once talked about a crisis you went through."

He sits down and then leans back in the chair like he's going to be there a while. "I spent half my twenties burning through life, fucking angry at everything, my dad, a girl named Patty O'Toole who dumped me in high school when I got injured. I was mad at the whole world and I was hell-bent on destroying myself."

Slumping down into a chair, I pretend to tighten and tune my guitar while taking his story in. It's familiar, hitting close to home. Very close. "So what changed?"

"Me. I met a woman."

I don't fail to notice the Patty chick was called a girl, his wife a woman. What if the woman is the same as the girl? I can't say she dumped me for Reggie, but the hookup still surprises me. Tumultuous. That's what she called their relationship. I've treaded carefully when it comes to the topic. My ego took more than a wallop over that bombshell, but I can tell it's a sensitive subject for her. She has a kid she has to put first.

Johnny adds, "I met the right woman at the right time. I was over groupies and drugs. I wanted a clear mind and clear conscience. The only way to get where I needed to be was to take a step back. I wanted it to be about the music, the art, the fans, the rhyme, the rhythm. I was lonely though. It's strange how you can be surrounded by twenty thousand people, but at night you still walk into an empty hotel room and nothing. Silence. It plays tricks on you." He sits forward and rests his arms on his legs. "I was sitting at a bar in Vegas pretending to be someone I wasn't. That's when I met her. She knew exactly who she was and what she wanted."

"What was that?"

Shrugging, he cocks a smile. "That night? A hotel security manager, but she got a rock star instead. It was a win-win situation for both of us." He reaches over and cracks the lid off of a bottle of water and drinks. "You guys," he says, looking between Kaz and me, "find who you want to be and fight for it. Everyone outside this room is looking to tear you down or replace you."

Kaz says, "Dex and Tommy are outside this room."

Johnny chuckles. "Like I said . . . Anyway." After making his joke, he stands and blows out a big breath. "We've been there or gone through it, so if you are or are going to, we're here. The five of us, no matter where we are in the world or in our lives, we've got your back." Before he walks out the door, he says, "Go after the woman, Derrick. You'll find out fast as fuck if she's into you or not. If she is, you're gonna score for the romance. If she's not, eh, you'll get your ass kicked to the curb, but we leave tomorrow anyway. There's always a groupie waiting in every city ready to heal your broken heart." *They're not there for my heart.*

Before Johnny leaves, Kaz asks, "The burning question is, are your feet bigger or smaller than John Wayne's?"

"Bigger, but I wouldn't say otherwise." He laughs and signals to Tommy in the other room with the producer.

Tommy gets up and makes his way in. Taking Johnny's guitar and picking up Dex's drumsticks, he looks at me, and says, "Buy ya a beer?"

"You got it. Kaz, you coming?"

"Yeah, but only for one."

KAZ AND TOMMY ARE DRUNK.

Man, Kaz's tolerance has gone downhill since we moved into our own places. He says he has Russian mafia ties if I ever need something taken care of. I'm not in a good mental state because I actually start considering this option in regard to Reggie. Tommy's been whining about love for forty-five minutes and Kaz has his arm wrapped around him agreeing wholeheartedly about Tommy getting older and needing to settle down. Have some kids.

The last part drags me back into their inebriated bromance of self-help. That's when it dawns on me. I whack Kaz in the chest. Oops. I didn't mean to knock him off the stool. Reaching down, I give him a solid hand and pull his ass up. "What the fuck was that for?" he slurs.

"Accident. Sorry." It was all him, but I'll take the blame. His balance is as drunk as he is. "You told Tommy he should have kids."

He stares at me blankly. So I say, "That he should settle down and have kids."

Still nothing. "Is that what you want?"

"Of course," he says, shrugging like this is common knowledge.

"What do you mean *of course*?"

"Don't you? Isn't that what living the dream really means?"

"No," I say, shaking my head. "Living the dream means we are literally living out our dreams. Playing to sold-out shows, millions of fans, traveling the world, making money doing what we love."

"Sure, there's that answer." I can practically see the beer slosh in his eyes when he rolls them. "But like Outlaw said, what do we come home to? That's up to us. When the tours stop and the records aren't gold anymore, what do we have? I'll tell you what we have. A warm bed with a hot woman. Family. Friends. People who love you because of who you are on the inside, not because we're famous or slept with a bevy of princesses. No. We'll have a home where they leave the light on for you."

"Dude, I think you're confusing your argument with a motel commercial."

"Whatever. What were we talking about?"

"Lara and how you need to get home to her."

"Yup. I do. I'll see you chaps tomorrow." He pats my back and grabs Tommy by the shirt. "Come on, Tommy. Your ass can sleep at mine."

I look down at the beer in front of me. I don't think I even finished a pint.

The guys are right. This is bullshit. The emotions and Jaymes are messing with my head. I'm a fucking rock star. I can have any girl I want.

While I wait for valet to pull my car around like the fucking LA pussy I've become, I drop the act. Being a rock star is awesome, better than any dream I ever had. But I don't want just any girl. Nope. Now that I've spent time with Jaymes again, she's the only woman I want.

I get in my car and use my not-so-secret weapon. The phone rings and before she can speak, I say, "Mom, I need a favor."

THE LIGHTS ARE STILL on inside, but it's almost ten at night, so I knock lightly. The creak of the floor signals someone is looking through the peephole. One lock and then another. The door opens and Jaymes is there looking like an angel in her nightgown. It's not sexy, but it's cotton and a little see-through. She looks younger, almost like I remember, with her hair down and loose around her shoulders. The deep color a stark contrast to the nightgown. I'm starting to think she can't look anything but stunning every time I see her.

"Hi." She gazes up at me, and asks, "What are you doing here?"

"I wanted to see you before I left."

"You leave tomorrow?"

"Yeah."

A pink tongue dips out and wets her bottom lip before it's dragged under her top teeth. The war is waging. Her nightgown blowing in the gentle breeze signals her surrender. "I'm glad you came by." The door is opened and I walk on in.

She closes the curtains, but then peeks out before tugging hard in the middle for privacy. When she turns around, she asks, "Would you like something to drink?"

"Water would be great."

That makes her smile for some reason. I follow her into the kitchen and watch as she gets the glass and fills it with ice and then water from a container in the fridge. "Thanks."

Leaning against the other counter, her arms are crossed, but not hiding her chest or body from me. More just waiting to hear why I'm there. "So what really brings you by this late?"

"The other night. It was great. I wanted you to know how much it meant to me that you came over."

"It's sex, Derrick. You get it all the time," she says, walking back to the living room.

"It wasn't just sex for me. It was more. I think it was for you too, but you're just stubborn enough to not give in when you see a good thing."

Sitting down on the opposite end of the couch that I do, she scoffs. "You think I want to deny myself pleasure? Why would I do that?"

"I haven't figured that out yet, but I can tell how determined you are to deny yourself having me."

"Oh God." She stands. "There it is. Rebel and his infamous ego return. I'm so glad you felt the need to stop by and share this, but if you'll excuse me, I have an early start tomorrow."

I stand too. "That's not what I meant."

"What did you mean then?"

"You keep acting like there's nothing between us. There is. I know I can't be the only one to feel it."

Her sighs feel put on, like a show just for me, not something she truly feels when she looks into my eyes. It's an act to resist what I can tell deep down she doesn't want to. "If you're feeling it, how long did you wait once you were gone last time to be with someone else?"

"Don't ask me that."

"That bad, huh?" Her laugh is sardonic, and then she rolls her eyes, causing my blood to start to boil.

Fuck that. I'm not letting her sidetrack this conversation. "What you're doing is a distraction of what's happening between us and you know it."

"I'm just a distraction, a temporary one at that." There's that sigh again.

"You're not a distraction, you're the main attraction. C'mon, baby, say it."

I move to her end of the couch and sit down. Taking her by the hips I coax her to sit on my lap. When she does, it feels like a win. When she wraps her arm around my neck, it feels like a victory of epic proportions. But when she relaxes into me and says, "I feel it," I feel like a fucking rock star.

19

JAYMES

"WHAT ARE YOU DOING TO ME?" I ask as if Derrick will actually answer with complete honesty.

"I decided since I can't get you to fall madly in love with me, I'll go for wearing you down."

That's pretty darn honest. Laughing, I lean my head against his. "It's working."

His smile grows. He may not be looking right at me, but I can see the lift in his cheeks. "Which is working?"

While damning my heart to hell for being so honest with him, I whisper, "Both."

Strong, caring arms tighten around me and I close my eyes. The smell of his hair is clean, soapy, but his neck has a subtle hint of sweat. I'm reminded how he used to smell and how protected I felt being with him. My body finds peace while inhaling the masculinity of everything about him again. He was always so alpha without knowing how much it turned me on.

He's grown patience over the years, something that's come with age, I suppose. Like me, there are things that have changed and some that remain. For better, and I'm sure in some ways, for worse. I'm not in a position to judge. I just know that I like the way he smells. "Why did you really come over?"

Sliding me to the side, my ass hits the couch cushion, but my upper body is left balancing in his arms. Madly in love—him or me or both? I'm starting to feel it strongly. He says, "I want you to come see me on tour. I've left two tickets at the Virgin Airlines counter. Open ended. For any city. First class. One in your name and one in Ace's."

The surprises never seem to cease with him, my lack of any response other than shock is my initial reaction. He lifts my jaw and kisses my lips lightly. "It will be fun. You can stay as long as you want or a night or two. Whatever works best for your life. A month is too damn long to go without seeing you."

"We just went years."

"Exactly. I'm not losing any more time with you."

There's nothing to argue. There's just this amazing man holding me like I'm the most precious thing he's ever held in his hands.

I kiss him.

I kiss him.

I kiss him.

And for the next few minutes, I forget about my daily struggles and making ends meet. I forget about all the bad and just feel the good. Running my hand down his cheek, I caress it, and lean my forehead against his. "It feels so good to be with you again."

"I've missed you. I've missed this, and your lips. Come see me on tour."

"I don't kn—"

Leaning back, and looking me in the eyes, he says, "I know you will have a million good reasons to say no or to not come. I respect every last one of them. Just please, when I leave here, I want you to remember this—*us*—and how we're a good reason too." He kisses me, then adds, "The other night wasn't a one-off kind of night. We're just getting started, baby. We were always meant to have this second chance. You don't have to answer tonight. You can look at your schedule and see if there's a free weekend or whenever, but consider us when deciding. If you decide against the trip or us, I won't come back and pressure you. I'll want to, but I won't."

"That's disappointing."

That brings a smile, even if it lacks true happiness, back to his handsome face. "Tell me about it." The pile of blankets and pillow on the chair catches his eyes. "Are you sleeping out here on the couch?"

"Yes. I sold our stuff and threw most of the rest away. We really didn't have much worth keeping and I knew we'd only have my old bedroom to store it in. Ace sleeps in there."

"Why did you move home?"

"To save money. You've come back into my life in the middle of so much upheaval. I'm sure it's hard for you to understand."

"No, what I don't understand is why you won't let me help you."

"Because that would only be a temporary fix. I can't just be given a house and then expected to take it at face value. There's always more to it."

"What if there's not?"

"Derrick, don't kid yourself. How can I say no to a date if you buy me a house? Or what if we do date and you bought me a house and then we break up. It leaves me helpless and in the same situation I'm already in. I have to do this on my own."

The palms of his hands scrub his eyes as he sighs. When he looks back at me, he doesn't rush his words. They come with that patience and empathy he's developed. "Maybe we're not the same people anymore, though I hate that you think I would ever ask for something I gave you as a gift back."

"It's not that I think you would. It just complicates things."

"I don't want to be another burden in your life, Jaymes. I care about you. I want to make things better. If I'm not, then just tell me and I'll go."

"You don't listen very well." I tap his nose once. "When I'm with you, I want to be with you. That's easy for me to see and feel. You feel good. I see the possibility of an *us* again. But when we're apart, I see my reality. I'm not sure I want to drag you back down into it again." *Back here to this world.*

"We'll take it slow."

"How about we start now?" I grab the remote and flick on a home improvements show. "Want to watch some TV with me?"

"Absolutely."

My smile goes wide and goofy and my bones almost feel soft like my heart for this man. We rearrange so I'm snuggled against him. His arm comes around my shoulders and the smile I don't bother hiding anymore brings one to his face. "Please tell me it's me and not the DIY show that's making you smile like a loon."

Rubbing his leg, I reply, "It's you. All you."

"Good. I like that."

"I like this. Thank you."

He kisses the top of my head and we watch the show and another after this one.

Sniffling, I wipe my tears from my cheeks. His arm is around me, but I find no comfort. Something is off. Reggie is tense, his tone fake. I take a deep breath and decide I'd rather be alone. "I'm sorry I called you. I thought—"

"It's okay, Jamie. I'm glad you did. He's been my best friend since I was ten. I can't believe he left like this. Your mom home?"

"No, she's still at work." His hand is on my leg and I cover it like I'm killing a bug. My brows knit in confusion. "What are you doing?"

"He's gone. Rebel left you."

My heart screams for relief from the sting of his words, but I know I won't get any because he's right. Derrick left me. I might have told him to go, but he still left.

"Guess you didn't mean as much to him as you thought."

"You're cruel." His hand is still on my leg, so I try to scoot down the couch away from him, but his arm around me tightens, his fingers digging into my upper arm. His other holds my wrist. "I think you should go."

"Did you know that Rebel stole from me?"

Reggie's pupils are wide with evil darkness centering in them. My heart starts pounding in my chest, my breathing becoming uneven as panic sets in. He knows we're alone. He knows my mom won't be home anytime soon. Oh fuck. In one swift move I pull away and say, "You should go now, I remembered my mom will be home early—"

I don't get the chance to finish my sentence. A hand is slapped over my mouth and I'm shoved back into the couch, my head hitting the threadbare arm. I'm dazed for a moment, spots clouding my vision. His rough hands are under my skirt when I come to. Scrambling to push him off, I yell, "Get off me, Reggie. What are you doing?"

But my questions, my plea fall on deaf ears. His focus is on one thing. "He owes me. Rebel owes me."

I land on my feet and run to the other side of the room. "Go! I mean it. I don't know what has gotten into you, but you need to go. Now."

"What has gotten into me?" The grin he tries for turns into a snarl as he stands. The only thing dividing us is a coffee table. "Your fucking boyfriend stole from me. Didn't you know? That's why he skipped town. Fucking loser. He used to be great. He was in line to lead this fucking gang, until he met you. You made him weak."

"I'm not going to ask you again. Leave, Reggie."

"I thought we were friends, Jamie. I thought you cared about me." His tone is mocking. "Isn't that what friends do? Take care of one another? Let me take care of you. You can be my main bitch."

My head is shaking, my thoughts running around the kitchen trying to remember if I put the knife in the sink after I used it earlier or if it's still on the counter. Shit. "No. Derrick's not gone for good. You know he'll be back. Then what will he do to you if you touch me again? He'll kill you."

His laughter rings out, echoing through the pit in my stomach. That's when I know. There is no out. He's not going to leave. He's come here to collect. I run for my bedroom. I can be out the window in seconds, a skill I mastered when I would meet Derrick late at night. The door, I make it to the door before I'm tackled to the hard floor, his weight crushing my soul as much as my body.

My tears come, but I fight.

I hit.

I kick.

I try to escape. There is none.

I'm hit.

I'm kicked.

My arms are held to the side, pain shooting through my veins. My underwear is ripped. My cries don't matter. Reggie is muttering how I am his payment for Rebel fucking him over.

Collateral damage.

"Jaymes, wake up."

My body shakes, my stomach turning. I scream, but no sound comes out. My heart lands in my throat when I'm grabbed. Like a bolt, I'm out of Reggie's arms and land on the floor. My eyes flying open. I scatter across heading for the kitchen. Knife. I must get the knife. I won't make the same mistake twice.

"Jaymes!"

I stop, knowing that voice. It's the voice of the one I love and trust. It's security wrapped in a velvet tone. *Derrick.* Looking back over my shoulder, he's standing, a look of horror on his face, matching the humiliation inside me thicker than blood. I turn back and look down at the floor and my whitened knuckles as I piece together the full picture. Crawling. I am crawling. I sit up and try to steady my thundering heart. My back is too him. I can't bear to see that look on his face again.

"Are you okay?" he asks. I hear the caution in his question. I've revealed myself in ways I never wanted, especially not to him. He tries again, "Please tell me you're all right."

Staring into the kitchen, I suddenly remember the knife was on the counter that night. I should have gone for the knife, not my bedroom. It's a choice that changed everything, that changed me forever. "I'm not all right."

I'm not scared. Not with Derrick. Mortified that I let it happen, but not scared of him now. Footfalls trail up to my back and he sits down in front of me, his back against the doorway to the kitchen. Despite my revelation, the expression of horror is gone, wiped clean and replaced not by sympathy, but empathy.

My mom's door opens and she looks out. "Jamie, are you okay? I heard you yell."

I put on the brave face I wear so often I have it down to a science and reply, "I'm okay. Derrick's here."

"Oh. Hi, Derrick. Well, if you need anything, honey, just call."

"I don't. Go to sleep. I'm fine. You have an early morning."

"Okay. Good night."

"Night," Derrick replies.

We wait, listening for the door to close. When it does, he says, "That was one hell of a nightmare you had there. Want to talk about it?" *Being completely honest with myself, my answer is no. I don't want to talk about it. I don't want to dredge up that pain again.* But now I know Derrick wants more from me, possibly a future, I don't think it's right to hold back. I hope he will still want me when I'm done.

"I guess it's time."

20

DERRICK

There are always two options.

Two roads.

Two paths.

Right and wrong.

Left and right.

Yin and yang.

Good and evil.

Choices.

Decisions.

Outcomes.

So much goes into deciding where this life leads. Some fate. Some destiny. Some great. Some bad. But we have to learn from those bad decisions, learn from our mistakes and hope we don't make them again.

Devastation should never exist in Jaymes Grenier's world, but it does. I control my expressions—my eyes, my mouth, my breathing, my whole body—except for my hands. As I stare into her mossy-green eyes, watch her tears fall to the floor, I can't control my hands. Tightening. Loosening. Fisting to the point of my bones aching.

"Blink, Derrick."

I blink.

She says, "Breathe."

I fill my lungs and then blow slowly out.

"Say something. Please. You're scaring me."

I blink and breathe, then ask, "I'm scaring you?"

Sucking in a jagged breath, she whips it out in a flurry of words. "I didn't mean it like that. You don't scare me. Not like that. I meant I was worried. By your silence. By your hands. I can see you're upset."

"Upset? Yes, Jaymes. I'm upset because you're upset."

Inching closer to me, she says, "If I tell you this, I need you to make me a promise."

"I can't do that and you're going to tell me anyway."

She stands, and I get up off the floor. Hugging me, she tilts her head down against my chest. When I bring my arms around her, she whispers, "You need to keep your voice down. Ace is sleeping and I don't want to worry my mom." She looks up, resting her chin on me. "Can you do that for me?"

For you? Anything for you. "Okay."

She leads me back to the couch and we sit down. I don't know if I'm blinking or breathing or what I'm doing. I know I'm imagining the worst. Her tears have dried and I failed to be the one to dry them. I failed. I failed her.

"I got away. I thought I could make it to my bedroom." She stops to reflect or to remember. "I made the wrong choice. I should have gone for the knife in the kitchen, but he was high, so I thought maybe he would be slow."

The beat of my heart rumbles through my ears.

What the fuck?

What the fuck?

What the fuck?

She continues, her eyes focused on me, her voice not trembling or upset, but matter-of-fact. No emotion, just retelling the facts of the night. I touch her arm, which seems to shake her into the present. "Hey," I say, "you only have to tell me if you want to. If you can't, I'll understand."

"I've carried this a long time. Too long. I'm tired. I'm tired of the power it has over me. I'm tired of the power *he* has over me."

"Jaymes, you need to tell me what happened."

"He was fast. He caught me before I could get the door closed. Tackled me to the floor and pinned me." She peeks over at me with shame filling her eyes. "I fought, Derrick. I promise you. I fought."

What the fuck is happening? What the fuck happened to my girl? A sickening fills me, bile rising until the taste of metal replaces it. "Are you telling me he raped you?"

I. Will. Fucking. Kill. Him.

"Keep your voice low. Please calm—"

"I never promised to stay calm," I whisper-fucking-yell. I'm on my feet and pacing, but I want to punch the fucking wall or better yet, Reggie.

"Please don't wake Ace. He has nightmares sometimes. Tonight he's sleeping. He needs it."

In my anger, I find clarity.

Ace.

My eyes flash to hers. The air stalls around us, the truth suffocating. When she looks down, I know. "Don't say it, Derrick." It's not a threat, but it's a warning.

We're in uncharted territory. I don't say a word. I can't for fear my voice will crack under the heartbreak.

She was violated, violated by someone she should have never trusted. Violated because I left. Fuck.

She didn't betray me by sleeping with him. I should have known better the minute I heard the news. "I should have come back for you. I should have called. I should hav—"

"You wouldn't be here if you had, so despite all I've been through, you're safe."

"I could have handled him."

"He doesn't play with toy guns, Derrick. He's shot people. He just hasn't been caught. Fortunately, they lived, but he's made everyone well aware that he's got a bullet with your name on it." When she continues, she says, "I know you're blaming yourself, but don't. We all played a part, made decisions—good or bad—that got us here today."

Four steps divide us, but not for long. I walk right over and sit next to her, pull her against me, and hold her. "We can change the future, Jaymes. Leave your job. Let me help you."

"No. You're not giving me your money or buying me a house. I'm still considering the plane tickets." She looks up and a small smile is there.

"Get away from this place for just one weekend."

"What about us?"

"Give me one weekend. That's all I ask."

"You make it very tempting."

"Just say yes. Come away with me. You and Ace."

Leaning back, she looks tired. Her eyes are on mine but she's drained emotionally, the weight of this conversation dragging her under. She lifts her legs and sets them across my lap. Gravitating to her, I rub up and down her soft skin a few times before lifting her right up and settling next to her with her back to my chest. Her hands are cold when she covers mine, but her words are warm. "We'll come see you."

I kiss the back of her head. "I'm happy about that, but I need you to know that I'm sorry for leaving like I did. I'm more sorry for what happened. If I would have stayed—"

Spinning around in my arms, her finger covers my mouth. "He would have killed you. And how would I have gone on after that?"

She's letting me off the hook, but I know what I did was wrong, even if what I did to him was right. My eyes home in on hers. "Just like you did. You're the strongest person I know."

"Your mother is a strong woman."

"So is yours, but you, you're special. Ace is so lucky to have you."

A gentle smile sweeps across her lips. "I'm lucky to have him. He's the best result one could ever get from what I went through." The tips of her fingers run along my jaw. "Promise me you'll never see him again."

I don't have to ask whom. I know who she's talking about and I can't make that promise. "It's not a promise I can keep. Not now."

Sitting up, she angles toward me. "Derrick, don't go starting trouble on my behalf. I've got enough as it is. Things are mostly peaceful. We rarely see him."

"Tumultuous. That's how you described your relationship with him. Has he ever touched you again?" The memories scroll through her thoughts. I see the hesitation in her eyes. "You don't have to answer. Your silence says enough."

"I don't want you involved."

"Too late."

"Because I told you?"

"No, because you didn't. You've been fighting that fucker for five years. You don't have to fight him alone. How does he even have any visitation much less custody rights? He's a fucking gang leader. A known criminal."

"I'm tired. I stayed up until three a.m. last night working on a paper due tomorrow. Please. Can we please not do this tonight?"

She's tough. Damn tougher than I am. I'm all about the physical, but she's got inner strength. I relent and let it go for tonight. For her. As for Reggie Rogers, he's about to have his world flipped upside down. Again.

LEAVING Jaymes last night was pure bullshit. I don't think I slept at all after she sent me home. It's now catching up with me on the plane. I'm out before we even take off.

I'm awoken by Tommy calling us sorry fucks for partying so hard the night before a tour. Kaz laughs. "I think you might be responsible for that."

Tommy joins in, laughing. "I can't help that the girls love me."

I've missed a part of this conversation, but don't care to catch up. Looking at the time, it's late enough for me to text Jaymes. *Hey, we left, but if you have a chance, maybe you can call me sometime.*

Okay, I'm officially a pussy because when she texts me back right away, I'm rereading every word over and over and smiling from ear to ear. *I'll call you on my break.*

She'll call me on her break. Yes!

I fist-pump, but when I look up, Kaz is shaking his head and laughing to himself. "I'm not going to say a word."

"Good."

"Except I told you so."

"Go ahead."

"I already did. My work here is done."

Leaning forward, I say, "Hey."

He looks up from his phone. "What?"

"If I tell you some shit, will you keep it between us?"

Kaz looks half-offended that I even preface my question like that. The other half has to be curious. His hand comes out and we shake. "You know you can tell me anything. We're friends. You're my best friend. You've always had my back. I'll always have yours."

"Thanks." Scanning the plane, I spot Tommy with his eyes closed and his earbuds in. Dex is asleep on the couch. Johnny is in the bedroom. When I feel it's sufficiently safe to open up, I say, "I used to be in a gang."

Staring at me, he asks, "Like a band gang?"

Annoyed, I lean back in my chair. "What the fuck is a band gang?"

He shrugs and chuckles. "I have no idea. What do you mean?"

"Drugs and guns and shit like that."

"You sold drugs?"

"No, but the others did." My defenses go up. They shouldn't, but I feel judged. "Look, we can't all be fucking princes."

"Don't be an asshole. I was trying to understand. You've never mentioned this before." I look out the window. We're stuck in the clouds, lost in the gray. "Why are you telling me this?" he asks. "And why now?"

"I saw Jaymes last night and found out some stuff that drudged up old feelings."

"Gang feelings?"

"Fuck you," I say, laughing. "Yes, my delicate gang feelings."

He drinks his Gatorade as soon as it's served. When the flight attendant returns to the front of the plane, he says, "Whatever nest has been disturbed, you better hope the snakes stay put. Don't get the band mixed up in some old mess."

"That's what I'm trying to keep in mind."

"Don't keep it in mind, man. Stay focused. The band is all that matters."

"Bullshit. Lara matters to you. Jaymes matters to me. The band matters."

He nods, and I continue, "But what would you do if Lara was being threatened?"

"You know what Lara and I have been through, so I've been there. How is Jaymes being threatened?"

"I can't say."

"What can you say?"

"Not much. I just need to get her out of the situation she's in."

"And what does she say?"

"She doesn't want my charity."

"One thing I learned with Lara was the more patience I showed, the more she opened up. Trust is huge. You need it or you're sunk before you even have a chance." He starts putting his headphones on, but stops and says, "Really, I just fought for her and she was worth it."

So is Jaymes. I didn't fight for her before, but now I'll do whatever I have to do for her and Ace. Despite what happened to her, that kid is like his mother—a fighter, and a hugger. He hugged me twice the first day I met him. We were instant buds. I'm glad they have each other. I still don't know how she does everything she does with such grace, not asking for a thing. She's got her life together way more than me. I've just been luckier in a few ways.

When we're landing, Kaz looks around like we're part of some secret agent shit, then says, "So the tattoo . . . Rebel—"

"It was an initiation, hazing kind of thing."

"And here I thought you were just that badass."

"It was the tattoo or lose the second finger on my left hand." I unsnap my seatbelt and stand. "There was no fucking way I was going to lose that finger."

"You wouldn't have been able to play guitar."

"Oh I'd figure out a way to play. It's my ring finger though. Once I'm married, that shit is getting shown off."

His eyes go wide. "The burn out is getting to you, man. You realize you're talking about long-term commitment, right? You definitely need a few days off."

Laughing, I reply, "Just had the best break of my life. I'm good." Better than I've been in ages. As soon as I'm in the SUV heading to the hotel in Sacramento, I get the text I've been waiting for.

I can't wait to see you again.

If I thought I was lucky before, finding fame and fortune, I know I'm the damn luckiest guy in the world now.

21

DERRICK

The lights are out.

Dex is center stage.

His solo starts and the spotlight hits him.

Johnny looks back at Kaz and me while we wait on the stairs that lead to the stage. It feels like we've done this a million times, but the excitement and nerves never go away. It always feels like the first time. "Break a leg."

"Break a leg," we repeat.

The arena goes dark and we head up, following the small lights hidden behind the equipment that lead to our places. I swing the strap over my head and tap the pedal twice. My fingers find their position on the fretboard of my guitar and we wait again. Live shows are about more than the music. It's about the performance, the entertainment, the showmanship.

A single spotlight hits Johnny, who is standing at the front of the stage behind his microphone. He sings without music or instruments to back him up. The crowd falls silent, every last fan taking in the song and his haunting voice. Even the band stands there in awe. He pulls emotion from deep within in every note. Watching a legend live is awe-inspiring. Watching him perform at this level of talent night after night is a privilege.

Four.

Three.

Two.

One.

I kick into the chorus, singing back up as I play my guitar. Glancing over, Kaz is leaning back, his bass guitar settled over his hips as he joins in. The audience goes wild and the show begins.

Three songs in, I'm already starting to sweat. I change guitars and plug in before tapping the pedal. Tommy stands just off stage with his arms crossed, his eyes analyzing each of us. Kaz moves to my side and we kick into the riff Dex has been bitching about, and nail it.

Exhilarating.

The thrill of it hits me and I look out at the audience. It's dark, but if I squint, I can see fans forever. *How is this my life?* Kaz and I sing before popping back and challenging each other. It's a long-standing argument—bass or rhythm guitar. He knows I win when I'm on lead.

Best damn job in the world.

After the twelfth song, Johnny tells the audience we're having technical difficulty with three speakers down front and we'll be back for the encore when they're fixed. We leave the stage and head for the dressing room. Tommy calls out, "Twenty-minutes."

The guys filter around the large room—Johnny sits on the counter, the Hollywood lights surrounding him as he calls his woman. Dex is smiling as he FaceTimes with Rochelle. Tommy is dragging Kaz to the table full of posters and paraphernalia. Kaz sits with a sharpie in hand and starts autographing everything from hats to posters.

I probably shouldn't bother her, but I do it anyway. Jaymes answers after one ring, and whispers, "Hey, I'm in class right now. Can I call you later?"

"Yeah, call me when you can."

I'm about to hang up, but she adds, "How's the show?"

"Issues with speakers, but we'll be going back out soon for the encore."

There's a pause before she says, "I haven't expressed this enough, but I want you to know that I'm so proud of you."

The emotion heard in her words catches me off-guard, the softness of her tone. I think she's caught a little off-guard too. "Thanks. Hey Jaymes?"

"Yeah?"

"I'm proud of you, too."

"Thanks, Dare. I've gotta go. I'll call you later."

Smiling from hearing the nickname she used to call me sometimes, I feel like there's a chance for this to happen—me and her—again. "Bye."

Last night we broke through some tall-as-the-sky barriers I don't think she believed we could. With the truth out there, she trusts me. Like Kaz said, that's the basis. Now we can move forward together. I'm high as that sky now and I haven't even had a sip of alcohol.

We kill the encore, the energy rising and the crowd whipped into a frenzy. Then the darkness comes. The arena goes black and we run down the stairs. I grab my phone as soon as we enter the dressing room. *One missed call.*

With the guys hollering about the awesome show, I call Jaymes back and plug one ear. When I can't even hear the ringing, I walk into the bathroom and lock the door. Sitting on the back of the toilet with my Doc Martens propped on the seat, I smile when she answers, "Hello?"

"Hi."

"Hi. Is the concert over?"

"No. I just thought I'd call you from stage."

"No you aren't," she replies in a panic.

Laughing, I shake my head. "No, I'm not. We just finished. We'll be leaving shortly. I need to sign some stuff and then we'll go back to the hotel."

"Not out?"

"I'm not sure. I don't think so. We were up late last night. I'm gonna crash."

"Sorry about everything last night. I know you didn't need all that dumped on your lap like that."

"Don't. Don't apologize. I'm glad you trusted me enough to tell me. You know, I've been thinking about it. I know we said we'll take it slow, but does that feel as wrong to you as it does to me?"

"Last night was a lot." Her voice lowers. "My mom is the only other one who knows because she's the one who found me . . . after." My smile is gone thinking about what happened to her as she takes a moment to gather herself before adding, "I don't want to talk about this on the phone. I'm sorry. Maybe when we see each other."

"It's okay. You set the pace and I'll follow your lead."

Happiness bubbles up when she says, "I was looking at your tour dates."

"Oh yeah?"

Banging on the door makes me jump. Tommy yells, "I need the toilet, Derrick. Get out."

Jaymes laughs. "You're talking to me in the bathroom?"

"I'm not using it. I just wanted privacy."

"Well, I love that, but I think your friend might not appreciate it as much. You can call me later if you want."

This. This is what I've missed. A connection to someone who knows me well enough to not have to worry about small talk. "I do want. I'll call you from the hotel."

"I look forward to it. Talk later."

"Later."

I push the door open and push Tommy on the chest. "Fuck, there's got to be another toilet around, dude."

"Eh, you're just gabbing like a girl in there anyway."

Flipping him off, I grab a bottle of soda and a Twix. "Is the car here?"

Kaz says, "Just got here. C'mon."

"Hey, how real are those connections?"

"What connections?"

Being drunk the other night, he probably doesn't even remember the conversation. I wouldn't involve him anyway, but it's good to know it's an option.

***

I flop on the bed, call Jaymes, and rest my arm over my eyes. When she answers, she sounds like she was sleeping. "Did I wake you?"

"It's okay. It's good to hear your voice."

"I like this change."

"What change would that be?"

Rolling over to my stomach, I whisper, "The one where you talk to me like we're friends, like there's been no time or distance separating us."

"I like it too. I know I've given you a hard time and been resistant to a lot of your kindness—"

"Don't apologize again. We could spend years searching for forgiveness for everything that's happened. Let's just skip to the present and start fresh."

"When did you become the reasonable one between us?"

"Ha. Yeah, go figure. Anyway, how was your day?"

Her breathing is deep and relaxed. "Busy. Tomorrow might be worse, so if I don't answer, you'll know why."

"Earlier, you said you were looking at tour dates. Want to elaborate?"

"A girl can dream."

"It's a dream we share."

"I need to be upfront with you on this, Dare. I don't know that I can make this happen. I have so many balls in the air that I'm afraid I'll drop them and instead of bouncing, they'll break."

I'm close to begging. I need more time with her. Selfishly, I need to explore these feelings between us. Are they lingering from the past or developing in the present? Can it be as easy as seeing her again that has calmed the inner turmoil I've had? Is all of this leading to the most obvious conclusion—it's her I've been missing all along? If I were to answer today . . . "Please come."

"No guarantees. Yet. I thought I would check in with you first and find out what you were thinking. We don't want to be a burden."

"You guys could never be."

She begins to whisper, "This is so fast."

And yet not fast enough.

"But—"

My breath stops waiting for her to finish this sentence. "But?"

"I want to see you again too."

Yes!

Score!

Goal!

Touchdown!

This victory feels better than when we won a Grammy.

"Is there a date you prefer? I won't know until last minute due to work and school, but I can start checking into it."

Now. I wish you were here with me now. "The soonest."

"Las Vegas next weekend? That's five days."

"Four shows."

"I'm not sure that Vegas is a place for Ace."

"It can be what we make it. If you're serious, I'll get us the best suite in the city with two bedrooms. Ace can have his own and we can have another." Too much? Too fast? "Unless you want your own private room. I can book that for you."

"No, a suite for all of us sounds amazing. Thank you."

"Thanks for coming."

"Five days. I'll get back with you, but I'm excited."

"Me too. I look forward to seeing you both."

"I should go, but thanks for always thinking of Ace."

That cute kid is hers. It doesn't matter that his dad is a fuck-up of epic proportions. Ace deserves the best chance at a future outside that neighborhood. If I can play a part in that, I will. "He's important to you, so he's important me, Jaymes."

"Thanks."

"No thanks needed. Good night."

"Good night."

Reaching over, I push the button closing the curtains and turning off the lights. Lying there, I remember so much about us when we thought we owned the world . . .

A rare night in LA—the stars shine above. Resting back on a pile of pillows in the bed of my truck, I stare up. Miles of universe make me feel small. Jaymes is strumming the guitar I gave her, singing softly along with the radio.

Glancing over at her, I say, "You're better."

"You only say that so you can get laid."

I laugh. "Put the guitar down."

With an all-knowing smile on her face, she passes it through the open window of the cab, setting it safely on the seat. I immediately grab her and swing her under me until I'm leaning over her. "I'm gonna get laid anyway, so when I tell you something, it's the truth, baby."

Her fingers zigzag into my hair and then stop. Full lips are licked, her eyes telling me everything she wants. I press my mouth to hers lightly at first. Running my tongue over her bottom lip, I then take it between my teeth with just enough pressure to feel her bated breath exhale. I need all of her—her breath, her kisses, her love, her soul. Our tongues touch as I rub her thigh under the little floral dress she wore to tease. I stole her innocence years ago, but the sweet little dresses she wears remind me of when I met her.

She tugs my shirt over my head and I lift up to remove my jeans. Her dress comes off next. Seeing her body highlighted in the moonlight, she's an angel here on Earth, the whole of my beating heart. Pert tits barely covered in purple lace beckon me. Dipping one cup down, I cover her nipple with my mouth, tonguing until chill bumps cover her and her fingers tighten in my hair. Peeking up, I see her eyes watching me while her mouth is open. "I want your underwear off." She lifts and I want to rip, but I pull them down instead. I can read her mood by the music she was playing and by the soft kisses.

Gentle. She wants love and romance. I can do that.

Her legs part for me and I run my fingers higher. Centered at the apex of her thighs, I rub small circles and tease until she's coming on me. Her moans echo through the trees and I lean down to devour her.

Fingers grapple with my shoulders to pull me up higher. "I need you," she says, her whisper whipped away on the wind. "Make love to me, Derrick."

When I move up, her hands push my boxers down. Moving to where we'll both feel so good, I hold myself above her. "See those stars in the sky?" She nods, her gaze heading high. "We're going to fly higher and shine brighter. Together we'll win the world over and conquer the universe."

"I'd settle for your heart."

"You already own it." I move and her head dips back. Pushing slowly in until my lips caress the underside of her jaw. My breath escapes as ecstasy takes over. Thrusting my body, my heart is pulled—all of me under her spell. I drop my head down next to hers.

Sliding her arms around me, she kisses my temple, and says, "Promise me life will always be this good."

"I promise you it will be better. I'll make sure of it."

Our lips embrace as our bodies come together in all ways.

. . . Wonder if we can conquer the universe this time around. I promised her a better life, and right now, I feel as though I've failed her. *I did fail her. Why did I believe she would want to be with Reggie? Why did I let my stupid pride stop me from checking the facts? Idiot.*

I promised her the world, and now I intend to give it to her.

22

———————

JAYMES

"Pack the pink dress. You look so pretty in that one."

I send a glare my mom's way. "What you think is pretty and what Derrick will find sexy are two different things."

She's smiling and yes, I showed my feelings, but if I can't share my happiness with her, then who can I? She'll also help me when the time comes. The time will come when I have to deal with certain *other* people. Some guy I didn't recognize with a large lettered tattoo peeking out the back of his wife-beater was loose-lipped to Leann at the convenience store on the corner. "Reggie was picked up. He's in for the weekend. No judge will see him until Monday."

That's when I knew I had to go. I could see Derrick without fear of being caught. Two nights and I would be back before anyone noticed I was even gone. The smile hasn't left my face since I called him to confirm.

Ace has effectively taken out the four shirts I've packed for him and messed up the jeans and shorts. "Hey buddy, can you help pack your suitcase while Mommy packs hers?"

"What does sexy mean?" he asks.

My mom grabs the pink dress and throws it at me. "Pack it." Tugging on Ace's sleeve, she adds, "Come help me make dinner."

Down the hall I hear him ask, "Where is Derrick going to find sexy, Grandma?"

A laugh escapes from the relief I feel that I don't have to answer that. Looking at the pink dress, it's so pink, but when I glance over at the closet, I don't have much of a selection for sexy. I pack the dress and then decide I'll win him over with sexy lingerie, except I don't have any. I've had no reason to want to feel or look sexy for anyone in a long time. I find my best underwear instead and pack it along with two pretty bras.

"Jamie."

"Mommy!"

I dash out of the room and into the living room. "What?"

Ace points at the TV and says, "Look. It's Derrick."

Following where he's pointing, I watch the TV. The bleach-blonde reporter is wearing a skin-tight red sweater dress. She shoves the microphone toward the lead singer who ignores her question. Security rushes around clearing the paparazzi away. One of the guys with sandy-blond hair wraps his arm around Derrick's neck and drags him over to the reporter. "Single? We sure are. What's your number?"

The dark sunglasses hide Derrick's eyes but when a flash goes off, I catch a glimpse of his annoyance. And then they're escorted into waiting cars and drive away.

Ace turns back and says, "You colored the box that said single when we went to school."

"Huh?" I'm not sure what he's talking about, but then I remember. "When I registered you for kindergarten?"

He nods and smiles before pointing back to the TV. "Derrick is single too."

Laughing, I agree. "He sure is."

"Mommy, what is single?"

Oh Lordy, here we go.

MY MOM ADJUSTS Ace's backpack on his shoulders. "You be good for your mommy, okay?"

"Yes, ma'am."

She squeezes him in a tight hug while I pull our suitcases from the trunk of her car. How a carry-on for only two days weighs this much is beyond me. Oh wait, no it's not. I packed everything I could fit in there. As soon as I close the trunk, my mom is hugging me just as hard. I comfort her. "We'll be all right."

"First plane ride for you both."

I take Ace's hand. "We're gonna do this together, aren't we, bud?"

"Yup. I'll take care of her, Grandma, like I promised."

"Good boy, Ace." She kisses my cheek, and whispers, "Try to have some fun and enjoy the time away."

"I will. I promise. Thanks for driving us."

"Call me when you land."

I hug her once more and then stack Ace's small case on mine and take his hand again. When we check in we're told we can wait in a lounge. I'm not sure where she says it is. It's like trying to find a secret door in the middle of an enchanted forest and Ace is sidetracked by the pretzel place. "Please, can I have one?"

"I don't know, Ace. I have some snacks with me. Two Granola bars and two apples. Do you want one of those instead?"

"No, it's a treat on our adventure. Please?"

They do look good and it will tide him over until dinner if he eats the whole thing. "Okay. But you know we have to be careful with money. This is an adventure, but not too many treats. Deal?"

"Deal." We shake on it and I give him a five-dollar bill. He steps up to the counter and orders cinnamon pretzel bites like a big man. I rub his back as he waits for his change. Twenty-three cents. Instead of handing it to me, he drops it all in the tip jar on the counter. I say a silent prayer right there that the world never ruins the good that is my son.

We never do find that lounge, but we find our terminal and gate easily. The flight attendant calls us to the stand and greets us with a smile. "I heard you're first-time fliers?"

Ace answers, "We are."

"Well, you are going to love first class. We'll make sure to take extra special care of you." She looks at me and says, "You may board now."

"Thank you."

We find our seats and I let Ace sit by the window. I try to keep my mouth from falling open at how fancy this is. Derrick outdid himself. Ace and I are officially spoiled.

The flight is short but I'm served champagne and berries. Ace fell asleep after the orange juice and his cookies and took a quick nap. I feel like we can ask for anything and they'll have it. Flying is amazing.

I sip a cup of coffee while Ace stares out the window, excited we're landing soon. Reading my phone, I check the messages from Derrick again just to make sure I understand. *A driver will be there to greet you in baggage claim. He'll bring you to the hotel where we're staying.* Okay. I can do this.

The landing was a bit rough. Ace got scared, but so was I. I'm amazed how Derrick can fly all the time. Wonder if he gets anxious like I was?

A guy in a black suit, just like in the movies, is holding a sign up for us. He takes our carry-ons and we follow him to the private car waiting area. "Thank you," I say when he opens the door. Ace springs in and I duck in after, but am surprised. "You're here?"

Derrick melts me to the seat with his killer smile. "I couldn't wait to see you."

The door is closed and I'm brought in for a kiss, but right before we get to follow through, he peeks between us and laughs. "Hey there, Ace, my man. How's it going?"

"I got cookies on the plane and Mom bought me pretzel bites."

"Your mom's the best."

Ace nods and I laugh. "Thank you for all this. The flight was incredible. A little rough at the end, but nothing I couldn't handle." When I look back into his eyes, they darken and I realize what I just said. We used to play around, a little rough sometimes, but so comfortable with each other that we didn't have to hide any of our desires. That feels like another life. But I won't be too quick to judge.

Optimism fills the car, and while looking into those oceanic eyes, I start to believe it's possible to capture the past. *Or maybe this is not about recapturing our past. Maybe this is about finding our future. Should I think that?*

Derrick reaches his arm around the top of the seat, over Ace's head, and rests his hand on my shoulder. His fingers tap and tickle. Looking into his cheerful expression, I know it's possible.

The hotel comes into view. Gold windows and grand statues welcome us, and as soon as we step out, Ace says, "Whoa."

"Come on," Derrick says, putting his sunglasses on.

His body is tense and I feed off his reaction, taking Ace's hand. "Are we safe?"

The question seems to surprise him. "We're safe. I just don't want to draw any attention."

"Neither do I."

The left side of his lips slides up and he takes my free hand. "Elevator's this way. They'll bring the bags up."

In the elevator, he pushes the button and I stand next to him, giddy as can be to be here with him. He sneaks a hand behind my back and rubs. "You look beautiful."

Touching my cheeks, I tilt my head down, knowing I'm blushing, and whisper, "Thank you."

The doors open and he leads us down the hall and opens the door. "Hey Ace, check out that view."

Ace runs to the window and presses his nose against it. "Whoa."

"I think we're going to hear a lot of that this weekend. He's never been anywhere like this before. I haven't either for that fact." *But this is now Derrick's norm. Surreal.*

Taking my hand, Derrick says, "Then let me give you a tour." We only make a few feet inside the bedroom before he tracks Ace's whereabouts and then presses me to the wall and kisses me hard. "God, I'm so glad you're here."

"Me too."

Ace runs in and we jump apart. "Mommy, you have to see the pool. It looks so small with ants around it." He grabs me and tugs me into the living room. I sneak a glance back at Derrick who's laughing and joins us at the floor-to-ceiling windows.

"Those are people, not ants." All three of us are pressed against the glass—biggest to smallest. Derrick reaches over and takes my hand. I reach over and take Ace's. *This.* This is all I ever wanted. "I don't need the view or the fancy suite."

Derrick looks over, and asks, "What?"

"That out there. Or this fancy hotel. It's nice, don't get me wrong, but this," I say, holding up our clasped hands, "is all I ever dreamed of."

The delivery of the bags interrupts a kiss to my cheek. We laugh and Derrick goes to the door. I remain while Ace points out all the things he sees, which is a lot. "I'm hungry," he says, looking up at me.

"Okay, let me grab an apple for you." I grab my purse to rummage through it until I find the Granola bars and the apples, and then set them on the table.

Derrick comes up behind me and his hands start to touch me, but he sees Ace and moves around to the other side of the table. "What's all this?"

"Ace is hungry, so I was getting him something to eat."

Holding up an apple, he asks, "You brought your own food?"

My defenses go up, but then I realize how this looks, how it appears to him. Lowering my voice and those defenses that popped up too fast for my own liking, I reply, "We don't have much money. We may be here on vacation, but I still need to be responsible."

He takes the apple and tosses it to Ace. When he turns back to me, he says, "You don't need your own food. Charge anything you want to the room and if you want anything in the hotel, just charge it to me. I've got you both covered. Anything you want, it's yours."

"This is so much. I don't want to take advantage of your generosity."

"Please. Take advantage. I have my mom. Other than that, I don't have anyone to spend all this money on. Let me spend some on you, and that guy over there."

"Were you always this charming, Derrick Masters?"

"More. You've just forgotten."

"Well, you're doing a darn good job reminding me."

"I try, sweet Jaymes. I try."

Another knock draws our attention away from each other. I join Ace by the window and we continue to look at The Strip and all the twinkling lights. I look back and see Derrick hugging a woman and welcoming a man I recognize from the band. Two kids run in and up to the windows next to us. "Hi," I say to the oldest. He's older than Ace, so I ask, "What's your name?"

"Neil." Not looking to carry on a conversation, he nudges Ace, and I smile. "This is a better view than ours. We got a parking lot. How old are you?"

Ace is shy at first, so he glances to me, but then replies, "Five."

"I'm eight. My brother's five like you. His name is CJ. Are you Uncle Derrick's kid?"

My heart sinks. This time Ace looks to me for more than a long second. He looks to me for answers. I'm about to step in and reply for him, but he beats me to it. "Yes."

23

JAYMES

SADNESS OVERTAKES HIS SMALL FRAME. His shoulders sag and his sweet little brown eyes are aimed down. I want to say something, but I'm not sure what and I don't want to embarrass him by correcting him in front of the others. "Ace?"

A tiny hand rests on my knee, and when we look into each other's eyes, he whispers, "Don't be sad, Mommy."

Neil taps him on the shoulder. "Tag. You're it."

They take off running and I'm left with the shame of what I've caused him.

I fought.

I didn't fight hard enough, but if I had stopped Reggie, I wouldn't have Ace.

"Jaymes?" My attention shifts toward my name. Derrick is a few feet away with the others. All three are staring at me, expecting something from me. A hand is held out and a gentle smile welcomes me. "I want you to meet my friends."

Friends. Friends from a life I know nothing about.

I stand, and join them.

"This is Jaymes Grenier." Pride is heard in the introduction as Derrick wraps his arm around my back. "Dex Caggiano, our drummer, and this is Rochelle Floros. Rochelle keeps the band running from our brand to our image and everything in between, including helping to organize the tour."

They're holding hands, but reach to shake mine before finding each other so effortlessly again. I don't think I've ever seen two more beautiful people. Rochelle asks, "How old is Ace, Jaymes?"

"You can call me Jamie."

She glances to Derrick and smiles with a raised eyebrow. "These guys seem to have an affinity for full names. I don't know what it is, but I just kind of love it, so Dex and I will call you Jamie, and leave Jaymes for Derrick."

It's funny what you learn when you finally open your eyes. I had forgotten, it always just felt right hearing my full name from him. Derrick even called me Jaymes when he was Rebel and everyone else called me Jamie. It seems the habit is rampant among the band. Or do all rock stars prefer the formality of birth given names? It's not important, but I still like the way it feels special that only he calls me Jaymes. "Ace is five. Are those your sons?"

"Yes. Neil and CJ. Sorry for the invasion. They tend to make themselves right at home wherever we are. I guess that's what all this traveling over the years has done."

"It's fine. Neil was very nice. He introduced himself and CJ to us."

"That's good to hear. He usually does most of the talking. CJ owns being the baby of the family, from tantrums to his curiosity, so sometimes he forgets his manners. I think he's been hanging around Dex too much," she teases, wrapping her arm around him. His arm comes around her shoulders as they tease. The conversation is lost as I witness the way he holds her so casually and comfortably that it makes me wonder if Derrick and I can ever get back to that place.

Not if Reggie has his way. Fortunately, I find some comfort that he isn't brave enough to come to my mom's house. It's not just me he'll be messing with, but my mom as well.

Damn it. I had managed to put him out of my mind, to take the trip, promising myself to get lost for a while in happiness and live in a fantasy world for two days. I don't think it's going to be possible. Not with the dark clouds of guilt hovering above us. Looking up at Derrick, his innocent gesture, his want to be with me and mine for him puts all three of us at risk. I need to talk to him this weekend.

"So what do you think?"

My eyes flash to Rochelle's. Staring dumbly at her, I ask, "What?"

The group laughs, except for Derrick, who looks concerned. He steps in to save me. "Jaymes flew for the first time today. She and Ace had never been on a plane or to Vegas. It's a lot to take in."

Running my hand through my hair, I push it back. "Yeah, it's exciting too. I'm so grateful Derrick did this for us."

Rochelle's expression is kind with trustworthy eyes. I'm comfortable around her, something I'm not used to being in my regular life. Are rich people genuine or am I being played? She says, "We came up here because Dex needed to talk to Derrick about the show tomorrow night. Why don't you show me around the fancy suite."

"I haven't seen much of it. We can take a tour together." Giving the guys privacy, we walk to the windows. I've not gotten to really look at the view. I helped Ace pinpoint a few things, but standing in silence in front of these large windows, I feel like we're on top of the world.

It's not silent for long. The boys are running from one end of the suite to the other chasing each other and giggling. I love the sound of their happiness and fun. CJ is acting like a total goofball, cracking jokes as he chases them. Rochelle says, "He loves to play. He's the happiest kid all the time and will do anything to make someone laugh. He's a lot like his father."

Dex and Derrick have moved to the dining table and both have their phones out. Music is playing and they appear to be breaking down the song, note by note.

"I'm a fan of their music, and I've heard great things about Dex."

Rochelle looks my way. "Dex isn't their biological father, but he is their dad. For CJ, he's practically the only one he's ever known."

Doing a double take, I look at her thinking of Ace. Reggie. Derrick. "I don't mean to pry—"

"It's not prying." She goes on to tell me how Dex stepped in when she needed someone most. How he was the one who was there for her and the boys. We stroll from room to room, stopping to take in the view from each.

Her story resonates with me, giving me hope that maybe we'll be out from under the dirty thumb of *him*, and accepted openly and cherished as part of a family. Ace deserves a family and a man who is a true role model.

And I want that too. A man in my life for me. It's as though I've hidden myself for years. Busy as a mom, as a daughter, as a student and a worker. Life has been about working what feels like twenty-four seven. I've *survived*. But not necessarily lived.

"Jaymes?" Walking back into the living room, Derrick and Dex are standing there looking more like the cats that ate the canaries than brooding rock stars.

I go to him. I wrap my arms around his middle and embrace him. In front of Dex. With Rochelle watching. With the kids running circles around us and weaving between the furniture, I hug him, so tight. "Yes?"

Strong arms envelop me. "Will you go on a date with me tonight?"

He doesn't even whisper it. Just asks like that for everyone to hear, and my heart is his all over again. That simple. Before I answer, Rochelle drags Dex over to the windows and thus starts the worst game of *not-eavesdropping* I've ever seen played. Tilting my head up, I grin, my pants practically charmed right off me from the sweetness of his question. "I would love to. I have to warn you though, Ace doesn't eat in fancy restaurants so we might want to keep it kid-friendly."

"Not with Ace, though I'd like to take him to do some stuff while you're here. Tonight, just you and me."

"He's five, Derrick. I can't leave him here by himself."

"I actually offered to watch him," Rochelle says, "I was thinking since I have my boys here and they're all getting along so well that maybe Ace could spend some time with us. Maybe even have a sleepover."

How are these people so nice? "Who are you and how did I get so lucky to meet you?" I joke.

Derrick's playful jealousy is showing when his arms tighten reminding me he's here. "Hey, what am I?"

"A dream come true. I'd love to go out with you, but he's never had a sleepover before."

Rochelle offers, "Of course no pressure. The boys have been getting along so well that—"

Derrick adds, "Only what you're comfortable with."

"He spends the night with my mom sometimes. It's not like I have to be there every night, but he needs to feel safe. That I'm okay and he's okay."

"Do you want to talk to Ace?"

"Yes. Let me talk to him and see how he feels about it."

It's so hard to let go when being in his arms is my favorite place to be, but I pull myself off of him and find Ace and the other boys jumping on the beds in his room. "Jump to me, buddy."

When he lands in my arms, I crouch with a grunt, setting his feet on the floor. "You're getting so big, Ace."

"Derrick told me if I keep eating healthy stuff and exercise I'll be bigger than you when I grow up." I kneel down so I'm eye level, but he continues, "He said I might even be as big as him one day. That's gigantic."

"You're growing fast. I think he might be right. So, I can tell you really like Derrick." He nods, his eyes glancing between me and the other boys, anxious to get back to playing. "I like Derrick, too."

"I know, Mommy. Grandma says when you weren't single that you weren't single with him."

As much as I want to be irritated at my mom for talking about Derrick and me with Ace, I'm struggling to muster the anger. Technically, what she said is true and the only time I've ever lied to Ace is to protect him from Reggie. I'm not going to lie about Derrick. Not to Ace. "Yes, we used to go on dates. That's when two people like each other and hang out."

"Like we do."

I smile. "Yes, like we do. So tonight Derrick wants to hang out with me and Neil and CJ's mommy thought it would be fun if you could hang out with them, maybe even have a sleepover."

"Whoa. Yes," he says, jumping up and down. "Yes. Yes. Yes. Please. Please. Please."

"I thought that might be your answer. I'll let them know." I stand and he's about to dive back on to the bed, but I grab him and hug him tight. "I love you, buddy."

"I love you."

He's so wiggly to get back that I let him loose. Standing there, I watch for a minute as the boys play, daring each other to jump off and land on their feet. "Be careful, guys." When I return to the others, I point at Derrick. "I'm all yours." Smiling to Rochelle and Dex, I say, "They're all yours. You sure it's okay?"

"Totally. We'll have a great time."

"Thank you so much."

"You're welcome. We'll let you guys settle in and come by around six for Ace. Does that work?"

"He'll be bouncing off the walls until then."

"I hear ya. With this wild crew, Dex is teaching them drums and guitar, so he's heading to the stage to let me nap. I have a feeling we're going to have a busy night."

"I think so, but I appreciate it so much."

"No problem at all," she replies.

Minutes later, they're gone and Derrick and I are left standing there. It's eerily quiet, so we sneak back to the bedroom where the kids were playing and find Ace zonked out on the bed. Derrick's hand is pressed lightly to my back, and I lean my head against the doorframe. This just all feels so good. So . . . *right*. That same *right* Derrick was talking about. We've already fallen into a little bubble of comfort and I don't know if I should go with it or be leery.

My shoulders are tense and his hand slides up, massaging me. He says, "Let him sleep. If I know Neil and CJ, which I do, he's going to need all the energy he can store."

Quietly, we go back to the living room and keep walking. It's been driving me crazy not to kiss this man. As soon as we enter the master bedroom, I grab him and press him to the wall. My lips are on him, my body against his Rock. Hard. Body. "We can stay in tonight," I suggest, hopeful.

"Ha. My oh my. I kind of like you all wound tight." He slips out of my grasp and backs toward the bed. "Call me cruel—"

"Cruel."

He snickers. "I'm thinking I might tease you a bit tonight. Wind you even tighter."

Stalking toward him, I cock an eyebrow. "That would be cruel. You shouldn't be so mean."

"I'm mean now? Hmmm . . ." He taps his chin. "C'mere, baby." I rush into his arms. With a kiss to the top of my head, and while stroking my hair, he whispers, "Let me take you. Wine and dine you good and proper and then we have the whole night to do all the dirty, fucking sexy things you want to do. How does that sound?"

"Sublime. Where have you been all my life?"

"Right here waiting for this moment with you."

24

DERRICK

She's going to kill me dead.

Right here.

Right now.

Rubbing up against me.

In a hotel room in Vegas.

With her hot body and dirty talk.

I pry her sexy little self off me and kick myself for asking her to wait. I'd be more than happy to fuck the night away. But that's not the memory I want her to have of our time together. Well, I do want that, but in addition, I also want to romance her and make this weekend the most unforgettable time of her life.

With the life I've been leading the last couple years, I forget she's still leading one I left in the past.

Her first flight.

Her first time out of LA.

Her first time to leave California.

Her first trip to Las Vegas.

Shit.

So many firsts. In my life, cities blur together without a second thought. I'm barely aware of where I am these days, much less appreciating where I've been.

Walking across the room, she lies on the bed and asks, "Do I get to sleep in here?"

"I wouldn't have it any other way."

"Where are you going to sleep?"

"Funny girl with all the jokes." She's laughing, completely amused. Me too. I sit at the end of the bed and take one of her shoes off and then the other. Rubbing her feet, I lean back on my elbow.

Her moan goes straight to my cock. *Fuck.* I get up and walk into the bathroom. While I readjust, she comes in. "Sorry. Didn't know you were so easily turned on."

"I think you knew."

"Maybe." She laughs just as our gazes catch in the reflection of the mirror The way she leans with her hip kicked out and a look on her face, that come-hither smirk, that used to have me begging, I see the girl I fell in love with the moment I laid eyes on her . . .

Reggie pulls a pack of cigs out of his jacket pocket and pops one up in offering.

Instead of taking one, I lean forward, resting my arms on my knees atop the picnic table. "You've got balls as big as San Francisco, dude."

We just got busted by Coach Thorne smoking behind the gym, scored one week of detention, and here this fucker is smoking on school property not even five minutes later. With an unlit cigarette hanging from the corner of his mouth, he says, "San Francisco isn't that big."

"And your point is?"

"Fuck you . . ."

I'm too busy laughing at my own joke to hear what he says next, but when he hits me in the chest, I take notice. "What the fuck?"

"There she is."

"Who?" I ask. When I follow his stare, I sit up.

Oh.

Dark hair. Almost black on this cloudy day.

Wow.

The wide eyes of innocence shining.

Shit.

Tits. Not huge, but enough to satisfy a tit guy. I guess that's what I am. I wasn't just knocked on my ass. I was knocked completely out of my orbit and straight off my axis. I didn't know her name, but Reggie did. "Jamie Grenier."

My throat felt dry and my chest hurt from the sight of her. Fuck. Am I having a heart attack at fifteen? "Give me a cigarette."

"Now you want one?"

"Yeah."

I light up—fire to the flame. My nerves settle, but my chest still aches. Then she looks my way. Reggie catcalled her and got flipped off in return. I try a different approach. "Hey."

When she realizes I'm talking to her, she replies, "What?"

"Did I see you at the mall the other day?" I never go to the mall.

"I don't think so."

"Maybe over at Ernie's?" The best sandwich shop in LA.

There it is. She smiles. "Maybe. They've got the best sandwiches in the city."

Damn, I knew I liked her. And then Fate played her hand—Reggie hits me from behind. "Call her over here. I want to meet her."

It's not just an ache I feel but more in that moment, something bigger, stronger, something I've never felt before. There's no way I'm walking away from this girl. And less chance I'm giving Reggie a shot at her. No, that's not gonna happen. "Hey Jamie, c'mere."

Reggie is so excited his hands are shaking. Or it might be from the drugs he took after we were busted. Who knows? The dude is fucked up. I've known him since I was ten and he was the only kid I was told to stay away from. Naturally he was the most fascinating. Five years later, I'm almost as deep into this gang shit as him. I've learned to protect myself and my home. No one else will do it for you. We're the small-time lackeys right now, but we're moving up the ranks fast. In two years, I'll get my tat. That will be the beginning of the end of all those dreams my mom once had, but I'll own these streets. Nothing's gonna change that course now.

She walks with purpose, not afraid of us like some of the chicks at this school. Crossing her arms over her chest, she stops right in front of me—all badass attitude wrapped in a bombshell body. "What's your name?" she asks.

"Rebel."

Reaching forward, she pushes some of the hair fallen over my forehead to the side, and takes my cigarette. Dropping it to the ground, she says, "You can call me Jaymes."

I realize right then that I'm not just a tit guy. I'm a Jaymes Grenier guy. She stole my cigarette and my heart that day.

. . . And she's never given it back. Our eyes are still locked, both of us caught up in memories that feel more real than this life sometimes. "You changed my course."

Sadness befalls her. "You changed mine." The doorway is vacated and I'm left with the damage I've done. While she gave me her best, I gave her my worst.

Walking back into the bedroom, I find her standing at the window staring out. Her arms are still crossed and her dark hair covers half her face. I join her, our arms pressed together as we both look out over Vegas. "He liked you," I say.

When her green eyes look into mine, she asks, "Who?"

"Reggie."

I see the change. It's instant. The softness in her body hardens. The kindness in her eyes turns to hate. The patience of her usual tone is gone. "I don't want to talk about *him*. Not tonight."

"I know, but I think we should."

"Why? Why ruin this?"

"I'm not trying to ruin it, Jaymes. I'm trying to make it better. We all have secrets and I know that mine did more damage than I ever realized."

"So this is a confessional now?" Walking to the bed, she sits at the end, her body closed off with arms wrapped around her and knees crossed. "Well, guess what? I don't want to hear it. I don't want to hear anything about him ever again."

"Please."

The plea pulls her gaze back to mine. Her breathing has changed

—harshness taking over. "Fine. Whatever makes you feel better, Derrick. Go for it."

"It's not that I'll feel better. I will never feel better because of how he hurt you."

Moving higher on the bed, she grabs a pillow and hugs it to her chest. Her back is to the headboard and her knees protecting her. I can't see her face and it's killing me that she won't look up. "Just say it."

"The day I met you, he told me to call you over so he could talk to you." We can't be more than what we've been without honesty and the purest of truths, even if it hurts to reveal them. "I didn't."

"You didn't what?" she asks.

"I didn't call you over for him. I betrayed him and called you over for me."

"Oh Derrick." Her words are trapped in the palm of her hands as she covers her face.

Moving to the bed, I sit down next to her and roll her to the side so she's cradled to me. "I couldn't stop myself. I never knew what love was until I saw you that day. I didn't know what a heart felt like until it started beating for the first time for you. I know now that it wasn't my chest aching. The moment I saw you, it was my soul trying to escape to be with you." I see her struggling emotionally and hold her.

"Why are you telling me this now?"

"Because he may have liked you, but I loved you. I loved you before I knew you." With tears building in the corner of her eyes, she sits up and angles her body. As soon as one falls, I wipe it away. "I'm sorry. What happened to you was because I fucked him over. I'm sorry, Jaymes." Her arms are around me as I lean my head on her shoulder. "I'm so sorry."

Quiet murmurs and warm breath cover my neck. "You're not to blame. I would have never been with him." She stalls and then corrects herself, "Not by choice." God, what have I done to this woman? She raises my head up until I'm looking at the face of the angel I destroyed. She adds, "The day I saw you, my heart knew I'd never survive you." Releasing a long breath, her face changes back to the one I know, the one I recognize so well—beauty and strength. "But I will survive *him*." She kisses me.

I don't deserve forgiveness or sweetness, but I receive, crave it, and am given it anyway. Rolling to the side, she manages to smile. "God, it's such a weight off, right?"

"Yeah."

"Since we're confessing, I kind of already told you, but thank you for being so gentle the other night. It was the first time since . . . Anyway, it meant a lot to me that you treated me with such care."

"It's how I feel about you."

"I know and I feel the same about you. One day, the horrors of our past won't haunt us any longer, but until that day, I'm glad we can be so open. It's the only way we can forgive ourselves and each other and move on."

I hadn't realized how much guilt I've carried until I saw her tears. Jaymes has always been so strong, so amazing. Knowing she was broken because of me hasn't sat well since we talked that night. Now it's her forgiveness I need. I don't deserve it. *I left her and a monster took her.* "Do you forgive me?"

"Silly man, there's nothing to forgive. Our love story was already set in motion. Our destiny was just waiting for us to meet." *Thank God.*

"I never sat at the picnic tables at lunch. We were usually behind the gym."

"I heard some guys got busted behind the gym by Coach Thorne."

My eyebrows rise in surprise. "You came to see me get in trouble?"

"Yeah, but we were too late."

"I'd say you were right on time."

25

JAYMES

Mom wins.

I pull the pink dress from my suitcase. It's the prettiest dress I own and I think Derrick will like it on me. I hope, at least.

When I finish showering, I go to check on Ace, but stop and hide behind the bedroom wall. Peeking into the living room, Derrick and Ace are sitting on the couch rubbing their stomachs. I listen carefully since their voices are low. Derrick pokes Ace in the tummy, making him giggle, but then says, "Go for the gusto, my friend. It starts low and then builds as it comes up. Watch and learn." Derrick belches so loud that even I'm impressed. Ace is super-impressed and a giggly mess on the couch.

With a towel on my head and a fluffy robe from the closet over me, I stand in the doorway with my hands on my hips. "You're teaching my son how to burp?"

"I figured you weren't going to. Yup, we're doing man stuff out here so take your time getting ready."

The way his lips curl at the sides and the lamp's light sparkles in his eyes, he's a sight to behold. Sexier than sin and seeing him play with Ace is all kinds of goodness. Pointing my finger, I say, "Ace, keep him out of trouble. Okay?"

"Ten-four, Mommy."

I'm taking it that Derrick taught him that too.

Rochelle shows up on time to pick up Ace. We go over a few things and I tell her to call me if she needs anything or if Ace needs me. As much as I'm excited to have a whole night off, I'm also worried. He's never been away from me. Rochelle hugs me like we're old friends. "I'll take the best care of him. I promise. We have lots of popcorn, and pizza, and candy. Games and movies. So you go have fun and enjoy your night off. I remember what it's like to be a single parent and these nights are rare." Maybe that's why I feel so easy around her. She does understand. She probably understands the loneliness too.

I say goodbye to my little man and then head back into the bathroom to finish getting ready. Derrick's in the shower, but he reads me well. "He's going to be all right. Rochelle's a great mother."

My baby's not here or in the other room. He's not with me or with my mom. I thought it would be easy to let him go, but I'm finding I'm a bit too choked up to speak. Peeking out from the shower, he says, "Hey, babe."

Turning to look over my shoulder, I see wet skin and strong muscles, but when I reach his eyes, I only see concern. "You okay?"

"I'll be fine. I'm just not used to Ace being away from me, except with my mom. My friend Leah in certain circumstances."

"You don't know Rochelle, but I do. I trust her completely. I also want you to have fun tonight, so we can check in with her."

"You don't mind?"

"Why would I mind?" He dips back under the shower spray.

I take my makeup bag and dig out my eyeliner. "It's supposed to be our night and all."

"Because it's a night for us doesn't mean we pretend that he's not a part of you." He's scrubbing his hair when he adds, "Call her anytime you need. I'd rather have you relaxed than stressed and worried." Two weeks ago, my life was bleak. I functioned on little input, little sleep, little . . . joy. Except for Ace. But now? With a man who was once my whole life, concerned about me and the welfare of my son as well? This is heaven.

Moving the shower curtain to the side, I surprise him. "You coming in?"

"No, but I needed to see you when I say this."

With a bar of soap in one hand, he stops lathering. "All right."

"Thank you for everything. You've been truly amazing to both me and Ace and it means more to me than you'll ever know."

"Hey, stop thanking me and get in here." With his hands on the belt of my robe, he pulls me close.

Squealing I spin right out of it. "No. No. I've already done most of my makeup and hair."

With a wink and a toss of the robe, "That's okay. I prefer you naked anyway."

"Uh-uh. You chose the rules for tonight. I'm going to hold you to that good and proper wining and dining you promised me."

"You got it, beautiful."

"And don't forget the big ending." This time I send him a wink.

"I'll give you the biggest and the happiest ending you've ever experienced."

Pointing my hairbrush at him, I say, "I'm going to hold you to that."

"Kinky. I like it." He laughs.

My chest reddens just thinking about later. "I'm getting warm in here. I'm going to get dressed."

"After seeing you naked, I might be a few more minutes." I love that. I love that I can still turn him on. I don't want to know how many women he's been with all these years, but knowing it's me he's chosen? It makes me *feel* beautiful. *And cheeky.* And it's been a long time since I've felt that.

"Noooo. Save it all for me. It will give you something to look forward to." I give him the evil eye, though I'm being playful, before walking out. I'm ironing the dress when he comes out. I almost burn my dress. Wow. He has an incredible body. Toned abs, lean body, strong muscles with veins that run the length of his forearms anchored by a large silver and black watch. But it's the V made of muscles leading down under that captures my attention. The towel is barely holding on by a thread. The slightest breeze or touch could send it falling to the floor. Tempting.

"Did you notice how we've fallen back into us so quickly?" he asks.

I stop ironing again and he tugs on a pair of boxer briefs. "Fallen back quickly or picking up where we left off?"

"Both."

I agree, but it doesn't bother me at all. "I like this, and how natural it feels." Disappearing into the bathroom, I tell him, "I'll be out in a minute." He may have seen me in my undies and less, but I'm hoping to look pretty for him too.

"I'm going to make a drink. Can I get you something?"

"White wine?"

"You got it."

The zipper is tough to get up, so I put it on but leave it open in the back. Once I slip on my flats, I check how I look in the mirror, and then head out of the bedroom to find him.

I stop suddenly, my hand covering my heart in awe of the sight before me. I've never felt more grown-up than standing here looking at this man that was once the same boy I loved. With his back to me, I let my gaze linger over the man he's become. Maybe I hadn't done this properly since we've reconnected, because I'm in awe. Dark jeans, black shoes that aren't scuffed or worn out. A black button-up shirt with the sleeves rolled expose his bare arms just enough to see the strength of the moving muscles from his forearms to his hands when he takes a sip of a brown liquid I can guess might be whiskey or bourbon. I wonder if the black and silver watch is something he bought for himself or was a gift from someone else, someone special maybe. It looks expensive. Everything about Derrick Masters these days looks expensive.

Confidence stretches through the width of his shoulders. Standing at the window as if he rules the world. I'm starting to believe he rules mine again. But now I start to doubt my attire. Looking down, I don't want to look dowdy next to him.

"Wow, Jaymes," I hear and look up to see nothing less than adoration in his eyes. "Just wow."

I'm quite sure my cheeks match the shade of the dress. Holding the skirt of the dress out, I ask, "You sure?"

"More than sure." He sets his glass down and comes to hug me. "Gorgeous girl, always be mine."

"I always was."

We come together as he hugs me and my zipper slides up my back. "Tell me I'm not dreaming. Tell me you're really here."

"If we are dreaming, let's stay asleep."

"I'll happily stay in bed with you."

Tapping him on the chest, I laugh softly. "I didn't say anything about bed, and by the way, you look very handsome. Did you get dressed up for me?"

"I did," he replies, popping his collar.

A glass of wine is handed to me and Derrick toasts, "To the past and that girl I met in the schoolyard. To the present and tonight being amazing. To you and me and the incredible future I intend to give you." *I think I want to hear that every day for a while.*

"I'll toast to that," I whisper, not wanting to ruin this dream. He might be right and I'm not ready wake up. Raising our glasses, we tap them together and then seal it with a kiss.

Derrick Masters is a rock star.

Derrick Masters is a rock star.

Derrick Masters *is a* rock star.

Derrick Masters *is a* rock *star.*

Holy shit.

Derrick, *my* Derrick, well, kind of my Derrick, is a rock star.

That has never been more apparent than it is right now. Doesn't matter that I've seen him on TV, or heard him on the radio. Nope. It's when we walk through the hotel with security flanking our sides, walkie-talkies preparing security to be on high alert that it hits me. Really hits me, like straight in the face.

My Derrick is a rock star. He's famous. Everyone knows who he is.

This may be normal protocol for him, but I'm terrified. My hand is safely tucked in his. Nothing can separate the hold he has on me, which calms my nerves just a little. "Is it always like this?" I ask.

"Yes." His response is clipped, but to the point.

I don't take it as an insult. He looks like he's in a zone, focused ahead and yet, well aware of what his presence does, the commotion he stirs.

We're escorted to a large black SUV with the hotel logo shining in gold on the back panel. Everything is fancy here. I climb in and he's quick behind me. The door shuts and his shoulders drop with the release of a harsh breath. Ensuring I'm fine, his hand covers my knee. "You okay?"

"I'm okay. Are you?"

A surprised grin checks in. "I'm all good, baby. Don't worry about me."

"So that always happens—the stares and people pointing? Some asking for pics, fans calling your name?"

"Pretty much."

Sitting back, his reality sets in. "You were once Rebel—"

"I don't like that name."

"The press calls you that sometimes."

"They don't know the history. We do."

"Have you ever thought about sharing it?"

"No." Clipped. His lips are tight, his answer succinct. Turning to look out the window as we leave The Strip, I can see how much of the past still weighs on him. He may be in a different league these days, but no one can ever fully leave the past in the past. It shapes who we are in the present. He's quiet a few minutes. Sometimes I need a little peace, so I give him the same courtesy, and then he speaks. "If I could scrub it off, I would. It's a part of me. My skin. My body. My shell, but not who I am. It never was."

"You got it when you didn't see another way. There were no outs. Just big talk of dreams and following them." Resting my hand on his, I add, "But you did it. You made it, Derrick. You got out and it wasn't just talk with you. So all that back then was just leading you to greater things. The whole world loves you now."

"But I only care about how you feel." He angles his legs my way and leans in. "You think I forgot you. I didn't. I never stopped thinking about you, Jaymes. I thought you meant what you said when you told me to not look back. I looked back but you were gone." *I hate that he thought that, but it was better for him that he did.*

"I was always with you. You just couldn't see me."

"I see you now and I never want to close my eyes again for fear you'll disappear." *I won't disappear. Can't.*

"I'm right here. Right here with you."

26

JAYMES

THE CAR COMES to a stop and Derrick looks out his window. It all happens so fast that I follow his lead. The door is unlocked and then opened. We shuffle out and are whisked in a door on the backside of a hotel from what it looks like. Following a man in a suit, he speaks to Derrick as if I'm not even here. Despite my growing frustration, I remain quiet, but my thoughts spin on the matter. We're brought into a dimly lit restaurant decorated in heavy blues and golds, booths and tables. It's small and I catch the name, Hugo's Cellar at the top of a wine list when we pass a waiter.

The waiter stops and offers us a booth in the corner. It's dimmer than most of the tables and I like it. The place is busy but not overly so for being such a quaint restaurant. It feels intimate and it's definitely romantic. "Are you romancing me?" I ask, sitting in the middle of the booth so I'm close to him.

"I am. How'd you figure it out?"

Shrugging, I wink. "Wild guess."

The service is quick and attentive. We have wine in front of us within minutes of sitting down. I take several sips of mine before we just look at each other. It's been five years, but he's changed so much, the boy I once knew buried under masculine features. He was always fit and muscular, but now he commands his body instead of the reverse. His eyes tell of the life he's led. Scarred fingertips from playing a guitar instead of illegal activity. "Your hair used to be lighter, dark blond."

Smoothing it back, he says, "Yeah, it's getting darker the older I get. One day I guess I'll be salt and pepper."

"You'll look so distinguished." The attention seems to affect him and he glances down. "What?" I ask, surprised he seems shy under the compliment.

His glass is pushed forward until it taps mine. "I can't believe I'm sitting here with Jaymes Grenier."

"I'm more than a name. I'm a real girl," I tease like Pinocchio.

Deep blues drink me in and when they land on my eyes, he says, "You're more than a girl these days."

"Be careful. I might actually start to believe this is real."

"Me too," he whispers, looking away.

The waiter comes and takes our order and when we're alone, I reach over and slip my hand under his. "I'm sorry about earlier. I didn't mean to sound cold when you wanted to talk. I just don't want bombshells dropped every time we're alone. We have so much more to say to each other. I do, for sure, but can it just wait until tomorrow?"

His fingers curl around mine and he brings my hand to his mouth and kisses it. "Do you trust me?"

"Yes."

"Then let me in. I only have the best intentions when it comes to you and Ace. I will never hurt you. I will help you in any way I can, but you have to trust me. I can see you're hiding from me as if I haven't loved you my whole life. As if I'd even know how to love anyone else. This may come off as a surprise to you. It does to me. But it's also so obvious. I've never stopped feeling forever with you. We have a second chance. Please give me that chance."

"Why do you even want it? Knowing what dating me drags you back into, why do you want to lower yourself when you're so much better off without me?"

"Lower myself?" He shakes his head. "Is that what you think? That I'm better than you?"

"You are. You proved it."

"Bullshit. Just like the bullshit reasons you gave me that day. I should have never believed you." The words are bitter as he spews them. "I fell for your lies, but I was too dumb to see the truth." When his tone softens, I dare look into his eyes again. "I see it now. I know what you did and I know you did it for me."

He's right. As much as I want to continue lying, I don't want to lie to him. Not anymore. But what could I do to protect someone that I loved more than life itself? How could I make him save himself? "I couldn't leave my mom behind."

"You said that, yes, but I know there's more to it. Your mom would have been rejoicing that you got out of that shithole, away from the gangs that were trying to take over."

My wine has become the most interesting thing I've ever seen. Avoidance is a good tactic. I think . . . except when you're the only two in the conversation. It gets very hard to distract him to another topic. His gaze is fixed. He's definitely not letting me out of this. "What do you want me to say?"

"Admit the truth."

"Remember when I said I will tell you anything and everything, just not tonight? Can we do that? Please?"

"Tell me I'm wrong. Tell me I'm right. Just promise to tell me the truth."

"Were you always this pushy?" I ask, nudging his knee with mine.

"Yes."

"It's all coming back to me now. Romance me. We will share all of our inner demons tomorrow. Just smile for me tonight."

A smile pops onto his face. It's fake and I laugh because he's wonderful to try for me, even if jokingly. I finish my wine and the waiter is quick with a refill. Looking around, I remark, "This place is very nice. Thank you for bringing me here."

"Remember how you used to make us sandwiches and we'd picnic in the back of the truck?"

"You gave me that guitar and we played together, making music under the stars."

"Do you still play?"

The question makes me sad. Maybe one day it won't, but knowing how hard he worked to buy me that guitar, I feel bad. "I haven't played in a long time."

"Just busy?"

I made a promise not to lie, but if I tell him Reggie took it, it will ruin what we have now. Does this lie matter in the scheme of things? His feelings are more important. I want him happy. "Something like that."

"You should play and sing. You were always way more talented than me."

I laugh. "Funny."

"Not funny at all. The truth. If you had a guitar right now, could you still play?"

"Is that a challenge?"

"Maybe."

"I can still play." I take a gulp of the deep red liquid. "Probably."

"Maybe we can play together sometime."

"Maybe."

Our food arrives. After three bites, I don't talk at all. This steak is the most delicious thing I've ever eaten. I catch Derrick watching me a few times, but I don't even care how I look to him. I devour it and the side dishes. If I could lick the dishes, I would. When my dress feels tighter around the middle, I sit back and exhale. "Whatever you want, I'll give it to you."

He chuckles. "So I feed you a good meal and now I get whatever I want in return?"

"Yep," I reply confidently.

"I'm gonna take you up on that offer, Ms. Grenier."

Rubbing my stomach, I bite my lip, then say, "I hope so." My phone chirps with a text and I pull it from my purse. It's Rochelle: *Boys are having a blast. Hope you two are.*

"Rochelle's pretty great, right?"

Derrick nods. "She's been to hell and back, but she's come out the other side stronger, not by choice, but by determination. For her boys."

I text her: *Thanks for the update. Can Ace call me for a quick good night?*

My phone rings within seconds. I slip out of the booth and answer it, keeping my voice down, "Hey buddy, is that you?"

"Hi, Mommy. We had pizza and strawberries."

"Together?" I ask, walking toward the restrooms. I stay outside the door to take my call.

"Ew. No. The strawberries were dinner. Then we got pizza for dessert."

Laughing, I love it. Hearing him makes me miss him. "Are you having fun?"

"It's like whoa, the best time. Ms. Rochelle said we can watch *Moana* if we aren't tired."

"Are you tired?"

"No. Where are you?"

"I'm at dinner. Are you okay?"

"Yeah," he replies and then yawns. "I'm good. I'm having fun."

"You still want to stay?"

"Yes. We get waffles in the morning."

"Sounds yummy. I should go, but I love you, buddy. Sweet dreams."

"Sweet dreams. Love you."

Rochelle takes the phone, then says, "Hi, he's doing great. How are you?"

"Great. Stuffed but great."

"Good. Tell Derrick I'll kick his ass if he steps out of line."

I laugh. "What if I want him to?"

Now she's laughing. "Well that's something different entirely. I won't keep you. Call or text me if you need anything."

"Thanks again."

"You're welcome. Now go have some fun and don't worry about Ace. He's a great kid and in good hands. Good night."

"Good night."

I find myself leaning against the wall smiling to myself when I get company. Derrick in all his darkness sure is a sight to behold when he comes around the corner. "Everything okay with Ace?"

"Yes," I say going up to him. "He's having the time of his life."

"That's good."

Fisting the front of his shirt, I turn us around until his back is against the wall and I'm firmly against him. "So am I."

"That's even better." Lifting my chin, he bends down and kisses me. "Do you want dessert?"

"Hell yes, I want dessert."

"Okay, maybe I shouldn't have ordered dessert," I moan, leaning my head back against the leather seat and closing my eyes in the SUV.

"Don't fall asleep on me."

"I make no promises. This food coma is intense."

"Ten minutes and we'll be back, but I was hoping to take you somewhere. Can you stay awake long enough for a quick stop?"

"How can I say no to you? I can't."

Five minutes later we're dropped off on a side street. Derrick takes my hand and we hurry around the corner. "The Bellagio Fountains," I say as if he didn't know.

"Come on. It's about to start." We hurry over to a spot in the corner and he maneuvers me in front of him because of the crowds. His arms cage me in resting his hands on the railing. With my back to his front, I feel safer than I've felt in years. I love how much bigger he is than me. I love the way our bodies fit no matter which way we're put together. A loud boom signals the start of the show reminding me of times that weren't so safe . . .

"Get down," Derrick yells at me.

I'm leveled to the ground, my cheek against the sparse grass in the park. Kids are still in school, but we decided to skip. I thought we'd be making out at one of our houses, but the second Reggie found out we were leaving after lunch, he was waiting for us at Derrick's truck. "Looking good, Jamie. If you and Derrick don't work out—"

"Fuck you," I say, flipping him off.

Derrick is laughing, but I'm not. It's been a few days since I've been alone with my boyfriend and I'm starting to think Reggie's invading our party of two on purpose.

Reggie gets in the cab, but I stand outside waiting for him to get back out. "What are you doing?" I ask him.

"Let's go. We're meeting the guys at the park."

"No, Derrick and I are hanging out."

Derrick pounds the roof of the cab. "Get in before we're busted skipping out."

"Not until he moves." No way am I sitting with Reggie in the middle.

"C'mon, baby. I'll drop his ass off and it will just be us."

"No."

"Jaymes," he says, his tone firmer.

I'm about to because I want the time alone with him. I also want to have sex with him. But then Reggie says, "Get control of your woman, Derrick. She's making you look like an asshole."

I slam the door closed and start back to school, but I'm quickly caught. "Hey, ignore him and come on."

"Ignore him? He's a fucker."

"I'll happily ignore him, but will you?"

"You're gonna get us busted. Can we finish this conversation elsewhere?"

Looking back at the school, I'm surprised we haven't been busted yet. "Fine, but we're dropping him off first."

When I go back to the truck, he still refuses to move, so I get in and keep to myself by putting my headphones on. If I was smart, instead of listening to EDM, I would have been listening to what Reggie was saying, the plan that was going down.

We get to the park and I move to let Reggie get out, but then he leans back in to talk to Derrick. Derrick's jaw is tense, ticking on the side, something he only does when he's stressed or angry. I'm guessing angry by the way he's staring at Reggie. The engine is cut and I whip off my headphones. "What are you doing?"

"Five minutes. That's all."

"You're kidding me?"

"Look—"

"You've got to handle her fucking mouth. The guys are talking about how pussy-whipped you are."

I know what he's doing. He's trying to turn Derrick against me. I can argue with him, but in the heat of the moment, Derrick needs to decide if he's choosing to listen to that asshole or if he's going to treat me with respect.

Derrick says, "Shut the fuck up, Reggie, or I'll shut you up. Don't talk about her like that. Ever."

My pride in the stand he took shines and I smile. So what if I'm grinning in gratification, he deserved to be put in his place. But then Derrick says, "I still have some business to handle. I'll be right back, babe."

He and Reggie walk across the park before I can convince him otherwise. "Screw them." I head in the direction of my house. It's only four blocks from here.

Rapid-fire shots sound out and I'm tackled to the ground before the loud boom sends woodchips flying around us. "Stay down," is whispered in my ear. "You're okay, baby."

. . . I will never forget the weight of his body on mine from that afternoon. "You're okay, baby."

"What?" The water bursts into the air as Celine Dion is piped through hidden speakers.

"You froze, your body tensed, your eyes seem to be focused somewhere far away. Not here."

"Yeah," I reply. "Just a bad memory popped up."

Derrick's arms are around me, his body molded to me from behind. "It's okay. We can go."

"I'm sorry. I had a flashback to that time in the park around the corner from our houses."

"God, Jaymes, what have I done?"

"Don't. You're not to blame any more than I am." I take his hand and pull him out of the crowd. They are so mesmerized by the fountains and show that no one notices the star amongst them. We rush around the corner and find our car waiting for us. As soon as we're safe inside, I say, "He's ruined so much. Let's not let him ruin tonight."

"What do you want, Jaymes?" And then I kiss him. He's responsive and embraces me. Our hands are frenzied and bodies anxious with anticipation.

Stopping to look him in the eyes, I reply, "You, only you."

27

DERRICK

THE DOOR FLIES open and I can't pull myself away from her long enough to care that it's slamming open and just took out a section of the sheetrock. I kick it closed and keep kissing her. My shirt didn't stay buttoned once we made it into the elevator. My belt was unhooked and lost somewhere between the suite and the elevator. The fly of my jeans is hanging open and I have her dress unzipped before we reach the bedroom.

Shoes are off and the dress drops to the floor on the way to the bed. My jeans and boxer shorts are discarded while her bra joins the party on the floor. "Holy fuck, you're so damn sexy."

"Come here. I'm cold."

I reach into my suitcase, grab a condom from my toiletry bag, and toss it on the bed next to her. "I'll warm you up." I crawl up and nudge her knees apart so I can rest my body on top of her.

Her arms come around my neck and she's smiling. "I was hoping you'd say that." Her smile is so damn easy. Seeing it makes my heart hurt. I want her to always feel this safe, this comfortable, this happy. I want her life to be this easy. I don't care what I have to do, I'll do it. For her, I'd do anything.

Stealing one kiss and then another, I lower more of my weight on her. Brushing my fingers through her hair, we stop kissing. She looks shy, a little rejected, so I say, "I just want to look at you a minute."

That really brings about a natural blush that I wish I could keep there always. I'll settle for the memory. She's nervous under my gaze, not liking the attention. Sliding her hand down my middle, I catch it and bring it up to my lips for a kiss. Then I hold it, keeping her still. "What are you looking at?" she asks, whispering.

"All that matters."

The smile slips away and something else, something heavier with a thump moves in. Her heart beats against mine and without going any further I already know she's mine. Just like I'm hers.

Instead of words, we kiss, our devotion shared through touch and feel. I angle my body to the side. Moving our joined hands lower, I position mine on top of hers between our hips. "How do you like it? How do you get off, baby? Show me."

"I don't know if I can."

"It's just us. We used to know everything about each other. You've done this for me before. Do it again. Just for me."

Her fingers lower and while looking me in the eyes, she says, "Touch yourself and let me watch."

I don't normally jerk off when I have a beautiful woman beneath me, but her request is only fair. Wrapping my hand around my dick, I look down between her legs and watch as her fingers manipulate her body. "Are you wet for me?"

"So much."

Turning my hand down, I drag my fingers between her pussy lips —slowly until her breath catches. Then leave her to finish and spread her wetness over my cock as I slide my hand up and down. "I'm so fucking hard for you."

"Kiss me."

Leaning over, I kiss her how I want to fuck her—deep, possessive, passionate. "You know how incredibly hot it is watching you get off for me?" A soft moan echoes from her into me. Knowing she's close, I reach down and take her hand in mine, pulling it up to my mouth. I bite her bottom lip and pull back until it releases. Holding her hand to my lips, I lick the tips while keeping my eyes on hers that have opened. Her body moves beneath me, her breath coming out jagged and wanton.

Fuck. Condom. I've got one on in seconds and the tip of my cock is against her entrance. It would be so easy to fuck her, but the torture is too sweet to rush it. One inch enters and her lips part. Pulling two of her fingers from my mouth, I whisper, "I'll go slow every time if that's what you like."

"I don't want slow. I just want you."

Her legs bend around me and I run my hand on the outside of her thigh and lift under her knee. Sliding in, her body conforms to me, embracing me in her welcoming heat. The tightness causes my eyelids to dip close momentarily, the sensation of her overwhelming. "I'm not gonna last."

"You don't have to last, babe. I just want you to feel so good."

"I do. So good. You feel too good, baby. Too good." My body moves against hers and we find a rhythm, moving until our pleasure ignites into a flame. Thrusting faster, I pursue that dark bliss that escapes me. It's not about fucking to get off with her. It's about that bond that builds, the connection being reinforced. I want it all with her. I have it all with her. Only her.

"Fuck." My hips move on their own, my mind lost to the sensation. When she cries my name, I let go and get dragged under with her. I drop when my body is exhausted and sated. Turning my head, my nose is behind her ear, her hair tickling. The scent of her skin a mixture of sex and the last lingering notes of her perfume. She's intoxicating.

Pushing forward, I place three kisses on her neck while ridding myself of the condom in a tissue from the nightstand. Arms come around me, and I close my eyes, teetering on sleep. I rest exactly where I landed.

Whispers and the smell of heaven urge me awake. I open my eyes slowly, the dim light from the lamp still too bright. Squinting, I see a sight to behold. With my cheek against her chest, I only see naked Jaymes. Perfection. "I wish I could wake up like this every day."

Her soft laughter rattles my head. I lift and roll off her. Running my hands through my hair, I close my eyes and then scrub over my face. "What time is it?"

"Late. Sorry to wake you. You are really heavy."

My eyes pop open and I sit up on my elbow. "Oh, I'm sorry. Did I hurt you?"

"No, you didn't, but it was getting hard to breathe."

She lifts up and kisses my forehead. "And I need to use the restroom."

Watching her sweet little ass as she pads to the bathroom, I fall back and ask, "How long was I out?"

"Not that long. Like an hour or so."

"Really?"

I hear her laughing from the other room. "Yeah, you just fell asleep right where you finished."

"Did you?"

"What?"

"Finish?"

She laughs again. Peeking out of the bathroom, she replies, "I did. Don't worry about me. I loved every minute being with you."

It's my turn to smile. "Sorry for falling asleep on you."

"You're tired. It's okay. You obviously needed it. I'm going to shower." She waggles a condom between her fingers. "Want to join me?"

I don't even bother waiting to answer. I'm up and in that bathroom in seconds. Once we're under the warm water, she's already soaping her body and I help her out by taking over. Running the bar all over her breasts, I then go lower and soap between her legs. Her breathing picks up. She's fighting it, making me chuckle, when she asks, "Do you like touring?"

"I like playing for the fans. I like the high I get." Cleaning my own body, I watch her watching me.

Her eyes are questioning but she doesn't ask what she's wondering, so I give her my answer, "It's better than drugs."

"Do you still smoke or do any?"

"I haven't in a while." Wetting my hair under the spray, I reply, "I partied. Hard. But when I joined the band, I couldn't keep doing that shit. Touring is hard on the body, but it's harder on your mind."

Turning us around, I put her under the water. While I stroke her hair under the shower spray, she asks, "What do you mean?"

I pour shampoo into the palm of my hands and start washing her hair. "I'm doing what I never thought I'd get to do—be in a band, tour the world, make money, but that's only fulfilling in some ways. Not in others."

"Money doesn't make everything better?" She almost seems disappointed.

"Money makes things easier, not necessarily better. When I meet people, I don't know if they want something from me, want to use me in some way, or if they're genuine. It's just easier to stick to those we already know."

"Is that why you invited me? Because it's easier?"

"No." I rinse her hair. When she opens her eyes again, I cup her face and kiss her. "I invited you because I never stopped thinking about you, never stopped caring about you, never stopped . . ."

"Never stopped what, Derrick?"

Somewhere between her telling me she was full from dinner and standing in the after of our lovemaking, I lost all reason and rationale. I need this woman. Not just tonight, but always. "I never stopped loving you."

Her hands caress my face and she lifts up on her toes. "You taught me what love was, you've shown me I can have it in my life again. I've never stopped loving you either."

The pull between us sends our bodies against the wall. I spin and let her press to my warmth while I take the cold wall. My voice is low, and direct. "Turn around."

When she does, I move her forward and drag my hands down her arms before taking her wrists raising them up and against the wall. I harden just from looking at her—the curve of the sides of her breasts and then inward to her waist. I appreciate the way her hips curve out and then kneel down to confess the sins I want to commit against her. As the shower rains down over us, I fuck her with my mouth, my tongue taking her until her legs are shaking and her orgasm subsides, I stand up behind her. "Hold on."

Slipping the condom down over my hardness, I then push between her legs. She adjusts and I slide inside her without production, just need, just instinct to tie myself to her in every way I can. I cover her hands and thrust. "I fuck my hand imagining it's you."

Her head falls back on my shoulder, exposing her neck. Nipping, licking, kissing, I savor her. With her eyes closed, she says, "I touch myself wishing it was your hands on me."

"I'll make all your wishes come true, baby." I slide my hands down her wet skin, over her shoulders, and around to her breasts. Taking hold, I fuck and thrust, love her body like she wants, like I need. Moving even lower, I slip my hand between her legs and appreciate her clit. She jolts, sensitive to my touch, but presses against my hand.

I run the end of my nose behind her hair, and whisper, "Come for me. Show me how good this feels."

"Fuck me, Derrick. I need you. So much. Harder. Make it so I only feel you. Only you."

"Always me." I speed up and then pinch lightly.

"Always you." Her body tremors, squeezing around me.

"Oh fuck. Yes." Grabbing her hips, I start thrusting hard, her body taking and giving until I feel the rush and can't hold back. A few lingering pumps and I drop my forehead on her shoulder. "Jaymes." I release. Release everything holding me back from realizing what she is to me. Release my fears of opening up and letting her in. I release myself to her, my soul bowing at her feet. "I love you."

28

DERRICK

I promised her tonight.

No questions.

Just sharing our bodies.

For me, sharing so much more.

Jaymes didn't tell me she loves me. She doesn't toss around words with that much importance without care. I know how she feels though. She told me she never stopped loving me. That's enough. For tonight, that's enough.

Sun's coming up. The Nevada sky lit up. She's been asleep on me for a few hours. The peace she's found in my arms makes me wish we could stay like this forever. She's given me the same peace. Dragging my fingers down her back lightly, I stare out the window.

The new day will give me the answers I need, but I fear what the repercussions of this new information will bring. Reggie has a hold over her. It doesn't seem he's in the picture, but he's definitely in her life.

Her phone chirps with a text. I reach over to the nightstand and grab it before it wakes her. There's a message from Rochelle: *Ace is crying. I've been holding him for a while, but I think you might want to come down. Suite 12447.* Glancing to the time, it's not quite six a.m.

I hate disturbing Jaymes. She's sleeping like she hasn't slept in years. Maybe she hasn't. I reply: *This is Derrick. I'll be there in a few minutes.*

Setting her phone back down, I very carefully, extra slowly extricate myself out from under Jaymes. She readjusts but doesn't wake. I kiss her cheek and then get dressed pulling jeans and a T-shirt on. Slipping on my black Adidas, I don't bother with socks or tying the laces. I just grab the room key and my phone and go.

Dex answers the door. "Come on in." I follow him inside as he continues, "He's a great kid."

"Yeah."

But then Dex stops and turns back to me. Crossing his arms, he says, "Something's going on."

"What do you mean?"

He whispers, "We found him hiding in the closet crying, but he was dead silent. Rochelle got up an hour or so ago just to check on them. CJ and Neil were in one bed. Ace in the other when we tucked them in. But he was gone. She freaked out and we searched everywhere. She found him in the closet. He wasn't afraid of her, but he wouldn't talk about why he was there either."

"Shit." I see the concern etched in his face. I'm sure it matches mine. He also looks as tired as I feel.

We start walking again. "They're in our room."

When we enter, Rochelle is sitting in bed and smiles sympathetically. Ace is curled on her lap, resting his head on her chest. Her arms are around him, but his eyes are wide open. He sits up when he sees me. "Derrick."

"Hey buddy, I came to get you and take you to your mom."

He comes running to me and my arms go out automatically. Throwing himself into my arms, he hugs me tight. I place a kiss on the side of his head before I realize what I'm doing. Damn. Like his mother, all I want to do is protect him from whatever scares him. I catch a glimpse of Rochelle whose smile was once filled with sympathy is now full of pride. Standing all the way up, I bring Ace with me. He wraps around me like a little monkey and I carry him to the door. Before I leave, I tell Ro and Dex, "Thanks for last night. We'll touch base with you guys later."

Ace gives Rochelle a side hug and fist-bumps Dex before we leave. They're only three floors down from us, so I manage to avoid being seen. Back in the suite, I ask him, "You hungry or tired?"

"I'm sleepy," he responds with a giveaway by rubbing his eyes.

"Okay." I glance toward the other room and then to the one I'm sharing with Jaymes. "Hey, go take a piss and meet me right back here."

"You said a bad word. Mommy's gonna be mad."

"Then let's not tell her, kid." I nod my head toward the bathroom. "Now go and don't forget to wash your hands." I sound like my mother.

As soon as he runs along, I go into the room and kick off my shoes. I should have put my boxers back on earlier, so I strip my pants off and slip those on in a hurry. Rushing to meet him, we both come out at the same time. Kneeling down, I say, "So, I'm going to let you decide where you want to sleep. In that room with the two beds or in that room with the one big bed and your mommy."

He rubs his chin while looking between the two options. I have to admit, this kid is seriously fucking cute. He points to the room with two beds and I smile. "That one."

"All right. Let's go tuck you in then. I have a show tonight and need to get some sleep."

"What's a show?" he asks while we're walking in the bedroom.

"It's a concert. A show." He doesn't look satisfied with that answer. "I play in a band. We play music live for people to enjoy."

"Ohhhh. What do you play?"

"I play guitar and I sing."

"Like Mommy, but she doesn't play anymore. I play guitar. I got one for Christmas once."

Now this is something I can work with, we can bond over. "Really?"

"Yeah, it's blue and white. One of the strings is broken, but Mommy fixed it with duck tape."

"Duct. T," I sound out.

"Yeah, that stuff." He climbs into bed and sits there expectantly.

So I pull the covers up and say, "Lie down. You can't sleep sitting up."

"Aren't you going to sleep?"

"Yeah. I'm tired too." I can't wait to climb back in bed with Jaymes and hold her again. This weekend is flying by too fast.

"You're sleeping here?"

"No, in there."

"My mom's in there."

"Right."

"But I thought . . ." Tears the size of puddles pool in his brown eyes and his bottom lip pops out.

Oh shit. "You thought I was staying in here?"

He nods, pulling the covers up to his nose. Looking down at him like that I see so much of his mother in him. Not Reggie, thank fuck. Well, shit. There go my plans. "Do you want me to stay in here?" He nods again. This is news. I'm not sure what to do, but I know I don't want him to cry. "Where do you want me to sleep?"

With a huge smile, he pats the bed that he's in. "Will you stay here, Derrick? Please?"

As much as I want to wake up next to Jaymes, this kid needs me more. "Sure." I climb in on the other side and he immediately rolls to his side, so I match his position. "Have you ever played a real guitar, not a toy?"

He nods excitedly. I think he's happy to please me. I rub my hand over his head and then pull the covers up a little higher making sure he's comfy. "Snug as a bug."

"My mommy says that too."

"You've got a great mommy."

"She likes you. She told me."

"I like her, too."

"I used to play Mommy's guitar. She kept it in the living room." As much as I'd like to say his thoughts are scattered like a kid's, I know a few adults who act the same.

It's a nice segue back to a topic I think Jaymes might be happier that we're discussing. My curiosity gets the best of me, and I ask, "Where does she keep it now?"

"The mean man took it."

I wasn't prepared for that. My heart stops beating and I find I stop breathing for a second. Trying to control my facial reaction, I fist the blanket. "What mean man?"

His demeanor is so commonplace that I start questioning what he's lived through, what he and Jaymes have had to survive. "The one that hurts Mommy."

Narrowing my eyes at him, I lean up. "Who's hurting your mommy?"

"She calls him Reggie. I hear her, but I hide in the closet and don't make a sound. Just like she told me."

Holy fuck.

Fuck.

Fuck.

FUCK.

Flopping back down, I stare up at the ceiling. I cover my face with my hands not wanting Ace to see my anger, his words ringing in my ears, *"The one that hurts Mommy."*

"Are you mad at me for not protecting Mommy?" *Oh, God. No. This incredible little man.*

My hands are down and I reach over and rub his shoulder. "No, buddy. I know you take care of her the best you can. I just . . . I don't know why someone wants to hurt her."

"She says for money. And drugs. I heard him say he got money for her guitar for drugs. That made me sad, so she told Santa to bring me a new one. I meant for her. She thought I wanted one for me."

Damn. This kid. He's going to be the death of me. "You did that for her?"

"She used to sing and play for me. That made her happy. It made me happy too. She has to work a lot now and has school. She doesn't smile as much."

I'm going to fucking kill Reggie. I contain my rage for Ace. He deserves to be happy. So does Jaymes. What kind of shit are they caught in?

"When I play the blue guitar it doesn't sound like the other one, but even with the duck . . . duct tape, she smiles."

"I bet she does."

There is so much to process through the innocence of this kid who struggles to make his mom smile. He reminds me so much of myself. I remember doing the same for my mom, through the abuse, the alcohol and fights with my father. The day he left was one of the best days of my life. When I turn back to Ace, his eyes are closed and his breathing is already evening.

Wish I could fall asleep like that. His little arm is outstretched toward me and his hand is palm up. I roll back to my side to face him and cover his hand with mine.

THE ROOM IS PITCH BLACK. Confused, I look at the clock. 1:25. I'm not even sure if that's a.m. or p.m. Much less what city I'm in.

I fucking love blackout curtains. *Jaymes. Ace.*

I sit up and feel next to me for Ace. The bed is empty so I throw the covers off and make a break for the door. Swinging it open, Jaymes and Ace look up from a game of checkers they're playing on the coffee table. She smiles. "Hello, sunshine."

"Hi," I reply, not fully with it yet. My body feels sluggish and I don't know if it's from the sexual activities all night or the tour catching up with me.

Ace asks, "Wanna play winner?"

"Sure. Just give me a few minutes, okay?"

He doesn't say anything, his attention back on the game. But Jaymes is staring at me, trying to hold a silent conversation.

Is something wrong?

Are you all right?

You're worrying me.

I love you.

I love you.

Please still love me.

I mouth, "I love you."

She smiles, though it's more relief flickering across her face than happiness. Happy. Smiles. Ace.

Fuck.

"I'm going to get dressed." I have to talk to her about everything he said to me early this morning. How do I even broach that topic? When I enter the other bedroom, I rub the bridge of my nose. I'm fucking starving and can't have that heavy of a conversation on an empty stomach. I need strength. The kind of strength she's shown she had to have to endure the life she's been living. The life where her daily worry is if she's protecting her son from "the mean man." I don't know much about what's going on with them when it comes to Reggie, but I do know that Reggie Rogers is a dead man. *No one hurts my family and gets away with it. No. One.*

29

JAYMES

DERRICK MOVES from one bedroom back to the one we were sharing last night. With a mighty fine itch the way he's rubbing the back of his neck. Something's wrong. Something's off. I woke up to an empty bed and Ace playing with his cars along the living room windowsill. He told me Derrick got him from downstairs and then they had to go to bed to rest for the show.

I also got a long, very excited explanation about what a "show" is and a lot about how Derrick plays guitar like we do. That part made me smile, but the rest of the story's pieces haven't been put together yet. As much as I'd like to follow him into the room and barrage him with questions, he just woke up, so I'll give him some time.

"Jaymes?"

I finish my move, my red checker jumping over one of Ace's pieces, and look up. Derrick's near the door. I get the signal to come to him, one nod into the bedroom, and get up. Maybe he's ready for those questions after all. "I'll be back in a few minutes to play. Can you watch a little TV until then?"

"Yeah." Ace gets up and climbs onto the couch. I turn the volume up so he can hear the show we had playing in the background.

When I walk into the bedroom, Derrick is holding the door. He closes it enough to leave a crack open. It's thoughtful of him to do that so we can hear if Ace needs me. He turns and comes to me where I've stopped. "Hi."

"Hi." Then I'm hugged awkwardly, like he's forgotten how to do it. "Umm . . . Is something wrong?"

"Can we talk?"

"Wow, okay. Of course." I walk to the chair by the window and sit, and wait.

Sitting on the corner of the bed, he drops his head in hands and scrubs his face. When his eyes meet mine again, he says, "Have you talked to Rochelle?"

"I texted a quick thank you, but I wanted to tell her in person today. Why? What's going on? You're starting to scare me."

"Stop saying that."

"I don't mean—"

"I know you don't mean I actually scare you, but if Ace hears you he won't know the difference."

"The difference in what?"

He stands, all six foot one of him, all muscle and attitude. All Rebel. My heart quickens, a feeling I haven't had in years coming back. Love and fear mixed together. That's what Rebel was. I knew he'd never hurt me, but I knew the damage he could do.

"The difference between Reggie and me."

Now I'm standing, my arms crossed, my defenses in full-effect. "Why would he confuse the two of you? Ever?"

"I don't want to be the mean man who scares his mother."

Our gazes lock in a standoff. My breathing shallows. The dust particles glisten in the stilling air and all the wonderful from last night is lost to the past like everything else good in my life. "What did he tell you?"

The sadness. The sympathy. The way people look at me like I'm pathetic for bringing a child into this world, or worse, like I'm a bad mom. I've seen that look before. The seconds ticking by are scorching my ears in the silence and I can't take it. "Tell me." I run forward and push him as hard as I can, but he doesn't budge. So I do it again. And again. "Tell me." I keep pushing him until he reacts.

Grabbing my wrists, his hold is firm, and he stops me. "What are you doing?"

Trying to free myself, I demand, "Tell me what he said right now, damn it."

"He said a mean man hurts you." And then I stop when my world falls from beneath my feet. "He hasn't seen him, but he hears him. Ace hears him hurting you and he knows his name is Reggie. Fucking Reggie. What the fuck is going on, Jaymes?"

"Keep your voice down. He'll hear you."

"He hears you. He's not dumb."

"You think I don't know he hears? We talk about it. I know what he hears. But do you know what he hears? His mother fighting to protect him, so don't come judging me like I've done something wrong—"

"Judging you?" My wrists are lowered, the grip loosened, but not released. "That's the last thing I'm doing. I'm not judging you, but if you think I'm letting you two go back to that hellhole to be hurt, or worse, you're wrong."

"I can't leave my mom."

"Five years ago you told me the same thing, but guess what? I'm not walking away this time. This time I'm here to stay."

The fight in me escapes when his commitment is unleashed. "What are you saying, Derrick?"

"I've already said it. I love you, Jaymes. I can see how you keep that wall half opened when we're together, ready to throw it back up at the first sign of trouble. But there's no trouble here with me. Don't you see? You could have always come to me. Always."

"I came to you this weekend."

"Now I'm asking *you* to stay."

I exhale a long sigh and look toward the door. When I seek his blues for comfort, I move in, wanting to believe what he says, wanting to hide from my life and live in his for a while.

His arms come around me and mine around him. He whispers into my hair, "I'm never going to let him hurt you again."

The tears only come when I finally give in, wholly, to him, to his love, when I finally give in to hope again. He holds me while they fall wetting our shirts and he lets me cry five years worth of tears between us.

"Mommy?" Squeezing my eyes closed, I dip my head down and wipe away my tears. He'll know. Despite my best efforts to shelter him from the bad, Ace has seen me cry enough to know. "Don't cry, Mommy."

When I look at him, I raise my chin high. He looks scared as his eyes dart between Derrick and me. I kneel down. "Come here. I want to talk to you about some stuff."

Silently he comes to me. "Derrick is a good guy. I might be crying, but they're happy tears. You and Derrick make Mommy so happy."

Suspicious eyes turn jolly and trusting again. "Like when you used to play guitar."

I tap his nose. "Yes, like that."

Derrick bends down and asks, "Hey buddy, want to come to sound check with me and we'll give your mom a little time to herself?"

Arms fly into the air and he jumps up and down. "Yes."

"How about it . . . Mommy? Can he hang with the guys for a few hours?"

We both stand up and I lean my head on Derrick's chest. "Sure. That sounds great all around." Turning to face Derrick, I add, "Please remember, he's five. He can't be left to his own devices."

"I've got him covered. As for you, you can get a massage or more sleep."

"I've never had a massage."

"Charge everything to the room. Even the gratuity. I don't want you paying for a thing."

"You're spoiling me. How am I supposed to go back to LA after living the best weekend of my life here?" Ace is bored and runs back into the living room.

The back of Derrick's hand rubs my cheek and all the playfulness in his eyes is gone. "I meant what I said. I'm going to help take care of you guys. We can talk about it more tonight because I need to get going soon, but think about what that means to you and I'll think about what it means to me. We can come together on it. I want you comfortable with how we move forward, but I also want you and Ace and your mom safe. That's a priority."

Safe. That isn't a word I've felt since that night. Vulnerable. Weak. Frightened. But safe? I need that. Lifting up on my toes, I kiss him. "Thank you."

"You've done this all on your own. You don't have to anymore. I'm here for you and Ace however you'll let me."

I repeat, for lack of anything befitting his words coming to my mind, "Thank you. You've given me a lot to think about."

"I hope so. Now, there's a button on the phone for the spa. Just call down and make an appointment and we'll leave you to it."

I roll my eyes at myself, but I need to say it. "Thank you again."

This time he laughs. "Stop thanking me. It's my pleasure." I'm swatted on the ass as he walks away, leaving me to squeak I'm so giddy.

The button to the speaker is pushed and I choose spa from the options and am answered immediately by a sultry sounding vixen. "Good afternoon, Mr. Masters, may I book you in for a spa appointment?"

"Hi," I say, feeling squeaky still and a lot uncomfortable. Visions of what she must think when she hears me run through my head—groupie, one-night stand, hooker. I try to block the names and mortification creeping up my spine, and sound strong, like I belong.

Belong.

Looking around the fancy room, is this where I belong?

Through the doorway, I see Derrick bent down on the floor tying Ace's shoe and I know where I belong. I belong with him. But I'll take a massage first. "Hi, I'd like to book a massage in the next two hours if possible."

The accommodating voice that answered is replaced with the ice queen. "I'm sorry. I made a mistake. We're completely full today, *Mssss*?"

"Grenier."

"I see you're not listed on the room, so unfortunately we wouldn't be able to book that appointment anyway. Registered guests only."

"Hello, this is Mr. Masters. Ms. Grenier is my guest for the weekend. Can you double-check your schedule please? I can pay extra if we need to bring someone in."

"Oh. Great news. We had something open up. We can accommodate your guest in fifteen minutes. Is that sufficient time?"

With a gleam in his eyes, he says, "She'll take it. Oh, and make sure to take good care of her. Whatever she wants, make sure she gets it."

"Yes, sir. We'll see you shortly, Ms. Grenier."

"Thank you," I call out, but I think she hangs up too fast to hear.

Hovering over me, I lean back and he comes closer. "When you're with me, you're treated like a queen. Don't ever settle for less, baby."

"Perks of being with a rock star?" I run my nails lightly over the exposed skin of his neck.

"You say that as if you're the lucky one when it's me who's fortunate to have you back in my life."

"You always were so damn charming."

"What can I say, you bring out the best in me."

With his lower half pressed to mine, I raise an eyebrow. "And other things it seems. I think you have sound check, Mr. Masters, if I'm not mistaken."

This time he sighs, blowing out a big breath. Pushing up and off me, he says, "We'll pick up where we left off later."

"Promise?"

"Definitely."

Ace runs in as Derrick walks out. We give each other a big hug and I tell him to stay with Derrick. "No wandering off. Okay?"

"Okay."

"Be good."

"I will. Love you."

"Love you, buddy."

When they leave, I hurry around and get dressed to head to the spa. Before I walk out, I see Ace's toys mixed with my stuff and Derrick's shoes. It looks like a family lives here. I have to be careful of getting my hopes up too high. Derrick and I will talk later, but I love how at home I feel with him. Seriously, my heart can't take much more goodness. I want to believe it will last. I want to believe that I somehow deserve it, but I'm skeptical. Not *of* Derrick. But *for* us. For my baby boy. Surely all good things must come to an end. I just hope it's not a fiery one when it does.

Reggie

"It's city, not county jail. Bail me out, bitch, or I'm kicking your ass to the street." I slam the phone back on the receiver, and turn. "Open," I command.

The button is pushed, the door buzzes and I walk through with my favorite escort, Guard Derails. He's a rookie. Easy to manipulate. Easier to bribe. Especially since he uses and I'm his hookup. Under his breath, he places his order, "A quarter on Tuesday."

He's a great customer. A regular. Fuck, I'd be druggin' up too if I had to work in this place. Being busted for a pipe in a random traffic stop doesn't feel so random. The cops needed a bust; I happen to be their victim. Now I'm in for three days before I face the court. The LA scene is everything you hear it is—overpopulated. I'm banking I'll be out by morning. Two nights in and it's already getting old. Shayna is scraping money together. Sure as shit not telling her where my stash is. Bitch can use her own money on me.

My hands are freed once we reach the common area. It's small and familiar. I've been here a few times. Petty shit. They can't nail me for anything substantial. I've got too much on these dirty cops. When I walk to a table, the other inmates get up and move. My reputation precedes me. They know I'm on the verge of making a big step in the underground scene. They just aren't sure who I'm taking out to take that step. They don't want it to be them, so the keep away from me.

The TV is on. Some entertainment celebrity show. "Who gives a fuck? Turn it."

"To what?" some brave soul asks.

My silence should be answer enough. It seems it is. He's up and about to turn the dial when I see the ghost I've been chasing for years. "Turn it up."

"I thought you wanted me to turn the channel?"

"Turn it up and fuck off."

*THE RESISTANCE IS **in Las Vegas as part of The Rebellion Tour. Last night the band members were seen at various locations around the small city. Johnny Outlaw lay low, but Kaz Fabian and his girlfriend were spotted taking in Cirque du Soleil's Love at Mirage. Derrick Masters and an unidentified date were seen briefly at Hugo Cellar's. The band performs live tonight but unfortunately, the concert is sold out.***

AN UNIDENTIFIED DATE.

The story has ended, but I stare at the old TV set, my fingers aching from the grip. I knew the second I saw her who she was.

The image of that motherfucker is burned in my brain. I vowed to kill him. He's always been my most wanted. But now, now he has the nerve to come into my neighborhood, my territory, fuck my woman, and mess with my family.

He's dead, but before I fucking kill him, he's going to watch me fuck the one thing he loves most—Jamie Grenier. I'm fucking pissed she lied to me. Told me she doesn't know where he is. The bitch will beg me for her life after I've finished with his. *The betrayer and the bitch.* Yeah, they're both mine.

30

JAYMES

WHEN I COME out of the spa treatment room, I'm led to the lounge with the hot tubs and these cool room experiences like a salt room and a chilled room. I'm also handed a cup of coconut water on the way. It's so decadent here, I wish I had more time.

In the hot tub room, I spot a familiar face. "Rochelle, hi. I didn't expect to see you here."

"Yes, Holli and I snuck away since the guys have the kids with them."

Dropping my robe on a lounge chair, I step into the large whirlpool. "Derrick has Ace."

"Yes, I saw them on their way out. Jamie, this is Holli Hughes."

The woman with Rochelle swims a little closer with a smile. "Dalton. I did change it, but I go by Hughes. I've heard about you."

"Oh really?"

"You're prettier than they let on and they said you were gorgeous."

Touching my hands to my cheeks, I remark, "I probably have marks on my face from the massage and look awful, but thanks. You're with Johnny, right?"

"Yes." The smile on her face says it all. *She knows how much she's loved.* "How's being out on the road treating you? Or more importantly, how's Derrick treating you?"

My face heats and I try to play it off like it's the steamy room, most likely to no avail.

"He's good . . . We're good," I reply shyly. "It's moving fast, but it's good. We have a million things to talk about and not enough time it seems."

Rochelle says, "Well, he's so smitten that I think you'll have years to come. Not to be nosy, but how are you feeling about things? The crazy that surrounds the band can be overwhelming."

"I don't know how you guys do it. I just had a small taste last night and I'm amazed by how well Derrick handles all the attention."

Holli leans back, resting her arms on the side and kicks her feet up. "It comes with the job. They know that, but there's an aspect, their egos, that thrive on it too. Derrick's really come into his own in the last year. I think he struggled the first year, but he understands what they trade to be at the level they're at."

"What about you?" I ask.

"I owe nothing to the public because of the band. I don't owe them photos of my family or personal memorabilia. I share what I want, but I control it. I have to. No one will protect my family like I will. That goes for Dalton as well. If he's on that stage, he's fair game. When he's home, he's mine."

Rochelle is nodding, and adds, "You have a child to protect. You don't owe the press any answers when it comes to Ace. If they ask about Derrick, that's up to you what you share." *I hadn't thought about that. It must have been hard when Rochelle first started dating Dex. How fortunate am I to have someone to help me feel the way?*

"There is more to think about than I thought."

Climbing out, Rochelle wraps a towel around her and sits on the edge with her feet in the water. "We're not trying to scare you, but I know you're not used to the attention. It can be intense and aggressive. Both Holli and I have been there. If you ever need to talk to someone, we understand, and we're here for you. Just like the guys are experiencing their fame together, as the women behind the band, we share a similar experience. Have you met Lara?”

“No, not yet, but I’ve heard about her.”

“I’ve known Lara for years. She’s great. You’ll meet her tonight.”

“What’s tonight?”

Holli climbs out and suddenly after seeing her incredible body, I want to remain hidden in the water until they’re gone. Holli says, “The concert. The four of us are going together.”

“Oh I can’t,” I reply. “I have Ace, my five-year-old with me.”

This time Holli, standing in a bikini, towel dries her hair, and smiles. “We have two nannies to watch the kids. They’re great. Ace would love it. I heard he’s a wonderful boy.” Walking toward the changing area, she adds, “Come on. Let’s get some shopping in.”

Rochelle winks. “Don’t worry. I’ve got Derrick’s credit card. Let’s go spend some money.”

I would ask how she has it, but somehow, I know he won’t mind. He might have even given it to her. I’ll find out soon enough. I climb out and start drying off because there is no way I’m missing this opportunity. I have my friend, Leah, at home, but I’d love more girl-friends, especially ones that Derrick trusts and adores, and I know he does with these two. *And they him. Perhaps I’m a little biased, but how could they not?*

“At what point do you throw in the towel?” Holli asks lounging on a red leather chair just outside the dressing room, where I’m trying on probably my thirtieth dress.

“I’m not sure because you guys refuse to let me.” I can hear them laughing from the other side of the curtain currently dividing my nakedness from the entire fancy schmancy store. They told me to not look at the prices, but I did. Once, and then about had a heart attack and took their advice.

A black dress is shoved through the crack between the curtain and the wall and Holli says, "Try this last one on. I think it's going to be our winner."

"Why do I need a dress and heels? I have flats and jeans and blouses."

They burst out laughing again. Rochelle says, "Which is fantastic most of the time, but tonight we're going to knock Derrick right on his ass when he sees you."

I pull the skin-tight dress on and adjust the straps on my shoulders. Bending forward I cup my left boob and lift it and then repeat with my right. I back out of the dressing room and ask, "Zip?"

Holli is right there ready to help. When I'm zipped, I turn around. "Ta-da!"

"Wow." She steps back and looks me over. "Wow, Jamie. You look just . . . Wow. He is going to die when he sees you. Spin for us."

Rochelle comes out of her room with a dress hanging off her shoulder and tags in her hand. "I found this one—Wow, Jamie."

Holli smiles, taking pride in her work. "That's what I said. That's definitely the one."

With her long brown hair off to one side, Rochelle, says, "You look incredible. How do you feel?"

"Incredible."

They both smile.

At the counter, Rochelle slaps down Derrick's credit card. "He gave it to me and told me to make sure you spend lots of money."

"Why would he do that?"

"Because he knew you wouldn't." The clerk takes the card, the dress from me, and some lingerie the girls insisted I get for later.

Leaning on the counter, I say, "He knows me well."

"You've got a good heart, Jamie. I can tell from spending time with you and with Ace. I also know a little about your background, Derrick's *shared* background. I'm not going to pretend to understand what you've gone through, but he says you work hard and are going to school. That's amazing. So try to enjoy the few days here if you can."

"Derrick makes it easy."

"Ace has really taken to him. When Derrick came and got him this morning, he ran right to him. It was like they've known each other forever."

"What time did he pick up Ace?"

The clerk hands the receipt back for me to sign. I catch a glimpse of the total and gasp. "I can't spend that."

Rochelle takes the pen and scribbles Derrick's name. "You're not. He is," she replies all sassy. I'm handed the dress, which is left on the hanger and a nice bag with fabric straps. I'll save it and carry my lunch in it when I return home.

Holli's already in Christian Louboutin when we leave the dress store. Rochelle says, "Derrick got him around six a.m."

I stop. "What? Why?"

Eyeing me, she asks, "He didn't tell you?"

"Tell me what?"

"Well, I'm only telling you. Please know I'm not making any judgments."

"Okay," I reply even more worried now.

She goes on to tell me how she found Ace in the closet crying. My heart hurts and I feel sick to my stomach. "I need to sit a minute."

We sit outside the shoe store. Holli is inside trying on a pair of red-soled shoes, and Rochelle sits with me. "Look, there's a story there. Obviously," Rochelle says. "If you need help, I'm here for you and Ace. I'll help however I can."

"There's no helping us. It is what it is." My son is damaged because of me. "Derrick and I spoke earlier. This is why he offered to help us. He knows some stuff." Angling her way, I say, "Ace's father is a very bad man. That's all I can say."

Her hand covers mine. "Derrick has been through a lot. I'm sure you might have heard the same about Dex. They're a lot alike, those two. Not just the past partying, but their hearts are gold and when they love, they love with their entire soul." She stands, rearranging her shopping bags on her arm. "That man loves you, which means he'll do anything for you. All you have to do is let him in."

"You make it sound easy."

"Not easy, but worth the effort." Walking toward the store, she turns back when she realizes I'm not with her. "Well, come on. Holli has ten pairs of shoes for you to try on. Let's complete that outfit."

Two pairs of beautiful shoes, a designer handbag from another store, and a sparkly clutch later, we are done shopping. I didn't bother going to the counters. I knew I'd never be able to sign the receipt. Rochelle looks at her watch. "Sound check is almost over. Let's go sneak a peek."

We work our way through the maze of back hotel hallways and Rochelle flashes her badge to get backstage. My breath lodges in my throat when we enter through a set of doors and I see the band on stage, when I see Derrick on stage. I watch, mesmerized by what I'm seeing. I've seen footage online and videos, interviews and performances on shows, but never in person. I move to sit in a seat hidden in the darkness of the arena.

I'm about to sit down, but Holli says, "We should go say hi. Dalton will figure out I'm here if I don't. He has a sixth sense."

Rochelle laughs. "He has a Holli sense."

The band stops mid-song and Dex stands. "I'm getting water. You guys figure out your riff shit."

Johnny walks to Derrick and they both start playing. Derrick says, "That's where I come in and then sing the chorus."

"That'll work," Johnny replies. "One more time."

They sync up their guitars and go through the part again. Derrick adds, "That's it."

"Hey," Holli says, leaning against the edge of the stage. "Look who I brought with me."

The three guys look over her head and right at me. Derrick's expression lights up and I love that a little too much. "Hey, babe," he says, walking to the front of the stage and kneeling down. "Ace is with Tommy."

I love that he tries to ease my worries first. "And Tommy is?"

Rochelle says, "I'll take you back to the dressing room. Dex is back there too."

Johnny lifts Holli onto the stage and they kiss under the spotlight.

I'm such a voyeur, but I can't stop myself from staring. I'm not sure if it's relationship goals I'm jealous of or that their lives just seem so much easier and freer than mine. Either way, I want that.

Derrick has set his guitar down and hops off the stage. "Hey, beautiful."

"Derrick?"

"Yeah?"

I'm overtaken with emotion—I think all that shopping has made me lose my mind. This is not my world and has never been my world. Holli and Rochelle are so lovely, and although I feel bonded with them, I still feel out of my league. This is outside of my norm. I don't want to embarrass myself, but I especially don't want to embarrass Derrick. Leaning against him, I whisper, "Do you think I'll fit in your world?"

"What? Of course, but you don't need to fit in. You are my world, my love."

31

DERRICK

AFTER WE BUSTED Tommy teaching the boys how to play blackjack, we wrapped sound check. Everyone went back to Dex and Rochelle's, but I stayed and asked Ace and Jaymes to wait a few minutes for me.

On stage, I unplug my electric guitar and bring in my acoustic. Holding it out for Jaymes, I ask, "Will you play for me?"

"For you?" Every reason not to flickers through her eyes, but she pleasantly surprises me when she replies, "Can I play with you?"

"Sure," I reply, grabbing another acoustic in the rack to the side of the stage.

Ace had been running around, but he stopped and sat on the stage floor. I think he knows how momentous this is.

Jaymes settles on a stool that I was using and I pull Kaz's over. Facing her, I ask, "What song?"

"Ours."

"You remember it?"

"How could I forget?"

"That's my girl. Want me to start?" I ask, watching her adjust the guitar on her lap.

"Yes, you lead."

Counting off, I tap my foot and start playing. Her part won't kick in until the second verse, but she looks like a natural sitting across from me, her fingers positioned. The first chords she plays, she nails. Not sure how long it's been, but it's like she's never stopped playing. Her sweet voice sings the melody with me, her eyes on me, but occasionally peeking over at Ace, who's grinning from ear to ear watching his mom perform.

When the song comes to the end, she strums and holds the note just like she used to sitting in the back of my old pickup truck. Clapping echoes from the audience. We can't see beyond the spotlight, but Johnny and Holli step back into the light. Johnny says, "Why are we not performing that song on tour?"

"I only perform it with Jaymes."

Holli is smiling at my girl. "Your voice is amazing," she says to her.

This time looking to Jaymes, Johnny asks, "Like I said, why aren't we performing it?"

"Me? Oh I can't tour. I'm in school and have a full-time job at a dealership. Ace is in school too."

I don't step in. She can handle herself just fine, but I see the cogs turning in Johnny's head. Wrapping his arm around Holli's shoulders, he adds, "We'll get Tommy to talk to Rochelle and see if we can work out a few dates. You think you can perform live in front of an audience?"

"I've never tried."

"Think about it and get back to us."

"I will. Thanks."

They return to the darkness and this time we hear the double doors slam closed. Jaymes jumps up, and asks, "Did that just happen? For real?"

"It really happened. A few years later than it should have for me," I say, popping a smirk that I hope makes her a little weak in the knees. "But he liked you right away. He doesn't give out praise unless he means it."

A roadie sneaks on stage and signals with his hand that he'll handle the clean up. I set the guitar back on the rack and hand him the guitar Jaymes played of mine. Ace has run around and is now running down in front of the stage. We've got to get some of that energy out. Maybe I'll take him for ice cream or a few laps around the parking garage. "We should get going. The crew needs to do some stuff that they can't when we're in the middle of it."

We weave our way back to the empty hallways, both of us watching Ace run ahead. "You still have the guitar."

I take her hand. "I use it in the show this tour."

"Just surprised me."

"I guess you were always with me, even when you weren't."

She brings my hand up and kisses each of my knuckles. "You know what I've learned most being here this weekend?"

"What?"

"You've found the family you always wanted." She's right. But she's also wrong. Until I found my Jaymes again, I wasn't complete. Now? Now I have my family. But only because of her and Ace.

"Not all of it."

***

Jaymes

Looking down, I'm tempted to see that heart on his sleeve that he wears so openly. He used to be more protective of his feelings, not when it came to me, but when it came for anyone else to see. Along with success he found freedom. It's amazing to see the man he's become.

"I've been thinking about what you said earlier, about what I wanted, how I saw us moving forward." He's addicting. Derrick Masters is better and takes me higher than any drug ever could. Not that I ever did them, but I imagine being around him is similar. I want more, another love fix. A second chance at a life we should have had the first time.

"And?" he asks.

"I never want you to think of me as someone who used you for gain." I watch him carefully, look for his tell that he believes me. His jaw doesn't tense, his eyes stay soft on mine, so I continue, "You said you don't trust people when you meet them. I don't want to be that in your eyes."

"You can't because of the simple fact that we have a past that wasn't easy, but you loved me anyway. You loved me despite my flaws and poor judgment. You loved me for me. It's the same with you. I don't have to spend years dating you to know where your heart lies. I know you, Jaymes. I know who you are and where you came from. I know why you fight so hard to give Ace the life that you didn't get. Let me do that with you."

"I've got to be careful."

"I know. I respect that, but you can't keep putting your own life at risk to protect his. If you're gone, who does he have? Your mom? Can she protect him?"

Ace is standing at the end of the corridor, excited to push through the doors. We stop a few feet back and lower our voices. I ask, "You're taking on *his* child when you take me on. Do you understand the magnitude of that? You'll have new responsibilities to him, as a father figure, Derrick. You're still young—"

"You were younger," he snaps back.

"I don't care how he was conceived, there was never an alternative for me."

"Why is that?" There's no judgment in his tone and I don't blame him for asking. It's a fair question considering the circumstances and one I've asked myself many times, but never answered.

Looking down, the tips of my sneakers between his well worn brown Doc Martens. "I don't like to think about it because if I do, I betray Ace."

He brings me in, holding me against him. With a kiss to my head, he then lingers there. "Then don't answer it. You don't owe anyone anything when it comes to your life or the decisions you've made."

"Rochelle said something similar."

"Rochelle's heart is as big as the ocean."

"I could say the same about you."

He chuckles. "Only when it comes to you." Stepping back, he

turns to Ace, and adds, "And this cool kid. Want a ride back to the room?"

"Yes." Ace comes running into his arms and that's when I see it.

I'm always seeing the boy and the man, but it's not about the past and the present when it comes to Derrick. It's about the future. "Yes."

With Ace now situated on Derrick's shoulders, they look my way. Derrick asks, "You want a ride too? That will be later." His signature smirk and a wink follows. Sexy bastard.

I sock him on the arm. "Ha ha. I meant yes to everything with us."

"You'll let me move you out of your mom's?"

Nodding, I rub where I playfully hit him, enjoying every second of being with him, Ace and Derrick and me, being together like a family. I also find it over the moon sexy that his hard muscle never even flinched. "We've got nothing to lose but more time and I don't want to lose anymore of that with you."

"Ms. Grenier, you're going to make me blush. Who's the charmer now?"

"I am. I learned from the best." Sending him my own brand of a wink and smirk, I say, "Let's go. I've got stuff to do."

"Fine. Bossy. Bossy."

Ace pipes in. "She's always like that." We open the doors and enter the hotel. We're going to have to hurry before his fans spot him, but at least I know Ace is safe sitting atop his shoulders. I may not be on his shoulders, but I've never felt safer myself than standing by his side. Looking up, Derrick's smirk is gone. Focused. He's ready for anything. He may not claim to like any part of being Rebel but watching him now, I realize that was good training for what he was to become. *He learned to become impenetrable.*

I'm thinking those star-crossed lovers in the sky really do have a hand in our destiny. Here we are, years later, being the family we were always meant to be.

Without incident, we make it back to the suite. As soon as we come off the elevator we see Rochelle and Holli waiting outside the door. I laugh. I can already tell I'm in for some adventure, most likely, against my will. I whisper to Derrick, "I really like them."

"That makes me happy."

Holli has champagne in one hand and three glasses in the other. Rochelle looks guilty and starts speaking really fast, "So we know we promised to leave you alone earlier, but we've been having so much fun that we thought we could get ready together."

"I brought drinks," Holli adds, holding the goods up.

Derrick sets Ace down and opens the door. Once we're inside, he says, "I've been wanting to spend some time with Ace and we have a few hours before dinner, so why don't you go with them and we'll hold down the fort." Ace looks up at him and smiles. "What do you say, buddy? You want to hang out with me?"

Ace asks, "I thought you were hanging out with Mommy?"

I snort. "Different kind of hanging out, bud."

He pops his pretend collar and says, "Yeah, I could use some dude time."

My head jerks in surprise. "Dude time?"

"Derrick taught me *dude time* and to pretend I had a collar up high."

Rochelle and Holli are laughing, but Rochelle says, "Sounds about right."

Holli takes my bags and says, "We're stealing her. You get her back for dinner and prepare to die when you see her."

Ace runs to Derrick and clings to his leg. "I don't want him to die. Don't die, Derrick."

I think it takes us all a second to even realize what happened, but then I see Holli's expression fall. Heartbroken and worried. "Oh no," she says, squatting down in front of him. "I didn't mean he would die. It's a bad saying. I'm sorry. I just meant he's going to love seeing your mommy."

"He doesn't now?"

I step in and tap her on the shoulder. "It's okay." Turning to Ace, I say, "He—"

Derrick's hand rubs over the top of Ace's head, and he says, "Your mom is beautiful, Ace. She always looks beautiful. Don't you think?"

Nodding, he looks up at him, a smile appearing. "My mommy is the most beautiful. Everyone says that." I smile listening to my sweet boy. Then he adds, "Even the mean man."

The words punch me in the chest. My heart plummets to the pit of my stomach and for a split second I lose my balance. My arm is grabbed by Derrick and I'm steadied from behind by Holli. "Are you okay, Jamie?"

All I see is the fear in Ace's eyes. *What if something happens to me? Who will protect him?* Derrick's questions come ringing back. Tears fill my eyes and my hand covers my mouth hoping I can hold back the sob. I'm not sure if it's embarrassment that I have failed to protect him fully in front of Derrick's friends or that I'm realizing I will never be free from Reggie, but I snap at Ace, "Don't talk about him. Ever."

His arms tighten around Derrick's leg and tears well in his eyes matching mine. The room is quiet, no one daring to speak a word, except Derrick. "Come with me, Ace. I got you a present." He takes his hand and they walk to the bedroom. Ace peeks back over his shoulder and my heart shatters that I just snapped at him.

I gulp, and look up at the two women standing there in all of the awkwardness I caused. "Cards on the table."

They repeat, "Cards on the table."

Holli adds, "Stays between us."

Not sure why I decide to tell them, but it doesn't feel wrong to talk about it, not with them. "His father is not a good person. Think of the worst qualities you would ever want in a father and he owns them proudly. Drugs, running guns, gang activity, illegal activity, abuse—emotional and physical." Then I whisper, "rape."

Beyond the fun I've been missing in life, these women are who I wish I could be. They don't pander to the easy answers. They're strong, like I want to be. Holli, with her hands full of champagne and glasses, says, "Fuck him. He'll never come near you and that little boy again. I'll help you fight this battle."

"Me too. Anything we have to do, we'll do."

Tears fill my eyes for different reasons now. Camaraderie. Do you know those moments where you finally realize just how alone you've felt? How overwhelmed and out of control? But somehow, in Las

Vegas of all places, I feel safe. I don't know these women, they don't know me, but they've taken me in. I suspect just how they've taken Derrick in too, and helped him not feel so alone. "Why? Why would you do that for me?"

Rochelle replies, "Because if Derrick loves you, which he clearly does, we love you."

And then Holli says, "The women of The Resistance always stick together."

32

DERRICK

ACE IS BOUNCING in the chair while I dig through my suitcase. I can hear them talking in the living room. Although Jaymes probably shouldn't have snapped at Ace, I understand why she did. Those damn defenses of hers I've tried to keep lowered popped back up in an instant.

I don't fault her in the least. I still struggle with the same. When you've been hurt like she has or lived on the edge like I did, you're always ready to fight. Like it took me, it will take her time to change that, but I have no doubt that with enough support and love, she will be fine.

Pulling out the toy, I say, "Here it is."

He stands to get a gander. I rip the package open, and say, "This is a yo-yo. Have you ever had one?"

"No," he replies, coming closer. "What is it?"

Drugs, running guns, illegal . . . her voice trails off and I bring my attention back to Ace. "So you tie a loop like this and then slip it on your finger."

"Then what?"

"I'll show you. Stand back and watch the magic." He steps back.

When I flick the yo-yo out and it comes rolling back in, I catch it in my palm.

"Whoa. Let me try. Let me try."

"Sure." I slip the loop on his finger. "It's all in the wrist. Quick flip and then steady."

The yo-yo just dangles above the floor. The disappointment is seen in his sad eyes. "I can't do it."

"It's okay. Like the guitar, it takes practice. I'll teach you and then soon you'll be a pro."

"And we can yo-yo together."

Laughing, I reply, "Yep, we can yo-yo together. But first, how about we go get some ice cream?"

"Yay!" He runs into the living room. "Derrick's taking me to get ice cream."

Maybe he doesn't need any more sugar. When I walk out of the bedroom, I flick the yo-yo mindlessly. "Are we all good?"

I'm only looking at Jaymes, but Rochelle and Holli answer, "Yeah, we're good."

"Go potty, Ace. Then we'll go."

When I turn back to the ladies, they're gawking. I catch the yo-yo, and ask, "What?"

After they exchange looks with each other complete with smiles and mischievous looks in their eyes, Rochelle says, "Oh nothing. We'll meet you at the elevator, Jaymes." Another all-telling expression on her face that I can't tell jack-shit the meaning of. They seem to get it though.

With Ace out of the room and the others gone, I go to her. "Don't beat yourself up. I can see that's what you're doing."

"I just, I can't. I don't want to do that to him."

"He's a happy boy. You gave him that happiness. We all fuck up. What you said was a real and raw reaction. He didn't take it personally. He was all smiles in the other room, so don't stress about it."

She's going to anyway because she cares so deeply, but maybe when she steps back from the situation she'll realize she's allowed to be human. Looking quickly over her shoulder to make sure the coast is clear, she turns to me and says, "I haven't told you everything."

Now I find myself looking to make sure Ace isn't coming. "Wash your hands, too." Looking into the softer sides of emerald, I ask, "Is this something you want to do now or later?"

Dropping her head to match her sagging shoulders, she whispers, "There's so much more I haven't told you."

"Go easy on yourself, Jaymes. You're doing the best you can. It's what we're all doing."

Ace runs in and she lifts up. "You be good for Derrick and listen to him, okay?"

"Okay."

He runs to the door, but I stop him. "Give your mom a hug, Ace."

Her sweet smile returns and she dips down into his wide-open arms. "I love you."

"Love you." Dashing for the door, he says, "I'm ready."

"Coming."

I follow him, but when I start to open the door, he says, "Give my mom a hug, Derrick."

Just the exact right thing we needed to break up the heavy. The kid's got great timing and Jaymes and I both start laughing. But when I start walking back to her, my feet slow just as my world does. Jaymes with the bright eyes and raven hair, sweet pink lips with the bow at the top. Jaymes Grenier with the sassy mouth and good grades, the girl who kept me alive by demanding my time. Standing right in front of me waiting for a hug. I hug her when I'd rather give her forever.

She owns me.

When I reach her, I take hold of her hips first and let her question me with her eyes. Her arms come up and around and I slide my hands higher to her waist, keeping the distance between us. "What are you doing?" she asks.

"Looking at you."

"What do you see?"

Life. Love. Hope. Fulfillment. Joy. Perfection. "Forever." I close the gap and run my fingers into the hair at the nape of her neck. "Close your eyes, Ace." That makes her smile, but I'm kissing her and she's receiving and then kissing me right back.

Her body is putty in my hands when she looks up at me. "That was some kiss."

"There are more where that came from."

"I hope so."

"I know so."

Ace asks, "Can I open my eyes now?" Making us laugh again.

"I'm going to take this kid out. You have fun and I'll see you later."

She blows me a kiss and then one to Ace who catches his. "Good trick, my man. The ladies love that."

A sideways glance was earned from her on that one, but the door closes, so it's all good.

We head down to the shops and past the restaurants to find the small little Gelateria. After a few minutes of explaining that gelato is Italian ice cream, Ace orders Stracciatella. I didn't even know what gelato was until last year when we toured Italy, and here's this kid ordering the most Italian one from the bunch. He makes me grin with pride.

We sit in the corner of the shop eating and talking about the yo-yo. I pull out some of my best tricks to his amazement. Eyes are on us. Whisperings heard. He looks around a few times, adept at being aware of his surroundings, but doesn't say anything. I try to keep his attention on me and enjoy our time together.

Leaning forward, I ask, "So what do you think about me dating your mom?"

"She likes to hang out with you. She smiles. That's always her tell."

"What do you know about tells?"

"Tommy told us everyone has a tell. Mommy's smile is hers."

I'm going to kick Tommy's ass when I see him next. "I like seeing her smile too."

"Will we see you again when we go home?"

Valid question and one I'm more than happy to answer. "Yes. I'm on tour with the band for three more weeks, but then I'll be home and we can hang out again."

"I can practice the yo-yo and show you my tricks."

"I'd like that."

"Me too."

After gelato, we go to this grassy area near the pool. It's surrounded by bushes and appears to be a no man's land, or secret garden as Ace calls it. I like the privacy and the fresh air. Ace loves the freedom to run. We don't have a lot of time but I lie down in the grass anyway. It's been a long time since I felt at peace enough to do so when I'm not home. Ace lies next to me and it reminds me of the first time I met him and the first time I saw Jaymes again. It's only been a few weeks, not quite a month, but life without them feels foreign to me now. They feel like they've been a part of my life forever, their presence slowly erasing the difference.

Ace asks, "Are we moving?"

Turning my head to the side, I see the curiosity in his eyes. "I hope so."

"With you?"

I'd like that. "I don't know. What would you think about that?"

He shrugs. "What's it like where you live?"

"Really nice. I have a house and there's a pool."

"I don't know how to swim."

"You can learn."

"Will you teach me?"

Guitar. Yo-yo. To swim. It's a lot to take on when I'm used to being single, but I've watched Dex adapt to being a father. And like how it was for him, it's an easy adjustment. *That's love.* I answer without hesitation, and I mean it, "Sure."

"You're rich."

"Why do you say that?"

"Everything is nice and there are no mean people."

I roll over on my stomach and lift up on my elbows. "I'd like to say that there aren't, but you're a wise little man, Ace. You know there are bad people. But there are also good people."

"Am I good?"

"You're the best."

Sitting up, he fidgets with my watch. "Does that mean goodest?"

"That does mean the goodest."

"So if I'm the goodest and my mom is the goodest, you'd want the best in your life."

"Absolutely."

"So it only makes sense that we should live in the house with the pool."

"Ahhh. I see how you worked that in your favor, and I like your style, kid."

"I like yours too."

WE KNOCK on Dex's door an hour before we need to leave for dinner if we want to eat before the show. Neil answers, but Rochelle is right behind him telling us to come in. Ace tags Neil and takes off. "Have you seen Jaymes?"

"In the bedroom, but I think she wants to surprise you. Let me go check on her."

Holli comes out of the room, but shuts the door behind her. When she sees me, she says, "You did good. She's smart and funny, and gorgeous."

"She was all those things before she met me."

"Well what can we say? Every girl loves a bad boy."

Rochelle peeks out from the bedroom. "Come in here." I shove my hands in my pockets not sure what to expect. Will she look different? Or the same? What have they been doing to her? The door is opened wide and now I see—my throat goes dry and my pants fit a lot tighter. This is not the same demure girl in a pink dress that showed up yesterday. This is a vixen who likes to dominate. Black dress that shows off all her sexy curves, tits pushed up, begging for my mouth, shapely legs, and fuck-me heels. "Fuck me." I mean it one way. They think a different way. Jaymes rolls her eyes, but I can tell it's only because she's anxious. "You look stunning."

"Really?" she asks, running her hands over her stomach. "I feel different."

While I come into the room, Rochelle slips out, and shuts the door behind her. "How do you feel?"

"Beautiful."

I slide my palm on the underside of her jaw and then cup her cheek. Leaning in, I kiss her gently, and whisper, "You should always feel as beautiful as you do right now." This time I kiss her not so gently. My need ravenous.

Her hands slide under my shirt and slip in the back of my jeans, pushing my hips against hers. Our panting breaths reveal our desires. Her lips are on my neck and against my ear. "Fuck me, baby," she whispers.

I spin her around and push her head down. "This dress is hot, but I want it off." I take the zipper pull and slide from high on her back all the way down to her ass and then slip the straps off her shoulders.

She steps out of the dress and I'm left with my mouth agape. Holy fuck me. With see-through lace stretched over her body, this lingerie number is about to be ripped to fucking shreds. "You look so sexy all my plans to love on you—just fuck those."

"No, fuck me, hot stuff." She walks with confidence to the door and turns the little lock on the knob. Coming back, she stands in front of me and says, "Drop your pants and sit on the bed."

I fucking move at the speed of light. With my cock on full display, I lean back on my elbows. The tips of her red nails glide over my erection and then spread the drop at the tip, coating my head before she takes her fingers in her mouth and slowly slides back out between ruby lips. "You make me want to do such naughty things to you." *Oh shit. This girl. Need. Her. Now.*

"I won't stop you."

She smiles, but I see the determination in her eyes. She's not going to be distracted from what she wants. Bending at the waist, she takes my dick into her mouth and slides down, slicking it between her lips.

Falling back on the bed, I want to close my eyes, but I can't take them off her as she takes me. She speeds up like my breath—her mouth and throat taking me slowly, but fully inside. Pausing, she closes her eyes and swallows around me and I almost shoot my fucking load. "Fuck," is muttered repeatedly and she obeys, picking up her pace. I watch with rapt fascination as she pulls my soul from the depths of my core, tighter and tighter I coil. Reaching up, I put a little pressure on the back of her head, but when she sucks me ever harder, I lose focus. Stars and darkness, Andromeda and Perseus, and midnight songs sung in the back of trucks blind me as I explode, letting her take everything she wants, everything she desires. I give my all to her. I always will.

33

JAYMES

I'VE MADE a mess of him and by the red lipstick all over his penis I can only imagine how I must look. I attempt to slink away to the bathroom and clean up before he has a chance to look at me, but I'm caught by the waist and pulled to the mattress beside him. "Don't hide. I want to see how fucking beautiful you are after making me come."

His dirty words elicit a soft whimper that I regret the second after I realize I did it. All my boldness, my empowerment from the clothes and makeup and hair is disappearing and I realize I just want him to love me for me. So I roll toward him and let him take me in—messy and disastrous I'm sure, but this is me after being together so intimately. "You're the most gorgeous woman I've ever seen. That has never changed from the moment I saw you in that short dress with the flowers on it and that denim jacket."

"You remember that?"

"I remember everything about you. You wore thick wool socks and a pair of deep-red combat boots."

"They were knock-offs. We couldn't afford Doc Martens. I found them at a resale shop for three dollars because the heel had split from the shoe. I used to use super glue to keep them together."

"I liked them on you."

She pushes against my chest. "I think you would say just about anything right now."

"You're wrong. I don't have to say stuff to impress you. I just have to be honest."

"You have me all figured out, do you?"

"No, I wish I did, but I do know that the truth goes a long way with you these days, so I won't lie to you, Jaymes."

Reaching between us, I find his hand and our fingers entwine. "When you left that day, Reggie was pulled over the same evening on an anonymous tip the cops had received." He stiffens between us, but doesn't say a word. "He wasn't taken in."

"What?"

"I won't lie to you either. Not anymore. I went by your house that afternoon, but you were turning the corner, driving erratic, so I followed you worried you had finally succumbed to doing what you swore to me you wouldn't."

"I wouldn't do heroine. No way."

"But I didn't know that."

"I told you. I gave you my word I wouldn't. Was my word worth nothing?"

"Your word was as good as your actions and you were acting strange the previous few days. I know what you did. I saw how you set Reggie up to take the fall."

"God, Jaymes." His hands slide over his face and he starts pacing. "What did you do?"

"I thought I was helping. Like I said, I thought you weren't thinking clearly."

Stopping in front of me on the bed, his words are tight. "What. Did. You. Do?"

Panic rises, making it hard to breathe. "I . . . I waited for you to leave and found the package under his seat. I took it and flushed it all down my toilet."

"Why?" he yells. "It was the perfect fucking plan. He would have gone down for life."

Crawling back on the bed away from him, my words come stuttering out, "I didn't know that. I, I thought, I thought he'd be released and he'd come for you."

"Instead he came for you."

Lies don't separate us anymore. Neither do omissions.

Here we are caught in the middle of the hurricane we created.

Coming around to the side of the bed, he sits next to me. The heaviness of our exposed acts weigh his throat down and I hear him swallow. "It was a good plan."

"A great plan. I just wish I would have been in on it."

"Me too."

A light knock is followed by Dex asking, "Everything okay?"

I look up at Derrick and sigh. He nods, understanding the weight of the world I've been carrying around with me all these years. Taking my hand in his, our fingers entwine again, and he replies, "All's good."

Helping me off the bed, he pulls me into the bathroom, and positions himself behind me. My makeup isn't as messy as I thought it would be. My hair is messier. But his arms slide around me and he's kissing my temple, so all that superficial stuff fades away. At the end of the day, we made a decision, took a path, and paid the price. Now, all we can do is live with it. Having that off my shoulders gives me peace. Peace I've needed for a long time.

SITTING in a private dining room at the hotel's sushi restaurant, I look around at the four couples and Tommy. Introductions have been made and conversation is lively. I have finally met the man Derrick refers to as his best friend. This is huge.

Kaz Fabian has his own very intriguing story to tell, and so opposite of Derrick's, but I see how they get on—teasing and joking, but honestly and genuine. His fiancée and I hit it off right off the bat. Lara Kessler has been telling me how she's been decorating Derrick's mom's house and that his mom just adores me and has these photos of Derrick and me in frames that she wants to keep out even with the new décor. She says, "So I talked her into new frames."

"I can't wait to see."

She leans in and whispers, "Between us, I've heard a lot about you in the last year. I don't even think Derrick realizes how much a part of his life you've been."

"What do you mean?"

"I'm sure you know about the guitar, but Kaz said Derrick used to mumble about a James in his sleep. He thought he was referring to a man and just wasn't ready to come out yet."

"I'm surprised Kaz never asked."

"Oh God, no. Kaz is all about being who you are and supporting that. Heaven knows I went through hell and he was right there however I needed him to be. Derrick's that way too. He has the biggest heart. A little hot tempered, but who doesn't want a friend willing and ready to fight for you?"

"That's Derrick. He used to hit first and ask questions after."

"Once at an awards show he punched my ex-boyfriend just to back Kaz up." I watch as her eyes drift to something I can't see in the distance, her memories. "I think he would have punched the world if he could because of all the anger he had tied up in him."

"But?"

Her attention turns to me. "But?"

"I thought there would be a but."

Smiling, she says, "But you came back."

Into his life. I came back. "I'm starting to think there's a conspiracy to see Derrick with somebody, especially when I look around this table."

"Not somebody. *You.*"

"You're making me feel special and you don't even know me."

She laughs and sips her glass of wine. "We may not know *you*, but we all know about you. There was never going to be anyone else even if he thought it possible."

"How possible did he think it would be?"

"Don't even go there, honey. Trust me, it's a no-win situation. Just know where his heart lies now. That's all that matters."

"What if I'm as temporary as the other possibilities?"

"You sitting here tonight should put your mind at ease."

This is new information. "He's never brought a date to dinner with you?"

"No. He hasn't. This dinner, he organized."

Derrick's hand covers my thigh and begins to rub. When I look to the other side of me, he's chatting with Tommy about some equipment, but his hand continues mindlessly. He won't know how that makes me feel, warm and cared for, or how he's treating me the exact opposite of temporary. He's treating me like we do this all the time, like we're together every day. It's natural and comforting.

This dinner, he organized. I cover his hand, and hold it until he looks my way. Leaning over, I kiss him. "Thank you."

"For what?"

"This weekend, brunch with the moms, coming by that night to pick up your mom just to see me. For lying in the grass with me when I obviously made a fool of myself and tried to play it off. For bringing my textbook up to my work when we were only seventeen because I forgot it at home the night before a test." The lines soften around his eyes and it's funny, but I never noticed before. I love that I'm sitting here witnessing another stage of his life with him. "For remembering what I was wearing the first time you saw me. And for making love to me with care but not treating me like I'll break."

"Any time."

"I have one more." His hand flips over so our palms are together. "Thank you for accepting my son and treating him like he's your own. If that scares you that I'm voicing that, I totally understand, and I won't do it again. I just need you to know that I see how you treat him and I see how taken he is with you. Thank you."

"It's been my complete pleasure to spend years of my life with you. I would never pass up a chance to spend more time with you and your son. I can make you that promise, Jaymes, and keep it."

"I don't want to go home tomorrow and I don't want you to leave to wherever the band is off to. Call me selfish, but I feel like I just got you back and now you have to go away again. I shouldn't feel this way, I know, but I'm already starting to miss you."

"Three weeks and then you'll be sick of me hanging all over you, following you around like a lovesick puppy. You know, pathetically head over heels in love kind of stuff. I might even write a few love songs and serenade you. I can already tell it's not going to be pretty."

"I'll take pathetically head over heels in love kind of stuff any day over not seeing your face at all."

"We can FaceTime. And get a sitter when I come back. I guarantee you a reunion you'll never forget." My hand is brought to his lips again, a small smile locked in his kiss.

"I like the sound of that."

"In the meantime, we have tonight."

WHEN THE GUYS head off for the concert, we all head back to change clothes. There's no way I'm standing around in five-inch heels and a dress at a concert. I'll break my ankle. Jeans and a T-shirt it is!

But not just any.

I scored a band shirt from Holli. What I didn't expect to find was a gift from Derrick waiting in the suite. I haven't opened a gift all by myself in years. Usually Ace sticks out his bottom lip and guilts me into letting him open it. So I rip the paper off like it's Christmas morning and open the lid.

That sweet man.

The burgundy of the leather is pristine, the size of the combat boots perfect. I may not be fifteen anymore, but I can't believe I finally have my first pair of Doc Martens.

He is so getting laid later.

I get dressed and touch up my makeup before going to say good night to Ace, who is with the other kids and a nanny for a few hours. "I'll come get you later, but go to bed when they tell you to, okay?"

"Okay," he agrees begrudgingly, looking sad.

"What's wrong, buddy?"

"I want to stay with CJ and Neil."

"You want to sleepover again?" Does it make me a horrible person that I wouldn't mind one more night with Derrick? Mom guilt. "Did you ask Rochelle and Dex?"

"They said it was up to you."

"I think it would be good for him to try again." I look over at Rochelle and she's nodding. "We're happy to have him if you're okay with it."

"As long as you are."

"The boys would love it and I think it's good for you and Ace as well."

"That sounds like a yes, Ace."

He hugs me tight, and says, "I love you."

"Love you, too. You have a fun night and I'll see you in the morning, okay?"

"'Kay."

Rochelle meets me at the door and we walk out together. "Ready to see that hot rocker of yours?"

"More than ready."

34

———————

JAYMES

"Wʜᴀᴛ ɪs this life I'm living?"

Lara laughs. "It's a nice gig if you can get it."

"Dating a rock star or being the rock star?"

"Either. Want a drink? I'm going to get a bourbon and Coke."

"I'll have whatever you're having."

Holli waves me down from the far end of the hall. When I reach her, she opens the door for me. "Come in. We usually hang out until right before they go on stage."

Peeking in, the whole band's there. Rochelle and Tommy are discussing something on an iPad and Holli holds the door open for Lara after me. I round the corner and there's Derrick. He glances up, but from the delayed response he was caught up in whatever he was listening to. Standing, he sets his guitar down and takes the ear buds out. "I didn't know if you'd be here before we went out."

"I'm glad I am."

"Me too." Running his hand around my neck, I tilt back and kiss him. Even though we're in a room full of people, I don't hold back. Now that I've found him again, I don't want to waste a second together.

Until the catcalls come.

Then we stop and laugh. I can feel my cheeks heating, but he whispers, "Ignore them. They're just jealous."

When I look back all three are kissing their guys and I elbow Derrick in the gut. "Yeah, I have a feeling they're not jealous."

Tommy says, "I am." Spreading his arms, he asks, "Any takers?"

We all laugh and it feels so good to laugh so freely, our problems left in another state entirely. Or at least mine.

Someone knocks on the door and says, "Five minutes."

Derrick gives me a quick kiss. "I'll see you out there."

"Break a leg."

I shake my ass for him, and he calls after me, "Nice shirt by the way."

Kicking my boots up, I say, "Nice boots. Thank you."

"No problem."

Holli slaps Johnny's ass and Rochelle says, "I'll see you out there. I have a few emails I need to send."

Lara hands me my drink and we're escorted backstage by a guy with a headset who's holding a clipboard. Behind a curtain and through a door, we're led to the VIP seating. Tapping Lara on the shoulder, I say, "I've never been so close to the stage during a concert before."

Standing in front of the seats, she laughs. "You do realize you're dating a member of The Resistance?"

"No. I don't think it's sunk in at all."

The stage goes black with the rest of the arena. From where we're standing I can see tiny flashing lights on the floor.

"Well, get ready."

I'm not sure if she means for the performance or for dating Derrick, which seems to be almost the same as dating the band by how close they all are.

The drums kick off and a spotlight hits Dex. Droplets fly from the impact when his sticks hit the set. His arms are sculpted and on display in a sleeveless Journey T-shirt that has seen better days. "I wish Rochelle could see him."

"She's watching backstage. She always watches his kickoff."

Not even two minutes in and he stops, and the lights go out. I hear shuffling about on stage but can't see a thing.

The spotlight comes on and Johnny is standing at the microphone. His guitar swung around on his back. He caresses the mic like he would caress a woman. Glancing to the other side of Lara, Holli stands mesmerized. He's wearing sunglasses, but I could bet money he's singing to her. It doesn't matter that thousands have spent money to see the band tonight, he only sees her.

She closes her eyes and sways to his sultry and entrancing voice, but it's not him who holds my attention. Another spotlight kicks in and Derrick joins the chorus and then Kaz. Dex starts in with a backbeat and the guitars are added.

I spend the next hour screaming in excitement, dancing, and flirting with the sexiest guitarist I've ever seen. Derrick steps to the edge several times and once while changing out guitars, he fell into a push-up and kissed me. He didn't miss a beat and Johnny laughed.

Lara screamed in excitement with me, then said, "You just won the most hated woman in America banner. I'm happy to hand the title over."

"What do you mean?"

"Derrick was the only one left. His single status gave fans hope they'd get a hookup. After that very public display of affection, you've earned it fair and square after me."

"I can't say the honor is all mine." I laugh anyway, but I have most definitely taken Derrick Masters off the market.

Looking down at my phone, a text catches my attention: *Ace is in bed and had a great time. Have fun tonight.*

I'm so happy to hear Ace is safe and sleeping.

The band rushes off stage and Holli zooms past me flashing her backstage pass and through the doors. We're hot on her tail, just as excited as she is. She bounds toward the band. Johnny turns and just like that she jumps into his arms. His sunglasses are off his face and she's smothering him with kisses.

Lara whispers, "They are the horniest couple ever."

I'm too busy laughing to reply, but I'm competitive by nature. "I bet I've got them beat."

"Hey Masters," I call.

Derrick looks back and then turns with a damn sexy smirk on his face. "You talkin' to me."

"Sure am."

"Why don't you bring that conversation in a little closer."

"How close?" I ask with only five feet left between us.

"Close. I want to show you something."

I shrug to Lara and she rolls her eyes, then says, "Kaz, wait up."

I think Lara might have a competitive streak too. But back to Derrick and how he's kissing me with abandon in the middle of the crew rushing around us setting up for the encore performance. "Where are the restrooms?"

"This way." He shoves a door open and we almost fall inside. Shutting the door, he locks it, and then stalks me against the sink. With one hand against the wall above my head, he leans down. "What do you need, baby?"

"Remember how good I made you feel?"

"Yes, I have a red dick to prove it."

Red? Oh right. The lipstick. "I want you to make me feel the same."

"Right now?"

"Right now."

"I've got fifteen minutes until I have to be back on that stage. Get to stripping, woman."

My jeans are too tight and my boots are a bitch to take off. I do it anyway and I'm like Speed Racer doing it. Standing there in socks and a T-shirt I can't say I'm on top of my sexy game, but he sure does seem to like it. "Do you know how hot you look in that shirt?"

"I feel even hotter. Twelve minutes."

He chuckles and lifts me onto the counter next to the sink. "Lean back and spread your legs for me."

I'd like to say this was uncomfortable or awkward, but once my panties were removed, I forgot what happened next. I just remember singing the Star-Spangled Banner and seeing stars from the ecstasy.

The knock comes with five minutes to spare. "I'll just stay here with bones made of jelly. Go on. Save yourself. The world can have you for thirty minutes. Then you're mine again."

He's laughing. "I really do have to go, babe." He kisses me and it's erotic and sensual. Careful not to expose me, he slips out of the room, but stops to add, "That was dinner. You tasted so good that I can't wait to eat you again for dessert later."

My vagina clenches in anticipation. Good Lord, that man's mouth —skilled and dirty. The perfect combination.

Managing to get dressed on shaky legs, I slip my jeans on after an exhaustive search for my underwear. I have no idea where they went. Probably to the same place that only single socks go to die. Once I come out of the bathroom, all three women are shaking their heads. "You know we could hear you?"

"What? No? Hear what?" I play the innocent.

Rochelle says, "Let's go. They're already lined up to start the encore."

We start walking, but I hear Lara say, "Girl's got some lungs on her."

"No," I reply mortified.

Holli whispers, "Don't worry. We've all done it. We're just teasing." That's a relief. *I think.*

"I lost my underwear though. I couldn't find it anywhere in there." She says, "That's odd."

"Yeah, it sucks. I just got those today."

We find our seats again and the band starts playing one of their biggest hits, but there's no sitting when it comes to one of their concerts. I've been revived and seeing him on stage . . . Gah! He's so incredibly hot up there. But then he shows me why his name is Masters. He licks his lips and tastes his finger. Holli, Rochelle, and Lara all look at me. I just nod. I'm not going to deny it. Everyone can see right through us, so I'll just own it.

Hollie's arm shoots straight out at Derrick. "There."

"What?"

"I think I found your underwear."

"Where?"

"Front right pocket."

Following her finger, my mouth drops open in shock. "Oh my God." The black lace is barely showing but we see it easily. "I'm going to kill him." After I have sex with him for that. Dirty boy. I love it and I've never been more turned on by something so naughty.

He knows I know too and flashes that signature smile that makes all of us go wild.

When the show is over, the band leaves the stage and a security guard escorts us to the back again. There are lots of people rushing around, breaking down the equipment and stands. We walk into the dressing room and the guys are so quiet, but when they see us, it erupts into a room of chaos, each couple sectioning off for privacy. I grab my handsome man's face, and say, "I'm so damn proud of you. You are incredible."

With a cocky smile, he asks, "So you liked the show then?"

"God, I loved it. It was amazing from beginning to end."

Lifting up so no one else hears me, I whisper into his ear, "I need to fuck you then make love to you all night."

His arm comes around my back and he pulls me against his hard body. "Fuck. Yes."

And we did.

Twice.

For both.

35

JAYMES

EXHAUSTED, I lie on the bed and watch him at the window. The lights from The Strip light up the room even with the interior lamps off. I roll to my side and tuck my hands under my head. "Where do you fly off to?"

Languidly he looks my way. All the tension from his body has disappeared. For someone made of solid muscles, he looks at ease. Peace looks good on him. "I'm not sure. I usually send Tommy a text and ask. Or not. Does it matter?"

"Yes."

He comes back to bed and we readjust until my head is resting on his legs as he leans against the headboard. "Why?" Fingertips dance across my skin, my body his instrument to create his own music.

"I want you to be present in your life, to feel the difference between the salty air of Florida and the mountain air of Colorado. Then when you come home to me, I want you to tell me all about standing in Times Square at midnight and eating BBQ in Kansas City. Is the water around Hawaii as blue as your eyes or is it more sea green? Watch the fog roll over the hills of Sausalito and then tell me how long it takes before it disappears into the ocean. I need you to experience everything you can and remember for me."

"Come with me. Come with me and let me show you how the Eiffel Tower sparkles at night. There's a little Mom and Pop restaurant just outside Rome that's worth the trip to eat their homemade pasta. And when you're in the Maldives, you can sit on the beach and forget that everyone else exists in the world. Standing at the base of Christ the Redeemer in Rio, you suddenly feel small enough to believe there just might be something bigger than us out there. Let me show you the world, my love."

"Just like Andromeda and Perseus, we can outrun our fates."

"Because they ended up in the heavens doesn't mean they didn't fulfill their destinies."

I slide up and sit next to him. His arm around my shoulder holds me close and I drop my head on his. "Guess we'll see how tomorrow turns out."

"I'm not willing to risk it. You can move into my house."

"No, I can't. We didn't take it slow, but I think taking that kind of leap might be too fast for all of us."

"I'll be back in three weeks. I want you to find a place, somewhere safe, somewhere he can't find you."

"I'm at my mom's."

"That's not safe. If he wants to get to you, he will, and you know it."

Rearranging, I turn to face him, pulling the sheet over my lap and crossing my legs. "It's not something I like to talk about, but you need to know what you're getting into when you decide if you want to see me beyond this weekend."

"There's no if, Jaymes. Not for me."

"You always were too stubborn for your own good."

"I can say the same about you."

"I need to say this, though, and I need you to hear me, really hear me. Reggie will be in our lives forever." Despite my constant wishing for his early demise. "There's no changing that." And then the floodgate of questions is opened.

"How often does he come around?"

"Not often. Every few months."

"Why does he come around?"

"Who knows? Money. To keep me scared. To make sure you're not there. Not for Ace."

"Is that why he doesn't know about me coming to your mom's?"

"He never goes over there. Like I said, my mom has made it very clear to him."

"So he has a vendetta against me. What will happen if I show up?"

"He said he'd kill you. I'm surprised he hasn't gotten a whiff of you visiting those two times."

"How would he?"

"He has guys, druggies who will snitch for a hit. The thing about Reggie is that he's the same guy you knew. He's a lot bark, but not much bite. His ego is what keeps him in charge. He's not afraid to hurt someone or worse, so no one messes with him. But he's still small-time in the grand scheme of LA."

"So when you return to your mom's house, do you think he'll come around?"

"He was arrested before we left. I should have told you. I know I'm a chickenshit to come here under the threat being lifted, but his arrest is our reprieve. He's threatened our lives so many times, I think he's capable of following through. With him in jail, I knew we could slip away and be back and he wouldn't be the wiser."

His hand warms my knee. "I wish I would have known what you've been going through."

"You don't need my troubles. You don't need anyone dragging you down."

"You don't drag me down. I love you. I love Ace. Heck, I love your mom. We may not be married, but we're family."

Not *a* family, but family. It's silly to notice such a slight variation of words but it means more than what was said. "Yeah," I say, sighing. "Family."

I scoot under the covers and lie down.

"Hey, did I say something wrong?"

"No." I'm the worst actress ever. "I'm just tired. I'm going to get a little more sleep before morning comes."

"So that's it?"

"I think so."

"You go back to that place and I go on tour and we go our separate ways or what? I'm confused what just happened here?"

"That makes two of us." My eyes are closed, but I can feel the burn of his gaze.

When I finally open mine, he asks, "What are you doing?"

"Trying to sleep."

"You know what I mean. Why are you pulling away from me?"

I don't want us to leave on bad terms and I don't want to hide how his words made me feel. Sitting up, I face him again. "Because we're *like* family, we're not your family."

"Is that what you want? You want us to be a family? I'll go down to that Elvis chapel right now and marry you if that's what you want."

"Derrick, don't say things you don't mean."

"I mean it." And by the look of determination in his eyes, he does.

"You're still drunk."

"I only had two drinks last night, so nope, not drunk."

"You're tired. You said yourself you're exhausted from traveling so much."

"I am tired. Fucking tired, but I'm not tired right now. I feel pretty damn awake actually."

Biting my lip, I analyze every little feature on his face, searching for the crack in his composure, the lie that I'll surely find. The trouble is, I'm not finding any. I actually find the opposite—the truth. "You mean it, don't you?"

"I do. I'd marry you right now, Jaymes."

"Do you understand what you're saying?"

"I do."

"Do you understand how insane it is that we're even talking about this?"

"I do."

"Do you have a fever?"

"I do. I'm hot for you."

"You can't just be hot for me. Sure the sex is great, we get along well. We always did. Ace clearly adores you, but this is crazy talk. Don't you think?"

"I do. And I still want to marry you." Reaching out, he picks me up by my ass and pulls me onto his lap. With his arms around me, and a smile that confirms he really means everything he said, he asks, "Do you think I'd make a good dad?"

"I do." Kissing his temple, I whisper, "The best dad."

"Do you think I could make you happy?"

"I do." I place another kiss on his cheek. "The happiest."

"Do you trust me to take care of you and your family?"

"I do." I kiss the corner of his mouth. "Implicitly."

"Do you love me?"

"I do." Kissing his lips, I stay, and say, "With my whole heart."

"Jaymes Grenier, will you be my forever and marry me?" I'm about to answer, but his finger presses to my lips, and he says, "Save it for the ceremony. What time's your flight?"

Okay, that was so sexy I'm melty inside. Wait . . . "Today?"

"Yes. Today."

"Noon."

"Perfect. You get some sleep. I'll take care of the rest."

I land on the bed with a little bounce after he rolls me off him. Lifting up on my elbows, I protest, "What? No. How am I supposed to sleep now?"

"I don't know. Try closing your eyes and being very quiet."

"Your sarcasm is not appreciated, but duly noted."

"Sweet dreams, sweetheart." He's chuckling as he walks out of the room with his phone to his ear.

The door is shut behind him, but I'm too giddy to sleep because I just said yes to marrying Derrick Masters, the first and only man I've ever loved. Well, kind of. He wouldn't let me actually say yes, but I'm definitely not saying no.

I grab my phone from the nightstand to call my mom, but it's only three in the morning. I huff, wanting to tell someone, but damn it, why did he have to go and ask me in the middle of the night? I have too much energy to lie still. I get up and emulate my five-year-old. Yup, I jump on the bed and touch the ceiling twice before the door opens and he peeks back in.

Getting the smile that would make me say yes a thousand more times, he adds, "Go to sleep. You're gonna need it."

This time I listen to him and flop down. When I'm covered up, he comes and tucks me in and kisses me on the head. "I'll wake you in a few hours."

"What are you going to do?"

"Plan a wedding."

"You won't let me help?"

"It's just boring phone calls tonight. You can plan the fun stuff when you get up."

He starts to get up to leave. "Hey." When he turns back, I ask, "Are you sure?"

"I can give you the boring phone calls if you prefer?"

"Not about that or the planning or me sleeping. Are you sure about us, and getting married?"

Sitting back down, his body leans to mine and he kisses me on the lips this time. "Never more sure about anything in my life. Now get some rest. I don't want you yawning at the altar." With that smile back in place, he winks, and leaves the room.

I lie there in the room with the lights outside the window still shining bright like the stars in the sky. Like Derrick and me.

We're getting married.

BOLTING UPRIGHT, I exclaim, "I'm getting married."

7:56 a.m. How is it possible that I fell asleep and slept like a baby for five hours on the morning of my wedding?

"Good morning, sunshine," Derrick says, pushing in a room service cart full of food. "Hungry?"

"Famished."

He goes back out and pushes another back in. "Me too, so I ordered the whole menu and two pots of coffee."

"I might love you more for this."

Laughing, he says, "Your love doesn't come cheap."

"Yeah, you must have spent a pretty penny or thousands to appease my appetite when all you had to do was come back to bed."

Diving on the mattress next to me, he lies there like a starfish. "I did. I got a few good hours surprisingly."

I reach over and grab some bacon from a platter piled high, and then I just decide to pull the cart up like it's a TV tray. Makes getting to the scrambled eggs a lot easier. "You don't mind me just eating off the plates?"

"Nope, go right ahead."

He pours me a cup of coffee and brings it to what I am now staking claim to as my tray. "So how do you feel now that the sun's up?"

"Are you asking if I've changed my mind about getting married?"

"Might be."

"Stop giving me outs. I don't need them. Do you?"

With a mouth full of egg-deliciousness, I shake my head. After I swallow, I say, "Not me, but I'm eating like a queen so really you got me at my weakest."

"So food is the key to your heart?" He pretends to be jotting this down on his phone. "Good to know."

"It's not everyone's?"

"I think your great tits are my kryptonite."

Taking my phone, I mimic him and laugh. "So maybe I can entice you back to bed for a quickie." I lower the sheet and flash him.

"Pre-wedding sex, Ms. Grenier? You know we'll go to Hell for that sin." *Yes, and I'm going to enjoy every moment of it.*

"We've already been. It's only up from here. Now come over here and show me what heaven's like."

36

JAYMES

HE TRICKED ME WITH FOOD. I don't know how I didn't remember I'd need to find a dress for the big day. But when a rack of beautiful dresses showed up at our suite, it was apparent by two dresses in, I shouldn't have had the waffle.

The saleswoman from the bridal shop downstairs is kind. "Twenty minutes. That's all we need and you'll feel less bloated. You just need to digest." Lowering her voice, even though we're alone, she whispers, "Or maybe try going number two."

I laugh, wondering how many times she's tried to settle bride's worries by telling them to go poop.

She adds, "Coffee always works for me."

Annnnnd apparently it works for me. Twenty-three minutes later, I'm slipping into the dresses with a lot more ease.

Rochelle texts me at nine when the kids wake to tell me she'll bring Ace to the ceremony, so not to worry. And it's not that I haven't thought about him and how marrying Derrick will affect him, but watching them together, Ace is happy. In fact, he's more relaxed than I've ever known him to be. Part of me feels guilty for the weight he's unknowingly had on his shoulders. But I can't feel guilty about that. *That belongs to Reggie.* Should I go and *ask* Ace if he's okay with me—

well, us—marrying Derrick? In some senses, yes. But, I consider my own mom and the choices she made *for* me when I was younger to help me feel safe. Wanting to be as wise and strong as my mom, I know this is okay. This decision is for us. For Ace and me. And as much as I am over the moon to have Derrick back in my life, and so thankful for all he's done to make that happen, I know Ace is happier too.

Holli shows up with more lingerie, white this time, and perfect under the dress I've chosen. "Did you just have this handy?" I tease. When I hold it up, my breath catches. "This is beautiful."

"To match the bride. Your dark against the white lace—you're a campaign dream come true."

"I don't know what you mean."

"An ad campaign. This lingerie set is from my line. I'm a designer."

"You're a clothing designer?" I ask, shocked.

"Amongst other things."

"Wait, so let me get this straight. You're a designer, you're married to Johnny Outlaw, and you look like this? I'll be honest, I can't keep up with that."

She gives my hand a little squeeze. "It's not a competition, Jamie. You just have to be you and from what I've seen, you're amazing."

"Thank you. That means a lot to me." I give her a hug and while standing there, I think of the life and friends I've missed out on from being under the watchful eye of Reggie. He's kept me down and held me back.

No more.

10:30 a.m.

My palms are sweating. I flap my arms several times to cool down. Is the air on in this place? After checking the thermostat and veri-fying that the air is indeed on and set to a comfortable seventy-three degrees, I realize it's just me. Even after pushing my flight back to the afternoon and going down to file for a marriage certificate with him, I'm nervous. And sweating.

I'm about to run and spritz more perfume on, but I detour when there's a knock on the door. Peeking through the hole, I see Rochelle. The door swings open and my heart bursts with pride and love and just all the wonderful things in life when I see my little man. Kneeling down, I hug Ace so tight. "You look so handsome in your suit, buddy."

I take his hand and Rochelle closes the door behind her. "I told him dapper."

"That means fancy," he says. "You look like a princess, Mommy."

Twirling for him, I ask, "Do you think Derrick will think so too?"

"No, he'll say you look pretty. He always says that."

"Does he now?"

Ace nods and says, "Whoa. This place is a mess."

With my hands on my hips, I can't argue otherwise. "Hair and makeup just left and yeah, with the food trays and stuff around, it's a mess all right."

When Ace runs to the windows to look out again, Rochelle says, "You make for a beautiful bride, Jamie."

"Thank you. Derrick did everything from the ceremony to my dress and shoes to setting up my hair and makeup for me. I definitely feel like a princess. I just wish I could do something for him."

"Do you have rings?"

"No," I confess. "I feel terrible, but I can't afford one. I was thinking we could pick one out when he gets back, something he likes that I can give to him."

"Getting married is a big step, but your anchor is love. Don't let things that don't matter break the chain. I know Derrick well enough to know that he doesn't need anything expensive. He'd be happy just having you, but I'd put a ring on it if you know what I mean. So, I've still got his credit card."

"And he did tell me to charge anything I want to the room."

"I'll call downstairs and have them bring some rings up in his size."

"I don't know his size."

She sits at the desk and scrolls her phone. "I do. He once did an ad campaign for a watch company and they wanted a ring on him. Let me find the email. You just have some champagne and relax for a few minutes."

How did I get this lucky to not just win Derrick's heart but to inherit his friends, who are his family? It's better than winning a jackpot at the casino. With the puzzle pieces of life clicking into place, I'm definitely the luckiest girl ever. Joining Ace at the window, I sit on an ottoman next to where he stands. His hands are in his pockets and his brow is furrowed. "Got a lot on your mind?" I ask, rubbing his back.

"Some." He shrugs.

"Want to talk about it?"

"I don't know."

"It's a lot and very fast. Is the wedding upsetting you?"

He sits on the ottoman next to me. His gaze stays out in the distance through the glass. "What does it mean? Derrick said it means he becomes your hubsand."

"*Hus*-band, buddy. Yes. It means we become partners." Taking his hand in mine, I hold it. "We'll always be partners too. Just like always."

"So I'll be your husband too?"

"No," I reply, amused. "You'll always be my son. Look at me, Ace." When he does, I lean down a little more to make sure he understands what I'm saying. "You'll always be the best thing in my life."

His head leans on my arm. "What happens when we go home? Derrick said he's going to Denver." Looking back up at me, he asks, "Does he not want to be with us?"

"It's not like that at all, Ace. He does want to be with us. That's why we're becoming a family so we can be together. His job means sometimes he has to travel. I wish we could go back to LA together, but he'll be back in three weeks."

Popping up, he points outside. "Helicopter."

"So awesome." I never see the helicopter because I'm too busy taking in my son. "You know, Ace, I'm the luckiest mommy in the whole wide world because I get to be your mommy."

He turns and hugs me. "Derrick said he was lucky that he gets to be my daddy." I exhale slowly, the sweet sentiment hitting me hard on that one. "Is Derrick my daddy?"

"He is, now and forevermore."

A tissue is dragged out of the box on the desk and Rochelle wipes her eyes. I'd forgotten she was there. Wiggling Ace by the waist back and forth, I say, "Why don't you go brush your teeth and go potty. We need to leave in a few minutes."

When he runs off, Rochelle sniffles. "That was beautiful and heartwarming. Ace is fortunate to have such an amazing mom."

"Thank you and thank you for being so good to me and Ace."

She stands and shakes off the emotions, but I could use a friend since I don't have my mom here and she didn't answer her phone earlier. "Am I making a mistake? Woman to woman. Mother to mother. Be honest with me."

"I think he made a mistake the first time he let you go. He's smart enough not to do it again, but let me ask you. We don't know each other well, but I get a vibe from people."

"And what vibe did you get from me?"

"You're a survivor, Jamie. I have a feeling you didn't just let him go, let him leave and then stop feeling anything for him. I see how you look at him. I see how much you care. I see the love you both share. I don't need the details, but I do know there's more to this story. The good part is, your story's just begun and it's starting with the happily ever after. So if you're asking if you should marry him, my answer will never change. Hell, yes. Derrick's a great guy. He just needed the right woman to remind him of that. You bring out the best in him. I have a feeling he does the same for you."

"He does. He's good for my soul."

"Then don't question what you already know the answer to. Just listen to your inner voice, the one that's telling you he's the one." I swear we're interrupted more by knocks on the door than anything else. Rochelle adds, "Let's buy that soon-to-be husband of yours a ring."

THE FLOWERS ARE BEAUTIFUL. I'm handed a bouquet of perfect roses with the lightest touch of pink. The card read *"To match your cheeks"* and was given to me when I arrived at the private wedding garden. Derrick had more sweet surprises up his sleeve. When I peeked outside to see how the ceremony spot looked, my mom was standing there with his mom.

The moms come rushing to me and I start crying on the spot. The planner shoves tissues in my direction and the moms dab very carefully at my face. I thought it would be seeing Ace that caused the emotional tearjerker waterfall. He was just so cute and handsome, but it's seeing them here, together, and crying from happiness that does the trick.

So now, five minutes before I'm supposed to get married, I find myself standing in the bathroom salvaging my makeup. Usually when I'm happiest, flashbacks of terror come back to ruin it, but right now, as I look at myself in the mirror, I only see the good, remembering the best times I ever had were with the man I'm about to marry . . .

I sit up in the back of his truck and turn the flashlight back on so I can study a little more before I have to be home. "This math test is going to kill me."

"You'll ace it."

"You always say that."

"I'm always right."

I poke his side and laugh when he squirms. "So basically it's good luck when you tell me I'll ace it?"

Sitting up, he tugs the collar of my shirt down and kisses the exposed bare skin. "Yes, ace equals good luck."

I turn and sneak in a quick kiss. "Got it. Ace will always be good luck."

. . . The tears come fast this time as the memory brings me full circle. Derrick won't remember that conversation, so insignificant at the time, but one that I always carried with me. My mom comes in with my makeup bag and says, "Let me help you."

"We're late," I say.

"They'll wait."

While she touches up my makeup, she says, "He told me he wants us to stay at his house while he's gone. What do you think, dear daughter?"

"I think we should." We speak in hushed, conspiratorial tones. "I don't want Derrick going near the neighborhood."

"What about you?"

"You and Ace can wait at the house. I'll go back and pack our bags and hurry back. Just the basics. Enough to get us by for a few days and work out a plan."

"We'll figure it before we land. Diane wants to throw a party when Derrick returns."

Smiling, I reply, "That would be lovely."

She stands back and inspects my face. "Beautiful as always."

"Will you walk me down the aisle?"

Her sweet smile has always comforted me and continues to do so. "Of course. Let's go. I think you're ready." *I am ready, but hearing my mom's confidence is all I really needed.* She didn't question our decision. She just smiled and accepted and supported.

My man awaits. My future sealed. *Our* future sealed.

Stepping into the room that leads outside, I kiss my mom on the cheek and take her hand. "Here Comes My Girl" by Tom Petty starts playing and I laugh. "I'm ready."

Ace steps forward and grabs my hand and starts tugging. With a huge smile, he says, "Come on, Mommy, race you to Derrick."

I take his hand and slow him down. "I think we should do this together." With the two people I love more than anything in this world leading me to the man I love bigger than the universe, the three of us start walking.

37

DERRICK

DIPPING MY HEAD DOWN, I pretend I have something in my eyes. Guess it's not pretending, but tears are tough for me. You don't cry where I came from. Fame has made me soft. Nah, I think it's just made me grateful. The guys are laughing, though, and I may be wrong but when I look at my best man, Kaz seems a little choked up himself. "You sad I beat you to the altar?" I make a lame joke.

He gets it, but being Kaz, he sees through the act and pats me on the back. "It's only fair. This has been a long time coming."

It's been eight years since I saw the girl that would become my wife.

Three of the best and worst years of my life spent together. She was the only saving grace I had. The only reason I fought to stay alive.

Five years since I looked backed. Even in that time, I knew I'd made the biggest mistake of my life. I can try to not blame my eighteen-year-old self, but I knew I was wrong and living in regret for years makes this moment so much sweeter.

The music starts—some cheesy, but traditional wedding march and everyone stands. The wooden doors to the garden open and there is the reason I'm standing here today. I will be the man she deserves. My angel floats to me in white, her dark hair flowing around her shoulders. Ace holding one hand and her mom holding the other. Her support. I hope I can bear the burdens she carries from now on. She blinks and then tilts her head down, her emotions getting the best of her. Tears escape the barrier of my lids and damn my male ego as they slip down my cheeks.

Her eyes go wide when she sees Leah standing near the altar, her friend and a confidante that I thanked for taking care of Jaymes and Ace in my absence when I called.

When her mom gifts me Jaymes's hand, I kiss both of them on the cheek before turning fully to Jaymes, my beauty. And then vows are exchanged.

". . . The one who will stand by your side, the one who will stay this time. I vow to be the man your son will look up to, not in height, but in character."

Ace is standing beside his mother because he wanted to be a part of this union, just where he belongs. I fist-bump him before turning back to the woman who has brought tears to my eyes. "I stand before you, my sweet Jaymes, and promise you my love in this life and beyond because you are the only woman my soul knows how to love, to breathe, to protect, and to cherish. I vow my life, trust, honesty, and love to you evermore." I slide a diamond-encrusted platinum band onto her delicate finger. I love when I take her breath away. Leaning down, I whisper, "We'll get you any diamond you want, but I thought I'd start with the band today."

"It's perfect. More than I could ever wish for."

My muse for music, for life, for laughter, for love speaks of hardship and sacrifice—two things she knows more about than she should.

She hasn't had weeks to think these up. They are in and from her heart. *Fucking lucky man.* " . . . You are not just the man I love with my entire being, you are the only man worthy of being a father to my son. There is no one else I'd rather him model himself after than the person you have become, the person I always knew you to be. So with this ring, I thee wed for this lifetime and every life after."

A sleek black and silver band is pressed onto my finger and I smile, admiring the way it looks and feels. I don't wear any rings now, but I'm never fucking taking this one off. I couldn't have picked a more *me* ring than the one she chose.

I'm kind of proud of myself for holding it together as well as I have. I've avoided looking at my mom though. She'll make me cry. In a lot of ways, today is her day as much as mine. When I'm told to kiss my wife, I don't waste the opportunity. In front of friends and family and friends who are family, I kiss my wife like we're the only ones in the world. I kiss her until she's breathless, and then I kiss her again so she remembers it when we're apart.

But to my surprise, she doesn't hold back. She doesn't even worry that we're in front of the band, the moms, her friend, or even Ace. She gives me a kiss like I'm the last man alive and her life depends on it. Damn my wife's hot.

She drags that bottom lip under her teeth and then cocks an eyebrow. "Promise me you'll always kiss me like that."

"I always keep my promises."

"That you do." And we kiss again just because we can.

***

A SMALL BALLROOM has been set with a long table full of flowers. China settings and crystal glasses fill it nicely. We only have time for a luncheon today. The tour can't wait. Twenty thousand tickets sold out in Denver in fifteen minutes. I have a feeling they'd be happy for me, but not to the point of letting me bail a night or two to celebrate my nuptials.

I watch Jaymes. The smile is there for others, but I can see the sadness underneath. She can barely eat and isn't really drinking. I know what she's thinking, what she feels deep down inside. I feel it too. "I don't want to leave you," I whisper while everyone at the table celebrates around us.

Our hands clasp between us and she angles her body toward me, our knees touching. "You've made me weak."

"You're the strongest person I know."

"I only had one to lose before. Now I have two and my heart hurts."

"You're not losing me. Three weeks. You can come to any show, any city. You can be with me."

"I can't," she says and I hear the tremble in her voice. "I have work and school—"

"Don't work anymore. Just go to school."

"I have Ace and he has school."

"You can fly out next weekend. To . . . ummm . . . to. Oh, fuck it. I have no idea. Tommy, where are we next weekend?"

We both look down the table at him and wait while he scrolls his phone. I cover her hand and thigh with my hand, hoping I can comfort her in some way. It's not going to be easy to leave her, especially knowing that maniac is in the same city, but at least he's locked away. *For now.*

Rochelle leans across the table and says, "Chicago."

Tommy gripes and puts his phone away.

I ask Jaymes, "Want to go to Chicago?"

Ace tells her, "I want to go to Chicago," but turns to Rochelle to ask, "What's Chicago?"

Rochelle laughs. "It's a city in Illinois, but you know, I've been wanting to take Neil and CJ to Disneyland. It's been a while since we've gone. I was thinking you might want to join us and stay the weekend at our house."

His expression is thoughtful when he turns to me, and asks, "What would you choose? Disneyland or Chicago?"

"Dude, Disney hands down."

To Rochelle, he says, "Disney!"

Dex leans over and says, "Make sure she takes you on the Peter Pan ride. It's my favorite."

"Disney! Disney!"

"Ace. Shhhh. Keep it down, buddy."

"How can I keep it down? I've always wanted to go to Disney."

CJ starts in too. "Disney!"

Neil rolls his eyes. "Kids."

The table erupts in laughter and my sweet bride is finally smiling again. "So Chicago?"

"Yes. Chicago."

My flight's at four, so while the cake is being served, I excuse my wife and myself with the lamest reason ever, but it's now or never. "We forgot we haven't packed. So we're going to go do that. Pack. For our flights."

Everyone is staring at me, including Jaymes, but she's the best, so she says, "Stuff everywhere. Yes, we must go pack. We'll see you guys in a little while."

It's when the moms burst out laughing that we turn and hightail out. Her dress is beaded and tight through the body and does this fluffing out thing at the bottom. She said mermaid. Again, I have no idea what she's talking about, but I want it the fuck off her. "Can I rip these tiny buttons off in the back?"

"No!"

My back hits the elevator and my hands go up in surrender. "Okay."

She takes a deep breath and says, "You don't even want to know how much this dress cost, so there will be no ripping of buttons or anything else off it."

Back in the suite and ten minutes later, the tips of my fingers are killing me and I'm a fucking guitarist. "What are these little torture devices and why'd you pick a dress with a hundred of them?"

"They're pearl buttons and I fell in love with the dress. Don't you love it?"

I see the telltale signs of a setup as soon as she asks the question. Her bottom lip even looks a little pouty. "You look gorgeous in that dress. I just wanted it off for comparison."

"Really?"

"No, Jaymes. I want to fucking consummate our nuptials before I have to fly out of here and not see you for the next five days."

"Your sarcasm is not warranted—"

"I know and it's duly noted, but please, baby. I'm begging you. We have thirty minutes until I have to leave for the airport."

"I kinda like you begging. And trust me, I want this as much as you do. That's why I packed our suitcases earlier. I'm all yours for the next twenty-eight minutes. I'll leave two minutes for you to catch your car ride downstairs."

"Unzip me please."

My patience is gone. If she wasn't so damn sexy standing there, shit, who am I kidding? "What do you mean unzip you? I just undid all those little fuckers to get you out of this dress and now you're telling me there's a zipper?"

"Well, you looked so determined and eager to figure them out that I didn't want to ruin the illusion."

"Show me the zipper."

She lifts her arm and I find the metal bastard and pull it down with lightning speed. Smart enough not to mess with a horny husband, she steps out of the dress and stands there for me like she just walked off a Victoria's Secret runway show. "Holy fuck. How'd I get so lucky?"

And there's that pale pink blush I ordered the flowers to match. Gorgeous.

She taps my watch. "Twenty-five minutes. Time's a ticking."

Over my shoulder in a flash, she squeals in delight and whacks my ass. When I toss her on the bed, I have my breath stolen right from my lungs. *Whoosh* and it was gone from the very sight of her.

The laughter stops and she stretches her arms above her head. "What is it?"

My mouth opens, needing air. Her beauty astounds me, but it's a life of memories from the past that I see before me. My mind flashing between her lying in bed wearing white lace on our wedding day and back to her in white cotton underwear the first time I stole them and her virginity.

"Derrick?"

Twenty-two minutes and I'd happily spend them looking at her. I start on my shirt, not rushing, just watching her. A soft smile slips into place and I recognize that one—she's happy. She's in love. She's happy in love with me.

Twenty minutes. I lie down and bring her atop me. When she bends down, she kisses me.

Eighteen minutes. I take down one of her straps and then the other. "You look incredible, but we're running out of time."

She slips it off and rolls a condom down the length of my cock.

Sixteen minutes. I was wrong. I thought I could watch her lying on the bed all day. Nope. *This.* I can watch her riding me well into next week. I hold tight to her hips, not wanting to let her go. Her tits bounce as her body moves steady. Her mouth opens.

Thirteen minutes. I flip her over and as much as I want to *make love* to my wife, I want to fuck her more. So I do.

Taking her by the wrists, I slide her arms back in that position from earlier. Call me selfish, but she looks fucking amazing open for me. She lifts her legs and I place her ankles over my shoulders. "Hold on, baby." With her hands pressed against the headboard, I take hold of her body and thrust. Pounding every ounce of sensation out of us until we're left pulsing together, electrified in our connection.

Alive.

Her legs are still up when I lay my head on her chest, panting for air. Her heart beats strong, so strong and vibrant. I want to listen to it forever. I close my eyes while she runs her fingers through my hair. She whispers, "Four minutes."

I think she's fine, still lost to her bliss, but her body shakes, wracked with a slight cry. When I look up, her eyes match mine. "There's no getting around the sadness, just distracting ourselves from it temporarily. Five days."

She holds back her tears, but I see her breath jagged in her chest. "Five days." It feels as though I've only had her back in my life for five minutes. The pain I'm feeling now resembles what I felt when I first moved away. I was desperately lonely. Desperately wanted to go back and get her. But then I heard she was with Reggie, and my heart broke. If only I'd ignored her wishes, swallowed my pride, and gone to her to find out the truth. *She was trying to protect me when she sent me away, when she was the one who needed protecting.*

And now I'm leaving her again. At least I know where we stand this time. And she'll be safe. Their driver is trained in covert operations and my bodyguard when I attend events, when needed. He'll make sure they're safe. The security system on the house is operating with a guard just inside the gate. They'll be safe and I can rest easy.

"I don't want to leave. You know that, right?"

"I know." She looks toward the window and I go to the bathroom and clean up.

She doesn't have to count down. Two minutes. I go back and pull on my clothes. Sad eyes watch me and then she gets up to hug me. Her naked body as bare as my soul as I have to tell her goodbye. I feel raw on the inside, my emotions hidden there.

"I love you. I love you. I love you," I whisper, hoping it sinks deep into her skin and deeper into her veins. I want her not just feeling my love, but breathing it deep within.

"I love you."

I turn and grab my leather duffel bag in one hand and pull my suitcase in the other.

Time's up.

38

JAYMES

*T*HE *NIGHT IS SO* quiet up here at the observatory that I can hear traffic *from a mile away. Lying in the back of his truck, I reach above my head and strum across the strings of the guitar he gave me.*

"What if I gave you the world?" Derrick asks, turning my way.

Finding his hand between us, our fingers weave together. "I don't need the world. I just need you."

When I squeeze lightly, his body cringes, tensing as if he's in pain. "Are you okay?"

"I'm fine."

. . . I found out a few months later that he had gotten in a fight with my father the night his hand was hurt. He never told me and never complained about the pain. Not while I was at work and not that night in the back of that pickup. But I know him. It takes a lot to upset him, much less make him violent. Violence toward women is at the top of his shit list. So if he threw one punch, he most likely threw another, but my father had gone too far when he pushed my mother.

She told me one night after a rough day. Told me to never love a man like my father. To stick to the ones that are brave when no one is watching. To marry a man that will defend your mother and not need the credit. That's the kind of man that will always protect, will always put you first.

Derrick Masters always did care more about me than he did himself. Today he proved it once again.

Leah takes my hand and spins the ring around my finger. "You're like Cinderella."

Laughing, I ask, "Did I just get married?"

Now she's laughing. "You did."

I sigh. "I miss my Prince Charming."

"Maybe that castle will keep you warm while he's gone."

"Ha ha. So how did you end up in Vegas?"

"Private jet, baby. He flew your moms and me in."

"What?" I sit up, staring at her.

"Yup. Now close your mouth. You got to marry the rock star. We just got to live like one for a day." Tilting her seat back, she closes her eyes, but I see the braggy grin she can't hide. "By the way, first class is the only way to travel when you're not traveling by private jet."

"You're lucky I like you so much."

"After flying today in the fanciest ways, I agree I'm lucky you like me so much."

I snort while laughing. "I can't believe he did that for me."

"He wanted to surprise you. How romantic is that?"

"The most."

"I'm not understanding the boots with that designer purse, Jamie. Not to judge, but that is a Gucci purse. You're really doing it an injustice with those shoes."

It doesn't matter that my Docs don't go with the purse the girls picked. Derrick gave them to me and that's enough for me to feel like the prettiest girl on the plane. I don't hear the rest of what she says because my mind is caught up in my morning. I'm married.

I'm married to Derrick.

I'm Mrs. Derrick Masters.

Mrs. Masters.

Wow.

My heart quickens and I look over at Ace sitting on the inside next to my mom. They are finding shapes in the clouds and laughing. The sound is so light and free, airy without care that I wonder if this new life will seal that beautiful sound forever. No more crying in closets or hiding when the banging starts. No more coded texts to my mom when the monster comes around. *When the monster won't know how to find me.*

The vise around my chest loosens and I feel like I can breathe with ease for the first time in years. That's the best gift anyone could give me.

THE FLIGHT IS FAST, which is good since it's a school night for Ace and me both. I'll turn in my resignation later this week. I want to find a replacement first and not leave them in a lurch. It's been a steady job and one I could rely on despite David hitting on me.

As soon as we land, I'm in action texting Rochelle and hurrying my mom and Ace to baggage claim. Rochelle was on a different flight but the arrival times were close. They shouldn't have to wait long, then Rochelle can get them set up in a car and off to Derrick's.

I hug Ace, and tell him, "Listen to Grandma. It's going to be late by the time you get home, so take your bath and brush your teeth. When I get home, I'll come tuck you in and kiss you good night. Be a good boy."

"I will."

Straightening up, I turn to my mom. "Rochelle will be here in the next ten minutes or so. I'm going, so I hopefully beat some traffic. You good?" She smiles at me, and as usual, I feel her strength.

"Yes, daughter. Be safe, Jamie."

"I will. In and out. I'll call you when I leave." A quick hug bonds us before I have to break away and catch a cab.

I rush to find cars for hire and catch one with relative ease considering the crowds coming out. Traffic still sucks. It's LA after all, so I make use of the time and do the one thing I've been wanting to do since we landed.

Derrick picks up on the first ring. "Hello there, wife."

"Hello, dear husband. Where are you?"

"Denver. We landed about thirty minutes ago. And you?"

"Somewhere in LA."

"Is it only me who thinks it's really fucked up that we got married this morning and now we're in different cities tonight?"

I laugh under my breath. It's not funny at all, but I'm trying not to cry. "It's messed up."

"Five days."

"Only five days and I'll be counting every hour until I see you again."

"You can be quite charming, Mrs. Masters, when you want to be."

Mrs. Masters.

And I swoon. Closing my eyes, I savor his voice, the deep richness that echoes through me when he sings, embedding itself into my soul. "I miss you," I whisper.

"I miss you more."

Flexing my fingers, I admire my ring. "Derrick, I love you."

"I know, sweetheart. God, it's so good to hear that from you. I never thought I would. When I see you next I'm going to show you how much I love you. How much having you in my life makes me so fucking happy."

"You already have. Years ago. I've never forgotten the way you always took care of me. Thank you. I know I've said it, but I need you to know that I feel it."

"I want you in my bed tonight and to call me before you fall asleep. I'll be in bed, wishing I was in bed with you, and we can fall asleep to the sound of each other."

I thought I swooned before, but this man . . . this man . . . this man. I'm so in love with him. "Next best thing."

"Yes, next best thing to falling asleep with you here." His voice returns to its regular tone and he adds, "I texted you the gate code and the house alarm code."

"Don't worry. I gave them to my mom with the instructions you gave me," I reply mindlessly while staring out the window.

"Why?"

"Why what?"

"Why did you give her the instructions?"

Shit. "Oh ummm . . ."

"What are you doing, Jaymes?" He sounds alarmed. *Shit.*

"I'm in a cab."

"Going where?"

I can't tell him, but I can't lie. Shoot. What to do? I panic and sit up, looking to see where I am and figure out how much time I have. "Derrick—"

"Don't *Derrick* me. You're going back, aren't you?"

"I just need to get Ace's and my school stuff and then I'll be out of there lickety-split."

"What the fuck are you thinking?"

"Don't talk to me like that."

"Your feelings aren't what I'm worried about right now. Your safety is. Is Ace with you?"

"No, he's with my mom. They're heading to your house."

"I could have sent someone over there. This isn't good. You need to turn around and go to the house with your mom and son."

"I get your concern. I do, but he's locked up. His guys won't mess with me. They just report back to him. Even if they do, I'll be long gone."

"I don't want you going there at all."

Too late. The cab turns down our street. "I'll grab the backpacks and be out and I'll call you as soon as I leave. I'm here. Five minutes max."

"No, Jaymes—"

"I love you. Five minutes." I hang up just as the cab pulls to the curb. Reaching forward, I ask the driver, "Will you wait? I'll only be a few minutes."

"Sure. Be quick. It's not a good neighborhood."

"You're telling me."

I pop the door open and hurry across the lawn and up the porch. As soon as the front door's open, I drop my purse and run to grab

Ace's backpack from his room. I shove a few books he loves and a stuffed dog he likes to sleep with sometimes into the bag as well. Opening his dresser, I pull out a few shirts and shorts, socks, and underwear. I don't even know if they match, but I don't have the time to worry about it. I'm just as quick in my mom's room, scrambling to get two of her dresses and shoes for work and putting them in a grocery bag I find in the kitchen. I have plenty of clothes in my carry-on so I run to get my backpack. With both on my back, the grocery bag in my hands along with my purse, I'm ready to leave, I open the door and turn to lock it, but then I spot a folder that has my essays in it. Dang it.

I run in and grab it and then back out the door to lock it. When I turn around, I scream, the bags in my hands and my essays falling to the porch.

"Where you going, Jamie?" Reggie is pale and his eyes are curious as he takes me in. Glancing down, he says, "Looks like somewhere with all these clothes."

"It's mostly school stuff. The rest are clothes for my mom," I lie. To save my life, I lie. "She spilled something on herself at work and she needs to change."

"So you wadded the pretty shirt up in a ball and shoved it in a grocery sack? Tsk. Tsk. Surely, you can do bet—"

That little voice in your head that guides your gut, reaffirms that your instincts are correct, and keeps you safe—mine grew louder once he left after raping me. Bending down slowly, I pick up the bag, careful to hide my ring.

But it's too late.

Reggie doesn't look high. He's calculating my demise.

"So the rumors on TV are true. Rebel came into my neighborhood, as if he still had the right to—" He walks to the far side of the porch, leaving me room to run.

"Reg—" I take one step before I see the cab is gone and Reggie's friends—two cars, four guys—are there instead. *Oh fuck.*

"Silence!"

My heart sinks. I just want to get home to Ace and fall asleep to the sound of Derrick.

His glare is deadly. I don't want to find out what else he's capable of. Walking back to me, he says, "The real problem is not that he came back. I would welcome him with open arms. I would allow him to beg for my forgiveness and be my right-hand man. But that's not what he did or seems to intend to do. Noooo, he came back to take what is clearly mine and make it his." Standing not six inches from me, he asks, "How did you always manage to go unscathed in this mess?"

"Unscathed? Hardly."

I turn away, but he grabs my jaw, squeezing so hard that tears spring to my eyes, and forces me to face him. "Don't you ever turn away from me." He pushes me free and I stumble back. "Shayna says I should put you to work for me on the streets."

"No."

"No? You don't tell me no. Not ever. Here's the thing with Shayna. She's never liked you. Nope. I'm not saying it to hurt your feelings. Just stating the facts. She's jealous of you like I used to be jealous of Rebel. So I see where her hate breeds for you. But luckily for you, I see the potential. She gives a solid blow, but she's not so great in the brains. You are, but I never tested your blowing skills. I can imagine they're decent if Rebel kept you around. Oops, I meant married you. It doesn't seem quite fair that I got arrested and you got married. I'm feeling a little left out that I didn't get invited." His expression perks up. "I know. We can have another reception for you." Though I'm shaking my head no, he says, "Yes. This is perfect."

Pacing across the porch again, he adds, "We can plan the reception, but it's no good unless we have the guest of honor in attendance. So, here's what we're going to do. You will call your husband and tell him that you are with me until he comes to the party. That's it. He only has to show up and you're all his again. And don't forget to bring my son." Dipping his head down to see my lowered eyes, he asks, "Maybe I need to inspire you to make that call. See, Pinkard, back there? He's always had a thing for you."

"Give me the damn phone."

Laughing like a hyena, he mimics me while digging through my purse, " 'Give me the damn phone, she says.' " He puts it in my hand and says, "If the cops show, you're dead."

I've taken too long. Derrick will be worried. I put the phone to my ear as soon as it starts ringing. "Are you—"

Reggie grabs the phone. "Hey, old buddy. Long time no talk. So, I was hanging out with your wife and we decided to have a little party. Similar to last time when I fucked her, but this time we thought—Eh. Eh. Eh. Let me finish. We thought we'd extend the invitation for you to join us. Well, that's a poor choice of words. Watch us might fit better. Yeah, I think it does. What is that you're saying?"

He stares at me, a snarl for a smile distorting his lips. "No, you've got it wrong. You left. I stayed. This is my territory and if you want something of mine in my territory you come see me. We'll be waiting." He hangs up and drops the phone in my bag. "Now all we do is wait."

Then the world goes black.

39

JAYMES

My breath comes slow, loud in my ears as I exhale. My vision is blurry when I first open my eyes, but clears as my hearing does.

"... it's a very nice purse, but she has no style. I'll carry it around and everyone will think you gave it to me." Shayna's shrill voice. I close my eyes again, hoping to escape this nightmare and wake up. But this is it.

"I did." The voice that follows is harsh and full of hate. *Reggie.* "Anything she has is mine. I wonder how much this ring is worth?"

My heart stops dead in my chest. I want to see my hand, look at my finger, but I fear I'm safer asleep. Like a spinning Rolodex, my thoughts roll out of control.

Derrick.

Ace.

My mom.

Phone.

Ring.

Pen.

Keys.

Nothing.

I've got nothing. It was all in my purse.

I've got nothing to fight with, nothing to protect myself with. *Nothing.*

Shayna's voice is close when she says, "Let me have the ring, Reggie. We'll get married—"

"Shut up. I can't hear myself think. Go clean something."

"You're such an asshole sometimes." By the clapping of her heels against the floor, she storms out.

He yells, "Leave the purse."

My foot is hit and I can hear the jingle of my stuff falling out of the bag.

Once we're alone again, he says, "I know you're awake."

I slowly open my eyes and see what I was dreading—my hand in front of my face, my finger bare. Tilting to look where his voice came from, he's sitting on a short stool near my knees.

Rubbing his forehead, he says, "Sit up." His voice is calm, unaffected by drugs, the way I remember from high school.

Slowly, I push up, the shooting pain blinds the left side of my skull and I reach to cover it, hoping pressure relieves it.

A long exhale is blown in my direction, and he says, "This ring makes us even." I'd argue, but I know it's of no use. "Rebel was my idol. He was the last person I ever expected to betray me. You, definitely." He laughs to himself. "I knew you would. That's why this whole situation is so ironic. He did and you didn't. You took his debt for that drug drop like a champ."

"I had no choice."

"You see, that's where you're wrong. You did. You had a choice, but you stood by him even when he didn't stand by you."

"What do you want?"

"This ring is a good start, but nothing you do will take away his betrayal. Did he really think I wouldn't find out? I would have done life for that crime. He wanted me gone and for what? So he could play guitar in some pansy-ass band? Fuck that." He tosses my phone at me and hits me in the arm. When it lands, the screen lights—Ace.

"Have you ever had déjà vu, Jamie? Fuck, I just had it. You look a lot like your dad."

Death. I will kill him if he continues. "Don't."

"Don't? Ha! Fuck, that's exactly what I told him, but he never did listen. Fucking drug addict. I saw him after Rebel beat the shit out of him. He came by my ma's place before she died. Looking for a hit, anything he said. I told him to go clean up. As a favor to you. I told him to go home and don't go take that next hit. Fucker didn't listen. Did you know they found his body?"

"Reggie, please, if we ever had any nice thoughts toward one another, I beg you to not finish this story."

"This is what you're begging for? I've got to give you credit. You're a lot tougher than Rebel ever was. So as I was saying, he was found under the highway. Clothes stolen. Everything gone."

Numbness has a feeling and it spreads. It creeps through the veins icing them over along the way. Sometimes it bypasses the heart leaving you vulnerable to the things that shouldn't matter. Making them matter more. My father is dead. Numb. Tears for a man that never loved me enough to raise me come forward, the ice of my heart thawing under the mess of the situation I've found myself in.

Shayna comes in and says, "I see the bitch is awake. That's a nasty bruise you got there." She crosses her arms and stares down at me from behind Reggie.

Just when I thought I could reason with Reggie, his usual disgusting self returns. "He never replied. I think there might be trouble in paradise. Fucking groupies takes time, time he doesn't have to take your call. So, how are we going to do this? We can make another baby together?"

He's pushed from behind and Shayna leaves again, the slam of a door down the hall reflecting her anger. My body convulses, rejecting even the words from his mouth, and I throw up.

"Gross. Guess kissin's out. How about me and Shayna raise *my* son? She wants a baby awful bad."

"I will die before I let you take him."

"You're gonna die anyway, so let the games begin." The stool flies out from under him and slides across the kitchen floor. I scramble to my feet but am grabbed under my arms and slammed against the wall near the door, making the door rattle. I push off his chest as he pins me. One hit to his ear shakes him, but he laughs. Lifting my knee in the space between, I keep him at a distance while I claw the side of his face.

In a hit to my left side, the pain explodes and my vision goes black. But still I fight. I fight for me. I fight for Ace. I fight for Derrick. I fight for the life I deserve. My vision is blurry as color comes back. Swinging my right, I land a hit that sends him down. With my boots, I kick him so hard that he falls the rest of the way to the floor. I kick him again before turning and opening the door.

I run. Jumping down the steps, gunfire rings out, and I fall to the grass.

"Drop your weapon." Commotion surrounds me—red and blue lights flashing. Another shot is fired after the warning.

I'm not sure at first if I'm shot or not, but I lie there frozen as police swarm the lawn and the house.

"Roll over," I'm commanded.

When I do, the officer has a radio to his mouth. "Victim has been identified."

Through the police telling me to lie there until the ambulance arrives and being lifted on a gurney, I stare into the clear night sky, searching for something to hold on to in my mind.

Peace is found.

Andromeda and Perseus.

I stay there until the paramedics arrive, decide I need further examination, and that they need to transport me. I'm lifted into the ambulance and taken to the hospital. When the doors close, I ask, "Is he dead?"

The paramedic sitting next to me doesn't make me work for it. He knows who I'm talking about. "No. He's being taken to the hospital." When I look away, he adds, "Gunshot wound. Shot by the police."

Even though I've prayed for Reggie's death many times, I don't wish for it now. Something about a life dying always goes hand in hand with sadness. It's not sadness I feel for him, it's not sympathy or respect. I'm numb when it comes to my emotions regarding him. It was always going to be him or me. I need to live for Ace. For Derrick, and for me. So sympathy is not something I can garner for Reggie Rogers.

I have no idea what time it is or even which hospital I'm going to. They confiscated my phone but called my mom for me. She must be beside herself. I'm hoping she stayed home with Ace though. I don't want him to see me in the hospital. It would terrify him.

I'm pulled from the back of the ambulance and pushed into the bright lights of the hospital corridor. I stopped listening to the medical words being tossed around when I was told I'd be all right. It was hard to decipher the other words, my thoughts fuzzier as time moves on . . .

Derrick is my most favorite thing to do, and watch, and listen to. No one plays the guitar like he does. He compliments me, but I've been slow to learn. Getting better every day since he gave me my guitar. I've been messing around with a song I hope to play on his birthday. Return the favor and all that. I've already got the guitar that cost more than I should have spent, but he'll do wonders with it. I just know it.

. . . a familiar melody travels through my thoughts, notes I cherish every time I hear them. My throat is dry when I swallow, so I cough. "Drink this."

Opening my eyes, I smile, then leave it behind. It hurts too much. "You're here?"

Derrick's hand caresses my cheek, that look of concern I hate seeing on his face ever present. "Drink first." A fire burns down my throat and I take a sip from the straw. "Why'd you have to go and be the hero?" The concern renders itself to a smile that I find comfort in. "I could have used some of that glory."

"Your ego's big enough. You are a rock star after all."

"Yeah, guess it was your turn." He kisses my head and says, "Reggie's dead."

"I had a feeling, but I didn't ask. He took my ring."

"He took my girl. The ring is replaceable. You're not."

"I just got it though."

He laughs out loud and in it I find the peace I need. "We'll get you a better one."

A nurse walks in and smiles when she sees us. "I'm glad you're awake."

She examines me, and then says, "The doctor will be by shortly." After adjusting the bed so I'm angled up, she says, "The man they brought in right before you didn't make it."

I nod. She continues, "He died in the ambulance on the ride over."

"I don't want to hear about him. Not ever again."

"I understand but I was hoping you could piece together a mystery for me."

Derrick takes hold of my hand, and asks, "What is it?"

"The paramedics called ahead for plasma for a potential transfusion. We're short, so we searched our area blood banks for the type we needed, and a nurse checked his file for next of kin. Your son Ace was—"

"No." Anger surges and I sit up, dizziness striking quick. "Please tell me they didn't touch my son to try to save him?"

The nurse and Derrick gently press me back. She says, "Everything is okay. We need to keep your blood pressure from spiking like it just did."

"I don't care about that. I care about Ace. What about my son?"

"You had his blood tested at birth? It's not that common to do."

"My mother said I should just in case there was an emergency. She had done the same with me."

"Smart. It's always good to know and most don't have that information. Your son's medical record shows he's blood type AB."

"Yes, I know. And?" I press her like I'm pulling teeth.

She stops messing with my covers and looks me in the eyes. "The man they were bringing in was blood type O. That's not a match."

"That's not a match?"

Derrick releases my hand and rests his hands on the bed. Staring at her, he asks, "Not a match?"

"There's no way he can be his father. O doesn't make an AB in any combination."

Dropping back against the bed, I look at Derrick. "Oh."

"Not to pry, but if I can help you in any way, I will."

When Derrick turns to me, our eyes meet and the air between us stills. "What have I done?" I close my eyes, wanting to disappear, hoping to wash away the image of Reggie forever. When I open them, I say, "They told me. When I went to my first appointment. I prayed. I begged God. I wished on the stars that he was yours. But the math. They counted back and told me. There was no way."

The nurse's cold hand covers mine, but I welcome the cooling relief. "Mistakes are made. I'm so sorry this one was made with you."

"Mr. Masters, do you know your blood type by chance?"

"I have a medical card."

"If you'd like I can find out."

The humiliation of the situation makes me feel hot and uncomfortable, exposed. "I wasn't with anyone else."

She smiles. "There are no judgments here. Just science."

"He raped me." Even now, I can barely get the words out.

A gasp followed by sympathetic eyes come. "I'm so sorry."

Derrick intervenes, "You did nothing wrong, Jaymes. You don't owe us anything."

"I owe you everything." When I dare look in his eyes, they're glassy. "Ace."

Reaching over me, he embraces me carefully, dropping his head on my shoulder. As I hug this big muscle of a man, I feel his tears through the thin cotton. The nurse leaves quietly and he says, "I'm a dad."

"You're a dad." My heart aches for him and what was stolen away. "I'm so sorry."

His head jerks back and he sits down on the edge. "Sorry for what?"

"For the last five years."

"You sure know how to make up for it. I got married and became a father all in the same day. That's a damn good day."

I inhale, my breath jagged. "Stop being so nice."

Tilting his head, a small smile plays on his lips. "Nice? I'm not being nice, I'm happy to be married to my dream girl and be a daddy to Ace. But Jaymes, seeing that the fucker hurt you not once but twice is killing me. Knowing he touched you today, or ever . . . He's dead, so he never will again. That also makes this the best day of my life." He wipes the tears away with the pads of his thumbs and teases, "Now stop raining on my parade."

Covering his hands with mine, I ask, "Are you really happy?"

"The happiest I've ever been. First, I get the honor of marrying my soul mate. Then I find out I'm a dad to the coolest kid I've ever met." Shrugging, he laughs. "I mean, I guess we could have figured this out just by knowing Ace. We took the long route, but we got there in the end." Leaning down, he kisses me. *He should be angry. He lost the first five years of his son's life. How he can see the good in this is beyond me.*

"How are you this good?"

I'm given that signature wink and a smirk. "Oh baby, I was always this good, but I'm happy to remind you for the rest of your life."

40

DERRICK

TWO MONTHS LATER ...

"We'll go over it again when we get home. Don't worry."

Looking in the rearview mirror, I see my son in the backseat. He's in his car seat and worrying about a science project he has due in a few days. Blood types. We've been working on it all week. His attitude is better than mine considering he's in kindergarten. This private school we enrolled him in is way more advanced than the school I went to.

I can hear him singing a song that might be weird to some, but I kind of love. "A plus AB equals me."

It does.

I could get hung up about losing five years of his life, but I get the distinct pleasure of calling him mine for the rest of it. I can't turn back time, and sure as shit don't want to speed it up. I finally feel good, at peace, and since the tour ended, I even miss performing live.

The embrace of my love, my lover, and my forever warms my arm when Jaymes reaches over and rests her hand on my leg. Tom Petty comes on and Jaymes sighs, and starts to change the station, but I stop her. "It's my favorite song."

"It's your theme song. All the girls always felt so special when Derrick Masters used to sing this song in the school parking lot."

"Is that what you think? Oh baby, you've got it all wrong. I only ever sang it for you. You're my girl. My only girl."

"Come on. You're pulling my leg."

"Nope. Full truth. I never sang it for anyone else."

"In that case." Leaning back in the seat, she turns the song up and we sing it together.

When we round the corner to my mother's house, I say, "Ace, remember what we talked about?"

"About the surprise for Mommy?"

I glare into the rearview mirror. "Nooooo. I meant you being on your best behavior. CJ said you took his drumsticks last time and wouldn't give them back. You know how attached he is to them."

Ace's face scrunches in annoyance. "Yeah. Whatever."

"Not whatever, buddy. Don't take them this time. Don't even touch them."

"But I want to play the drums. It's not fair he gets to."

My eyes flash to Jaymes. Our minds in sync. In a much calmer voice than I'll be able to put on, she asks, "Buddy, don't you want to play guitar? Daddy's been teaching you, and you play so well." She pats my leg.

"No. I want drums."

Damn. "Why do all kids want drums?" I ask rhetorically.

She answers with a laugh, "Because they get to bang on them. Don't worry, he'll come back around."

"Let's hope. I'm really not wanting to lose street cred by raising a drummer."

That makes her laugh harder. "I think your Hollywood Hills street cred is safe."

WE'RE LATE, but we're the guests of honor so everyone lets it slide. My mom is the first to hug me . . . after she hugs Ace and Jaymes. I've been relegated to third in the lineup. But third place to them is a beautiful place to be.

The wedding celebration is in full swing and Lara has given us the tour of my mom's newly furnished home, and this time no one's in a hurry to leave. She's got a new roommate. Jaymes's mom moved in a month ago. They have so much fun together.

The band is here, their families, Leah and Jose from the dealership, too. I turn him down on a "Cherry-red Ford Minivan with only 70,000 miles on it," but I like his determination. He got me once. Not going for another. I found out later that Kaz got suckered into a lime-green 2006 VW Beetle that Lara fell in love with for tootling around on the weekends. Kaz was not amused by the car or the tootling part, but he bought it anyway. For her. Apparently. But thanks to Jose, I've been given a whole lot of teasing material.

I come in from outside and see Jaymes talking to Katerina, Kaz's sister. Swerving left into the kitchen, I'm caught before I have a chance to duck behind the counter. "Derrick?"

I pop up above the deviled eggs with a plastered smile on my face. "Yes, dear?"

Her head tilts and a hand goes to the hip. Busted. "Come over here."

Deadman walking. I make my way over with a deviled egg in each hand and pop one in my mouth, hoping to not have to talk much, or avoid it altogether.

Katerina laughs. It's not her fault. Well, it kind of mostly is, but what's a guy to say to a hot chick dragging you to bed? Exactly. She says, "Jaymes is lovely. Congratulations on the marriage."

With a full mouth, I nod. Jaymes thanks her and then says, "Katerina tells me you two used to date."

Egg bits fly from my mouth . . . oh wait, did she say date or fuck? The relish in this egg is crunchy. "Derrick! Gross," Jaymes exclaims stepping back, making sure none landed on her.

Katerina's laughing, but all in good fun. "Relax, she knows, but I told her that you always only had a heart for one woman—her." Turning to Jaymes, she adds, "I never stood a chance, but life works in mysterious ways. I met someone recently that I'm quite intrigued by. Kaz will scare him off soon enough so I'm keeping him a secret." She moves to leave. "Congratulations again. I'm truly happy for you both."

Jaymes turns my way, with questions in her eyes, so I go ahead and spew it, not the egg, "That's another story from the past that doesn't need to be dredged up. My favorite story is ours. Deviled egg?"

Lifting up, she kisses my cheek. "No, it's all yours. Just like me. Now about that surprise Ace spilled the beans over." She waits expectantly.

I kiss her cheek this time. "Give me a few minutes. I'll be right back."

Heading to the guest bedroom, I find the guitar where my mom hid it for me. I double-check that the scratches are gone and strum a few times to tune it again. I want it to be perfect, like her. Something about this guitar—it's resilient, like her . . .

"Come on, Tank," I haggle. "You know this is for Jaymes. It's something good when she's been through so much bad. Cut me a deal."

"This might have worked on me once when you were a scrawny-ass punk, but now you're a freaking man. No deals today."

"That's a lie. I was never scrawny." I slap five big bills down on the counter. "She's worth it."

He shakes my hand. "It's a pleasure doing business with you. And take my advice, learn to play the drums. Chicks dig it."

"I think I'm doing all right in that department."

"You've made us proud, man."

He hands me the guitar just as some teenager walks in. "Oh man, you sold it, Tank? I got the two hundred you wanted and everything."

I send darts with my glare to Tank. "You overcharged me?" Covering my heart, I say, "I thought you loved me, man."

"I do. I just love a sucker and his money. Deal's done, sucker."

Laughing, I look back to the kid, and then behind the pawnshop counter at the last guitar hanging there. "It's not acoustic like this one, but it's a nice electric."

"That's three hundred. I can't afford that one. It took me two months to save up for this one."

"Solid fretboard from what I can see. You play?"

"I play. You?"

"Dabble." Tank chuckles. I add, "What's your favorite band?"

"Tom Petty and the Heartbreakers. He's the best."

Smiling, I say, "Get 'im the guitar, Tank. On me."

"No way!" The kid runs to the counter with his hands out as Tank passes it over. "No freaking way." Looking at me with his mouth open, he says, "Thanks. This is the best gift ever. Thank you."

"You're welcome. Just keep playing and don't ever let anyone stop you from dreaming."

"I won't. Thanks, mister."

The music softly playing in the background is familiar. It's a song I play every time I play live. "Hey, turn it up, Tank," I say, walking to the door. He obliges with a knowing nod.

I overhear the kid say, "That band sucks," and laugh while pushing through the door. Shrugging, I know—can't please everyone.

. . . I cover Jaymes's eyes hoping to please her. We walk forward until she's positioned right where I want her. When I remove my hands, her mouth drops open and she runs to Ace. "Oh my God. How did you get this?" She immediately puts the strap over her head and starts to strum as if it's second nature. "Ace? Where did this come from?"

"Daddy."

Everyone turns toward me. Yup, they know I'm Ace's dad, but this just might be the first time they've witnessed him calling me one of the two best names in the world—Daddy and husband. Rebel can fuck right off. Although, even that name has been tempered a bit. It's a remnant of a past life, but one that led me here. My own personal rebellion that turned into a transformation. So maybe it doesn't need to fuck off. Maybe I just need to see how it fits into my life now.

Jaymes comes to me. "How did you find it?"

"I went to the most obvious place. Tank's Pawnshop."

Her smile is prettier than blue skies and sunshine, and better than a stadium full of screaming fans any day. Okay, not better, okay, yes, better. For sure better. I do miss the chant of my name sometimes. Maybe she'll do it for me later. "Thank you." With the guitar between us, I bend down and kiss her. "I didn't get you a wedding gift."

"Are you kidding me? You made me a dad. Best gift ever. Hey Ace, c'mere." Ace runs over and I lift him up into my arms. "I got you something too, buddy." The troublesome twosome and mischievous matchmakers themselves, the grandmas, come outside carrying a big box. It's wiggling and eventually barks and pushes the open flap back and pops it's head up. Ace screams, "A puppy."

The kid's got some vocals. Maybe we should get him singing lessons. Beats drums. The golden lab puppy was too cute to pass up outside of the grocery store, crying in that box to get out. They had five in the litter and we got the last one. He was the runt, but I don't see it. He's a big puppy. "What should we name him, buddy?" Ace is on the ground with the dog, who is currently licking the crumbs from his face.

Ace looks up as if he's known the answer his whole life. "Rebel, like your back."

My brow furrows as I process what he just said. I glance to Jaymes who's about to tell him to pick something else, but I stop her. I wasn't exactly thinking this was how the name would fit into our lives, but the more I think about it, the more I like it. "I think that's a great name, son."

Ace smiles, and then pets Rebel.

Jaymes leans on my shoulder, and says, "Well, that's one way to turn it into something good."

Something good. A stupid tattoo doesn't define me. It came close, but it's not me. I'm the dad in the pickup line on the mornings when my wife stays up studying too late. I'm the guy who now buys tampons because my wife promised me sexual favors in return. I'd do it anyway, but I'm not going to say no to sex with my wife. Have you seen her?

Damn luckiest guy in the world. I wrap my arms around her

shoulders and hold her to me. She whispers, "How do you like being a dad?"

"It's the best." Kaz hands me a beer and we tap our bottles together and drink.

Jaymes asks, "How do you feel about two?"

Two minutes later I'm still cleaning the beer I spewed on Kaz and Lara. "I'm sorry," I say, laughing.

Jaymes is laughing harder. I toss them a roll of paper towels and turn to take my wife off to the side. Once we're alone, I ask, "Are you pregnant?"

"I am."

Sweet pink cheeks, bright green eyes. My heart skips a beat just looking at her. Grabbing her into my arms, I hold her. The guitar on her back makes it a little awkward, but we manage. "I thought I was lucky before, but you just topped that."

"I was thinking you might want to name the baby."

"Oh man, too bad Rebel is taken by the dog."

"Your sarcasm is duly noted."

Laughing, I reply, "Good to know." With my arm around my wife, we start walking back toward the other guests. "So how do you feel about Spade?"

"Ha. Ha. Very funny."

"In all seriousness, I think we should wait to see what the baby looks like."

She stops in her tracks. "Then they'd all be named Winston or Maude."

"I think we've got time."

"We do have time on our side."

Before we get too far into the party again, Rochelle pulls us aside. "How does your schedule look next week for lunch?"

I cross my arms over my chest and shrug. "Good."

"I meant Jaymes. I want to go over the contract for the song and do a test recording."

"Wow, it's moving fast."

"The guys are off to Australia in a few weeks. If we're incorporating the song, we've got to get the legal stuff handled."

Jaymes looks to me. "It's your song. What do you think?"

"It's your song. It was a gift for your birthday. Anyway, it was always written for you to sing. I've seen the contract. It's a good deal."

Turning back to Rochelle, she says, "Tuesday works."

They hug and Rochelle says, "Get ready for the time of your life."

"Wait, it's only one song, right?"

She shrugs. "Guess we'll see."

Later, we leave a party of guests who were yo-yoing for prizes, but I had to steal my family away. I have more up my sleeve and it's late afternoon. I watch the sky turn from blue to orange then pinks and yellows as I drive. Ace says, "It looks like the sky is on fire," right before he's giggling from puppy kisses.

The setting sun is getting lower and radiates beauty from its core. Reaching over, I hold Jaymes's hand, never happier than this moment right here. She asks, "Where are we going?"

"You'll see."

She does soon enough, and a smile rivaling the sun shines, and she gives my hand a gentle squeeze. "I haven't been here in years. Not since I was here with you. Is that why you bought this truck from Jose?"

"I needed a truck bed."

Our hands rest in Ace's lap, who's situated between us on the bench seat, and he couldn't be more pleased. The puppy sticks his head out the window and my raven-haired beauty smiles into the wind. I park in our old spot and we pile out. In the back, I take off the tarp and straighten the pillows. Ace and Jaymes are chasing the puppy. I bring out her guitar and set it next to mine before I climb up. Ace runs in the grassy area while Jaymes leans against the side of the truck. She's smiling when she says, "We could be arrested for trespassing."

Hopping down over the side, I land next to her. After a swift kiss, I waggle my eyebrows. "That's what makes coming up to the Observatory fun." I paid the guard off last night when I said I was going out for ice cream. I brought her three flavors home and she never asked why I was gone so long. Trust is good like that, or maybe she's onto me. Either way, it worked out.

I lift her up into the back of the truck and then chase the puppy and then Ace until he *lets me* catch him and set him up there too. I hop back up and take my guitar in hand. Ace has a kid's guitar now and is getting pretty decent. For a five-year-old. By fifteen, those wrong chords aren't gonna fly in our house. I start to rethink my stance on that as I strum. I'd rather him play guitar than drums though, so I guess I need to learn patience. He'll get there one way or another, just like his dad. I'm just glad he doesn't have to spend fifteen years fighting his way out like I did. He's slept soundly through the night since we told him the mean man died and that he'll never come around again. He'll never have to be scared again, especially not with me around. I'll always protect my family.

Rebel settles down on one of the pillows and the three of us play a song together. Eventually, Jaymes cuddles with Ace and they watch me play another. When I finish, Jaymes says, "I notice when you're home for more than a few weeks, you start missing the stage and the fans. Your name being screamed—"

"And the pulse," I add. "But I miss you guys more when I'm away."

"We can't chant your name here or we might get caught, but know we're always cheering for you, even when you can't hear us."

She looks to Ace and it seems they are in on a plan together. With their hands fisted, they start whisper chanting, "Derrick. Daddy. Derrick. Daddy."

I have to admit, this beats any concert I've ever played.

Best fans ever.

Lying down, I rest my head on her lap next to Ace who is sprawled out the other way. We don't get many clear nights here, but tonight, as if it heard my wish, we can see beyond the universe. I'm about to point out the constellations, but when her fingers run mindlessly through my hair, she whispers, "Derrick and Jaymes."

"Forever destined to be together."

EPILOGUE
DERRICK

THE NIGHT SKY IS OVERCAST. *Bummer.* It's not raining, so whatever. I can still work with this weather. Our fingers are intertwined, but I was idly spinning her ring around her finger moments earlier. I love seeing that band on her hand.

Jaymes Anne-Marie Masters.

I'll never tire of seeing that name on documents or hearing it spoken. We've not been married but six months, but it's been the best six months of my life. The band traveled Europe over the summer. She, Ace, and I had a blast exploring the cities during the day. Our nights were completely our own or booked with concerts. She opened our shows by performing three songs live. One song was ours that we performed together acoustically. A song written when I was seventeen and in love with a raven-haired girl with tranquility found in her eyes that settled the raging waters of my soul. The other two songs were all her. Written by and sung by her, sitting on a stool in the middle of a big stage.

She's the bravest soul I know. Not because she has no fear in performing solo, but because she has no fear when it comes to things and people she loves.

Her wounds healed, leaving a small scar up near her eyebrow. I tell her it makes her look tough. She says being tough makes her tired. I think it's the baby. Reaching over, I rub my hand over her round belly. A little fist or hand follows mine and I smile. Jaymes says, "You woke her up."

"I only touched your belly."

"She's already a daddy's girl."

Chuckling, I rub again. "Could be a boy. I think that's a fist I feel."

"It's probably a heel. And since we don't know if it's a girl or boy, I'm going with it's a she. I need to combat some of the testosterone in our home."

Home.

She's my home. Ace is my home. This baby is my home.

Family.

It was the missing link to happiness. Who knew? I somehow knew it wasn't the bevy of one-night stands that slipped out the next morning. To think Jaymes was in the same city, her soul waiting for mine to return . . . I wish I would have seen things clearer, seen through the lies she told to protect me, sooner. It took a lot of living for me to discover what I'd been searching for was here all along. I know it now. I see her and that amazing heart of hers at work, at play, at love, at life every day. It took us going through hell to find our own heaven. Now that we're here, I'm never leaving.

A guard meets us when we arrive. We're let on to the private property and I pull into the lot to park. She knows. There's no hiding the surprise now.

"The Hollywood Bowl? What are we doing here?"

Getting out of the car, I say, "You'll see." When I come around, I help her out. I grab our guitars from the back of the car and watch her smile grow. "I know."

"I know you know. You never forget anything."

"That's not true. I just remember the best of things."

Walking with a guitar in each hand, I ask, "How do you feel about playing a few songs with me?"

Her arm wraps around mine and she rests her head on my bicep. I pop it, flexing so she thinks I'm still as sexy as she did when we reunited. I've gotten a little mushy since she got pregnant. Ice cream. I've never eaten so much as I have in the last six months. Mushy by my standards. I'll add two more days back into the current workout schedule.

The side door is opened for us and I thank the manager for making this happen. We're led to the stage and look out. The moment is quiet, the feeling mutual and overwhelming—so much has gotten us to this point. When your dream comes true, it's good to take some time to appreciate the journey and savor the reward.

I set the guitars down and get two chairs off to the side for us as my words come echoing back. *"I'm going to play that stage one day. Just you wait, baby."* I set one down for her, and kiss the top of her head when she sits. *"You, my songbird, are going to sing for the world."*

"I was right."

Her eyes flick to mine, her lips swept up in a smile. "You've sung for the world. Just like you were born to do."

"That's where you're wrong."

This time, I look her way. With my guitar across my lap, I say, "That's highly unlikely."

"I wasn't born to sing. I was born to love you, to make babies with you, to live a happy life with my family."

My smile comes, just like it always does for her. "Are you happy?"

"The happiest." She glances out at the empty seats, and says, "Not even eight years later and here we are. Your dreams were big enough for the both of us and carried us here."

Spinning my ring around, the engraved ace symbol comes to the top. "I used to think my dream was to play this stage, but now that I'm here, I realize my dream already came true the day I got busted behind the gym smoking."

"You're always so charming. Keep it up and I might believe you one day."

"Your sarcasm, Mrs. Masters, has been duly noted."

"Fine," she says, rolling her eyes. "I'm a sucker for that story. Tell it to me again." She strums down the strings and watches me.

So I say, "Hey—"

"No. No. No skipping over the good parts. Start from the very beginning."

"I'll sing instead," I say, laughing. I start playing my new song, the one where I get to sing about a girl in a flower-covered dress and a name that starts with J. I move my chair closer to hers and look into her eyes.

My forever.

She's always been my muse, but now she's the melody that plays in my heart, the one that made it worthwhile to go back to the start.

The End

HARD TO RESIST

If you enjoyed The *Redemption*, *The Revolution*, and *The Rebellion*, make sure to check out Johnny Outlaw's journey, which started it all, in *The Resistance* and *The Reckoning*.

Hard to Resist Series

ABOUT THE AUTHOR

To keep up to date with her writing and more, visit S.L. Scott's
website: https://geni.us/slscott

To receive the newsletter about all of her publishing adventures, free
books, giveaways, steals and more:
https://geni.us/intheknow

ALSO BY S.L. SCOTT

To keep up to date with her writing and more, visit her website: www.slscottauthor.com

To receive the Scott Scoop about all of her publishing adventures, free books, giveaways, steals and more:

https://geni.us/intheknow

Join S.L.'s Facebook group: S.L. Scott Books

https://www.slscottauthor.com/audiobooks/

"Best Book of the Year!"

"Best I Ever Read!"

Packed with emotion, heart, and angst, this book will leave you swooning. *Best I Ever Had* is live in Kindle Unlimited, ebook, paperback, and audio.

Best I Ever Had

Read the Bestselling Book that's been called "**The Most Romantic Book Ever**" by readers and have them raving. We Were Once is now available and FREE in Kindle Unlimited.

We Were Once

Hard to Resist Series (Stand-Alones)

The Resistance

The Reckoning

The Redemption

The Revolution

The Rebellion

The Crow Brothers (Stand-Alones)

Spark

Tulsa

Rivers

Ridge

The Crow Brothers Box Set

DARE - A Rock Star Hero (Stand-Alone)

The Everest Brothers (Stand-Alones)

Everest - Ethan Everest

Bad Reputation - Hutton Everest

Force of Nature - Bennett Everest

The Everest Brothers Box Set

New York Love Stories (Stand-Alones)

Never Got Over You

The One I Want

Crazy in Love

Head Over Feels

It Started with a Kiss

The Kingwood Series

SAVAGE

SAVIOR

SACRED

FINDING SOLACE - Stand-Alone

The Kingwood Series Box Set

Emotional Stand-alones

We Were Once

Missing Grace

Finding Solace

Until I Met You

Playboy in Paradise Series

Falling for the Playboy

Redeeming the Playboy

Loving the Playboy

Playboy in Paradise Box Set

Talk to Me Duet (Stand-Alones)

Sweet Talk

Dirty Talk

Stand-Alone Books

Drunk on Love

Naturally, Charlie

A Prior Engagement

Lost in Translation

Sleeping with Mr. Sexy

Morning Glory

From the Inside Out